EVERYMAN,
I WILL GO WITH THEE,
AND BE THY GUIDE,
IN THY MOST NEED
TO GO BY THY SIDE

# The Arabian Nights

Translated by Husain Haddawy

Based on the text of the
Fourteenth-Century Syrian Manuscript
edited by Muhsin Mahdi

E V E R Y M A N ' S   L I B R A R Y

First included in Everyman's Library, 1907
This translation first published in Everyman's Library, 1992
Copyright © 1990 by W. W. Norton & Company
Published by arrangement with W. W. Norton & Company, Inc.,
New York

ISBN 1-85715-087-2

A catalogue record for this book is available from the British Library

Published by David Campbell Publishers Ltd., 79 Berwick Street,
London W1V 3PF

Distributed by the Random Century Group Ltd.,
20 Vauxhall Bridge Road, London SW1V 2SA

Printed and bound in Germany

الف ليلة وليلة

# Contents

For Mike, for Myriam, Peter,
Christopher, and Mark, and for
Diana and Shahrazad

الف ليلة وليلة

# Introduction

Bless thee, Bottom! Bless thee! Thou art translated.
—*A Midsummer Night's Dream*

## The World of *The Arabian Nights*

It has been some years now since as a little boy in Baghdad I used to listen to tales from *The Thousand and One Nights*. It sometimes seems like yesterday, sometimes like ages ago, for the Baghdad I knew then seems now closer to the time of the *Nights* than to our own times. It was on long winter nights, when my grandmother was visited by one lady or another, Um Fatma or Um Ali, always dressed in black, still mourning for a husband or a son, long lost. We would huddle around the brazier, as the embers glowed in the dim light of the oil lamp, which cast a soft shadow over her sad, wrinkled face, as if to smooth out the sorrows of the years. I waited patiently, while she and my grandmother exchanged news, indulged in gossip, and whispered one or two asides. Then there would be a pause, and the lady would smile at me, and I would seize the proffered opportunity and ask for a story—a long story. I used to like romances and fairy tales best, because they took me to a land of magic and because they were long.

The lady would begin the story, and I would listen, first apprehensively, knowing from experience that she would improvise, depending on how early or late the hour. If it was early enough, she would spin the yarn leisurely, amplifying here and interpolating there episodes I recognized from other stories. And even though this sometimes troubled my childish notions of honesty and my sense of security in reliving familiar events, I never objected, because it prolonged the action and the pleasure. If the hour was late, she would, in spite of my entreaties, tell either a brief story or one of normal length, summarizing here and omitting there. If I knew the story, I would protest, reminding her of what she had left out, and she, smilingly, would promise to tell me the story in its entirety the next time. I would then entreat her to narrate at least such and such an episode. Sometimes my grandmother, out of love for me and her own delight in the story, would add her voice to mine, and the lady, pleased to be appreciated and happy to oblige, would consent to go on, narrating in a gentle, steady voice, except when she impersonated a man or woman in a moment of passion or a demon in a fit of anger, at times getting up to act out the part. Her pauses were just as delicious as her words, as we waited, anticipating a pleasure certain to come. At last, with the voice still steady but the pauses shorter and less frequent, she would reunite the lovers or reconcile the hero to fate, bringing the story, alas, to an end and leaving me with a feeling of nostalgia, a sense at once of fulfillment and of loss. Then I would go to sleep, still living with magic birds and with demons who pursued innocent lovers and haunted my dreams, and often dreaming, as I grew older, of a face in Samarkand that glowed with love and blessed my waking hours.

So has the drab fabric of life been transformed into the gossamer of romance, as these stories have been spun for centuries in family gatherings, public assemblies, and coffeehouses, in Baghdad, Damascus, or Cairo. (Indeed, on a recent trip to Marrakech, I came across storytellers in a public square, mesmerizing their audiences.) Everybody has loved them, for they enchanted the young and the old, alike, with their magic.

In the *Nights* themselves, tales divert, cure, redeem, and save lives. Shahrazad cures Shahrayar of his hatred of women, teaches him to love, and by doing so saves her own life and wins a good man; the Caliph Harun al-Rashid finds more fulfillment in satisfying his sense of wonder by listening to a story than in his sense of justice or his thirst for vengeance; and the king of China spares four lives when he finally hears a story that is stranger than a strange episode from his own life. Even angry demons are humanized and pacified by a good story. And everyone is always ready to oblige, for everyone has a strange story to tell.

The work consists of four categories of folk tales — fables, fairy tales, romances, and comic as well as historical anecdotes, the last two often merging into one category. They are divided into nights, in sections of various lengths, a division that, although it follows no particular plan, serves a dual purpose: it keeps Shahrayar and us in suspense and brings the action to a more familiar level of reality. The essential quality of these tales lies in their success in interweaving the unusual, the extraordinary, the marvelous, and the supernatural into the fabric of everyday life. Animals discourse and give lessons in moral philosophy; normal men and women consort or struggle with demons and, like them, change themselves or anyone else into any form they please; and humble people lead a life full of accidents and surprises, drinking with an exhalted caliph here or sleeping with a gorgeous girl there. Yet both the usual incidents and the extraordinary coincidences are nothing but the web and weft of Divine Providence, in a world in which people often suffer but come out all right at the end. They are enriched by the pleasure of a marvelous adventure and a sense of wonder, which makes life possible. As for the readers, their pleasure is vicarious and aesthetic, derived from the escape into an exotic world of wish fulfillment and from the underlying act of transformation and the consequent pleasure, which may be best defined in Freudian terms as the sudden overcoming of an obstacle.

Such an effect, which is contingent on merging the supernatural and the natural and securing a willing suspension of disbelief, the storyteller of the *Nights* produces by the precise and concrete detail that he uses in a matter-of-fact way in description, narration, and conversation, bridging the gap between the natural and supernatural situations. It is this quality, by the way, that explains the appeal of these tales to the romantic imagination. For instance, the demon is a serpent as thick as the trunk of a palm tree, while the she-demon is a snake as thin as a spear and as long as two; the transparent curtain hiding the gorgeous girl in the bed is red-speckled; and the seductive girl from Baghdad buys ten pounds of mutton, while the pious gardener buys two flagons of wine for the mysterious lovers. Thus the phantasmagoric is based on the concrete, the supernatural grounded in the natural.

## Dissemination and Manuscripts

The stories of the *Nights* are of various ethnic origins, Indian, Persian, and Arabic. In the process of telling and retelling, they were modified to conform to the general life and customs of the Arab society that adapted them and to the particular conditions of that society at a particular time. They were also modified, as in my own experience, to suit the role of the storyteller or the demand of the occasion. But different as their ethnic origins may be, these stories reveal a basic homogeneity resulting from the process of dissemination and assimilation under Islamic hegemony, a homogeneity or distinctive synthesis that marks the cultural and artistic history of Islam.

No one knows exactly when a given story originated, but it is evident that some stories circulated orally for centuries before they began to be collected and written down. Arab historians of the tenth century, like al-Mas'udi and ibn al-Nadim speak of the existence of such collections in their time. One was an Arabic work called *The Thousand Tales* or *The Thousand Nights*, a translation from a Persian work entitled *Hazar Afsana* (A thousand legends). Both works

are now lost, but although it is not certain whether any of these
stories or which of them were retained in subsequent collections,
it is certain that the *Hazar Afsana* supplied the popular title as well
as the general scheme — the frame story of Shahrazad and Shahrayar
and the division into nights — to at least one such collection, namely
*The Thousand and One Nights*.

The stories of the *Nights* circulated in different manuscript copies
until they were finally written down in a definite form, or what may
be referred to as the original version, in the second half of the thirteenth century, within the Mamluk domain, either in Syria or in
Egypt. That version, now lost, was copied a generation or two later
in what became the archetype for subsequent copies. It too is now
lost, but its existence is clearly attested to by the remarkable simi-
larities in substance, form, and style among the various early copies,
a fact that points to a common origin. Specifically, all the copies
share the same nucleus of stories, which must have formed the
original and which appear in the present translation. The only exception is the "Story of Qamar al-Zaman," of which only the first
few pages are extant in any Syrian manuscript, and for this reason
I have not included it in the present translation.

From the archetype there evolved two separate branches of manuscripts, the Syrian and the Egyptian. Of the Syrian branch four
manuscripts are known to exist. The first is the copy in the *Bibliothèque
Nationale* in Paris, in three volumes (nos. 3609–3611). It is of all
existing manuscripts the oldest and the closest to the original, having been written sometime during the fourteenth century. The other
three Syrian manuscripts were copied much later, in the sixteenth,
eighteenth, and nineteenth centuries, respectively. They are, however, very close to the fourteenth-century manuscript and simi-
larly contain only the nucleus and the very first part of "Qamar
al-Zaman."

If the Syrian branch shows a fortunately stunted growth that
helped preserve the original, the Egyptian branch, on the contrary,
shows a proliferation that produced an abundance of poisonous fruits
that proved almost fatal to the original. First, there exists a plethora
of Egyptian copies all of which, except for one written in the seventeenth century, are late, dating between the second part of the eighteenth and the first part of the nineteenth century. Second, these
copies delete or modify passages that exist in the Syrian manuscripts,
add others, and indiscriminately borrow from each other. Third,
the copyists, driven to complete one thousand and one nights, kept
adding folk tales, fables, and anecdotes from Indian, Persian, and
Turkish, as well as indigenous sources, both from the oral and from
the written traditions. One such example is the story of Sindbad,

which, though early in date, is a later addition. What emerged, of course, was a large, heterogeneous, indiscriminate collection of stories by different hands and from different sources, representing different layers of culture, literary conventions and styles tinged with the Ottoman cast of the time, a work very different from the fundamentally homogeneous original, which was the clear expression of the life, culture, and literary style of a single historical moment, namely, the Mamluk period. This is the more significant because the Ottoman period is marked by a sharp decline in Arabic culture in general and literature in particular.

The mania for collecting more stories and "completing" the work led some copyists to resort even to forgery. Such is the case of none other than "The Story of Aladdin and the Magic Lamp." This story is not among the eleven basic stories of the original work, nor does it appear in any known Arabic manuscript or edition, save in two, both written in Paris, long after it had appeared in Galland's translation. Galland himself, as his diaries indicate, first heard the story in 1709 from Hanna Diab, a Maromite Christian of Aleppo, who may have subsequently written it down and given it to Galland for his translation. The first time the story appeared in Arabic was in 1787, in a manuscript written by a Syrian Christian priest living in Paris, named Dionysius Shawish, alias Dom Denis Chavis, a manuscript designed to complete the missing portions of the fourteenth-century Syrian manuscript. The story appeared again in a manuscript written between 1805 and 1808, in Paris, by Mikhail Sabbagh, a Syrian collaborator of Silvestre de Sacy. Sabbagh claimed to have copied it in turn from a Baghdad manuscript written in 1703. Such good fortune, in retrieving not one but two versions of a lost wonderful tale, might be cause for rejoicing, as it indeed was among the scholars. However, a careful examination of the two versions, both in the light of the general style of the *Nights* and in the light of Galland's translation, leads to a less joyful conclusion. Chavis fabricated the text by translating Galland back into Arabic, as is manifest from his French syntax and turns of phrase, and Sabbagh perpetuated the hoax by improving Chavis's translation and claiming it to be a Baghdad version. And this forgery was the source used by Payne and Burton for their own translations of the story.

# The Printed Editions

If the history of the manuscripts is a confusing tale, that of the printed editions of *The Thousand and One Nights* is a sad comedy of errors. The first edition was published by Fort William College in

Calcutta, in two volumes comprising the first two hundred nights (vol. 1 in 1814; vol. 2 in 1818). The editor was one Shaikh Ahmad ibn-Mahmud Shirawani, an instructor of Arabic at the college. He pieced this edition together from a late Syrian manuscript and a work containing classical anecdotes, choosing the texts at random. He deleted, added, and modified numerous passages and tried to change, whenever he could, the colloquial to literary expressions. He edited as he pleased. Then came the Breslau edition, the first eight volumes of which were published by Maximilian Habicht, between 1824 and 1838, and the last four by Heinrich Fleischer, between 1842 and 1843. For reasons known only to himself, Professor Habicht claimed to have based his edition not on a Syrian or an Egyptian but on a Tunisian manuscript, thus confusing the scholars until they finally disproved the claim by discovering that he had patched the text together from copies of the fourteenth-century Syrian manuscript and late Egyptian ones.

It was on such a late Egyptian manuscript that the first Bulaq edition of 1835 was exclusively based. It is a manuscript whose copyist, by culling, collecting, and interpolating numerous tales of recent vintage and written in a late style, swelled the old text, and by subdividing the material, obtained one thousand and one nights, thus producing a "complete" version of the *Nights*, a version very different from the Mamluk original in substance, form, and style. The Bulaq editor, Abd al-Rahman al-Safti Al-Sharqawi, not content to edit and print an accurate text of the manuscript, took it upon himself to correct, emend, and improve the language, producing a work that was in his judgment superior in literary quality to the original. Then came the second Calcutta edition, published in four volumes by William Macnaghten, between 1839 and 1842. Edited by several hands, it was based on a late Egyptian manuscript copied in 1829, with interpolations and with "corrections" in the substance and the style, according to the first Calcutta and the Breslau editions. Thus "thoroughly edited" and "completed," as its editors claimed, it has ever since vied with the Bulaq edition in the estimation of scholars and general readers, not to mention all the major translators. Thus authentic came to mean complete and, ironically, spurious. (For a full history of the manuscripts and printed editions, see Muhsin Mahdi's Arabic introduction to his edition of the text of the *Nights, Alf Layla wa Layla*, Leiden, 1984, and his English introduction in the forthcoming third volume.)

# The Mahdi Edition

It is one of the curiosities of literary history that a work that has
been circulating since the ninth century, that has been heard and
read for centuries by young and old everywhere, and that has become a world classic should wait until very recently for a proper
edition. This is curious yet understable as one of the anomalies of
comparative cultural studies. While the history of textual scholar-
ship in the West has been, since the Renaissance, increasingly one
of keen accuracy and authenticity, its counterpart in the East,
especially in the case of the *Nights*, has been one of error and cor-
ruption, at the hands of Eastern and Western scholars alike, the
result of ignorance and contempt. It is all the more gratifying,
therefore, that the most recent edition of the Arabic text of the *Nights*
should be by far the best. After years of sifting, analyzing, and col-
lating virtually all available texts, Muhsin Mahdi has published the
definitive edition of the fourteenth-century Syrian manuscript in
the *Bibléothèque Nationale* (*Alf Layla wa Layla*, Leiden, 1984). Mahdi
fills lacunae, emends corruptions, and elucidates obscurities; however, he refrains from providing punctuation and diacritical marks
or corrected spellings. What emerges is a coherent and precise work
of art that, unlike other versions, is like a restored icon or musical
score, without the added layers of paint or distortions, hence, as
close to the original as possible. Thus a long-standing grievance
has been finally redressed, and redressed with a sense of poetic justice, not only because this edition redeems all others from a general
curse, but also because it is the work of a man who is at once the
product of East and West. And it is particularly gratifying to me personally, because it has provided me with the text for my translation.

# Past Translations

Not so fortunate were the major translators of the work into English,
Edward Lane (1839–41), John Payne (1882–84), and Richard Burton (1885–86). Lane based his translation on the Bulaq, the first
Calcutta and the Breslau; Payne on the second Calcutta and the
Breslau; and Burton on the Bulaq, the second Calcutta, and the
Breslau editions. These translators did not, as one might expect,
compare the various editions to establish an accurate text for their
translations (assuming that, given what they had, such a task was
possible); instead they deleted and added at random, or at will, from
the various sources to piece together a text that suited their individual purposes: in the case of Lane, a detailed but expurgated ver-

sion; in the case of Payne and Burton, versions that are as full and complete as possible. In effect, they followed the same Arabic editorial tradition, except that whereas the editors of Bulaq and Calcutta produced a corrupt text in Arabic, the translators of London produced an even more corrupt text in English. Even the two less significant twentieth-century translations followed this pattern. Edward Poweys Mather based his English version (Routledge, 1937) on a French translation by J. C. Mardrus, which was based on the Bulaq and second Calcutta editions. Since he knew no Arabic, he altered the French text, ignorant of what he was doing to the Arabic or how far he had strayed from it. And N. J. Dawood, who translated a selection of tales (Penguin, 1956), which includes less than three of the eleven basic stories of the *Nights*, followed the second Calcutta, "editing" and "correcting" here and there in the light of the Bulaq edition.

Interestingly, the only exception to this pattern is Galland himself, the very first to translate the work in Europe (1704–17). His French translation of the basic stories was based on none other than the fourteenth-century Syrian text, as well as other sources. But instead of following the text faithfully, Galland deleted, added, and altered drastically to produce not a translation, but a French adaptation, or rather a work of his own creation. He did succeed, however, in establishing the work as a classic, for no sooner had his translation begun to appear than a Grub Street English version followed (1706–8), went into many editions, and was itself followed by other translations, pseudotranslations, and imitations, so numerous that by 1800 there were more than eighty such collections. It was such hack versions that inflamed the imagination of Europe, of general readers and poets alike, from Pope to Wordsworth. The *Nights* could shine in the dark.

These translators did not deviate from the letter of the original because they did not know sufficient Arabic. On the contrary, a careful comparison between any given Arabic passage and their own respective translation of it reveals an admirable command of Arabic diction, grammar, and syntax, except where the text itself poses severe problems, as it often does. Although the tales are generally written in the conversational style of the storyteller, they modulate between the colloquial and the literary, and even ornate, within a given passage, from passage to passage, and from story to story, and both types pose problems in regards to diction, grammar, and syntax. A great many words are thirteenth-century Syrian and Egyptian colloquial idioms, which have long since disappeared from usage or whose meanings have been altered; and many others are of Persian origin, either used without alteration or Arabized. The sentences are often ungrammatical, hence capable of several different and often contradictory readings. The typical structure is that of an interminable running sentence, consisting of brief coordinated clauses, often without apparent regard for place, time, or causality. The translator is therefore forced to interpret and reorder the clauses in a subordinated and logical sequence, in order to suit the European habits of reading and thinking, if his reader is to understand the passage at all. To make matters worse, the text, including Mahdi's, normally bears neither diacritical nor punctuation marks. In Arabic, the diacritical marks distinguish one letter from another, thus differentiating between words that share the same letters but have different roots and therefore different meanings. Thus a word may offer two very different readings in a given sentence. This is not a problem when one of the meanings is unlikely in the context, but when both are possible, the translator must choose a single interpretation. The diacritical marks also indicate the forms of conjugation and declension. Their absence, therefore, coupled with the faulty grammar of some sentences, makes every sentence an encounter, assuming, that is, that one always knows where a sentence or a unit of expression begins or ends, for the Arabic text uses no punctuation, not even question marks.

What makes a coherent reading or translation of such a text possible is an eye familiar with Arabic prose and an ear attuned to the rhythm of the spoken language, ideally the eye and ear of someone who reads, writes, and speaks Arabic like a native. It is a wonder, therefore, that foreign translators, like Lane, Payne, and Burton, made so few mistakes, yet no wonder that they made them. In diction, for instance, when they met words they could not understand, they often dropped them from their text. In grammar, a misreading, for instance, of the conjugation of the verb "to overtake," which also means "to realize," leads Burton to translate the refrain "But morning overtook Shahrazad, and she lapsed into silence," as "And Shahrazad perceived the dawn of day and ceased saying her permitted say." This example would seem innocuous enough were it not that it is repeated one thousand times and were it not that it spoils the dramatic poignancy of the situation, when the morning, the hour of her execution, finally catches up with Shahrazad. In syntax, reordering the clauses for a coherent reading often requires knowledge of Arab life and culture. For example, the following passage, translated literally, reads:

> After a while, our mother also died, and left us three thousand dinars, which we divided equally among ourselves. I was the youngest. My two sisters prepared their dowries and got married.

Burton translates it as follows:

> After a while my mother also deceased, leaving me and my sisters-german three thousand dinars; so each daughter received her portion of a thousand dinars and I the same, albe the youngest. In due course of time, my sisters married with the usual festivities.

But it should read:

> After a while, our mother also died, leaving us three thousand dinars, which we divided equally among ourselves. Since I was the youngest of the three, my two sisters prepared their dowries and got married before me.

For what is at issue here is not the Islamic law of inheritance but marriage customs in Arab society.

Moreover, the problem for the translators was compounded in that, as often as not, a given passage had already been altered by the editor of a manuscript or a printed edition or by both. For the tales, for all their popularity among the people, were regarded with condescension and contempt by the Arab literati of the eighteenth and nineteenth centuries. These included the editors themselves, self-appointed men of taste and judgment, who, trained during the period of the decline of Arabic literature, had little judgment and no taste. They regarded these folk tales as entertaining in substance but vulgar in style, and they undertook to improve them according to their own light.

Their method was to condense, amplify, or alter. They took a given passage, summarized it, and recast it in correct, polite, or literary Arabic, often sacrificing vivid details vital to the art of the storyteller for empty academic phrases or poetic diction. For instance, "The Story of the Hunchback" opens with this passage:

> It is related, O King, that there lived once in China a tailor who had a pretty, compatible, and loyal wife. It happened one day that they went out for a stroll to enjoy the sights at a place of entertainment, where they spent the whole day in diversions and fun, and when they returned home at the end of the day, they met on the way a jolly hunchback. He was smartly dressed in a folded inner robe and an open outer robe, with gathered sleeves and an embroidered collarband, in the Egyptian style, and sporting a scarf and a tall green hat, with knots of yellow silk stuffed with ambergris. The hunchback was short, like him of whom the poet 'Antar said:
>
> > Lovely the hunchback who can hide his hump,
> > Like a pearl hidden in an oyster shell,

> A man who looks like a castor oil branch,
> From which dangles a rotten citric lump.

He was busy playing on the tambourine, singing, and improvising all kinds of funny gestures. When they drew near and looked at him, they saw that he was drunk, reeking of wine. Then he placed the tambourine under his arm and began to beat time by clapping his hands, as he sang the following verses:

> Go early to the darling in yon jug;
> Bring her to me,
> And fete her as you fete a pretty girl,
> With joy and glee,
> And make her as pure as a virgin bride,
> Unveiled to please,
> That I may honor my friend with a cup
> Of wine from Greece.
> If you, my friend, care for the best in life,
> Life can repay,
> Then at this moment fill my empty cup,
> Without delay.
> Don't you, my tantalizer, on the plain
> The gardens see?

. . . [W]hen the tailor and his wife saw the hunchback in this condition, drunk and reeking of wine, now singing, now beating the tambourine, they were delighted with him and invited him home to sup and drink with them that night. He accepted gladly and walked with them to their home.

I have deliberately chosen this lengthy passage in order to show how drastically the Egyptian editor reduces and excises (in this case two entire poems) and to show the extent of the substance and flavor the reader misses as a result. Payne's translation is accurate, but he uses the edited version, and so he reads:

> There lived once in the city of Bassora a tailor, who was open-handed and loved pleasure and merrymaking: and he was wont, he and his wife, to go out by times, a-pleasuring, to the public places of recreation. One day they went out as usual and were returning home in the evening, when they fell in with a hunchback, the sight of whom would make the disappointed laugh and dispel chagrin from the sorrowful. So they went up to look at him and invited him to go home and make merry with them that night. He consented and accompanied them to their house.

Or else the editors altered some details and thereby showed insensitivity to psychological subtlety or dramatic nuance. In "The

Story of the Slave-Girl Anis al-Jalis and Nur al-Din ibn-Khaqan,"
the passage in which the caliph throws off his disguise reads:

> I heard, O happy King, that the old man went into a storeroom
> to fetch a stick with which to beat the fisherman, who was the
> caliph, while the caliph cried out from the window, "Help, help!"
> and was at once joined by Ja'far and the officers, who dressed
> him in his royal suit, seated him on a chair, and stood in atten-
> dance. When the old man came out of the storeroom with the
> stick, rushing toward the fisherman, he was stunned to see in-
> stead the caliph seated on a chair and Ja'far standing in atten-
> dance. He began to bite his nails in bewilderment and to exclaim,
> "Am I asleep or awake?" The caliph turned to him and said, "O
> Shaikh Ibrahim, what state do I see you in?" The old man became
> sober at once and, rolling on the ground, recited the following
> verses.

The Egyptian editor alters the passage to read, again in Payne's
translation:

> When the Khalif heard this, he cried out at him and made a sign
> to Mesrour, who discovered himself and rushed upon him. Now
> Jaafer had sent one of the gardeners to the doorkeeper of the
> palace for a suit of the royal raiment for the Commander of the
> Faithful; so he went and returning with the suit, kissed the earth
> before the Khalif and gave it to him. Then he threw off the clothes
> he had on and dressed himself in those which the gardener had
> brought, to the great amazement of Gaffer Ibrahim, who bit his
> nails in bewilderment and exclaimed, 'Am I asleep or awake?'
> 'O Gaffer Ibrahim,' said the Khalif, 'what state is this in which
> I see thee?' With this, he recovered from his drunkenness and
> throwing himself on the ground, repeated the following verses:

Or they inserted some details, often exaggerating action, description, or emotion and thereby weakening the literary effect. Again
in a passage in "Anis al-Jalis," for instance, the added details change
the delicate humor of high comedy to the coarse humor of low comedy. After the caliph exchanges his clothes with the fisherman, he
takes the salmon and returns to the garden in disguise to surprise
Ja'far, who has been waiting for him there. But the Egyptian editor
inserts the following passage, which reads, this time in Burton's
translation:

> Hardly had the fisherman ended his verse, when the lice began
> to crawl over the Caliph's skin, and he fell to catching them on
> his neck with his right and left throwing them from him, while
> he cried, 'O fisherman, woe to thee! What be this abundance of

lice on thy gaberdine? 'O my lord,' replied he, 'They may annoy thee just at first, but before a week is past thou wilt not feel them nor think of them'. The Caliph laughed and said to him, 'Out on thee! Shall I leave this gaberdine of thine so long on my body?' Quoth the fisherman, 'I would say a word to thee but I am ashamed in presence of the Caliph!' and quoth he. 'Say what thou hast to say'. 'It passed through my thought, O Commander of the Faithful', said the fisherman, 'that since thou wishest to learn fishing so thou mayest have in hand an honest trade whereby to gain thy livelihood, this my gaberdine besitteth thee right well.' The Commander of the Faithful laughed at this speech, and the fisherman went his way.

Thus the translators, by adhering to such sources, deviate not only from the letter but also from the spirit of the original, particularly since the letter and the spirit are often inextricable. But such adherence is not the only cause of their violation of the spirit; another and more fundamental cause lay in their respective views of the work itself, their objectives in translating it, and their strategies and styles, all of which may be explained by the fact that they simply failed to see that fidelity to the precise detail was crucial to achieve the essential quality of the *Nights*, by bridging the gap between the natural and the supernatural.

From Galland to Burton, translators, scholars, and readers shared the belief that the *Nights* depicted a true picture of Arab life and culture at the time of the tales and, for some strange reason, at their own time. Time and again, Galland, Lane, or Burton claimed that these tales were much more accurate than any travel account and took pains to translate them as such. For this purpose, each of them adopts a specific strategy, depending on his other intentions. Lane translates the work as a travel guide to Cairo, Damascus, and Baghdad. In order to substantiate this claim, he adds compendious notes intended to explain a given passage and to introduce the reader to various aspects of Arab culture, such as social customs, mythology, religion, and ethics, without asking himself whether such substantiation would be necessary if the claims were true. Consequently, he proceeds to depict this life in an accessibly plain style, much more faithful to the conversational style of the original than, say, the style of Burton. But instead of being faithful to the life depicted in the tales, Lane omits sometimes a few details, sometimes whole passages, curiously because he finds them inconsistent with his own observations of life in Cairo. For instance, he omits the details of the drinking scene in "The Story of the Porter and the Three Ladies," because he has never seen Cairene ladies drink, but, to make sure that the reader is properly informed, he appends a twenty-page footnote dealing with drinking habits among the Arabs. Then he goes on to explain that such passages, like the one he has omitted, "seem as if they were introduced for the gratification of the lowest class of auditors of a public reciter of a coffee-shop. These passages exhibit to us persons of high rank, both men and women, as characterized by a grossness which is certainly not uncommon among Arabs of the inferior classes" (ch.10, n. 87). He also omits the verse passages, except for a token line here and there, because he finds them to be for the most part either worthless or obscure, and because in truth they do not suit his sociological purpose. He is an orientalist or a sociologist, rather than a storyteller.

If Lane attempts to guide the prudish Victorian reader through Cairo by introducing him to a higher class of Egyptian society, Burton attempts to bring Cairo, in all its color, to England. But unlike Lane, who is interested in what he considers to be typical manifestations of Arab culture, Burton is interested in the exotic, the quaint, and the colorful. He too appends copious notes, but these are meant to appeal to Victorian prurience or to shock prudish sensibility. Typical is the note on the passage in the "Prologue," in which Shahrayar's wife lies on her back and invites the black slave Mas'ud to make love to her while ten other black slaves are busy making love to ten of her female attendants; Burton explains the white woman's predilection for black men by expatiating on the efficacy of the enormous male organs in Zanzibar, promising the reader to regale him on the retention of the semen, in due course.

Burton declares in the introduction that his purpose is to produce a "full, complete, unvarnished, uncastrated copy of the great original." That original, as I have mentioned earlier, uses a style that modulates between the colloquial and the literary. The literary is marked by metaphors and similes, formulaic epithets, parallelisms, and rhymed prose, and Burton literally preserves all this, including the jingling rhymes, merrily telling the reader that he has "carefully Englished the picturesque turns and novel expressions of the original in all their outlandishness." And outlandish, indeed grotesque, they appear, both to English and to Arabic eyes. Having gone so far, Burton is unable to retrench in his rendering of the colloquial passages; therefore, he renders them in a pseudo-archaic style dear to the heart of many a Victorian translator, a style that is totally alien both to the style of the Arabic original and to any recognizable style in English literature. One may suppose that Burton follows a general Victorian tendency to archaize and make more colorful the "rude" works of primitive times and places; and subsequently one may trace the same tendency in the style of Payne's translation of the *Nights*, in which Burton detects and admires a "sub-flavor of the Mabinogianic archaism." But even a cursory comparison easily shows that the style of Payne's translation, which was unfortunately published in a limited edition of five hundred copies and was therefore unavailable to the general reader, is by far more successful than Burton's in reproducing both the letter and the spirit of the original. But what is more to the point here is that a careful and thorough comparison between Burton and Payne explains another reason for Burton's choice of style. He himself admits in the introduction that Payne "uses the exact vernacular equivalent of the foreign word so happily and so picturesquely that all future translations must perforce use the same expression." Burton consistently follows Payne's translation, copying it almost verbatim but adding his own sauce and spices.

Thus Burton's translation is akin to that of Galland, at least in one respect, for it is not so much a true translation of the *Nights* as it is a colorful and entertaining concoction. For instance, a passage that reads:

> The curtain was unfastened, and a dazzling girl emerged, with genial charm, wise mien, and features as radiant as the moon. She had an elegant figure, the scent of ambergris, sugared lips, Babylonian eyes, with eyebrows as arched as a pair of bent bows, and a face whose radiance put the shining sun to shame, for she was like a great star soaring in the heavens, or a dome of gold, or an unveiled bride, or a splendid fish swimming in a fountain, or a morsel of luscious fat in a bowl of milk soup,

becomes in Burton's hands:

> Thereupon sat a lady bright of blee, with brow beaming brilliancy, the dream of philosophy, whose eyes were fraught with Babel's gramarye and her eyebrows were arched as for archery; her breath breathed ambergris and perfumery and her lips were sugar to taste and carnelian to see. Her stature was straight as the letter I and her face shamed the noon-sun's radiancy; and she was even as a galaxy, or a dome with golden marquetry or a bride displayed in choicest finery or a noble maid of Araby.

Another passage, which reads:

> When I saw that he was dead and realized that it was I who had killed him, I let out a loud scream, beat my face, tore my clothes, and cried, "O people, O God's creatures, there remained for this young man only one day out of the forty, yet he still met his death at my hand. O God, I ask for your forgiveness, wishing that I had died before him. These my afflictions I suffer, draught by bitter draught, 'so that God's will may be fulfilled.' "

becomes almost a parody or rather a self-parody:

> When I saw that he was slain and knew that I had slain him,
> maugre myself, I cried out with an exceeding loud and bitter cry
> and beat my face and rent my raiment and said, 'Verily we be
> Allah's and unto Him we be returning, O Moslems! O folk fain
> of Allah! there remained for this youth but one day of the forty
> dangerous days which the astrologers and the learned had foretold
> for him; and the predestined death of this beautiful one was to
> be at my hand. Would Heaven I had not tried to cut the water
> melon. What dire misfortune is this I must bear lief or loath?
> What a disaster! What an affliction! O Allah mine, I implore
> thy pardon and declare to Thee my innocence of his death. But
> what God willeth let that come to pass.'

Burton, having raised his style to such a pitch, is forced, when
he comes to the more ornate verse passages, to raise it yet to a higher
pitch, adopting an even more artificial and more tortured expression that is forced to slide downward. For instance, a humorous
poem that reads:

> Wail for the crane well-stewed in tangy sauce;
> Mourn for the meat, either well baked or fried;
> Cry for the hens and daughters of the grouse
> And the fried birds, even as I have cried.
> Two different kinds of fish are my desire,
> Served on two loaves of bread, zestful though plain,
> While in the pan that sizzles o'er the fire
> The eggs like rolling eyes fry in their pain.
> The meat when grilled, O what a lovely dish,
> Served with some pickled greens; that is my wish.
> 'Tis in my porridge I indulge at night,
> When hunger gnaws, under the bracelets' light.
> O soul, be patient, for our fickle fate
> Oppresses one day, only to elate.

becomes:

> Wail for the little partridges on porringer and plate;
> Cry for the ruin of the fries and stews well marinate:
> Keen as I keen for loved, lost daughters of the Kata-grouse,
> And omelette round the fair enbrowned fowls agglomerate:
> O fire in heart of me for fish, those deux poissons I saw,
> Bedded on new-made scones and cakes in piles to laniate.
> For thee, O vermicelli! aches my very maw! I hold
> Without thee every taste and joy are clean annihilate.
> Those eggs have rolled their yellow eyes in torturing pains of
>    fire

Ere served with hash and fritters hot, that delicatest cate.
Praised be Allah for His baked and roast and ah! how good
This pulse, these pot-herbs steeped in oil with eysill
    combinate!
When hunger sated was, I elbow-propt fell back upon
Meat-pudding wherein gleamed the bangles that my wits
    amate.
Then woke I sleeping appetite to eat as though in sport
Sweets from brocaded trays and kickshaws most elaborate.
Be patient, soul of me! Time is haughty, jealous wight;
Today he seems dark-lowering and tomorrow fair to sight.

Burton hoped, by adapting such a procedure and such a style
for his translation, by writing "as the Arab would have written in
English," to create a work that would be added to the treasures of
English literature, for "the translator's glory is to add something
to his native tongue." What Burton bequeathed to the nation, however, was no more than a literary Brighton Pavilion.


# The Present Translation

## The Guiding Principles

Three centuries have gone by since Antoine Galland first introduced
the *Nights* to Europe, and a full century since Richard Burton translated the work, in the last serious attempt to introduce it to the
English reader. Much has happened in the world since then, a world
in which, though technology seems hostile to romance, the ventures
of science have become as fantastic as the adventures of fiction, and
illusion and reality have become almost one. Nonetheless, it is
science that has been largely responsible for the demand for authenticity, or truth, in facing our world, which is becoming threaten-
ingly small, recognizing the value of other cultures, and exploring
their treasures. Now the flamboyant Victorian distortions of Burton
seem closer to the disarming neoclassical liberties of Galland than
to our modern functionalism, which needs a style more suited to
our modern sensibility than the styles of Burton or Galland, the
one still circulating as a Victorian relic, the other, though lively
in its own day, now lying buried in the archives of literary history.

The failure of past translations lies in assuming the work to be
other than what it was intended to be, a collection of tales told to
produce aesthetic pleasure in the Arabic reader. In translating the
work as they did, they violated its integrity — Lane by emasculating
it; Burton by reproducing its Arabic peculiarities and adding other

idiosyncrasies of his own; and Galland by altering it to suit French taste, although this method comes the closest to producing the intended effect. Translation is the transfer of a text from one cultural context to another by converting its language into the language of the host culture. This requires command of the languages involved and of the literary idioms and conventions of both cultures. In converting the meaning of the text, the translators, who must act both as editors and as interpreters, offer a reading of it, designed for a given reader in a given language, and in the context of a given culture. They try to achieve equivalency, but since, due to the untranslatable difference in cultural connotations, associations, and other nuances, full equivalency is impossible, the translators try to achieve approximation by securing a willing suspension of disbelief that allows the reader to believe that the translated text is the original text. This is possible, especially since in literature, the translators must convey not only the meaning of the text but also its aesthetic effect on readers. They respond to the text as natives would, by identifying the means by which this effect is produced, and by finding the comparable linguistic and literary means available in the host culture to produce a comparable effect in the intended reader. Therefore, they should not, as translators from Dryden to Burton have advocated, try to write as the original author would have written in the host language, for such a creature can never be; instead, they should try to produce an equivalent text that will produce an effect on the intended reader comparable to the effect the original text produces on the native reader. For the aesthetic effect, which is grounded in human nature and which can be achieved by our knowledge of and skill in using the tools of the respective literary conventions, is the common denominator between the native and the host culture and the principal means of success in transferring the literary work from one context to another.

## The Prose

In translating the *Nights*, whose principal function is not to express the subtle nuances of experience and of our perceptions of it but to produce a certain kind of aesthetic pleasure, mainly by grounding the supernatural in the natural, adherence to the aesthetic effect becomes paramount. Such adherence has been the underlying principle of my translation. This does not mean, however, that I have taken liberties with the text; on the contrary, I have been as faithful as possible, except for very few interpolations (placed in brackets) without which the gaps would have rendered the narrative illogical, and except when literal fidelity would have meant deviating from the limits of idiomatic English and consequently violating the spirit or the intended effect of the original. Thus, for instance, "O my liver," becomes, "O my heart" or "O my life"; "Allah" becomes "God"; and "God the Most High," the most familiar epithet for God in Arabic, becomes "The Almighty God." I have, unlike the other translators, who use the same style regardless of level, adopted a plain narrative as well as a conversational style that modulates with the original between the colloquial and the literary, according to speaker or situation, yet I have used colloquialisms and slang terms sparingly because the English equivalents are certain to disappear sooner or later, thus rendering the translation obsolete before its time. Likewise, I have used literary ornament judiciously because what appealed to Arabic thirteenth- or fourteenth-century literary taste does not always appeal to the taste of the modern English reader. For instance, I have avoided the rhymed prose of the original because it is too artificial and too jarring to the English ear.

Furthermore, I have varied the level of the style to suit the level of a given story, a lower level for some of the comic tales of "The Story of the Hunchback," and a higher level for "The Story of Nur al-Din ibn-Bakkar and the Slave-Girl Shams al-Nahar," a story written in thirteenth-century Baghdad, with literary echoes from the highly euphuistic and popular *Maqamat* of Hariri. Finally, I have avoided the temptation to add a distinctive color or stamp a personal manner or mannerism on the original in order to appeal to the reader. Burton's case is sobering enough; besides, the intention of the style of the *Nights* is to provide the storyteller or the reader with the opportunity to tell or read the story in his own voice and to dramatize the action and dialogue in his own way, very much as the actors do when they bring their written parts to life. Neutrality is crucial here.

## *The Verse*

One of the distinctive features of the *Nights* is that the prose narrative is interspersed with verse passages, some of which were interpolated by the original editor, some by subsequent copyists. They are inserted to suit the occasion, and whether adding color to the description of a place or a person, expressing joy or grief, complimenting a lady, or underscoring a moral, they are intended to heighten the action, raise the literary level, and intensify the emotional effect. Yet a great number of these passages fail to achieve such effects because they are too mediocre, for less than one-half are anthologized from the classical poets of the period down to the fourteenth century, while the rest are composed by lesser versifiers, including hacks and even the copyists themselves.

In general, the verse is characterized by poetic diction, compari-

sons, metaphors, conceits, and all kinds of parallelisms, especially
balanced antitheses. For this reason, I have adopted a style similar
to that of neoclassic poetry, particularly because, like its Arabic
counterpart, it was ultimately derived from the same source, namely
the Greco-Roman tradition; besides, a traditional Arabic poem consists of lines, each of which comprises two equal halves and follows
the same rhyme throughout, thus producing an effect akin to that
of the heroic couplet. I have, however, used an abab rhyme scheme
for greater freedom and flexibility in reproducing both the sense
and the stylistic ornaments of the original. In the case of the love
lyrics, I have drawn on the tradition of courtly compliment, imi-
tating one type or another depending on the freedom or emotional
intensity of the Arabic lyric in question.

My main problem was how to render the turgid or vapid verse
passages of the lesser versifiers, which are marked by artificial word
order, forced rhymes, inexact parallelisms, and hackneyed metaphors. The choice was either to purify them through the filter of
translation and avoid the charge of inept English renderings, or to
be consistent with my aim of adhering both to the letter and to the
spirit of the original. I have decided in favor of the latter and have
rendered each passage as it is, making it appear neither better nor
worse. Thus the original discrepancy between the good and the bad
is maintained. For instance, a classic passage reads:

> If you suffer injustice, save yourself,
> And leave the house behind to mourn its builder.
> Your country you'll replace by another,
> But for yourself you'll find no other self.
> Nor with a mission trust another man,
> For none is as loyal as you yourself.
> And did the lion not struggle by himself,
> He would not prowl with such a mighty mane.

while that of a hack versifier reads:

> If I bemoan your absence, what will you say?
> If I pine with longing, what is the way?
> If I dispatch someone to tell my tale,
> The lover's complaint no one can convey.
> If I with patience try to bear my pain,
> After the loss of love, I can't endure the blow.
> Nothing remains but longing and regret
> And tears that over the cheeks profusely flow.
> You, who have long been absent from my eyes,
> Will in my loving heart forever stay.
> Was it you who have taught me how to love,
> And from the pledge of love never to stray?

And thus the English reader, like his discerning Arab counterpart. can see for himself both the faults and the felicities of the work.

# Conclusion

For all a given translator's knowledge and skill, a translation is essentially a matter of sensitivity and taste, applied in one thousand and one instances. As such, for the translator, who stands astride two cultures, possesses two different sensibilities, and assumes a double identity, a translation is a journey of self-discovery. And the road to truth is, like the road to fairyland, fraught with perils and requires an innocent suspension of disbelief in the self and what it creates. By translating the work, one translates oneself; the little Arab boy who listened to the *Thousand and One Nights* has become the English storyteller. He may have produced a strange creature, a man with an ass's head, or may even, like Bottom, sport an ass's head of his own. What does it matter, so long as he has dreamed, in one Baghdad or another, a dream in the lap of a fairy queen.

HUSAIN HADDAWY
Reno 1988

## Acknowlegments

My thanks to John Benedict, Marian Johnson, Muhsin Mahdi, Ann Ronald, and Jennings Woods for their generous reading of the text and their valuable suggestions. Thanks also to Dia Azzawi and N. Ramzi for the Arabic calligraphy.

## A Note on the Transliteration

For the transliteration of Arabic words, the Library of Congress system is used, without diacritical marks except for the " ' ", as in " 'Ajib," which is an "a" pronounced from the back of the throat.

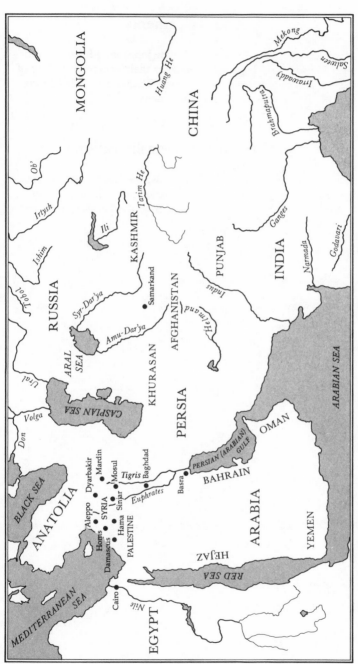

The World of the *Nights*: Places Mentioned in the Stories

الفليلة وليلة

# The
# Arabian Nights

# FOREWORD

In the Name of God the Compassionate, The Merciful.
In Him I Trust

Praise be to God, the Beneficent King, the Creator of the world and man, who raised the heavens without pillars and spread out the earth as a place of rest and erected the mountains as props and made the water flow from the hard rock and destroyed the race of Thamud, 'Ad, and Pharaoh of the vast domain.[1] I praise Him the Supreme Lord for His guidance, and I thank Him for His infinite grace.

To proceed, I should like to inform the honorable gentlemen and noble readers that the purpose of writing this agreeable and entertaining book is the instruction of those who peruse it, for it abounds with highly edifying histories and excellent lessons for the people of distinction, and it provides them with the opportunity to learn the art of discourse, as well as what happened to kings from the beginnings of time. This book, which I have called *The Thousand and One Nights*, abounds also with splendid biographies that teach the reader to detect deception and to protect himself from it, as well as delight and divert him whenever he is burdened with the cares of life and the ills of this world. It is the Supreme God who is the True Guide.

---

1. No specific Egyptian pharaoh is referred to here. Thamud and 'Ad were two neighboring tribes of the Arabian peninsula that were destroyed by natural disasters. They are referred to in pre-Islamic poetry and the Quran, and their destruction is cited as an example of God's wrath against blasphemy.

# PROLOGUE:
## [THE STORY OF KING SHAHRAYAR AND SHAHRAZAD, HIS VIZIER'S DAUGHTER]

It is related — but God knows and sees best what lies hidden in the old accounts of bygone peoples and times — that long ago, during the time of the Sasanid dynasty,[2] in the peninsulas of India and Indochina, there lived two kings who were brothers. The older brother was named Shahrayar, the younger Shahzaman. The older, Shahrayar, was a towering knight and a daring champion, invincible, energetic, and implacable. His power reached the remotest corners of the land and its people, so that the country was loyal to him, and his subjects obeyed him. Shahrayar himself lived and ruled in India and Indochina, while to his brother he gave the land of Samarkand to rule as king.

Ten years went by, when one day Shahrayar felt a longing for his brother the king, summoned his vizier[3] (who had two daughters, one called Shahrazad, the other Dinarzad) and bade him go to his brother. Having made preparations, the vizier journeyed day and night until he reached Samarkand. When Shahzaman heard of the vizier's arrival, he went out with his retainers to meet him. He dismounted, embraced him, and asked him for news from his older brother, Shahrayar. The vizier replied that he was well, and that he had sent him to request his brother to visit him. Shahzaman complied with his brother's request and proceeded to make preparations for the journey. In the meantime, he had the vizier camp on the outskirts of the city, and took care of his needs. He sent him what he required of food and fodder, slaughtered many sheep in his honor, and provided him with money and supplies, as well as many horses and camels.

For ten full days he prepared himself for the journey; then he appointed a chamberlain in his place, and left the city to spend the night in his tent, near the vizier. At midnight he returned to his palace in the city, to bid his wife good-bye. But when he entered the palace, he found his wife lying in the arms of one of the kitchen boys. When he saw them, the world turned dark before his eyes and, shaking his head, he said to himself, "I am still here, and this

---

2. A dynasty of Persian kings who ruled from c. A.D. 226 to 641.
3. The highest state official or administrator under a caliph or a king (literally, "one who bears burdens").

is what she has done when I was barely outside the city. How will it be and what will happen behind my back when I go to visit my brother in India? No. Women are not to be trusted." He got exceedingly angry, adding, "By God, I am king and sovereign in Samarkand, yet my wife has betrayed me and has inflicted this on me." As his anger boiled, he drew his sword and struck both his wife and the cook. Then he dragged them by the heels and threw them from the top of the palace to the trench below. He then left the city and going to the vizier ordered that they depart that very hour. The drum was struck, and they set out on their journey, while Shahzaman's heart was on fire because of what his wife had done to him and how she had betrayed him with some cook, some kitchen boy. They journeyed hurriedly, day and night, through deserts and wilds, until they reached the land of King Shahrayar, who had gone out to receive them.

When Shahrayar met them, he embraced his brother, showed him favors, and treated him generously. He offered him quarters in a palace adjoining his own, for King Shahrayar had built two beautiful towering palaces in his garden, one for the guests, the other for the women and members of his household. He gave the guest house to his brother, Shahzaman, after the attendants had gone to scrub it, dry it, furnish it, and open its windows, which overlooked the garden. Thereafter, Shahzaman would spend the whole day at his brother's, return at night to sleep at the palace, then go back to his brother the next morning. But whenever he found himself alone and thought of his ordeal with his wife, he would sigh deeply, then stifle his grief, and say, "Alas, that this great misfortune should have happened to one in my position!" Then he would fret with anxiety, his spirit would sag, and he would say, "None has seen what I have seen." In his depression, he ate less and less, grew pale, and his health deteriorated. He neglected everything, wasted away, and looked ill.

When King Shahrayar looked at his brother and saw how day after day he lost weight and grew thin, pale, ashen, and sickly, he thought that this was because of his expatriation and homesickness for his country and his family, and he said to himself, "My brother is not happy here. I should prepare a goodly gift for him and send him home." For a month he gathered gifts for his brother; then he invited him to see him and said, "Brother, I would like you to know that I intend to go hunting and pursue the roaming deer, for ten days. Then I shall return to prepare you for your journey home. Would you like to go hunting with me?" Shahzaman replied, "Brother, I feel distracted and depressed. Leave me here and go with God's blessing and help." When Shahrayar heard his brother, he thought that his dejection was because of his homesickness for his country. Not wishing to coerce him, he left him behind, and set out with his retainers and men. When they entered the wilderness, he deployed his men in a circle to begin trapping and hunting.

After his brother's departure, Shahzaman stayed in the palace and, from the window overlooking the garden, watched the birds and trees as he thought of his wife and what she had done to him, and sighed in sorrow. While he agonized over his misfortune, gazing at the heavens and turning a distracted eye on the garden, the private gate of his brother's palace opened, and there emerged, strutting like a dark-eyed deer, the lady, his brother's wife, with twenty slave-girls, ten white and ten black. While Shahzaman looked at them, without being seen, they continued to walk until they stopped below his window, without looking in his direction, thinking that he had gone to the hunt with his brother. Then they sat down, took off their clothes, and suddenly there were ten slave-girls and ten black slaves dressed in the same clothes as the girls. Then the ten black slaves mounted the ten girls, while the lady called, "Mas'ud, Mas'ud!" and a black slave jumped from the tree to the ground, rushed to her, and, raising her legs, went between her thighs and made love to her. Mas'ud topped the lady, while the ten slaves topped the ten girls, and they carried on till noon. When they were done with their business, they got up and washed themselves. Then the ten slaves put on the same clothes again, mingled with the girls, and once more there appeared to be twenty slave-girls. Mas'ud himself jumped over the garden wall and disappeared, while the slave-girls and the lady sauntered to the private gate, went in and, locking the gate behind them, went their way.

All of this happened under King Shahzaman's eyes. When he saw this spectacle of the wife and the women of his brother the great king—how ten slaves put on women's clothes and slept with his brother's paramours and concubines and what Mas'ud did with his brother's wife, in his very palace—and pondered over this calamity and great misfortune, his care and sorrow left him and he said to himself, "This is our common lot. Even though my brother is king and master of the whole world, he cannot protect what is his, his wife and his concubines, and suffers misfortune in his very home. What happened to me is little by comparison. I used to think that I was the only one who has suffered, but from what I have seen, everyone suffers. By God, my misfortune is lighter than that of my brother." He kept marveling and blaming life, whose trials none can escape, and he began to find consolation in his own affliction and forget his grief. When supper came, he ate and drank with relish and zest and, feeling better, kept eating and drinking, enjoying himself and feeling happy. He thought to himself, "I am no longer alone in my misery; I am well."

For ten days, he continued to enjoy his food and drink, and when his brother, King Shahrayar, came back from the hunt, he met him happily, treated him attentively, and greeted him cheerfully. His brother, King Shahrayar, who had missed him, said, "By God, brother, I missed you on this trip and wished you were with me." Shahzaman thanked him and sat down to carouse with him, and when night fell, and food was brought before them, the two ate and drank, and again Shahzaman ate and drank with zest. As time went by, he continued to eat and drink with appetite, and became lighthearted and carefree. His face regained color and became ruddy, and his body gained weight, as his blood circulated and he regained his energy; he was himself again, or even better. King Shahrayar noticed his brother's condition, how he used to be and how he had improved, but kept it to himself until he took him aside one day and said, "My brother Shahzaman, I would like you to do something for me, to satisfy a wish, to answer a question truthfully." Shahzaman asked, "What is it, brother?" He replied, "When you first came to stay with me, I noticed that you kept losing weight, day after day, until your looks changed, your health deteriorated, and your energy sagged. As you continued like this, I thought that what ailed you was your homesickness for your family and your country, but even though I kept noticing that you were wasting away and looking ill, I refrained from questioning you and hid my feelings from you. Then I went hunting, and when I came back, I found that you had recovered and had regained your health. Now I want you to tell me everything and to explain the cause of your deterioration and the cause of your subsequent recovery, without hiding anything from me." When Shahzaman heard what King Shahrayar said, he bowed his head, then said, "As for the cause of my recovery, that I cannot tell you, and I wish that you would excuse me from telling you." The king was greatly astonished at his brother's reply and, burning with curiosity, said, "You must tell me. For now, at least, explain the first cause."

Then Shahzaman related to his brother what happened to him with his own wife, on the night of his departure, from beginning to end, and concluded, "Thus all the while I was with you, great King, whenever I thought of the event and the misfortune that had befallen me, I felt troubled, careworn, and unhappy, and my health deteriorated. This then is the cause." Then he grew silent. When King Shahrayar heard his brother's explanation, he shook his head, greatly amazed at the deceit of women, and prayed to God to protect him from their wickedness, saying, "Brother, you were fortunate in killing your wife and her lover, who gave you good reason to feel troubled, careworn, and ill. In my opinion, what happened to you has never happened to anyone else. By God, had I been in your place, I would have killed at least a hundred or even a thousand women. I would have been furious; I would have gone mad. Now praise be to God who has delivered you from sorrow and distress. But tell me what has caused you to forget your sorrow and regain your health?" Shahzaman replied, "King, I wish that for God's sake you would excuse me from telling you." Shahrayar said, "You must." Shahzaman replied, "I fear that you will feel even more troubled and careworn than I." Shahrayar asked, "How could that be, brother? I insist on hearing your explanation."

Shahzaman then told him about what he had seen from the palace window and the calamity in his very home—how ten slaves, dressed like women, were sleeping with his women and concubines, day and night. He told him everything from beginning to end (but there is no point in repeating that). Then he concluded, "When I saw your own misfortune, I felt better—and said to myself, 'My brother is king of the world, yet such a misfortune has happened to him, and in his very home.' As a result I forgot my care and sorrow, relaxed, and began to eat and drink. This is the cause of my cheer and good spirits."

When King Shahrayar heard what his brother said and found out what had happened to him, he was furious and his blood boiled. He said, "Brother, I can't believe what you say unless I see it with my own eyes." When Shahzaman saw that his brother was in a rage, he said to him, "If you do not believe me, unless you see your misfortune with your own eyes, announce that you plan to go hunting. Then you and I shall set out with your troops, and when we get outside the city, we shall leave our tents and camp with the men behind, enter the city secretly, and go together to your palace. Then the next morning you can see with your own eyes."

King Shahrayar realized that his brother had a good plan and ordered his army to prepare for the trip. He spent the night with his brother, and when God's morning broke, the two rode out of the city with their army, preceded by the camp attendants, who had gone to drive the poles and pitch the tents where the king and his army were to camp. At nightfall King Shahrayar summoned his chief chamberlain and bade him take his place. He entrusted him with the army and ordered that for three days no one was to enter the city. Then he and his brother disguised themselves and entered the city in the dark. They went directly to the palace where Shahzaman resided and slept there till the morning. When they awoke, they sat at the palace window, watching the garden and chatting, until the light broke, the day dawned, and the sun rose. As they watched, the private gate opened, and there emerged as usual the wife of King Shahrayar, walking among twenty slave-girls. They made their way under the trees until they stood below the palace window where the two kings sat. Then they took off their women's clothes, and suddenly there were ten slaves, who mounted the ten girls and made love to them. As for the lady, she called, "Mas'ud, Mas'ud," and a black slave jumped from the tree to the ground, came to her, and said, "What do you want, you slut? Here is Sa'ad al-Din Mas'ud." She laughed and fell on her back, while the slave mounted her and like the others did his business with her. Then the black slaves got up, washed themselves, and, putting on the same clothes, mingled with the girls. Then they walked away, entered the palace, and locked the gate behind them. As for Mas'ud, he jumped over the fence to the road and went on his way.

When King Shahrayar saw the spectacle of his wife and the slave-girls, he went out of his mind, and when he and his brother came down from upstairs, he said, "No one is safe in this world. Such doings are going on in my kingdom, and in my very palace. Perish the world and perish life! This is a great calamity, indeed." Then he turned to his brother and asked, "Would you like to follow me in what I shall do?" Shahzaman answered, "Yes. I will." Shahrayar said, "Let us leave our royal state and roam the world for the love of the Supreme Lord. If we should find one whose misfortune is greater than ours, we shall return. Otherwise, we shall continue to journey through the land, without need for the trappings of royalty." Shahzaman replied, "This is an excellent idea. I shall follow you."

Then they left by the private gate, took a side road, and departed, journeying till nightfall. They slept over their sorrows, and in the morning resumed their day journey until they came to a meadow by the seashore. While they sat in the meadow amid the thick plants and trees, discussing their misfortunes and the recent events, they suddenly heard a shout and a great cry coming from the middle of the sea. They trembled with fear, thinking that the sky had fallen on the earth. Then the sea parted, and there emerged a black pillar that, as it swayed forward, got taller and taller, until it touched the clouds. Shahrayar and Shahzaman were petrified; then they ran in terror and, climbing a very tall tree, sat hiding in its foliage. When they looked again, they saw that the black pillar was cleaving the sea, wading in the water toward the green meadow, until it touched the shore. When they looked again, they saw that it was a black demon, carrying on his head a large glass chest with four steel locks. He came out, walked into the meadow, and where should he stop but under the very tree where the two kings were hiding. The demon sat down and placed the glass chest on the ground. He took out four keys and, opening the locks of the chest, pulled out a full-grown woman. She had a beautiful figure, and a face like the full moon, and a lovely smile. He took her out, laid her under the tree, and looked at her, saying, "Mistress of all noble women, you whom I carried away on your wedding night, I would like to sleep a little." Then he placed his head on the young woman's lap, stretched his legs to the sea, sank into sleep, and began to snore.

Meanwhile, the woman looked up at the tree and, turning her head by chance, saw King Shahrayar and King Shahzaman. She lifted the demon's head from her lap and placed it on the ground. Then she came and stood under the tree and motioned to them with her hand, as if to say, "Come down slowly to me." When they realized that she had seen them, they were frightened, and they begged her and implored her, in the name of the Creator of the heavens, to excuse them from climbing down. She replied, "You must come down to me." They motioned to her, saying, "This sleeping demon is the enemy of mankind. For God's sake, leave us alone." She replied, "You must come down, and if you don't, I shall wake the demon and have him kill you." She kept gesturing and pressing, until they climbed down very slowly and stood before her. Then she lay on her back, raised her legs, and said, "Make love to me and satisfy my need, or else I shall wake the demon, and he will kill you." They replied, "For God's sake, mistress, don't do this to us, for at this moment we feel nothing but dismay and fear of this demon. Please, excuse us." She replied, "You must," and insisted, swearing, "By God who created the heavens, if you don't do it, I shall wake my husband the demon and ask him to kill you and throw you into the sea." As she persisted, they could no longer resist and they made love to her, first the older brother, then the younger. When they were done and withdrew from her, she said to them, "Give me your rings," and, pulling out from the folds of her dress a small purse, opened it, and shook out ninety-eight rings of different fashions and colors. Then she asked them, "Do you know what these rings are?" They answered, "No." She said, "All the owners of these rings slept with me, for whenever one of them made love to me, I took a ring from him. Since you two have slept with me, give me your rings, so that I may add them to the rest, and make a full hundred. A hundred men have known me under the very horns of this filthy, monstrous cuckold, who has imprisoned me in this chest, locked it with four locks, and kept me in the middle of this raging, roaring sea. He has guarded me and tried to keep me pure and chaste, not realizing that nothing can prevent or alter what is predestined and that when a woman desires something, no one can stop her." When Shahrayar and Shahzaman heard what the young woman said, they were greatly amazed, danced with joy, and said, 'O God, O God! There is no power and no strength, save in God the Almighty, the Magnificent. 'Great is women's cunning.'" Then each of them took off his ring and handed it to her. She took them and put them with the rest in the purse. Then sitting again by the demon, she lifted his head, placed it back on her lap, and motioned to them, "Go on your way, or else I shall wake him."

They turned their backs and took to the road. Then Shahrayar turned to his brother and said, "My brother Shahzaman, look at this sorry plight. By God, it is worse than ours. This is no less than a demon who has carried a young woman away on her wedding night, imprisoned her in a glass chest, locked her up with four locks, and kept her in the middle of the sea, thinking that he could guard her from what God had foreordained, and you saw how she has managed to sleep with ninety-eight men, and added the two of us to make a hundred. Brother, let us go back to our kingdoms and our cities, never to marry a woman again. As for myself, I shall show you what I will do."

Then the two brothers headed home and journeyed till nightfall. On the morning of the third day, they reached their camp and men, entered their tent, and sat on their thrones. The chamberlains, deputies, princes, and viziers came to attend King Shahrayar, while he gave orders and bestowed robes of honor, as well as other gifts. Then at his command everyone returned to the city, and he went to his own palace and ordered his chief vizier, the father of the two girls Shahrazad and Dinarzad, who will be mentioned below, and said to him, "Take that wife of mine and put her to death." Then Shahrayar went to her himself, bound her, and handed her over to the vizier, who took her out and put her to death. Then King Shahrayar grabbed his sword, brandished it, and, entering the palace chambers, killed every one of his slave-girls and replaced them with others. He then swore to marry for one night only and kill the woman the next morning, in order to save himself from the wickedness and cunning of women, saying, "There is not a single chaste woman anywhere on the entire face of the earth." Shortly thereafter he provided his brother Shahzaman with supplies for his journey and sent him back to his own country with gifts, rarities, and money. The brother bade him good-bye and set out for home.

Shahrayar sat on his throne and ordered his vizier, the father of the two girls, to find him a wife from among the princes' daughters. The vizier found him one, and he slept with her and was done with her, and the next morning he ordered the vizier to put her to death. That very night he took one of his army officers' daughters, slept with her, and the next morning ordered the vizier to put her to death. The vizier, who could not disobey him, put her to death. The third night he took one of the merchants' daughters, slept with her till the morning, then ordered his vizier to put her to death, and the vizier did so. It became King Shahrayar's custom to take every night the daughter of a merchant or a commoner, spend the night with her, then have her put to death the next morning. He continued to do this until all the girls perished, their mothers mourned, and there arose a clamor among the fathers and mothers, who called the plague upon his head, complained to the Creator of the heavens, and called for help on Him who hears and answers prayers.

Now, as mentioned earlier, the vizier, who put the girls to death, had an older daughter called Shahrazad and a younger one called Dinarzad. The older daughter, Shahrazad, had read the books of literature, philosophy, and medicine. She knew poetry by heart, had studied historical reports, and was acquainted with the sayings of men and the maxims of sages and kings. She was intelligent, knowledgeable, wise, and refined. She had read and learned. One day she said to her father, "Father, I will tell you what is in my mind." He asked, "What is it?" She answered, "I would like you to marry me to King Shahrayar, so that I may either succeed in saving the people or perish and die like the rest." When the vizier heard what his daughter Shahrazad said, he got angry and said to her, "Foolish one, don't you know that King Shahrayar has sworn to spend but one night with a girl and have her put to death the next morning? If I give you to him, he will sleep with you for one night and will ask me to put you to death the next morning, and I shall have to do it, since I cannot disobey him." She said, "Father, you must give me to him, even if he kills me." He asked, "What has possessed you that you wish to imperil yourself?" She replied, "Father, you must give me to him. This is absolute and final." Her father the vizier became furious and said to her, "Daughter, 'He who misbehaves, ends up in trouble,' and 'He who considers not the end, the world is not his friend.' As the popular saying goes, 'I would be sitting pretty, but for my curiosity.' I am afraid that what happened to the donkey and the ox with the merchant will happen to you." She asked, "Father, what happened to the donkey, the ox, and the merchant?" He said:

# [The Tale of the Ox and the Donkey]

There was a prosperous and wealthy merchant who lived in the countryside and labored on a farm. He owned many camels and herds of cattle and employed many men, and he had a wife and many grown-up as well as little children. This merchant was taught the language of the beasts, on condition that if he revealed his secret to anyone, he would die; therefore, even though he knew the language of every kind of animal, he did not let anyone know, for fear of death. One day, as he sat, with his wife beside him and his children playing before him, he glanced at an ox and a donkey he kept at the farmhouse, tied to adjacent troughs, and heard the ox say to the donkey, "Watchful one, I hope that you are enjoying the comfort and the service you are getting. Your ground is swept and watered, and they serve you, feed you sifted barley, and offer you clear, cool water to drink. I, on the contrary, am taken out to plow in the middle of the night. They clamp on my neck something they call yoke and plow, push me all day under the whip to plow the field, and drive me beyond my endurance until my sides are lacerated, and my neck is flayed. They work me from nighttime to nighttime, take me back in the dark, offer me beans soiled with mud and hay mixed with chaff, and let me spend the night lying in urine and dung. Meanwhile you rest on well-swept, watered, and smoothed ground, with a clean trough full of hay. You stand in comfort, save for the rare occasion when our master the merchant rides you to do a brief errand and returns. You are comfortable, while I am weary; you sleep, while I keep awake."

When the ox finished, the donkey turned to him and said, "Greenhorn, they were right in calling you ox, for you ox harbor no deceit, malice, or meanness. Being sincere, you exert and exhaust yourself to comfort others. Have you not heard the saying 'Out of bad luck, they hastened on the road'? You go into the field from early morning to endure your torture at the plow to the point of exhaustion. When the plowman takes you back and ties you to the trough, you go on butting and beating with your horns, kicking with your hoofs, and bellowing for the beans, until they toss them to you; then you begin to eat. Next time, when they bring them to you, don't eat or even touch them, but smell them, then draw back and lie down on the hay and straw. If you do this, life will be better and kinder to you, and you will find relief."

As the ox listened, he was sure that the donkey had given him good advice. He thanked him, commended him to God, and invoked His blessing on him, and said, "May you stay safe from harm, watchful one." All of this conversation took place, daughter, while the merchant listened and understood. On the following day, the plowman came to the merchant's house and, taking the ox, placed the yoke upon his neck and worked him at the plow, but the ox lagged behind. The plowman hit him, but following the donkey's advice, the ox, dissembling, fell on his belly, and the plowman hit him again. Thus the ox kept getting up and falling until nightfall, when the plowman took him home and tied him to the trough. But this time the ox did not bellow or kick the ground with his hoofs. Instead, he withdrew, away from the trough. Astonished, the plowman brought him his beans and fodder, but the ox only smelled the fodder and pulled back and lay down at a distance with the hay and straw, complaining till the morning. When the plowman arrived, he found the trough as he had left it, full of beans and fodder, and saw the ox lying on his back, hardly breathing, his belly puffed, and his legs raised in the air. The plowman felt sorry for him and said to himself, "By God, he did seem weak and unable to work." Then he went to the merchant and said, "Master, last night, the ox refused to eat or touch his fodder."

The merchant, who knew what was going on, said to the plowman, "Go to the wily donkey, put him to the plow, and work him hard until he finishes the ox's task." The plowman left, took the donkey, and placed the yoke upon his neck. Then he took him out to the field and drove him with blows until he finished the ox's work, all the while driving him with blows and beating him until his sides were lacerated and his neck was flayed. At nightfall he took him home, barely able to drag his legs under his tired body and his drooping ears. Meanwhile the ox spent his day resting. He ate all his food, drank his water, and lay quietly, chewing his cud in comfort. All day long he kept praising the donkey's advice and invoking God's blessing on him. When the donkey came back at night, the ox stood up to greet him, saying, "Good evening, watchful one! You have done me a favor beyond description, for I have been sitting in comfort. God bless you for my sake." Seething with anger, the donkey did not reply, but said to himself, "All this happened to me because of my miscalculation. 'I would be sitting pretty, but for my curiosity.' If I don't find a way to return this ox to his former situation, I will perish." Then he went to his trough and lay down, while the ox continued to chew his cud and invoke God's blessing on him.

"You, my daughter, will likewise perish because of your miscalculation. Desist, sit quietly, and don't expose yourself to peril. I advise you out of compassion for you." She replied, "Father, I must go to the king, and you must give me to him." He said, "Don't do it." She insisted, "I must." He replied, "If you don't desist, I will do to you what the merchant did to his wife." She asked, "Father, what did the merchant do to his wife?" He said:

# [The Tale of the Merchant and His Wife]

After what had happened to the donkey and the ox, the merchant and his wife went out in the moonlight to the stable, and he heard the donkey ask the ox in his own language, "Listen, ox, what are you going to do tomorrow morning, and what will you do when the plowman brings you your fodder?" The ox replied, "What shall I do but follow your advice and stick to it? If he brings me my fodder, I will pretend to be ill, lie down, and puff my belly." The donkey shook his head, and said, "Don't do it. Do you know what I heard our master the merchant say to the plowman?" The ox asked, "What?" The donkey replied, "He said that if the ox failed to get up and eat his fodder, he would call the butcher to slaughter him and skin him and would distribute the meat for alms and use the skin for a mat. I am afraid for you, but good advice is a matter of faith; therefore, if he brings you your fodder, eat it and look alert lest they cut your throat and skin you." The ox farted and bellowed.

The merchant got up and laughed loudly at the conversation between the donkey and the ox, and his wife asked him, "What are you laughing at? Are you making fun of me?" He said, "No." She said, "Tell me what made you laugh." He replied, "I cannot tell you. I am afraid to disclose the secret conversation of the animals." She asked, "And what prevents you from telling me?" He answered, "The fear of death." His wife said, "By God, you are lying. This is nothing but an excuse. I swear by God, the Lord of heaven, that if you don't tell me and explain the cause of your laughter, I will leave you. You must tell me." Then she went back to the house crying, and she continued to cry till the morning. The merchant said, "Damn it! Tell me why you are crying. Ask for God's forgiveness, and stop questioning and leave me in peace." She said, "I insist and will not desist." Amazed at her, he replied, "You insist! If I tell you what the donkey said to the ox, which made me laugh, I shall die." She said, "Yes, I insist, even if you have to die." He replied, "Then call your family," and she called their two daughters, her parents and relatives, and some neighbors. The merchant told them that he was about to die, and everyone, young and old, his children, the farmhands, and the servants began to cry until the house became a place of mourning. Then he summoned legal witnesses, wrote a will, leaving his wife and children their due portions, freed his slave-girls, and bid his family good-bye, while everybody, even the witnesses, wept. Then the wife's parents approached her and said, "Desist, for if your husband had not known for certain that he would die if he revealed his secret, he wouldn't have gone through all this." She replied, "I will not change my mind," and everybody cried and prepared to mourn his death.

Well, my daughter Shahrazad, it happened that the farmer kept
fifty hens and a rooster at home, and while he felt sad to depart
this world and leave his children and relatives behind, pondering
and about to reveal and utter his secret, he overheard a dog of his
say something in dog language to the rooster, who, beating and
clapping his wings, had jumped on a hen and, finishing with her,
jumped down and jumped on another. The merchant heard and
understood what the dog said in his own language to the rooster,
"Shameless, no-good rooster. Aren't you ashamed to do such a thing
on a day like this?" The rooster asked, "What is special about this
day?" The dog replied, "Don't you know that our master and friend
is in mourning today? His wife is demanding that he disclose his
secret, and when he discloses it, he will surely die. He is in this
predicament, about to interpret to her the language of the animals,
and all of us are mourning for him, while you clap your wings and
get off one hen and jump on another. Aren't you ashamed?" The
merchant heard the rooster reply, "You fool, you lunatic! Our
master and friend claims to be wise, but he is foolish, for he has
only one wife, yet he does not know how to manage her." The dog
asked, "What should he do with her?"

The rooster replied, "He should take an oak branch, push her
into a room, lock the door, and fall on her with the stick, beating
her mercilessly until he breaks her arms and legs and she cries out,
'I no longer want you to tell me or explain anything.' He should
go on beating her until he cures her for life, and she will never
oppose him in anything. If he does this, he will live, and live in
peace, and there will be no more grief, but he does not know how
to manage." Well, my daughter Shahrazad, when the merchant
heard the conversation between the dog and the rooster, he jumped
up and, taking an oak branch, pushed his wife into a room, got
in with her, and locked the door. Then he began to beat her mercilessly on her chest and shoulders and kept beating her until she cried
for mercy, screaming, "No, no, I don't want to know anything.
Leave me alone, leave me alone. I don't want to know anything,"
until he got tired of hitting her and opened the door. The wife
emerged penitent, the husband learned good management, and
everybody was happy, and the mourning turned into a celebration.

"If you don't relent, I shall do to you what the merchant did to
his wife." She said, "Such tales don't deter me from my request.
If you wish, I can tell you many such tales. In the end, if you don't
take me to King Shahrayar, I shall go to him by myself behind your
back and tell him that you have refused to give me to one like him
and that you have begrudged your master one like me." The vizier
asked, "Must you really do this?" She replied, "Yes, I must."

Tired and exhausted, the vizier went to King Shahrayar and, kissing the ground before him, told him about his daughter, adding that he would give her to him that very night. The king was astonished and said to him, "Vizier, how is it that you have found it possible to give me your daughter, knowing that I will, by God, the Creator of heaven, ask you to put her to death the next morning and that if you refuse, I will have you put to death too?" He replied, "My King and Lord, I have told her everything and explained all this to her, but she refuses and insists on being with you tonight." The king was delighted and said, "Go to her, prepare her, and bring her to me early in the evening."

The vizier went down, repeated the king's message to his daughter, and said, "May God not deprive me of you." She was very happy and, after preparing herself and packing what she needed, went to her younger sister, Dinarzad, and said, "Sister, listen well to what I am telling you. When I go to the king, I will send for you, and when you come and see that the king has finished with me, say, 'Sister, if you are not sleepy, tell us a story.' Then I will begin to tell a story, and it will cause the king to stop his practice, save myself, and deliver the people." Dinarzad replied, "Very well."

At nightfall the vizier took Shahrazad and went with her to the great King Shahrayar. But when Shahrayar took her to bed and began to fondle her, she wept, and when he asked her, "Why are you crying?" she replied, "I have a sister, and I wish to bid her goodbye before daybreak." Then the king sent for the sister, who came and went to sleep under the bed. When the night wore on, she woke up and waited until the king had satisfied himself with her sister Shahrazad and they were by now all fully awake. Then Dinarzad cleared her throat and said, "Sister, if you are not sleepy, tell us one of your lovely little tales to while away the night, before I bid you good-bye at daybreak, for I don't know what will happen to you tomorrow." Shahrazad turned to King Shahrayar and said, "May I have your permission to tell a story?" He replied, "Yes," and Shahrazad was very happy and said, "Listen":

THE FIRST NIGHT

# [THE STORY OF THE MERCHANT AND THE DEMON]

It is said, O wise and happy King, that once there was a prosperous merchant who had abundant wealth and investments and commitments in every country. He had many women and children and kept many servants and slaves. One day, having resolved to visit another country, he took provisions, filling his saddlebag with loaves of bread and with dates, mounted his horse, and set out on his journey. For many days and nights, he journeyed under God's care until he reached his destination. When he finished his business, he turned back to his home and family. He journeyed for three days, and on the fourth day, chancing to come to an orchard, went in to avoid the heat and shade himself from the sun of the open country. He came to a spring under a walnut tree and, tying his horse, sat by the spring, pulled out from the saddlebag some loaves of bread and a handful of dates, and began to eat, throwing the date pits right and left until he had had enough. Then he got up, performed his ablutions, and performed his prayers.

But hardly had he finished when he saw an old demon, with sword in hand, standing with his feet on the ground and his head in the clouds. The demon approached until he stood before him and screamed, saying, "Get up, so that I may kill you with this sword, just as you have killed my son." When the merchant saw and heard the demon, he was terrified and awestricken. He asked, "Master, for what crime do you wish to kill me?" The demon replied, "I wish to kill you because you have killed my son." The merchant asked, "Who has killed your son?" The demon replied, "You have killed my son." The merchant said, "By God, I did not kill your son. When and how could that have been?" The demon said, "Didn't you sit down, take out some dates from your saddlebag, and eat, throwing the pits right and left?" The merchant replied, "Yes, I did." The demon said, "You killed my son, for as you were throwing the stones right and left, my son happened to be walking by and was struck and killed by one of them, and I must now kill you." The merchant said, "O my lord, please don't kill me." The demon replied, "I must kill you as you killed him — blood for blood." The merchant said, "To God we belong and to God we turn. There is no power or

strength, save in God the Almighty, the Magnificent. If I killed
him, I did it by mistake. Please forgive me." The demon replied,
"By God, I must kill you, as you killed my son." Then he seized
him and, throwing him to the ground, raised the sword to strike
him. The merchant began to weep and mourn his family and his
wife and children. Again, the demon raised his sword to strike, while
the merchant cried until he was drenched with tears, saying, "There
is no power or strength, save in God the Almighty, the Magnificent." Then he began to recite the following verses:

> Life has two days: one peace, one wariness,
> And has two sides: worry and happiness.
> Ask him who taunts us with adversity,
> "Does fate, save those worthy of note, oppress?
> Don't you see that the blowing, raging storms
> Only the tallest of the trees beset,
> And of earth's many green and barren lots,
> Only the ones with fruits with stones are hit,
> And of the countless stars in heaven's vault
> None is eclipsed except the moon and sun?
> You thought well of the days, when they were good,
> Oblivious to the ills destined for one.
> You were deluded by the peaceful nights,
> Yet in the peace of night does sorrow stun."

When the merchant finished and stopped weeping, the demon said,
"By God, I must kill you, as you killed my son, even if you weep
blood." The merchant asked, "Must you?" The demon replied, "I
must," and raised his sword to strike.

*But morning overtook Shahrazad, and she lapsed into silence,
leaving King Shahrayar burning with curiosity to hear the rest of
the story. Then Dinarzad said to her sister Shahrazad, "What a
strange and lovely story!" Shahrazad replied, "What is this compared with what I shall tell you tomorrow night if the king spares
me and lets me live? It will be even better and more entertaining."
The king thought to himself, "I will spare her until I hear the rest
of the story; then I will have her put to death the next day." When
morning broke, the day dawned, and the sun rose; the king left
to attend to the affairs of the kingdom, and the vizier, Shahrazad's
father, was amazed and delighted. King Shahrayar governed all
day and returned home at night to his quarters and got into bed
with Shahrazad. Then Dinarzad said to her sister Shahrazad,
"Please, sister, if you are not sleepy, tell us one of your lovely little
tales to while away the night." The king added, "Let it be the conclusion of the story of the demon and the merchant, for I would*

*like to hear it." Shahrazad replied, "With the greatest pleasure, dear, happy King":*

## THE SECOND NIGHT

It is related, O wise and happy King, that when the demon raised his sword, the merchant asked the demon again, "Must you kill me?" and the demon replied, "Yes." Then the merchant said, "Please give me time to say good-bye to my family and my wife and children, divide my property among them, and appoint guardians. Then I shall come back, so that you may kill me." The demon replied, "I am afraid that if I release you and grant you time, you will go and do what you wish, but will not come back." The merchant said, "I swear to keep my pledge to come back, as the God of Heaven and earth is my witness." The demon asked, "How much time do you need?" The merchant replied, "One year, so that I may see enough of my children, bid my wife good-bye, discharge my obligations to people, and come back on New Year's Day." The demon asked, "Do you swear to God that if I let you go, you will come back on New Year's Day?" The merchant replied, "Yes, I swear to God."

After the merchant swore, the demon released him, and he mounted his horse sadly and went on his way. He journeyed until he reached his home and came to his wife and children. When he saw them, he wept bitterly, and when his family saw his sorrow and grief, they began to reproach him for his behavior, and his wife said, "Husband, what is the matter with you? Why do you mourn, when we are happy, celebrating your return?" He replied, "Why not mourn when I have only one year to live?" Then he told her of his encounter with the demon and informed her that he had sworn to return on New Year's Day, so that the demon might kill him.

When they heard what he said, everyone began to cry. His wife struck her face in lamentation and cut her hair, his daughters wailed, and his little children cried. It was a day of mourning, as all the children gathered around their father to weep and exchange good-byes. The next day he wrote his will, dividing his property, discharged his obligations to people, left bequests and gifts, distributed alms, and engaged reciters to read portions of the Quran in his house. Then he summoned legal witnesses and in their presence freed his slaves and slave-girls, divided among his elder children their shares of the property, appointed guardians for his little ones, and gave his wife her share, according to her marriage contract.

He spent the rest of the time with his family, and when the year came to an end, save for the time needed for the journey, he performed his ablutions, performed his prayers, and, carrying his burial shroud, began to bid his family good-bye. His sons hung around his neck, his daughters wept, and his wife wailed. Their mourning scared him, and he began to weep, as he embraced and kissed his children good-bye. He said to them, "Children, this is God's will and decree, for man was created to die." Then he turned away and, mounting his horse, journeyed day and night until he reached the orchard on New Year's Day.

He sat at the place where he had eaten the dates, waiting for the demon, with a heavy heart and tearful eyes. As he waited, an old man, leading a deer on a leash, approached and greeted him, and he returned the greeting. The old man inquired, "Friend, why do you sit here in this place of demons and devils? For in this haunted orchard none come to good." The merchant replied by telling him what had happened to him and the demon, from beginning to end. The old man was amazed at the merchant's fidelity and said, "Yours ia a magnificent pledge," adding, "By God, I shall not leave until I see what will happen to you with the demon." Then he sat down beside him and chatted with him. As they talked . . .

*But morning overtook Shahrazad, and she lapsed into silence. As the day dawned, and it was light, her sister Dinarzad said, "What a strange and wonderful story!" Shahrazad replied, "Tomorrow night I shall tell something even stranger and more wonderful than this."*

### THE THIRD NIGHT

*When it was night and Shahrazad was in bed with the king, Dinarzad said to her sister Shahrazad, "Please, if you are not sleepy, tell us one of your lovely little tales to while away the night." The king added, "Let it be the conclusion of the merchant's story." Shahrazad replied, "As you wish":*

I heard, O happy King, that as the merchant and the man with the deer sat talking, another old man approached, with two black hounds, and when he reached them, he greeted them, and they returned his greeting. Then he asked them about themselves, and the man with the deer told him the story of the merchant and the demon, how the merchant had sworn to return on New Year's Day, and how the demon was waiting to kill him. He added that when he himself heard the story, he swore never to leave until he saw what would happen between the merchant and the demon. When the man with the two dogs heard the story, he was amazed, and he too swore never to leave them until he saw what would happen between them. Then he questioned the merchant, and the merchant repeated to him what had happened to him with the demon.

While they were engaged in conversation, a third old man approached and greeted them, and they returned his greeting. He asked, "Why do I see the two of you sitting here, with this merchant between you, looking abject, sad, and dejected?" They told him the merchant's story and explained that they were sitting and waiting to see what would happen to him with the demon. When he heard the story, he sat down with them, saying, "By God, I too like you will not leave, until I see what happens to this man with the demon." As they sat, conversing with one another, they suddenly saw the dust rising from the open country, and when it cleared, they saw the demon approaching, with a drawn steel sword in his hand. He stood before them without greeting them, yanked the merchant with his left hand, and, holding him fast before him, said, "Get ready to die." The merchant and the three old men began to weep and wail.

*But dawn broke and morning overtook Shahrazad, and she lapsed into silence. Then Dinarzad said, "Sister, what a lovely story!" Shahrazad replied, "What is this compared with what I shall tell you tomorrow night? It will be even better; it will be more wonderful, delightful, entertaining, and delectable if the king spares me and lets me live." The king was all curiosity to hear the rest of the story and said to himself, "By God, I will not have her put to death until I hear the rest of the story and find out what happened to the merchant with the demon. Then I will have her put to death the next morning, as I did with the others." Then he went out to attend to the affairs of his kingdom, and when he saw Shahrazad's father, he treated him kindly and showed him favors, and the vizier was amazed. When night came, the king went home, and when he was in bed with Shahrazad, Dinarzad said, "Sister, if you are not sleepy, tell us one of your lovely little tales to while away the night." Shahrazad replied, "With the greatest pleasure":*

It is related, O happy King, that the first old man with the deer
approached the demon and, kissing his hands and feet, said, "Fiend
and King of the demon kings, if I tell you what happened to me
and that deer, and you find it strange and amazing, indeed stranger
and more amazing than what happened to you and the merchant,
will you grant me a third of your claim on him for his crime and
guilt?" The demon replied, "I will." The old man said:

## [The First Old Man's Tale]

Demon, this deer is my cousin, my flesh and blood. I married her
when I was very young, and she a girl of twelve, who reached
womanhood only afterward. For thirty years we lived together, but
I was not blessed with children, for she bore neither boy nor girl.
Yet I continued to be kind to her, to care for her, and to treat her
generously. Then I took a mistress, and she bore me a son, who
grew up to look like a slice of the moon. Meanwhile, my wife grew
jealous of my mistress and my son. One day, when he was ten,
I had to go on a journey. I entrusted my wife, this one here, with
my mistress and son, bade her take good care of them, and was
gone for a whole year. In my absence my wife, this cousin of mine,
learned soothsaying and magic and cast a spell on my son and
turned him into a young bull. Then she summoned my shepherd,
gave my son to him, and said, "Tend this bull with the rest of the
cattle." The shepherd took him and tended him for a while. Then
she cast a spell on the mother, turning her into a cow, and gave
her also to the shepherd.

When I came back, after all this was done, and inquired about
my mistress and my son, she answered, "Your mistress died, and
your son ran away two months ago, and I have had no news from
him ever since." When I heard her, I grieved for my mistress, and
with an anguished heart I mourned for my son for nearly a year.
When the Great Feast of the Immolation[4] drew near, I summoned
the shepherd and ordered him to bring me a fat cow for the sacrifice.
The cow he brought me was in reality my enchanted mistress. When
I bound her and pressed against her to cut her throat, she wept
and cried, as if saying, "My son, my son," and her tears coursed

---

4. A four-day Muslim feast that celebrates the pilgrimage to Mecca and that is marked by the
slaughtering of sheep and cattle as sacrificial offerings to God.

down her cheeks. Astonished and seized with pity, I turned away and asked the shepherd to bring me a different cow. But my wife shouted, "Go on. Butcher her, for he has none better or fatter. Let us enjoy her meat at feast time." I approached the cow to cut her throat, and again she cried, as if saying, "My son, my son." Then I turned away from her and said to the shepherd, "Butcher her for me." The shepherd butchered her, and when he skinned her, he found neither meat nor fat but only skin and bone. I regretted having her butchered and said to the shepherd, "Take her all for yourself, or give her as alms to whomever you wish, and find me a fat young bull from among the flock." The shepherd took her away and disappeared, and I never knew what he did with her.

Then he brought me my son, my heartblood, in the guise of a fat young bull. When my son saw me, he shook his head loose from the rope, ran toward me, and, throwing himself at my feet, kept rubbing his head against me. I was astonished and touched with sympathy, pity, and mercy, for the blood hearkened to the blood and the divine bond, and my heart throbbed within me when I saw the tears coursing over the cheeks of my son the young bull, as he dug the earth with his hoofs. I turned away and said to the shepherd, "Let him go with the rest of the flock, and be kind to him, for I have decided to spare him. Bring me another one instead of him." My wife, this very deer, shouted, "You shall sacrifice none but this bull." I got angry and replied, "I listened to you and butchered the cow uselessly. I will not listen to you and kill this bull, for I have decided to spare him." But she pressed me, saying, "You must butcher this bull," and I bound him and took the knife . . .

*But dawn broke, and morning overtook Shahrazad, and she lapsed into silence, leaving the king all curiosity for the rest of the story. Then her sister Dinarzad said, "What an entertaining story!" Shahrazad replied, "Tomorrow night I shall tell you something even stranger, more wonderful, and more entertaining if the king spares me and lets me live."*

THE FIFTH NIGHT

*The following night, Dinarzad said to her sister Shahrazad, "Please, sister, if you are not sleepy, tell us one of your little tales." Shahrazad replied, "With the greatest pleasure":*

I heard, dear King, that the old man with the deer said to the demon and to his companions:

I took the knife and as I turned to slaughter my son, he wept, bellowed, rolled at my feet, and motioned toward me with his tongue. I suspected something, began to waver with trepidation and pity, and finally released him, saying to my wife, "I have decided to spare him, and I commit him to your care." Then I tried to appease and please my wife, this very deer, by slaughtering another bull, promising her to slaughter this one next season. We slept that night, and when God's dawn broke, the shepherd came to me without letting my wife know, and said, "Give me credit for bringing you good news." I replied, "Tell me, and the credit is yours." He said, "Master, I have a daughter who is fond of soothsaying and magic and who is adept at the art of oaths and spells. Yesterday I took home with me the bull you had spared, to let him graze with the cattle, and when my daughter saw him, she laughed and cried at the same time. When I asked her why she laughed and cried, she answered that she laughed because the bull was in reality the son of our master the cattle owner, put under a spell by his stepmother, and that she cried because his father had slaughtered the son's mother. I could hardly wait till daybreak to bring you the good news about your son."

Demon, when I heard that, I uttered a cry and fainted, and when I came to myself, I accompanied the shepherd to his home, went to my son, and threw myself at him, kissing him and crying. He turned his head toward me, his tears coursing over his cheeks, and dangled his tongue, as if to say, "Look at my plight." Then I turned to the shepherd's daughter and asked, "Can you release him from the spell? If you do, I will give you all my cattle and all my possessions." She smiled and replied, "Master, I have no desire for your wealth, cattle, or possessions. I will deliver him, but on two conditions: first, that you let me marry him; second, that you let me cast a spell on her who had cast a spell on him, in order to control her and guard against her evil power." I replied, "Do whatever you wish and more. My possessions are for you and my son. As for my wife, who has done this to my son and made me slaughter his mother, her life is forfeit to you." She said, "No, but I will let her taste what she has inflicted on others." Then the shepherd's daughter filled a bowl with water, uttered an incantation and an oath, and said to my son, "Bull, if you have been created in this image by the All-Conquering, Almighty Lord, stay as you are, but if you have been treacherously put under a spell, change back to your human form, by the will of God, Creator of the wide world." Then she sprinkled him with the water, and he shook himself and changed from a bull back to his human form.

As I rushed to him, I fainted, and when I came to myself, he told me what my wife, this very deer, had done to him and to his mother. I said to him, "Son, God has sent us someone who will pay her back for what you and your mother and I have suffered at her hands." Then, O demon, I gave my son in marriage to the shepherd's daughter, who turned my wife into this very deer, saying to me, "To me this is a pretty form, for she will be with us day and night, and it is better to turn her into a pretty deer than to suffer her sinister looks." Thus she stayed with us, while the days and nights followed one another, and the months and years went by. Then one day the shepherd's daughter died, and my son went to the country of this very man with whom you have had your encounter. Some time later I took my wife, this very deer, with me, set out to find out what had happened to my son, and chanced to stop here. This is my story, my strange and amazing story.

The demon assented, saying, "I grant you one-third of this man's life."

Then, O King Shahrayar, the second old man with the two black dogs approached the demon and said, "I too shall tell you what happened to me and to these two dogs, and if I tell it to you and you find it stranger and more amazing than this man's story will you grant me one-third of this man's life?" The demon replied, "I will." Then the old man began to tell his story, saying . . .

*But dawn broke, and morning overtook Shahrazad, and she lapsed into silence. Then Dinarzad said, "This is an amazing story," and Shahrazad replied, "What is this compared with what I shall tell you tomorrow night if the king spares me and lets me live!" The king said to himself, "By God, I will not have her put to death until I find out what happened to the man with the two black dogs. Then I will have her put to death, God the Almighty willing."*

THE SIXTH NIGHT

*When the following night arrived and Shahrazad was in bed with King Shahrayar, her sister Dinarzad said, "Sister, if you are not sleepy, tell us a little tale. Finish the one you started." Shahrazad replied, "With the greatest pleasure":*

I heard, O happy King, that the second old man with the two dogs said:

# [The Second Old Man's Tale]

Demon, as for my story, these are the details. These two dogs are my brothers. When our father died, he left behind three sons, and left us three thousand dinars,[5] with which each of us opened a shop and became a shopkeeper. Soon my older brother, one of these very dogs, went and sold the contents of his shop for a thousand dinars, bought trading goods, and, having prepared himself for his trading trip, left us. A full year went by, when one day, as I sat in my shop, a beggar stopped by to beg. When I refused him, he tearfully asked, "Don't you recognize me?" and when I looked at him closely, I recognized my brother. I embraced him and took him into the shop, and when I asked him about his plight, he replied, "The money is gone, and the situation is bad." Then I took him to the public bath, clothed him in one of my robes, and took him home with me. Then I examined my books and checked my balance, and found out that I had made a thousand dinars and that my net worth was two thousand dinars. I divided the amount between my brother and myself, and said to him, "Think as if you have never been away." He gladly took the money and opened another shop.

Soon afterward my seond brother, this other dog, went and sold his merchandise and collected his money, intending to go on a trading trip. We tried to dissuade him, but he did not listen. Instead, he bought merchandise and trading goods, joined a group of travelers, and was gone for a full year. Then he came back, just like his older brother. I said to him, "Brother, didn't I advise you not to go?" He replied tearfully, "Brother, it was foreordained. Now I am poor and penniless, without even a shirt on my back." Demon, I took him to the public bath, clothed him in one of my new robes, and took him back to the shop. After we had something to eat, I said to him, "Brother, I shall do my business accounts, calculate my net worth for the year, and after subtracting the capital, whatever the profit happens to be, I shall divide it equally between you and myself. When I examined my books and subtracted the capital, I found out that my profit was two thousand dinars, and I thanked God and felt very happy. Then I divided the money, giving him a thousand dinars and keeping a thousand for myself. With that money he opened another shop, and the three of us stayed together for a while. Then my two brothers asked me to go on a trading journey with them, but I refused, saying, "What did you gain from your ventures that I can gain?"

They dropped the matter, and for six years we worked in our

5. Gold coins, the basic Muslim money units.

stores, buying and selling. Yet every year they asked me to go on a trading journey with them, but I refused, until I finally gave in. I said, "Brothers, I am ready to go with you. How much money do you have?" I found out that they had eaten and drunk and squandered everything they had, but I said nothing to them and did not reproach them. Then I took inventory, gathered all I had together, and sold everything. I was pleased to discover that the sale netted six thousand dinars. Then I divided the money into two parts, and said to my brothers, "The sum of three thousand dinars is for you and myself to use on our trading journey. The other three thousand I shall bury in the ground, in case what happened to you happens to me, so that when we return, we will find three thousand dinars to reopen our shops." They replied, "This is an excellent idea." Then, demon, I divided my money and buried three thousand dinars. Of the remaining three I gave each of my brothers a thousand and kept a thousand for myself. After I closed my shop, we bought merchandise and trading goods, rented a large seafaring boat, and after loading it with our goods and provisions, sailed day and night, for a month.

*But morning overtook Shahrazad, and she lapsed into silence. Then her sister Dinarzad said, "Sister, what a lovely story!" Shahrazad replied, "Tomorrow night I shall tell you something even lovelier, stranger, and more wonderful if I live, the Almighty God willing."*

### THE SEVENTH NIGHT

*The following night Dinarzad said to her sister Shahrazad, "For God's sake, sister, if you are not sleepy, tell us a little tale." The king added, "Let it be the completion of the story of the merchant and the demon." Shahrazad replied, "With the greatest pleasure":*

I heard, O happy King, that the second old man said to the demon:

For a month my brothers, these very dogs, and I sailed the salty sea, until we came to a port city. We entered the city and sold our goods, earning ten dinars for every dinar. Then we bought other goods, and when we got to the seashore to embark, I met a girl who was dressed in tatters. She kissed my hands and said, "O my lord, be charitable and do me a favor, and I believe that I shall

be able to reward you for it." I replied, "I am willing to do you a
favor regardless of any reward." She said, "O my lord, marry me,
clothe me, and take me home with you on this boat, as your wife,
for I wish to give myself to you. I, in turn, will reward you for your
kindness and charity, the Almighty God willing. Don't be misled
by my poverty and present condition." When I heard her words,
I felt pity for her, and guided by what God the Most High had
intended for me, I consented. I clothed her with an expensive dress
and married her. Then I took her to the boat, spread the bed for
her, and consummated our marriage. We sailed many days and
nights, and I, feeling love for her, stayed with her day and night,
neglecting my brothers. In the meantime they, these very dogs, grew
jealous of me, envied me for my increasing merchandise and wealth,
and coveted all our possessions. At last they decided to betray me
and, tempted by the Devil, plotted to kill me. One night they waited
until I was asleep beside my wife; then they carried the two of us
and threw us into the sea.

When we awoke, my wife turned into a she-demon and carried
me out of the sea to an island. When it was morning, she said,
"Husband, I have rewarded you by saving you from drowning, for
I am one of the demons who believe in God. When I saw you by
the seashore, I felt love for you and came to you in the guise in
which you saw me, and when I expressed my love for you, you
accepted me. Now I must kill your brothers." When I heard what
she said, I was amazed and I thanked her and said, "As for destroying my brothers, this I do not wish, for I will not behave like them."
Then I related to her what had happened to me and them, from
beginning to end. When she heard my story, she got very angry
at them, and said, "I shall fly to them now, drown their boat, and
let them all perish." I entreated her, saying, "For God's sake, don't.
The proverb advises 'Be kind to those who hurt you.' No matter
what, they are my brothers after all." In this manner, I entreated
her and pacified her. Afterward, she took me and flew away with
me until she brought me home and put me down on the roof of
my house. I climbed down, threw the doors open, and dug up the
money I had buried. Then I went out and, greeting the people in
the market, reopened my shop. When I came home in the evening,
I found these two dogs tied up, and when they saw me, they came
to me, wept, and rubbed themselves against me. I started, when
I suddenly heard my wife say, "O my lord, these are your brothers."
I asked, "Who has done this to them?" She replied, "I sent to my
sister and asked her to do it. They will stay in this condition for
ten years, after which they may be delivered." Then she told me
where to find her and departed. The ten years have passed, and

I was with my brothers on my way to her to have the spell lifted, when I met this man, together with this old man with the deer. When I asked him about himself, he told me about his encounter with you, and I resolved not to leave until I found out what would happen between you and him. This is my story. Isn't it amazing?

The demon replied, "By God, it is strange and amazing. I grant you one-third of my claim on him for his crime."

Then the third old man said, "Demon, don't disappoint me. If I told you a story that is stranger and more amazing than the first two would you grant me one-third of your claim on him for his crime?" The demon replied, "I will." Then the old man said, "Demon, listen":

*But morning overtook Shahrazad, and she lapsed into silence. Then her sister said, "What an amazing story!" Shahrazad replied, "The rest is even more amazing." The king said to himself, "I will not have her put to death until I hear what happened to the old man and the demon; then I will have her put to death, as is my custom with the others."*

THE EIGHTH NIGHT

*The following night Dinarzad said to her sister Shahrazad, "For God's sake, sister, if you are not sleepy, tell us one of your lovely little tales to while away the night." Shahrazad replied, "With the greatest pleasure":*

I heard, O happy King, that the third old man told the demon a story that was even stranger and more amazing than the first two. The demon was very much amazed and, swaying with delight, said, "I grant you one-third of my claim on him for his crime." Then the demon released the merchant and departed. The merchant turned to the three old men and thanked them, and they congratulated him on his deliverance and bade him good-bye. Then they separated, and each of them went on his way. The merchant himself went back home to his family, his wife, and his children, and he lived with them until the day he died. But this story is not as strange or as amazing as the story of the fisherman.

*Dinarzad asked, "Please, sister, what is the story of the fisherman?" Shahrazad said:*

# [THE STORY OF THE FISHERMAN AND THE DEMON]

It is related that there was a very old fisherman who had a wife and three daughters and who was so poor that they did not have even enough food for the day. It was this fisherman's custom to cast his net four times a day. One day, while the moon was still up, he went out with his net at the call for the early morning prayer. He reached the outskirts of the city and came to the seashore. Then he set down his basket, rolled up his shirt, and waded to his waist in the water. He cast his net and waited for it to sink; then he gathered the rope and started to pull. As he pulled little by little, he felt that the net was getting heavier until he was unable to pull any further. He climbed ashore, drove a stake into the ground, and tied the end of the rope to the stake. Then he took off his clothes, dove into the water, and went around the net, shaking it and tugging at it until he managed to pull it ashore. Feeling extremely happy, he put on his clothes and went back to the net. But when he opened it, he found inside a dead donkey, which had torn it apart. The fisherman felt sad and depressed and said to himself, "There is no power and no strength save in God, the Almighty, the Magnificent," adding, "Indeed, this is a strange catch!" Then he began to recite the following verses:

> O you who brave the danger in the dark,
> Reduce your toil, for gain is not in work.
> Look at the fisherman who labors at his trade,
> As the stars in the night their orbits make,
> And deeply wades into the raging sea,
> Steadily gazing at the swelling net,
> Till he returns, pleased with his nightly catch,
> A fish whose mouth the hook of death has cut,
> And sells it to a man who sleeps the night,
> Safe from the cold and blessed with every wish.
> Praised be the Lord who blesses and withholds:
> This casts the net, but that one eats the fish.

*But morning overtook Shahrazad, and she lapsed into silence. Then her sister Dinarzad said, "Sister, what a lovely story!" Shahrazad replied, "Tomorrow night I shall tell you the rest, which is stranger and more wonderful, if the king spares me and lets me live!"*

## THE NINTH NIGHT

*The following night Dinarzad said to her sister Shahrazad, "Sister, if you are not sleepy, finish the fisherman's story." Shahrazad replied, "With the greatest pleasure":*

I heard, O happy King, that when the fisherman finished reciting his verses, he pushed the donkey out of the net and sat down to mend it. When he was done, he wrung it out and spread it to dry. Then he waded into the water and, invoking the Almighty God, cast the net and waited for it to sink. Then he pulled the rope little by little, but this time the net was even more firmly snagged. Thinking that it was heavy with fish, he was extremely happy. He took off his clothes and, diving into the water, freed the net and struggled with it until he reached the shore, but inside the net he found a large jar full of nothing but mud and sand. When he saw this, he felt sad and, with tears in his eyes, said to himself, "This is a strange day! God's we are and to God we turn," and he began to recite the following verses:

> O my tormenting fate, forbear,
> Or if you can't, at least be fair.
> I went to seek my daily bread,
> But they said to me it was dead.
> And neither luck nor industry
> Brought back my daily bread to me.
> The Pleiads[6] many fools attain,
> While sages sit in dark disdain.

Then the fisherman threw the jar away, washed his net, and, wringing it out, spread it to dry. Then he begged the Almighty God for forgiveness and went back to the water. For the third time, he cast the net and waited for it to sink. But when he pulled it up, he found nothing inside but broken pots and bottles, stones, bones, refuse, and the like. He wept at this great injustice and ill luck and began to recite the following verses:

> Your livelihood is not in your own hands;
> Neither by writing nor by the pen you thrive.
> Your luck and your wages are by lot;
> Some lands are waste, and some are fertile lands.
> The wheel of fortune lowers the man of worth,

6. Cluster of stars in the constellation of Taurus.

Raising the base man who deserves to fall.
Come then, O death, and end this worthless life,
Where the ducks soar, while the falcons are bound to earth.
No wonder that you see the good man poor,
While the vicious exalts in his estate.
Our wages are alloted; 'tis our fate
To search like birds for gleanings everywhere.
One bird searches the earth from east to west,
Another gets the tidbits while at rest.

Then the fisherman raised his eyes to the heavens and, seeing that the sun had risen and that it was morning and full daylight, said, "O Lord, you know that I cast my net four times only. I have already cast it three times, and there is only one more try left. Lord, let the sea serve me, even as you let it serve Moses."[7] Having mended the net, he cast it into the sea, and waited for it to sink. When he pulled, he found that it was so heavy that he was unable to haul it. He shook it and found that it was caught at the bottom. Saying "There is no power or strength save in God, the Almighty, the Magnificent," he took off his clothes and dove for the net. He worked at it until he managed to free it, and as he hauled it to the shore, he felt that there was something heavy inside. He struggled with the net, until he opened it and found a large long-necked brass jar, with a lead stopper bearing the mark of a seal ring.[8] When the fisherman saw the jar, he was happy and said to himself, "I will sell it in the copper market, for it must be worth at least two measures of wheat." He tried to move the jar, but it was so full and so heavy that he was unable to budge it. Looking at the lead stopper, he said to himself, "I will open the jar, shake out the contents, then roll it before me until I reach the copper market." Then he took out a knife from his belt and began to scrape and struggle with the lead stopper until he pried it loose. He held the stopper in his mouth, tilted the jar to the ground, and shook it, trying to pour out its contents, but when nothing came out, he was extremely surprised.

After a while, there began to emerge from the jar a great column of smoke, which rose and spread over the face of the earth, increasing so much that it covered the sea and rising so high that it reached the clouds and hid the daylight. For a long time, the smoke kept

7. When Moses and the Jews fled from Egypt, pursued by the pharaoh and his army, Moses struck the water of the Red Sea with his stick, and the sea parted, so that he and his people were able to cross safely into Sinai, while his pursuers were drowned. Moses is a prophet in Islam, as well.
8. A ring that houses a precious or semiprecious stone (usually agate) engraved with the name of a person and used to imprint a signature, or in other instances engraved with talismanic words and used as a charm.

rising from the jar; then it gathered and took shape, and suddenly it shook and there stood a demon, with his feet on the ground and his head in the clouds. He had a head like a tomb, fangs like pincers, a mouth like a cave, teeth like stones, nostrils like trumpets, ears like shields, a throat like an alley, and eyes like lanterns. In short, all one can say is that he was a hideous monster. When the fisherman saw him, he shook with terror, his jaws locked together, and his mouth went dry. The demon cried, "O Solomon,[9] prophet of God, forgive me, forgive me. Never again will I disobey you or defy your command."

*But morning overtook Shahrazad, and she lapsed into silence. Then Dinarzad said, "Sister, what a strange and amazing story!" Shahrazad replied, "Tomorrow night I shall tell you something stranger and more amazing if I stay alive."*

### THE TENTH NIGHT

*The following night, when Shahrazad was in bed with King Shahrayar, her sister Dinarzad said, "Please, sister, finish the story of the fisherman." Shahrazad replied, "With the greatest pleasure":*

I heard, O happy King, that when the fisherman heard what the demon said, he asked, "Demon, what are you saying? It has been more than one thousand and eight hundred years since the prophet Solomon died, and we are now ages later. What is your story, and why were you in this jar?" When the demon heard the fisherman, he said, "Be glad!" The fisherman cried, "O happy day!" The demon added, "Be glad that you will soon be put to death." The fisherman said, "You deserve to be put to shame for such tidings. Why do you wish to kill me, I who have released you and delivered you from the bottom of the sea and brought you back to this world?" The demon replied, "Make a wish!" The fisherman was happy and asked, "What shall I wish of you?" The demon replied, "Tell me how you wish to die, and what manner of death you wish me to choose." The fisherman asked, "What is my crime? Is this my reward from you for having delivered you?" The demon replied, "Fisherman, listen to my story." The fisherman said, "Make it short, for I am at my rope's end."

The demon said, "You should know that I am one of the rene-

9. The Old Testament king and son of David.

gade, rebellious demons. I, together with the giant Sakhr, rebelled
against the prophet Solomon, the son of David, who sent against
me Asif ibn-Barkhiya, who took me by force and bade me be led
in defeat and humiliation before the prophet Solomon. When the
prophet Solomon saw me, he invoked God to protect him from me
and my looks and asked me to submit to him, but I refused. So
he called for this brass jar, confined me inside, and sealed it with
a lead seal on which he imprinted God's Almighty name. Then he
commanded his demons to carry me and throw me into the middle
of the sea. I stayed there for two hundred years, saying to myself,
'Whoever sets me free during these two hundred years, I will make
him rich.' But the two hundred years went by and were followed
by another two hundred, and no one set me free. Then I vowed
to myself, 'Whoever sets me free, I will open for him all the treasures
of the earth,' but four hundred years went by, and no one set me
free. When I entered the next hundred years, I vowed to myself,
'Whoever delivers me, during these hundred years, I will make him
king, make myself his servant, and fulfill every day three of his
wishes,' but that hundred years too, plus all the intervening years,
went by, and no one set me free. Then I raged and raved and
growled and snorted and said to myself, 'Whoever delivers me from
now on, I will either put him to the worst of deaths or let him choose
for himself the manner of death.' Soon you came by and set me
free. Tell me how you wish to die."

When the fisherman heard what the demon said, he replied, "To
God we belong and to Him we return. After all these years, with
my bad luck, I had to set you free now. Forgive me, and God will
grant you forgiveness. Destroy me, and God will inflict on you one
who will destroy you." The demon replied, "It must be. Tell me
how you wish to die." When the fisherman was certain that he was
going to die, he mourned and wept, saying, "O my children, may
God not deprive us of each other." Again he turned to the demon
and said, "For God's sake, release me as a reward for releasing you
and delivering you from this jar." The demon replied, "Your death
is your reward for releasing me and letting me escape." The fisherman said, "I did you a good turn, and you are about to repay me
with a bad one. How true is the sentiment of the following lines:

> Our kindness they repaid with ugly deeds,
> Upon my life, the deeds of men depraved.
> He who the undeserving aids will meet
> The fate of him who the hyena saved."

The demon said, "Be brief, for as I have said, I must kill you."
Then the fisherman thought to himself, "He is only a demon, while

I am a human being, whom God has endowed with reason and thereby made superior to him. He may use his demonic wiles on me, but I will use my reason to deal with him." Then he asked the demon, "Must you kill me?" When the demon replied, "I must," the fisherman said, "By the Almighty name that was engraved on the ring of Solomon the son of David, will you answer me truthfully if I ask you about something?" The demon was upset and said with a shudder, "Ask, and be brief!"

*But morning overtook Shahrazad, and she lapsed into silence. Then Dinarzad said, "Sister, what an amazing and lovely story!" Shahrazad replied, "What is this compared with what I shall tell you tomorrow night if the king spares me and lets me live! It will be even more amazing."*

## THE ELEVENTH NIGHT

*The following night Dinarzad said to her sister Shahrazad, "Sister, if you are not sleepy, finish the story of the fisherman and the demon." Shahrazad replied, "With the greatest pleasure":*

I heard, O King, that the fisherman said, "By the Almighty name, tell me whether you really were inside this jar." The demon replied, "By the Almighty name, I was imprisoned in this jar." The fisherman said, "You are lying, for this jar is not large enough, not even for your hands and feet. How can it be large enough for your whole body?" The demon replied, "By God, I was inside. Don't you believe that I was inside it?" The fisherman said, "No, I don't." Whereupon the demon shook himself and turned into smoke, which rose, stretched over the sea, spread over the land, then gathered, and, little by little, began to enter the jar. When the smoke disappeared completely, the demon shouted from within, "Fisherman, here I am in the jar. Do you believe me now?"

The fisherman at once took out the sealed lead stopper and hurriedly clamped it on the mouth of the jar. Then he cried out, "Demon, now tell me how you wish to die. For I will throw you into this sea, build a house right here, and sit here and stop any fisherman who comes to fish and warn him that there is a demon here, who will kill whoever pulls him out and who will let him choose how he wishes to die." When the demon heard what the fisherman said and found himself imprisoned, he tried to get out but could not, for he was prevented by the seal of Solomon the son of David.

Realizing that the fisherman had tricked him, the demon said, "Fisherman, don't do this to me. I was only joking with you." The fisherman replied, "You are lying, you the dirtiest and meanest of demons," and began to roll the jar toward the sea. The demon shouted, "Don't, don't!" But the fisherman replied, "Yes, yes." Then in a soft and submissive voice the demon asked, "Fisherman, what do you intend to do?" The fisherman replied, "I intend to throw you into the sea. The first time you stayed there for eight hundred years. This time I will let you stay until Doomsday. Haven't I said to you, 'Spare me, and God will spare you. Destroy me, and God will destroy you'? But you refused, and persisted in your resolve to do me in and kill me. Now it is my turn to do you in." The demon said, "Fisherman, if you open the jar, I will reward you and make you rich." The fisherman replied, "You are lying, you are lying. Your situation and mine is like that of King Yunan and the sage Duban." The demon asked, "What is their story?" The fisherman said:

# [The Tale of King Yunan and the Sage Duban]

Demon, there was once a king called Yunan, who reigned in one of the cities of Persia, in the province of Zuman.[1] This king was afflicted with leprosy, which had defied the physicians and the sages, who, for all the medicines they gave him to drink and all the ointments they applied, were unable to cure him. One day there came to the city of King Yunan a sage called Duban. This sage had read all sorts of books, Greek, Persian, Turkish, Arabic, Byzantine, Syriac, and Hebrew, had studied the sciences, and had learned their groundwork, as well as their principles and basic benefits. Thus he was versed in all the sciences, from philosophy to the lore of plants and herbs, the harmful as well as the beneficial. A few days after he arrived in the city of King Yunan, the sage heard about the king and his leprosy and the fact that the physicians and the sages were unable to cure him. On the following day, when God's morning dawned and His sun rose, the sage Duban put on his best clothes, went to King Yunan and, introducing himself, said, "Your Majesty, I have heard of that which has afflicted your body and heard that many physicians have treated you without finding a way to cure you. Your Majesty, I can treat you without giving you any medicine to drink or ointment to apply." When the king heard this, he said,

1. Modern Armenia.

"If you succeed, I will bestow on you riches that would be enough for you and your grandchildren. I will bestow favors on you, and I will make you my companion and friend." The king bestowed robes of honor on the sage, treated him kindly, and then asked him, "Can you really cure me from my leprosy without any medicine to drink or ointment to apply?" The sage replied, "Yes, I will cure you externally." The king was astonished, and he began to feel respect as well as great affection for the sage. He said, "Now, sage, do what you have promised." The sage replied, "I hear and obey. I will do it tomorrow morning, the Almighty God willing." Then the sage went to the city, rented a house, and there he distilled and extracted medicines and drugs. Then with his great knowledge and skill, he fashioned a mallet with a curved end, hollowed the mallet, as well as the handle, and filled the handle with his medicines and drugs. He likewise made a ball. When he had perfected and prepared everything, he went on the following day to King Yunan and kissed the ground before him.

*But morning overtook Shahrazad, and she lapsed into silence. Then her sister Dinarzad said, "What a lovely story!" Shahrazad replied, "You have heard nothing yet. Tomorrow night I shall tell you something stranger and more amazing if the king spares me and lets me live!"*

### THE TWELFTH NIGHT

*The following night Dinarzad said to her sister Shahrazad, "Please, sister, finish the rest of the story of the fisherman and the demon." Shahrazad replied, "With the greatest pleasure":*

I heard, O King, that the fisherman said to the demon:

The sage Duban came to King Yunan and asked him to ride to the playground to play with the ball and mallet. The king rode out, attended by his chamberlains, princes, viziers, and lords and eminent men of the realm. When the king was seated, the sage Duban entered, offered him the mallet, and said, "O happy King, take this mallet, hold it in your hand, and as you race on the playground, hold the grip tightly in your fist, and hit the ball. Race until you perspire, and the medicine will ooze from the grip into your perspiring hand, spread to your wrist, and circulate through your entire body. After you perspire and the medicine spreads in your body, return to your royal palace, take a bath, and go to sleep. You will wake up cured, and that is all there is to it." King Yunan took the mallet from the sage Duban and mounted his horse. The attendants threw the ball before the king, who, holding the grip tightly in his fist, followed it and struggled excitedly to catch up with it and hit it. He kept galloping after the ball and hitting it until his palm and the rest of his body began to perspire, and the medicine began to ooze from the handle and flow through his entire body. When the sage Duban was certain that the medicine had oozed and spread through the king's body, he advised him to return to his palace and go immediately to the bath. The king went to the bath and washed himself thoroughly. Then he put on his clothes, left the bath, and returned to his palace.

As for the sage Duban, he spent the night at home, and early in the morning, he went to the palace and asked for permission to see the king. When he was allowed in, he entered and kissed the ground before the king; then, pointing toward him with his hand, he began to recite the following verses:

> The virtues you fostered are great;
> For who but you could sire them?
> Yours is the face whose radiant light
> Effaces the night dark and grim.
> Forever beams your radiant face;
> That of the world is still in gloom.
> You rained on us with ample grace,
> As the clouds rain on thirsty hills,
> Expending your munificence,
> Attaining your magnificence.

When the sage Duban finished reciting these verses, the king stood up and embraced him. Then he seated the sage beside him, and with attentiveness and smiles, engaged him in conversation. Then the king bestowed on the sage robes of honor, gave him gifts and endowments, and granted his wishes. For when the king had looked at himself the morning after the bath, he found that his body was clear of leprosy, as clear and pure as silver. He therefore felt exceedingly happy and in a very generous mood. Thus when he went in the morning to the reception hall and sat on his throne, attended by the Mamluks[2] and chamberlains, in the company of the viziers and the lords of the realm, and the sage Duban presented himself, as we have mentioned, the king stood up, embraced him, and seated him beside him. He treated him attentively and drank and ate with him.

2. Literally "slaves," members of a military force, originally of Caucasian slaves, who made themselves masters of Egypt in A.D. 1254 until their massacre in 1811.

*But morning overtook Shahrazad, and she lapsed into silence. Then her sister Dinarzad said, "Sister, what a lovely story!" Shahrazad replied, "The rest of the story is stranger and more amazing. If the king spares me and I am alive tomorrow night, I shall tell you something even more entertaining."*

### THE THIRTEENTH NIGHT

*The following night Dinarzad said to her sister Shahrazad, "Sister, if you are not sleepy, tell us one of your lovely little tales to while away the night." Shahrazad replied, "With the greatest pleasure":*

I heard, O happy King who is praiseworthy by the Grace of God, that King Yunan bestowed favors on the sage, gave him robes of honor, and granted his wishes. At the end of the day he gave the sage a thousand dinars and sent him home. The king, who was amazed at the skill of the sage Duban, said to himself, "This man has treated me externally, without giving me any draught to drink or ointment to apply. His is indeed a great wisdom for which he deserves to be honored and rewarded. He shall become my companion, confidant, and close friend." Then the king spent the night, happy at his recovery from his illness, at his good health, and at the soundness of his body. When morning came and it was light, the king went to the royal reception hall and sat on the throne, attended by his chief officers, while the princes, viziers, and lords of the realm sat to his right and left. Then the king called for the sage, and when the sage entered and kissed the ground before him, the king stood up to salute him, seated him beside him, and invited him to eat with him. The king treated him intimately, showed him favors, and bestowed on him robes of honor and many other gifts. Then he spent the whole day conversing with him, and at the end of the day he ordered that he be given a thousand dinars. The sage went home and spent the night with his wife, feeling happy and thankful to God the Arbiter.

In the morning, the king went to the royal reception hall, and the princes and viziers came to stand in attendance. It happened that King Yunan had a vizier who was sinister, greedy, envious, and fretful, and when he saw that the sage had found favor with the king, who bestowed on him much money and many robes of honor, he feared that the king would dismiss him and appoint the sage in his place; therefore, he envied the sage and harbored ill will against him, for 'nobody is free from envy.' The envious vizier approached the king and, kissing the ground before him, said, "O excellent King and glorious Lord, it was by your kindness and with your blessing that I rose to prominence; therefore, if I fail to advise you on a grave matter, I am not my father's son. If the great King and noble Lord commands, I shall disclose the matter to him." The king was upset and asked, "Damn you, what advice have you got?" The vizier replied, "Your Majesty, 'He who considers not the end, fortune is not his friend.' I have seen your Majesty make a mistake, for you have bestowed favors on your enemy who has come to destroy your power and steal your wealth. Indeed, you have pampered him and shown him many favors, but I fear that he will do you harm." The king asked, "Whom do you accuse, whom do you have in mind, and at whom do you point the finger?" The vizier replied, "If you are asleep, wake up, for I point the finger at the sage Duban, who has come from Byzantium." The king replied, "Damn you, is he my enemy? To me he is the most faithful, the dearest, and the most favored of people, for this sage has treated me simply by making me hold something in my hand and has cured me from the disease that had defied the physicians and the sages and rendered them helpless. In all the world, east and west, near and far, there is no one like him, yet you accuse him of such a thing. From this day onward, I will give him every month a thousand dinars, in addition to his rations and regular salary. Even if I were to share my wealth and my kingdom with him, it would be less than he deserves. I think that you have said what you said because you envy him. This is very much like the situation in the story told by the vizier of King Sindbad[3] when the king wanted to kill his own son.

*But morning overtook Shahrazad, and she lapsed into silence. Then her sister Dinarzad said, "Sister, what a lovely story!" Shahrazad replied, "What is this compared with what I shall tell you tomorrow night! It will be stranger and more amazing."*

### THE FOURTEENTH NIGHT

*The following night, when the king got into bed and Shahrazad got in with him, her sister Dinarzad said, "Please, sister, if you are not sleepy, tell us one of your lovely little tales to while away the night." Shahrazad replied, "Very well":*

3. Not to be confused with Sindbad the Sailor.

I heard, O happy King, that King Yunan's vizier asked, "King of the age, I beg your pardon, but what did King Sindbad's vizier tell the king when he wished to kill his own son?" King Yunan said to the vizier, "When King Sindbad, provoked by an envious man, wanted to kill his own son, his vizier said to him, 'Don't do what you will regret afterward.'"

# [The Tale of the Husband and the Parrot]

I have heard it told that there was once a very jealous man who had a wife so splendidly beautiful that she was perfection itself. The wife always refused to let her husband travel and leave her behind, until one day when he found it absolutely necessary to go on a journey. He went to the bird market, bought a parrot, and brought it home. The parrot was intelligent, knowledgeable, smart, and retentive. Then he went away on his journey, and when he finished his business and came back, he brought the parrot and inquired about his wife during his absence. The parrot gave him a day-by-day account of what his wife had done with her lover and how the two carried on in his absence. When the husband heard the account, he felt very angry, went to his wife, and gave her a sound beating. Thinking that one of her maids had informed her husband about what she did with her lover in her husband's absence, the wife interrogated her maids one by one, and they all swore that they had heard the parrot inform the husband.

When the wife heard that it was the parrot who had informed the husband, she ordered one of her maids to take the grinding stone and grind under the cage, ordered a second maid to sprinkle water over the cage, and ordered a third to carry a steel mirror and walk back and forth all night long. That night her husband stayed out, and when he came home in the morning, he brought the parrot, spoke with it, and asked about what had transpired in his absence that night. The parrot replied, "Master, forgive me, for last night, all night long, I was unable to hear or see very well because of the intense darkness, the rain, and the thunder and lightning." Seeing that it was summertime, during the month of July, the husband replied, "Woe unto you, this is no season for rain." The parrot said, "Yes, by God, all night long, I saw what I told you." The husband, concluding that the parrot had lied about his wife and had accused her falsely, got angry, and he grabbed the parrot and, taking it out of the cage, smote it on the ground and killed it. But after the parrot's death, the husband heard from his neighbors that the parrot

had told the truth about his wife, and he was full of regret that he
had been tricked by his wife to kill the parrot.

King Yunan concluded, "Vizier, the same will happen to me."

*But morning overtook Shahrazad, and she lapsed into silence.
Then her sister Dinarzad said, "What a strange and lovely story!"
Shahrazad replied, "What is this compared with what I shall tell
you tomorrow night! If the king spares me and lets me live, I shall
tell you something more amazing." The king thought to himself,
"By God, this is indeed an amazing story."*

THE FIFTEENTH NIGHT

*The following night Dinarzad said to her sister Shahrazad,
"Please, sister, if you are not sleepy, tell us one of your lovely little
tales, for they entertain and help everyone to forget his cares and
banish sorrow from the heart." Shahrazad replied, "With the greatest
pleasure." King Shahrayar added, "Let it be the remainder of the
story of King Yunan, his vizier, and the sage Duban, and of the
fisherman, the demon, and the jar." Shahrazad replied, "With the
greatest pleasure":*

I heard, O happy King, that King Yunan said to his envious
vizier, "After the husband killed the parrot and heard from his
neighbors that the parrot had told him the truth, he was filled with
remorse. You too, my vizier, being envious of this wise man, would
like me to kill him and regret it afterward, as did the husband after
he killed the parrot." When the vizier heard what King Yunan said,
he replied, "O great king, what harm has this sage done to me?
Why, he has not harmed me in any way. I am telling you all this
out of love and fear for you. If you don't discover my veracity, let
me perish like the vizier who deceived the son of the king." King
Yunan asked his vizier, "How so?" The vizier replied:

# [The Tale of the King's Son and
the She-Ghoul]

It is said, O happy King, that there was once a king who had a
son who was fond of hunting and trapping. The prince had with
him a vizier appointed by his father the king to follow him wherever

he went. One day the prince went with his men into the wilderness, and when he chanced to see a wild beast, the vizier urged him to go after it. The prince pursued the beast and continued to press in pursuit until he lost its track and found himself alone in the wilderness, not knowing which way to turn or where to go, when he came upon a girl, standing on the road, in tears. When the young prince asked her, "Where do you come from?" she replied, "I am the daughter of an Indian king. I was riding in the wilderness when I dozed off and in my sleep fell off my horse and found myself alone and helpless." When the young prince heard what she said, he felt sorry for her, and he placed her behind him on his horse and rode on. As they passed by some ruins, she said, "O my lord, I wish to relieve myself here." He let her down and she went into the ruins. Then he went in after her, ignorant of what she was, and discovered that she was a she-ghoul, who was saying to her children, "I brought you a good, fat boy." They replied, "Mother, bring him to us, so that we may feed on his innards." When the young prince heard what they said, he shook with terror, and fearing for his life, ran outside. The she-ghoul followed him and asked, "Why are you afraid?" and he told her about his situation and his predicament, concluding, "I have been unfairly treated." She replied, "If you have been unfairly treated, ask the Almighty God for help, and he will protect you from harm." The young prince raised his eyes to Heaven . . .

*But morning overtook Shahrazad, and she lapsed into silence. Then her sister Dinarzad said, "What a strange and lovely story!" Shahrazad replied, "What is this compared with what I shall tell you tomorrow night! It will be even stranger and more amazing."*

THE SIXTEENTH NIGHT

*The following night Dinarzad said, "Please, sister, if you are not sleepy, tell us one of your lovely little tales." Shahrazad replied, "I shall with pleasure":*

I heard, O King, that the vizier said to King Yunan:

When the young prince said to the she-ghoul, "I have been unfairly treated," she replied, "Ask God for help, and He will protect you from harm." The young prince raised his eyes to Heaven and said, "O Lord, help me to prevail upon my enemy, for 'everything is within your power.'" When the she-ghoul heard his invocation, she gave up and departed, and he returned safely to his father and told him about the vizier and how it was he who had urged him to pursue the beast and drove him to his encounter with the she-ghoul. The king summoned the vizier and had him put to death.

The vizier added, "You too, your Majesty, if you trust, befriend, and bestow favors on this sage, he will plot to destroy you and cause your death. Your Majesty should realize that I know for certain that he is a foreign agent who has come to destroy you. Haven't you seen that he cured you externally, simply with something you held in your hand?" King Yunan, who was beginning to feel angry, replied, "You are right, vizier. The sage may well be what you say and may have come to destroy me. He who has cured me with something to hold can kill me with something to smell." Then the king asked the vizier, "My vizier and good counselor, how should I deal with him?" The vizier replied, "Send for him now and have him brought before you, and when he arrives, strike off his head. In this way, you will attain your aim and fulfill your wish." The king said, "This is good and sound advice." Then he sent for the sage Duban, who came immediately, still feeling happy at the favors, the money, and the robes the king had bestowed on him. When he entered, he pointed with his hand toward the king and began to recite the following verses:

> If I have been remiss in thanking you,
> For whom then have I made my verse and prose?
> You granted me your gifts before I asked,
> Without deferment and without excuse.
> How can I fail to praise your noble deeds,
> Inspired in private and in public by my muse?
> I thank you for your deeds and for your gifts,
> Which, though they bend my back, my care reduce.

The king asked, "Sage, do you know why I have had you brought before me?" The sage replied, "No, your Majesty." The king said, "I brought you here to have you killed and to destroy the breath of life within you." In astonishment Duban asked, "Why does your Majesty wish to have me put to death, and for what crime?" The king replied, "I have been told that you are a spy and that you have come to kill me. Today I will have you killed before you kill me. 'I will have you for lunch before you have me for dinner.'" Then the king called for the executioner and ordered him, saying, "Strike off the head of this sage and rid me of him! Strike!"

When the sage heard what the king said, he knew that because he had been favored by the king, someone had envied him, plotted against him, and lied to the king, in order to have him killed and get rid of him. The sage realized then that the king had little wisdom, judgment, or good sense, and he was filled with regret, when it was useless to regret. He said to himself, "There is no power and no strength, save in God the Almighty, the Magnificent. I did a good deed but was rewarded with an evil one." In the meantime, the king was shouting at the executioner, "Strike off his head." The sage implored, "Spare me, your Majesty, and God will spare you; destroy me, and God will destroy you." He repeated the statement, just as I did, O demon, but you too refused, insisting on killing me. King Yunan said to the sage, "Sage, you must die, for you have cured me with a mere handle, and I fear that you can kill me with anything." The sage replied, "This is my reward from your Majesty. You reward good with evil." The king said, "Don't stall; you must die today without delay." When the sage Duban became convinced that he was going to die, he was filled with grief and sorrow, and his eyes overflowed with tears. He blamed himself for doing a favor for one who does not deserve it and for sowing seeds in a barren soil and recited the following verses:

> Maimuna was a foolish girl,
> Though from a sage descended,
> And many with pretense to skill
> Are e'en on dry land upended.

The executioner approached the sage, bandaged his eyes, bound his hands, and raised the sword, while the sage cried, expressed regret, and implored, "For God's sake, your Majesty, spare me, and God will spare you; destroy me, and God will destroy you." Then he tearfully began to recite the following verses:

> They who deceive enjoy success,
> While I with my true counsel fail
> And am rewarded with disgrace.
> If I live, I'll nothing unveil;
> If I die, then curse all the men,
> The men who counsel and prevail.

Then the sage added, "Is this my reward from your Majesty? It is like the reward of the crocodile." The king asked, "What is the story of the crocodile?" The sage replied, "I am in no condition to tell you a story. For God's sake, spare me, and God will spare you. Destroy me, and God will destroy you," and he wept bitterly.

Then several noblemen approached the king and said, "We beg your Majesty to forgive him for our sake, for in our view, he has done nothing to deserve this." The king replied, "You do not know the reason why I wish to have him killed. I tell you that if I spare

him, I will surely perish, for I fear that he who has cured me externally from my affliction, which had defied the Greek sages, simply
by having me hold a handle, can kill me with anything I touch.
I must kill him, in order to protect myself from him." The sage
Duban implored again, "For God's sake, your Majesty, spare me,
and God will spare you. Destroy me, and God will destroy you."
The king insisted, "I must kill you."

Demon, when the sage realized that he was surely going to die,
he said, "I beg your Majesty to postpone my execution until I return
home, leave instructions for my burial, discharge my obligations,
distribute alms, and donate my scientific and medical books to one
who deserves them. I have in particular a book entitled *The Secret
of Secrets*, which I should like to give you for safekeeping in your
library." The king asked, "What is the secret of this book?" The
sage replied, "It contains countless secrets, but the chief one is that
if your Majesty has my head struck off, opens the book on the sixth
leaf, reads three lines from the left page, and speaks to me, my head
will speak and answer whatever you ask."

The king was greatly amazed and said, "Is it possible that if I
cut off your head and, as you say, open the book, read the third
line, and speak to your head, it will speak to me? This is the wonder
of wonders." Then the king allowed the sage to go and sent him
home under guard. The sage settled his affairs and on the following day returned to the royal palace and found assembled there the
princes, viziers, chamberlains, lords of the realm, and military officers, as well as the king's retinue, servants, and many of his
citizens. The sage Duban entered, carrying an old book and a
kohl[4] jar containing powder. He sat down, ordered a platter, and
poured out the powder and smoothed it on the platter. Then he
said to the king, "Take this book, your Majesty, and don't open
it until after my execution. When my head is cut off, let it be placed
on the platter and order that it be pressed on the powder. Then
open the book and begin to ask my head a question, for it will then
answer you. There is no power and no strength save in God, the
Almighty, the Magnificent. For God's sake, spare me, and God
will spare you; destroy me, and God will destroy you." The king
replied, "I must kill you, especially to see how your head will speak
to me." Then the king took the book and ordered the executioner
to strike off the sage's head. The executioner drew his sword and,
with one stroke, dropped the head in the middle of the platter, and
when he pressed the head on the powder, the bleeding stopped.
Then the sage Duban opened his eyes and said, "Now, your

4. Cosmetic, used by Eastern, especially Muslim, women to darken the eyelids.

Majesty, open the book." When the king opened the book, he found the pages stuck. So he put his finger in his mouth, wetted it with his saliva, and opened the first page, and he kept opening the pages with difficulty until he turned seven leaves. But when he looked in the book, he found nothing written inside, and he exclaimed, "Sage, I see nothing written in this book." The sage replied, "Open more pages." The king opened some more pages but still found nothing, and while he was doing this, the drug spread through his body — for the book had been poisoned — and he began to heave, sway, and twitch.

*But morning overtook Shahrazad, and she lapsed into silence. Then her sister Dinarzad said, "Sister, what an amazing and entertaining story!" Shahrazad replied, "What is this compared with what I shall tell you tomorrow night if the king spares me and lets me live!"*

## THE SEVENTEENTH NIGHT

*The following night Dinarzad said to her sister Shahrazad, "Please, sister, if you are not sleepy, tell us one of your lovely little tales to while away the night." The king added, "Let it be the rest of the story of the sage and the king and of the fisherman and the demon." Shahrazad replied, "Very well, with the greatest pleasure":*

I heard, O King, that when the sage Duban saw that the drug had spread through the king's body and that the king was heaving and swaying, he began to recite the following verses:

> For long they ruled us arbitrarily,
> But suddenly vanished their powerful rule.
> Had they been just, they would have happily
> Lived, but they oppressed, and punishing fate
> Afflicted them with ruin deservedly,
> And on the morrow the world taunted them,
> "'Tis tit for tat; blame not just destiny."

As the sage's head finished reciting the verses, the king fell dead, and at that very moment the head too succumbed to death. Demon, consider this story.

*But morning overtook Shahrazad, and she lapsed into silence. Then her sister Dinarzad said, "Sister, what an entertaining story!" Shahrazad replied, "What is this compared with what I shall tell you tomorrow night if I live!"*

THE EIGHTEENTH NIGHT

*The following night, Dinarzad said to her sister Shahrazad, "Please, sister, if you are not sleepy, tell us one of your lovely little tales to while away the night." The king added, "Let it be the rest of the story of the fisherman and the demon." Shahrazad replied, "With the greatest pleasure":*

I heard, O King, that the fisherman said to the demon, "Had the king spared the sage, God would have spared him and he would have lived, but he refused and insisted on destroying the sage, and the Almighty God destroyed him. You too, demon, had you from the beginning agreed to spare me, I would have spared you, but you refused and insisted on killing me; therefore, I shall punish you by keeping you in this jar and throwing you into the bottom of the sea." The demon cried out, "Fisherman, don't do it. Spare me and save me and don't blame me for my action and my offense against you. If I did ill, you should do good. As the saying goes, 'Be kind to him who wrongs you.' Don't do what Imama did to 'Atika." The fisherman asked, "What did Imama do to 'Atika?" The demon replied, "This is no time and this narrow prison is no place to tell a story, but I shall tell it to you after you release me." The fisherman said, "I must throw you into the sea. There is no way I would let you out and set you free, for I kept imploring you and calling on you, but you refused and insisted on killing me, without any offense or injury that merits punishment, except that I had set you free. When you treated me in this way, I realized that you were unclean from birth, that you were ill-natured, and that you were one who rewards good with ill. After I throw you into the sea, I shall build me a hut here and live in it for your sake, so that if anyone pulls you out, I shall acquaint him with what I suffered at your hands and shall advise him to throw you back into the sea and let you perish or languish there to the end of time, you the dirtiest of demons." The demon replied, "Set me free this time, and I pledge never to bother you or harm you, but to make you rich." When he heard this, the fisherman made the demon pledge and covenant that if the fisherman released him and let him out, he would not harm him but would serve him and be good to him.

After the fisherman secured the demon's pledge, by making him swear by the Almighty Name, he opened the seal of the jar, and the smoke began to rise. When the smoke was completely out of the jar, it gathered and turned again into a full-fledged demon, who kicked the jar away and sent it flying to the middle of the sea. When the fisherman saw what the demon had done, sure that he was going to meet with disaster and death, he wet himself and said, "This is a bad omen." Then he summoned his courage and cried out, "Demon, you have sworn and given me your pledge. Don't betray me. Come back, lest the Almighty God punish you for your betrayal. Demon, I repeat to you what the sage Duban said to King Yunan, 'Spare me, and God will spare you; destroy me, and God will destroy you.'" When the demon heard what the fisherman said, he laughed, and when the fisherman cried out again, "Demon, spare me," he replied, "Fisherman, follow me," and the fisherman followed him, hardly believing in his escape, until they came to a mountain outside the city. They climbed over to the other side and came to a vast wilderness, in the middle of which stood a lake surrounded by four hills.

The demon halted by the lake and ordered the fisherman to cast his net and fish. The fisherman looked at the lake and marveled as he saw fish in many colors, white, red, blue, and yellow. He cast his net, and when he pulled, he found four fish inside, one red, one white, one blue, and one yellow. When he saw them, he was full of admiration and delight. The demon said to him, "Take them to the king of your city and offer them to him, and he will give you enough to make you rich. Please excuse me, for I know no other way to make you rich. But don't fish here more than once a day." Then, saying, "I shall miss you," the demon kicked the ground with his foot, and it opened and swallowed him. The fisherman, O King, returned to the city, still marveling at his encounter with the demon and at the colored fish. He entered the royal palace, and when he offered the fish to the king, the king looked at them . . .

*But morning overtook Shahrazad, and she lapsed into silence. Then Dinarzad said, "Sister, what an amazing and entertaining story!" Shahrazad replied, "What is this compared with what I shall tell you tomorrow night if the king spares me and lets me live!"*

### THE NINETEENTH NIGHT

*The following night Dinarzad said to her sister Shahrazad, "Sister, tell us the rest of the story and what happened to the fisherman." Shahrazad replied, "With the greatest pleasure":*

I heard, O King, that when the fisherman presented the fish to the king, and the king looked at them and saw that they were colored, he took one of them in his hand and looked at it with great amazement. Then he said to his vizier, "Take them to the cook whom the emperor of Byzantium has given us as a present." The vizier took the fish and brought them to the girl and said to her, "Girl, as the saying goes, 'I save my tears for the time of trial.' The king has been presented these four fish, and he bids you fry them well." Then the vizier went back to report to the king, and the king ordered him to give the fisherman four hundred dirhams.[5] The vizier gave the money to the fisherman, who, receiving it, gathered it in the folds of his robe and went away, running, and as he ran, he stumbled and kept falling and getting up, thinking that he was in a dream. Then he stopped and bought some provisions for his family.

So far for the fisherman, O King. In the meantime the girl scaled the fish, cleaned them, and cut them into pieces. Then she placed the frying pan on the fire and poured in the sesame oil, and when it began to boil, she placed the fish in the frying pan. When the pieces were done on one side, she turned them over, but no sooner had she done this than the kitchen wall split open and there emerged a maiden with a beautiful figure, smooth cheeks, perfect features, and dark eyes. She wore a short-sleeved silk shirt in the Egyptian style, embroidered all around with lace and gold spangles. In her ears she wore dangling earrings; on her wrists she wore bracelets; and in her hand she held a bamboo wand. She thrust the wand into the frying pan and said in clear Arabic, "O fish, O fish, have you kept the pledge?" When the cook saw what had happened, she fainted. Then the maiden repeated what she had said, and the fish raised their heads from the frying pan and replied in clear Arabic, "Yes, yes. If you return, we shall return; if you keep your vow, we shall keep ours; and if you forsake us, we shall be even." At that moment the maiden overturned the frying pan and disappeared as she had come, and the kitchen wall closed behind her.

When the cook came to herself, she found the four fish charred, and she felt sorry for herself and afraid of the king, saying to herself, "'He broke his lance on his very first raid.'" While she remonstrated with herself, the vizier suddenly stood before her, saying, "Give me the fish, for we have set the table before the king, and he is waiting for them." The girl wept and told the vizier what she had seen and witnessed and what had happened to the fish. The vizier was astonished and said, "This is very strange." Then he sent an officer after the fisherman, and he returned a while later with the fisherman.

5. Small silver coins; in Iraq the dirham is one-twentieth of a dinar.

The vizier shouted at him, saying, "Bring us at once four more fish like the ones you brought us before, for we have had an accident with them." When he followed with threats, the fisherman went home and, taking his fishing gear, went outside the city, climbed the mountain, and descended to the wilderness on the other side. When he came to the lake, he cast his net, and when he pulled up, he found inside four fish, as he had done the first time. Then he brought them back to the vizier, who took them to the girl and said, "Fry them in front of me, so that I can see for myself." The girl prepared the fish at once, placed the frying pan over the fire, and threw them in. When the fish were done, the wall split open, and the maiden appeared in her elegant clothes, wearing necklaces and other jewelry and holding in her hand the bamboo wand. Again she thrust the wand into the frying pan and said in clear Arabic, "O fish, have you kept the pledge?" and again the fish raised their heads and replied, "Yes, yes. If you return, we shall return; if you keep your vow, we shall keep ours; and if you forsake us, we shall be even."

*But morning overtook Shahrazad, and she lapsed into silence. Then Dinarzad said, "What an entertaining story!" Shahrazad replied, "What is this compared with what I shall tell you tomorrow night if I live, the Almighty God willing!"*

### THE TWENTIETH NIGHT

*The following night Dinarzad said to her sister Shahrazad, "Please, sister, if you are not sleepy, tell us one of your lovely little tales to while away the night." Shahrazad replied, "With the greatest pleasure":*

I heard, O happy King, that after the fish spoke, the maiden overturned the frying pan with the wand and disappeared into the opening from which she had emerged, and the wall closed behind her. The vizier said to himself, "I can no longer hide this affair from the king," and he went to him and told him what had happened to the fish before his very eyes.

The king was exceedingly amazed and said, "I wish to see this with my own eyes." Then he sent for the fisherman, who came after a little while, and the king said to him, "I want you to bring me at once four more fish like the ones you brought before. Hurry!" Then he assigned three officers to guard the fisherman and sent him away. The fisherman disappeared for a while and returned with four fish, one red, one white, one blue, and one yellow. The king commanded, "Give him four hundred dirhams," and the fisherman, receiving the money, gathered it in the folds of his robe and went away. Then the king said to the vizier, "Fry the fish here in my presence." The vizier replied, "I hear and obey," and he called for a stove and a frying pan and sat to clean the fish. Then he lit the fire and, pouring the sesame oil, placed the fish in the frying pan.

When they were almost done, the palace wall split open, and the king and vizier began to tremble, and when they looked up, they saw a black slave who stood like a towering mountain or a giant descendant of the tribe of 'Ad.[6] He was as tall as a reed, as wide as a stone bench, and he held a green palm leaf in his hand. Then in clear but unpleasant language, he said, "O fish, O fish, have you kept the pledge?" and the fish raised their heads from the frying pan and said, "Yes, yes. If you return, we shall return; if you keep your vow, we shall keep ours; and if you forsake us, we shall be even." At that moment, the black slave overturned the frying pan, in the middle of the hall, and the fish turned into charcoal. Then the black slave departed as he had come, and the wall closed behind him. When the black slave disappeared, the king said, "I cannot sleep over this affair, for there is no doubt a mystery behind these fish." Then he bade the fisherman be brought before him again.

When the fisherman arrived, the king said to him, "Damn you, where do you catch these fish?" The fisherman replied, "My lord, I catch them in a lake that lies among four hills, on the other side of the mountain." The king turned to the vizier and asked, "Do you know this lake?" The vizier replied, "No, by God, your Majesty. For sixty years, I have hunted, traveled, and roamed far and wide, sometimes for a day or two, sometimes for a month or two, but I have never seen or known that such a lake existed on the other side of the mountain." Then the king turned to the fisherman and asked him, "How far is this lake from here?" The fisherman replied, "King of the age, it is one hour from here." The king was astonished, and he ordered his soldiers to be ready. Then he rode out with his troops, behind the fisherman, who led the way under guard, muttering curses on the demon as he went.

They rode until they were outside the city. Then they climbed the mountain, and when they descended to the other side, they saw a vast wilderness that they had never seen in all their lives, as well as the four hills and the lake in whose clear water they saw the fish in four colors, red, white, blue, and yellow. The king stood marveling; then he turned to the vizier, princes, chamberlains, and

6. Tribe supposedly destroyed by God's wrath; see n. 1, p. 2.

deputies and asked, "Have any of you ever seen this lake before?"
They replied, "Never." He asked, "And none of you knew where
it was?" They kissed the ground before him and replied, "By God,
your Majesty, till now we have never in our lives seen this lake
or known about it, even though it is close to our city." The king
said, "There is a mystery behind this. By God, I shall not return
to the city until I find the answer to the mystery behind this lake
and these fish in four colors." Then he ordered his men to halt and
pitch the tents, and he dismounted and waited.

When it was dark, he summoned the vizier, who was an experienced and wise man of the world. The vizier came to the king,
without being seen by the soldiers, and when he arrived, the king
said, "I wish to reveal to you what I intend to do. At this very hour,
I shall go all by myself to look for an answer to the mystery of this
lake and these fish. Early tomorrow morning you shall sit at the
entrance of my tent and tell the princes that the king is indisposed
and that he has given you orders not to let anyone be admitted to
his presence. You must not let anyone know about my departure
and absence, and you must wait for me for three days." The vizier,
unable to disobey him, abided by the order, saying, "I hear and
obey."

Then the king packed, prepared himself, and girded himself with
the royal sword. Then he climbed one of the four hills, and when
he reached the top, he journeyed on for the rest of the night. In
the morning, when the sun rose and steeped the mountaintop with
light, the king looked and sighted a dark mass in the distance. When
he saw it, he was glad, and he headed in its direction, saying to
himself, "There may be someone there to give me information."
He journeyed on, and when he arrived, he found a palace, built
under a lucky star, with black stones and completely overlaid with
iron plates. It had double doors, one open, one shut. Pleased, the
king knocked gently at the door and waited patiently for a while
without hearing any reply. He knocked again, this time more loudly
than before, but again waited without hearing any reply or seeing
anyone. He knocked for the third time and kept knocking repeatedly
but once more waited without hearing any reply or seeing anyone.
Then he said to himself, "There is no doubt that there is no one
inside, or perhaps the palace is deserted." Summoning his courage,
he entered and shouted from the hallway, "O inhabitants of the
palace, I am a stranger and a hungry traveler. Have you any food?
Our Lord will requite you and reward you for it." He shouted a
second and a third time but heard no reply. Feeling bold and determined, he advanced from the hallway into the center of the palace
and looked around, but saw no one.

*But morning overtook Shahrazad, and she lapsed into silence. Then Dinarzad said, "Sister, what an amazing and entertaining story!" Shahrazad replied, "What is this compared with what I shall tell you tomorrow night if I live, the Almighty God willing!"*

### THE TWENTY-FIRST NIGHT

*The following night Dinarzad said to her sister Shahrazad, "For God's sake, sister, if you are not sleepy, tell us one of your lovely little tales to while away the night." Shahrazad replied, "With the greatest pleasure":*

I heard, O King, that the king walked to the center of the palace and looked around, but saw no one. The palace was furnished with silk carpets and leather mats and hung with drapes. There were also settees, benches, and seats with cushions, as well as cupboards. In the middle there stood a spacious courtyard, surrounded by four adjoining recessed courts facing each other. In the center stood a fountain, on top of which crouched four lions in red gold, spouting water from their mouths in droplets that looked like gems and pearls, and about the fountain singing birds fluttered under a high net to prevent them from flying away. When the king saw all this, without seeing anyone, he was astonished and regretted that he found none to give him any information. He sat pensively by one of the recessed courts, when he heard sad moans and lamentations and the following plaintive verses:

> My soul is torn between peril and toil;
> O life, dispatch me with one mighty blow.
> Lover, neither a bankrupt nor a noble man
> Humbled by love's law do you pity show.
> Ev'n from the breeze I jealously used to guard you,
> But at the blow of fate the eyes blind go.
> When, as he pulls to shoot, the bowstring breaks
> What can the bowman facing his foes do?
> And when the foes begin to congregate
> How can he then escape his cruel fate?

When the king heard the lamentation and the verses, he rose and moved toward the source of the voice until he came to a doorway behind a curtain, and when he lifted the curtain, he saw at the upper end of the room a young man sitting on a chair that rose about twenty inches above the floor. He was a handsome young man, with a full figure, clear voice, radiant brow, bright face, downy beard, and ruddy cheeks, graced with a mole like a speck of amber, just as the poet describes it:

> Here is a slender youth whose hair and face
> All mortals envelope with light or gloom.
> Mark on his cheek the mark of charm and grace,
> A dark spot on a red anemone.

The king greeted the seated young man, pleased to see him. The young man wore a long-sleeved robe of Egyptian silk with gold embroidery, and on his head he wore an Egyptian conical head covering, but his face showed signs of grief and sorrow. When the king greeted him, the young man greeted him back courteously and said, "Pardon me, sir, for not rising, for you deserve even a greater honor." The king replied, "Young man, you are pardoned. I myself am your guest, having come to you on a serious mission. Pray tell me the story behind the lake and the colored fish, as well as this palace and the fact that you sit alone and mourn with no one to console you." When the young man heard this, his tears began to flow over his cheeks until they drenched his breast. Then he sang the following *Mawwaliya* verses:[7]

> Say to the man whom life with arrows shot,
> "How many men have felt the blows of fate!"
> If you did sleep, the eyes of God have not;
> Who can say time is fair and life in constant state?

Then he wept bitterly. The king was astonished and asked, "Young man, why do you cry?" The young man replied, "Sir, how can I refrain from crying in my present condition?" Then he lifted the skirt of his robe, and the king saw that while one half of the young man, from the navel to the head, was human flesh, the other half, from the navel to the feet, was black stone.

*But morning overcame Shahrazad, and she lapsed into silence. Then King Shahrayar thought to himself, "This is an amazing story. I am willing to postpone her execution even for a month, before having her put to death." While the king was thinking to himself, Dinarzad said to her sister Shahrazad, "Sister, what an entertaining story!" Shahrazad replied, "What is this compared with what I shall tell you tomorrow night if I live, the Almighty God willing!"*

---

7. Poems in colloquial language, often sung to the accompaniment of a reed pipe.

*The following night Shahrazad said:*

I heard, O King, that when the king saw the young man in this
condition, he felt very sad and sorry for him, and said with a sigh,
"Young man, you have added one more worry to my worries. I
came to look for an answer to the mystery of the fish, in order to
save them, but ended up looking for an answer to your case, as
well as the fish. There is no power and no strength save in God,
the Almighty, the Magnificent. Hurry up, young man, and tell me
your story." The young man replied, "Lend me your ears, your eyes,
and your mind." The king replied, "My ears, my eyes, and my mind
are ready." The young man said:

# [The Tale of the Enchanted King]

My story, and the story of the fish, is a strange and amazing one,
which, if it could be engraved with needles at the corner of the
eye,[8] would be a lesson to those who would consider. My lord, my
father was the king of this city, and his name was King Mahmud
of the Black Islands. For these four hills were islands. He ruled for
seventy years, and when he died, I succeeded him and married my
cousin. She loved me very much, so much so that if I was away
from her even for a single day, she would refuse to eat and drink
until I returned to her. In this way, we lived together for five years
until one day she went to the bath and I ordered the cook to grill
meat and prepare a sumptuous supper for her. Then I entered this
palace, lay down in this very spot where you are sitting now, and
ordered two maids to sit down, one at my head and one at my feet,
to fan me. But I felt uneasy and could not go to sleep. While I lay
with my eyes closed, breathing heavily, I heard the girl at my head
say to the one at my feet, "O Mas'uda, what a pity for our poor
master with our damned mistress, and him so young!" The other
one replied, "What can one say? May God damn all treacherous,
adulterous women. Alas, it is not right that such a young man like
our master lives with this bitch who spends every night out."
Mas'uda added, "Is our master stupid? When he wakes up at night,

---

8. I.e., if a master calligrapher could by a miracle of his art write the entire story at the corner
of an eye, it would then be read as a double miracle, one for the extraordinary events, one for
the extraordinary art.

doesn't he find that she is not by his side?" The other replied, "Alas, may God trip the bitch our mistress. Does she leave our master with his wits about him? No. She places a sleeping potion in the last drink he takes, offers him the cup, and when he drinks it, he sleeps like a dead man. Then she leaves him and stays out till dawn. When she returns, she burns incense under his nose, and when he inhales it, he wakes up. What a pity!"

My lord, when I heard the conversation between the two maids, I was extremely angry and I could hardly wait for the night to come. When my wife returned from the bath, we had the meal served but ate very little. Then we retired to my bed and I pretended to drink the contents of the cup, which I poured out, and went to sleep. No sooner had I fallen on my side than my wife said, "Go to sleep, and may you never rise again. By God, your sight disgusts me and your company bores me." Then she put on her clothes, perfumed herself with burning incense and, taking my sword, girded herself with it. Then she opened the door and walked out. My lord, I got up . . .

*But morning overtook Shahrazad, and she lapsed into silence. Then Dinarzad said, "O my lady, what an amazing and entertaining story!" Shahrazad replied, "What is this compared with what I shall tell you tomorrow night!"*

THE TWENTY-THIRD NIGHT

*The following night Dinarzad said to her sister Shahrazad, "Please, sister, if you are not sleepy, tell us one of your lovely little tales." Shahrazad replied, "With the greatest pleasure":*

It is related, O King, that the enchanted young man said to the king:

Then I followed her, as she left the palace and traversed my city until she stood at the city gate. There she uttered words I could not understand, and the locks fell off and the gate opened by itself. She went out, and I followed her until she slipped through the trash mounds and came to a hut built with palm leaves, leading to a domed structure built with sun-dried bricks. After she entered, I climbed to the top of the dome, and when I looked inside, I saw my wife standing before a decrepit black man sitting on reed shavings and dressed in tatters. She kissed the ground before him and

he raised his head and said, "Damn you, why are you late? My
black cousins were here. They played with the bat and ball, sang,
and drank brewed liquor. They had a good time, each with his own
girlfriend, except for myself, for I refused even to drink with them
because you were absent."

My wife replied, "O my lord and lover, don't you know that I
am married to my cousin, who finds me most loathsome and detests
me more than anyone else? Were it not for your sake, I would not
have let the sun rise before reducing his city to rubble, a dwelling
place for the bears and the foxes, where the owl hoots and the crow
crows, and would have hurled its stones beyond Mount Qaf."[9] He
replied, "Damn you, you are lying. I swear in the name of black
chivalry that as of tonight, if our cousins visit me and you fail to
be present, I will never befriend you, lie down with you, or let my
body touch yours. You cursed woman, you have been playing with
me like a piece of marble, and I am subject to your whims, you
cursed, rotten woman." My lord, when I heard their conversation,
the world started to turn black before my eyes, and I lost my senses.
Then I heard my wife crying and imploring, "O my lover and my
heart's desire, if you remain angry at me, whom else have I got,
and if you turn me out, who will take me in, O my lord, my lover,
and light of my eye?" She kept crying and begging until he was
appeased. Then, feeling happy, she took off her outer garments,
and asked, "My lord, have you anything for your little girl to eat?"
The black man replied, "Open the copper basin," and when she
lifted the lid, she found some leftover fried rat bones. After she ate
them, he said to her, "There is some brewed liquor left in that jug.
You may drink it." She drank the liquor and washed her hands and
lay beside the black man on the reed shavings. Then she undressed
and slipped under his tatters. I climbed down from the top of the
dome and, entering through the door, grabbed the sword that my
wife had brought with her, and drew it, intending to kill both of
them. I first struck the black man on the neck and thought that
I had killed him.

*But morning overtook Shahrazad, and she lapsed into silence.*
*Then Dinarzad said, "Sister, what an entertaining story!" Shahrazad*
*replied, "Tomorrow night I shall tell you something more enter-*
*taining if I live!"*

9. Legendary mountain cited for its remoteness.

## THE TWENTY-FOURTH NIGHT

*The following night Dinarzad said to her sister Shahrazad, "For God's sake, sister, if you are not sleepy, tell us one of your lovely little tales." Shahrazad replied, "With the greatest pleasure":*

I heard, O King, that the enchanted young man said to the king:

My lord, I struck the black man on the neck, but failed to cut the two arteries. Instead I only cut into the skin and flesh of the throat and thought that I had killed him. He began to snort violently, and my wife pulled away from him. I retreated, put the sword back in its place, and went back to the city. I entered the palace and went to sleep in my bed till morning. When my wife arrived and I looked at her, I saw that she had cut her hair and put on a mourning dress. She said, "Husband, don't reproach me for what I am doing, for I have received news that my mother has died, that my father was killed in the holy war, and that my two brothers have also lost their lives, one in battle, the other bitten by a snake. I have every reason to weep and mourn." When I heard what she said, I did not reply, except to say, "I don't reproach you. Do as you wish."

She mourned for an entire year, weeping and wailing. When the year ended, she said to me, "I want you to let me build inside the palace a mausoleum for me to use as a special place of mourning and to call it the house of sorrows." I replied, "Go ahead." Then she gave the order, and a house of mourning was erected for her, with a domed mausoleum and a tomb inside. Then, my lord, she moved the wounded black man to the mausoleum and placed him in the tomb. But, although he was still alive, from the day I cut his throat, he never spoke a word or was able to do her any good, except to drink liquids. She visited him in the mausoleum every day, morning and evening, bringing with her beverages and broth, and she kept at it for an entire year, while I held my patience and left her to her own devices. One day, while she was unaware, I entered the mausoleum and found her crying and lamenting:

> When I see your distress,
> It pains me, as you see.
> And when I see you not,
> It pains me, as you see.
> O speak to me, my life,
> My master, talk to me.

Then she sang:

> The day I have you is the day I crave;
> The day you leave me is the day I die.
> Were I to live in fear of promised death,
> I'd rather be with you than my life save.

Then she recited the following verses:

> If I had every blessing in the world
> And all the kingdom of the Persian king,
> If I see not your person with my eyes,
> All this will not be worth an insect's wing.

When she stopped crying, I said to her, "Wife, you have mourned and wept enough and further tears are useless." She replied, "Husband, do not interfere with my mourning. If you interfere again, I will kill myself." I kept quiet and left her alone, while she mourned, wept, and lamented for another year. One day, after the third year, feeling the strain of this drawn-out, heavy burden, something happened to trigger my anger, and when I returned, I found my wife in the mausoleum, beside the tomb, saying, "My lord, I have not had any word from you. For three years I have had no reply." Then she recited the following verses:

> O tomb, O tomb, has he his beauties lost,
> Or have you lost yourself that radiant look?
> O tomb, neither a garden nor a star,
> The sun and moon at once how can you host?

These verses added anger to my anger, and I said to myself, "Oh, how much longer shall I endure?" Then I burst out with the following verses:

> O tomb, O tomb, has he his blackness lost,
> Or have you lost yourself that filthy look?
> O tomb, neither a toilet nor a heap of dirt,
> Charcoal and mud at once how can you host?

When my wife heard me, she sprang up and said, "Damn you, dirty dog. It was you who did this to me, wounded my beloved, and tormented me by depriving me of his youth, while he has been lying here for three years, neither alive nor dead." I said to her, "You, dirtiest of whores and filthiest of all venal women who ever desired and copulated with black slaves, yes it was I who did this to him." Then I grabbed my sword and drew it to strike her. But when she heard me and realized that I was determind to kill her, she laughed and said, "Get away, you dog. Alas, alas, what is done cannot be undone; nor will the dead come back to life, but God has delivered into my hand the one who did this to me and set my heart ablaze with the fire of revenge." Then she stood up, uttered words I could not understand, and cried, "With my magic and cunning, be half man, half stone." Sir, from that instant, I have been as you now see me, dejected and sad, helpless and sleepless, neither living with the living nor dead among the dead.

*But morning overtook Shahrazad, and she lapsed into silence. Then Dinarzad said, "Sister, what an amazing and entertaining story!" Shahrazad replied, "Tomorrow night I shall tell you something more entertaining if the king spares me and lets me live!"*

### THE TWENTY-FIFTH NIGHT

*The following night Dinarzad said to her sister Shahrazad, "Sister, if you are not sleepy, tell us one of your lovely little tales to while away the night." Shahrazad replied, "With the greatest pleasure":*

It is related, O King, that the enchanted young man said to the king:

"After my wife turned me into this condition, she cast a spell on the city, with all its gardens, fields, and markets, the very place where your troops are camping now. My wife turned the inhabitants of my city, who belonged to four sects, Muslims, Magians,[1] Christians, and Jews, into fish, the Muslims white, the Magians red, the Christians blue, and the Jews yellow. Likewise, she turned the islands into four hills surrounding the lake. As if what she has done to me and the city is not enough, she strips me naked every day and gives me a hundred lashes with the whip until my back is lacerated and begins to bleed. Then she clothes my upper half with a hairshirt like a coarse rug and covers it with these luxurious garments." Then the young man burst into tears and recited the following verses:

> O Lord, I bear with patience your decree,
> And so that I may please you, I endure,
> That for their tyranny and unfair use
> Our recompense your Paradise may be.
> You never let the tyrant go, my Lord;
> Pluck me out of the fire, Almighty God.

---

1. Zoroastrian priests. Zoroastrianism is the religion of ancient Persia, based on the recognition of the dual principle of good and evil or light and darkness.

The king said to the young man, "Young man, you have lifted one anxiety but added another worry to my worries. But where is your wife, and where is the mausoleum with the wounded black man?" The young man replied, "O King, the black slave is lying in the tomb inside the mausoleum, which is in the adjoining room. My wife comes to visit him at dawn every day, and when she comes, she strips me naked and gives me a hundred lashes with the whip, while I cry and scream without being able to stand up and defend myself, since I am half stone, half flesh and blood. After she punishes me, she goes to the black slave to give him beverages and broth to drink. Tomorrow at dawn she will come as usual." The king replied, "By God, young man, I shall do something for you that will go down in history and commemorate my name." Then the king sat to converse with the young man until night fell and they went to sleep.

The king got up before dawn, took off his clothes, and, drawing his sword, entered the room with the domed mausoleum and found it lit with candles and lamps and scented with incense, perfume, saffron, and ointments. He went straight to the black man and killed him. Then he carried him out and threw him in a well inside the palace. When he came back, he put on the clothes of the black man, covered himself, and lay hiding at the bottom of the tomb, with the drawn sword hidden under his clothes.

A while later, the cursed witch arrived, and the first thing she did was to strip her husband naked, take a whip, and whip him again and again, while he cried, "Ah wife, have pity on me; help me; I have had enough punishment and pain; have pity on me." She replied, "You should have had pity on me and spared my lover."

*But morning overtook Shahrazad, and she lapsed into silence. Then Dinarzad said, "Sister, what an amazing and entertaining story!" Shahrazad replied, "What is this compared with what I shall tell you tomorrow night if I live!" King Shahrayar, with a mixture of amazement, pain, and sorrow for the enchanted youth, said to himself, "By God, I shall postpone her execution for tonight and many more nights, even for two months, until I hear the rest of the story and find out what happened to the enchanted young man. Then I shall have her put to death, as I did the others." So he said to himself.*

## The Twenty-Sixth Night

*The following night Dinarzad said to Shahrazad, "Sister, if you are not sleepy, tell us one of your lovely little tales to while away the night." Shahrazad replied, "With the greatest pleasure":*

I heard, O King, that after the witch punished her husband by whipping him until his sides and shoulders were bleeding and she satisfied her thirst for revenge, she dressed him with the coarse hair-shirt and covered it with the outer garments. Then she headed to the black man, with the usual cup of drink and the broth. She entered the mausoleum, reached the tomb, and began to cry, wail, and lament, saying, "Lover, denying me yourself is not your custom. Do not be stingy, for my foes gloat over our separation. Be generous with your love, for forsaking is not your custom. Visit me, for my life is in your visit. O my lord, speak to me; O my lord, entertain me." Then she sang the following verses of the *Mufrad* [2] variety:

> For how long is this cruel disdain,
> Have I not paid with enough tears?
> O lover, talk to me,
> O lover, speak to me,
> O lover, answer me.

The king lowered his voice, stammered, and, simulating the accent of black people, said, "Ah, ah, ah! There is no power and no strength save in God the Almighty, the Magnificent." When she heard him speak, she screamed with joy and fainted, and when she came to herself, she cried, "Is it true that you spoke to me?" The king replied, "Damn you, you don't deserve that anyone should speak to you or answer you." She asked, "What is the cause?" He replied, "All day long you punish your husband, while he screams for help. From sunset till dawn he cries, implores, and invokes God against you and me, with his deafening and enervating cries that deprive me of sleep. If it had not been for this, I would have recovered a long time ago, and this is why I have not spoken to you or answered you." She said, "My lord, if you allow me, I shall deliver him from his present condition." He replied, "Deliver him and rid us of his noise."

She went out of the mausoleum, took a bowl, and, filling it with water, uttered a spell over it, and the water began to boil and bub-

---

2. Literally "single," a verse form.

ble as in a caldron over fire. Then she sprinkled the young man with the water and said, "By the power of my spell, if the Creator has created you in this form, or if he has turned you into this form out of anger at you, stay as you are, but if you have been transformed by my magic and cunning, turn back to your normal form, by the will of God, Creator of the world." The young man shook himself at once and stood up, erect and sound, and he rejoiced and thanked God for his deliverance. Then his wife said to him, "Get out of my sight and don't ever come back, for if you do and I see you here, I shall kill you." She yelled at him, and he went away.

Then she returned to the mausoleum and, descending to the tomb, called out, "My sweet lord, come out and let me see your handsome face." The king replied in a muffled voice, "You have rid me of the limb, but failed to rid us of the body." She asked, "My sweet lord, what do you mean by the body?" He replied, "Damn you, cursed woman, it is the inhabitants of this city and its four islands, for every night at midnight, the fish raise their heads from the lake to implore and invoke God against me, and this is why I do not recover. Go to them and deliver them at once; then come back to hold my hand and help me rise, for I am beginning to feel better already." When she heard him, she rejoiced and replied joyfully, "Yes, my lord, yes, with God's help, my sweetheart." Then she rose, went to the lake, and took a little of its water.

*But morning overtook Shahrazad, and she lapsed into silence. Then Dinarzad said, "What an amazing and entertaining story!" Shahrazad replied, "What is this compared with what I shall tell you tomorrow night if the king spares me and I live!"*

### THE TWENTY-SEVENTH NIGHT

*The following night Dinarzad said to her sister Shahrazad, "If you are not sleepy, tell us one of your lovely little tales to while away the night." Shahrazad replied, "With the greatest pleasure":*

It is related, O King, that the wife uttered some words over the lake, and the fish began to dance, and at that instant the spell was lifted, and the townspeople resumed their usual activities and returned to their buying and selling. Then she went back to the palace, entered the mausoleum, and said, "My lord, give me your gracious hand and rise." The king replied in a muffled voice, "Come closer to me." She moved closer, while he urged her "Come closer still," and she moved until her body touched his. Then he pushed her back and with one stroke of the sword sliced her in half, and she fell in two to the ground.

Then the king went out and, finding the enchanted young man waiting for him, congratulated him on his deliverance, and the young man kissed his hand, thanked him, and invoked God's blessing on him. Then the king asked him, "Do you wish to stay here or come with me to my city?" The young man replied, "King of the age, and Lord of the world, do you know the distance between your city and mine?" The king replied, "It is a half-day journey." The young man said, "O King, you are dreaming, for between your city and mine it is a full year's journey. You reached us in half a day because the city was enchanted." The king asked, "Still, do you wish to stay here in your city or come with me?" The young man replied, "O King, I shall not part from you, even for one moment." The king was happy and said, "Thank God who has given you to me. You shall be a son to me, for I have never had one." They embraced, holding each other closely, and felt happy. Then they walked together back to the palace, and when they entered the palace, the enchanted young king announced to the eminent men of his kingdom and to his retinue that he was going on a journey.

He spent ten days in preparation, packing what he needed, together with the gifts that the princes and merchants of the city had given him for his journey. Then he set out with the king, with his heart on fire to be leaving his city for a whole year. He left, with fifty Mamluks and many guides and servants, bearing one hundred loads of gifts, rarities, and treasures, as well as money. They journeyed on, evening and morning, night and day, for a whole year until God granted them safe passage and they reached their destination. Then the king sent someone to inform the vizier of his safe return, and the vizier came out with all the troops and most of the townspeople to meet him. Having given him up for lost, they were exceedingly happy, and the city was decorated and its streets were spread with silk carpets. The vizier and the soldiers dismounted and, kissing the ground before the king, congratulated him on his safety and invoked God's blessing on him.

Then they entered the city, and the king sat on his throne and, meeting with the vizier, explained to him why he had been absent for an entire year. He told him the story of the young man and how he, the king, had dealt with the young man's wife and saved him and the city, and the vizier turned to the young man and congratulated him on his deliverance. Then the princes, viziers, chamberlains, and deputies took their places, and the king bestowed on them robes of honor, gifts, and other favors. Then he sent for the fisherman, who was the cause of saving the young man and the city, and when the fisherman stood before the king, the king bestowed on him robes of honor, and then asked him, "Do you have any children?" The fisherman replied that he had one boy and two girls. The king had them brought before him, and he himself married one of the girls, while he married the other to the enchanted young man. Moreover, the king took the fisherman's son into his service and made him one of his attendants. Then he conferred authority on the vizier, appointing him king of the city of the Black Islands, supplied him with provisions and fodder for the journey, and ordered the fifty Mamluks, who had come with them, as well as a host of other people, to go with him. He also sent with him many robes of honor and many fine gifts for all the princes and prominent men there. The vizier took his leave, kissed the king's hand, and departed. The king, the enchanted young man, and the fisherman lived peacefully thereafter, and the fisherman became one of the richest men of his time, with daughters married to kings.

*But morning overtook Shahrazad, and she lapsed into silence. Then Dinarzad said, "What an amazing and entertaining story!" Shahrazad replied, "What is this compared with what I shall tell you tomorrow night if the king spares me and lets me live!"*

### THE TWENTY-EIGHTH NIGHT

*The following night Dinarzad said to her sister Shahrazad, "Sister, if you are not sleepy, tell us one of your lovely little tales." Shahrazad replied, "With the greatest pleasure":*

# [THE STORY OF THE PORTER
# AND THE THREE LADIES]

I heard, O happy King, that once there lived in the city of Baghdad[3] a bachelor who worked as a porter. One day he was standing in the market, leaning on his basket, when a woman approached him. She wore a Mosul[4] cloak, a silk veil, a fine kerchief embroidered with gold, and a pair of leggings tied with fluttering laces.

---

3. Then and now capital of Iraq, at that time capital of the Abbasid caliphate and its empire, situated on the Tigris River. It is the scene of several of the stories of the *Nights*.
4. Then and now an important city in northern Iraq.

When she lifted her veil, she revealed a pair of beautiful dark eyes graced with long lashes and a tender expression, like those celebrated by the poets. Then with a soft voice and a sweet tone, she said to him, "Porter, take your basket and follow me." Hardly believing his ears, the porter took his basket and hurried behind her, saying, "O lucky day, O happy day." She walked before him until she stopped at the door of a house, and when she knocked, an old Christian came down, received a dinar from her and handed her an olive green jug of wine. She placed the jug in the basket and said, "Porter, take your basket and follow me." Saying, "Very well, O auspicious day, O lucky day, O happy day," the porter lifted the basket and followed her until she stopped at the fruit vendor's, where she bought yellow and red apples, Hebron peaches and Turkish quinces, and seacoast lemons and royal oranges, as well as baby cucumbers. She also bought Aleppo jasmine and Damascus lilies, myrtle berries and mignonettes, daisies and gillyflowers, lilies of the valley and irises, narcissus and daffodils, violets and anemones, as well as pomegranate blossoms. She placed everything in the porter's basket and asked him to follow her.

Then she stopped at the butcher's and said, "Cut me off ten pounds of fresh mutton." She paid him, and he cut off the pieces she desired, wrapped them, and handed them to her. She placed them in the basket, together with some charcoal, and said, "Porter, take your basket and follow me." The porter, wondering at all these purchases, placed his basket on his head and followed her until she came to the grocer's, where she bought whatever she needed of condiments, such as olives of all kinds, pitted, salted, and pickled, tarragon, cream cheese, Syrian cheese, and sweet as well as sour pickles. She placed the container in the basket and said, "Porter, take your basket and follow me." The porter carried his basket and followed her until she came to the dry grocer's, where she bought all sorts of dry fruits and nuts: Aleppo raisins, Iraqi sugar canes, pressed Ba'albak figs, roasted chick-peas, as well as shelled pistachios, almonds, and hazelnuts. She placed everything in the porter's basket, turned to him, and said, "Porter take your basket and follow me."

The porter carried the basket and followed her until she came to the confectioner's, where she bought a whole tray full of every kind of pastry and sweet in the shop, such as sour barley rolls, sweet rolls, date rolls, Cairo rolls, Turkish rolls, and open-worked Balkan rolls, as well as cookies, stuffed and musk-scented kataifs, amber combs, ladyfingers, widows' bread, Kadi's tidbits, eat-and-thanks, and almond pudding. When she placed the tray in the basket, the porter said to her, "Mistress, if you had let me know, I would have

brought with me a nag or a camel to carry all these purchases."
She smiled and walked ahead until she came to the druggist's, where
she bought ten bottles of scented waters, lilywater, rosewater scented
with musk, and the like, as well as ambergris, musk, aloewood,
and rosemary. She also bought two loaves of sugar and candles and
torches. Then she put everything in the basket, turned to the porter,
and said, "Porter, take your basket and follow me." The porter carried the basket and walked behind her until she came to a spacious
courtyard facing a tall, stately mansion with massive pillars and
a double door inlaid with ivory and shining gold. The girl stopped
at the door and knocked gently.

*But morning overtook Shahrazad, and she lapsed into silence.*
*Then her sister said, "Sister, what a lovely and entertaining story!"*
*Shahrazad replied, "What is this compared with what I shall tell*
*you tomorrow night if the king spares me and lets me live! May*
*God grant him long life."*

## THE TWENTY-NINTH NIGHT

*The following night Dinarzad said to her sister Shahrazad, "Sister,*
*if you are not sleepy, tell us one of your little tales to while away*
*the night." Shahrazad replied, "I hear and obey":*

I heard, O wise and happy King, that as the porter stood with
the basket, at the door, behind the girl, marveling at her beauty,
her charm, and her elegant, eloquent, and liberal ways, the door
was unlocked, and the two leaves swung open. The porter, looking
to see who opened the door, saw a full-bosomed girl, about five
feet tall. She was all charm, beauty, and perfect grace, with a forehead like the new moon, eyes like those of a deer or wild heifer,
eyebrows like the crescent in the month of Sha'ban,[5] cheeks like
red anemones, mouth like the seal of Solomon, lips like red car-
nelian, teeth like a row of pearls set in coral, neck like a cake for
a king, bosom like a fountain, breasts like a pair of big pomegranates
resembling a rabbit with uplifted ears, and belly with a navel like
a cup that holds a pound of benzoin ointment. She was like her
of whom the poet aptly said:

> On stately sun and full moon cast your sight;
> Savor the flowers and lavender's delight.

5. The eighth month of the lunar Muslim year.

Your eyes have never seen such white in black,
Such radiant face with hair so deeply dark.
With rosy cheeks, Beauty proclaimed her name,
To those who had not yet received her fame.
Her swaying heavy hips I joyed to see,
But her sweet, slender waist brought tears to me.

When the porter saw her, he lost his senses and his wits, and the basket nearly fell from his head, as he exclaimed, "Never in my life have I seen a more blessed day than this!" Then the girl who had opened the door said to the girl who had done the shopping, "Sister, what are you waiting for? Come in and relieve this poor man of his heavy burden." The shopper and the porter went in, and the doorkeeper locked the door and followed them until they came to a spacious, well-appointed, and splendid hall. It had arched compartments and niches with carved woodwork; it had a booth hung with drapes; and it had closets and cupboards covered with curtains. In the middle stood a large pool full of water, with a fountain in the center, and at the far end stood a couch of black juniper wood, set with gems and pearls, with a canopylike mosquito net of red silk, fastened with pearls as big as hazelnuts or bigger. The curtain was unfastened, and a dazzling girl emerged, with genial charm, wise mien, and features as radiant as the moon. She had an elegant figure, the scent of ambergris, sugared lips, Babylonian eyes, with eyebrows as arched as a pair of bent bows, and a face whose radiance put the shining sun to shame, for she was like a great star soaring in the heavens, or a dome of gold, or an unveiled bride, or a splendid fish swimming in a fountain, or a morsel of luscious fat in a bowl of milk soup. She was like her of whom the poet said:

Her smile reveals twin rows of pearls
Or white daisies or pearly hail.
Her forelock like the night unfurls;
Before her light the sun is pale.

The third girl rose from the couch and strutted slowly until she joined her sisters in the middle of the hall, saying, "Why are you standing? Lift the load off this poor man." The doorkeeper stood in front of the porter, and the shopper stood behind him, and with the help of the third girl, they lifted the basket down and emptied its contents, stacking up the fruits and pickles on one side and the flowers and fresh herbs on the other. When everything was arranged, they gave the porter one dinar and said . . .

*But morning overtook Shahrazad, and she lapsed into silence.
Then Dinarzad said to her sister Shahrazad, "What an amazing
and entertaining story!" Shahrazad replied, "If I am alive tomorrow night, I shall tell you something stranger and more amazing
than this."*

### THE THIRTIETH NIGHT

*The following night Dinarzad said to her sister Shahrazad, "Sister,
tell us the rest of the story of the three girls." Shahrazad replied,
"With the greatest pleasure":*

I heard, O King, that when the porter saw how charming and
beautiful the girls were and saw how much they had stacked of wine,
meat, fruits, nuts, sweets, fresh herbs, candles, charcoal, and the
like for drinking and carousing, without seeing any man around,
he was very astonished and stood there, hesitant to leave. One of
the girls asked him, "Why don't you go? Do you find your pay too
little?" and, turning to her sister, said, "Give him another dinar."
The porter replied, "By God, ladies, my pay is not little, for I deserve
not even two dirhams, but I have been wondering about your situation and the absence of anyone to entertain you. For as a table needs
four legs to stand on, you being three, likewise need a fourth, for
the pleasure of men is not complete without women, and the
pleasure of women is not complete without men. The poet says:

> For our delight four things we need, the lute,
> . The harp, the zither, and the double flute,
> Blending with the scent of four lovely flowers,
> Roses, myrtles, anemones, and gillyflowers.
> Only in four such things join together,
> Money, and wine, and youth, and a lover.

You are three and you need a fourth, a man." His words pleased
the girls, who laughed and said, "How can we manage that, being
girls who keep our business to ourselves, for we fear to entrust our
secrets where they may not be kept. We have read in some book
what ibn al-Tammam[6] has said:

> Your own secret to none reveal;
> It will be lost when it is told.

---

6. Actually Abu-Tamman, an Arab poet of the ninth century, and author of the *Hamasa*.

> If your own breast cannot conceal,
> How can another better hold?"

When the porter heard their words, he replied, "Trust me; I am a sensible and wise man. I have studied the sciences and attained knowledge; I have read and learned, and presented my knowledge and cited my authorities. I reveal the good and conceal the bad, and I am well-behaved. I am like the man of whom the poet said:

> Only the faithful does a secret keep;
> None but the best can hold it unrevealed.
> I keep a secret in a well-shut house
> Of which the key is lost and the lock sealed."

When the girls heard what he said, they replied, "You know very well that this table has cost us a lot and that we have spent a great deal of money to get all these provisions. Do you have anything to pay in return for the entertainment? For we shall not let you stay unless we see your share; otherwise you will drink and enjoy yourself with us at our expense." The mistress of the house said, "'Without gain, love is not worth a grain.'" The doorkeeper added, "Have you got anything, my dear? If you are emptyhanded, go emptyhanded." But the shopper said, "Sisters, stop teasing him, for by God, he served me well today; no one else would have been as patient with me. Whatever his share will come to, I shall pay for him myself." The porter, overjoyed, kissed the ground before her and thanked her, saying, "By God, it was you who brought me my first business today and I still have the dinar you gave me; take it back and take me, not as a companion but as a servant." The girls replied, "You are very welcome to join us."

Then the shopper, girding herself, began to arrange this and that. She first tidied up, strained the wine, stacked up the flasks, and arranged the bowls, goblets, cups, decanters, plates, and serving spoons, as well as various utensils in silver and gold. Having prepared all the requisites, she set the table by the pool and laid it will all kinds of food and drink. Then she invited them to the banquet and sat down to serve. Her sisters joined her, as did the porter, who thought that he was in a dream. She filled the first cup and drank it, filled the second and offered it to one of her sisters, who drank it, filled a third and gave it to the other sister to drink, and filled a fourth and gave it to the porter, who held it in his hand and, saluting with a bow, thanked her and recited the following verses:

> Drink not the cup, save with a friend you trust,
> One whose blood to noble forefathers owes.

> Wine, like the wind, is sweet if o'er the sweet,
> And foul if o'er the foul it haply blows.

Then he emptied his cup, and the doorkeeper returned his salute and recited the following verses:

> Cheers, and drink it in good health;
> This wine is good for your health.

The porter thanked her and kissed her hand. After the girls had drunk again and had given the porter more to drink, he turned to his companion, the shopper, saying, "My lady, your servant is calling on you," and recited the following verses:

> One of your slaves is waiting at your door,
> With ample thanks for your ample favor.

She replied "By God, I will kiss you. Drink the wine and enjoy it in good health, for it relieves pain, hastens the cure, and restores health." The porter emptied his cup and, pouring out another, kissed her hand, offered it to her, and proceeded to recite the following verses:

> I gave her pure old wine, red as her cheeks,
> Which with red fire did like a furnace glow.
> She kissed the brim and with a smile she asked,
> "How can you cheeks with cheeks pay what you owe?"
> I said, "Drink! This wine is my blood and tears,
> And my soul is the fragrance in the cup."
> She said, "If for me you have shed your blood,
> Most gladly will I on this red wine sup."

The girl took the cup, drank it off, then sat by her sister.

Thus receiving the full and returning the empty, they went on drinking cup after cup until the porter began to feel tipsy, lost his inhibitions, and was aroused. He danced and sang lyrics and ballads and carried on with the girls, toying, kissing, biting, groping, rubbing, fingering, and playing jokes on them, while one girl thrust a morsel in his mouth, another flirted with him, another served him with some fresh herbs, and another fed him sweets until he was in utter bliss. They carried on until they got drunk and the wine turned their heads. When the wine got the better of them, the doorkeeper went to the pool, took off her clothes, and stood stark naked, save for what was covered of her body by her loosened hair. Then she said, "Whee," went into the pool, and immersed herself in the water.

*But morning overtook Shahrazad, and she lapsed into silence. Then Dinarzad said, "What an amazing and entertaining story!"*

*Shahrazad replied, "What is this compared with what I shall tell you tomorrow night!"*

THE THIRTY-FIRST NIGHT

*The following night Dinarzad said, "Sister, if you are not sleepy, tell us one of your lovely little tales to while away the night." Shahrazad replied, "With the greatest pleasure":*

I heard that the doorkeeper went into the pool, threw water on herself, and, after immersing herself completely, began to sport, taking water in her mouth and squirting it all over her sisters and the porter. Then she washed herself under her breasts, between her thighs, and inside her navel. Then she rushed out of the pool, sat naked in the porter's lap and, pointing to her slit, asked, "My lord and my love, what is this?" "Your womb," said he, and she replied, "Pooh, pooh, you have no shame," and slapped him on the neck. "Your vulva," said he, and the other sister pinched him, shouting, "Bah, this is an ugly word." "Your cunt," said he, and the third sister boxed him on the chest and knocked him over, saying, "Fie, have some shame." "Your clitoris," said he, and again the naked girl slapped him, saying, "No." "Your pudenda, your pussy, your sex tool," said he, and she kept replying, "No, no." He kept giving various other names, but every time he uttered a name, one of the girls hit him and asked, "What do you call this?" And they went on, this one boxing him, that one slapping him, another hitting him. At last, he turned to them and asked, "All right, what is its name?" The naked girl replied, "The basil of the bridges." The porter cried, "The basil of the bridges! You should have told me this from the beginning, oh, oh!" Then they passed the cup around and went on drinking for a while.

Then the shopper, like her sister, took off all her clothes, saying, "Whee," went into the pool, and immersed herself completely in the water. Then she washed herself under the belly, around the breasts, and between the thighs. Then she rushed out, threw herself in the porter's lap, and asked, "My little lord, what is this?" "Your vulva," said he, and she gave him a blow with which the hall resounded, saying, "Fie, you have no shame." "Your womb," said he, and her sister hit him, saying, "Fie, what an ugly word!" "Your clitoris," said he, and the other sister boxed him, saying, "Fie, fie, you are shameless." They kept at it, this one boxing him, that one slapping him, another hitting him, another jabbing him, repeating, "No, no," while he kept shouting, "Your womb, your cunt, your

pussy." Finally he cried, "The basil of the bridges," and all three
burst out laughing till they fell on their backs. But again all three
slapped him on the neck and said, "No, this is not its name." He
cried, "All right, what is its name?" One of them replied, "Why don't
you say 'the husked sesame'?" He cried out, "The husked sesame!
Thank God, we are finally there." Then the girl put on her clothes
and they sat, passing the cup around, while the porter moaned with
sore neck and shoulders.

They drank for a while, and then the eldest and fairest of the
three stood up and began to undress. The porter touched his neck
and began to rub it with his hand, saying, "For God's sake, spare
my neck and shoulders," while the girl stripped naked, threw herself into the pool, and immersed herself. The porter looked at her
naked body, which looked like a slice of the moon, and at her face,
which shone like the full moon or the rising sun, and admired her
figure, her breasts, and her swaying heavy hips, for she was naked
as God had created her. Moaning "Oh, oh," he addressed her with
the following verses:

> If I compare your figure to the bough,
> When green, I err and a sore burden bear.
> The bough is fairest when covered with leaves,
> And you are fairest when completely bare.

When the girl heard his verses, she came quickly out of the pool,
sat in his lap and, pointing to her slit, asked "O light of my eyes,
O sweetheart, what is the name of this?" "The basil of the bridges,"
said he, but she replied, "Bah!" "The husked sesame," said he, and
she replied, "Pooh!" "Your womb," said he, and she replied, "Fie,
you have no shame," and slapped him on the neck. To make a long
story short, O King, the porter kept declaring, "Its name is so,"
and she kept saying "No, no, no, no." When he had had his fill
of blows, pinches, and bites until his neck swelled and he choked
and felt miserable, he cried out, "All right, what is its name?" She
replied, "Why don't you say the Inn of Abu Masrur?" "Ha, ha, the
Inn of Abu Masrur," said the porter. Then she got up, and after
she put on her clothes, they resumed their drinking and passed the
cup around for a while.

Then the porter stood up, took off his clothes, and, revealing
something dangling between his legs, he leapt and plunged into the
middle of the pool.

*But morning overtook Shahrazad, and she lapsed into silence.
Then Dinarzad said to her sister Shahrazad, "Sister, what a lovely
and entertaining story!" Shahrazad replied, "What is this compared*

*with what I shall tell you tomorrow night if the king spares me and lets me live!" The king said to himself, "By God, I will not have her put to death until I hear the rest of the story. Then I shall do to her what I did to the others."*

THE THIRTY-SECOND NIGHT

*The following night Dinarzad said to her sister Shahrazad, "Sister, if you are not sleepy, tell us one of your lovely little tales." Shahrazad replied, "With the greatest pleasure":*

I heard, O King, that when the porter went down into the pool, he bathed and washed himself under the beard and under the arms; then he rushed out of the pool, planted himself in the lap of the fairest girl, put his arms on the lap of the doorkeeper, rested his legs in the lap of the shopper and, pointing to his penis, asked, "Ladies, what is this?" They were pleased with his antics and laughed, for his disposition agreed with theirs, and they found him entertaining. One of them said, "Your cock," and he replied, "You have no shame; this is an ugly word." The other said, "Your penis," and he replied, "You should be ashamed; may God put you to shame." The third said, "Your dick," and he replied, "No." Another said, "Your stick," and he replied "No." Another said, "Your thing, your testicles, your prick," and he kept saying, "No, no, no." They asked, "What is the name of this?" He hugged this and kissed that, pinched the one, bit the other, and nibbled on the third, as he took satisfaction, while they laughed until they fell on their backs. At last they asked, "Friend, what is its name?" The porter replied, "Don't you know its name? It is the smashing mule." They asked, "What is the meaning of the name the smashing mule?" He replied, "It is the one who grazes in the basil of the bridges, eats the husked sesame, and gallops in the Inn of Abu Masrur." Again they laughed until they fell on their backs and almost fainted with laughter. Then they resumed their carousing and drinking and carried on until nightfall.

When it was dark, they said to the porter, "Sir, it is time that you get up, put on your slippers, and show us your back." The porter replied, "Where do I go from here? The departure of my soul from my body is easier for me than my departure from your company. Let us join the night with the day and let each of us go his way early tomorrow morning." The shopper said, "By God, sisters, he is right. For God's sake and for my sake, let him stay tonight, so that we may laugh at him and amuse ourselves with him, for who will live to meet with one like him again? He is a clever and witty rogue." They said, "You cannot spend the night with us unless you agree to abide by our condition, that whatever we do and whatever happens to us, you shall refrain from asking for any explanation, for 'speak not of what concerns you not, lest you hear what pleases you not.' This is our condition; don't be too curious about any action of ours." He replied, "Yes, yes, yes, I am dumb and blind." They said, "Rise, then, go to the entrance, and read what is inscribed on the door and the entrance." He got up, went to the door, and found on the door and the entrance the following inscription written in letters of gold, "Whoever speaks of what concerns him not hears what pleases him not." The porter came back and said, "I pledge to you that I will not speak of what concerns me not."

Then the shopper went and prepared supper, and after they had something to eat, they lighted the lamps, and, sticking the aloewood and ambergris into the wax, they lighted the candles, and the incense burned, rose, and filled the hall. Then they changed the plates, laid the table with wine and fresh fruits, and sat to drink. They sat for a long time, eating, drinking, engaging in refined conversation, bantering, and laughing, and joking, when suddenly they heard a knocking at the door. Without showing much concern, one of the girls rose, went to the door, and returned after a while, saying, "Sisters, if you listen to me, you will spend a delightful night, a night to remember." They asked, "How so?" She replied, "At this very moment, three one-eyed dervishes[7] are standing at the door, each with a shaven head, shaven beard, and shaven eyebrows, and each blind in the right eye. It is a most amazing coincidence. They have just arrived in Baghdad from their travel, as one can see from their condition, and this is their first time in our city. Night overtook them and, being strangers with no one to go to and unable to find a place to sleep, they knocked at our door, hoping that someone would give them the key to the stable or offer them a room for the night. Sister, each one of them is a sight, with a face that would make a mourner laugh. Would you agree to let them in for this one time, so that we may amuse ourselves with them tonight and let them go early tomorrow morning?" She continued to persuade her sisters until they consented, saying, "Let them in, but make it a condition that they 'speak not of what concerns them not, lest they hear what pleases them not.'"

Pleased, she disappeared for a while and returned, followed by three one-eyed dervishes, who greeted them, bowed, and stood back.

7. Members of a Muslim order of mendicant monks, vowed to a life of poverty.

The three girls rose to greet them, extended welcomes, expressed
delight at their visit, and congratulated them on their safe arrival.
The three dervishes thanked them and again saluted with bows,
and when they saw the beautiful hall, the well-set table laden with
wine, nuts, and dried fruits, the burning candles, the smoking incense, and the three girls, who had thrown off all restraint, they
exclaimed with one voice, "By God, this is fine." When they turned
and looked at the porter, who, sore from the beating and slapping
and intoxicated with the wine, lay almost unconscious, they said,
"Whether an Arab or a foreigner, he is a brother dervish." The
porter sat up and, fixing his eyes on them, said, "Sit here without
meddling. Haven't you read the inscription on the door, which is
quite clearly written, 'Speak not of what concerns you not, lest you
hear what pleases you not'? Yet as soon as you come in you wag
your tongues at us." They replied, "O mendicant, we ask for God's
forgiveness. Our heads are in your hands." The girls laughed and
made peace between the dervishes and the porter; then the shopper offered the dervishes something to eat, and after they ate, they
all sat down to carouse and drink, with the doorkeeper replenish-
ing the cups as they passed them around. Then the porter asked,
"Friends, can you entertain us with something?"

*But morning overtook Shahrazad, and she lapsed into silence.
Then her sister Dinarzad said, "Sister, what a lovely and entertain-
ing story!" Shahrazad replied, "What is this compared with what
I shall tell you tomorrow night if I live!"*

## THE THIRTY-THIRD NIGHT

*The following night Dinarzad said to her sister Shahrazad, "Sister,
if you are not sleepy, tell us one of your lovely little tales to while
away the night." Shahrazad replied, "With the greatest pleasure":*

I heard, O King, that the dervishes, heated with the wine, called
for musical instruments, and the doorkeeper brought them a tambourine, a flute, and a Persian harp. The dervishes rose, and one
took the tambourine, another the flute, another the Persian harp,
tuned their instruments, and began to play and sing, and the girls
began to sing with them until it got very loud. While they were
thus playing and singing, they heard a knocking at the door and
the doorkeeper went to see what was the matter.
Now the cause of that knocking, O King, was that it happened

on that very night that the Caliph Harun al-Rashid and Ja'far[8] came into the city, as they used to do every now and then, and as they walked through, they passed by the door and heard the music of the flute, the harp, and the tambourine, the singing of the girls, and the sounds of people partying and laughing. The caliph said, "Ja'far, I would like to enter this house and visit the people inside." Ja'far replied, "O Prince of the Faithful, these are people who are intoxicated and who do not know who we are, and I fear that they may insult us and abuse us." The caliph said, "Don't argue; I must go in and I want you to find a pretext to get us in." Ja'far replied, "I hear and obey." Then Ja'far knocked at the door, and when the doorkeeper came and opened the door, he stepped forward, kissed the ground before her, and said, "O my lady, we are merchants from the city of Mosul, and we have been in Baghdad for ten days. We have brought with us our merchandise and have taken lodgings at an inn. Tonight a merchant of your city invited us to his home and offered us food and drink. We drank and enjoyed ourselves and sent for a troop of musicians and singing women and invited the rest of our companions to join us. They all came and we had a good time, listening to the girls blow on the flutes, beat the tambourines, and sing, but while we were enjoying ourselves, the prefect of the police raided the place, and we tried to escape by jumping from walls. Some of us broke our limbs and were arrested, while some escaped safely. We have come now to seek refuge in your house, for, being strangers in your city, we are afraid that if we continue to walk the streets, the prefect of the police will stop us, discover that we are intoxicated, and arrest us. If we go to the inn, we shall find the door locked for, as is the rule, it is not to be opened till sunrise. As we passed by your house, we heard the sounds of music and the noise of a lovely party and hoped that you would be kind enough to let us join you to enjoy the rest of the night, giving us the chance to pay you for our share. If you refuse our company, let us sleep in the hallway till the morning, and God will reward you. The matter is in your magnanimous hands and the decision is yours, but we will not depart from your door."

After the doorkeeper had listened to Ja'far's speech, looked at their dress, and seen that they were respectable, she went back to her sisters and repeated Ja'far's story. The girls felt sorry for them and said, "Let them in," and she invited them to come in. When the caliph, together with Ja'far and Masrur,[9] entered the hall, the en-

8. Harun al-Rashid was the fifth Abbasid caliph, who ruled from A.D. 786 to 809; his rule is considered to be the golden age of the Arab empire, and his court in Baghdad is idealized in the *Nights*. Ja'far al-Barmaki was Harun al-Rashid's vizier and frequent companion, to whose family Harun delegated the administrative duties of the empire until, grown suspicious of their rising power, he had Ja'far and virtually the entire clan exterminated.
9. A black eunuch who was Harun al-Rashid's executioner and bodyguard.

tire group, the girls, the dervishes, and the porter, rose to greet them, and then everyone sat down.

*But morning overtook Shahrazad, and she lapsed into silence. Then Dinarzad said, "What a lovely and entertaining story!" Shahrazad replied, "What is this compared with what I shall tell you tomorrow night if I stay alive!"*

### THE THIRTY-FOURTH NIGHT

*The following night Dinarzad said to her sister Shahrazad, "Please, if you are not sleepy, tell us the rest of the story of the three girls." Shahrazad replied, "Very well":*

It is related, O King, that when the caliph, together with Ja'far and Masrur, entered and sat down, the girls turned to them and said, "You are welcome, and we are delighted to have you as our guests, but on one condition." They asked, "What is your condition?" The girls replied, "That you will be eyes without tongues and will not inquire about whatever you see. You will 'speak not of what concerns you not, lest you hear what pleases you not.'" They replied, "Yes, as you wish, for we have no need to meddle." Pleased with them, the girls sat to entertain them, drinking and conversing with them. The caliph was astonished to see three dervishes, all blind in the right eye, and he was especially astonished to see girls with such beauty, charm, eloquence, and generosity, in such a lovely place, with a music band consisting of three one-eyed dervishes. But he felt that at that moment he could not ask any questions. They continued to converse and drink, and then the dervishes rose, bowed, and played another round of music; then they sat down and passed the cup around.

When the wine had taken hold, the mistress of the house rose, bowed, and, taking the shopper by the hand, said, "Sister, let us do our duty." Both sisters replied, "Very well." The doorkeeper got up, cleared the table, got rid of the peels and shells, replenished the incense, and cleared the middle of the hall. Then she made the dervishes sit on a sofa at one side of the hall and seated the caliph, Ja'far, and Masrur on another sofa at the other side of the hall. Then she shouted at the porter, saying, "You are very lazy. Get up and lend us a hand, for you are a member of the household." The porter got up and, girding himself, asked, "What is up?" She replied, "Stand where you are." Then the shopper placed a chair in the middle of the hall, opened a cupboard, and said to the porter, "Come and help me." When the porter approached, he saw two black female hounds with chains around their necks. He took them and led them to the middle of the hall. Saying, "It is time to perform our duty," the mistress of the house came forward, rolled up her sleeves, took a braided whip, and called to the porter, "Bring me one of the bitches." The porter dragged one of the bitches by the chain and brought her forward, while she wept and shook her head at the girl. As the porter stood holding the chain, the girl came down on the bitch with hard blows on the sides, while the bitch howled and wept. The girl kept beating the bitch until her arm got weary. Then she stopped, threw the whip away, and, taking the chain from the porter, embraced the bitch and began to cry. The bitch too began to cry, and the two cried together for a long time. Then the girl wiped the bitch's tears with her handkerchief, kissed her on the head, and said to the porter, "Take her back to her place, and bring me the other." The porter took the bitch to the cupboard and brought the other bitch to the girl, who did to her as she had done to the first, beating her until she fainted. Then she took the bitch, cried with her, kissed her on the head, and asked the porter to take her back to her sister, and he took her back. When those who were present saw what happened, how the girl beat the bitch until the bitch fainted, and how she cried with the bitch and kissed her on the head, they were completely amazed and began to speak under their breath. The caliph himself felt troubled and lost all patience as he burned with curiosity to know the story of these two bitches. He winked to Ja'far, but Ja'far, turning to him, said with a sign, "This is not the time to inquire."

O happy King, when the girl finished punishing the two bitches, the doorkeeper said to her, "My lady, go and sit on your couch, so that I in turn may fulfill my desire." Saying, "Very well," the girl went to the far end of the hall and seated herself on the couch, with the caliph, Ja'far, and Masrur seated in a row to her right and the dervishes and the porter, to her left, and although the lamps glowed, the candles burned, and the incense filled the place, these men were depressed and felt that their evening was spoiled. Then the doorkeeper sat on the chair.

*But morning overtook Shahrazad, and she lapsed into silence. Then Dinarzad said to her sister, "Sister, what an amazing and entertaining story!" Shahrazad replied, "What is this compared with what I shall tell you tomorrow night if I live!"*

## THE THIRTY-FIFTH NIGHT

*The following night, Dinarzad said to her sister Shahrazad,*
*"Sister, if you are not sleepy, tell us one of your lovely little tales*
*to while away the night." Shahrazad replied, "Very well":*

I heard, O happy King, that the doorkeeper sat on the chair and
said to her sister the shopper, "Get up and pay me my due." The
shopper rose, entered a chamber, and soon brought back a bag of
yellow satin with two green silk tassels ornamented with red gold
and two beads of pure ambergris. She sat in front of the doorkeeper,
drew a lute out of the bag, and with its side resting on her knee,
held it in her lap. Then she tuned the lute and, plucking the strings
with her fingertips, began to play and sing the following verses of
the *Kan wa Kan* variety:[1]

> My love, you are my aim,
> And you are my desire.
> Your company is constant joy,
> Your absence, hellish fire.
> You are the madness of my life,
> My one infatuation,
> A love in which there is no shame,
> A blameless adoration.
> The shirt of agony I wore
> Revealed my secret passion,
> Betrayed my agitated heart
> And left me in confusion.
> My tears to all declared my love,
> As o'er my cheeks they flowed,
> My treacherous tears betrayed me
> And all my secrets showed.
> O, cure me from my dire disease;
> You are the sickness and the cure,
> But he whose remedy you are
> Will suffer evermore.
> Your brilliant eyes have wasted me,
> Your jet-black hair has me in thrall,
> Your rosy cheeks have vanquished me
> And told my tale to all.

1. A verse form in quatrains, which originated in Baghdad. At first the subject matter con-
sisted of narratives that began with the word "kan," meaning "once upon a time"; later the form
included love lyrics and maxims.

My hardship is my martyrdom,
The sword of love, my death.
How often have the best of men
This way ended their breath?
I will not cease from loving you,
Nor unlock what is sealed.
Love is my law and remedy,
Whether hid or revealed.
Blessed my eyes that gazed on you,
O treasured revelation;
Which has left me confused, alone,
In helpless adoration.

When the girl finished the poem, her sister let out a loud cry and moaned, "Oh, oh, oh!" Then she grabbed her dress by the collar and tore it down to the hem, baring her entire body, and fell down in a swoon. When the caliph looked at her, he saw that her whole body, from her head to her toe, bore the marks of the whip, which left it black and blue. Seeing the girl's condition and not knowing the cause, he and his companions were troubled, and he said to Ja'far, "By God, I will not wait a moment until I get to the bottom of this and ask for an explanation for what has happened, the flogging of the girl, the whipping of the two bitches, then the crying and the kissing." Ja'far replied, "My lord, this is not the time to ask for an explanation, especially since they have imposed on us the condition that we speak not of what concerns us not, for 'he who speaks of what concerns him not hears what pleases him not.'"

Then the shopper rose and, entering the chamber, came out with a fine dress that she put on her sister, replacing the one her sister had torn, and sat down. The sister said to the shopper, "For God's sake, give me some more to drink," and the shopper took the cup, filled it, and handed it to her. Then the shopper held the lute in her lap, improvised a number of measures, and sang the following verses:

If I bemoan your absence, what will you say?
If I pine with longing, what is the way?
If I dispatch someone to tell my tale,
The lover's complaint no one can convey.
If I with patience try to bear my pain,
After the loss of love, I can't endure the blow.
Nothing remains but longing and regret
And tears that over the cheeks profusely flow.
You, who have long been absent from my eyes,
Will in my loving heart forever stay.
Was it you who have taught me how to love,
And from the pledge of love never to stray?

When the sister finished her song, the girl cried out, "Oh, oh, oh!" and, overcome by passion, again grabbed her dress by the collar and tore it to the hem. Then she shrieked and fell down in a swoon. Again the shopper entered the chamber and came out with a dress even better than the first. Then she sprinkled her sister's face with rosewater, and when her sister came to herself, she put the dress on her. Then the sister said, "For God's sake, sister, pay me and finish off, for there remains only this one song." "With the greatest pleasure," replied the shopper, and she took the lute and began to play and sing the following verses:

> How long shall I endure this cruel disdain?
> Have I not paid enough with tears of woe?
> For how long suffer your willful neglect,
> As if it were a vengeful, envious foe?
> Be kind! Your cruel ways inflict a cruel pain,
> Master, 'tis time to me you pity show.
> O gentlemen, avenge this thrall of love,
> Who neither sleep nor patience does now know.
> Is it the law of love that one my love enjoys,
> While I alone do emptyhanded go?
> My lord, let him my unjust tyrant be;
> Many the toils and trials I undergo.

When she finished her song . . .

*But morning overtook Shahrazad, and she lapsed into silence. Then Dinarzad said, "Sister, what an amazing and entertaining story!" Shahrazad replied, "Tomorrow night I shall tell you something stranger, more amazing, and more entertaining if the king spares me and lets me live!"*

THE THIRTY-SIXTH NIGHT

*The following night Dinarzad said to her sister Shahrazad, "Sister, tell us the rest of the girls' story." Shahrazad said:*

It is related, O King, that when the girl heard the third song, she cried out, "By God, this is good." Then she grabbed her dress and tore it, and, as she fell down in a swoon, she revealed on her chest marks like welts from a whip. The dervishes muttered. "We wish that we had never entered this house, but had rather spent the night on the rubbish mounds outside the city, for our visit has been spoiled by such heartrending sights." The caliph turned to them and asked, "How so?" and they replied, "O distinguished gentleman, our minds are troubled by this matter." The caliph asked, "But you are members of the household; perhaps you can explain to me the story of these two black bitches and this girl." They replied, "By God, we know nothing and we have never laid eyes on this place until tonight." Surprised, the caliph said, "Then this man who sits beside you should know the explanation." They winked at the porter, questioning him, but he replied, "By the Almighty God, 'In love all are alike,' for even though I have been raised in Baghdad, never in my life have I entered this house until today. I did spend an amazing day with them. Still, I kept wondering that they were all women without men." They said to him, "By God, we took you to be one of them, but now we find that you are in the same predicament as we are."

Then the caliph said, "Adding Ja'far and Masrur, we are seven men, and they are only three women, without even a single man. Let us ask them for an explanation; if they don't answer by choice, they will answer by force." They agreed to proceed with this plan, but Ja'far said, "This is not right; let them be, for we are their guests and, as you know, they made a condition that we promised to keep. It is better to keep silent about this matter, for little remains of the night, and soon each of us will go his own way." Then he winked at the caliph and whispered to him, "O Commander of the Faithful, be patient for this one last hour of the night, and tomorrow morning I will come back and bring them before you to tell us their story." But the caliph yelled at him, saying, "Damn you, I can no longer wait for an explanation. Let the dervishes question them." Ja'far replied, "This is not a good idea." Then they talked at length and disputed as to who should first put the question, and at last all agreed on the porter.

When the girls heard their clamor, one of them asked, "Men, what is the matter?" The porter approached her and said, "My lady, these men express the wish that you acquaint them with the story of the two black bitches and why you punish them and then weep over them, and they wish to know the story of your sister and how it was that she got flogged with the whip, like a man. That is all; that is what they want to know." Turning to them, the girl asked, "Is it true what he says about you?" They all replied, "Yes," except Ja'far, who remained silent. When the girl heard their reply, she said, "O guests, you have wronged us. Have we not told you of our condition, that 'he who speaks of what concerns him not will hear what pleases him not'? We took you into our home and fed you with our food, but after all this you meddled and did us wrong. Yet the fault is not so much yours as hers who let you in and brought you to us." Then she rolled up her sleeves and struck the floor three

times, crying out, "Come at once," and a door opened and out came
seven black men, with drawn swords in their hands. Then with the
palm of the sword, each man dealt one of the men a blow that threw
him on his face to the ground, and in no time they had the seven
guests tied by the hands and bound each to each. Then they led
them in a single file to the center of the hall, and each black man
stood with his sword drawn above the head of his man. Then they
said to the girl, "O most honorable and most virtuous lady, permit
us to strike off their heads." She replied, "Wait a while until I question them, before you strike off their heads." The porter cried, "God
protect me. O lady, slay me not for another's sin. All these men
have sinned and offended, except me. By God, we had a delightful
day. If only we could have escaped these one-eyed dervishes, whose
entrance into any city blights it, destroys it, and lays it waste!" Then
he began to weep and recite the following verses:

> Fair is the forgiveness of mighty men,
> And fairest when to weakest men 'tis shown.
> Break off not the first friendship for the last,
> By the bond of the love that has between us grown.

The girl, despite her anger, laughed, and, coming up to the
group, said, "Tell me who you are, for you have only one hour to
live. Were you not men of rank or eminent among your people or
powerful rulers, you would not have dared to offend us." The caliph
said to Ja'far, "Woe unto you, tell her who we are, lest we be slain
by mistake." Ja'far replied, "This is part of what we deserve." The
caliph yelled at him, saying, "This is no time for your witticisms."
Then the lady approached the dervishes and asked, "Are you
brothers?" They replied, "No, by God, mistress, we are not, nor
are we mendicants." Then she asked one of them, "Were you born
blind in one eye?" and he replied, "No, by God, my lady. It was
an amazing event and a strange mischance that caused me to lose
my eye, shave off my beard, and become a dervish. Mine is a tale
that, if it were engraved with needles at the corner of the eye, would
be a warning to those who wish to consider." Then she questioned
the second dervish, and he said the same, and questioned the third,
and again he replied like the other two. Then they added, "By God,
lady, each one of us comes from a different city, and each one of
us is the son of a king, a prince sovereign over land and people."
The girl turned to the black men and said, "Whoever tells us his
tale and explains what has happened to him and what has brought
him to our place, let him stroke his head and go,[2] but whoever
refuses, strike off his head."

---

2. I.e., stroke your head in satisfaction, or in appreciation that you still have it, and go.

*But morning overtook Shahrazad, and she lapsed into silence. Then Dinarzad said to her sister, "What an amazing and entertaining story!" Shahrazad replied, "What is this compared with what I shall tell you tomorrow night if I stay alive!"*

## THE THIRTY-SEVENTH NIGHT

*The following night Dinarzad said to her sister Shahrazad, "Sister, if you are not sleepy, tell us one of your lovely little tales to while away the night." Shahrazad replied, "With the greatest pleasure":*

I heard, O King, that after the girl spoke, the first to come forth was the porter, who said, "Mistress, you know that the reason I came to this place was that I was hired as a porter by this shopper, who led me from the vintner to the butcher, and from the butcher to the greengrocer, and from the greengrocer to the fruit vendor, and from the fruit vendor to the drygrocer, then to the confectioner, to the druggist, and finally to this house. This is my tale." The girl replied, "Stroke your head and go." But he replied, "By God, I will not go until I hear the tales of the others."

Then the first dervish came forward and said:

# [The First Dervish's Tale]

My lady, the cause of my eye being torn out and my beard being shaved off was as follows. My father was a king, and he had a brother who was also a king and who had a son and a daughter. As the years went by and we grew up, I used to visit my uncle every now and then, staying with him for a month or two and returning to my father. For between my uncle's son and myself there grew a firm friendship and a great affection. One day I visited my cousin, and he treated me with unusual kindness. He slaughtered for me many sheep, offered me clear wine, and sat with me to drink. When the wine got the better of us, my cousin said, "Cousin, I would like to acquaint you with something that I have been preparing a whole year for, provided that you do not try to hinder me." I replied, "With the greatest pleasure." After he made me take a binding oath, he got up and quickly disappeared, but a while later came back with a woman wearing a cloak, a kerchief, and a headdress, and smelling of a perfume so sweet as to make us even more intoxicated. Then he said, "Cousin, take this lady and go before me to a sepul-

cher in such and such a graveyard," describing it so that I knew
the place. Then he added, "Enter with her into the sepulcher and
wait for me there." Unable to question or protest because of the
oath I had taken, I took the lady and walked with her until we
entered the graveyard and seated ourselves in the sepulcher. Soon
my cousin arrived, carrying a bowl of water, a bag of mortar, and
an iron adze. He went straight to a tomb, broke it open with the
adze, and set the stones to one side. Then he went on digging into
the earth of the tomb until he came upon an iron plate, the size
of a small door, that covered the length and width of the tomb.
He raised the plate, and there appeared below it a vaulting, winding staircase. Then turning to the lady, he said with a sign, "Make
your choice," and she went down the staircase and disappeared.
Then he turned to me and said, "Cousin, there is one last favor
to ask." I asked, "What is it?" He said, "After I descend into this
place, place the iron plate and the earth back over us."

*But morning overtook Shahrazad, and she lapsed into silence.
Then her sister said, "Sister, what an entertaining story!" Shahrazad
replied, "What is this compared with what I shall tell you tomorrow night!"*

### THE THIRTY-EIGHTH NIGHT

*The following night Dinarzad said to her sister Shahrazad, "For
God's sake, sister, if you are not sleepy, tell us one of your lovely
little tales." King Shahrayar added, "Tell us the rest of the story
of the king's son." Shahrazad replied, "With the greatest pleasure":*

I heard, O happy King, that the first dervish said to the girl:

After I followed his instructions, I returned, suffering from a
hangover, and spent the night in one of my uncle's houses, which
he had given me to use before he went on a hunting trip. When
I woke up in the morning and recalled the events of the previous
night, I thought that it was all a dream. Being in doubt, I inquired
about my cousin, but no one could tell me anything about him.
Then I went to the graveyard and searched for the sepulcher, but
I could not find it or remember anything about it. I kept wander-
ing from sepulcher to sepulcher and from tomb to tomb, without
stopping to eat or drink, until night set in. I was getting worried
about my cousin, and as I wondered where the vaulted staircase

led to, I began to recall the events little by little, as one recalls what happens in a dream. Finally I went back to the house, ate a little, and spent a restless night. Having recollected everything he and I did that night, I returned the following morning to the graveyard and wandered about, searching till nightfall, without finding the sepulcher or figuring out a way that might lead me to it. I went back to the graveyard for a third day and a fourth and searched for the sepulcher from early morning till nightfall without success, until I almost lost my sanity with frustration and worry. At last, realizing that I had no other recourse, I resolved to go back to my father's city.

When I arrived there and entered the city gate, I was immediately set upon, beaten, and bound. When I inquired, asking, "What is the cause?" I was told, "The vizier has plotted against your father and betrayed him. Being in league with the entire army, he has killed your father and usurped his power and ordered us to lie in wait for you." Then they carried me off in a swoon and brought me before him. O great lady, it so happened that the vizier and I were bitter enemies, for I was the cause of tearing out one of his eyes. Being fond of shooting with the crossbow, I stood one day on my palace roof, when a bird alighted at the palace of the vizier, who by coincidence also stood on his palace roof. When I shot at the bird, the missile missed him and instead hit the vizier and pierced the corner of his eye, and that was the cause of his grudge against me; therefore, when they brought me before him, he thrust his finger into my eye, gouged it out, and made it ooze over my cheek. Then he bound me, placed me in a chest, and handed me over to my father's swordsman, saying, "Ride your horse, draw your sword, and take this one with you into the wilderness. Then kill him and let the beasts and vultures devour his flesh." The executioner followed the vizier's order and led me into the wilderness. Then he dismounted, taking me out of the chest, and looked at me and was about to kill me. I wept bitterly over what had happened to me until I made him weep with me. Then looking at him, I began to recite the following verses:

> My shield I deemed you from the foeman's dart,
> But you did prove to be that very dart.
> I counted on your aid in all mishaps,
> Just as the left hand comes to aid the right.
> Stand then as one absolved, away from me,
> And let the foes at me their arrows aim,
> For if our friendship you cannot maintain,
> Between yourself and me there is no claim.

When the executioner heard my verses, he felt pity for me, and he spared me and set me free, saying, "Run with your life and never return to this land, for they will kill you and kill me with you." The poet says:

> If you suffer injustice, save yourself,
> And leave the house behind to mourn its builder.
> Your country you'll replace by another,
> But for yourself, you'll find no other self.
> Nor with a mission trust another man,
> For none is as loyal as you yourself.
> And did the lion not struggle by himself,
> He would not prowl with such a mighty mane.

Hardly believing in my escape, I kissed his hand and thought that losing my eye was certainly better than dying.

Then I journeyed slowly until I reached my uncle's city. When I went to him and told him about my father's death and the loss of my eye, he said to me, "I too have enough woes, for my son is missing, and I do not know what has happened to him, nor do I have any news about him." Then he wept bitterly, reviving my old grief and arousing my pity. Unable to remain silent, I acquainted him with what his son had done, and he was exceedingly happy and said, "Come and show me the sepulcher." I replied, "By God, uncle, I have lost the way to it, and I no longer know which one it is." He said, "Let us go together." Then he and I went secretly to the graveyard, and when I came to the center, I suddenly recognized the sepulcher and was exceedingly happy at the prospect of finding out what lay below the staircase and what had happened to my cousin. We entered the sepulcher, opened the tomb, and, removing the earth, found the iron plate. My uncle led the way, and we descended about fifty steps, and as we reached the bottom of the staircase, we met a great cloud of smoke that almost blinded our eyes. My uncle cried, "There is no power and no strength, save in God, the Almighty, the Magnificent." Then we saw a hallway, and as we advanced a little, we came to a hall resting on pillars and lighted by very high skylights. We wandered about and saw a cistern in the center, saw large jars and sacks full of flour, grains, and the like, and at the end of the hall saw a bed covered with a canopy. My uncle went up to the bed, and when he lifted the curtain, he found his son and the lady who had gone down with him, lying in each other's arms, but saw that the two had turned to black charcoal. It was as if they had been cast into a raging fire, which burned them thoroughly until they were reduced to charcoal. When my uncle saw this spectacle, he expressed satisfaction and spat in his son's face, saying, "This is your punishment in this world, but there remains your punishment in the world to come." Then he took off his shoe and struck his son, hard on the face.

*But morning overtook Shahrazad, and she lapsed into silence. Then her sister Dinarzad said to her, "Sister, what an entertaining story!" Shahrazad replied, "What is this compared with what I shall tell you tomorrow night if I stay alive!"*

### THE THIRTY-NINTH NIGHT

*The following night Dinarzad said to her sister Shahrazad, "Sister, if you are not sleepy, tell us one of your lovely little tales to while away the night." The king added, "Let it be the completion of the first dervish's tale." Shahrazad replied, "With the greatest pleasure":*

I heard, O happy King, that the first dervish said to the girl:

My lady, when my uncle struck his son's face with the shoe, as he and the lady lay there in a charred heap, I said to him, "For God's sake, uncle, don't make me feel worse; I feel worried and sorry for what happened to your son; yet as if he has not suffered enough, you strike him on the face with your shoe." He replied, "Nephew, you should know that this son of mine was madly in love with his sister, and I often forbade him from seeing her but went on saying to myself, 'They are only children.' But when they grew up, they did the ugly deed and I heard about it, hardly believing my ears. I seized him and beat him mercilessly, saying, 'Beware, beware of that deed, lest our story spread far and wide even to every remote province and town and you be dishonored and disgraced among the kings, to the end of time. Beware, beware, for this girl is your sister, and God has forbidden her to you.' Then, nephew, I secluded her from him, but the cursed girl was in love with him, for the devil had possessed her and made the affair attractive in her eyes. When they saw that I had separated them from each other, he built and prepared this subterranean place, dug up the well, and brought whatever they needed of provisions and the like, as you see. Then, taking advantage of my going to the hunt, he took his sister and did what you saw him do. He believed that he would be enjoying her for a long time and that the Almighty God would not be mindful of their deed." Then he wept, and I wept with him. Then he looked at me and said, "You are my son in his place," and when he thought of what had happened to his two children, his brother's murder, and the loss of my eye, he wept again and I wept with him over the trials of life and the misfortunes of this world. Then we climbed out of the tomb and I replaced the iron plate cover over my cousin and his sister, and without being detected by anyone, we returned home.

But hardly had we sat down when we heard the sounds of kettle-drums, little drums, and trumpets, the din of men, the clanking of bits, the neighing of horses, and the orders to line up for battle, while the world became clouded with dust raised by the galloping of horses and the tramping of men. We were bewildered and startled, and when we asked, we were told that the vizier who had usurped my father's kingdom had levied his soldiers and prepared his armies, and taking a host of bedouins[3] into service, had invaded us with armies like the desert sand, whom no one could count and no one could withstand. They took the city by surprise, and the citizens, being unable to oppose them, surrendered the place to the vizier. My uncle was slain and I escaped to the outskirts of the city, thinking to myself, "If I fall into the vizier's hands, he will kill me and kill Sayir, my father's swordsman." My sorrows were renewed and my anxiety grew, as I pondered over what had happened to my uncle and my cousins and over the loss of my eye, and I wept bitterly. I asked myself, "What is to be done? If I show myself in public, the people of my city and all my father's soldiers will recognize me as they recognize the sun and will try to win favor with the vizier by killing me." I could think of no way to escape and save my life except to shave my beard and eyebrows. I did so, changed my clothes for those of a mendicant, and assumed the life of a dervish. Then I left the city, undetected by anyone, and journeyed to this country, with the intention of reaching Baghdad, hoping that I might be fortunate to find someone who would assist me to the presence of the Commander of the Faithful, the Vice Regent of the Supreme Lord, so that I might tell him my tale and lay my case before him. I arrived this very night, and as I stood in doubt at the city gate, not knowing where I should go, this dervish by my side approached me, showing the signs of travel, and greeted me. I asked him, "Are you a stranger?" and when he replied, "Yes," I said, "I too am a stranger." As we were talking, this other dervish by our side joined us at the gate, greeted us, and said, "I am a stranger." We replied, "We are strangers too." Then the three of us walked as night overtook us, three strangers who did not know where to go. But God drove us to your house, and you were kind

3. Arab nomads of the desert.

and generous enough to let us in and help me forget the loss of my eye and the shaving off of my beard.

The girl said to him, "Stroke your head and go." He replied, "By God, I will not go until I hear the tales of the others."

*But morning overtook Shahrazad, and she lapsed into silence. Then Dinarzad said, "Sister, what an entertaining story!" Shahrazad replied, "What is this compared with what I shall tell you tomorrow night if the king spares me and lets me live!" The king said to himself, "By God, I shall postpone her execution until I hear the tales of the dervishes and the girls, then have her put to death like the rest."*

## THE FORTIETH NIGHT

*The following night Dinarzad said to her sister Shahrazad, "Sister, if you are not sleepy, tell us one of your lovely little tales." Shahrazad replied, "With the greatest pleasure":*

It is related, O happy King, that those who were present marveled at the tale of the first dervish. The caliph said to Ja'far, "In all my life I have never heard a stranger tale." Then the second dervish came forward and said:

## [The Second Dervish's Tale]

By God, my lady, I was not born one-eyed. My father was a king, and he taught me how to write and read until I was able to read the Magnificent Quran in all the seven readings. Then I studied jurisprudence in a book by al-Shatibi[4] and commented on it in the presence of other scholars. Then I turned to the study of classical Arabic and its grammar until I reached the height of eloquence, and I perfected the art of calligraphy until I surpassed all my contemporaries and all the leading calligraphers of the day, so that the fame of my eloquence and calligraphic art spread to every province and town and reached all the kings of the age.

One day the king of India sent my father gifts and rarities worthy of a king and asked him to send me to him. My father fitted me

---

4. Well-known writer on Muslim jurisprudence. "Seven readings": a "reading" is a distinct manner of reciting, punctuating, and vocalizing a text of the Quran.

with six riding horses and sent me along with the posted couriers.
I bade him good-bye and set out on my journey. We rode for a
full month until one day we came upon a great cloud of dust, and
when a little later the wind blew the dust away and cleared the air,
we saw fifty horsemen who, looking like glowering lions in steel
armor . . .

*But morning overtook Shahrazad, and she lapsed into silence.
Then her sister said, "Sister, what an amazing and entertaining
story!" Shahrazad replied, "What is this compared with what I shall
tell you tomorrow night if I stay alive!"*

THE FORTY-FIRST NIGHT

*The following night Dinarzad said, "Sister, if you are not sleepy,
tell us one of your lovely little tales to while away the night." Shahrazad replied, "Very well":*

I heard, O happy King, that the second dervish, the young son
of the king, said to the girl:

When we looked at them closely, we discovered that they were
highwaymen, and when they saw that we were a small company
with ten loads of goods—these were gifts—they thought that we
were carrying loads of money, drew their swords, and pointed their
spears at us. We signaled to them, saying, "We are messengers to
the great king of India; you cannot harm us." They replied, "We
are neither within his dominions nor under his rule." Then they
killed all my men and wounded us. But while the highwaymen were
scrambling for the gifts that were with us, I escaped and wandered
away without knowing where I was heading or in which direction
to go. I was mighty and became lowly; I was rich and became poor.

*But morning overtook Shahrazad, and she lapsed into silence.
Then her sister said, "What a strange and entertaining story!"
Shahrazad replied, "What is this compared with what I shall tell
you tomorrow night if the king spares me and lets me live!"*

## THE FORTY-SECOND NIGHT

*The following night Shahrazad said,*

I heard, O happy King, that the second dervish said to the girl:

After I was robbed, I fared on, and when night approached, I
climbed the side of a mountain and took shelter for the night in
a cave till daybreak. Then I journeyed till nightfall, feeding on the
plants of the earth and the fruits of the trees, and slept till daybreak.
For a month I traveled in this fashion until I came to a fair, peaceful, and prosperous city, teeming with people and full of life. It was
the time when winter had departed with its frost and spring had
arrived with its roses. The streams were flowing, the flowers blooming, and the birds singing. It was like the city of which the poet said:

> Behold a peaceful city, free from fear,
> Whose wonders make it a gorgeous heaven appear.

I felt both glad and sad at the same time, glad to reach the city,
sad to arrive in such a wretched condition, for I was so tired from
walking that I was pale with exhaustion. My face and my hands
and feet were chapped, and I felt overwhelmed with worry and grief.
I entered the city, not knowing where to go, and chanced to pass
by a tailor sitting in his shop. I greeted him, and he returned my
greeting, and detecting in me traces of better days, he welcomed
me and, inviting me to sit with him, talked freely to me. He asked
me who I was, and I told him about myself and what had happened
to me. He felt sad for me and said, "Young man, do not reveal
your secret to anyone, for the king of this city is your father's greatest
enemy, and there is a blood feud between them." Then he brought
some food, and we ate together. When it was dark, he gave me
a recess next to his in the shop, and brought me a blanket and other
necessities.

It stayed with him for three days; then he asked me, "Don't you
have any skill with which you can earn your living?" I replied, "I
am a jurist, a man of letters, a poet, a grammarian, and a calligrapher." He said, "Such skills are not much in demand in our city."
I replied, "By God, I have no other skills, save what I have mentioned to you." He said, "Gird yourself, take an axe and a rope,
and go and hew wood in the wilderness for your livelihood. But
lest you perish, keep your secret to yourself and don't let anyone
know who you are, until God sends you relief." Then he bought

me an axe and a rope and put me under the charge of certain wood-cutters. I went out with them, cut wood all day long, and came back, carrying my bundle on my head. I sold the wood for half a dinar and brought the money to the tailor. In such work I spent an entire year.

One day I went out into the wilderness, and having penetrated deep, I came to a thick patch of trees in a meadow irrigated by running streams. When I entered the patch, I found the stump of a tree, and when I dug around it with my axe and shoveled the earth away, I came upon a ring that was attached to a wooden plank. I raised the plank and beneath it I found a staircase. I descended the steps, and as I reached the bottom, I came to a subterranean palace, solidly built and beautifully designed, a palace so splendid that a better one I have never seen. I walked inside and saw a beautiful girl who looked as radiant as a brilliant pearl or the shining sun and whose speech banished all sorrow and captivated even the sensible and the wise. She was about five feet tall, with a beautiful figure, firm breasts, soft cheeks, and a fair complexion. Through the night of her tresses, her face beamed, and above her smooth bosom, her mouth gleamed, as the poet said of one like her:

> Four things that never meet do here unite
> To shed my blood and to ravage my heart,
> A radiant brow and tresses that beguile
> And rosy cheeks and a glittering smile.

*But morning overtook Shahrazad, and she lapsed into silence. Then Dinarzad said, "Sister, what a strange and entertaining story!" Shahrazad replied, "What is this compared with what I shall tell you tomorrow night if the king spares me and lets me live!"*

THE FORTY-THIRD NIGHT

*The following night, Dinarzad said to her sister Shahrazad, "Sister, if you are not sleepy, tell us one of your lovely little tales to while away the night." Shahrazad replied, "Very well":*

I heard, O happy King, that the second young dervish said to the girl:

When the girl looked at me, she asked, "What are you, a man or a demon?" I replied, "I am a human being." She asked, "What brought you here? I have lived in this place for twenty-five years without ever seeing any human being. I said—for I found her words sweet and touching and she captivated my heart—"My good fortune brought me here to dispel my care, or perhaps your good fortune, to banish your sorrow." Then I related to her my mishaps, and she felt sad for me and said, "I too shall tell you my tale. I am the daughter of Aftimarus, king of the Ebony Island. He married me to one of my cousins, but on my wedding night a demon snatched me up, flew away with me, and a while later set me down in this place. Then he brought me all I needed of food and drink and sweets and the like. Once every ten days he comes to spend a night with me—for he took me after he had already a family. If ever I need him for anything by night or by day, I have only to touch the two lines engraved on the doorstep, and he will be with me before I lift my fingers. He has been away for four days, so there remain only six days before he comes again. Would you like to spend five days with me and leave on the day before he arrives?" I replied, "Yes, indeed, 'if only dreams were true!'"

She was pleased and she rose and took me by the hand through an arched doorway that led to a bath. She took off my clothes and took off hers and, entering the bath, she bathed me and washed me. When we came out, she dressed me with a new gown, seated me on a couch, and, giving me a large cup of juice to drink, sat conversing with me for a while. Then she set some food before me, and I ate my fill. Then she offered me a pillow, saying, "Lie down and rest, for you are tired." I lay down and slept, forgetting every care in the world and regaining my energy. When I awoke, some time later, I found her massaging me. I sat up, thanked her, and commended her to God, feeling very much refreshed. Then she asked, "Young man, are you ready to drink?" I replied, "Yes, let us drink," and she went to a cupboard and took out a sealed flask of old wine and, setting a sumptuous table, began to sing the following lines:

> Had we known of your coming, our dark eyes
> Or throbbing heart for you we would have spread,
> Or with our cheeks would have covered the earth,
> So that over the eyelids you might tread.

My love for her began to possess my whole being and my sorrow departed. We sat drinking till nightfall, and I spent with her a delightful night the like of which I never spent in all my life. When we awoke, delight followed delight till midday, and I was so drunk that I almost lost consciousness and began to stagger right and left. I said, "My beautiful one, let me carry you up and deliver you from this prison." She laughed and replied, "O my lord, sit still, hold your peace, and be content, for of every ten days only one is for the demon and nine for you." I said—as drink had got the better of me—"This very instant I shall smash the doorstep with the engraved inscription and let the demon come, so that I may kill him, for I am used to killing demons by the tens." When she heard my words, she grew pale and said, "No, for God's sake, don't do it." Then she recited the following lines:

> You, who seek separation, hold your reins,
> For its horses are much too swift and free.
> Hold, for betrayal is the rule of life
> And severance the end of amity.

But in my drunkenness, I kicked the step with my foot.

*But morning overtook Shahrazad, and she lapsed into silence. Then Dinarzad said, "What a strange and entertaining story!" Shahrazad replied, "What is this compared with what I shall tell you tomorrow night if the king spares me and lets me live!"*

THE FORTY-FOURTH NIGHT

*The following night Dinarzad said, "Sister, if you are not sleepy, tell us one of your lovely little tales to while away the night." Shahrazad replied, "Very well":*

It is related, O happy King, that the second dervish said to the girl:

As soon as I kicked the step, there was thunder and lightning, and the earth began to tremble and everything turned dark. I became sober at once and cried out to her, "What is happening?" She replied, "The demon is coming. O my lord, get up and run for your life." I fled up the staircase, but in my great terror I left my sandals and my iron axe behind. I had not reached the top when I saw the palace floor split asunder and the demon appear, saying, "What disaster has led you to trouble me like this?" She replied, "My lord, today I felt depressed and took a little wine to lighten my heart. Then I got up to go and relieve myself, but I felt tipsy and fell against the step." The demon cried, "You are lying, you whore," and, looking about, saw my sandals and my axe, and asked, "Whose are these?" She replied, "I have never set eyes on them till this moment. They must have stuck to your clothes and you brought them with you." The demon said, "I will not be deceived by this ruse, you slut." Then he seized her, stripped her naked and, binding her hands and feet to four stakes, proceeded to torture her and make her confess."

O lady, it was not easy for me to hear her cries, but trembling with fear, I climbed the staircase slowly until I was outside. Then I placed the trapdoor as it was before and covered it with earth. I felt very sad and extremely sorry, as I thought of the girl, her beauty, her kindness, and her generous treatment, how she had lived quietly for twenty-five years and how in one night I had brought her this calamity. And when I remembered my father and my country, how life turned against me and I became a woodcutter, and how for a brief moment it befriended me and punished me again, I wept bitterly, blamed myself, and repeated the following verses:

> My fate does fight me like an enemy
> And pursues helpless me relentlessly.
> If once it chooses to treat me kindly,
> At once it turns, eager to punish me.

Then I walked on until I came to my friend the tailor, whom I found most anxiously waiting for me. He was glad to see me and asked, "Brother, where did you stay last night? I was worried about you; praise be to God for your safety." I thanked him for his friendly concern and, retiring to my recess, sat thinking about what had happened to me, blaming myself for my rashness, for had I not kicked the step, nothing would have happened. As I sat, absorbed in such thoughts, my friend the tailor came to me and said, "There is outside an old Persian gentleman, who has your iron axe and your sandals. He had taken them to the woodcutters, saying, 'I went out this morning to answer the call to prayer and stumbled on this axe and these sandals. Take a look at them and tell me to whom they belong and where I may find him.' The woodcutters recognized your axe and told him where to find you, saying, 'This axe belongs to a young man, a foreigner who lives with the tailor.' At this very moment he is sitting at the entrance of the shop. Go to him and take your axe from him." When I heard what he said, I felt faint and turned pale and, while we stood there talking, the floor of my recess split asunder and there emerged the old Persian gentleman, who was that very demon. He had tortured the girl almost to her death, but she did not confess. So he took the axe and the sandals, saying, "If I am truly the son of Satan's daughter, I shall bring you back the owner of the axe." Then he assumed the guise of a Persian gentleman and came to find me. When the ground split asunder and he emerged . . .

*But morning overtook Shahrazad, and she lapsed into silence.*
*Then Dinarzad said, "Sister, what a strange and entertaining story!"*
*Shahrazad replied, "What is this compared with what I shall tell*
*you tomorrow night if the king spares me and lets me live!"*

### THE FORTY-FIFTH NIGHT

*The following night Dinarzad said to her sister Shahrazad, "Sister,*
*if you are not sleepy, tell us one of your little tales." Shahrazad*
*replied, "Very well":*

It is related, O King, that the second dervish said to the girl:

As soon as the demon emerged, he snatched me up from my
recess, soared high in the sky, and flew away with me. When he
landed a while later, he kicked the ground with his foot, split it
asunder, and, carrying me in a swoon, plunged under the earth
and emerged with me in the middle of the palace where I had spent
the night. There I saw the girl stripped naked, her limbs tied, and
her sides bleeding, and my eyes filled with tears. The demon untied
her and, covering her, said, "You slut, isn't it true that this man
is your lover?" Looking at me, she replied, "I don't know this man
at all and I have never laid eyes on him till this very moment." He
said, "Damn you, all this torture, and you refuse to confess!" She
said, "I don't know this man, and I cannot tell lies about him and
let you kill him." He replied, "If you don't know him, take this sword
then and strike off his head." She took the sword and, coming up
to me, stood facing me. I signaled her with my eyes, and she understood and winked back, meaning, "Aren't you the one who has
brought all this upon us?" I signaled again, "This is the time for
forgiveness," and she replied with words written with tears on her
cheeks:

> My eyes spoke for my tongue to let him know,
> And love betrayed what I tried to conceal.
> When we last met and shed our thoughts in tears,
> Tongue-tied, I let my eyes my heart reveal.
> He signed with his eyes, and I understood;
> I winked, and he knew what my eyes did say.
> Our eyebrows carried out our task so well,
> As mute we stood and let love have its sway.

Then the girl threw the sword away and stepped back, saying,
"How can I strike the neck of one I do not know and be guilty of

his blood?" The demon said, "You cannot bear to kill him because he has slept with you. You have suffered all this torture, yet you have not confessed. It is clear that only like feels for and pities like." Then he turned to me and said, "You human being, do you too not know this woman?" I replied, "Who may she be, for I have never laid eyes on her till this very moment?" He said, "Then take this sword and strike her head off, and I will believe that you do not know her and let you go free." I replied, "I will do it," and I took the sword and sprang toward her.

*But morning overtook Shahrazad, and she lapsed into silence. Then Dinarzad said, "Sister, what an entertaining story!" Shahrazad replied, "What is this compared with what I shall tell you tomorrow night if I stay alive!"*

### THE FORTY-SIXTH NIGHT

*The following night Dinarzad said to her sister Shahrazad, "Tell us the rest of the story." Shahrazad replied, "Very well":*

I heard, O happy King, that the second dervish said to the girl:

When I took the sword and went up to her, she winked at me, meaning, "Bravo! This is how you repay me!" I understood her look and pledged with my eyes, "I will give my life for you." Then we stood for a while, exchanging looks, as if to say:

> Many a lover his beloved tells
> With his eyes' language what is in his heart.
> "I know what has befallen," seems to say,
> And with a glance he does his thoughts impart.
> How lovely are the glances of the eyes,
> How graceful are the eyes with passion fraught.
> One with his looks a lover's message writes,
> Another with his eyes reads what his lover wrote.

I threw the sword away, stepped back, and said, "Mighty demon, if a woman, who is befuddled, thoughtless, and inarticulate, refuses to strike off the head of a man she does not know, how can I, a man, strike off the head of a woman I do not know? I can never do such a deed, even if I have to die for it." The demon replied, "You two are conniving against me, but I am going to show you the result of your misdeeds." Then he took the sword and struck the girl, severing her arm from her shoulder and sending it flying. Then he struck again and severed the other arm and sent it flying. She looked at me, as she lay in the throes of death, and with a glance bade me good-bye. O my lady, at that moment I longed for death, and for a moment I fell into a swoon. "This is the punishment of those who deceive," said the demon and, turning to me, added, "O human being, it is in our law that if a wife deceives her husband, she is no longer lawful to him, and he must kill her and get rid of her. I snatched this woman away on her wedding night, when she was merely a girl of twelve who knew no man but myself. I used to come to her every ten days in the semblance of a Persian gentleman, to spend a night with her. When I became certain that she had deceived me, I killed her, for she was no longer lawful to me. As for you, even though I am not certain whether you are the culprit, I cannot let you go unharmed. Tell me into what animal you wish me to turn you with my magic, a dog, an ass, or a lion. Do you prefer to be a bird or a beast?" I replied, hoping that he might spare me, "O demon, it is more befitting to you to pardon me, even as the envied pardoned the envier." The demon asked, "And how was that?" and I began to tell him:

## [The Tale of the Envious and the Envied]

It is related, O demon, that there lived in a certain city two men who dwelt in adjoining houses separated by a common wall. One of them envied the other, gave him the evil eye, and did his utmost to hurt him. He was so obsessed that his envy grew until he could hardly eat or enjoy the pleasure of sleep. But the envied did nothing but prosper, and the more the envious strove to injure him, the more he throve and flourished. At last the envy and malice of his neighbor came to his attention, and he left the neighborhood and moved to another city, saying, "By God, because of him, I will even depart from this world." There he bought himself a piece of land that had an old irrigation well, built a hermitage that he furnished with straw mats and other necessities, and devoted himself to the worship of the Almighty God. The mendicants began to flock to him from every quarter, and his fame spread throughout the city.

Soon the news reached his envious neighbor, how he had prospered and how even the eminent men of the city called on him. So the neighbor journeyed to that city, and when he entered the hermitage, the envied received him with cheerful greetings, warm welcome, and great respect. Then the envious said, "I would like to acquaint you with something that has caused me to come to you. Let us walk aside in the hermitage, so that I may tell you what it is." The envied got up, and as the envious held him by the hand, they walked to the far end of the hermitage. Then the envious said, "Friend, bid your mendicants enter their cells, for I will not tell you, except in private, so that none may hear us." Accordingly, the envied said to the mendicants, "Retire to your cells," and they did so. Then the envious said, "Now, as I was telling you, my tale . . ." and he walked with him slowly until they reached the edge of the old well. Suddenly the envious pushed the envied and, without being seen by anyone, sent him tumbling into the well. Then he left the hermitage and went away, believing that he had killed him.

*But morning overtook Shahrazad, and she lapsed into silence. Then Dinarzad said, "Sister, what a strange and entertaining story!" Shahrazad replied, "What is this compared with what I shall tell you tomorrow night if I stay alive!"*

### THE FORTY-SEVENTH NIGHT

*The following night Dinarzad said to her sister Shahrazad, "Sister, if you are not sleepy, tell us what happened to the envious after he pushed the envied into the well." Shahrazad replied, "Very well":*

It is related, O King, that the second dervish said to the girl that he told the demon:

Demon, I heard that the envious threw the envied into the ancient well. That well happened to be haunted by a group of demons who caught him and, letting him down little by little, seated him on a rock. Then they asked each other, "Do you know who this man is?" and the answer was "No." But one of them said, "This man is the envied who, flying from the envious, came to live in our city, built this hermitage, and has ever since delighted us with his litanies and his recitals of the Quran. But the envious journeyed until he rejoined him, tricked him, and threw him into this well where you now are. It so happens that this very night the fame of this man has come to the attention of the king of this city, and he is planning to visit him tomorrow morning, on account of his daughter." Someone asked him, "What is the matter with her?" He replied, "She is possessed, for the demon Maimun ibn-Damdam is madly in love with her, but if this man knew the remedy, her cure would be as easy as can be." One of them asked, "What is the remedy?" He replied, "This man has in the hermitage a black cat with a white spot the size of a dirham at the end of its tail. If he plucks seven white hairs from the white spot, burns them, and fumigates her with the smoke, the demon will depart from her head, never to return, and she will be cured that very instant." O demon, all of this conversation took place while the envied listened. When the day dawned, the mendicants came out in the morning and found the holy man climbing out of the well, and he grew even greater in their esteem. Then the envied endeavored to look for the black cat and, when he found it, he plucked seven hairs from the white spot on its tail and kept them with him.

In the meantime hardly had the sun risen when the king arrived with his troops. He dismounted with the lords of the realm, bidding the rest of his troops stand outside. When he entered the hermitage, the envied welcomed him and, seating him by his side, asked, "Shall I tell you the cause of your visit?" The king replied, "Yes." The envied continued: "You have come to visit me with the intention of consulting me about your daughter." The king said, "O man of God, you're right." The envied said, "Send someone to fetch her, and God the Almighty willing, she will recover presently." The king gladly sent for his daughter, and they brought her in, bound and fettered. The envied made her sit behind a curtain and, taking out the hairs, burned them and fumigated her with the smoke. At that moment he who was in her head cried out and departed from her, and she instantly recovered her sanity and, veiling her face, asked, "What has happened to me and who brought me here?" The king felt unequaled joy, and he kissed his daughter's eyes and kissed the holy man's hand. Then turning to the great lords of the realm, he asked, "What do you say to this, and what does he who has cured my daughter deserve?" They answered, "He deserves to have her for a wife." The king said, "You are right." Then he married her to him, and the envied became son-in-law to the king. A short time later the vizier died, and the king asked, "Whom shall I make vizier?" They answered, "Your son-in-law," and the envied became vizier. And a short time later, the king also died, and his men asked each other, "Whom shall we make king?" The answer was, "The vizier," and the envied became a monarch, a sovereign king.

One day, as he was riding with his equipage . . .

*But morning overtook Shahrazad, and she lapsed into silence. Then Dinarzad said, "What a strange and entertaining story!" Shahrazad replied, "What is this compared with what I shall tell you tomorrow night if the king spares me and lets me live!"*

## THE FORTY-EIGHTH NIGHT

*The following night Dinarzad said, "Sister, if you are not sleepy, tell us what happened to the envious and the envied." Shahrazad replied, "Very well":*

I heard, O King, that the second dervish said to the girl that he told the demon:

One day, as the envied rode with his royal equipage at the head of his princes, viziers, and lords of the realm, his eyes fell on the envious. He turned to one of his viziers and commanded, "Bring me that man, but do not alarm him or frighten him." The vizier left and came back with the envious neighbor. The king said, "Give him one thousand weights of gold from my treasury, provide him with twenty loads of goods he trades in, and send him with an escort to his own town." Then the envied bade him farewell and went away without reproaching him for what he had done to him.

I said to the demon, "O demon, consider the mercy of the envied on the envious, who had envied him from the beginning, borne him great malice, pursued him, followed him, and thrown him into the well to kill him. Yet the envied did not respond in kind, but instead of punishing the envious, he forgave him and treated him magnanimously." Then, O my lady, I wept until I could weep no more and recited the following verses:

> Pardon my crime, for every mighty judge
> Is used to mercy some offenders show.
> I stand before you guilty of all sins,
> But you the ways of grace and mercy know.
> For he who seeks forgiveness from above,
> Should pardon the offenders here below.

The demon replied, "I will not kill you, but in no way will I pardon you and let you go unharmed. I have spared you from death, but I will put you under a spell." Then he snatched me up and flew with me upward until the earth appeared like a white cloud. Soon he set me down on a mountain and, taking a little dust, mumbled some incantation and sprinkled me with the dust, saying, "Leave your present form and take the form of an ape." At that very instant, I became an ape, and he blew away and left me behind.

When I saw that I was an ape, I wept for myself and blamed life, which is fair to none. Then I descended the mountain and found a vast desert, over which I journeyed for a month until I reached the seashore. As I stood on the shore, looking at the sea, I saw in the offing a ship sailing under a fair wind and cleaving the waves. I went to a tree and, breaking off a branch, began to signal the ship with it, running back and forth and waving the branch to and fro, but being unable to speak or cry out for help, I began to despair. Suddenly the ship turned and began to sail toward the shore, and when it drew near, I found that it was a large ship, full of merchants and laden with spices and other goods. When the merchants saw me, they said to the captain, "You have risked our lives and property for an ape, who brings bad luck with him wherever he goes." One of them said, "Let me kill him." Another said, "Let me shoot him with an arrow." And a third said, "Let us drown him." When I heard what they said, I sprang up and held the hem of the captain's gown like a suppliant, as my tears began to flow over my face. The captain and all the merchants were amazed, and some of them began to feel pity for me. Then the captain said, "Merchants, this ape has appealed to me for protection, and I have taken him under my care. Let none of you hurt him in any way, lest he become my enemy." Then he treated me kindly, and I understood whatever he said and did his bidding, although I could not respond to him with my tongue.

For fifty days the ship sailed on before a fair wind until we came to a great city, vast and teeming with countless people. No sooner had we entered the port and cast anchor than we were visited by messengers from the king of that city. They boarded the ship and said, "Merchants, our king congratulates you on your safe arrival, sends you this roll of paper, and bids each of you write one line on it. For the king's vizier, a man learned in state affairs and a skilled calligrapher, has died, and the king has sworn a solemn oath that he will appoint none in his place, save one who can write as well as he could." Then they handed the merchants a roll of paper, ten cubits long and one cubit wide, and each of the merchants who knew how to write wrote a line. When they came to the end, I snatched the scroll out of their hands, and they screamed and scolded me, fearing that I would throw it into the sea or tear it to pieces, but I signed to them that I wanted to write on it, and they were exceedingly amazed, saying, "We have never yet seen an ape write." The captain said to them, "Let him write what he likes, and if he merely scribbles, I will beat him and chase him away, but if he writes well, I will adopt him as my son, for I have never seen a more inteligent or a better-behaved ape. I wish that my son had this ape's understanding and good manners." Then I held the pen, dipped it in the inkpot, and in Ruqa' script[5] wrote the following lines:

> Time's record of the favors of the great
> Has been effaced by your greater favor.
> Of you your children God will not deprive,
> You, being to grace both mother and father.

Then under these, in Muhaqqiq script I wrote the following lines:

> His pen has showered bounty everywhere
> And without favors favored every land.
> Yet even the Nile, which destroys the earth,
> Cannot its ink use with such mighty hand.

And in Raihani script I wrote the following lines:

> I swore, whoever uses me to write,
> By the One, Peerless, Everlasting God,
> That he would never any man deny
> With one of the pen's strokes his livelihood.

Then in Naskhi script I wrote the following lines:

> There is no writer who from death will flee,
> But what his hand has written time will keep.
> Commit to paper nothing then, except
> What you would like on Judgment Day to see.

Then in Thuluth script I wrote the following lines:

> When the events of life our love condemned
> And painful separation was our end,
> We turned to the inkwell's mouth to complain,
> And voiced with the pen's tongue our parting's pain.

Then in Tumar script I wrote the following lines:

> When you open the inkwell of your boon
> And fame, let the ink be munificence and grace.
> Write good and generous deeds while write you can;
> Both pen and sword such noble deeds will praise.

Then I handed them the scroll, and they took it back in amazement.

*But morning overtook Shahrazad, and she lapsed into silence. Then Dinarzad said, "Sister, what an amazing and entertaining story!" Shahrazad replied, "What is this compared with what I shall tell you tomorrow night if I stay alive!"*

---

5. The scripts named are all calligraphic varieties of the cursive, curvilinear Arabic script.

## THE FORTY-NINTH NIGHT

*The following night Dinarzad said, "Sister, tell us the rest of the story." Shahrazad replied, "Very well":*

It is related, O happy King, that the second dervish said to the girl:

The messengers took the scroll and returned with it to the king, and when he looked at it, my writing pleased him and he said, "Take this robe of honor and this she-mule to the master of these seven scripts." The men smiled, and seeing that their smiling had made the king angry, they said, "O King of the age and sovereign of the world, the writer of these lines is an ape." The king asked, "Is it true what you say?" They replied, "Yes, by your bounty, the writer is an ape." The king was greatly amazed and said, "I wish to see this ape." Then he dispatched his messengers with the she-mule and the robe, "Dress him with this robe, place him on the she-mule, and bring him to me, together with his master."

As we sat on board, we saw the king's messengers suddenly appear again. They took me from the captain, dressed me with the robe, and, placing me on the she-mule, walked behind me in a procession, which caused a great commotion in the city. Everyone came out, crowding to gaze at me and enjoy the spectacle. By the time I reached the king, the whole city was astir, and the people were saying to each other, "The king has taken an ape for vizier."

When I entered into the presence of the king, I prostrated myself and then stood up and bowed three times. Then I kissed the ground once, before the chamberlains and statesmen and knelt on my knees. Those who were present marveled at my fine manners, most of all the king himself, who said, "This is a wonder." Then he gave permission to his retinue to leave, and everyone left, save for the king, one servant, one little Mamluk,[6] and myself. Then he ordered a table of food set before him, and motioned to me to eat with him. I rose, kissed the ground before him, and, after I washed my hands seven times, I sat back on my knees and, as good manners require, took only a little to eat. Then I took a pen and an inkwell and over a board wrote the following lines:

> Wail for the crane well-stewed in tangy sauce;
> Mourn for the meat, either well baked or fried;

6. See n. 2, p. 38.

Cry for the hens and daughters of the grouse
And the fried birds, even as I have cried.
Two different kinds of fish are my desire,
Served on two loaves of bread, zestful though plain,
While in the pan that sizzles o'er the fire
The eggs like rolling eyes fry in their pain.
The meat when grilled, O what a lovely dish,
Served with some pickled greens; that is my wish.
'Tis in my porridge I indulge at night,
When hunger gnaws, under the bracelets' light.
O soul, be patient, for our fickle fate
Oppresses one day, only to elate.

The king read the verses and pondered. Then they removed the food, and the butler set before us a choice wine in a glass flagon. The king drank first and offered me some. I kissed the ground before him, took a sip, and wrote the following lines over the flagon:

For my confession they burned me with fire
And found that I was for endurance made.
Hence I was borne high on the hands of men
And given to kiss the lips of pretty maid.

When the king read the verses, he marveled and said, "If a man had such cultivation, he would excel all the men of his time." Then he set before me a chessboard and with a sign asked, "Do you play?" I kissed the ground before him and nodded "Yes." Then the two of us arranged the pieces on the board and played a game, and it was a draw. We played a second game, and I won. Then we played for the third time, and I attacked and won again, and the king marveled at my skill. Once more I took the inkwell and the pen and over the chessboard wrote the following lines:

Two armies all day long with arms contend,
Bringing the battle always to a head.
But when night's cover on them does descend
The two go sleeping in a single bed.

As the king read these lines, he was overwhelmed with admiration and delight, and said to the servant, "O Muqbil, go to your lady, Sitt al-Husn, and tell her that her father the king summons her to come and look at this strange ape and enjoy this wonderful spectacle."

The eunuch disappeared and came back a while later with the king's daughter. When she entered and saw me, she veiled her face and said, "O father, have you lost your sense of honor to such a degree that you expose me to men?" Astonished, the king asked, "Daughter, there is no one here, save this little Mamluk, this your mentor who brought you up, and I your father. From whom do you veil your face?" She replied, "From this young man who has been cast under a spell by a demon who is the son of Satan's daughter. He turned him into an ape after he killed his own wife, the daughter of Aftimarus, king of the Ebony Island. This whom you think an ape is a wise, learned, and well-mannered man, a man of culture and refinement." The king was amazed and, looking at me, asked, "Is it true what my daughter said?" I replied with a nod, "Yes." Then he turned to his daughter and asked, "For God's sake, daughter, how did you know that he is enchanted?" She replied, "O father, there was with me from childhood a wily and treacherous old woman who was a witch. She taught me witchcraft, and I copied and memorized seventy domains of magic, by the least of which I could within the hour transport the stones of your city beyond Mount Qaf and beyond the ocean that surrounds the world." The king was amazed and said to his daughter, "O daughter, may God protect you. You have had such a complete power all this time, yet I never knew it. By my life, deliver him from the spell, so that I may make him vizier and marry you to him." She replied, "With the greatest pleasure." Then she took a knife . . .

*But morning overtook Shahrazad, and she lapsed into silence. Then Dinarzad said, "Sister, what a strange and entertaining story!" Shahrazad replied, "What is this compared with what I shall tell you tomorrow night, if the king spares me and lets me live!"*

### THE FIFTIETH NIGHT

*The following night Dinarzad said to her sister Shahrazad, "Sister, if you are not sleepy, tell us one of your lovely little tales." Shahrazad replied, "Very well":*

I heard, O King, that the second dervish said to the girl:

The king's daughter took a knife engraved with names in Hebrew characters and, drawing a perfect circle in the middle of the palace hall, inscribed on it names in Kufic letters,[7] as well as other talismanic words. Then she muttered charms and uttered spells, and in a short time the world turned dark until we could no longer see anything and thought that the sky was falling on our heads. Suddenly we were startled to see the demon descending in the semblance

---

7. The rectilinear Arabic script characteristic of the early Qurans.

of a lion as big as a bull, and we were terrified. The girl cried, "Get away, you dog!" The demon replied, "You traitor, you have betrayed me and broken the oath. Have we two not taken an oath that neither would cross the other?" She said, "Cursed one, how could I keep a pledge with one like you?" The demon cried, "Then take what you have brought on yourself," and with an open mouth he rushed toward the girl, who quickly plucked a hair from her head and as she waved the hair in the air and muttered over it the hair turned into a keen sword blade with which she struck the lion, cutting him in half. But while the two halves went flying, the head remained and turned into a scorpion. The girl quickly turned into a huge serpent, and the two fought a bitter battle for a long time. Then the scorpion turned into a vulture and flew outside the palace, and the girl changed into an eagle and flew after the vulture. The two were gone for a long time, but suddenly the ground split asunder, and there emerged a piebald tomcat, which meowed, snorted, and snored. He was followed by a black wolf, and the two battled in the palace for a long time, and when the cat saw that he was losing to the wolf, he screamed, turned into a worm, and crept into a pomegranate that was lying beside the fountain. The pomegranate swelled until it was as big as a striped watermelon, and the wolf turned immediately into a snow white rooster. The pomegranate flew in the air and fell on the marble floor of the raised hall, breaking to pieces, and as the seeds scattered everywhere, the rooster fell to picking them. He picked them all, save for one that lay hidden at the edge of the fountain. Then the rooster began to cry and crow, flap his wings, and motion with his beak, as if to ask us, "Are there any seeds left?" But we did not understand, and he let out such a loud shriek that we thought that the palace was falling on our heads. Then the rooster chanced to turn and saw the seed at the edge of the fountain. He rushed to pick it . . .

*But morning overtook Shahrazad, and she lapsed into silence. Then Dinarzad said, "Sister, what an amazing and entertaining story!" Shahrazad replied, "What is this compared with what I shall tell you tomorrow night if the king spares me and lets me live!"*

### The Fifty-First Night

*The following night Dinarzad said to her sister Shahrazad, "Sister, if you are not sleepy, tell us the rest of the story." Shahrazad replied, "With the greatest pleasure":*

I heard, O King, that the second dervish said to the girl:

O lady, the rooster, glad to see the seed, rushed to pick it, when it rolled into the fountain, became a fish, and dove into the water. The rooster turned immediately into a bigger fish and plunged after it, and the two disappeared into the bottom of the fountain for a very long time. Then we heard loud shouts, shrieks, and howls, which made us tremble, and a while later the demon came out as a burning flame, followed by the girl, who was also a burning flame. The demon blew fire and sparks from his mouth, nostrils, and eyes and battled the girl for a long time until their flames engulfed them, and the smoke filled the palace until we were resigned to suffocate, as we stood stricken by fear for our lives, certain of disaster and perdition, and, as the fire raged and became more intense, we cried, "There is no power and no strength save in God, the Almighty, the Magnificent." Suddenly, before we could notice, the demon darted as a flame out of the fire, and with one leap stood in the hall before us, blowing fire in our faces, and the girl pursued him, with a loud cry. As the demon blew fire at us, the sparks flew, and, as I stood there in the semblance of an ape, one of them hit my right eye and destroyed it. A second spark hit the king, burning half of his face, including his beard and chin, and knocking out a row of his teeth. A third spark hit the servant in the chest and killed him instantly. At that moment, as we felt certain of destruction and gave ourselves up for lost, we heard a cry, "God is great, God is great! He has conquered and triumphed; He has defeated the infidel." It was the cry of the king's daughter, who had at that very moment defeated the demon. We looked and saw a heap of ashes.

Then the girl came up to us and said, "Bring me a bowl of water," and crying, "In the name of the Almighty God and His covenant, be yourself again," she sprinkled me with the water, and I shook and stood "a full-fledged man." Then she cried out, "The fire! The fire! O father, I am going to miss you, for I have been wounded by one of the demon's arrows, and I shall not live much longer. Although I am not used to fighting demons, I had no trouble until the pomegranate broke to pieces and I became a rooster. I picked all the seeds but overlooked the one that contained the very soul of the demon. Had I picked it up, he would have died instantly, but I overlooked it. I fought him under the earth and I fought him in the sky, and every time he initiated a domain of magic, I countered with a greater domain and foiled him until I opened the domain of fire. Few open it and survive, but I exceeded him in cunning, and with God's help I killed him. God will protect you in my place." Then she implored again, "The fire! The fire!"

*But morning overtook Shahrazad, and she lapsed into silence. Then Dinarzad said, "Sister, what an entertaining story!" Shahrazad replied, "What is this compared with what I shall tell you tomorrow night if I stay alive!"*

THE FIFTY-SECOND NIGHT

*The following night Dinarzad said to her sister Shahrazad, "Sister, if you are not sleepy, tell us one of your little tales." Shahrazad replied, "Very well":*

I heard, O King, that the second dervish said to the girl:

When the king's daughter implored, "The fire! The fire!" her father said, "Daughter, it would be a wonder if I too do not perish, for this your servant died instantly, and this young man has lost an eye." Then he wept and made me weep with him. Soon the girl implored again, "The fire! The fire!" as a spark shot at her legs and burned them, then flew to her thighs, then to her bosom, while she kept crying out, "The fire! The fire!" until all of her body burned to a heap of ashes. By God, mistress, I grieved sorely for her, wishing to have been a dog, an ape, or even a dead man, instead of seeing that girl fight, suffer, and burn to ashes. When the father saw that his daughter was dead, he beat his face, and as I did likewise and cried, the statesmen and the servants came in and were amazed to see two heaps of ashes and the king in a bad way. Then they attended him, and when he regained consciousness and told them about his daughter's calamity, their grief grew greater and they mourned for her for seven days. Then the king bade a vaulted tomb be built over his daughter's ashes, but the demon's ashes he bade be scattered to the wind.

Then the king lay ill for a full month, but when God granted him recovery and he regained his health and his beard grew again, he summoned me before him and said, "Young man, listen to what I have to say to you, and don't disobey me, lest you perish." I replied, "My lord, tell me, for I shall never disobey an order of yours." He said, "We have enjoyed the happiest of lives, safe from the misfortunes of the world, until you came with your black face and brought disaster with you. My daughter died for your sake, my servant perished, and I myself barely escaped destruction. You were the cause of all this, for ever since we laid eyes on you, we have been unfortunate. Would that we never saw you, for we have paid for your deliverance with our destruction. Now I want you to leave our city and depart in peace, but if I ever see you again, I will kill you." Then he yelled at me, and I went forth from his presence, dumbfounded and deaf and blind to everything.

Before leaving the city, I went to the bath and shaved off my beard and eyebrows, and when I came out, I put on a black woolen robe and departed. I left the king's capital in dismay and tears, not knowing where I should go, and when I recalled everything that had happened to me, how I had entered the city and in what condition I was leaving it, my grief grew worse. O mistress, every day I ponder my misfortune, the loss of my eye and the death of the two girls. I weep bitterly and repeat these verses:

> The Lord of Mercy sees me stand perplexed,
> Beset by ills, whence came I cannot see.
> I will endure until I patience tire
> And God fulfills my wish by His decree.
> I will endure until God sees that I
> Bitterness worse than aloes have endured.
> Nor would I have tested such bitterness,
> Had my weak patience such a taste endured.
> Nor would I have endured such bitterness,
> Had my weak patience endured such decree.
> He who says that life is made of sweetness
> A day more bitter than aloes will see.

Then I journeyed through many regions and visited many countries, with the intention of reaching Baghdad and the hope of finding someone there who would help me to the presence of the Commander of the Faithful, so that I might tell him my tale and acquaint him with my misfortune. I arrived here this very night and found this man my brother standing about. I greeted him and asked, "Are you a stranger?" and he replied, "Yes, I am a stranger." Soon this other man joined us and said, "I am a stranger," and we replied, "We too are strangers like you." Then the three of us walked on, as night descended on us, until God brought us to your house. Such then is the cause of losing my eye and shaving off my beard.

The girl said to him, "Stroke your head and go," but he replied, "By God, I will not leave until I hear the tales of the others." Then the black men untied him, and he stood by the side of the first dervish.

*But morning overtook Shahrazad, and she lapsed into silence. Then her sister said, "Sister, what a strange and entertaining story!" Shahrazad replied, "What is this compared with what I shall tell you tomorrow night if I stay alive!"*

*The following night Dinarzad said, "Please, sister, if you are not sleepy, tell us a tale to while away the night." The king added, "Finish the dervishes' tale." Shahrazad replied, "Very well":*

It is related, O King, that the third dervish said:

# [The Third Dervish's Tale]

O great lady, the story behind the shaving off of my beard and the loss of my eye is stranger and more amazing than theirs, yet it is unlike theirs, for their misfortune took them by surprise, whereas I knowingly brought misfortune and sorrow upon myself. My father was a great and powerful king, and when he died, I inherited the kingdom. My name is 'Ajib ibn-Khasib, and my city stood on the shore of a vast sea that contained many islands. My fleet numbered fifty merchantmen, fifty small pleasure boats, and one hundred and fifty ships fitted for battle and holy war. One day I decided to go on an excursion to the islands, and I carried with me a month's supply and went there, enjoyed myself, and came back. A while later, driven by a desire to give myself to the sea, I fitted ten ships, carried two months' supply, and set out on my voyage. We sailed for forty days, but on the night of the forty-first, the wind blew from all directions, the sea raged with fury, buffeting our ships with huge waves, and a dense darkness descended upon us. We gave ourselves up for lost and said, "'Even if he escapes, the foolhardy deserves no praise.'" We prayed to the Almighty God and implored and supplicated, but the blasts continued to blow and the sea continued to rage till dawn. Then the wind died down, the waves subsided, and the sea became calm and peaceful, and when the sun shone on us, the sea lay before us like a smooth sheet.

Soon we came to an island, where we landed and cooked and ate some food. We rested for two days and we set out again and sailed for ten days, but as we sailed, the sea kept expanding before us and the land kept receding behind us. The captain was puzzled and said to the lookout man, "Climb to the masthead and look." The lookout man climbed, and after he looked for a while, came down and said, "I looked to my right and saw nothing but sky and water, and I looked to my left and saw something black looming before me. That is all I saw." When the captain heard what the lookout man said, he threw his turban to the deck, plucked out his beard, beat his face, and said, "O King, I tell you that we are all going to perish. There is no power and no strength save in God, the Almighty, the Magnificent," and he began to weep and made us weep with him. Then we said to him, "Captain, explain the matter." He replied, "My lord, we lost our course on the night of the storm, and we can no longer go back. By midday tomorrow, forced by the currents, we will reach a black mountain of a metal called the magnetic stone. As soon as we sail below the mountain, the ship's sides will come apart and every nail will fly out and stick to the mountain, for the Almighty God has endowed the magnetic stone with a mysterious virtue that makes the iron love it. For this reason and because of the many ships that have been passing by for a long time, the mountain has attracted so much iron that most of it is already covered with it. On the summit facing the sea, there is a dome of Andalusian brass, supported by ten brass pillars, and on top of the dome there is a brass horse with a brass horseman, bearing on his breast a lead tablet inscribed with talismans. O King, it is none but this rider who destroys the people, and they will not be safe from him until he falls from his horse." Then, O my lady, the captain wept bitterly, and certain that we would perish, we too wept for ourselves with him. We bade each other good-bye, and each of us charged his friend with his instructions, in case he was saved.

We never slept a wink that night, and in the morning we began to approach the magnetic mountain, so that by midday, forced by the currents, we stood below the mountain. As soon as we arrived there, the planks of the ship came apart, and the nails and every iron part flew out toward the mountain and stuck together there. Some of us drowned and some escaped, but those who did escape knew nothing about the fate of the others. As for me, O my lady, God spared me that I might suffer what He had willed for me of hardship and misery. I climbed on one of the planks of the ship, and it was thrown immediately by the wind at the foot of the mountain. There I found a path leading to the summit, with steps carved out of the rock.

*But morning overtook Shahrazad, and she lapsed into silence. Then Dinarzad said, "Sister, what a strange and entertaining story!" Shahrazad replied, "What is this compared with what I shall tell you tomorrow night if I stay alive!"*

## THE FIFTY-FOURTH NIGHT

*The following night Dinarzad said to her sister Shahrazad,
"Please, sister, if you are not sleepy, tell us the rest of the story of
the third dervish." Shahrazad replied, "Very well":*

O my lord, I heard that the third dervish said to the girl:

When I saw the path on the side of the mountain, I invoked the
name of the Almighty God, hung against the rock, and began to
climb little by little. And the Almighty God bade the wind be still
and helped me with the ascent, so that I reached the summit safely
and went directly to the dome. Glad at my safe escape, I entered
the dome, performed my ablutions, and prayed, kneeling down
several times in thanksgiving to the Almighty God for my safety.
Then I fell asleep under the dome overlooking the sea and heard
in a dream a voice saying, "O 'Ajib, when you wake from your sleep,
dig under your feet, and you will find a brass bow and three lead
arrows inscribed with talismans. Take the bow and arrows and shoot
at the horseman to throw him off the horse and rid mankind of this
great calamity. When you shoot at him, he will fall into the sea,
and the horse will drop at your feet. Take the horse and bury it
in the place of the bow. When you do this, the sea will swell and
rise until it reaches the level of the dome, and there will come to
you a skiff carrying a man of brass (a man other than the man you
will have thrown), holding in his hands a pair of paddles. Ride with
him, but do not invoke the name of God. He will row you for ten
days until he brings you to the Sea of Safety. Once there, you will
find those who will convey you to your native land. All this will
be fulfilled, providing that you do not invoke the name of God."
    Then I awoke and eagerly sprang up to do the voice's bidding.
I shot at the horseman, and he fell from the horse into the sea, while
the horse dropped at my feet, and when I buried the horse in the
place of the bow, the sea swelled and rose until it came up to me.
Soon I saw a skiff in the offing, coming toward me, and I praised
and thanked the Almighty God. When the skiff came up to me,
I saw there a man of brass, bearing on his breast a lead tablet
inscribed with names and talismans. I climbed into the skiff without
uttering a word, and the boatman rowed with me through the first
day and the second and on to the ninth, when I happily caught
sight of islands, hills, and other signs of safety. But in my excess
of joy, I praised and glorified the Almighty God, crying, "There

is no god but God." No sooner had I done that than the skiff turned upside down and sank, throwing me into the sea. I swam all day until my shoulders were numb with fatigue and my arms began to fail me, and when night fell and I was in the middle of nowhere, I became resigned to drown. Suddenly there was a violent gust of wind, which made the sea surge, and a great wave as tall as a mountain swept me and with one surge cast me on dry land; for God had willed to preserve my life. I walked ashore, wrung out my clothes, and spread them to dry. Then I slept the whole night.

In the morning I put on my clothes and went to scout and see where I was. I came to a cluster of trees, circled around them, and as I walked further, I found out that I was on a small island in the middle of the sea. I said, "There is no power and no strength save in God, the Almighty, the Magnificent," and while I was thinking about my situation, wishing that I was dead, I suddenly saw in the distance a ship with human beings on board, making for the island. I climbed a tree and hid among the branches. Soon the ship touched land, and there came ashore ten black men, carrying shovels and baskets. They walked on until they reached the middle of the island. Then they began to dig into the ground and to shovel the earth away until they uncovered a slab. Then they returned to the ship and began to haul out sacks of bread and flour, vessels of cooking butter and honey, preserved meat, utensils, carpets, straw mats, couches, and other pieces of furniture — in short, all one needs for setting up house. The black men kept going back and forth and descending through the trapdoor with the articles until they had transported everything that was in the ship. When they came out of the ship again, there was a very old man in their middle. Of this man nothing much was left, for time had ravaged him, reducing him to a bone wrapped in a blue rag through which the winds whistled east and west. He was like one of whom the poet said:

> Time made me tremble; ah! how sore that was
> For with his might does time all mortals stalk.
> I used to walk without becoming tired;
> Today I tire although I never walk.

The old man held by the hand a young man who was so splendidly handsome that he seemed to be cast in beauty's mold. He was like the green bough or the tender young of the roe, ravishing every heart with his loveliness and captivating every mind with his perfection. Faultless in body and face, he surpassed everyone in looks and inner grace, as if it was of him that the poet said:

> With him to make compare Beauty they brought,
> But Beauty hung his head in abject shame.

They said, "O Beauty, have you seen his like?"
Beauty replied, "I have ne'er seen the same."

My lady, they walked until they reached the trapdoor, went
down, and were gone for a long time. Then the old man and the
black men came out without the young man and shoveled the earth
back as it was before. Then they boarded the ship, set sail, and
disappeared.

I came down from the tree and, going to the spot they had
covered, began to dig and shovel away. Having patiently cleared
the earth away, I uncovered a single millstone, and when I lifted
it up, I was surprised to find a winding stone staircase. I descended
the steps, and when I came to the end, I found myself in a clean,
whitewashed hall, spread with various kinds of carpets, beddings,
and silk stuffs. There I saw the young man sitting on a high couch,
leaning back on a round cushion, with a fan in his hand. A banquet was set before him, with fruits, flowers, and scented herbs,
as he sat there all alone. When he saw me, he started and turned
pale, but I greeted him and said, "My lord, set your mind at ease,
for there is nothing to fear. I am a human being like you, my dear
friend, and like you, the son of a king. God has brought me to you
to keep you company in your loneliness. But tell me, what is your
story, and what causes you to dwell under the ground?"

*But morning overtook Shahrazad, and she lapsed into silence.
Then Dinarzad said, "Sister, what a strange and entertaining story!"
Shahrazad replied, "What is this compared with what I shall tell
you tomorrow night if I stay alive!"*

THE FIFTY-FIFTH NIGHT

*The following night Dinarzad said to her sister Shahrazad,
"Please, sister, if you are not sleepy, tell us the rest of the story of
the king's son and the young man under the ground." Shahrazad
replied, "With the greatest pleasure":*

I heard, O King, that the third dervish said to the girl:

My lady, when I asked the young man to tell me his story, and
he was assured that I was of his kind, he rejoiced and regained his
composure. Then he made me draw near to him and said, "O my
brother, my case is strange and my tale is amazing. My father is
a very wealthy jeweler, who deals even with kings and who has many

black and white slaves as well as traders who travel on ships to trade for him. But he was not blessed with a child. One night he dreamt that he was going to have a son who would be short-lived, and he woke up in the morning, feeling depressed. My mother happened to conceive on the following night, and my father noted the date of her conception. When the months passed and her time came, she gave birth to me, and my father was exceedingly happy. Then the astrologers and wise men, noting my birth date, read my horoscope and said, 'Your son will live fifteen years, after which there will be a conjunction of the stars, and if he can escape it, he will live. For there stands in the salty sea a mountain called the magnetic mountain, on top of which stands a brass horseman riding on a brass horse and holding in his mouth a lead tablet. Fifty days after this horseman falls from the horse, your son will die, and his killer will be the man who will have thrown the horseman off the horse, a man named 'Ajib, son of King Khasib.' My father was stricken with grief. But he raised me and educated me as the years went by until I was fifteen. Ten days ago, the news reached my father that the brass horseman has been thrown into the sea by a man called King 'Ajib, son of King Khasib. When my father heard the news, he wept bitterly at our impending separation and became like a madman. Then for fear that 'Ajib, son of King Khasib, would kill me, my father built me this house under the ground and brought me in the ship with everything I need for the duration of fifty days. Ten days have already passed, and there remain only forty days until the conjunction of the stars is over and my father comes back to take me home. This is my story and the cause of my loneliness and isolation."

My lady, when I heard his narrarive and strange tale, I said to myself, "I am the one who overthrew the brass horseman, and I am 'Ajib, son of King Khasib, but by God, I will never kill him." Then I said to him, "O my lord, may you be spared from death and safe from harm. God willing, there is nothing to worry about or fear. I will stay with you to serve you and entertain you these forty days. I will help you and go home with you, and you in turn will help me to return to my native land, and God will reward you." My words pleased him, and I sat to chat with him and entertain him.

When night came, I got up and, lighting a candle, I filled and lit three oil lamps. Then I offered him a box of sweets, and after we both ate and savored some, we sat and chatted most of the night. When he fell asleep, I covered him, and then I too lay down and slept. When I woke up in the morning, I heated some water for him and gently woke him up, and when he awoke, I brought him the hot water, and he washed his face and thanked me saying, "God bless you, young man. By God, when I escape the man who is called 'Ajib, son of Khasib, and God saves me from him, I will make my father reward you and grant you every favor." I replied, "May all your days be free from harm, and may God set my appointed day before yours!" Then I offered him something to eat, and after the two of us ate I rose and cut pieces of wood for checkers and set the pieces on the checkerboard. We diverted and amused ourselves, playing and eating and drinking till nightfall. Then I rose, lit the lamps, and offered him some sweets, and after we ate and savored some, we sat and chatted, then went to sleep.

My lady, in this way we passed many days and nights, and I became an intimate friend of his, felt a great affection for him, and forgot my cares and sorrows. I said to myself, "The astrologers lied when they told his father, 'Your son will be killed by one called 'Ajib, son of Khasib.' for by God, this is I and in no way will I kill him," and for thirty-nine days I kept serving him, entertaining him, and carousing with him through the night. On the night of the fortieth day, feeling glad at his safe escape, he said, "Brother, I have now completed forty days. Praise be to God who has saved me from death by your blessed coming. By God, I shall make my father reward you and send you to your native land. But, brother, kindly heat some water for me, so that I may wash my body and change my clothes." I replied, "With the greatest pleasure." Then I rose, heated some water, and took the young man into a little room where I gave him a good bath and put on him fresh clothes. Then I spread for him a high bed, covered with a leather mat, and there he lay down to rest, tired from his bath. He said to me, "Brother, cut me up a watermelon and sweeten the juice with sugar." I rose and, bringing back a fine watermelon, set it on a platter, saying, "My lord, do you know where the knife is?" He replied, "Here it is, on the high shelf over my head." I sprang up and, reaching over him in haste, drew the knife from the sheath, and as I stepped back, I slipped on the leather mat, as had been foreordained, and fell prostrate on the young man, and the knife, which was in my hand, pierced his heart and killed him instantly. When I saw that he was dead and realized that it was I who had killed him, I let out a loud scream, beat my face, tore my clothes, and cried, "O people, O God's creatures, there remained for this young man only one day out of the forty, yet he still met his death at my hand. O God, I ask for your forgiveness, wishing that I had died before him. These my afflictions I suffer, draught by bitter draught, 'so that God's will may be fulfilled.'"

*But morning overtook Shahrazad, and she lapsed into silence.
Then Dinarzad said, "What a strange and entertaining story!"
Shahrazad replied, "What is this compared with what I shall tell
you tomorrow night if I stay alive!"*

## THE FIFTY-SIXTH NIGHT

*The following night Dinarzad said to her sister Shahrazad, "Sister,
if you are not sleepy, tell us the rest of the story of the third dervish." Shahrazad replied, "With the greatest pleasure":*

I heard, O King, that the third dervish said to the girl:

My lady, when I was sure that I had killed him, as the God above
had foreordained, I rose and, ascending the stairs, replaced the trapdoor and covered it with earth. Then I looked toward the sea and
saw the ship that had brought him, cleaving the waters toward the
island to fetch him. I said to myself, "The moment they come and
see their boy slain and find that I am his slayer, they will surely
kill me." I headed toward a nearby tree and, climbing it, hid among
the branches, and hardly had I done so when the ship reached the
island and touched the shore, and the black servants came out with
the old father of the young man I had killed. They came to the spot,
and when they removed the earth, they were surprised to find it
soft. They went down and found the young man lying down, with
his face still glowing after the bath, dressed in clean clothes and
the knife deep in his heart. When they examined him and found
that he was dead, they shrieked, beat their faces, wept, wailed, and
invoked awful curses on the murderer. His father fell into such a
deep swoon that the black servants thought that he was dead. At
last he came to himself, and they wrapped the young man in his
clothes and carried him up, together with the old man. Then one
of the slaves went and came back with a seat covered with silk, and
they carried the old man, laid him there, and sat by his head. All
this took place under the tree in which I hid, watching everything
they did and listening to everything they said. My heart felt hoary
before my head turned gray because of the afflictions, misfortunes,
calamities, and sorrows I had suffered. O my lady, the old man
remained in a swoon till close to sunset. When he came to himself,
looked at his son, and recalled what had happened—that what he
feared had come to pass—he wept, beat his face, and recited the
following verses:

By my life, hurry; they have gone away,
And my tears from my eyes profusely flow.
Their resting place is far, O far away;
What shall I say of them, what shall I do?
I wish that I had never seen their sight.
Helpless I stand and no solution know.
Comfort and consolation can I find
When burning sorrow sets my heart aglow?
O luck, off with me to their dwelling place;
Cry out to them about my tears that flow
They died and left my heart with burning pain,
The fire that in the loving breast did glow.
I wish that death would take me to their place;
Forever lasts the bond between us two.
For God's sake, luck, be careful with our fate,
Our pending union, careful be and slow.
How blessed we lived together in one home,
A life of bliss that did not hindrance know,
Until with parting's arrow we were shot,
And who can of such arrows bear the blow?
By death was felled the noblest of the tribe,
The age's pearl, with beauty on his brow.
I mourned or silently I seemed to say,
"I wish that death had not hastened the blow.
On me and mine did envy fix his eye,
O son, I'd have given my life for you.
How can I meet you soon, my only one,
My son, for whom I would my soul bestow?
Your gifts you lavished like the bounteous moon,
And like the moon your fame did rise and grow.
If moon I call you, no, the moon goes down,
And if I call you sun, the sun sinks low.
O you, whose beauties were on every tongue,
You whom the virtues did with grace endow,
For you I will forever grieve and mourn;
No other love but you I'll ever know.
Longing for you your father has consumed,
But helpless now he stands since death felled you.
Some evil eyes on you have had their feast,
Would they were pierced or black and blind did grow."

Then the old man took a breath, and with a deep sigh his soul left his body. The black servants shrieked and, throwing dust on their heads and faces, wailed and cried bitterly. Then they carried the old man and his son to the ship and laid them down side by side. Soon they set sail and vanished from my sight. Then I descended from the tree and went back to the underground dwelling. When I entered, I saw some of the young man's belongings, which reminded me of him, and I repeated the following verses:

> I see their traces and with longing pine
> In their empty dwelling, and my tears flow.
> And Him who has their loss decreed I beg,
> That He may on me their return bestow.

*But morning overtook Shahrazad, and she lapsed into silence. Then her sister said, "Sister, what a strange and entertaining story!" Shahrazad replied, "What is this compared with what I shall tell you tomorrow night if I stay alive!"*

### THE FIFTY-SEVENTH NIGHT

*The following night Dinarzad said to her sister Shahrazad, "If you are not sleepy, tell us the rest of the dervish's story." Shahrazad said:*

I heard, O King, that the third dervish said to the girl:

My lady, for a month I lived on the island, spending my day in the open and my night in the underground hall, until one day I noticed that the water on the west side of the island was receding little by little. By the end of the month dry land appeared on the east side, and I felt happy and certain of my safety. I waded through the shallow water, and when I reached permanent dry land, I saw nothing but sand as far as the eye can see. Then I noticed a great fire raging in the distance, and I gathered my energy and braved the sand toward the fire, saying to myself, "Someone must surely have kindled such a fire, and there perhaps is where I can find help," and I repeated the following verses:

> Perhaps my fate will his own bridle turn
> And bring good fortune, O my fickle fate,
> Replacing past ills with present good deeds,
> My needs to answer and my hopes elate.

When I drew near, I found out that the fire was in reality a palace overlaid with copper plates that, as the sun shone on them, glowed and from a distance appeared like a fire. I was glad to see the palace and sat down to rest, but hardly had I done so when I was approached by ten neatly dressed young men accompanied by an old

man, and I was astonished to see that each young man was blind
in the right eye, and marveled at this coincidence. When they saw
me, they greeted me, delighted to see me, and when they asked
me about myself, I told them about my misfortunes. Marveling at
my tale, they took me into the palace, where I saw ranged around
the hall ten couches, each with blue bedding and blue coverlet, with
a smaller couch in the middle, covered likewise in blue. We entered
and each young man took his seat on a couch, and the old man
seated himself on the smaller couch in the middle, saying to me,
"Young man, sit down on the floor and do not inquire about our
situation or the loss of our eyes." Then he rose and one by one set
before each of them his own food and did the same for me. After
we ate, he offered us wine, each in his own cup, and they sat to
carouse and ask me about my extraordinary case and strange adventures, and I told them my tale until most of the night was gone.
Then the young men said to the old man, "Old man, will you give
us our due, for it is time to go to bed?" The old man rose, entered
a chamber, and came back, carrying on his head ten trays, each
covered with a blue cover. He set a tray before each young man
and, lighting ten candles, stuck one on each tray. Then he drew
off the covers, and there appeared on each tray nothing but ashes,
powdered charcoal, and kettle soot. Then rolling up their sleeves,
every young man blackened his face and smeared his clothes with
soot and ashes, beat his breast and face, and wept and wailed, crying out again and again, "'We would be sitting pretty but for our
curiosity.'" They carried on like this until it was close to sunrise.
Then the old man rose and heated some water for them, and the
young men ran, washed themselves, and put on clean clothes.

My lady, when I saw what the young men had done and how
they had blackened their faces, I was filled with bewilderment and
curiosity and forgot my own misfortunes. Unable to remain silent,
I asked them, "What brought this on, after we frolicked and enjoyed
ourselves? You seem, God be praised, perfectly sane, and such
actions befit only madmen. I ask you by all that is dearest to you
to tell me your tale and the cause of losing your eyes and smearing
your faces with soot and ashes." They turned to me and said, "Young
man, don't let our youth and our behavior deceive you. It is better
for you not to ask." Then they laid out some food, and we began
to eat, but my heart was still on fire and I burned with curiosity
to find out the cause of their action, especially after having eaten
and drunk with them. Then we sat to converse until late afternoon,
and when it got dark, the old man offered us wine, and we sat drinking till past midnight. Then the young men said, "Give us our due,
old man, for it is time to go to bed." The old man rose, disappeared,

then came back a while later with the same trays, and the young men repeated what they had done the previous night.

My lady, to make a long story short, I stayed with them for a full month, and every night they did the same thing and washed themselves early in the morning, while I watched, marveling at their action, until my curiosity and my anxiety increased to the point that I was no longer able to eat or drink. At last I said to them, "Young men, if you don't relieve me and tell me why you blacken your faces and repeat, 'We would be sitting pretty but for our curiosity,' let me relieve myself of such sights by leaving you and going home, for as the saying goes, 'Better for me and meet to see you not, for if the eye sees nought, the heart grieves not.'" When they heard my words, they came up to me and said, "Young man, we have kept our secret from you only out of pity for you, so that you would not suffer what we have suffered." I replied, "You must tell me." They said, "Young man, listen to our advice and don't ask, lest you become one-eyed like us." I repeated, "I must know the secret." They replied, "Young man, when you find out the secret, remember that we will no longer harbor you nor let you stay with us again."

Then they fetched a ram, slaughtered it, skinned it, and made the skin into a sack. Then they said, "Take this knife and get into the sack, and we shall sew you up in it. Then we shall go away and leave you alone. Soon a bird called Rukh[8] will pick you up with his talons, fly with you high in the air for a while; then you will feel that he has set you down on a mountain and moved away from you. When you feel that the bird has done so, rip the skin open with this knife and come out, and when the bird sees you, he will fly away. Proceed immediately and walk for half a day, and you will see before you a towering palace, built with sandal- and aloewood and covered with plates of red gold, studded with emeralds and all kinds of precious stones. Enter the palace, and you will have your wish, for we have all entered that palace, and that was the cause of losing our eyes and blackening our faces. It would be too tedious to tell you the whole story, for each of us has his own tale for losing his right eye."

*But morning overtook Shahrazad, and she lapsed into silence. Then Dinarzad said, "Sister, what a strange and entertaining story!" Shahrazad replied, "What is this compared with what I shall tell you tomorrow night if I stay alive!"*

8. The phoenix, a mythological bird.

### THE FIFTY-EIGHTH NIGHT

*The following night Dinarzad said to her sister Shahrazad, "Please, sister, if you are not sleepy, tell us the rest of the story of the third dervish." Shahrazad replied, "With the greatest pleasure":*

It is related, O King, that King 'Ajib, the third dervish, said:

When the young men finished their explanation, they let me into the skin sack, sewed me up, and returned to the palace. Soon I felt the white bird approach, and snatching me up with his talons, he flew away with me for a while and set me down on the mountain. I ripped the skin open and came out, and when the bird saw me, he flew away. I proceeded immediately to walk until I reached the palace and found it to be exactly as they had described it. The door stood open, and when I entered, I found myself in a spacious and lovely hall as vast as a playground. It was surrounded by forty chambers with doors of sandal- and aloewood, covered with plates of red gold and graced with silver handles. At the far end of the hall, I saw forty girls, sumptuously dressed and lavishly adorned. They looked like moons, so lovely that none could tire of gazing on them. When they saw me, they said in one voice, "O lord, welcome, O master, welcome! and good cheer to you, lord! We have been expecting one like you for months. Praised be God who has sent us one who is as worthy of us as we are of him." Then they raced toward me and made me sit on a high couch, saying, "This day, you are our lord and master, and we are your maids and servants, at your beck and call." Then while I sat marveling at their behavior, they rose, and some of them set food before me; others warmed water and washed my hands and feet and changed my clothes; others mixed juice and gave me to drink; and they all gathered around me, joyful at my coming. Then they sat down to converse with me and question me till nightfall.

*But morning overtook Shahrazad, and she lapsed into silence. Then Dinarzad said, "Sister, what a strange and entertaining story!" Shahrazad replied, "What is this compared with what I shall tell you tomorrow night if the king spares me and lets me live!"*

## The Fifty-Ninth Night

*The following night Dinarzad said to her sister Shahrazad, "Sister, if you are not sleepy, tell us the rest of the story." Shahrazad replied, "Very well":*

It is related, O King, that the third dervish said to the girl:

My lady, the girls sat around me, and when night came, five of them rose and set up a banquet with plenty of nuts and fragrant herbs. Then they brought the wine vessels and we sat to drink, with the girls sitting all around me, some singing, some playing the flute, the psalter, the lute, and all other musical instruments, while the bowls and cups went round. I was so happy that I forgot every sorrow in the world, saying to myself, "'This is the life; alas, that it is fleeting.'" I enjoyed myself with them until most of the night was gone and we were drunk. Then they said to me, "O our lord, choose from among us whomever you wish to spend this night with you and not return to be your bedfellow again until forty days will have passed." I chose a girl who had a lovely face and dark eyes, with black hair, joining brows, and a mouth with slightly parted teeth. Perfect in every way, like a willow bough or a stalk of sweet basil, her beauty struck the eye and bewildered the mind. She was like the one of whom the poet said,

> She bent and swayed like a ripe willow bough,
> O more lovely, sweet, and delicious sight!
> She smiled and her glittering mouth revealed
> The flashing stars that answered light with light.
> She loosened her black tresses, and the morn
> Became a dusky, black, and darkling night,
> And when her radiant face shone in the dark,
> From east to west the gloomy world turned bright.
> 'Tis foolish to compare her to a roe;
> How can such fledgling thing such beauties show,
> Such lovely body, such honeydew lips,
> Such sweet nectar to drink, such joy to know,
> Such wide eyes that with the arrows of love
> The tortured victim pierce; how can the roe?
> I loved her madly like a pagan boy,
> No wonder when with love one is laid low.

That night I slept with her and spent the best of nights.

*But morning overtook Shahrazad, and she lapsed into silence.*
*Then her sister said, "Sister, what a strange and entertaining story!"*
*Shahrazad replied, "What is this compared with what I shall tell*
*you tomorrow night if I stay alive!"*

### THE SIXTIETH NIGHT

*The following night Dinarzad said to her sister Shahrazad,*
*"Please, sister, tell us the rest of the story of the third dervish."*
*Shahrazad replied, "Very well":*

I heard, O King, that the third dervish said to the girl:

When it was morning, the girls took me to a bath in the palace,
and after they bathed me, they dressed me in fine clothes. Then
they served food, and after we ate they served wine, and as the cup
was passed around, we drank into the night. Then they said,
"Choose from among us whomever you wish to spend the night with;
we are your maids, awaiting your command." I chose a girl with
a lovely face and a soft body, like her of whom the poet said:

> I saw two caskets on her bosom fair,
> Shielded with musk seals from lovers' embrace.
> Against assault she guarded them with darts
> And arrowy glances from her lovely face.

I spent with her a lovely night, and when morning came, I bathed
and put on new clothes.

My lady, to make a long story short, for a full year I lived with
them a carefree life, eating and drinking, carousing, and spending
every night with one of them. But one day, at the beginning of the
new year, they began to wail and cry, bidding me farewell, cling-
ing to me, and weeping. Amazed at their behavior, I asked, "What
is the matter, for you are breaking my heart?" They replied, "We
wish that we had never known you, for we had lived with many
men but never met one more pleasant than you. May God never
deprive us of you," and they wept. I asked, "Why do you weep,
for to me your tears are gall?" They replied with one voice, "The
reason is our separation from you, of which none other than you
yourself is the cause. If you listen to us, we will not be separated,
but if you disobey us, we will. Our hearts tell us that you will not
obey and that it will happen, and this is the cause of our weeping."
I said, "Explain the matter." They replied, "Our lord and master,

we are the daughters of kings, and we have lived together here for many years. It has been our custom to go away once a year for forty days and return to live here for the rest of the year, eating and drinking and taking our pleasure and enjoying ourselves here. Now this is how you will disobey us. We are about to leave for forty days. We commit to you now all the keys to this palace, which contains one hundred chambers. Eat and drink and enjoy looking around in every chamber, for each one you open will occupy you a full day, but there is one chamber you must never open or even approach, for it is its opening that will cause our separation. You have ninety-nine chambers to open and to enjoy looking at what is in them as you please, but if you open the one with the door of red gold, that will cause our separation."

*But morning overtook Shahrazad, and she lapsed into silence. Then Dinarzad said, "Sister, what a strange and entertaining story!" Shahrazad replied, "What is this compared with what I shall tell you tomorrow night if I stay alive!"*

## THE SIXTY-FIRST NIGHT

*The following night Shahrazad said:*

I heard, O happy King, that the third dervish said to the girl:

My lady, the forty girls said, "O our lord, the cause of our separation is in your hand. For God's sake and for our sake, enjoy looking into all ninety-nine chambers, but don't open the hundredth, lest we be separated. Be patient for forty days, and we shall come back to you." Then one of them came up to me, embraced me, wept, and repeated the following verses:

> When she drew near to bid adieu, her heart
> Burning with love and longing in her breast,
> Her tears and mine, wet pearls and carnelians,
> A necklace made for her and came to rest.

I bid her farewell, saying, "By God, I will never open that door." Then the girls left, shaking at me admonishing fingers.

When they departed and I was left alone in the palace, I said to myself, "By God, I will never open that door and never cause our separation." Then I went and opened the first chamber, and when I entered, I found myself in a garden with streams, trees, and abundant fruits. It was a garden like Paradise, with tall trees, intertwining branches, ripe fruits, singing birds, and running waters. Pleased with the sight, I walked through the trees, enjoying the perfume of the flowers and the song of the birds, which hymned together the glory of the Almighty One. I saw apples like those of which the poet said:

> Two colors, in one apple joining, seemed
> Two cheeks in the embrace of love's desire,
> Two cheeks that, as from sleep they startled stood,
> One yellow turned with fright, one burned with fire.

And I saw pears sweeter than sugar and rosewater and more aromatic than musk and ambergris and saw quinces like those of which the poet said:

> The quince has gathered every pleasing taste,
> Thereby the queen of fruits she has been crowned.
> Her taste is wine, a waft of musk her scent.
> Her hue is gold, her shape, like the moon, round.

And I saw plums so lovely that they dazzled the eyes like polished rubies. At last I went out of the garden and closed the door.

The following day I opened another door, and when I entered, I found myself in a large field full of palm trees and encircled by a running stream whose banks were covered with roses, jasmine, mignonettes, irises, daffodils, narcissus, violets, daisies, gillyflowers, and lilies of the valley; and as the breeze blew over these aromatic plants, the whole field was filled with the sweet aroma. After I enjoyed and diverted myself there for a while, I went out and closed the door. Then I opened a third door and found myself in a large hall covered with all kinds of colored marble, rare metals, and precious stones and hung with cages of aloe- and sandalwood, full of all kinds of singing birds, such as nightingales, thrushes, pigeons, ringdoves, turtledoves, silver doves, and Nubian doves. There I enjoyed myself, felt happy, and forgot my cares.

Then I went to sleep, and in the morning I opened a fourth door and found myself in a large hall, surrounded by forty chambers whose doors stood open. I entered every chamber and found them full of jewels, such as pearls, emeralds, rubies, corals, and carbuncles, as well as gold and silver. I was amazed at such abundance and said to myself, "Such wealth could belong only to the greatest of kings, for no ordinary monarch could assemble such a fortune, not even if all the monarchs of the world joined together." I felt happy and carefree, saying to myself, "I am the king of the age, for these jewels and this wealth are mine, and these girls belong to me and to me alone." O my lady, I enjoyed myself in chamber after chamber until thirty-nine days had passed and there remained only one day and one night. During that time, I had opened all ninety-nine chambers, and there remained only the hundredth, the one the girls had cautioned me not to open.

*But morning overtook Shahrazad, and she lapsed into silence. Then Dinarzad said to her sister, "Sister, what an amazing and entertaining story!" Shahrazad replied, "What is this compared with what I shall tell you tomorrow night if the king spares me and lets me live!"*

## THE SIXTY-SECOND NIGHT

*The following night Shahrazad said:*

I heard, O happy King, that the dervish said:

There remained only that one chamber to complete the hundred, and I began to feel obsessed and tempted with it, as Satan urged me to open it and cause my undoing. Even though there remained but one night for the appointed time for the girls to return and spend a whole year with me, I was no longer able to restrain myself and, succumbing to the devil, at last opened the door plated with gold. As soon as I entered, I was met by a perfume that, as I smelled it, sent me reeling to the floor and made me swoon for a long time. When I came to myself, I summoned my courage and entered the chamber. I found the floor strewn with saffron and saw lamps of gold and silver, fed with costly oils, and saw fragrant candles burning with aloes and ambergris. I also saw two incense burners, each as large as a kneading bowl, full of glowing embers in which burned the incense of aloewood, ambergris, musk, and frankincense, and as the incense burned, the smoke rose to blend with the odors of the candles and the saffron, filling the chamber with perfume.

O my lady, I then saw a deep-black horse as black as the darkest night, bridled and ready with a saddle of red gold, as it stood before two mangers of clear crystal, one filled with husked sesame, the other with rosewater scented with musk. When I saw the horse, I was exceedingly amazed, and said to myself, "There is something of great importance about this horse." Then the devil took hold of me again, and I took the horse from his place and led him outside the palace. I got on his back and tried to ride him, but he refused to move. I kicked him, but he did not stir. Then I took the whip and hit him angrily, and as soon as he felt the blow, he neighed with a sound like roaring thunder and, spreading a pair of wings, flew up with me and disappeared in the sky. A while later he landed on the roof of another palace and, throwing me off his back, lashed my face with his tail with a blow so hard that it gouged out my eye and made it roll on my cheek, leaving me one-eyed. I cried, "There is no power and no strength save in God, the Almighty, the Magnificent. I have taunted the one-eyed young men until I became one-eyed like them."

I looked down from the terrace of the palace and saw again the ten couches with the blue bedding and realized that the palace was the same one that belonged to the ten one-eyed young men who had admonished me and whose admonition I had refused to follow. I went down from the roof and sat down amid the couches, and hardly had I done so when I saw the young men and their old companion approaching. When they saw me, they cried, "You are not welcome or wanted here. By God, we will not let you stay. May you perish." I replied, "All I wanted to know was why you smeared your faces with blue and black soot." They said, "Each of us suffered the same misfortune as you did. We all lived the best of lives in bliss, feeding on chicken, sipping wine from crystal cups, resting on silk brocade, and sleeping on the breasts of fair women. We had to wait one more day to gain a year of pleasures, such food and drink and such entertainment, but because of our curious eyes, we lost our eyes, and now, as you see, we are left to mourn our misfortune." I said, "Do not blame me for what I did, for I have become like you. Indeed, I want you to bring me all ten black trays to blacken my face," and I burst into bitter tears. They replied, "By God, by God, we will never harbor you or let you stay with us. Get out of here, go to Baghdad, and find someone to help you there."

When I saw that there was no avail against their harsh treatment and when I recalled the miseries written on my forehead, how I killed the young man and how 'I would be sitting pretty but for my curiosity,' I could no longer stand it. I shaved off my beard and eyebrows, renounced everything, and roamed the world, a one-eyed dervish. Then God granted me safe passage and I reached Baghdad on the evening of this very night. Here I met these two men standing at a loss, and I greeted them and said, "I am a stranger," and they replied, "We are strangers like you." We formed an extraordinary group, for by coincidence, all three of us happened to be blind in the right eye. This, my lady, was the cause of losing my eye and shaving off my beard.

It is related, O happy King, that after the girl heard the dervishes' tales, she said to them, "Stroke your heads and go your way," but they replied, "By God, we will not go until we hear our companions' tales." Then, turning to the caliph, Ja'far, and Masrur, the girl said, "Tell us your tales." Ja'far stood forth and said, "O my lady, we are citizens of Mosul who have come to your city for trade. When we arrived here, we took lodgings in the merchants' inn and we traded and sold our goods. Tonight a merchant of your city held a party and invited all the merchants in the inn, including our group, to his house, where we had a good time, with choice wine, entertainment, and singing girls. Then there was argument and yelling among some of the guests, and the prefect of police raided the place. Some of us were arrested and some escaped. We were among those who escaped, and when we went to the inn, late at night, we found the door locked, not to be opened again till sunrise. We wandered helplessly, not knowing where to go, for fear that the police would catch up with us, arrest us, and humiliate us. God drove us to your house, and when we heard the beautiful singing and the sound of carousing, we knew that there was a company having a party inside and said to ourselves that we would enter at your service and spend the rest of our night with you to entertain you and to make our pleasure complete. It pleased you to offer us your hospitality and to be generous and kind. This was the cause of our coming to you."

The dervishes said, "O our lady and mistress, we wish you to grant us as a favor the lives of these three men and to let us depart with gratitude." Looking at the entire group, the girl replied, "I grant you your lives, as a favor to all." When they were outside the house, the caliph asked the dervishes, "Men, where are you going, for it is still dark?" They replied, "By God, sir, we do not know where to go." He said, "Come and sleep at our place." Then, turning to Ja'far, the caliph said, "Take these men home with you for the night and bring them before me early tomorrow morning, so that we may chronicle for each his adventure that we have heard tonight." Ja'far did as the caliph bade him, while the caliph returned to his palace. But the caliph was agitated and stayed awake, pondering the mishaps of the dervishes and how they had changed from being sons of kings to what they were now, and burning with curiosity to hear the stories of the flogged girl and the other with the two black bitches. He could not sleep a wink and waited impatiently for the morning.

No sooner had the day dawned than he sat on his throne, and when Ja'far entered and kissed the ground before him, he said, "This is no time for dawdling. Go and bring me the two ladies, so that I may hear the story of the two bitches, and bring the dervishes with you," yelling at him, "Hurry!" Ja'far withdrew and came back soon with the three girls and the three dervishes. Then placing the dervishes next to him and the girls behind a curtain, he said, "Women, we forgive you because of your generosity and kindness to us. If you do not know who is the one sitting before you, I shall introduce him. You are in the presence of the seventh of the sons of 'Abbas, al-Rashid, son of al-Mahdi son of al-Hadi and brother of al-Saffah son of Mansur. Take courage, be frank, and tell the truth and nothing but the truth, and do not lie, for 'you should be truthful even if the truth sends you to burning Hell.' Explain to the caliph why you beat the two black bitches, why you weep after you beat them, and why they weep with you."

*But morning overtook Shahrazad, and she lapsed into silence. Then Dinarzad said, "Sister, what a strange and amazing story!" Shahrazad replied, "What is this compared with what I shall tell you tomorrow night if the king spares me and lets me live!"*

### THE SIXTY-THIRD NIGHT

*The following night Shahrazad said,*

I heard, O happy King, that when the girl who was the mistress of the house heard what Ja'far said to her on behalf of the Commander of the Faithful, she said:

## [The Tale of the First Lady, the Mistress of the House]

My case is so strange and my tale is so amazing that were it engraved with needles at the corner of the eye, it would be a lesson for those who wish to consider. The two black bitches are my sisters by the same mother and father. These two girls, the one whose body bears the marks of the rod and the other who is the shopper are sisters by another mother. When our father died and the inheritance was divided, the three of us lived with our mother, while the other two sisters lived with their own mother. After a while, our mother also died, leaving us three thousand dinars, which we divided equally among ourselves. Since I was the youngest of the three, my two sisters prepared their dowries and got married before me.

The husband of the eldest sister bought merchandise with his money and hers, and the two of them set out on their travels. They were absent for five years, during which time he threw away and wasted all her money. Then he deserted her, leaving her to wander alone in foreign lands, trying to find her way back home. After five years she returned to me, dressed like a beggar in tattered clothes and a dirty old cloak. She was in a most miserable plight. When I saw her, I was stunned, and I asked her, "Why are you in this condition?" She replied, "Words are useless, for 'the pen has brought to pass that which had been decreed.'" O Commander of the Faithful, I took her at once to the bath, dressed her with new clothes, prepared for her some broth, and gave her some wine to drink. I took care of her for a month, and then I said to her, "Sister, you are the eldest, and you have now taken the place of our mother. You and I will share my wealth equally, for God has blessed my share of the inheritance, and I have made much money by spinning and producing silk." I treated her with the utmost kindness, and she lived with me for a whole year, during which time our minds were on our other sister." Shortly she too came home in a worse plight than the first. I treated her just as I had treated the other, clothing her and taking care of her.

A little later, they said to me, "Sister, we would like to get married, for it is not fitting that we live without husbands." I replied, "Sister, there is little good in marriage, for it is hard to find a good man. You got married, but nothing good came of it. Let us stay together and live by ourselves." But, O Commander of the Faithful, they did not listen to my advice and married again without my consent. This time I was obliged to provide them with dowries from my own pocket. Soon their husbands betrayed them; they took what they could, cleared out, and left their wives behind. My two sisters came to me with apologies, saying, "Sister, although you are younger than the two of us in years, you are older in wisdom. We will never mention marriage again. Take us back, and we shall be your servants to earn our upkeep." I replied, "Sisters, none is dearer to me than you." I took them in and treated them even more generously than before. We spent the third year together, and all that time my wealth kept increasing, and my circumstances kept getting better and better.

One day, O Commander of the Faithful, I resolved to take my merchandise to Basra.[9] I fitted a large ship and loaded it with merchandise, provisions, and other necessities. Then we set out, and for many days we sailed under a fair wind. Soon we discovered that we had strayed from our course, and for twenty days we were lost on the high seas. At the end of the twentieth day, the lookout man,

9. Then and now a port city in southern Iraq, situated on the Shat al-Arab, a waterway formed by the confluence of the Tigris and the Euphrates and going into the Arabian, or Persian, Gulf.

climbing the masthead, cried out, "Good news!" Then he joyfully came down, saying, "I have seen what seems to be a city that looks like a fat pigeon." We were happy, and in less than an hour our ship entered the harbor, and I disembarked to visit the city. When I came to the gate, I saw people standing there with staves in their hands, but as I drew nearer, I saw that they had been turned by a curse into stone. I went into the city and saw that all the people in their shops had been turned into stone. 'Not one of them breathed or gave a sign of life.' I walked through the streets and found out that the entire city had been turned into hard stone. When I came to the upper end of the city, I saw a door plated with red gold, draped with a silk curtain, and hung with a lamp. Saying to myself, "By God, this is strange! Can it be that there are human beings here!" I entered through the door and found myself in a hall that led to another and then another, and as I kept going from hall to hall all alone, without meeting anyone, I became apprehensive. Then I entered the harem quarters and found myself in an apartment bearing the royal insignia and hung throughout with drapes of gold brocade. There I saw the queen, the king's wife, wearing a dress decorated with opulent pearls, each as big as a hazelnut, and a crown studded with precious stones.

*But morning overtook Shahrazad, and she lapsed into silence. Then Dinarzad said to her sister, "Sister, what an entertaining story!" Shahrazad replied, "What is this compared with what I shall tell you tomorrow night if the king spares me and lets me live!"*

### THE SIXTY-FOURTH NIGHT

*The following night Shahrazad said:*

I heard, O King, that the girl who was the mistress of the house said to the caliph:

O Commander of the Faithful, the queen wore a crown studded with all kinds of gems, and the apartment was spread with silk tapestries embroidered with gold. In the middle of the hall I saw an ivory bed plated with burnished gold, set with two bosses of green emeralds, and draped with a canopylike net strung with pearls. I saw something glitter, sending rays through the net, and when I approached and put my head in, I saw there, O Commander of the Faithful, set on a pedestal, a gem as big as an ostrich egg, with an incandescent glow and a brilliant light that dazzled the eyes. I also saw silk bedding and a silk coverlet, and beside the pillow, I saw two lighted candles. But there was nobody in the bed. I marveled at the sight, and astonished to find the gem and the two lighted candles, I said to myself, "Someone must have lighted these candles." Then I proceeded to other rooms and came to the kitchen, then the wine cellar, then the king's treasure chambers. I continued to explore the palace, going from room to room, absorbed in the wonderful sights and the amazing state of the city's inhabitants, until I forgot myself and was surprised by the night. I searched for the gate of the castle, but I lost my way and could not find it, and for a long time I wandered in the dark without finding a place of refuge save the canopied bed with the candles. I lay down there, covered myself with the coverlet, and tried to go to sleep, but I could not.

At midnight I heard a sweet voice chanting the Quran. I rose, glad to hear someone, and followed the voice until I came to a chamber, whose door stood ajar. I peered through and saw what looked like a place of worship and recitation, with a prayer niche lighted with hanging lamps and two candles. On a prayer carpet stood a section of the Quran set on a stand, and on the carpet sat a handsome young man reciting the Holy Book. I was amazed to find that this young man was the only one among the people of the city to have escaped the curse and thought that there was a mystery behind this. I opened the door and, entering the chamber, greeted him and said, "Blessed be God who has granted you to me, to be the cause of our deliverance and help our ship return to our native land. O holy man, by the Holy Book you are reciting, answer my question." He looked at me with a smile and said, "O good woman, tell me first what caused you to come here, and I shall relate to you what happened to me and to the people of this city and why they were cursed while I was not." I told him our story and how our ship had strayed for twenty days. Then I questioned him again about the city and its people, and he replied, "O sister, be patient, and I shall tell you." Then he closed the Quran, put it aside, and seated me, O Commander of the Faithful . . .

*But morning overtook Shahrazad, and Dinarzad said, "O sister, what a strange and entertaining story!" Shahrazad replied, "Sister, what is this compared with what I shall tell you tomorrow night if the king spares me and lets me live!"*

### THE SIXTY-FIFTH NIGHT

*The following night Shahrazad said:*

It is related, O happy King, that the girl who was the mistress of the house said to the caliph:

O Commander of the Faithful, the young man placed the Quran in the prayer niche and seated me by his side. When I looked at him, I saw a face as beautiful as the full moon, like the one of whom the poet said:

> The stargazer one night charted the stars
> And saw his fair form shining like a moon
> Who vied in brilliance with the hiding sun
> And left in darkness the bewildered moon.

It was a face on which the supreme God has bestowed the robe of beauty, which was embroidered with the grace of his perfect cheeks. He was like the one of whom the poet said:

> By his enchanting eyelids and his slender waist,
> By his beguiling eyes so keen, so fair,
> By his sharp glances and his tender sides,
> By his white forehead and his jet black hair,
> By eyebrows that have robbed my eyes of sleep
> And made me subject to their mighty will,
> By lovely sidelocks that curl, coil, and charm
> And all rejected lovers with their beauty kill,
> By the soft myrtle of his rosy cheeks,
> By his carnelian lips and mouth of pearls,
> Which sends the fragrance of the honey breath,
> And the sweet wine which in its sweetness purls,
> By his graceful neck and his boughlike frame,
> Which bears two pomegranates on the breast,
> By his charming, tender, and slender waist,
> And hips that quiver while they move or rest,
> By his soft silky skin and charming touch
> And all the beauty that his own does seem,
> By his open hand and his truthful tongue,
> And noble pedigree and high esteem,
> By these I swear that his life-giving breath
> Gives the musk being and perfumes the air,
> That the sun pales before him and the moon
> Is nothing but a paring of his nail; I swear.

O Commander of the Faithful, I looked at him and sighed, for he had captivated my heart. I said to him, "O my dear lord, tell me the story of your city." He said, "O woman of God, this city is the capital of my father the king whom you must have seen turned into black stone inside this cursed palace, together with my mother the queen whom you found inside the net. They and all the people of the city were Magians[1] who, instead of the Omnipotent Lord, worshiped the fire, to which they prayed and by which they swore. My father, who had been blessed with me late in life, reared me in affluence, and I grew and throve. It happened that there lived with us a very old woman who used to teach me the Quran, saying, "'You should worship none but the Almighty God,'" and I learned the Quran without telling my father or the rest of my family. One day we heard a mighty voice proclaiming, 'O people of this city, leave your fire worship and worship the Merciful God.' But they refused to obey. A year later the voice cried out again and did the same the following year. Suddenly one morning the city turned into stone, and none was saved except myself. Here I sit now, as you see, to worship God, but I have grown weary of loneliness, for there is none to keep me company."

I said to him (for he had captured my heart and mastered my life and soul), "Come with me to the city of Baghdad, for this girl standing before you is the head of her family, mistress over servants and slaves, and a businesswoman of considerable wealth, part of which is on the very ship that, after straying, now anchors outside your city, by the will of God who drove us here that I might meet you." I continued to press him, O Commander of the Faithful, until he consented. I spent that night, hardly believing my fortune, asleep at his feet. When morning dawned, we rose and, taking from his father's treasure chambers whatever was light in weight and great in worth, the two of us went from the castle to the city and found the captain, my sisters, and my servants looking for me. When they saw me, they were happy, and when I related to them the story of the young man and the city, they were amazed. But when my two sisters, these very bitches, saw the young man with me, they envied me, O Commander of the Faithful, and harbored ill feelings toward me. Then we went aboard, all of us feeling happy at our gain, most of all I, because of the young man, and sat waiting for the wind to blow before setting sail.

*But morning overtook Shahrazad, and she lapsed into silence. Then Dinarzad said, "O sister, what a strange and entertaining*

---

1. Zoroastrian priests; see n. 1, p. 61.

*story!"* Shahrazad replied, *"What is this compared with what I shall tell you tomorrow if the king spares me and lets me live!"*

## THE SIXTY-SIXTH NIGHT

*The following night Shahrazad said,*

It is related, O happy King, that the girl who was the mistress of the house said to the caliph:

O Commander of the Faithful, when the wind began to blow, we set sail, and, as we sat chatting, my sisters asked me, "Sister, what will you do with this young man?" I replied, "I will make him my husband." Then I turned to him and said, "O my lord, I want you to follow my wish that when we reach Baghdad, our native city, I offer you myself in marriage as your maidservant, and we will be husband and wife." The young man replied, "Yes, indeed, for you are my lady and my mistress, and I will obey you in everything." Then I turned to my sisters and said, "Whatever goods we have brought are yours; my only reward is this young man; he is mine and I am his." But my sisters turned green with envy over him and harbored ill feelings toward me. We sailed on under a fair wind until we entered the Sea of Safety and began to approach Basra. When night came, and the young man and I fell asleep, my two sisters, who had been waiting patiently, carried me with my bed and threw me into the sea. They did the same thing to the young man. He drowned, but I was saved; I wish that I had drowned with him. I was cast on a raised island, and when I came to myself and saw myself surrounded by water, I realized that my sisters had betrayed me, and I thanked God for my safety. Meantime, the ship sailed on like a flash of lightning, while I stood alone through the night.

When morning dawned, I saw a dry strip of land connecting the island to the shore. I crossed it; then I wrung out my clothes and spread them to dry in the sun. When they were dry, I ate some dates and drank some fresh water I had found there; then I proceeded to walk until there remained only two hours between me and the city. As I sat to rest, I suddenly saw a long serpent, as thick as the trunk of a palm tree, gliding sideways and sweeping the sand in her way, as she speeded toward me. When she drew near, I saw that she was being pursued by a long and slender dragon, as slender as a spear and as long as two. He had seized her by the tail, while she, with a tongue about ten inches long, rolling in the dust, and eyes streaming with tears, wriggled right and left, trying to escape. Feeling pity for her, O Commander of the Faithful, I ran toward a big stone, picked it up, and calling on God for help, hit the dragon with it and killed him. As soon as the dragon rolled dead, the serpent opened a pair of wings, flew up, and disappeared from my sight.

Then I sat down to rest and dozed off, and when I awoke, I saw a black girl, together with two bitches, sitting at my feet, massaging them. Sitting up, I asked, "O friend, who are you?" She replied, "How soon you have forgotten me. I am she for whom you have done the good deed and sowed the seed of gratitude. I am the serpent who was in distress until it pleased you, with the help of the Almighty God, to kill my foe. In order to reward you, I hurried after the ship and carried to your house everything that belonged to you. Then I ordered my attendants to sink the ship, for I knew how you had been kind to your sisters all your life and how they had treated you, how out of envy over the young man, they threw you both into the sea and caused him to drown. Here they are, these two black bitches, and I swear by the Creator of the heavens that if you disobey my command, I will take you and imprison you under the earth." Then the girl shook and, turning into a bird, picked up me and my two sisters and flew up with us until she set us down in my house, where I found all my property, which she had brought from the ship. Then she said to me, "I swear by 'Him who made the two seas flow'—this is my second oath—that if you disobey my command, I will turn you into a bitch like them. I charge you to give them every night three hundred blows with the rod, as a punishment for what they did." I replied, "I shall obey," and she departed and left me. Since that time, I have been forced to punish them every night until they bleed. I feel very sorry for them, and, knowing that I am not to blame for their punishment, they forgive me. This is the cause of my beating them and crying with them, and this is my story and the end of my history.

When she finished, the caliph was greatly amazed. Then the Commander of the Faithful ordered Ja'far to ask the second girl to explain to them the cause of the rod marks on her sides and chest. She said:

O Commander of the Faithful, when my father died . . .

*But morning overtook Shahrazad, and she lapsed into silence. Then her sister said, "O sister, what an entertaining story!" Shahrazad replied, "What is this compared with what I shall tell you tomorrow night if the king spares me and lets me live!"*

*The following night Shahrazad said:*

I heard, O happy King, that the flogged girl said to the Commander of the Faithful:

# [The Tale of the Second Lady, the Flogged One]

When my father died, he left me a great deal of money. Shortly thereafter, I married the wealthiest man in Baghdad, and for a year I lived with him the happiest of lives. Then he too died and left me my legal share of the inheritance, which was ninety thousand dinars. I lived a prosperous life, buying so much gold jewelry, clothes, and embroideries that I had ten complete changes of clothes, each costing one thousand dinars, and my reputation spread in the city. One day, as I was sitting at home, an old woman came to me, and what an old woman she was, with a pallid, scabby skin; a bent body; matted gray hair; a gray, freckled face; broken teeth; plucked-out eyebrows; hollow, bleary eyes; and a runny nose. She was like the one of whom the poet said:

> Seven defects are planted in her face,
> The least of which is but the curse of fate
> A bleary frown that covers all the face,
> A mouth full of stones, or a mowed-down pate.

She greeted me and, kissing the ground before me, said, "My lady, I have an orphan daughter, and tonight is her unveiling and wedding night, but we are brokenhearted, for we are strangers in this city, and we do not know anyone. If you come to her wedding, you will earn a reward in Heaven, for when the ladies of this city will hear that you are coming, they too will come, and you shall honor us with your presence and make her happy." Then the old woman repeated the following verses:

> We own that your visit is an honor
> That cannot be performed by another.

She wept and implored me until I felt pity for her and agreed to her request. I said, "Yes, I shall do it for the sake of the Almighty God, and she will not be unveiled to her bridegroom, save in my clothes, ornaments, and jewelry." Overjoyed, the old woman bent and kissed my feet, saying, "May God reward you and comfort you, as you have comforted me, but my lady, do not trouble yourself yet. Be ready at suppertime, and I shall come and fetch you." When she left, I proceeded to string the pearls, assemble the embroideries, and pack the ornaments and jewelry, not knowing what God had in store for me. At nightfall the old woman arrived with a happy smile and, kissing my hand, said, "Most of the ladies of the city are already assembled in our house, and they are waiting for you and looking forward to your coming." I rose, put on my outer garment, and, wrapping myself in my cloak, followed the old lady with my maids behind me. We walked on until we came to a well-swept and -watered alley and stood before a door draped with a black curtain hung with a lamp covered with gold filigree, bearing the following inscription in letters of gold:

I am the house of mirth
And eternal laughter.
Inside a fountain flows
With a healing water,
With myrtle, daisy, rose,
And clove pink for border.

The old woman knocked at the door, and when it was opened we entered and saw silk carpets covering the floor and saw two rows of lighted candles that formed an avenue leading from the door to the upper end of the hall. There stood a couch of juniper wood, encrusted with gems and hung with a canopylike red-speckled silk curtain. Suddenly, O Commander of the Faithful, a girl came out from behind the curtain, shining like the half moon. Indeed, her face was as radiant as the full moon or the rising sun, just like her of whom the poet said:

To her inferior Caesar she was sent,
A gift nobler than all her Persian kings.
The roses blossomed on her rosy cheeks,
Staining with crimson dye such lovely things.
Slender and sleepy-eyed and languorous,
She won from Beauty all of Beauty's ploys,
As if her forelock sat upon her brow
A night of gloom before a dawn of joys.

The girl came down from the couch and said to me, "Welcome and greetings to my dear and illustrious sister." Then she recited the following verses:

If the house could know who has visited,
It would rejoice and kiss the very dust,

> As if to say, "Only the generous
> Has by his gifts such welcome merited."

Then she came up to me, O Commander of the Faithful, and said, "O my lady, I have a brother who is more handsome by far than I. He has noticed you at some wedding feasts and other festive occasions, and, seeing your great beauty and charm and hearing that, like him, you are the head of your clan, he has decided that he would like to tie his knot with you, so that you may become husband and wife." I replied, "Yes, I hear and obey." O Commander of the Faithful, no sooner had I uttered these words than she clapped her hands and a door opened and out came a finely dressed young man in the bloom of youth, all beauty and perfect grace. He was sweetly coquettish, with a fine figure, eyebrows arching like a bow, and eyes that bewitched the heart with their holy magic. He was like him of whom the poet said:

> He has a face as bright as the young moon,
> And joys as pearls he scatters as a boon.

As soon as I looked at him, I was attracted to him. He sat beside me and chatted with me for a while; then the girl clapped her hands a second time, and a door opened and out came a judge and four witnesses, who sat and wrote the marriage contract. Then the young man made me pledge that I would not look at any other man, and he was not satisfied until I took a solemn oath. I was feeling very happy and impatient for the night to come. When it finally came, we retired to our room, and I spent with him the best of nights. In the morning he slaughtered many sheep in thanksgiving, showed me favors, and treated me lovingly. For a full month thereafter, I lived with him a most happy life.

One day, wishing to buy certain fabric, I asked him for permission to go to the market. He consented, and I went with the old woman and two maids. When we entered the silk-mercers' market, the old woman said, 'O my lady, here is a very young merchant who has a large stock of goods and every kind of fabric you may desire, and no one in the market has better goods. Let us go into his shop, and there you can buy whatever you wish." We entered his shop, and I saw that he was slender, handsome, and very young, like him of whom the poet said:

> Here is a slender youth whose hair and face
> All mortals envelope with light or gloom.
> Mark on his cheek the mark of charm and grace,
> A dark spot on a red anemone.

I said to the old lady, "Let him show us some nice fabric." She replied, "Ask him yourself." I said, "Don't you know that I have sworn not to speak to any man except my husband?" So she said to him, "Show us some fabric," and he showed us several pieces, some of which I liked. I said to the old woman, "Ask him for the price." When she asked him, he replied, "I will sell them for neither silver nor gold but for a kiss on her cheek." I said, "God save me from such a thing." But the old woman said, "O my lady, you needn't talk to him or he to you; just turn your face to him and let him kiss it; that is all there is to it." Tempted by her, I turned my face to him. He put his mouth on my cheek and bit off with his teeth a piece of my flesh. I fainted, and when I came to myself, a long time later, I saw that he had locked the shop and departed, while the old woman, in a display of grief, sorrowed over my bleeding face.

*But morning overtook Shahrazad, and she lapsed into silence.*

THE SIXTY-EIGHTH NIGHT

*The following night Shahrazad said:*

I have heard, O happy King, that the flogged girl said to the Commander of the Faithful:

The old woman, expressing anguish, grief, and sorrow, said, "O my lady, God has saved you from something worse. Take heart and let us go, before the matter becomes public. When you get home, pretend to be sick, and cover yourself up, and I will bring you powders and plasters that will heal your cheek within three days. I rose, and we walked slowly until we reached the house, where I collapsed on the floor with pain. Then I lay in bed, covered myself up, and drank some wine.

In the evening my husband came in and asked, "O my darling, what is the matter with you?" I replied, "I have a headache." He lighted a candle and, coming close to me, looked at my face and, seeing the wound on my cheek, asked, "What caused this?" I replied, "When I went today to the market to buy some fabric, a camel driver with a load of firewood jostled me in a narrow passage, and one of the pieces tore my veil and cut my cheek, as you see." He said, "Tomorrow I shall ask the governor of the city to hang every camel driver in this city." I replied, "O my lord, this does not warrant hanging innocent men and bearing the guilt of their death." He asked, "Then who did it?" I replied, "I was riding a rented donkey, and when the donkey driver drove it hard, it stumbled and threw me to the ground, and I fell on a piece of glass that happened to be there and cut my cheek." He said, "By God, I shall not let the sun rise before I go to Ja'far the Barmakid[2] and ask him to hang every donkey driver and every sweeper in this city." I said, "By God, my lord, this is not what really happened to me. Don't hang people because of me." He asked, "What then is the real cause of your wound?" I replied, "I suffered what God had foreordained for me." He kept pressing me relentlessly, and I kept mumbling and resisting him until he drove me to speak rudely to him. At that moment, O Commander of the Faithful, he cried out and a door opened and out came three black slaves who, at his bidding, dragged me out of my bed and threw me down on my back in the middle of the room. Then he ordered one slave to sit on my knees, the other to hold my head, and the third to draw his sword, saying to him, "You, Sa'd, strike her and with one blow cut her in half and let each of you carry one half and throw it into the Tigris river for the fish to feed upon. This is the punishment of those who violate the vow." Then he grew angrier and recited the following verses:

> If there be one who shares the one I love,
> I'll kill my love even though my soul dies,
> Saying, "Better nobly to die, O soul,
> Than share a love for which another vies."

Then he ordered the slave to strike me with the sword. When the slave was sure of the command, he bent down to me and said, "O my lady, have you any wish, for this is the last moment of your life?" I replied, "Get off me, so that I may tell him something." I raised my head and, thinking of my condition and how I had fallen from high esteem into disgrace and from life into death, I wept bitterly and choked with sobs. But my husband looked at me angrily and recited the following verses:

> Tell her who for another lover left,
> Bored with me, and repaid me with disdain,
> That even though I suffered first, I found
> Contentment in what was between us twain.

When I heard his words, O Commander of the Faithful, I wept and, looking at him, replied with the following verses:

> You set my poor heart burning with your love
> And left my eyes to smart and went to sleep,

2. Harun al-Rashid's vizier; see n. 3, p. 3.

> While all alone I thought of you and wept
> And in my sorrow did a vigil keep.
> You promised to be faithful to the end,
> But when you had my heart, you broke the vow.
> I loved you in all childish innocence;
> Kill not that love, for I am learning now.

But when he heard my verses, O Commander of the Faithful, he grew even angrier and, giving me a furious look, recited the following verses:

> 'Twas not boredom that bid me leave my love,
> But a sin that imposed such fate on me.
> She wished to let another share our love,
> But faith forbade me such a blasphemy.

I wept and implored and, looking at him, recited the following verses:

> You left me burdened with the weight of love,
> Being too weak even a shirt to wear.
> I marvel not that my soul wastes away
> But that my body can your absence bear.

When he heard my words, he cursed me and scolded me. Then looking at me, he recited the following verses:

> You left me to enjoy another love
> And showed disdain, a deed I could not do.
> If you dislike my presence, I will leave
> And rue the end of love, as you did rue,
> And take another lover for myself,
> For love was killed not by me but by you.

Then he yelled at the slave, saying, "Cut her in half and rid me of her, for her life is worthless." O Commander of the Faithful, as we argued in verse, I grew certain of death and gave up myself for lost, but suddenly the old woman rushed in and, throwing herself at my husband's feet, said tearfully, "O son, by the rights of rearing you up, by the breasts that nursed you, and by my service to you, pardon her for my sake. You are still young, and you should not bear the guilt of her death, for as it is said, 'Whoever slays shall be slain.' Why bother with such a worthless woman? Drive her out of your hearth and heart." She kept weeping and imploring until he relented and said, "But I must brand her and leave a permanent mark on her." Then he ordered the slaves to strip me of all my clothes and stretch me on the floor, and when they sat on me to pin me down, he rose and, fetching a quince rod, fell with blows on my sides until I despaired of life and lost consciousness. Then he bade the slaves take me to my own home as soon as it was dark and let the old woman show them the way.

Following their master's command, they took me away, threw me into my house, and departed. I remained unconscious till the morning. Then I treated myself with ointments and drugs, but my body remained disfigured from the beating and my sides bore the marks of the rod. I lay sick in bed for four months, and when I recovered and was able to get up, I went to look for my husband's house but found it in ruin. The entire alley, from beginning to end, was torn down, and on the site of the house stood piles of rubbish. Unable to find out how this had come about, I went to this woman, my sister on my father's side, and found her with these two black bitches. I greeted her and told her my story, and she said, "O my sister, who is safe from the accident of life and the misfortunes of the world?" Then she repeated the following verses:

> Such is the world; with patience it is best
> The loss of wealth or loss of love to breast.

Then, O Commander of the Faithful, she told me her story, what her sisters had done to her, and what had become of them.

We lived together without thinking of any man, and everyday, this girl, the shopper, would come by and go to the market to buy for us what we needed for the day and the night. We lived like this for a long time until yesterday, when our sister went to shop as usual and returned with the porter, whom we allowed to stay to divert us. Less than a quarter of the night had passed when these three dervishes joined us, and we sat to converse, and when a third of the night had gone by, three respectable merchants from Mosul joined us and told us about their adventures. We had pledged the guests to accept a condition, and when they broke the pledge, we treated them accordingly. Then we questioned them about themselves, and when they told us their tales, we pardoned them and they departed. This morning we were unexpectedly summoned to your presence. This is our story.

The caliph, O happy King, marveled at their tales and their adventures.

*But morning overtook Shahrazad, and she lapsed into silence. Then Dinarzad said, "O sister, what a strange, amazing, and entertaining story!" Shahrazad replied, "What is this compared with what I shall tell you tomorrow night if the king spares me and lets me live!"*

## THE SIXTY-NINTH NIGHT

*The following night Shahrazad said:*

It is related, O glorious King, that the caliph, marveling at these adventures, turned to the first girl and said, "Tell me what happened to the demon serpent who had cast a spell on your sisters and turned them into bitches. Do you know her whereabouts, and did she set with you the date of her return to you?" The girl replied, "O Commander of the Faithful, she gave me a tuft of hair, saying 'Whenever you need me, burn two of the hairs, and I will be with you at once, even if I am beyond Mount Qaf.'" The caliph asked, "Where is the tuft of hair?" She brought it, and he took it and burned the entire tuft. Suddenly the whole palace began to tremble, and the serpent arrived and said, "Peace be with you, O Commander of the Faithful! This woman has sown with me the seed of gratitude, and I cannot reward her amply enough, for she killed my enemy and saved me from death. Knowing what her sisters had done to her, I felt bound to reward her by avenging her. At first, I was about to destroy them once and for all, but I feared that their deaths would be hard on her; therefore, I cast a spell on them and turned them into bitches. Now, if you wish me to release them, O Commander of the Faithful, I will do it gladly, for your wish is my command, O Commander of the Faithful!" The caliph replied, "O spirit, release them and let us deliver them from their misery. After you release them, I will look into the case of this flogged girl, and may the Almighty God help me and make it easy for me to solve her case and discover who wronged her and usurped her rights, for I am sure that she is telling the truth." The she-demon replied, "O Commander of the Faithful, not only will I release these two bitches, but I will also reveal to you who abused and beat this girl. In fact, he is the nearest of all men to you." Then she took, O King, a bowl of water, and muttering a spell over it in words no one could understand, sprinkled the two sisters with the water and turned them back into their original form.

Then the she-demon said, "O Commander of the Faithful, the man who beat this girl is your son al-Amin brother of al-Ma'mun. He had heard of her beauty and charm, and he tricked her into a legal marriage. But he is not to blame for beating her, for he pledged her and bound her by a solemn oath not to do a certain thing, but she broke the pledge. He was about to kill her but, reflecting on the sin of murder and fearing the Almighty God, contented himself with flogging her and sending her back to her home. Such is the story of the second girl, and God knows all." When the caliph heard what the she-demon said and found out who had flogged the girl, he was exceedingly amazed and said, "Praise be to the Almighty God who has blessed me and helped me to release these two women and deliver them from sorcery and torture and who has blessed me a second time and revealed to me the cause of that woman's misfortune. By God, I am now going to do a deed by which I will be remembered." Then the caliph, O King, summoned his son al-Amin and questioned him to confirm the truth of the story. Then he assembled together the judge and witnesses, the three dervishes, the first girl and her two sisters who had been cast under a spell, and the flogged girl and the shopper. When they were all assembled, he married the first girl and her sisters who had been cast under a spell to the three dervishes, who were the sons of kings. He made the three dervishes chamberlains and members of his inner circle, giving them money, clothes, horses, a palace in Baghdad, and everything they needed. He married the flogged girl to his son al-Amin, under a new marriage contract, showered her with wealth and ordered the house to be rebuilt and made even better than before. Then the Commander of the Faithful himself married the third girl, the shopper. The people marveled at the caliph's wisdom, tolerance, and generosity and, when all the facts were revealed, recorded these stories.

# [THE STORY OF THE THREE APPLES]

A few days later the caliph said to Ja'far, "I wish to go into the city to find out what is happening and to question the people about the conduct of my administrators, so that I may dismiss those of whom they complain and promote those they praise." Ja'far replied, "As you wish." When it was night, the caliph went into the city with Ja'far and Masrur and walked about the streets and markets, and as they made their way through an alley, they met a very old man carrying a basket and a fishnet on his head and holding a staff in his hand. The caliph said to Ja'far, "This is a poor man in need." Then he asked the old man, "Old man, what is your trade?" and the old man replied, "My lord, I am a fisherman with a family, and I have been out fishing since midday without luck or anything with which to buy supper for my family; I feel helpless and disgusted with life, and I wish that I was dead." The caliph said to him,

"Fisherman, would you go back with us to the Tigris,[3] stand at the riverbank, and cast the net for me, and whatever you happen to catch, I shall buy from you for one hundred dinars?"

Delighted, the old fisherman replied, "Yes, my lord," and went back with them to the Tigris. He cast his net, and when he gathered his rope and pulled it up, he found inside the net a locked, heavy chest. The caliph gave the fisherman one hundred dinars and bade Masrur carry the chest back to the palace. When they broke it open, they found inside a basket of palm leaves sewn with a red woolen thread. Cutting the basket open, they saw inside a piece of carpet and, lifting it out, saw a woman's cloak folded in four. When they removed the cloak, they found at the bottom of the chest a girl in the bloom of youth, as fair as pure silver. She had been slain and cut to pieces.

*But morning overtook Shahrazad, and she lapsed into silence. Then Dinarzad said, "O sister, what an entertaining story!" Shahrazad replied, "What is this compared with what I shall tell you tomorrow night if I stay alive!"*

THE SEVENTIETH NIGHT

*The following night Shahrazad said:*

I heard, O happy King, that the girl had been cut into nineteen pieces. When the caliph looked at her, he felt sad and sorry for her, and with tears in his eyes turned to Ja'far and said angrily, "You dog of a vizier, people are being killed and thrown into the river in my city, while I bear the responsibility till Doomsday. By God, I will avenge this girl and put her murderer to the worst of deaths. If you do not find me her killer, I will hang you and hang forty of your kinsmen with you." He was exceedingly angry and cried a disquieting cry at Ja'far, who said, "O Commander of the Faithful, grant me three days' delay." The caliph replied, "Granted." Then Ja'far withdrew and went into the city, vexed and sad, not knowing what to do. He said to himself, "Where shall I find the murderer of this girl, so that I may bring him before the caliph? If I bring him one of the men from jail, I will be guilty of his blood. I don't know what to do, but there is no power and no strength, save in God, the Almighty, the Magnificent." He stayed at home the first

---

3. One of the two great rivers that cross Iraq from north to south, the other being the Euphrates.

day, and the second, and by noon of the third day the caliph sent
some of his chamberlains to fetch him. When he came into the
presence of the caliph, the caliph asked him, "Where is the murderer
of the girl?" Ja'far replied, "O Commander of the Faithful, am I
an expert in detecting a murder?" The caliph was furious at his
answer. He yelled at him and commanded that he be hanged before
the palace, bidding a crier to cry throughout Baghdad, "Whoever
wishes to see the hanging of the vizier Ja'far with forty of his Barmaki kinsmen let him come before the palace and look at the spectacle." Then the governor of the city and the chamberlains brought
Ja'far and his kinsmen and made them stand under the gallows.

But while they waited to see the handkerchief at the window (this
was the usual signal), and while the crowd wept for Ja'far and his
kinsmen, a neatly dressed young man pushed his way through the
crowd toward Ja'far. He had a bright face, with dark eyes, fair brow,
and rosy cheeks covered with a downy beard, and graced with a
mole like a disk of ambergris. When he finally made his way and
stood before Ja'far, he kissed his hand and said, "May I spare you
from such a horrible fate, O Grand Vizier, most eminent prince,
and refuge of the poor? Hang me for the murder of the girl, for
I am the one who murdered her." When Ja'far heard the young
man's confession, he rejoiced at his own deliverance but grieved
for the young man. But while Ja'far was talking to him, an old man,
well-advanced in years, pushed his way through the crowd until
he reached Ja'far and said, "O Vizier and mighty lord, do not believe
what this young man is saying, for none has murdered the girl but
I. Punish me for her death, for if you do not, I will call you to
account before the Almighty God." But the young man cried out,
"O Vizier, none murdered her but I." The old man said, "Son, you
are still very young, while I am an old man who has had enough
of life; I will give my life for you." And turning to Ja'far, he continued, "None murdered the girl but I. Hurry up and hang me,
for my life is over, now that she is dead."

When Ja'far heard the conversation, he was amazed, and he took
both the young man and the old man with him and went to the
caliph. After kissing the ground before him seven times, he said,
"O Commander of the Faithful, I have brought you the murderer
of the girl. Each of these two men, the young man and the old man,
claims that he is the murderer. Here they stand before you." The
caliph, looking at the young man and the old man, asked, "Which
of you killed the girl and threw her into the river?" The young man
replied, "I murdered her," and the old man said, "None killed her
but I." Then the caliph said to Ja'far, "Hang them both." But Ja'far
said, "O Commander of the Faithful, since only one of them is

guilty, it will be unjust to hang the other too." The young man said, "By Him who raised the firmament, I am the one who four days ago killed the girl, placed her in a basket of palm leaves, covered her with a woman's cloak, placed a piece of carpet over it, sewed the basket with a red woolen thread, and threw her into the river. In the name of God and His Judgment Day, I ask you to punish me for her death; do not let me live after her." The caliph, marveling at what the young man said, asked him, "What caused you to kill her wrongfully, and what caused you to come forward on your own?" The young man replied, "O Commander of the Faithful, our story is such that were it engraved with needles at the corner of the eye, it would be a lesson to those who would consider." The caliph said, "Relate to us what happened to you and her." The young man replied, "I hear and obey the command of God and the Commander of the Faithful." Then the young man . . .

*But morning overtook Shahrazad, and she lapsed into silence.*

### THE SEVENTY-FIRST NIGHT

*The following night Shahrazad said:*

I heard, O happy King, that the young man said:

O Commander of the Faithful, the murdered girl was my wife and the mother of my children. She was my cousin, the daughter of this old man, my uncle, who gave her to me in marriage when she was still a young virgin. We lived together for eleven years, during which time God blessed her and she bore me three sons. She was well-behaved toward me and served me exceedingly well, and I in turn loved her very much. On the first day of this month she fell gravely ill and kept getting worse, but I took great care of her until by the end of the month she slowly began to recover.

One day, before going to the bath, she said to me, "Husband, I want you to satisfy a desire of mine." I replied, "I hear and obey, even if it were a thousand desires." She said, "I have a craving for an apple. If I could only smell it and take a bite, I wouldn't care if I die afterward." I replied, "It shall be done." Then I went and looked for apples but could not find any anywhere in your whole city. Had I found any, I would have paid a dinar for one. Vexed at my failure to satisfy her craving, I went home and said, "Wife, I was unable to find any apples." She was upset and, being still

ill, suffered a relapse that night. As soon as it was morning, I went out and made the rounds of the orchards, one by one, but found no apples anywhere. At last a very old gardener answered my inquiry, saying, "Son, no apples can be found, except in the orchards of the Commander of the Faithful in Basra, where they are stored by the gardener. I went home and, driven by my love and solicitude for her, I prepared myself for the journey. For two full weeks, O Commander of the Faithful, I journeyed day and night, returning finally with three apples I had bought from the gardener for three dinars. But when I handed them to her, she showed no pleasure in them but laid them aside. Then she suffered another relapse, lay ill, and made me worried about her for ten days.

One day, as I sat in my shop, buying and selling fabrics, I suddenly saw an ugly black slave, as tall as a reed and as broad as a bench, passing by. He was holding in his hand one of the three apples for which I had journeyed for half a month. I called after him, saying, "My good slave, where did you get this apple?" He replied, "I got it from my mistress, for I went to see her today and found her lying ill with three apples by her side. She told me that her pimp of a husband had journeyed for half a month to bring them. After I ate and drank with her, I took one of the apples with me." When I heard what he said, O Commander of the Faithful, the world turned black before my eyes. I locked up my shop and went home, mad with resentment and fury. When I got home and looked for the apples, I found only two, and when I asked her, "Wife, where is the other apple?" she raised her head and replied, "By God, husband, I don't know." This convinced me that the slave had told the truth, and I took a sharp knife and, stealing behind her silently, knelt on her breast, worked the knife into her throat, and cut off her head. Then I quickly placed her in a basket, covered her with a woman's cloak, placed a piece of carpet on top of it, and sewed the basket. Then I placed the basket inside a chest, carried it on my head, and threw it into the Tigris. For God's sake, O Commander of the Faithful, avenge her on me and hang me quickly, or I will call you to account on her behalf before the Almighty God. For when I threw her into the river and went home, I found my eldest son crying, and when I asked him, "What is the matter with you?" he replied, "O father, this morning I stole one of the three apples you had brought back for my mother. I took it and went to the market, and as I was standing with my brothers, a tall black slave came by and snatched it from my hand. I protested, saying, 'For God's sake, good slave, this is one of the apples for which my father journeyed for half a month to Basra to bring back to my mother who was ill. Don't get me into trouble.' But he paid no attention to me, and when I begged him for a second and a third time, he slapped me and went off with it. Scared of my mother, I went with my brothers outside the city and we stayed there in fear until it started to get dark. For God's sake, father, say nothing to her of this, or her illness will get worse." When I heard my son's words and saw him trembling and weeping, O Commander of the Faithful, I realized that I had killed my wife wrongfully and that she had died unjustly; the accursed slave, hearing about the apples from my son, had slandered her and lied about her. When I realized that, I wept and made my sons weep with me, and when this old man, my uncle and her father, came in, I related to him what had happened, and he wept and made us weep with him till midnight, and for three days afterward we mourned for her and grieved over her unjust death, and all because of that black slave. This is the story of the murdered girl. So by your fathers and forefathers, I beg you to avenge her unjust death on me and kill me for my mistake, for I have no life left after her.

When the caliph heard his words . . .

*But morning overtook Shahrazad, and she lapsed into silence.*

THE SEVENTY-SECOND NIGHT

*The following night, Shahrazad said:*

I heard, O happy King, that when the caliph heard the young man's story, he was very much amazed and said, "By God, I will hang none but the accursed slave and I will do a deed that will quench the thirst for vengeance and please the Glorious King." Then he said to Ja'far, "Go into the city and bring me the slave, or I will strike your neck." Ja'far left in tears, saying to himself, "There is no escape from death this time, for 'the jar cannot be saved every time,' but the All-powerful and Omnipotent God who saved me the first time may save me yet a second time. By God, I will stay home for three days until God's will is accomplished." He stayed home the first day and the second, and by noon of the third day, giving himself up for lost, Ja'far summoned the judges and witnesses and made his will. Then he called his children to him, bade them farewell, and wept. Soon a messenger from the caliph arrived, saying, "The caliph is in a great rage and he swears that this day shall not pass before you are hanged." Ja'far wept and made all his slaves

and members of his household weep for him. After he bade his
children and all the members of his household farewell, his little
daughter, who was very pretty and whom he loved more than all
the others, came up to him, and he embraced her and kissed her,
as he wept at parting from his family and his children. But as he
embraced her to comfort her, pressing her hard to his aching heart,
he felt something round in her pocket. He asked her, "My little girl,
what is in your pocket?" and the little one replied, "It is an apple
with the name of our Lord the caliph written on it. Rayhan our
slave brought it, but he would not let me have it until I gave him
two dinars for it." When Ja'far heard her mention the apple and
the slave, he shrieked and, putting his hand in her pocket, took
out the apple and, recognizing it, cried out, "O Speedy Deliverer!"

Then he bade the slave be brought before him, and when the
slave came, Ja'far said, "Damn you, Rayhan, where did you get
this apple?" The slave replied, "Although 'a lie may save a man,
the truth is better and safer.' By God, my lord, I did not steal this
apple from your palace or from the palace of the Commander of
the Faithful or from his gardens. Four days ago, as I was walking
through one of the alleys of the city, I saw some children at play,
and when one of them dropped this apple, I beat him and snatched
it from him. He cried and said to me, 'Kind gentleman, this apple
belongs to my mother who is ill. She had told my father that she
had a craving for apples, and he journeyed for half a month to Basra
and brought her back three apples, of which I stole this one; give
it back to me.' But I refused to give it back to him; instead, I brought
it here and sold it to my little lady for two dinars. This is the story
of the apple." When Ja'far heard his words, he marveled at the story
and at the discovery that the cause of all the trouble turned out
to be none other than one of his own slaves. He rejoiced and, taking the slave by the hand, led him before the caliph and related
to him the whole story from beginning to end. The Commander
of the Faithful was greatly astonished and laughed until he fell on
his back. Then he asked Ja'far, "Do you mean to tell me that this
slave of yours is the cause of all the trouble?" Ja'far replied, "Yes,
Commander of the Faithful." Seeing that the caliph was greatly
struck by the coincidences of the story, Ja'far said to the Commander
of the Faithful, "Do not marvel at this story, for it is not as amazing as the story of the two viziers, Nur al-Din Ali al-Misri and Badr
al-Din Hasan al-Basri." The caliph asked, "O my vizier, is the story
of these two viziers truly more amazing than this one?" Ja'far replied,
"Yes, it is indeed more amazing and more extraordinary, but I will
not relate it to you, save on one condition." Eager to hear the story,
the caliph said, "Come on, my vizier, and let me hear it. If it is

indeed more amazing than the events we have just witnessed, I will
pardon your slave, but if it is not, I will kill him. Come on: tell
me what you know." Ja'far said:

# [The Story of the Two Viziers,
# Nur al-Din Ali al-Misri and
# Badr al-Din Hasan al-Basri][4]

I heard, O Commander of the Faithful, that a long time ago there
lived in the province of Egypt a just, trusted, kind, generous,
courageous, and powerful king, who associated with the learned
and loved the poor. He had a wise, experienced, and influential
vizier who was careful, cautious, and skilled in the affairs of state.
This vizier, who was a very old man, had two sons who were like
two moons or two lovely deer in their perfect elegance, beauty, and
grace. The elder was called Shams al-Din Muhammad, the younger,
Nur al-Din Ali. The younger surpassed his brother in beauty; indeed in his day God had created none more beautiful. One day
as it had been foreordained, their father the vizier died, and the
king mourned him and summoned the two sons, bestowed on them
robes of honor and other favors and said, "You shall take your
father's place and be joint viziers of Egypt." They kissed the ground
before him and withdrew and for a full month they performed the
ceremonial mourning for their father. Then they assumed their position, taking turns, each performing his duty for a week at a time,
and each accompanying the king on one journey at a time. The
two lived in the same house and their word was one.

It happened that one night, before the elder brother was to set
out on a journey with the king the next morning, the two brothers
sat chatting. The elder brother said, "Brother, I wish that you and
I would marry two sisters, draw our marriage contracts on the same
day, and go in to our wives on the same night." Nur al-Din replied,
"Brother, do as you wish, for this is an excellent idea, but let us
wait until you come back from your journey, and with God's blessing we shall seek two girls in marriage." The elder brother said to
Nur al-Din, "Tell me, brother, if you and I perform our wedding
on the same day and consummate our marriage on the same night
and if your wife and mine conceive on our wedding night and at
the end of their pregnancy give birth on the same day and if your
wife gives birth to a boy and my wife to a girl, tell me, will you

4. Fictitious names, like most of the names in the *Nights*. Al-Misri means "of Egypt" and al-
Basri means "of Basra."

marry your son to my daughter?" Nur al-Din replied, "Yes, brother
Shams al-Din," adding, "But what dowry will you require from my
son for your daughter?" The elder brother replied, "I will take at
least three thousand dinars, three orchards, and three farms in addition to an amount specified in the contract." Nur al-Din replied,
"Brother Shams al-Din, why such an excessive dowry? Are we not
brothers, and is not each of us a vizier who knows his obligations?
It behooves you to offer your daughter to my son without a dowry,
for the male is worthier than the female. But you treat me like the
man who said to another who came to ask for help 'Very well, I
will help you, but wait till tomorrow,' prompting the other to repeat
the following verses:

> When one postpones the favor for a day,
> The wise man knows that he has answered, 'Nay.'"

Shams al-Din said, "Enough of your comments. Damn you for com-
paring your son to my daughter and thinking that he is worthier
than she; by God, you lack understanding and wisdom. You say
that we are partners in the vizierate, without realizing that I let
you share it with me, only in order to spare your feelings by letting
you assist me. By God, I will never marry my daughter to your
son, not even for her weight in gold. I will never marry her to your
son and have him for a son-in-law, not even if I have to suffer death."
When Nur al-Din heard his brother's words, he became very angry
and asked, "Will you indeed not marry your daughter to my son?"
Shams al-Din replied, "No, I will never consent to that, for he is
not worth even a paring of her nail. Were I not on the eve of a
journey, I would make an example of you, but when I come back,
I will show you how I will vindicate my honor." Nur al-Din's anger
grew so great that he was beside himself with rage, but he hid what
he felt, while the brother sulked, and the two spent the night far
apart, each full of wrath against the other.

    As soon as it was morning, the king went to the pyramids, accom-
panied by the Vizier Shams al-Din, whose turn it was to go with
him. When Shams al-Din departed, Nur al-Din got up, still full
of anger, opened his treasure chamber and, taking gold only, filled
a small saddlebag. He recalled how his brother had scolded him
and insulted him, and he recited the following verses:

> Travel, and new friends will succeed the friends you lost,
> And toil, for life's sweets do through toil come.
> To stay wins you no honor nor from exile saves;
> Set out to roam the world and leave your home.
> When water stands, it stagnant turns and stinks
> But tastes so sweet when it does flow and run.

And if the sun stood in its orbit still,
Both Arabs and barbarians would tire of the sun,
And if the full moon did not wane and set,
No watchful eyes would the moon's rising mark.
If in the lair the lion stayed, in the bow the dart,
Neither would catch the prey, or hit the mark.
Deep in the mine, gold dust is merely dust,
And in its native ground, fuel aloewood.
Gold, when extracted, grows much in demand.
And when exported, aloe fetches gold.

When he finished reciting these verses, he ordered one of his pages to saddle his Arabian she-mule, with her sturdy saddle and saddle-cloth. She was a particularly fine riding animal, with dappled gray skin, ears like sharp reed pens, and legs like pillars. He ordered the page to saddle her with all her trappings, to place the saddle-bags on her back, and to cover them with a soft seat of silk carpeting. Then he said to his pages and slaves, "I am leaving the city on an excursion in the vicinity of Qalyubiya to divert myself for a night or two, for I have been very depressed lately. Let none of you follow me." Then he took some provisions, mounted the she-mule, and leaving Cairo,[5] entered the desert. At midday, he reached a town called Bilbis, where he dismounted to rest and have something to eat. Then he took some food for himself and forage for his she-mule and left the town and, spurring his she-mule, fared forth in the desert. By nightfall, he reached the town of al-Sa'idiya, where he dismounted to spend the night at the post station. He walked the she-mule seven or eight times, then gave her some fodder to eat, and after he himself ate some food, he spread the carpet he had used for a seat and, placing the saddlebags under his head, lay down, still seething with anger, saying to himself, "By God, I will ride on even if I wander as far as Baghdad." In the morning, he resumed his journey and, chancing to meet a courier, O Commander of the Faithful, he accompanied him on his she-mule, stopping whenever the courier stopped and riding whenever he rode, until God granted him safe passage and he reached the city of Basra.

It happened that as he approached the outskirts of the city, the vizier of Basra was also traveling on the same road, and when the vizier overtook him and saw that he was a handsome and well-mannered young man, he drew near him, greeted him, and inquired about his situation. Nur al-Din Ali told the vizier about himself and said, "I quarreled with my family and pledged myself not to go back until I visit all the countries of the world, even if I perish

5. Then and now the capital of Egypt, situated on the Nile River near the pyramids.

and meet my end before I achieve my aim." When the vizier of Basra heard his words, he said to him, "O my son, do not go any further, for most of the regions are waste, and I fear for your safety." Then he took Nur al-Din Ali home with him and treated him with kindness and generosity, for he was beginning to feel a great affection for him. Then the vizier said to him, "O my son, I am a very old man whom God has never blessed with a son, but I have a daughter who is your equal in beauty. Many wealthy and eminent men have asked for her hand, but I have rejected them all, but since I have affection for you, will you accept my daughter as your wife and maid and be a husband to her? If you marry her, I will go to the king and tell him that you are like a son to me and I will advance your cause and make you vizier in my place, so that I may be able to stay at home and rest. For by God, son, I am advanced in years and I am weary and worn out. You shall be a son to me and shall have control over my possessions and over the vizierate in the province of Basra." When Nur al-Din heard the vizier's words, he bowed his head a while, then finally looked up and said, "I hear and obey." The vizier was overjoyed, and he bade his servants prepare food and sweets and decorate the large hall used for wedding feasts, and they at once did as he bade. Then he gathered his friends and invited the prominent and the wealthy men of Basra, and when they were all assembled, he said, "I have a brother who is the vizier of Egypt. He has been blessed with a son and I, as you know, have been blessed with a daughter. When his son and my daughter reached the age of marriage, he sent his son to me, and now I would like to draw their marriage contract, so that he may consummate his marriage here. After the wedding, I shall prepare him for the journey and send him back with his wife." They replied, "This is an excellent idea and a happy and praiseworthy plan. May God crown your good fortune with happiness and may He keep your course blameless."

*But morning overtook Shahrazad, and she lapsed into silence.*

### THE SEVENTY-THIRD NIGHT

*The following night Shahrazad said:*

I heard, O happy King, that Ja'far said to the caliph:

The prominent men of Basra said, "May God keep your course blameless." Then the witnesses arrived, and the servants brought the tables and laid out the banquet, and the guests ate until they were satisfied, and when the sweets were offered, they enjoyed their fill. Then the servants cleared the tables, and the witnesses came forward and signed the marriage contract, and when the incense rose, the guests departed.

Then the vizier ordered his servants to take Nur al-Din Ali al-Misri to the bath and sent him a full attire worthy of a king, as well as towels, incense, and whatever he needed. A little later, Nur al-Din came back from the bath, looking like the full moon or the rising sun, like him of whom the poet said:

> The scent is musk, the cheek a rose,
> The teeth are pearls, the mouth is wine,
> The frame a bough, the hip a barge,
> The hair is night, the face a moon divine.

He went in to his father-in-law and kissed his hand, and the vizier stood up to greet him, treated him with respect, and seated him beside him. Then turning to him, he asked, "Son, I would like you to tell me why you left your family, and how it is that they allowed you to depart. Hide nothing from me and tell me the truth, for it is said:

> Be truthful, even though the truth
> May torment you with hellish fire,
> And please the Lord and not his slaves,
> In order to avoid His ire.

I wish to take you to the king and let you have my position." When Nur al-Din heard what his father-in-law said, he replied, "O great Vizier and mighty lord, I am not of humble origin, nor did I leave my family with their consent. My father was a vizier." And he told him about what happened after his father died and about the dispute between himself and his brother (but there is no point in repeating the story), adding "Finally, you were kind and gracious to me and you married me to your daughter. This is my story." When the vizier heard Nur al-Din's story, he was amazed and said with a smile, "My son, you quarreled even before getting married and having children! Now, son, go in to your wife, and tomorrow I shall take you to the king and acquaint him with our case, and I hope that God will grant you every blessing."

It so chanced, as God had willed and ordained, that on the very same night on which Nur al-Din consummated his marriage in Basra, his brother Shams al-Din Muhammad consummated his own marriage to a girl in Egypt. This is how it came about.

It is related that Ja'far said to the caliph:

I heard that at the time Nur al-Din set out from Egypt, his elder brother Shams al-Din journeyed with the king of Egypt, and they were absent for a month. When they returned, the king went to his palace, while Shams al-Din went home, and when he looked for his brother and could not find him, he asked his servants and was told, "O our lord, no sooner had the sun risen on the very morning you set out on your journey than he was already far away. He said that he would stay away for a night or two, but we have not heard from him ever since." When he heard what they said, he felt very sorry to lose his brother and said to himself, "He must have run away, and I must pursue him even to the remotest corners of the land." Then he sent couriers after Nur al-Din, who had already reached Basra. When the couriers reached Aleppo but heard no news about Nur al-Din, and returned empty handed, Shams al-Din despaired of finding him and said to himself, "There is no power and no strength, save in God, the Almighty, the Magnificent. I went too far in quarreling with him over the marriage."

Some time later, the Almighty God willed that Shams al-Din should seek in marriage the daughter of one of the merchants of Cairo, that he should draw up the marriage contract on the very same day that his brother drew up his in Basra and that he should consummate his marriage on the very same night that his brother consummated his own with the vizier's daughter in Basra. So the Almighty and Glorious God, in order that his decree over his creatures be fulfilled, for a purpose of his own, let it come to pass, O Commander of the Faithful, that these two brothers drew up their marriage contracts on the very same day and consummated their marriages on the very same night, one in Cairo and the other in Basra. Subsequently, the wife of Shams al-Din Muhammed, the vizier of Egypt, gave birth to a girl, and the wife of Nur al-Din Ali al-Misri, the vizier of Basra, gave birth to a boy, a boy who put to shame both the moon and sun. He had a neck as white as marble, a radiant brow, and rosy cheeks, and on the right cheek, he had a mole like a disc of ambergris. He was like one of whom the poet said:

> Here is a slender youth whose hair and face
> All mortals envelope with light and gloom.
> Mark on his cheek the mark of charm and grace,
> A dark spot on a red anemone.

That child, who had a figure as slender as a bough, was endowed by God with beauty, charm, and perfect grace, so that he captured the heart with his loveliness and captivated the mind with his perfection. He was so faultless in character and looks that the deer stole

from him their necks and eyes and every other grace. He was like
him of whom the poet said:

> With him to make compare Beauty they brought,
> But Beauty hung his head in abject shame.
> They said, "O Beauty, have you seen his like?"
> Beauty replied, "I have ne'er seen the same."

Nur al-Din Ali named him Badr al-Din Hasan, and his grandfathr
the vizier of Basra rejoiced in him and gave banquets in his honor
and distributed presents worthy of kings.

One day, the vizier took Nur al-Din Ali, the vizier of Egypt, with
him and went up to the king. When Nur al-Din entered before the
king, he kissed the ground before him and repeated the following
verses, for he was a cultivated, intelligent, generous, and gentle
man:

> May you long live in glory, night and day,
> And may eternal bliss attend your way.

The king thanked Nur al-Din for the compliment and asked his
vizier, "Who is this young man with you?" and the vizier repeated
Nur al-Din's story from beginning to end, adding, "O King, I would
like my lord Nur al-Din to take my place as vizier, for he is an eloquent man, and I your slave have become a very old man, weak
in body and mind. As a favor, in consideration of my service to
your Majesty, I beg you to appoint him vizier in my place, for he
is more qualified than I," and he kissed the ground before the king.
When the king looked at Nur al-Din, the vizier of Egypt, and
scrutinized him, he was pleased with him and took a liking to him.
So he granted the vizier's request, bestowed on Nur al-Din a full
robe of honor, presented him with one of his best she-mules, and
allotted him stipends and allowances. Then Nur al-Din and his
father-in-law went home, feeling happy and saying to each other,
"The newborn Hasan has brought us good fortune."

The next day Nur al-Din went up to the king and, sitting in the
vizier's seat, carried out all the usual duties of viziers, signing,
instructing, judging, and granting, for nothing was beyond him.
And the king took him into favor. Then Nur al-Din Ali al-Misri
went home, happy and pleased with his position as vizier and with
the powers and favors the king had bestowed on him.

The days and nights went by, and he continued to raise and
rejoice in his son Badr al-Din Hasan, who grew and thrived, becoming ever more beautiful and charming. When the boy was four years
old, his grandfather the old vizier, his mother's father, fell ill and
willed all his wealth to him, and when the grandfather died, they

mourned him and gave banquets for a whole month. Nur al-Din continued to be the vizier of Basra, as his son Badr al-Din continued to grow and thrive. When he was seven years old, Nur al-Din entered him in a school and charged the tutor to take care of him, saying, "Take care of this boy and give him a good education and teach him good manners." At school everybody was as pleased with Badr al-Din as could be, for he was intelligent, perceptive, sensible, well-mannered, and articulate, and for two full years, under his tutor's guidance, he continued to read and learn.

*But morning overtook Shahrazad, and she lapsed into silence.*

THE SEVENTY-FOURTH NIGHT

*The following night Shahrazad said:*

I heard, O King, that Ja'far said to the caliph:

By the time Badr al-Din was twelve years old, he had learned to read and write the Arabic language, as well as calligraphy, mathematics, and jurisprudence; furthermore, the Almighty God had bestowed on his fine figure the robe of beauty, charm, and perfect grace, so that he was like the one of whom the poet eloquently said:

> In perfect beauty he vies with the moon,
> In his fine figure, with the slender bough.
> The sun sets in his cheeks' anemones;
> The rising moon shines in his radiant brow.
> All grace is his, as if he does the earth
> With beauty from his boundless grace endow.

Yet while he was growing up, he never ventured into the city until one day his father Nur al-Din Ali had him fully attired, placed him on a she-mule, and went with him through the city, on his way to the king. When the people looked at him and saw his face, they invoked God to save his beauty from harm, raising their voices in prayer for him and his father, as they crowded around him to look at his beauty, charm, and perfect grace. From that time on he rode with his father every day, and everyone who saw him marveled at his loveliness, for he was like the one of whom the poet said:

> When he appeared, they said, "May he be blessed,
> And glory to the God who fashioned such a one."

Above all lovely men.he was the king,
And they his subjects all, excepting none.
The nectar of his mouth tasted so sweet,
And like a row of pearls his white teeth shone.
He garnered all the beauty of the world,
Leaving all mortals helpless and undone.
And on his cheeks beauty for all to see,
Proclaimed, "No one is beautiful but he."

He bent coquettishly like a willow bough, and his cheeks resembled roses and anemones. With sweet speech, and a smile so radiant as to put the full moon to shame, he was the lovers' trial and delight.

When he reached the age of twenty, his father Nur al-Din Ali, having grown feeble, summoned him and said, "Son, you should know that this world is temporary while the next is eternal. I wish to instruct you in what I have learned and understood. I have five admonitions for you." Then he recalled his home and country and, thinking of his brother Shams al-Din, began to weep over his separation from those he loved and from his distant home, and as passion raged within him, he sighed deeply and repeated the following verses:

I blame you and proclaim my ardent love.
My body is here, my heart with you still.
I did not wish to leave you, but our fate
And God's decree defeat the human will.

When he finished reciting the verses and stopped weeping, he said to his son, "Son, before I give you advice, you should know that you have an uncle who is a vizier in Egypt and whom I left without his consent, as it had been foreordained." Then he took a roll of paper and wrote down what had happened between him and his brother before his departure. Then he wrote down what had happened to him in Basra and how he had become a vizier, recording the date of the day on which he got married and the night on which he consummated the marriage, noting that he was less than forty years old on the day of the quarrel. He concluded by stating that this was his letter to his brother whom he commended to God's care. Then he folded and sealed the scroll, saying, "O Hasan, my son, keep this scroll, and don't ever part with it." Hasan took it and hid it by sewing it into the skullcap of his turban, while his eyes filled with tears for parting from his father, who was entering the throes of death.

But a while later his father opened his eyes and said, "O Hasan, my son, my first advice is that you should not mix or associate with anyone. If you do not, you will avoid trouble, for safety is in keeping aloof. I have heard the poet say:

> There is no man whose friendship you can trust,
> Nor is there true friend in adversity.
> Then live alone and lean for help on none.
> Let this advice of mine your lesson be.

Second, O my son, oppress no one, lest fortune oppress you, for fortune is for you one day but against you another, and its gifts are a loan to be repaid. I have heard the poet say:

> Be careful and restrain your hasty wish;
> Be merciful to all, and they will mercy show.
> The hand of God is above every hand,
> And every tyrant shall another know.

Third, hold your tongue and let your faults distract you from the faults of others. Preserve silence, for it is said, 'In silence safety.' I have heard the poet say:

> Silence is fair, safe taciturnity,
> So, if you speak, do not a babbler be.
> For if your silence may once bother you,
> Your uttered words you will forever rue.

Fourth, O my son, beware of drinking wine, for wine is the root of all evil, because it robs man of reason. Beware, beware of drinking wine. I have heard the poet say:

> I have all wine forsworn
> And joined its many detractors,
> For wine leads man astray
> And opens all the evil doors.

Last, O my son, protect your wealth, so that it may protect you, and watch over it, so that it may watch over you. Do not squander your substance, lest you become dependent on the meanest of men, and guard your money, for money is a salve. I have heard the poet say:

> When my wealth dwindles, all friends disappear;
> When it increases, all are friends to me.
> How many men for money were my friends,
> And when it went, how many left my company!

Follow my advice." He continued to exhort his son until his soul left his body. Then they burned incense around him and buried him.

*But morning overtook Shahrazad, and she lapsed into silence. Then Dinarzad said, "Sister, what an entertaining story!" Shahrazad replied, "What is this compared with what I shall tell you tomorrow night if I stay alive!"*

## THE SEVENTY-FIFTH NIGHT

*The following night Dinarzad said, "O sister, tell us the rest of the story." Shahrazad replied, "With the greatest pleasure":*

It is related, O King, that Ja'far said to the caliph:

After the vizier died, his son Badr al-Din sat in mourning for two full months, without riding out or attending on the king until the king finally grew angry at him, summoned one of his chamberlains, and made him vizier. Then he bade him take chamberlains and envoys, seize the assets of the deceased Vizier Nur al-Din Ali, confiscate all his money, and seal up all his houses, goods, and possessions, without leaving a penny. The new vizier took with him chamberlains, envoys, guards, clerks, and treasury inspectors, and proceeded to the house of the Vizier Nur al-Din Ali. It happened that there was among the troops a man who had been one of the Mamluks of the Vizier Nur al-Din Ali, and when he heard this order, he spurred his horse and hurried to Badr al-Din Hasan. He found him sitting at the gate of his house, with downcast head and broken heart. He dismounted and, kissing his hand, said, "O my lord and son of my lord, hurry up, hurry up before death catches up with you." Badr al-Din Hasan trembled and asked, "What is the matter?" The Mamluk replied, "The king is angry with you. He has ordered your arrest, and calamity is behind me on its way to you. Run for your life, and don't fall into their hands, for they will not spare you." Badr al-Din Hasan was terribly alarmed, and he paled and asked, "Brother, is there time for me to go into the house?" The Mamluk replied, "No, my lord. Rise this instant and flee your house." Badr al-Din rose, repeating the following verses:

> If you suffer injustice, save yourself,
> And leave the house behind to mourn its builder.
> Your country you'll replace by another,
> But for yourself you'll find no other self.
> Nor with a mission trust another man,
> For none is as loyal as you yourself.
> And did the lion not struggle by himself,
> He would not prowl with such a mighty mane.

He put on his shoes, and, covering his head with the hem of his outer robe, left in confusion, full of anxiety and fear, not knowing where he was proceeding or in which direction he was heading. At last he decided to go to his father's sepulcher, and as he made his way among the tombs, he let fall from his head the hem of his outer robe, which was adorned with bands of brocaded taffeta embroidered with the following lines in gold:

> You who with the dew and stars
> Do with face so radiant vie,
> May your fortune stay the same
> And your glory ever high.

As he was walking, he met a Jew on his way to the city. He was a moneychanger carrying a basket, and when he saw Badr al-Din, he greeted him.

*But morning overtook Shahrazad, and she lapsed into silence. Then Dinarzad said, "What an entertaining story!" Shahrazad replied, "What is this compared with what I shall tell you if I live!"*

### THE SEVENTY-SIXTH NIGHT

*The following night, Dinarzad said to her sister, "Tell us the rest of the story." Shahrazad said:*

It is related, O King, that Ja'far said to the caliph:

When the Jew saw Badr al-Din, he kissed his hand and said, "My lord, where are you going, for it is near the end of the day, and you are lightly dressed and you look unhappy?" Badr al-Din replied, "I was asleep a while ago and saw my father in a dream. I woke up and came to visit him before nightfall." The Jew replied, "My lord and master, before he died, your father had a seafaring trade, and many of his ships have just arrived with his goods. I would like to ask you as a favor not to sell the cargo to anyone but me." Badr al-Din Hasan replied, "Very well." The Jew said, "I will this instant buy from you the cargo of the first ship to arrive, for a thousand dinars." Then he took out of the basket a sealed purse, opened it, and, setting up the scales, weighed twice until he had a thousand dinars. Badr al-Din Hasan said, "It is sold to you." Then the Jew said, "My lord, write me an acknowledgment on a piece of paper." Badr al-Din Hasan took a piece of paper and wrote on it, "Badr al-Din Hasan al-Basri has sold to Isaac the Jew the cargo of the first ship to arrive, for a thousand dinars, and has received the money." The Jew said, "Put the paper into the purse," and Badr al-Din placed the paper into the purse, tied it, sealed it, and attached it to his belt. Then he left the Jew and continued to make his way

among the tombs until he reached his father's sepulcher. There he
sat and wept for a while and recited the following verses:

> Since you left me, home is no longer home,
> Nor is the neighbor neighbor, since you went away,
> Nor is the friend who kept me company
> The friend I knew, nor is the day bright day,
> Nor are the sun and moon that shone with light,
> The same, for they will never shine again.
> In desolation you have left the world,
> In gloomy darkness, every field and plain.
> O, may the crow that at our parting crowed
> His feathers lose and without shelter stand.
> My patience fails; my body wastes away;
> How many veils are torn my death's cruel hand!
> I wonder, will our nights come back again,
> And will the old home once more hold us twain?

Badr al-Din Hasan wept at his father's tomb for a full hour, thinking of his plight and feeling at a loss what to do or where to go.
As he wept, he laid his head on his father's tomb until he fell asleep—
Glory be to Him who sleeps not. He slept on till it was dark, when
his head rolled off the tomb and he fell on his back and, with arms
and legs outstretched, lay sprawling against the tomb.

   It happened that the cemetery was haunted by a demon who
sought shelter there in the daytime and flew to another cemetery
at night. When night came, the demon came out and was about
to fly away, when he saw a man, fully dressed, lying on his back.
When he drew near him and looked at his face, he was startled by
and amazed at his beauty.

   *But morning overtook Shahrazad, and she lapsed into silence.
Then Dinarzad said, "Sister, what an entertaining story!" Shahrazad
replied, "What is this compared with what I shall tell you tomorrow night if I stay alive!"*

### The Seventy-Seventh Night

*The following night Shahrazad said:*

It is related, O King, that Ja'far said to the caliph:

When the demon looked at Hasan al-Basri, who lay asleep on
his back, he marveled at his beauty, saying to himself, "This can
be none other than one of the children of Paradise, whom God has

created to tempt all mortals." He looked upon him for a long time; then he flew up in the air, rising until he was between the heaven and the earth, where he ran into a flying she-demon. He asked her, "Who are you?" and she replied, "I am a she-demon." Then he greeted her and asked her, "She-demon, will you come with me to my cemetery to see what the Almighty God has created among men?" She replied, "Very well." Then they both flew down to the cemetery, and as they stood there, the demon asked, "In all your life, have you ever seen a young man more beautiful than this one?" When the she-demon looked at Badr al-Din and examined his face, she said, "Glory be to Him who has no rival. By God, brother, by your leave, I will tell you about an extraordinary thing I witnessed this very night in the land of Egypt." The demon said, "Tell me." The she-demon said, "Demon, you should know that there is in the city of Cairo a king who has a vizier named Shams al-Din Muhammad. That vizier has a daughter who is about twenty years old and who bears the most striking resemblance to this young man, for with an elegant and fine figure, she is endowed with beauty, charm, and perfect grace. When she approached the age of twenty, the king of Egypt heard of her and, summoning the vizier her father, said to him, 'Vizier, it has come to my knowledge that you have a daughter, and I wish to demand her of you in marriage.' The vizier replied, 'O King, accept my apology and do not reproach me but grant me your indulgence. As you know, I had a brother called Nur al-Din, who shared the vizierate with me in your service. It happened that one night we sat discussing marriage and children, but the next morning he disappeared, and for twenty years I have never heard of him. Recently, however, I heard, O King of the age, that he had died in Basra, where he was a vizier, leaving behind a son. Having recorded the date of the day I got married, the night I went in to my wife, and the day she gave birth, I have reserved my daughter for her cousin; besides, there are plenty of other women and girls for our lord the king.' When the king heard the vizier's answer, he was angry."

*But morning overtook Shahrazad, and she lapsed into silence. Then Dinarzad said, "Sister, what an entertaining story!" Shahrazad replied, "What is this compared with what I shall tell you tomorrow night if I stay alive!"*

## THE SEVENTY-EIGHTH NIGHT

*The following night Shahrazad said:*

It is related, O King, that Ja'far said to the caliph:

The she-demon said to the demon, "The king, angry at the answer of his vizier Shams al-Din, said to him, 'Damn it, you. Someone like me asks the likes of you for his daughter in marriage, yet you put me off with a lame excuse,' and he swore to marry her to none but the meanest of his servants. It happened that the king had a hunchbacked groom with two humps, one behind and one in front, and he sent for the hunchback and, summoning witnesses, ordered the vizier to draw the marriage contract between his daughter and the hunchback that very day, swearing that he would have the hunchback led in procession and that he would have him go in to his bride that very night. I have just now left the princes and their Mamluks waiting for the hunchback at the door of the bath, with lighted candles in their hands, in order to lead him in procession when he comes out. As for the vizier's daughter, she has been dressed and decked out with jewelry by her attendants, while her father is placed under guard until the hunchback goes in to her. O demon, I have never seen anyone as beautiful or delightful as that girl." The demon replied, "You are lying; this young man is more beautiful than she." The she-demon said, "By the Lord of this world, none is worthy of her but this young man. It would be a pity to waste her on that hunchback." The demon replied, "Let us take him up, carry him in his sleep to the girl, and leave them alone together." She said, "Very well," and the demon carried Badr al-Din Hasan al-Basri and flew with him up in the air, while the she-demon flew by his side. Then he came down at the gate of Cairo and, setting Badr al-Din on a bench, awakened him.

When Badr al-Din woke up and found himself in an unknown city, he started to make inquiries, but the demon jabbed him and, handing him a thick candle, said to him, "Go to the bath, mix with the Mamluks and the crowd of people, and walk with them until you come to the wedding hall. Then press ahead and enter the hall as if you are one of the candle bearers. Stand at the right side of the hunchbacked bridegroom, and whenever the bride's attendants, the singing women, or the bride herself approaches you, take a handful of gold from your pocket and give it to the women. Don't hesitate, and whenever you put your hand in your pocket and take

it out, it will be full of gold. Take it and give it to those who approach
you. Do not wonder, for this is not by your power or strength but
by the power, the strength, and the will of God, so that His wise
decree may be fulfilled upon His creatures." Then Badr al-Din
Hasan rose, lighted the candle, and walked until he came to the
bath, where he found the hunchbacked bridegroom already on
horseback. So he mixed with the people in the guise and manner
already mentioned, wearing a double turban.

*But morning overtook Shahrazad, and she lapsed into silence.
Then Dinarzad said, "Sister, what an entertaining story!" Shahrazad
replied, "What is this compared with what I shall tell you tomorrow night if the king spares me and lets me live!"*

THE SEVENTY-NINTH NIGHT

*Shahrazad said:*

It is related, O King, that Ja'far said to the caliph:

Badr al-Din Hasan walked in the procession, and whenever the
singing women stopped to sing and collect money from the people,
he put his hand in his pocket and, finding it full of gold, took a
handfull and cast it in the singing women's tambourines until they
were full of dinars. The singing women and all the people were
amazed at his beauty and grace, and he continued in this fashion
until they reached the palace of the vizier (who was his uncle), where
the doormen drove back the people, and forbade them to enter.
But the singing women said, "By God, we will not enter unless this
wonderful young man enters with us, for in all our life we have
never seen anyone more beautiful or more generous, and we will
not unveil the bride except in his presence, for he has given out
a golden treasure in her honor." So they brought him into the wedding hall and seated him on the dais to the right of the hunchback.
The wives of the princes, viziers, chamberlains, and deputies, as
well as every other woman present, each veiled to the eyes and
holding a large lighted candle in her hand, lined up in two opposite
rows, extending from the dais to the bride's throne, which stood
in front of the door from which she was to emerge. When the women
saw Hasan al-Basri's beauty and grace and looked on his face, which
was as bright as the new moon and as dazzling as the full moon,
and looked on his body, which swayed like a willow bough, they

loved his charm and flirtatious looks, and when he showered them
with money, they loved him even more. They crowded around him
with their lighted candles and gazed on his beauty and envied him
his charm, winking at each other, for every one of them desired
him and wished that she was lying in his lap. Everyone said, "None
deserves our bride but this young man. What a pity to waste her
on the worthless hunchback! May God curse him who brought this
about!" and they cursed the king. The hunchback, who was wearing a brocaded robe of honor and a double turban, with his neck
buried between his shoulders, sat rolled up like a ball, looking more
like a toy than a man. He was like him of whom the poet said:

> O for a hunchback who can hide his hump
> Like a pearl hidden in an oyster shell,
> Or one who looks like a castor oil branch
> From which dangles a rotten citric lump.

Then the women began to curse the hunchback and to jeer at
him, while they prayed for Badr al-Din Hasan and ingratiated themselves with him.

Then the singing women beat their tambourines and played their
flutes, as the attendants emerged with the bride.

*But morning overtook Shahrazad, and she lapsed into silence.
Then Dinarzad said to her sister, "Sister, what an amazing and
entertaining story!" Shahrazad replied, "What is this compared with
what I shall tell you tomorrow night if the king spares me and lets
me live!"*

THE EIGHTIETH NIGHT

*The following night Shahrazad said:*

It is related, O King, that Ja'far said to the caliph:

As Badr al-Din Hasan sat on the bench next to the hunchback,
the attendants emerged with his cousin. They had combed her hair
and, inserting sacks of musk, braided her tresses, and after they
had perfumed her with the incense of cardamon and ambergris,
they decked her with robes and jewelry worthy of the Persian kings.
She paraded in a robe embroidered in gold with dazzling figures
of all kinds of birds and beasts, with eyes and bills of precious stones
and feet of rubies and green beryl. She wore a very rare and precious

necklace, set with large, round gems that dazzled the eye and stag-
gered the mind. As the attendants led the way with lighted camphor
candles, her face shone under the candlelight, looking more brilliant
than the full moon when it shines on the fourteenth night. With
eyes sharper than a bare sword, lashes that captivate the heart, rosy
cheeks, and a swinging gait, she advanced, dazzling the eyes with
beauty beyond description. The singing women received her by
playing on the tambourines and all sorts of musical instruments.
Meanwhile, Badr al-Din Hasan al-Basri sat while the women gazed
on him, like the moon among the stars, with a radiant brow, a neck
as white as marble, a face as bright as the moon, and a rosy cheek
graced with a mole like a disk of ambergris.

As the bride approached, swaying gracefully, and unveiled her
face, the hunchback rose and bent to kiss her, but she turned her
head from him, slipped away, and stood before Badr al-Din Hasan,
her cousin, causing the singing women to cry out aloud and the
people to clamor. Badr al-Din Hasan put his hand in his pocket
and, again finding it full of dinars, took out a handful and cast it
in the singing women's tambourines, and he kept taking out hand-
fuls and throwing them to them, while they commended him to God
and signaled to him with their fingers, meaning to say, "We wish
that this bride was yours." And as every woman at the wedding
gazed on him, he smiled, while the hunchback sat alone like a
monkey. Then Badr al-Din Hasan began to move excitedly, surrounded by servants and slave-girls, who were carrying on their
heads large trays full of gold pieces and dinars, part as a gift for
the bride, part for distribution to the public. When the bride made
her way to him and stood before him, he kept staring at her, con-
templating the beauty that God had bestowed on her alone, while
the servants scattered the gold pieces over the heads of the young
and the old. And he was happy and rejoiced at what he saw.

*But morning overtook Shahrazad, and she lapsed into silence.
Then Dinarzad said, "Sister, what a strange and entertaining story!"
Shahrazad replied, "What is this compared with what I shall tell
you tomorrow night if I stay alive!"*

THE EIGHTY-FIRST NIGHT

*The following night Shahrazad said:*

It is related, O King, that Ja'far said to the caliph:

The attendants presented the bride, in her first dress,[6] as she swayed coquettishly, to the delight and amazement of Badr al-Din Hasan and everyone present. When he looked at his cousin in her red satin dress and saw her blooming radiant face, he was happy and rejoiced at what he saw, for she was like the one of whom the excellent poet said:

> Like the sun above a reed in the dunes, she flamed,
> Clad in a pomegranate red attire,
> And offered me the bounty of her cheeks
> And her lips' wine to quench my burning fire.

Then they changed her dress and put on a blue one, and she reappeared like the shining moon, with jet black hair, soft cheeks, smiling mouth, swelling bosom, firm wrists, and opulent limbs. She was like her of whom the noble poet said:

> She came in lapis blue, O heavenly sight,
> A moon of summer on a winter's night.

Then they clad her with another dress and, letting down her long tresses, which were as black as the deep night, veiled her face with her abundant hair, save for her eyes, which pierced the hearts with their keen arrows. She was like her of whom the poet said:

> Veiling her cheeks with hair, she came to charm,
> And like a dove appeared to lovers' harm.
> I said, "You veil the morning with the night."
> Said she, "No, 'tis the moon that I veil from the light."

Then they clad her with the fourth dress, and she reappeared like the rising sun, swaying coquettishly, turning gracefully like a deer, and piercing the hearts with the arrows of her eyes. She was like her of whom the poet said:

> The sun of beauty she to all appears,
> With coy reserve and with coquettish grace.
> And when the sun beholds her radiant smile,
> He in the clouds hastens to hide his face.

Then they presented her in the fifth dress, which revealed her wonders, as she swayed her hips and shook her ringlets and curving sidetresses, like a willow bough or a deer bending to drink. She was like her of whom the poet said:

---

6. The custom still prevails in some parts of the Middle East to present the bride in different dresses to the bridegroom.

She comes like a full moon on a fair night,
With dainty limbs and with a slender waist,
With eyes that subdue all men with their charm,
With cheeks that vie with rubies at their best.
She trails her jet black hair over her hips;
Beware the serpents of her curls, beware!
Her sides are soft, but alas, alas!
A heart harder than stones lies hidden there.
From arching brows she sends her darting looks,
Which, although distant, never miss the mark.
When I embrace her waist to press her to my heart,
Her swelling breasts repel and push me back.
Ah, how her beauty all outshines, and how
Her fair shape puts to shame the tender bough.

Then they presented her in the sixth dress, which was green. In this she attained the height of beauty, shaming a bronze spear with her slender form and the bending bough with her softness and supple grace and outshining the rising moon with her radiant face. She surpassed every fair woman in the world and broke every heart, as the poet said of one like her:

There was a maid with such polish and grace
That e'en the sun seemed borrowed from her face.
Bedecked in green she came, fair to behold,
As a pomegranate bud the green leaves enfold.
And when we asked, "What do you call this dress?"
She answered in sweet words meant to impress,
"Since I have tortured many with my arts,
In this dress, I call it Breaker of Hearts."

*But morning overtook Shahrazad, and she lapsed into silence. Then her sister Dinarzad said, "Sister, what an amazing and entertaining story!" Shahrazad replied, "What is this compared with what I shall tell you tomorrow night if I stay alive!"*

THE EIGHTY-SECOND NIGHT

*The following night Shahrazad said:*

It is related, O King, that Ja'far said to the caliph:

Whenever the attendants presented the bride in a new dress and brought her before the hunchback, she turned her head from him and, moving away, stood before Badr al-Din Hasan, who took out a handful of gold from his pocket and gave it to the singing women. This went on until she was unveiled in all seven dresses, and the attendants signaled to the guests to depart. Everyone departed, except Badr al-Din and the hunchback, while the attendants took the bride inside to undress her and prepare her for the bridegroom. The hunchback turned to Badr al-Din and said, "You have favored us and cheered us with your presence. Would you please rise and leave us now?" Saying "Very well," Badr al-Din rose and made his way to the hallway where he was met by the demon and she-demon, who asked, "Where are you going? Wait here, and when the hunchback comes out to go to the privy to relieve himself, go back to the bedroom and lie in the canopied bed, and when the bride comes and speaks to you, say, 'It is I who am your husband, for the king has planned all this only to laugh at the hunchback, whom we hired for ten dirhams and a bowl of food and then got rid of.' Then proceed to take her virginity and consummate your marriage. We have no sympathy for the hunchback in this matter, for none but you deserves this young woman."

While they were talking, the hunchback came out and went into the privy. While he sat, defecating so much that the shit kept coming from his ass, the demon suddenly emerged from the water bowl in the privy, in the shape of a black tomcat, and said "Meow, meow." The hunchback cried, "Away with you, unlucky cat!" But the cat grew and swelled until he became as big as an ass-colt, braying, "Hee-haw, hee-haw!" The hunchback was startled, and in his fear, he smeared his legs with shit, screaming, "O people of the house, help me!" Then the ass grew even bigger and became a buffalo, and in a human voice said, "Damn you, hunchback!" The hunchback quaked and was so terrified that he slipped on the toilet with his clothes on, saying, "Yes, indeed, O king of the buffaloes!" The demon cried out, "Damn you, you mean hunchback! Is the world so small that you had to marry none but my mistress?" The hunchback replied, "My lord, I am not to blame, for they forced me to marry her, and I did not know that she had a buffalo for a lover. What would you like me to do?" The demon said, "I swear to you that if you leave this place or say anything before sunrise, I will wring your neck. As soon as the sun rises, depart and never return to this house or let us hear from you again." Then the demon seized the hunchback and turned him upside down, with his head stuck in the toilet and his feet up in the air, saying to him, "I will stand here to watch you, and if you try to leave before sunrise, I will seize you by the legs and dash your head against the wall. Be careful with your life."

So much for the hunchback. As for Badr al-Din Hasan, when the hunchback entered the privy, Badr al-Din went straightaway into the net covering the bed and sat there waiting. Soon the bride came in, accompanied by an old woman who stood at the opening of the net and said, "You misshapen man, take God's gift, you trash!" and departed, while the bride, whose name was Sit al-Husn, entered the bed, and when she saw Badr al-Din Hasan sitting there, she exclaimed, "O my dear, are you still here? By God, I wish that you and the hunchback were partners in me." When Badr al-Din heard her words, he said, "Sit al-Husn, why should the filthy hunchback share you with me?" Sit al-Husn replied, "Why shouldn't he? Is he not my husband?" Badr al-Din replied, "Lady, God forbid. The wedding was nothing but a masquerade. Haven't you noticed that the attendants, the singing women, and all your relatives presented you to me, while they laughed at him? Your father knows very well that we hired the hunchback for ten dirhams and a bowl of food and then got rid of him."

When Sit al-Husn heard his words, she laughed and said, "By God, my little lord, you have made me happy and put my heart at ease. Take me and hold me in your lap." She had no trousers on, so Badr al-Din also took off his trousers and, taking from his belt the purse containing the thousand dinars he had received from the Jew, he wrapped it in his trousers and laid them under the mattress. Then taking off his turban, which he laid over the wrapping cloth on the seat, he remained only in his shirt and skullcap and stood hesitating. But Sit al-Husn drew him to her, saying, "O my love, you are keeping me waiting. Quench my desire with your love and let me enjoy your loveliness!" Then she recited these verses:

> For God's sake, rest your legs between my thighs,
> For that is all I now want in the world,
> And let me hear your voice again, O love!
> For I long for you and await your word,
> While my right arm, like your own binding lace,
> My arm alone, enjoys the tight embrace.

*But morning overtook Shahrazad, and she lapsed into silence. Then Dinarzad said, "Sister, what an amazing and entertaining story!" Shahrazad replied, "What is this compared with what I shall tell you tomorrow night if I stay alive!"*

## THE EIGHTY-THIRD NIGHT

*The following night Shahrazad said:*

It is related, O King, that Ja'far said to the caliph:

Badr al-Din Hasan and Sit al-Husn embraced, and he took her
virginity and consummated the marriage. Then she placed one arm
under his neck and the other under his shoulder, and with neck
on neck and cheek on cheek they went to sleep, as if they seemed
to say:

> Cleave to the one you love and ignore calumny,
> For those who envy never favor love.
> Two lovers in one bed, no fairer sight
> Has mercy's Lord created from above.
> Bosom to bosom in each other's arm,
> They lie in bliss, clad in their own delight,
> For when two hearts unite in love's embrace,
> The world and all its chatter seem so trite.
> Therefore, if ever you your true love find,
> O rare occasion, you should never part,
> And you who chide the lovers for their love,
> Why not instead reform the wicked heart?

When they were fast asleep, the demon said to the she-demon,
"Take up the young man, and let us return him to the place where
he was asleep, before morning overtakes us." The she-demon took
up Badr al-Din Hasan, as he lay asleep without trousers clad only
in his thin sequin shirt with its Moroccan gold embroidery and in
his striped blue skullcap, and flew away with him, while the demon
flew by her side. But no sooner had the Glorious and Almighty God
bidden the day dawn and the announcers of prayer climbed to the
minaret tops to proclaim the Almighty One, than the angels shot
the two demons with shooting stars. The demon was consumed by
fire, while the she-demon was saved by the Almighty God and was
able to come down safety with Badr al-Din Hasan, at the very
moment when, as fate would have it, she had reached the city of
Damascus,[7] and there she left him by one of the city gates and
departed.

When the day dawned and it was light, the city gate was opened
and the people came out and, seeing a handsome young man clad

---

7. Then and now the capital of Syria.

in nothing but a light shirt and a skullcap and snoring as he lay in a deep sleep from the exhaustion of the previous night, the candle procession, the presentation of the bride, and his other activities, said, "Lucky is he with whom he spent the night! He should have waited until the boy put on his clothes." Another said, "What a pity for such young people! Look at this young man! Perhaps he came out of the tavern, seeking something and, being drunk, fell asleep without clothes, or perhaps he could not find the door of his house and wandered until he came to the city gate and, finding it shut, fell asleep here." As everyone offered an opinion, the breeze blew and raised his shirt, revealing legs and thighs and belly and navel as clear as crystal and softer than cream. The bystanders cried out, "O lovely, lovely!" and their cries awakened Badr al-Din Hasan al-Basri, who, finding himself lying at the city gate, surrounded by a huge crowd of people, asked in astonishment, "Good people, where am I, and why do you crowd around me?" They replied, "We found you lying here, at the time of the morning call to prayer, and this is all we know about you. Where did you sleep last night?" He replied, "By God, good people, I slept in Cairo last night." One of them said, "Listen to him!" Another said, "Give him a hard kick!" Another said, "Son, you are mad; how can you sleep in Cairo and wake up in Damascus?"

Badr al-Din replied, "By God, good people, last night I slept in the city of Cairo; yesterday I was in the city of Basra; and this morning I am in Damascus." One of them said, "By God, this is a good one; by God, this is a good one!" Another said, "Well, well!" Another said, "He is mad," and everybody began to shout, "He is mad," thus making him a madman in spite of himself and affirming to each other, "There is no doubt of his madness; what a pity for this young man!" Then they said to him, "Son, return to your senses. Who in the world could be in Basra yesterday, in Cairo last night, and in Damascus this morning?" Badr al-Din Hasan replied, "I was truly a bridegroom in Cairo last night." They said, "No doubt, you must have dreamt and seen all this in your sleep." Badr al-Din was no longer sure of himself and began to wonder, but finally said to them, "By God, brothers, it was not in a dream that I went to Cairo and they unveiled the bride before me and before the hunchback. If it was a dream, then where are my gold purse, my dagger, my turban, and my robe?" He was utterly confused.

*But morning overtook Shahrazad, and she lapsed into silence. Then Dinarzad said to her sister, "What an amazing and entertaining story!" Shahrazad replied, "What is this compared with what I shall tell you tomorrow night if the king spares me and lets me live!"*

## THE EIGHTY-FOURTH NIGHT

*The following night Shahrazad said:*

It is related, O King, that Ja'far said to the caliph:

When the people cried out, "He is mad," Badr al-Din began to run, and they followed him, shouting, "Madman! Madman!" He entered the city and ran through the markets, with the crowd pressing on him, until he took refuge in a cook's shop. This cook had been a scoundrel and a robber until he repented, became reformed, and opened a cookshop. Yet all the people of Damascus were still frightened by him and afraid of his mischief. When they saw Badr al-Din enter his shop, they retreated, dispersed, and went their ways. The cook looked at Badr al-Din and asked, "Young man, where do you come from?" Badr al-Din told him his story from beginning to end (but there is no point in repeating it here). The cook said, "This is a strange story. Keep it to yourself until God sends you relief, and stay with me in this shop, for I am childless and I will adopt you as my son." Badr al-Din replied, "Very well." Then the cook went to the market, bought him some clothes, and had him put them on. Then he took him before witnesses and adopted him formally, and from that day Badr al-Din became known in Damascus as the cook's son, living with him and sitting by the scales in the shop.

So much for Badr al-Din Hasan; as for his cousin Sit al-Husn, when she woke up at dawn and did not find Badr al-Din by her side, she thought that he had gone to the privy. While she was waiting, her father, the Egyptian vizier Shams al-Din Muhammad the brother of Nur Al-Din Ali who was the father of Badr al-Din Hasan, came out, feeling unhappy because of the wrong he had suffered at the hands of the king, who had forced him to marry his daughter to the meanest of servants, a lump of a hunchback. He walked about until he came to his daughter's bed and, standing by the net, called out to his daughter, "Sit al-Husn!" She replied, "Here I am, here I am," and she came out, with a face that had turned more radiant and beautiful from the embraces of that deerlike Badr al-Din, and kissed her father's hand. He said to her, "You cursed girl, you seem mighty pleased with that abominable hunchback!"

*But morning overtook Shahrazad, and she lapsed into silence. Then Dinarzad said, "Sister, what a strange and entertaining story!"*

Shahrazad replied, "What is this compared with what I shall tell you tomorrow night if I live!"

### THE EIGHTY-FIFTH NIGHT

*The following night Shahrazad said:*

It is related, O King, that Ja'far said to the caliph:

When Sit al-Husn heard her father say to her, "You seem mighty pleased with that abominable hunchback!" she smiled and said, "Stop, father! It was enough what I had suffered yesterday at the hands of the women who taunted me and mocked me with that mean hunchback, who is not worthy even to bring my husband his mule or his shoes. By God, in all my life I have never had a better night than last night. Stop mocking me with the hunchback, whom you had hired to ward off the evil eye from my young bridegroom!" When her father heard what she said, he glared at her and said, "Damn you, what is this talk! Hasn't the hunchback slept with you?" The girl replied, "Stop mentioning the hunchback, that worthless creature! May God curse him. I slept in the lap of none but my true husband, the one with the dark eyes and the arched black eyebrows." Her father yelled at her, "Damn you, shameless woman! Have you lost your senses?" She replied, "Ah, for God's sake, father, stop torturing me and being hard on me. I swear by God that my husband, who took my virginity and made me pregnant, is a handsome young man, who is in the privy at this very moment."

Her father went to the privy and there he found the hunchback standing upside down, with his head stuck in the toilet and his feet in the air. The vizier was taken aback and called out, "You hunchback!" The hunchback replied, "Yeah, yeah." The vizier asked, "Why are you in this position, and who did this to you?" The hunchback replied, "Couldn't you people have found anyone for me to marry except a girl who consorts with buffaloes and takes demons for lovers?"

*But morning overtook Shahrazad, and she lapsed into silence. Then Dinarzad said, "Sister, what a strange and entertaining story!" Shahrazad replied, "What is this compared with what I shall tell you tomorrow night if the king spares me and lets me live!"*

## THE EIGHTY-SIXTH NIGHT

*The following night Shahrazad said:*

It is related, O King, that Ja'far said to the caliph:

When the hunchback said to the father of the bride, "Couldn't you people have found anyone for me to marry except a girl who consorts with buffaloes and takes demons for lovers? May God curse the Devil and my wretched lot," the vizier said to him, "Get up and go!" But the hunchback said, "I am not crazy, for the sun has not risen yet, and I will not go from here until the sun rises. Yesterday I came here to relieve myself, when a black tomcat suddenly emerged and screamed at me. Then he kept getting bigger until he was as big as a buffalo and spoke to me in a way that made me obey him. Leave me and go your way, and may God reward you and curse the bride!" But the vizier took him out of the toilet, and the hunchback, in that same condition, went at once to the king and told him what had happened to him at the hands of the demon.

Meanwhile, the father of the bride went back inside the house, amazed and bewildered, not knowing what to make of his daughter. He went to her and said, "Damn it, tell me your secret!" She replied, "Ah, father, what secret? By God, last night I was presented to a young man who spent the night with me, took my virginity, and made me pregnant. Here on this chair is his turban, and here are his robe and his dagger, and here under the mattress are his trousers, wrapped around something. The vizier took his nephew's turban and, turning it in his hand, examined it and said, "By God, this is a vizier's turban, tied in the style of Mosul." When he examined it further, he felt inside it a scroll, folded, sealed, and sewn into the lining. Then he unfolded the trousers and found the purse with the thousand dinars and the piece of paper. When he unfolded the paper, he read, "Badr al-Din Hasan al-Basri has sold to Isaac the Jew the cargo of the first ship to arrive for a thousand dinars and has received the money," and as soon as he read it, he screamed and fell into a swoon.

*But morning overtook Shahrazad, and she lapsed into silence. Then Dinarzad said, "Sister, what a strange and entertaining story!" Shahrazad replied, "What is this compared with what I shall tell you tomorrow night if the king spares me and lets me live!"*

## THE EIGHTY-SEVENTH NIGHT

*The following night Shahrazad said:*

It is related, O King, that Ja'far said to the caliph:

O Commander of the Faithful, when the vizier Shams al-Din came to himself and recalled what he had discovered, he was amazed, and when he opened the sealed paper and saw that it was in his brother's handwriting, he was even more amazed and said, "Daughter, do you know who the man who took your virginity really was? By God, he is none other than your cousin, and these thousand dinars are your dowry. Glory be to the Omnipotent God who controls everything, for He has turned the cause of my quarrel with my brother Nur al-Din into a just resolution. I wonder how all this came about?" Then he looked at the letter again, and when he saw the date in his brother's handwriting, he kissed it many times, and as he kept looking at the handwriting, he wept, lamented, and repeated these verses:

> I see their traces and with longing pine
> In their empty dwelling, and my tears flow.
> And Him who had decreed their loss I beg
> That He may on me their return bestow.

Then he read the letter and saw the dates of his brother's arrival in Basra, the marriage contract, the consummation of the marriage, the birth of his son Badr al-Din Hasan, and the year of his death. When the vizier realized what these dates meant, he shook with amazement and delight, for when he compared the events of his life with those of his brother's, he found them parallel, and when he compared the dates of his brother's marriage in Basra, the consummation of that marriage, and the birth of his son, he found them to be identical with his own in Cairo, and when he pondered how shortly thereafter his nephew had arrived and consummated the marriage with his daughter, he concluded that all of this was planned by Providence. Then he took the letter and the piece of paper that he had found inside the purse, went at once to the king, and told him the whole story. The king was very much amazed and ordered that these events be dated and recorded.

Then the vizier went home and waited for his nephew all day long, but he did not show up, and when he waited a second and a third day and kept waiting until the seventh day, without any news or any trace of his nephew, he said, "By God, I will do what has never been done before." He took an inkwell and a sheet of paper and wrote down a description of the entire wedding chamber and its contents. Then he ordered everything put aside, including the turban, the trousers, and the purse.

*But morning overtook Shahrazad, and she lapsed into silence. Then Dinarzad said, "Sister, what a strange and entertaining story!" Shahrazad replied, "What is this compared with what I shall tell you tomorrow night if the king spares me and lets me live!"*

THE EIGHTY-EIGHTH NIGHT

*The following night Shahrazad said:*

I heard, O happy King, that Ja'far said to the caliph:

Days and months went by, and when her time came, the daughter of the vizier of Egypt gave birth to a boy, who had a face as round as the full moon or the rising sun, a radiant brow, and rosy cheeks. They cut his navel cord and applied kohl to his eyelids, and his grandfather named him 'Ajib and committed him to the care of the nurses, stewardesses, and servants.

'Ajib grew, and when he was seven, his grandfather sent him to school, bidding the tutor educate him and teach him good manners. 'Ajib remained at the school about four years. Then he began to bully, beat, and abuse the other children. At last they got together and complained to the monitor about their maltreatment at the hands of 'Ajib. The monitor said, "I will tell you what you should do tomorrow, so that he will stop coming to school and you will never see him again. When he comes tomorrow, gather around him to play a game and say to each other, 'No one can join us in this game, unless he tells us the names of his mother and father, for he who does not know the names of his parents is a bastard and shall not play with us.'" The children were pleased, and the next day they came to school, and when 'Ajib arrived, they gathered around him and one of them said, "We will play a game, but no one can join in unless he tells us the names of his mother and father." Everyone said, "Very well." Then one said, "My name is Majid, my mother's name is Sittita, and my father's name is 'Iz al-Din," and others said the like, until it was 'Ajib's turn. He said, "My name is 'Ajib, my mother's name is Sit al-Husn, and my father's name is Shams al-Din, the vizier." They said, "How can that be? By God, he is not your father!" He said to them, "Damn you, the Vizier Shams al-Din is indeed my father." But they laughed at him and clapped their hands and said, "May God help him! He does not know his father! By God, he cannot play or sit with us." Then they laughed, and dispersed, leaving him choking with tears. Then the monitor came to him and said, "'Ajib, don't you know that the Vizier Shams al-Din is your mother's father, your grandfather, and not your father? As for your father, neither you nor we know who he is. For the king married your mother to a hunchback, but the demons came and slept with her, and your father is unknown. Unless you find out who he is, you will not be able to face the schoolchildren, for they will treat you as a bastard. Don't you see that even though your grandfather is the vizier of Egypt, the merchant's son knows his own father and the grocer's son knows his, but you don't know your father? 'Ajib, this is a strange business!"

*But morning overtook Shahrazad, and she lapsed into silence. Then Dinarzad said, "Sister, what a strange and entertaining story!" Shahrazad replied, "What is this compared with what I shall tell you tomorrow night if I stay alive!"*

THE EIGHTY-NINTH NIGHT

*The following night Shahrazad said:*

I heard, O happy King, than Ja'far said to the caliph:

When 'Ajib heard the insulting remarks of the children and the monitor, he left at once and came crying to his mother Sit al-Husn. When she saw him, her heart was on fire for him, and she asked him, "Son, why do you cry? May God never let you cry again!" Sobbing, he told her what had happened; then he asked her, "Who, then, is my father?" She replied, "Your father is the vizier of Egypt." He said, "You are lying. The vizier is your own father; he is my grandfather. Who, then, is my father?" When Sit al-Husn heard him speak of his father, her cousin and husband Badr al-Din Hasan, and recalled her wedding night, she wept bitterly and recited these verses:

> Love in my breast he lit and went away
> And left behind an empty hearth and heart.

His shrine is too distant to visit now,
A distance that has kept us worlds apart!
And when he left, my patience also left,
So did endurance, so did self-control.
And when he went away, he took with him
My joy, my peace, my rest, all; he took all
And left me my tears of unhappy love,
Which from my burning eyes profusely flow.
And when I long to see him once again,
And with vain longing wait for him to show,
I trace his image in my empty heart,
Which wells with thoughts, longing, and deep passion.
You, whose remembrance wraps me in its warmth,
Whose love I show, a sign of devotion,
Is there no ransom for the captive heart,
And for the afflicted no remedy,
And for the sick with love no medicine,
And for the defeated no victory?
O my dear love, how long this coy disdain?
When will you come back and be mine again?

While she wept and made her son weep with her, the vizier came in, and when he saw them, he asked, "Why do you weep?" His daughter told him what had happened to her son, and when he remembered his brother and nephew and his daughter's puzzling story, he wept with them. Then he went at once to the king of Egypt and, kissing the ground before him, begged him leave to go eastward to the city of Basra to inquire about his nephew; he also begged him for royal edicts to all the provinces and cities, authorizing him to take custody of Badr al-Din wherever he found him. And he wept before the king, who took pity on him and wrote him letters and edicts to all the provinces and cities. The vizier rejoiced, thanked the king, and invoked God's blessing on him. Then he returned at once to his house, and after he made preparations for the journey, he took his daughter and her son 'Ajib with him and departed.

*But morning overtook Shahrazad, and she lapsed into silence. Then Dinarzad said, "Sister, what a strange and entertaining story!" Shahrazad replied, "What is this compared with what I shall tell you tomorrow night if the king spares me and lets me live!"*

## THE NINETIETH NIGHT

*The following night Shahrazad said:*

I heard, O happy King, that Ja'far said to the caliph:

The vizier of Egypt, the uncle of Badr al-Din Hasan, journeyed with his daughter and her son for twenty days until he came to the city of Damascus and saw its rivers and birds, just as the poet described them:

> Once in Damascus I spent such a night
> That time swore 't would never the like allow.
> We slept carefree under the wing of night
> Till morning smiled and beamed with dappled brow,
> And dewdrops on the branches hung like pearls,
> Then fell and scattered when the zephyr blew,
> And birds chanted the words traced on the lake,
> As the wind wrote and the clouds the points drew.

The vizier dismounted and pitched his tents at a place called the Plain of Pebbles, saying to his followers, "Let us rest here for two or three days." Then the pages and servants went on their errands into the city, this to sell, that to buy, another to go to the bath. 'Ajib too went into the city to see the sights, followed by a eunuch carrying a red club of knotted almondwood, 'with which if one hit a camel, it would go galloping as far as Yemen.'[8] When the people of Damascus saw 'Ajib, who in spite of his very young age was all beauty, charm, and perfect grace, just like him of whom the poet said:

> The scent is musk, the cheek a rose,
> The teeth are pearls, the mouth is wine,
> The frame a bough, the hip a barge,
> The hair is night, the face a moon divine,

they followed him, while others ran ahead and waited for him to pass by, so that they might gaze on him, until, as if it had been foreordained, the eunuch stopped in front of the shop of 'Ajib's father, Badr al-Din Hasan al-Basri.

Badr al-Din had been living in Damascus for twelve years, during which time the reformed cook died, leaving his shop and all his property to his adopted son, Badr al-Din. In the course of the

---

8. A country situated on the southwestern corner of the Arabian peninsula.

years Badr al-Din's beard had grown and his understanding had matured. When his son and the servants stood before him . . .

*But morning overtook Shahrazad, and she lapsed into silence. Then the king said to himself, "By God, I will not have her put to death until I find out what happened to the vizier Badr al-Din Hasan, his son, his uncle, and his cousin. Then I will have her put to death as I did the others."*

### The Ninety-First Night

*The following night Shahrazad said:*

I heard, O happy King, that Ja'far said to the caliph:

When 'Ajib and the servant stood before Badr al-Din's shop, and he gazed on his son's extraordinary beauty and grace, his heart began to throb, his stomach began to flutter, and he felt happy, as the blood hearkened to the blood, driven by instinctive sympathy and the divine mystery—Glory be to Him who controls everything. Looking at his son's outlandish attire and at his wonderful face, Badr al-Din said to him, "O my lord and master of my life and heart, you for whom I would shed my blood, would you enter my shop to taste my food and make me happy?" (That day he had prepared a pomegranate-seed dish cooked in sugar.) At that moment, he remembered his happy days as a vizier's son, and his eyes filled with tears and he recited the following verses:

> O my beloved, as I shed my tears,
> I should acquaint you with my sorry plight:
> When I avoid you, I yearn for you so
> And feel a passion that does burn and blight.
> 'Tis not that I hate or wish to forget,
> But that such love can such wisdom beget!

'Ajib felt tenderness for him, and his heart throbbed. He turned to the eunuch and said, "Tutor, I feel sympathy and pity for this cook, who seems to have lost a son or a brother. Let us enter his shop and by accepting his hospitality console him; perhaps God will reward this act by reuniting me with my father." When the eunuch heard his words, he was angry and said, "What a fine thing for a vizier's son to eat at a cookshop! While I stand here to protect you with this club even from people's looks, how can I let you enter their shops?" When Badr al-Din heard what the eunuch said, he turned to his son and recited the following verses:

> I marvel that they guard you with one slave,
> While many are enslaved by your own grace,
> The basil of the beard and jewels of the mouth,
> The mole of ambergris and rubies of the face.

Than Badr al-Din turned to the eunuch and said, "Noble lord, will you make me happy by entering my shop, you who are like a chestnut, black without but white within, just like him of whom the poet said?" The eunuch laughed and asked, "For God's sake, what did the poet say?" Badr al-Din recited the following verses:

> Were he not such a fine and trusty man,
> He would not in the court hold such a sway,
> Or guard the harem with such zeal and care
> That even the angels do him homage pay.
> In blackness he excels, but 'tis his deeds,
> His noble deeds that outshine the bright day.

This pleased the eunuch, who laughed and, taking 'Ajib by the hand, entered Badr al-Din's shop. Badr al-Din placed before them a sizzling bowl of pomegranate seeds conserved with almonds and sugar, and they ate and found it extremely delicious. 'Ajib turned to his father and said, "Sit down and eat with us, and may the Almighty God reunite me with the one for whom I long!" Badr al-Din said, "Son, have you too at your tender age suffered the loss of one you love?" 'Ajib replied, "Yes uncle, my heart bleeds for the loss of one I love, and my grandfather and I have been roaming the land in search of him. Alas, how I long to be reunited with him!" Then he wept and Badr al-Din wept at the sight of his son's tears and at the thought of his own separation from his home and mother, in a distant land, and he recited the following verses:

> If ever we meet each other again,
> I will have much about which to complain,
> For no letter can cure the ailing heart,
> Nor can another voice a lover's pain.
> The critics censure my abundant tears,
> But tears are little for lovers to pay.
> When will the Good Lord bring me back my love
> And let my care and sorrow go away?
> If we meet then, I will to you complain,
> For none but I myself can voice such pain.

The eunuch felt pity for Badr al-Din, and after they ate together, he took 'Ajib and departed. But when they left the shop, Badr al-Din felt as if his soul had left his body and had gone with them. He could not bear to be without them even for a single moment; so he closed his shop and followed them.

*But morning overtook Shahrazad, and she lapsed into silence.*
*Then Dinarzad said, "Sister, what a strange and entertaining story!"*
*Shahrazad replied, "What is this compared with what I shall tell*
*you tomorrow night if I stay alive!"*

THE NINETY-SECOND NIGHT

*The following night Shahrazad said:*

I heard, O happy King, that Ja'far said to the caliph:

Badr al-Din closed his shop and followed his son, without knowing that he was his son. He walked until he caught up with them
before they reached the city gate and kept following them. When
the eunuch looked behind and saw him, he said, "Damn it, what
do you want?" Badr al-Din replied, "Noble lord, when you departed,
I felt that my soul had left me and gone with you; besides, as I
have some business outside the Victory Gate, I thought that I would
come out to finish it and return." The eunuch was angry and said
to 'Ajib, "This is what I feared, and this is what you have done to
me. When one is blind, one does not see ahead. Because we entered
this fellow's shop and ate an unfortunate mouthful, he takes liberties with us and follows us from place to place." 'Ajib turned around
and, seeing the cook following him, reddened with anger and said
to the eunuch, "Let him walk like any Muslim, but if he turns in
the same direction when we come outside the city and turns toward
our tents, we will know that he is following us." Then he bowed
his head and walked on, with the eunuch behind him.

Badr al-Din followed them until they came to the Plain of Pebbles
and drew near their tents, and when 'Ajib turned around and saw
Badr al-Din still following him, he flushed and turned pale, angry
and afraid that his grandfather might find out that he had gone
into a cookshop and that he had been followed by one of the cooks;
and when 'Ajib saw Badr al-Din's eyes fixed on him, for he was
like a body without a soul, he thought that they were the eyes of
a treacherous or a lewd fellow, and his rage mounted. He bent to
the ground, picked up a granite stone weighing a pound, and threw
it at his father. It struck him on the forehead, cutting it open from
eyebrow to eyebrow, and he fell down in a swoon, with his blood
streaming down over his face, while 'Ajib and the eunuch headed
to their tents. When Badr al-Din came to himself, he wiped away
the blood and, taking off his turban, bandaged his wound with it,

blaming himself and saying, "I wronged the boy in closing my shop and following him, making him think that I was some treacherous or lewd fellow." Then he returned to his shop, where every now and then he would feel a bit of nostalgia for his mother in Basra, weep for her, and recite the following verses:

> If you ask fair play of fate, you wrong it,
> For blameless fate is not meant to be fair.
> Take what may please you and be not concerned,
> For in this life, one day is troubled, one day fair.

*But morning overtook Shahrazad, and she lapsed into silence. Then Dinarzad said, "Sister, what a strange and entertaining story!" Shahrazad replied, "What is this compared with what I shall tell you tomorrow night if the king spares me and I stay alive!"*

### THE NINETY-THIRD NIGHT

*The following night Shahrazad said:*

I heard, O happy King, that Ja'far said to the caliph:

Badr al-Din returned to his shop and resumed selling his food. Meanwhile the vizier, his uncle, stayed in Damascus for three days and departed for Homs, and after he arrived there and finished his search, he departed for Hama, where he spent the night. Again, after he finished his search, he departed, pressing on until he reached Aleppo,[9] where he stayed for two days. Then going through Dyarbakir, Mardin, Sinjar, and Mosul,[1] he fared on until he reached Basra. When he arrived, he went up to meet the king, who received him with honor and esteem and asked the reason for his coming. Shams al-Din related to him his story and told him that his vizier, Nur al-Din Ali of Egypt, was his brother. The king commended Nur al-Din's soul to the mercy of God and said, "My lord, he lived here for fifteen years; then he died, leaving a son, who stayed here only one month after his father's death and disappeared without any trace or news. But his mother, who was the daughter of my old vizier, is still with us." Shams al-Din asked the king for per-

---

9. Homs, Hama, and Aleppo: then and now cities in Syria.
1. Then and now cities in northern Iraq. Dyarbakir and Mardin: then and now cities in eastern Turkey.

mission to visit her and meet with her, and the king gave him permission.

He went to his brother Nur al-Din's house and looked around and kissed the threshold. And he thought of his brother Nur al-Din and how he had died in a foreign land, and he recited the following verses:

> I wander through the halls where Leyla lived,
> And in my sorrow kiss the stony walls.
> 'Tis not for the stones that I burn with love
> But for the dear one who dwelt in the halls.

Then he entered the main gate and found himself in a spacious courtyard, at the end of which stood an arched door vaulted over with granite inlaid with multicolored marble. He walked around the house and, casting his eyes on the walls, saw his brother Nur al-Din's name inscribed in letters of gold and Iraqi lapis lazuli.[2] He went up to the inscription and kissed it, and, thinking of his brother and his loss, he wept and repeated the following verses:

> I ask for news of you the rising sun
> And of the lightning's flash of you inquire
> And in the throes of passion pass my night,
> Without complaining of love's hellish fire.
> O my love, if our parting longer lasts
> My pining heart with pain will waste away,
> But if you bless my sad eyes with your sight,
> The day we meet will be a blessed day.
> Think not that I have found another love;
> There is no room for others in my heart.
> Pity a tortured lover, sick with love,
> Whose heart by parting has been torn apart.
> If fate should bless my sad eyes with your sight,
> I would that day offer my thanks to fate.
> May God defeat all those who wish us ill
> And thwart those who slander to separate.

Then he walked in and stopped at the door of the hall.

In the intervening years, his brother's widow, the mother of Badr al-Din Hasan of Basra, had, from the day of her son's disappearance, given herself up to weeping and lamentation, day and night, and after a long time went by, she made a tomb for her son in the middle of the hall and continued to weep there, day and night. When her brother-in-law reached the hall and stood at the door, he saw her draping the tomb with her flowing hair and heard her

2. Semiprecious stone of a bright blue color.

invoking her son Badr al-Din Hasan, weeping, and repeating these
verses:

> O tomb, O tomb, has he his beauties lost,
> Or have you lost yourself that radiant look?
> O tomb, neither a garden nor a star,
> The sun and moon at once how can you host?

Shams al-Din entered and, after greeting her, informed her that
he was her brother-in-law and told her what had happened.

*But morning overtook Shahrazad, and she lapsed into silence.
Then Dinarzad said, "What a strange and entertaining story!"
Shahrazad said, "What is this compared with what I shall tell you
tomorrow night if I am alive!"*

### THE NINETY-FOURTH NIGHT

*The following night, Shahrazad said:*

I heard, O happy King, that Ja'far said to the caliph:

Shams al-Din told her what had happened and how Badr al-Din
had spent a night at his house, ten years ago, but had disappeared
in the morning, how on that night the young man had gone in to
his daughter, taken her virginity, and made her pregnant, and how
when her time came, she gave birth to a boy, concluding, "This
boy with me here is the son of your son." When Badr al-Din's mother
heard this news of her son, that he was still alive, she looked at
her brother-in-law and threw herself at his feet, wept bitterly, and
recited the following verses:

> How good is he who tells me they have come,
> For he brings me the best of news to know!
> Were he content with worn-out robes, a heart,
> At parting torn, I would on him bestow.

Then she rose, embraced 'Ajib, pressing him to her heart, kissed
him and was kissed by him, and wept. But the vizier said to her,
"This is no time for weeping. Get yourself ready and come with
us to the land of Egypt, and we will perhaps be reunited with your
son, my nephew. This story should be written down!" She rose at
once and prepared herself for the journey, while the vizier went
to take his leave of the king, who provided him for the journey,
sending with him gifts to the king of Egypt, and bade him good-bye.

Shams al-Din set out of Basra on his journey homeward, and he fared on until he reached Aleppo, where he stayed for three days. Then he resumed his journey until he came to Damascus and halted, pitching his tents in the same place and saying to his men, "We shall stay here for two or three days to buy some fabrics, as well as other presents for the king." Then he went on his business. Meanwhile 'Ajib came out and said to the eunuch, "Tutor, let us go into the city to enjoy the sights and see what has become of the cook whose food we ate and whose head I cut, for he was kind to us, but we treated him badly." The eunuch replied, "Very well, let us." Then they left the tents, as the blood tie drew 'Ajib to his father, and walked until they entered the city through the Heavenly Gate. They spent the time at the Umayyad Mosque[3] till close to the time of the afternoon prayer; then they walked through the Grand Market[4] and continued walking until they came to the shop of Badr al-Din Hasan and found him standing there. He had prepared a pomegranate-seed dish, preserved in almonds and sweet julep and flavored with cardamom and rosewater, and the food was ready to serve. When 'Ajib looked at him and saw him marked from eyebrow to eyebrow with the dark scar he had given him with the blow, he felt tenderness for him and was overcome with pity. He said to his father, "Peace be with you! You have been on my mind." When Badr al-Din looked at him, his stomach began to flutter and his heart began to throb, as the blood hearkened to the blood. He bowed his head and tried to reply, but his tongue could not find the words. Then still overwhelmed, he raised his head, looked at his son sadly and imploringly, and recited the following verses:

> I longed to see the one I love, and when
> I did, I stood before him dumb and blind.
> I bowed my head in reverence and awe
> But failed to hide the love that seethed behind.
> My heart was full of troubles and concerns,
> But not a single word bespoke my mind.

Then he said to 'Ajib, "Perhaps you and the noble gentleman will enter my shop and eat my food to heal my broken heart, for by God, I cannot look at you without a throbbing in my heart. When I followed you, the other time, I was beside myself." 'Ajib replied . . .

*But morning overtook Shahrazad, and she lapsed into silence. Then Dinarzad said, "Sister, what a strange and entertaining story!"*

---

3. Then and now one of the great mosques of the Muslim world, built between A.D. 705 and 714.
4. The famous market of Damascus whose main street leads to the Umayyad Mosque.

*Shahrazad replied, "What is this compared with what I shall tell you tomorrow night if the king spares me and lets me live!"*

## THE NINETY-FIFTH NIGHT

*The following night Shahrazad said:*

I heard, O happy King, that Ja'far said to the caliph:

Badr al-Din said to his son, "When I followed you, I was beside myself." 'Ajib replied, "You must be very fond of us. You gave us a mouthful of food and, assuming that we owed you something, you tried to dishonor us. This time we will not eat anything unless you swear that you will not hold us under any obligation, follow us, or make any claim on us. Else we will not visit you again. We are staying here for about a week, so that my grandfather may buy presents for the king of Egypt." Badr al-Din said, "Very well, you may do as you please." 'Ajib and the eunuch entered the shop, and Badr al-Din ladled from the top of the pot a bowlful of food and placed it before them. 'Ajib said to him, "Sit down and eat with us," and Badr al-Din was glad and sat down and ate with his son, with his eyes fixed on him, for his whole being yearned for him. 'Ajib said, "Ha, ha, haven't I told you that you are an overbearing lover? Stop staring at my face!" Badr al-Din sighed and recited the following verses:

> Passion for you lies deeply in the heart,
> A secret sealed in darkness, seen by none.
> O you whose beauty shames the shining moon,
> Whose ample grace rivals the rising sun,
> Your radiant face frustrates the burning heart
> And with hopelessness afflicts love's desire.
> Your mouth is nectar, but I die of thirst;
> Your face is Heaven, but I burn in fire.

They ate together, and Badr al-Din kept putting morsels, now in 'Ajib's mouth, now in the eunuch's, until they were satisfied. They rose up, and Badr al-Din poured water on their hands and, loosening a towel from his waist, gave it to them to wipe their hands with, and sprinkled them with rosewater from a casting bottle. Then he ran out of the shop and rushed back with an earthenware pitcher containing a sweet drink, flavored with rosewater and cooled with snow. He set it before them, saying, "Complete your kindness to me." 'Ajib took the pitcher and drank and passed it to the eunuch, and they kept passing it around until they had had enough and their stomachs felt too full, for they had eaten much more than usual. Then they thanked him and, bidding him good-bye, hurried through the city until they came out through the East Gate and hastened to their tents.

'Ajib went to see his grandmother, Badr al-Din's mother, and she kissed him and, thinking of her son Badr al-Din and his days with her, sighed and wept, until her veil was wet, and recited the following verses:

> Had I not thought that we would meet again,
> I would have after you of life despaired.
> I swear my heart holds nothing but your love,
> By God who knows and has my secret shared.

Then she asked 'Ajib, "Son, where have you been?" and set food before him, and as it had been foreordained, they too had cooked a pomegranate-seed dish, except that this one had less sugar. She gave him a bowlful, together with some bread, and said to the eunuch, "Eat with him." Saying to himself, "By God, I can't even smell the bread," he sat down to eat.

*But morning overtook Shahrazad, and she lapsed into silence. Then Dinarzad said, "Sister, what a strange and entertaining story!" Shahrazad replied, "What is this compared with what I shall tell you tomorrow night if the king spares me and I stay alive!"*

THE NINETY-SIXTH NIGHT

*The following night Shahrazad said:*

It is related, O King, that Ja'far said to the caliph:

The eunuch sat down, though his belly was full with what he had already eaten and drunk. 'Ajib dipped a piece of bread in the pomegranate dish and took a bite but found the food insipid, for he too was full. He said, "Bah, what is this awful stuff?" His grandmother was astonished and said, "Son, do you find fault with my food? I cooked it myself, and no cook can compare with me, except my son Badr al-Din Hasan." 'Ajib replied, "Grandmother, we have just now found in the city a cook who had prepared a pomegranate-seed dish whose aroma delights the heart and whose flavor stimulates the appetite. Your food is nothing by comparison." When his grand-mother heard his words, she was angry and, turning to the eunuch, said, "Damn you, you are corrupting my son by taking him into the city and letting him eat in cookshops." When the eunuch heard her words, he was frightened and said, "No, by God, my lady, we did not eat anything; we only saw the cookshop in passing." But 'Ajib said, "By God, grandmother, we did enter the shop, and both this time and the other time we ate a pomegranate-seed dish that was better than yours." In her anger, she went and informed her brother-in-law, provoking him against the eunuch, at whom the grandfather yelled, saying, "Damn you, where did you take my grandson?" Afraid of being put to death, the eunuch denied every-thing, but 'Ajib told on him, saying, "Yes, by God, grandfather, we went into the cookshop and ate until the food came out of our nostrils, and the cook gave us an iced sweet drink." The vizier became angrier and said, "You ill-fated slave, did you take my grandson into a cookshop?" The eunuch continued to deny it until the vizier said to him, "My grandson says that the two of you ate until you were full. If you are telling the truth, then eat this bowlful of pomegranate seeds, which is before you." The eunuch said, "Very well," and took a morsel from the bowl and ate it, but unable to swallow a second, he spat it out and threw it away and, drawing away from the food, said, "By God, my lord, I am full ever since yesterday."

By this the vizier realized the truth and ordered his servants to throw the eunuch down and beat him. Smarting under the blows, the eunuch cried for mercy and said, "My lord, we did enter a cookshop and we did eat a pomegranate-seed dish that was indeed better than this one." His words angered Badr al-Din's mother, who said, "For God's sake, son, and may God reunite me with my own son, you must go and bring me back a bowl of pomegranate dish from that cook, so that your master may judge which is the better and tastier of the two, his or mine." The eunuch replied, "Indeed I will." Then she gave him a bowl and half a dinar, and he went out running until he came to the cookshop and said to Badr al-Din, "Excellent cook, I have made a wager about your cooking in my master's household. Give me half a dinar's worth of your pome-granate dish and it better be good, for I have had a bellyful of beating for entering your shop. Don't let me taste more beating with your food." Badr al-Din laughed and said, "By God, noble lord, no one can cook this dish as well but myself and my mother, and she is far away." Then he ladled out the food, choosing the best parts, covered the bowl, and gave it to the eunuch, who hastened back with it. Badr al-Din's mother took it, and when she tasted the food and noticed its excellent flavor, she knew who had cooked it, shrieked, and fell down in a swoon. The vizier was astonished and sprinkled water on her, and when she came to herself, she said, "If my son Badr al-Din is still in this world, none has cooked this dish but he."

*But morning overtook Shahrazad, and she lapsed into silence. Then Dinarzad said, "Sister, what a strange and entertaining story!" Shahrazad replied, "What is this compared with what I shall tell you tomorrow night if the king spares me and lets me live!"*

## THE NINETY-SEVENTH NIGHT

*The following night Shahrazad said:*

It is related, O King, that Ja'far said to the caliph:

Badr al-Din's mother said, "None has cooked this dish but my son Badr al-Din, for none knows how to cook it as well as he." When the vizier heard her words, he rejoiced and felt happy and said, "Alas for you, my nephew! I wonder whether God will ever reunite us with you!" Then he rose at once and called out to his followers, attendants, slaves, cameldrivers, and porters, about fifty in all, saying, "Take sticks, clubs, and the like and go to the cook's shop and demolish it by breaking everything inside, even the pots and dishes. Then tie him with his turban and, saying 'Are you the one who has cooked this awful pomegranate-seed dish,' bring him here. But let none of you beat him or do him any harm; just bind him and bring him here by force. In the meantime I will go to the vizier's palace and come back." They replied, "Very well."

Then the vizier mounted his horse, rode to the palace, and met with the viceroy of Damascus, showing him the king's edicts. The viceroy kissed them and, after reading them, asked, "Who is your adversary?" The vizier replied, "He is a cook." The viceroy ordered a chamberlain to go to the cookshop, and the chamberlain went with four captains, four palace guards, and six soldiers, leading the way. When they came to the cookshop, they found it in ruins and saw everything in it broken.

For while the vizier was at the palace, his servants rose and, taking sticks, tent poles, clubs, and swords, flew in a hurry until they reached the cookshop and, without speaking to Badr al-Din, fell with their weapons on his pots and utensils, broke his shelves, bowls, dishes, and trays, and destroyed his stoves. When Badr al-Din asked them, "O good people, what is the matter?" they replied by asking him, "Are you the one who cooked the pomegranate dish that the eunuch bought?" He replied, "Yes, I am the one who cooked it, and no one can cook anything like it." They yelled at him, abused him, and continued to demolish the shop until a crowd of people assembled and, seeing about fifty or sixty men demolishing the shop, said, "There must be a grave cause behind this!" Badr al-Din cried out, saying, "O fellow Muslims, what is my crime in cooking this food that you should treat me like this, breaking my dishes and ruining my shop?" They said, "Aren't you the one who cooked the pomegranate dish?" He replied, "Yes, indeed! What is wrong with it that you should do this to me?" But they kept yelling at him, scolding him, and cursing him. Then they surrounded him, took off his turban and, tying him with it, dragged him by force out of the shop, while he screamed, cried, and called for help.

*But morning overtook Shahrazad, and she lapsed into silence. Then Dinarzad said, "Sister, what a strange and entertaining story!" Shahrazad replied, "What is this compared with what I shall tell you tomorrow night if the king spares me and lets me live!"*

### The Ninety-Eighth Night

*The following night Shahrazad said:*

It is related, O King, that Ja'far said to the caliph:

Badr al-Din kept crying, calling for help, and asking, "What fault did you find with the pomegranate dish?" and they kept asking, "Aren't you the one who cooked the pomegranate dish?" while he kept answering, "Yes, indeed! But what is wrong with it that I should suffer like this?" As they drew close to the tents, the chamberlain, with his captains and other men, caught up with them. He pushed the vizier's servants aside to look at Badr al-Din and, hitting him on the shoulders with his stick, asked him, "You, are you the one who cooked the pomegranate seeds?" Badr al-Din cried with pain from the blow and replied, "Yes, my lord, but I ask you, in the name of God, what is supposed to be wrong with it?" But the chamberlain scolded him and cursed him, saying to his men, "Drag away this dog who has cooked the pomegranate dish." Badr al-Din felt miserable, wept, and said to himself, "What did they find wrong

with the pomegranate dish that they should abuse me to this extent?"
and he felt frustrated for not knowing what his fault was. The men
kept dragging him until they reached the tents, where they waited
until the vizier, having gotten the viceroy's permission to depart
and having bidden him good-bye, returned to the tents.

As soon as he dismounted, he asked, "Where is the cook?" and
they brought Badr al-Din before him. When Badr al-Din saw his
uncle the vizier Shams al-Din, he wept and said, "My lord, what
is my offense against you?" Shams al-Din replied, "Damn you, aren't
you the one who cooked the pomegranate dish?" With a cry of exasperation, Badr al-Din replied, "Yes my lord, and what a misfortune! Does my crime warrant cutting off my head?" Shams al-Din
replied, "That misfortune would be the least punishment." Badr al-
Din said, "My lord, will you not tell me my crime and what is wrong
with the pomegranate dish?" Shams al-Din replied, "Yes, presently,"
and he called out to his servants, shouting, "Pack up, and let us
go." The servants undid the tents at once and made the camels kneel
for loading. Then they put Badr al-Din in a chest, which they locked
and placed on a camel. Then they departed and journeyed until
nightfall, when they stopped to eat. Then they took Badr al-Din
out of the chest, fed him, and locked him up again.

They kept traveling in this way until they reached Cairo and dismounted outside the city. Then the vizier ordered the servants to
take Badr al-Din out of the chest, and they did so and brought him
before the vizier, who sent for wood and a carpenter and said to
him, "Make a wooden, crosslike figure." Badr al-Din asked, "What
will you do with it?" The vizier replied, "I will crucify you by nailing
you on it, and then I will parade you throughout the city, because
the pomegranate dish you cooked lacked pepper and tasted awful."
Badr al-Din said, "Haven't you done enough, and all because the
pomegranate dish lacked pepper?"

*But morning overtook Shahrazad, and she lapsed into silence.
Then Dinarzad said to her sister, "What a strange and entertain-
ing story!" Shahrazad replied, "What is this compared with what
I shall tell you tomorrow night if the king spares me and lets me live!"*

THE NINETY-NINTH NIGHT

*The following night Shahrazad said:*

It is related, O King, that Ja'far said to the caliph:

Badr al-Din said, "Because the pomegranate dish lacked pepper, you have beaten me, smashed my dishes, and ruined my shop, all because the pomegranate dish lacked pepper! Isn't it enough, O Muslims, that you have tied me and locked me up in this chest, day and night, fed me only one meal a day, and inflicted on me all kinds of torture, because the pomegranate dish lacked pepper? Isn't it enough, O Muslims, to have shackled my feet that you should now make a crosslike figure to nail me on, because I have cooked a pomegranate dish that lacked pepper?" Then Badr al-Din pondered in bewilderment and asked, "All right, suppose I did cook the dish without pepper, what should my punishment be?" The vizier replied, "To be crucified." Badr al-Din said, "Alas, are you going to crucify me because the pomegranate dish lacked pepper?" and he appealed for help, wept, and said, "None has been crushed as I have been, and none has suffered what I have suffered. I have been beaten and tortured, my shop has been ruined and plundered, and I am going to be crucified, all because I cooked a pomegranate dish that lacked pepper! May God curse the pomegranate dish and its very existence!" and as his tears flowed, he concluded, "I wish that I had died before this calamity."

When they brought the nails, he cried, lamented, and mourned over his crucifixion. But as night was falling and it was getting dark, the vizier took Badr al-Din, pushed him into the chest, and locked it, saying, "Wait till tomorrow morning, for tonight we have no time left to nail you." Badr al-Din sat inside the chest, crying and saying to himself, "There is no power and no strength, save in God, the Almighty, the Magnificent. Why do I have to be crucified and die? I have not killed anyone or committed any crime; nor have I cursed or blasphemed. My only offense is that I am supposed to have cooked a pomegranate dish that lacked pepper; that is all."

In the meantime the vizier placed the chest on a camel and followed it into the city, after the markets closed, until he came to his house. Later at night the servants arrived with the loaded camels and, making them kneel, carried the equipment and baggage inside. The first thing the vizier did was to say to his daughter Sit al-Husn, "Daughter, praised be God who has reunited you with your cousin and husband. Rise this instant and let the servants prepare the house and arrange the furniture as it was on your wedding night, twelve years ago." The servants replied, "Very well." Then the vizier called for candles, and when they lighted the candles and lanterns and brought him the sheet of paper on which he had written the exact description of the room on the wedding night, he began to read it out to them until everything was arranged as it had been on that night. They put everything in its place, lighting the candles as they

had been lighted, and placing the turban on the chair and the
trousers and the purse with the thousand dinars under the mattress,
as Badr al-Din had placed them on that night. Then the vizier came
to the hallway and said to his daughter, "Undress and go to bed,
as you did the night he came in to you, and when he comes in,
this time, say to him, 'My lord, you have stayed too long in the
privy.' Then let him lie beside you and engage him in conversation
till the morning, when we will tell him the whole extraordinary
story."

*But morning overtook Shahrazad, and she lapsed into silence.
Then Dinarzad said, "Sister, what a strange and entertaining story!"
Shahrazad replied, "What is this compared with what I shall tell
you tomorrow night if the king spares me and lets me live!"*

## THE ONE HUNDREDTH NIGHT

*The following night Shahrazad said:*

It is related, O King, that Ja'far said to the caliph:

I heard, O Commander of the Faithful, that the vizier went to
Badr al-Din, untied him, and, taking off all his clothes, save for
a shirt, led him slowly until he came to the door of the room from
which the bride had come out to be unveiled before him and in
which he had slept with her and taken her virginity. When he looked
at the room, he recognized it, and when he saw the bed, the net,
and the chair, he was amazed and bewildered. Advancing one foot
and drawing the other back, he rubbed his eyes and said to himself
in his confusion, "Glory be to the Almighty God! Am I awake or
asleep?" Sit al-Husn lifted the net and said to him "Ah, my lord,
will you not come in? You have stayed too long in the privy; come
back to bed!" When Badr al-Din heard her words and saw her face,
he smiled in amazement and said, "By God, you are right; I did
stay too long in the privy!" But as he entered the room, he recalled
the events of the last ten years, and as he kept looking at the room
and recalling those events, he was confounded and felt lost, not
knowing what to make of this. He looked at the turban, the robe,
and the dagger on the chair, went to the bed and felt the trousers
and the purse under the mattress, and finally burst out laughing,
and said, "By God, this is a good one; by God, this is a good one!"
Sit al-Husn asked, "My lord, why do you stare at the room and

laugh for no reason?" When he heard her words, he laughed again and asked, "How long have I been absent from you?" She replied, "Ah, may the Compassionate and Merciful God preserve you! Ah, haven't you gone out but a while ago to relieve yourself and come back? Have you lost your wits?"

Badr al-Din laughed and said, "By God, lady, you are right. I left you and, forgetting myself, fell asleep in the privy. I recall as if I dreamt that I lived in Damascus for ten years, working as a cook, and that one day a young boy and his servant visited my shop." Then, touching his forehead and feeling the scar from the blow, he cried out, "No, by God, it must have been true, for the boy hit me with a stone and cut my forehead open. By God, my friend, it would seem that it really happened." Then he reflected for a while and said, "By God, my lady, it seems to me that when I embraced you and we fell asleep, a little while ago, I dreamt that I went to Damascus without turban or trousers and worked there as a cook." Then he reflected again and said, "Yes, by God, my lady, it seems as if I dreamt that I cooked a pomegranate dish that lacked pepper. Yes, by God, my lady, I must have slept in the privy and seen all this in a dream, except that, by God, my lady, it was a long dream." Sit al-Husn said, "For God's sake, my lord, tell me what else you dreamed?" Badr al-Din replied, "My lady, had I not awakened, they would have crucified me." She asked, "For what reason?" He replied, "Because I cooked a pomegranate dish that lacked pepper. It seemed as if they smashed my dishes, ruined my shop, tied me and shackled me, and put me in a chest. Then they brought a carpenter to make a wooden crosslike figure to nail me on. It all happened because the pomegranate dish lacked pepper. Thank God that all of this happened to me in a dream and not in reality." Sit al-Husn laughed and pressed him to her bosom, and he returned her embrace. But he reflected again and said, "My lady, what happened to me must indeed have been real, but there is no power and no strength, save in God, the Almighty, the Magnificent. By God, what a strange story!"

*But morning overtook Shahrazad, and she lapsed into silence. Then Dinarzad said, "Sister, what a strange and entertaining story!" Shahrazad replied, "What is this compared with what I shall tell you tomorrow night if the king spares me and lets me live!"*

## The One Hundred and First Night

*The following night Shahrazad said:*

It is related, O King, that Ja'far said to the caliph:

That night Badr al-Din lay down in a state of confusion, now
saying, "I was dreaming," now, "I was awake." He kept looking in
astonishment at the room, the objects, and the bride, saying to
himself, "By God, till now I have not even completed one night
with her." Then he would reflect again and say, "It must have been
real," until it was morning and his uncle came in, bidding him good
morning. When Badr al-Din saw him, he recognized him and was
utterly confused. He said, "In fact, aren't you the one who gave
the orders to beat, tie, shackle, and crucify me because of the pomegranate dish?" The vizier replied, "Son, the truth is out, for what
was hidden has been revealed. You are my true nephew, and I did
all this only to be sure that you were indeed the one who had consummated the marriage with my daughter that night. You recognized your turban, your clothes, and your gold purse, as well as
the scroll written by my brother and hidden in the lining of your
turban. Had the man we brought here been other than you, he
would not have recognized these objects." Then he recited the following verses:

> Our fate is fickle, for such is our state
> That one day may depress, one day elate.

Then the vizier called for Badr al-Din's mother, and when she saw
her son, she threw herself at him, wept bitterly, and recited the
following verses:

> When we meet, we will complain
> Of our afflictions, that day,
> For the feelings of the heart
> No messenger can convey,
> Nor is the voicing of grief
> Keeping the feelings at bay.
> No messenger ever knows
> How to say what I can say.

Then she told him how she had endured after his departure, and
he too told her how he had suffered, and they thanked God for their
reunion. The following day the vizier went to the king and ac-

quainted him with the situation, and the king was exceedingly amazed and ordered that the story be recorded. Thereafter, the vizier and his nephew and daughter lived the best of lives in prosperity and ease, eating and drinking and enjoying themselves to the end of their days.

Ja'far concluded: This, O Commander of the Faithful, is what happened to the vizier of Basra and the vizier of Egypt." The caliph said, "By God, Ja'far, this is the wonder of wonders," and ordered that the story be recorded. Then he freed the slave and gave the young man one of his choice concubines, settled on him a sufficient income, and made him one of his companions to the end of his days.

THE ONE HUNDRED AND SECOND NIGHT

*The following night Shahrazad said:*

# [THE STORY OF THE HUNCHBACK]

It is related, O King, that there lived once in China a tailor who had a pretty, compatible, and loyal wife. It happened one day that they went out for a stroll to enjoy the sights at a place of entertainment, where they spent the whole day in diversions and fun, and when they returned home at the end of the day, they met on the way a jolly hunchback. He was smartly dressed in a folded inner robe and an open outer robe, with gathered sleeves and an embroidered collarband, in the Egyptian style, and sporting a scarf and a tall green hat, with knots of yellow silk stuffed with ambergris.[5] The hunchback was short, like him of whom the poet 'Antar[6] said:

> Lovely the hunchback who can hide his hump,
> Like a pearl hidden in an oyster shell,
> A man who looks like a castor oil branch,
> From which dangles a rotten citric lump.

He was busy playing on the tambourine, singing, and improvising all kinds of funny gestures. When they drew near and looked at

---

5. Waxy substance secreted by the intestinal tract of the sperm whale, often found floating in the sea, and used in the manufacture of perfume.
6. Pre-Islamic hero, and author of one the Arabic Golden Odes.

him, they saw that he was drunk, reeking of wine. Then he placed the tambourine under his arm and began to beat time by clapping his hands, as he sang the following verses:

> Go early to the darling in yon jug;
> Bring her to me,
> And fete her as you fete a pretty girl,
> With joy and glee,
> And make her as pure as a virgin bride,
> Unveiled to please,
> That I may honor my friend with a cup
> Of wine from Greece.
> If you, my friend, care for the best in life,
> Life can repay,
> Then at this moment fill my empty cup,
> Without delay.
> Don't you, my tantalizer, on the plain
> The gardens see?

*But morning overtook Shahrazad, and she lapsed into silence. Then Dinarzad said to her sister, "What a strange and entertaining story!" Shahrazad replied, "What is this compared with what I shall tell you tomorrow night if the king spares me and lets me live!"*

### THE ONE HUNDRED AND THIRD NIGHT

*The following night Shahrazad said:*

It is related, O King, that when the tailor and his wife saw the hunchback in this condition, drunk and reeking of wine, now singing, now beating the tambourine, they were delighted with him and invited him home to sup and drink with them that night. He accepted gladly and walked with them to their home.

Then the tailor went to the market — it was already dark — and bought bread, fried fish, radishes, lemons, and a bowl of honey, as well as a candle to give them light during their carousing. When he returned, he set the bread and fish before the hunchback, and the wife joined them for supper. The tailor and his wife were pleased to have the hunchback with them, saying to each other, "We will spend the night carousing, bantering, and amusing ourselves with this hunchback." They ate until they were satisfied. Then the tailor took a piece of fish and, cramming it in the hunchback's mouth, held it shut and said laughing, "By God, you must swallow the whole piece." The hunchback, unable to breathe, could not wait to chew, and he hastened to swallow the piece, which happened to have a large bone, which stuck in his throat and choked him. When the tailor saw the hunchback's eyes rolled up, he raised his hand and boxed him on the chest, and the hunchback's soul left his body and he slumped lifeless. The tailor and his wife were stunned and, trembling, said, "There is no power and no strength, save in God, the Almighty, the Magnificent. How soon was his appointed hour!" The wife said to her husband the tailor, "Why do you sit still and do nothing? Haven't you heard the poet say:

> How can you sit and let the fire rage on?
> Such idleness brings ruin and destruction."

The tailor asked, "What shall I do?" and she replied, "Rise, carry him in your arms, cover him with a silk shawl, and follow me. If anybody sees us in the dark, we shall say, 'This is our sick boy who took ill a short while ago, and since the doctor could not come to see him, we are taking him there.' If we do that . . ."

*But morning overtook Shahrazad, and she lapsed into silence. Then Dinarzad said to her sister, "What a strange and amusing story!" Shahrazad replied, "What is this compared with what I shall tell you tomorrow night if I stay alive!"*

### THE ONE HUNDRED AND FOURTH NIGHT

*The following night Shahrazad said:*

It is related, O King, that the tailor carried the hunchback in his arms, covered him with a silk shawl, and followed his wife, who led the way, wailing and saying, "O my boy, may you recover from your illness. Where has this smallpox been lying in wait for us?" so that whoever saw them said, "These two have a child stricken with the smallpox," until someone directed them to the house of a Jewish physician. When the wife knocked at the door, a maid came down, and when she opened the door, she saw a man carrying a sick child. The wife handed her a quarter-dinar and said, "Miss, give this to your master, and let him come down to see my child, who is gravely ill." As soon as the maid went upstairs, the wife went in, saying to her husband, "Let us leave the hunchback here and run." The tailor propped up the hunchback, leaving him standing in the middle of the Jew's staircase, and went away with his wife.

Meanwhile the maid went to the Jew and said to him, "Master, there are people downstairs, carrying a sick child, and they have sent you this quarter-dinar to go down to see him and prescribe for him." When the Jew saw the quarter-dinar as a fee for merely going downstairs, he was pleased and in his joy rose hastily in the dark, saying to the maid, "Bring me light," and descended hurriedly in the dark. But hardly had he taken a step when he stumbled on the hunchback, who fell and rolled to the bottom of the stairs. The Jew was startled and shouted to the maid, "Hurry with the light." When she brought it, he went down and, finding the hunchback dead, said, "O Esdras, O Moses, O Aaron, O Joshua son of Nun! It seems that I have stumbled against this sick fellow, and he has fallen downstairs and died. By the hoof of Esdras's ass, how shall I get this dead body out of my house?" Then he carried the body upstairs, and when he told his wife about it, she said to him, "Why do you sit still? If the day breaks and he is still here, we will both lose our lives. You are naïve and careless." Then she recited the following verses:

> You thought well of the days, when they were good,
> Oblivious to the ills life brings to one.
> You were deluded by the peaceful nights,
> Yet in the peace of night does sorrow stun.

*But morning overtook Shahrazad, and she lapsed into silence. Then Dinarzad said, "Sister, what a strange and entertaining story!" Shahrazad replied, "What is this compared with what I shall tell you tomorrow night if the king spares me and lets me live!"*

THE ONE HUNDRED AND FIFTH NIGHT

*The following night Shahrazad said:*

I heard, O King, that the Jew's wife said to him, "Why do you sit still? Rise at once and let us carry the body to the roof and throw it into the house of our neighbor, the Muslim bachelor." It happened that the Jew's neighbor was the steward of the king's kitchen, who used to bring home a great deal of cooking butter, which, together with everything else he brought, was eaten by the cats and mice, which caused considerable loss. The Jew and his wife took the hunchback up to the roof, carried him little by little to the steward's house and, holding him by the hands and feet, lowered him until he reached the ground. Then they propped him up against the wall and went away.

No sooner had they descended from the roof than the steward, who had been at a recitation of the Quran, came home in the middle of the night, carrying a lighted candle. He opened the door, and when he entered his house, he found a man standing in the corner, under the ventilator, and said, "By God, this is a fine thing! My food has been stolen by none other than a man. You kept taking the meat and the fat sheep tails and scooping out the cooking butter, and I kept blaming the cats and dogs and mice. I have killed many cats and dogs and have sinned against them, while you have been coming down the windshaft to steal my provisions, but now, by God, I will avenge myself on you with my own hands." Then he took a heavy club and with one leap stood before the hunchback and gave him a heavy blow on the rib cage, and as the hunchback fell, he gave him another blow on the back. Then looking at his face and seeing that he was dead, he cried out, saying, "Alas! I have killed him. There is no power and no strength, save in God, the Almighty, the Magnificent." Then he turned pale with fear for himself, saying, "May God curse the cooking butter and curse this night! To God we belong and to Him we return."

*But morning overtook Shahrazad, and she lapsed into silence. Then Dinarzad said to her sister, "What a strange and entertaining story!" Shahrazad replied, "What is this compared with what I shall tell you tomorrow night if the king spares me and lets me live!"*

THE ONE HUNDRED AND SIXTH NIGHT

*The following night Shahrazad said:*

It is related, O happy King, that when the steward saw that the man was a hunchback, he said, "O hunchback, O cursed man! Wasn't it enough for you to be a hunchback, but you had to turn thief too? What shall I do? O Protector, protect me!" Then as it was getting toward the end of the night, he carried the hunchback on his back and went out with him until he reached the entrance of the market, where he set him on his feet against a shop, at the corner of a dark alley, and went away.

Soon there came a prominent Christian tradesman, who had a workshop and was the king's broker. He was drunk, and in his drunkenness he had left home, heading for the bath, thinking that morning prayers were near. He came staggering along until he drew near the hunchback and squatted in front of him to urinate and, happening to look around, suddenly saw a man standing before him. It so happened that early that night, someone had snatched off the Christian's turban, so that when he saw the hunchback standing before him, he thought that he too was going to snatch off his turban. He clenched his fist and boxed the hunchback on the neck, knocking him down. Then crying out for the watchman, he fell in his drunkenness on the hunchback, pummeling him and choking him. When the watchman came up to the lamppost and saw a Christian kneeling on a Muslim and beating him, he asked, "What is the matter?" The Christian replied, "This man tried to snatch off my turban." The watchman said, "Get up from him," and when the Christian got up, the watchman drew close to the hunchback and, finding that he was dead, said, "By God, this is a fine thing, a Christian killing a Muslim!" Then he seized the Christian broker, bound him, and brought him in the night to the house of the chief of the police. The Christian was bewildered, wondering how he could have killed the fellow so quickly with one blow of the fist, as "drunkenness left him and reflection returned." Then he and the hunchback passed the night in the chief's house.

In the morning, the chief went up to the king and informed him that his Christian broker had killed a Muslim. The king ordered that the broker be hanged, and the chief went down and bade the executioner proclaim the sentence. Then the hangman set up a gallows, under which he made the Christian stand, put the rope around his neck and was about to hang him, when the steward of the king's kitchen made his way through the crowd and said to the executioner, "Stop! This man did not kill the fellow; I am the one who killed him." The chief asked, "What did you say?" The steward replied, "I am the one who killed him." Then he related to him his story, how he hit the hunchback with the club and how he carried him and propped him up in the market, adding, "Is it not enough for me to have killed a Muslim, without burdening my conscience with the death of a Christian too? On my own confession, hang no one but me."

*But morning overtook Shahrazad, and she lapsed into silence. Then Dinarzad said to her sister, "What a strange and entertaining story!" Shahrazad replied, "What is this compared with what I shall tell you tomorrow night if the king spares me and lets me live!"*

### THE ONE HUNDRED AND SEVENTH NIGHT

*The following night Shahrazad said:*

I heard, O happy King, that when the chief heard the steward's words, he said to the hangman, "Release the Christian, and hang this man, on the strength of his confession." The hangman, after releasing the Christian, made the steward stand under the gallows, put the rope around his neck, and was about to hang him, when the Jewish physician made his way through the crowd and cried out to the hangman, "Stop! This man did not kill the fellow; I am the one who killed him. Last night I was sitting at home after the markets closed, when a man and a woman knocked at the door. When the maid went down and opened the door, she found that they had a sick person with them. They gave the maid a quarter-dinar, and she brought it up to me and told me about them, but no sooner had she come up than they rushed in and placed the sick person at the top of the stairs. When I went down, I stumbled on him, and the two of us rolled to the bottom of the stairs, and he died instantly. No one was the cause of his death but I. Then my wife and I carried the dead hunchback to the roof and let him down, through the windshaft, into the house of this steward, which adjoins ours, and left him standing in the corner. When the steward came home, he found a man standing there and, thinking that he was a thief, hit him with a club, knocking him down flat on his face, and concluded that he had killed him, whereas in truth none killed him but I. Is it not enough for me to have involuntarily and unwillingly killed one Muslim, without burdening my conscience with the death of another Muslim? Don't hang him, for no one killed the hunchback but I."

*But morning overtook Shahrazad, and she lapsed into silence. Then Dinarzad said to her sister, "What a strange and entertaining story!" Shahrazad replied, "What is this compared with what I shall tell you tomorrow night if the king spares me and lets me live!"*

## THE ONE HUNDRED AND EIGHTH NIGHT

*The following night Shahrazad said:*

I heard, O happy King, that when the chief heard the Jew's words, he said to the hangman, "Release the steward and hang the Jew." The hangman seized the Jew and put the rope around his neck, when the tailor made his way through the crowd and said to the hangman, "Stop! This man did not kill him, and none killed him but I." Then turning to the chief, he said, "My lord, none killed the hunchback but I. Yesterday I went out to see the sights, and when I returned in the evening, I met the hunchback, who was drunk and singing and playing on the tambourine. I invited him home with me and then went out, bought fried fish for him, and brought it back. Then we sat to eat, and I took a piece of fish and crammed it down his throat, and he choked on a bone and died instantly. My wife and I were frightened, and we carried him to the Jew's house. We knocked at the door, and when the maid came down and opened the door, I said to her, 'Go up and tell your master that there are a man and a woman downstairs, with a sick person for him to see,' handing her a quarter-dinar to give to her master. As soon as she went up, I carried the hunchback to the top of the stairs, propped him up, and went down and ran with my wife. When the Jew came down, he stumbled against the hunchback and thought that he had killed him." Then the tailor turned to the Jew and asked, "Isn't this the truth?" The Jew replied, "Yes, this is the truth." Then turning back to the chief, the tailor said, "Release the Jew and hang me, since I am the one who killed the hunchback." When the chief heard the tailor's words, he marveled at the adventure of the hunchback and said, "There is a mystery behind this story, and it should be recorded in the books, even in letters of gold." Then he said to the hangman, "Release the Jew and hang the tailor on his own confession." The hangman released the Jew and placed the tailor under the gallows, saying to the chief, "I am tired of stringing up this man and releasing that, without any result." Then he put the rope around the tailor's neck and threw the other end over the pulley.

It happened that the hunchback was the favorite clown of the king of China, who could not bear to be without him even for the batting of an eye, so that when the hunchback got drunk and failed to make his appearance that night . . .

*But morning overtook Shahrazad, and she lapsed into silence. Then Dinarzad said, "Sister, what a strange and entertaining story!"*

*Shahrazad replied, "What is this compared with what I shall tell
you tomorrow night if the king spares me and lets me live!"*

THE ONE HUNDRED AND NINTH NIGHT

*The following night Shahrazad said:*

I heard, O happy King, that when the hunchback got drunk and
failed to make his appearance before the king that night, and when
the king waited for him in vain the next day until it was close to
noon, he at last inquired about him from one of those present, who
replied, "I heard, O King, that the chief of the police found a dead
hunchback and caught his murderer. But when he was about to
hang him, a second and a third man came forward, and each
claimed to be the murderer. They are still there, each telling the
chief how the hunchback died." When the king of China heard these
words, he called out to one of his chamberlains, saying, "Go down
and bring me everyone, the chief, the murdered man, and the
murderers." The chamberlain went down at once and arrived just
when the hangman had put the rope around the tailor's neck and
was about to hoist him up. He cried out to the hangman, "Stop!"
and, turning to the chief, relayed to him the king's order. The chief
took the tailor, the Jew, the steward, and the Christian, together
with the hunchback, carried on a litter, and brought them all before
the king. He kissed the ground before him and related to him their
adventures with the hunchback, from beginning to end. When the
king of China heard the story, he was very much amazed and moved
to mirth, and he ordered that the story be recorded, saying to those
around him, "Have you ever heard anything more amazing than
the adventure of the hunchback?" The Christian broker came forward and, kissing the ground before the king, said, "O King of the
age, with your leave, I will tell you a more amazing story that happened to myself, a story that will make even the stone weep." The
king replied, "Tell us your story." The Christian said:

# [The Christian Broker's Tale:
# The Young Man with the Severed Hand
# and the Girl]

O King, I came as a stranger to your country, bringing merchandise
with me, and was fated to stay here these many years. I was born

a Copt,[7] a native of Cairo. My father was a prominent broker, and when he died, I became a broker in his place and worked there for many years. One day, as I was sitting in the market of the fodder merchants in Cairo, a handsome and finely dressed young man, riding a tall ass, came up to me. He saluted me, and I rose in salute. Then he took out a handkerchief containing sesame and asked me, "How much is the measure worth?"

*But morning overtook Shahrazad, and she lapsed into silence. Then Dinarzad said, "Sister, what a strange and entertaining story!" Shahrazad replied, "What is this compared with what I shall tell you tomorrow night if the king spares me and lets me live!"*

THE ONE HUNDRED AND TENTH NIGHT

*The following night Shahrazad said:*

I heard, O happy King, that the Christian broker said to the king of China:

O King of the age, I replied to the young man, "It is worth a hundred dirhams." He said, "Take a measurer and some porters and come to the al-Jawli Caravansary,[8] by the Gate of Victory, where you will find me." I rose and went to find a buyer, making the rounds of the sesame merchants, confectioners, and fodder dealers, and got one hundred dirhams per measure. Then I took with me four teams of porters and went with them to the al-Jawli Caravansary, where I found the young man waiting for me. As soon as he saw me, he rose and led me to the storeroom, saying, "Let the measurer enter to measure, while the porters load the donkeys." The porters kept loading, one team coming and one team going, until they emptied the storeroom, carrying fifty measures in all, costing five thousand dirhams. Then the young man said to me, "Take ten dirhams per measure for your brokerage, and keep my share of four thousand and five hundred dirhams with you. When I finish selling the rest of my crop, I will come to you and take the money." I replied, "Very well," kissed his hand, and departed, surprised at his liberality.

For a month I sat waiting for him until he finally came and asked, "Where is the money?" I welcomed him and invited him to sit with

---

7. Egyptian Christian.
8. Inn with a large courtyard, where caravans could rest during the night.

me and have something to eat, but he refused and said, "Go and get the money, and in a little while I will come back to take it from you." Then he departed on assback, while I went and brought the money and sat waiting for him. But again he did not show up for a month, and I said to myself, "This is indeed a liberal young man. He has left four thousand and five hundred dirhams of his money with me, for two full months, without coming to take it." At last he came back, riding an ass, dressed in fine clothes, and looking as if he had just come from the bath.

*But morning overtook Shahrazad, and she lapsed into silence. Then Dinarzad said, "What a strange and entertaining story!" Shahrazad replied, "What is this compared with what I shall tell you tomorrow night if the king spares me and lets me live!"*

## THE ONE HUNDRED AND ELEVENTH NIGHT

*The following night Shahrazad said:*

I heard, O happy King, that the Christian broker said to the king of China:

The young man looked as if he had just come from the bath. When I saw him, I left the shop and went up to him, saying, "Sir, will you take your money back?" He replied, "What is the hurry? Wait until I sell the rest of my crop. Then I'll take it from you, next week." When he left, I said to myself, "When he comes back next time, I will invite him to eat with me."

He was absent for the rest of the year, during which I used his money, trading with it and making a great deal of profit. At the end of the year, he came back again, dressed in fine clothes. When I saw him, I went up to him and swore by the New Testament that he must eat with me as my guest. He agreed, saying, "On condition that what you spend on me will be from my own money." I replied, "Very well." Then I went in, prepared the place for him and seated him. Then I went to the market and, getting enough of beverages, stuffed chickens, and sweets, set them before him, saying, "Please help yourself." He came to the table and began to eat with his left hand.[9] I said to myself, "Only God is perfect. Here is a young man who is handsome and respectable yet so conceited

9. Considered a lapse in manners, since the left hand is used for toilet hygiene.

that he does not bother to use his right hand in eating with me."
But I ate with him.

*But morning overtook Shahrazad, and she lapsed into silence.
Then Dinarzad said, "What a strange and entertaining story!" Shahrazad replied, "What is this compared with what I shall tell you
tomorrow night if the king spares me and lets me live!"*

### The One Hundred and Twelfth Night

*The following night Shahrazad said:*

I heard, O happy King, that the Christian broker said to the king
of China:

When we finished eating, I poured water on his hand and gave
him something to wipe it with, and after I offered him some sweets,
we sat to chat. I asked him, "Sir, relieve my mind by telling me
why you ate with me with your left hand? Does something ail your
right hand?" When the young man heard my question, he wept and
recited the following verses:

> If Leyla[1] I have for Selma exchanged,
> 'Twas not at will but by necessity.

Then he drew his right arm from his bosom and showed it to
me. It was a stump, with the hand cut off at the wrist. I was astonished at this, and he said to me, "Don't wonder and say to yourself
that I am conceited and have eaten with my left hand out of con-
ceit. There is a strange story behind the cutting off of my hand."
I asked, "How came it to be cut off?" Sighing and weeping, he said:

I was a native of Baghdad and the son of one of its most prominent men. When I reached manhood, I heard travelers and other
people tell of the land of Egypt, and it stayed in my mind. When
my father died and I inherited his business, I prepared a load of
merchandise, taking with me all kinds of fabrics of Baghdad and
Mosul, including a thousand silk cloaks. Then I left Baghdad and
journeyed until I reached Egypt. When I entered Cairo, I unloaded
at the Masrur Caravansary, where I unpacked the goods and stored
them in the storerooms. Then I gave one of my servants money

---

1. Leyla: the beloved cousin of the Arabic poet Kais, known as "Majnun," who went mad because
of his unrequited love for her; she is a legendary figure in Arab and Persian poetry and art.

to prepare some food, and after I and my servants ate and I took
a rest, I went out for a walk along Bain al-Qasrain Street and then
came back and slept. When I arose, I opened the bales of fabric
and said to myself, "I will go to some good market and find out
the prices." I took samples and, giving them to one of my servants
to carry, put on my finest clothes and walked out until I came to
the Jerjes Market. When I entered, I was met by the brokers, who
had already heard of my arrival. They took my fabrics and auc-
tioned them, but the pieces failed to fetch even their cost. I was
vexed and said to the brokers, "My pieces did not fetch even their
cost." But they replied, "Sir, we can tell you how you can make
a profit without risk."

*But morning overtook Shahrazad, and she lapsed into silence.
Then Dinarzad said, "Sister, what a strange and entertaining story!"
Shahrazad replied, "What is this compared with what I shall tell
you tomorrow night if the king spares me and lets me live!"*

THE ONE HUNDRED AND THIRTEENTH NIGHT

*The following night Shahrazad said:*

I heard, O happy King, that the Christian broker told the king
of China that the young man said:

The brokers said, "We can tell you how you can make a profit
without risk. You should do what the other merchants do and sell
your goods on credit for a fixed period, on a contract drawn by
a scribe and duly witnessed, employ a money changer, and collect
your money, every Monday and Thursday. In this way you will
make a profit, while you spend your own time enjoying the sights
of Cairo and the Nile." I said, "This is a good idea," and took the
brokers and the porters with me to the caravansary, where I took
out the bales of fabric, and they carried them and went with me
to the market, where I sold them on credit, on a written and duly
witnessed contract, which I left with the banker. Then I left the
market and returned to the caravansary.

I lived there, breakfasting every morning on a cup of wine,
mutton, pigeons, and sweets, until a month went by, and the time
came when my receipts began to fall due. Then I began to go to
the market every Monday and Thursday and sit in the shop of one
or other of the merchants, while the scribe and money changer went

around to collect the money till past the afternoon prayer, when they would bring it, and I would count it and give them a receipt for it and take it and return to the caravansary.

I did this for six days, until one day, which happened to be a Monday, I went early to the bath. When I came out, I put on nice clothes and returned to my place in the caravansary, where I breakfasted on a cup of wine and then went to sleep. Then I arose, ate a boiled chicken and, perfuming myself, went to the market and sat at the shop of a merchant called Badr al-Din al-Bustani. We sat chatting for a while, when a lady, wearing a cloak and a magnificent headcloth and exhaling perfume, came up to the shop, and her beauty at once captured my heart. She saluted Badr al-Din, raising her upper veil and revealing a pair of large black eyes. He welcomed her and stood talking with her, and when I heard her speech, the love of her got hold of my heart, and I felt a sense of foreboding. Then she asked him, "Do you have a piece of silk fabric with hunting scenes?" He showed her one of the pieces he had gotten from me, and she bought it for one thousand and two hundred dirhams. Then she said to him, "With your permission, I will take it with me and send you the money next market day." He replied, "This is not possible, my lady, for this gentleman is the owner of the piece, and I have to pay him for it today." She said, "Shame on you, haven't I been buying much from you at whatever profit you wished, taking the fabric from you and sending you the money afterwards?" Badr al-Din replied, "Yes, indeed, but this time, I need the money today." She threw the piece of fabric back into the shop and said angrily, "You merchants don't respect anyone. May God blight you all." Then she turned to go.

*But morning overtook Shahrazad, and she lapsed into silence. Then Dinarzad said, "O sister, what a strange and entertaining story!" Shahrazad replied, "What is this compared with what I shall tell you tomorrow night if the king spares me and lets me live!"*

THE ONE HUNDRED AND FOURTEENTH NIGHT

*The following night Shahrazad said:*

I heard, O happy King, that the Christian broker told the king of China that the young man said:

When she threw the piece of fabric back into the shop and turned to go, I felt as if my soul was going with her and cried out to her,

"For God's sake, lady, do me a favor and come back." She turned
back, saying with a smile, "I am coming back for your sake," and
sat in the shop facing me. I asked Badr al-Din, "Sir, what was the
price we set for this piece of fabric?" He replied, "One thousand
and two hundred dirhams." I said, "I will give you one hundred
dirhams as a profit for it. Give me a piece of paper, and I will write
you a discharge." I wrote him a discharge, took the piece of fabric,
and gave it to the lady, saying to her, "Take it, my lady, and if
you wish, bring me the money next market day, or better yet, accept
it as a present from me to you." She replied, "May God reward
you and grant you a larger share of riches and a longer life than
mine." (And the gates of Heaven opened and received Cairo's
prayers.) I said to her, "My lady, this piece of fabric is yours, and
God willing, many like it, only let me see your face." She turned
her head and lifted her veil, and when I took one look, I sighed
and lost my senses. Then she let down the veil and, taking the piece
of fabric, said, "I will miss you," and departed, while I remained
in the shop till past the afternoon prayer, lost in another world.
When I asked Badr al-Din about the girl, he said, "She is a lady
of wealth, the daughter of a prince who died and left her a great
fortune." Then I took my leave of him and went to the caravansary, still thinking of her, and when they set supper before me, I
could not eat, and when I lay down, I could not sleep but lay awake
till dawn. Then I rose, changed my clothes and, swallowing something for breakfast, hurried to Badr al-Din's shop.

*But morning overtook Shahrazad, and she lapsed into silence.
Then Dinarzad said, "Sister, what a strange and entertaining story!"
Shahrazad replied, "What is this compared with what I shall tell
you tomorrow night if the king spares me and lets me live!"*

### THE ONE HUNDRED AND FIFTEENTH NIGHT

*The following night Shahrazad said:*

I heard, O happy King, that the Christian told the king of China
that the young man said:

Hardly had I been in Badr al-Din's shop, when the lady came
up, followed by a maid, and more richly dressed than before. She
greeted me, instead of Badr al-Din, and said to me, "Sir, let someone receive the money." I said, "What is the hurry for the money?"

She replied, "My dear, may I never lose you," and handed me the money. Then we sat talking, and I dropped some hints, by which she understood that I desired to have an affair with her. She rose hastily and went away, taking my heart with her. I left the shop and walked in the market, when suddenly a black maid came up to me and said, "My lord, my lady wishes to speak with you." I was surprised and said, "No one knows me here." She said, "My lord, how soon you seem to have forgotten her! My lady is the one who was in the merchant's shop today."

I walked with her until we came to the lane of the money-changers, and when the lady saw me, she drew me aside and said to me, "My dear, you have found a place in my heart, and from the day I first laid eyes on you, I have been unable to eat and drink." I replied, "I feel the same, and my condition speaks for my plight." She asked, "My dear, your place or mine?" I replied, "I am a stranger here and have no lodging but the caravansary."

*But morning overtook Shahrazad, and she lapsed into silence. Then Dinarzad said, "Sister, what a strange and entertaining story!" Shahrazad replied, "What is this compared with what I shall tell you tomorrow night if the king spares me and lets me live!"*

THE ONE HUNDRED AND SIXTEENTH NIGHT

*The following night Shahrazad said:*

It is related, O happy King, that the Christian broker told the king of China that the young man said:

"I have no lodging but the caravansary. Do me a favor and let me come to your place." She replied, "Very well, my lord. Tonight is Friday night, and nothing can be done, but tomorrow, after you perform the morning prayer, ride an ass and ask for the house of the syndic[2] Barqut abu-Shamah, in the Habbaniya quarter, and do not delay, for I will be waiting for you." I said, "Very well," and I bade her good-bye.

I waited impatiently for morning, and as soon as it was daylight, I arose, put on my clothes, and perfumed myself. Then I took fifty dinars in a handkerchief and walked from the Masrur Caravansary to the Zuwayla Gate, where I hired an ass, bidding the driver

---

2. Representative of a guild or corporation.

take me to the Habbaniya quarter. He set off with me and in no time brought me to a side street called al-Taqwa Lane. I bade him go in and inquire about the house of the syndic Barqut, known as abu-Shamah, and he disappeared and soon returned and said, "Very well, dismount." I dismounted and said to him, "Guide me to the house, so that you can find it when you return tomorrow to take me back to the Masrur Caravansary." He took me to the house, and I gave him a quarter-dinar and bade him go.

I knocked at the gate, and there came out two little white maids who said, "Please come in, for our mistress, being overjoyed with you, was unable to sleep last night." I walked through the hallway and came to a hall, raised seven steps above the ground and surrounded by windows, overlooking a garden that delighted the eye with running streams and all kinds of fruits and birds. In the middle of the hall there was a square fountain at whose corners stood four snakes made of red gold, spouting water, as if it were jewels and pearls.

*But morning overtook Shahrazad, and she lapsed into silence. Then Dinarzad said, "What a strange and entertaining story!" Shahrazad replied, "What is this compared with what I shall tell you tomorrow night if I stay alive!"*

THE ONE HUNDRED AND SEVENTEENTH NIGHT

*The following night Shahrazad said:*

I heard, O happy King, that the Christian broker told the king of China that the young man said:

I entered the hall, and hardly had I sat down, when the lady came up to me, bedecked in fine clothes and ornaments, with a diadem on her head. Her face was made up, and her eyes were penciled. When she saw me, she smiled at me, pressed me hard to her bosom and, setting her mouth to mine, sucked my tongue, and I did likewise. Then she said, "Can it be true, my little lord, that you have indeed come to me?" I replied, "Yes, I am with you and I am your slave." She said, "By God, since I first saw you, I have enjoyed neither food nor sleep." I said, "I have felt the same." Then we sat down to converse, while I kept my head bowed. Soon she set before me a tray with the most sumptuous dishes, such as ragout, fricassee,

fritters soaked in honey, and chickens stuffed with sugar and pistachio nuts, and we ate until we were satisfied. Then the servants
removed the tray, and after we washed our hands and they sprinkled
them with rosewater scented with musk, we sat down again to converse, and my love for her took such hold of me that all my wealth
seemed little to me in comparison with her. We passed the time
in dalliance till nightfall, when the servants set before us a banquet
of food and wine, and we sat drinking till midnight. Then we went
to bed, and I lay with her till the morning, having never spent a
better night. When it was day, I arose and, slipping under the mattress the handkerchief containing the fifty dinars, took my leave
of her. She wept and asked, "My lord, when shall I see you again?"
I replied, "I will be with you this evening." She saw me to the door
and said, "My lord, bring our supper with you."

When I stepped out, I found the driver with whom I had ridden
the previous day waiting for me, and I mounted, and he drove the
ass to the caravansary. I dismounted but did not pay him, saying,
"Come back for me at sunset," and he replied, "Very well," and went
away. After I had a little breakfast, I went out to collect the money
from the sale of my merchandise. In the meantime I ordered a
roasted lamb on a bed of rice, as well as some sweets and, giving
a porter directions to the lady's house, sent the food to her. Thus
I occupied myself with my business till the end of the day, and when
at sunset the driver came for me, I took fifty dinars in a handkerchief, adding two quarter-dinars, and rode the ass, spurring it until
in no time I reached the lady's house. I dismounted and gave the
driver half a dinar. Then I entered and found that the house was
better prepared than ever. When she saw me, she kissed me and
said, "I have missed you all day long." Then the servants set the
table, and we ate until we were satisfied. Then they brought us wine,
and we drank till midnight; then we went to the bedroom and lay
together till daylight. When I arose, I left with her the fifty dinars
in the handkerchief and went out, finding the driver waiting. I rode
to the caravansary, where I slept a while. Then I went out and
bought from a delicatessen a pair of home-grown geese on two
platters of peppered rice. I also bought colocassia roots, fried and
soaked in honey, fruits and nuts, as well as aromatic herbs and
candles, and sent them all with a porter to her house. Then I waited
impatiently till nightfall, when I again took fifty dinars in a handkerchief and rode with the driver to the house. Again she and I
conversed, ate, and lay together, and when I arose in the morning, I again left the handkerchief with her and rode back with the
driver to the Masrur Caravansary.

*But morning overtook Shahrazad, and she lapsed into silence.
Then Dinarzad said to her sister Shahrazad, "What a strange and
entertaining story!" Shahrazad replied, "What is this compared with
what I shall tell you tomorrow night, if the king spares me and lets
me live!"*

THE ONE HUNDRED AND EIGHTEENTH NIGHT

*The following night Shahrazad said:*

I heard, O happy King, that the Christian broker told the king
of China that the young man said:

I continued like this, eating and drinking and giving her fifty
dinars every night until one day I found myself penniless. Not knowing where to find money and saying to myself, "There is no power
and no strength save in God, the Almighty, the Magnificent. This
is Satan's doing," I left my lodging at the caravansary and walked
along Bain al-Qasran Street until I came to the Zuwayla Gate, where
it was so crowded that the gate was blocked up with people. As
it had been foreordained, I found myself pressed against a soldier,
so that my hand came upon his breast pocket and I felt a purse
inside. I looked and, seeing a green tassel hanging from the pocket,
realized that it was attached to the purse. The crush grew greater
every moment, and just then, a camel, bearing a load of wood,
jostled the soldier on the other side, and he turned to ward it off
from him, lest it should tear his clothes. And Satan tempted me,
and I pulled the tassel and drew out a little blue silk purse, with
something clinking inside. Hardly had I held the purse in my hand,
when the soldier felt something and, touching his pocket with his
hand, found it empty. He turned to me and, raising his mace, struck
me with it on the head. I fell to the ground, while the people
gathered around us and, holding the soldier back, asked him, "Is
it because he pushed you that you struck him with such a blow?"
But he shouted at them with curses and said, "This fellow is a thief!"
At that moment, I came to myself and got up, and the people looked
at me and said, "This nice young man would not steal anything."
Some believed him while others did not, and after much debate,
some of them were about to rescue me from him, when the chief
of the police and the captain and the watchmen entered through
the gate and saw the crowd gathered around me and the soldier.
The chief asked, "What is the matter?" and they told him what had

happened [and the soldier said, "He stole from my pocket a blue silk purse containing twenty dinars."]. The chief asked him, "Was there anyone else with him?" and the soldier replied, "No." Then the chief cried out to the captain, bidding him seize me. Then he said, "Strip him naked," and when they did so and found the purse hidden in my clothes, I fell into a swoon. When the chief saw the purse . . .

*But morning overtook Shahrazad, and she lapsed into silence. Then Dinarzad said, "Sister, what a strange and entertaining story!" Shahrazad replied, "What is this compared with what I shall tell you tomorrow night if the king spares me and lets me live!"*

## THE ONE HUNDRED AND NINETEENTH NIGHT

*The following night Shahrazad said:*

I heard, O happy King, that the Christian broker told the king of China that the young man said:

When the chief saw the purse, he seized it and took out the gold coins, and when he counted, he found twenty dinars. He was angry and, yelling at the officers to bring me before him, said to me, "Young man, there is no need to force it out of you if you tell me the truth. Did you steal this purse?" I bowed my head and said to myself, "I cannot deny it, for they found the purse in my clothes, but if I confess, I will be in trouble." At last I raised my head and said, "Yes, I took it." When the chief heard my words, he called for witnesses, and they attested my confession. (All of this took place at the Zuwayla Gate.) Then he summoned the executioner, who cut off my right hand, and he would have bidden him cut off my foot too, but as the people said to him, "This is a pitiful young man," and as I implored the soldier, who finally took pity on me and interceded for me with him, the chief left me and went away, while the people remained around me and gave me a cup of wine to drink. As for the soldier, he gave me the purse, saying, "You are a nice young man, and it does not become you to be a thief." Then he left me and went away.

I wrapped my hand in a rag, thrust it into my bosom, and walked until I reached my mistress's house and threw myself on the bed. When she saw that I was pale from the bleeding, she asked, "My darling, what ails you?" I replied, "I have a headache." Worried about me, she said, "Sit up and tell me what has happened to you today, for it is written on your face." When I wept without reply, she said, "It seems as if you are tired of me. For God's sake, tell me what is the matter with you." But even though I kept silent and did not reply, she continued to talk to me till nightfall. Then she brought me food, but I refused it, for fear that she would see me eat with my left hand, and I said to her, "I don't care to eat anything." Again she asked, "Tell me what happened to you today and what is troubling you." I said, "Must I tell you?" Then she gave me wine to drink, saying, "Drink it, for it will make you feel better and help you tell me what happened." I replied, "If I must, then give me the wine." She drank, gave me the cup, and I took it with my left hand.

*But morning overtook Shahrazad, and she lapsed into silence. Then Dinarzad said, "Sister, what a strange and entertaining story!" Shahrazad replied, "What is this compared with what I shall tell you tomorrow night if the king spares me and lets me live!"*

### THE ONE HUNDRED AND TWENTIETH NIGHT

I heard, O happy King, that the Christian broker told the king of China that the young man said:

When she gave me the cup, I took it with my left hand with tears in my eyes. She let out a loud cry and said, "My lord, why do you weep, and why do you hold the cup with your left hand?" I replied, "I have a boil on my right hand." She said, "Put it out, and I will lance it for you." I replied, "It is not ready yet." She kept forcing me to drink until I got drunk and fell asleep. Then she examined my right arm and found it a wrist without a hand, and when she searched me and found the purse and my severed hand wrapped in a handkerchief, she grieved for me and lamented till the morning.

When I awoke, I found that she had made me a dish of broth of five boiled chickens, and after I ate some and drank a cup of wine, I laid down the purse and was about to go out, when she said to me, "Where are you going? Sit down." Then she added, "Has your love for me been so great that you have spent all your substance on me until you finally lost even your hand? I pledge to you that I will die nowhere but at your feet, and you shall soon see the truth of my words." Then she sent for witnesses and drew up a marriage contract, saying, "Write down that everything I own belongs to this young man." After she paid the witnesses their fee, she took me by the hand and, leading me to a chest, said to me, "Look at all these handkerchiefs inside; they contain all the money you brought me. Take your money back, for I can never reward you enough for your precious and dear self," repeating, "Take your money." I locked the money in the chest, forgetting my sorrow and feeling happy, and thanked her. She said to me, "By God, even if I gave my life for you, it would be less than you deserve."

We lived together, but in less than a month, she fell ill and continued to get worse because of her grief for me, and in less than fifty days, she was dead. After I buried her, I found that she had left me countless bequests, including the storeroom and the crop of sesame that you, Christian, sold for me.

*But morning overtook Shahrazad, and she lapsed into silence. Then Dinarzad said, "Sister, what a strange and entertaining story!" Shahrazad replied, "What is this compared with what I shall tell you tomorrow night if the king spares me and lets me live!"*

THE ONE HUNDRED AND TWENTY-FIRST NIGHT

*The following night Shahrazad said:*

I heard, O happy King, that the Christian broker told the king of China that the young man said:

"It was because I was busy selling the rest of the goods that I did not have the time to pay attention to you and receive my money from you, but now I have at last sold everything she left me. This then is the reason why I ate with my left hand. Now, by God, Christian, you must not object to what I am about to do, for I have entered your home and eaten your food. I make you a present of all the money you are holding for me from the sale of the sesame, for it is only a portion of what the Supreme God has bestowed on me."

The young man added, "Christian, I have prepared a load of merchandise for trading; will you go aboard with me?" I replied, "Yes, indeed," and agreed to go with him at the beginning of the month. Then after I too bought merchandise, I set out with the young man until we came to your city, O King, where he bought merchandise and went back to Egypt. But it was my lot to stay here. This then is my adventure and strange story. Isn't it, O King, more amazing than the hunchback's story?

The king of China replied, "No, it is not more amazing than the hunchback's story, and I must hang all four of you for the hunchback's death."

Then the steward of the king's kitchen came forward and said to the king of China, "O happy King, if I tell you a story that happened to me last night, before I found the hunchback in my house, and you find it to be more amazing than the hunchback's story, will you grant us our lives and let us go?" The king of China replied, "Yes, if I find it to be more amazing than the story of the hunchback, I will grant all four of you your lives." The steward said:

## [The Steward's Tale: The Young Man from Baghdad and Lady Zubaida's Maid]

O King of the age, last night I was invited to hear a recitation of the Quran, where the doctors of the law, as well as a great many citizens of your city, were assembled. After the reciters finished their recitation, the table was spread, and among the dishes set before us there was a ragout spiced with cumin. But when one of the guests saw the ragout, he held back and abstained from eating. We entreated him to eat of the ragout, but he swore that he would not, and we pressed him until he said, "Don't force me to eat, for I have suffered enough from eating this dish." Then he repeated the following verses:

> Shoulder your drum, my man, and
> leave your home
> And use the kohl if 'tis the
> kohl you like.

We said to him, "Tell us the reason of your refusal to eat of the ragout," and as the host insisted, saying, "I swear that you must eat of it," the guest replied, "There is no power and no strength, save in God. If I must eat, then I will first have to wash my hands forty times with soap, forty times with potash, and forty times with galingale,[3] all in all one hundred and twenty times."

*But morning overtook Shahrazad, and she lapsed into silence. Then Dinarzad said, "What a strange and entertaining story!" Shahrazad replied, "What is this compared with what I shall tell you tomorrow night if the king spares me and lets me live!"*

---

3. Aromatic root of certain East Indian herbs of the ginger family; "potash": a crude potassium carbonate obtained from wood or other vegetable ashes.

THE ONE HUNDRED AND TWENTY-SECOND NIGHT

*The following night Shahrazad said:*

It is related, O happy King, that the steward said to the king:

O King of the age, the host ordered his servants to bring the guest water and all that he required to wash his hands, and he washed his hands as he had said. Then he came reluctantly and sat down with us, as if in fear, and dipping his hand into the ragout, began to eat, but with repugnance, while we looked at him with surprise, for his hand and indeed his whole body were shaking, and we noticed that his thumb was cut off and that he ate with four fingers only, so that the food kept slipping awkwardly from his hand. We asked him in amazement, "What happened to your thumb? Did God create you like this, or did you have an accident?" He replied, "By God, it is not only this thumb that is missing, but also that of the other hand, and the great toe of each of my feet, as you will see." Then he bared his left hand and his two feet, and we saw that the left hand was like the right and that each of his feet lacked the great toe. When we saw this, our amazement increased, and we said to him, "We are impatient to hear your story and the reason for cutting off your thumbs and toes and for washing your hands one hundred and twenty times." He said:

My father was one of the most prominent merchants of Baghdad, in the days of the caliph Harun al-Raschid, but he was fond of wine and the lute, so that when he died, he left me nothing. I held a mourning ceremony for him, arranged for recitations of the Quran, and continued to mourn for him for a long time. Then I opened the shop and found that he had left little substance and many debts. So I arranged with his creditors to pay them in installments, and I began to buy and sell and to pay the creditors week by week, until at last I paid off all his debts and began to increase my capital.

One day, as I was sitting in the shop early in the morning, there came to the market a beautiful young lady, the like of which I had never seen before, richly dressed and bedecked with jewelry. She was riding a she-mule, with one black slave walking before and another behind her. She dismounted and, leaving the she-mule by the entrance, entered the market. No sooner had she done so, when a well-groomed eunuch followed her and said, "My lady, go in, but don't let anyone recognize you, or we will be in trouble." Then he stood guard before her, while she looked at the shops and, finding none open but mine, came up to my shop, followed by the eunuch, greeted me, and sat down.

*But morning overtook Shahrazad, and she lapsed into silence. Then Dinarzad said, "Sister, what an entertaining story!" Shahrazad replied, "What is this compared with what I shall tell you tomorrow night if the king spares me and lets me live!"*

### THE ONE HUNDRED AND TWENTY-THIRD NIGHT

*The following night Shahrazad said:*

I heard, O happy King, that the steward told the king of China that the young merchant said:

She sat in my shop and unveiled her face, and when I saw it, I sighed. Then she asked me, "Do you have any fabrics?" I replied, "My lady, your servant is poor, but wait until the other merchants open their shops, and I will get you whatever you wish." We sat talking for a while, and I was beginning to feel an overwhelming passion for her. When the merchants opened their shops, I rose and got her everything she wished, to the value of five thousand dirhams. She gave the fabrics to the eunuch and went back to the slaves, who brought her the she-mule, and she mounted and rode away, without telling me where she lived. Being too embarrassed to mention money before such a beautiful woman, I vouched to the merchants for the value of the goods, incurring a debt of five thousand dirhams. Then I went home, drunk with love, and for a week was unable to eat or drink or sleep.

*But morning overtook Shahrazad, and she lapsed into silence. Then Dinarzad said, "Sister, what an entertaining story!" Shahrazad replied, "What is this compared with what I shall tell you tomorrow night if the king spares me and lets me live!"*

### THE ONE HUNDRED AND TWENTY-FOURTH NIGHT

*The following night Shahrazad said:*

It is related, O King, that the steward told the king of China that the young merchant said:

A week later the merchants came to me, asking for their money, but I persuaded them to wait, and as soon as another week passed, the lady came up, riding the she-mule and followed, as usual, by the eunuch and the two slaves. She greeted me and, sitting down in the shop, said, "I am late in bringing you the money for the fabrics. Fetch a money changer and receive the amount." I sent for the money changer, and the eunuch counted out the money and gave it to him. Then she and I sat talking until the shops opened, at which time I paid every merchant what I owed him. Then she said to me, "Sir, get me such and such," and I got her what she wanted from the merchants, and she took it and went away, without saying a word about payment. I began to regret what I had done, for the price of what I had bought for her was a thousand dinars, and I said to myself, "What a predicament! She has given me five thousand dirhams but has taken a thousand dinars' worth of goods, and the merchants know only me. There is no power and no strength, save in God, the Almighty, the Magnificent. This woman who tricked me must be a swindler, and I did not even ask her for her address."

She was gone for more than a month, and the merchants began to press me for their money and, finally despairing of ever seeing her again, I put up my property for sale. But one day, while I sat dejected and perplexed, she came in and, sitting in the shop, said, "Fetch the scales and take your money." Then she gave me the money and sat, conversing freely with me, until I was beside myself with joy. Then she asked me, "Do you have a wife?" I replied, "No, I have never been married," and began to weep. She asked, "Why do you weep?" I replied, "It is nothing." Then, giving the eunuch some money, I asked him to act as my go-between with her. But he laughed and said, "By God, she is more in love with you than you are with her. She had no need for the fabrics she bought from you, but she only did it out of love for you. Tell her yourself what you want." She had seen me giving the eunuch the money, so I said to her, "Be charitable and permit your servant to tell you what is on his mind." Then I told her what was on my mind, and she assented and said to the eunuch, "You shall carry my message to him," and saying to me, "Do whatever he asks you," went away. I paid the merchants what I owed them and spent a sleepless night.

A few days later the eunuch came to me . . .

*But morning overtook Shahrazad, and she lapsed into silence. Then her sister Dinarzad said, "Sister, what a strange and entertaining story!" Shahrazad replied, "What is this compared with what I shall tell you tomorrow night if the king spares me and lets me live!"*

### THE ONE HUNDRED AND TWENTY-FIFTH NIGHT

*The following night Shahrazad said:*

It is related, O King, that the steward told the king of China
that the young man said:

When the eunuch came, I treated him generously, and when I
asked him about his mistress, he replied, "She is pining with love
for you." Then I asked him, "Who is she?" and he said, "She is one
of the waiting-women who is charged with errands for the Lady
Zubaida, the wife of the caliph, who brought her up. By God, she
told her lady about you and begged her to marry her to you, but
the Lady Zubaida said, 'I will not marry you to him until I see
whether he is handsome and whether he is a match for you.' I will
take you to the palace at once, and if you succeed in entering without being seen, you may win her in marriage, but if you are found
out, you will lose your head. What do you say?" I replied, "I am
ready to go with you." Then he said, "As soon as it is night, go
to the mosque built by the Lady Zubaida on the Tigris River." I
replied, "Very well." Then I went to the mosque, where I performed
my evening prayer and passed the night.

Just before daybreak, there came up some servants in a boat,
with some empty chests, which they deposited in the mosque and
departed. But one of them stayed behind, and when I looked at
him closely, I found that he was the eunuch who had come to me
earlier. Soon, my lady herself came in, and when she drew near,
I rose to greet her, and she sat to converse with me, with tears in
her eyes. Then she made me get into one of the chests and locked
me in. Then the eunuchs came back with all sorts of things that
she kept stowing in the chests until she had filled them all and locked
them. Then the placed the chests in the boat and headed down-
stream to the palace of the Lady Zubaida. I soon began to regret
what I had done, saying to myself, "By God, I am undone," and
kept weeping and praying to God to deliver me until the boat
reached the gate of the caliph's palace. Then the eunuchs lifted out
the chests, including mine, and carried them past the eunuchs in
charge of guarding the harem until they came to a eunuch who
seemed to be their chief. He started up from sleep.

*But morning overtook Shahrazad, and she lapsed into silence.
Then her sister Dinarzad said, "Sister, what an entertaining story!"*

*Shahrazad replied, "What is this compared with what I shall tell you tomorrow night if the king spares me and lets me live!"*

THE ONE HUNDRED AND TWENTY-SIXTH NIGHT

*The following night Shahrazad said:*

I heard, O happy King, that the steward told the king of China that the young man said:

The chief of the eunuchs started up from sleep and cried out to the young lady, "Don't delay. You must open these chests." It so happened that the chest he was about to start with was the one in which I was, and when they brought it to him, I lost my senses and in my panic wet myself until my urine began to run out of the chest. Then the young lady said, "Chief, you have ruined me and ruined many merchants by spoiling the belongings of the Lady Zubaida, for the chest contains colored dresses and a jar of Zamzam water.[4] The jar has just tipped over and the water will make the colors run." The chief of the eunuchs said, "Take the chest and go." But hardly had the eunuchs carried me and hurried away with all the other chests, when I heard a voice crying, "O my, O my, the caliph, the caliph!" When I heard this, my heart died within me. Then I heard the caliph ask the young lady, "Hey you, what is in these chests of yours?" She replied, "Clothes for the Lady Zubaida." He said, "Open them and let me see," and when I heard this, I knew that I was undone. Then I heard the young lady say, "O Commander of the Faithful, these chests contain the clothes and belongings of the Lady Zubaida, and she does not wish their contents to be seen by anyone." But the caliph said, "You must open these chests, so that I may see what is in them. Bring them to me." When I heard the caliph say, "Bring them to me," I was sure of death. Then the eunuchs brought the chests up, opening them, one after another, and he kept looking at the clothes and belongings until there remained only the chest in which I was hiding. They carried me and let me down before him, and I bade life good-bye, being certain that I was going to lose my head and die. The caliph said, "Open the chest, so that I may see what is in it," and the eunuch rushed to open the chest.

4. From a sacred well in Mecca.

*But morning overtook Shahrazad, and she lapsed into silence.
Then Dinarzad said to her sister Shahrazad, "What a strange and
entertaining story!" Shahrazad replied, "What is this compared with
what I shall tell you tomorrow night if the king spares me and lets
me live!"*

THE ONE HUNDRED AND TWENTY-SEVENTH NIGHT

*The following night Shahrazad said:*

I heard, O King, that the steward told the king of China that
the young man said:

The caliph said to the eunuchs, "Open this chest, so that I may
see what is in it." But the young lady said, "O my lord, open it
in the presence of the Lady Zubaida, for that which is in it is her
secret, and she is more particular about this one than all the other
chests." When the caliph heard her explanation, he ordered the
eunuchs to carry the chests inside, and two of them came and carried
the chest in which I was hiding, while I could hardly believe that
I was still alive. As soon as the chest was inside the harem, where
my friend lived, she rushed in and, opening it, said, "Get out quickly
and take this stairway upstairs." I stood up and climbed out of the
chest, and hardly had she closed the lid and I climbed the stairs,
when the eunuchs came in with the other chests, followed by the
caliph. Then they opened everything again before him, while he
sat on the chest where I had been hiding. Then he got up and went
into the harem.

All this time I sat with my mouth dry from fear until the young
lady came upstairs and said to me, "There is no longer anything
to fear. Be cheerful and wait until the Lady Zubaida comes to see
you, and you may be fortunate and win me." I went downstairs,
and as soon as I sat down in the small hall, there came in ten maids,
like moons, and stood in two rows, and they were followed by twenty
high-bosomed virgins, with the Lady Zubaida, who could hardly
walk under the weight of her dresses and ornaments. When she drew
near, the maids dispersed and brought her a chair, on which she
sat. Then she cried out to the girls, who in turn cried out to me,
and I advanced and kissed the ground before her. She motioned
me to sit down, and I sat down before her, as she conversed with
me and I answered her questions about my condition. She was
pleased with me and finally said, "By God, I have not raised this

girl in vain. She is like my own child, a trust committed to you by God." Then she bade me stay for ten days in the palace.

*But morning overtook Shahrazad, and she lapsed into silence. Then Dinarzad said, "What a strange and entertaining story!" Shahrazad replied, "What is this compared with what I shall tell you tomorrow night if the king spares me and lets me live!"*

THE ONE HUNDRED AND TWENTY-EIGHTH NIGHT

*The following night Shahrazad said:*

I heard that the steward told the king of China that the young man said:

I stayed in the palace ten days and nights, without seeing the young lady. Then the Lady Zubaida consulted the caliph about the marriage of her waiting-woman, and he gave permission and assigned ten thousand dirhams for that purpose. Then the Lady Zubaida sent for the judge and witnesses, and they drew up the marriage contract, performed the ceremony, and for ten days thereafter celebrated our wedding with sumptuous meals and sweets. At the end of the ten days, the young lady entered the bath. In the meantime they set before me the supper tray, and as there was among the dishes a great platter of ragout cooked with pistachio nuts, white sugar, rosewater, and cumin, I did not hesitate but, by God, fell upon the ragout and ate until I was satisfied. Then I wiped my hands, for God had willed that I should forget to wash them.

I sat until it grew dark, when they lit the candles and all the musicians and singing women of the palace came in a procession, beating the tambourines and singing all kinds of melodies and songs. They kept parading from room to room, displaying the bride and receiving gifts of money and pieces of silk, until they made the round of the whole palace and brought her to my room. They disrobed her and left her with me, but no sooner did I enter the bed with her and embrace her, hardly believing that she was mine, than, smelling the ragout spiced with cumin on my hand, she let out such a loud scream that the maids rushed in from all sides and stood around her, while I sat alarmed and trembled from fear, not knowing why she had screamed. The maids asked her, "Sister, what is the matter with you?" She replied, "Take this madman away from me." I got up, afraid and bewildered, and asked her, "My lady, what makes you think me mad?" She replied, "Madman, didn't you eat the ragout spiced with cumin without washing your hands? By God, I will punish you for it. Shall the like of you consummate marriage with one like me, with a hand smelling of ragout spiced with cumin?" Then she yelled at the girls, saying, "Throw him to the ground," and they threw me to the ground, and she took a braided whip and fell with it on my back and buttocks until her arm was tired. Then she said to the girls, "Take him and send him to the chief of the police, so that he may cut off the hand with which he ate the ragout without washing it and sparing me the stench." When I heard this, still smarting from the blows, I said to myself, "There is no power and no strength, save in God, the Almighty, the Magnificent. What a calamity! What a great calamity! Did I suffer such a painful beating and will my hand be cut off, just because I ate the ragout spiced with cumin and forgot to wash my hands? May God curse this ragout and its very existence."

*But morning overtook Shahrazad, and she lapsed into silence. Then Dinarzad said, "Sister, what a strange and entertaining story!" Shahrazad replied, "What is this compared with what I shall tell you tomorrow night if the king spares me and lets me live!"*

THE ONE HUNDRED AND TWENTY-NINTH NIGHT

*The following night Shahrazad said:*

It is related that the steward told the king of China that the young man said:

The girls interceded with her, saying, "Our lady, this man does not know your worth. Forgive him for our sake." But she said, "He is a madman, and I must punish his hand, so that he may never again eat the ragout without washing it." When the girls interceded again and kissed her hands, saying, "Our lady, for God's sake, don't blame him for what he forgot to do," she yelled at me, cursed me, and went away, and they followed her.

She was gone for ten days, during which a maid brought me food and drink everyday and informed me that the lady was not feeling well because I had eaten the ragout without washing my hands. I was very much amazed and burst out with anger, saying to myself, "What a cursed temper!" adding, "There is no power and no

strength, save in God, the Almighty, the Magnificent." When the
ten days passed, the maid brought me the food and informed me that
the lady was going to the bath, adding, "Bear her anger patiently,
for tomorrow she will come to you." When the lady finally came
in, she looked at me and said, "May God shame you; couldn't you
be patient even for one moment? I will not make peace with you
until I punish you for eating the ragout without washing your
hands." Then crying out to the girls, who surrounded me and bound
me, she took out a sharp blade and, coming up to me, cut off my
two thumbs, as you people can see for yourselves, and I fell into
a swoon. Meanwhile, she sprinkled the wounds with powder and
a store of drugs to stop the flow of blood, and when the blood
stopped, the maids gave me wine to drink. As soon as I opened
my eyes, I said to her, "I pledge to you that I will never again eat
ragout spiced with cumin without washing my hands one hundred
and twenty times." The lady replied, "Bravo," and made me take
an oath to that effect. So when the food was brought in here, and
I saw the ragout spiced with cumin, I turned pale and said to myself,
"It was this dish that was the cause of cutting off my thumbs"; so
when you forced me to eat of it, I had to fulfill the oath.

*But morning overtook Shahrazad, and she lapsed into silence.*
*Then Dinarzad said to her sister Shahrazad, "What a strange and*
*entertaining story!" Shahrazad replied, "What is this compared with*
*what I shall tell you tomorrow night if the king spares me and lets*
*me live!"*

THE ONE HUNDRED AND THIRTIETH NIGHT

*The following night Shahrazad said:*

It is related that the steward told the king of China that the guests
asked the young man, "What happened to you after that?" and he
said:

When my wounds healed and I recovered, she came to me, and
I slept with her. Then I spent the rest of the month with her in
the palace until I began to feel depressed, and she finally said to
me, "Listen! The caliph's palace is no place for us to live. The Lady
Zubaida has given me fifty thousand dinars. Take some money with
you and go and buy us a good house." Then she gave me ten thousand dinars, and I took them and went out and bought a beautiful

house. Then she moved in with me, and for many years we lived like kings until she died. This then is the cause of the cutting off of my thumbs and the washing of my hands.

After we ate, the party ended and we departed, and afterward I had my adventure with the hunchback.

The king of China said, "By God, this is not more amazing than the story of the roguish hunchback." Then the Jewish physician rose and, kissing the ground before the king, said, "O my lord, I have a story to tell, which is more amazing than this one." The king said, "Let us hear it."

*But morning overtook Shahrazad, and she lapsed into silence. Then Dinarzad said, "Sister, what a strange and entertaining story!" Shahrazad replied, "What is this compared with what I shall tell you tomorrow night if the king spares me and lets me live!"*

THE ONE HUNDRED AND THIRTY-FIRST NIGHT

*The following night Shahrazad said:*

It is related, O King, that the Jew said:

# [The Jewish Physician's Tale: The Young Man from Mosul and the Murdered Girl]

O King of the age, the most amazing thing that ever happened to me occurred when I was studying medicine in Damascus. One day a Mamluk from the house of the governor came to take me there. I went to the house, and when I entered, I saw lying on a bed at the upper end of the hall a sick young man, so handsome that I have seen none handsomer. I sat at his head and offered a prayer for his recovery, and he responded by making a sign with his eyes. I said to him, "My lord, give me your hand, and may you recover speedily." He put forth his left hand, and I wondered and said to myself, "By God, it is strange that such a handsome young man of such a high family should lack good manners. How very strange!" I felt his pulse and wrote him a prescription, and for ten days I continued to visit him until he recovered and I took him to the bath. Then when I came out, the governor bestowed on me a robe of honor and appointed me superintendent of the hospital.

But when I was with him in the bath, which was cleared for our private use, and the servants and valets came in and took off his clothes, I saw that his right hand had been recently cut off and realized that this was the cause of his illness. When I saw this, I was filled with amazement, worry, and sorrow for him. I looked closely at his body and saw marks of beating with rods, for which he had used ointments, drugs, and plasters, leaving only faint traces on the sides. As my worry increased and began to show on my face, the young man looked at me and, reading my thought, said, "Doctor, don't wonder about my case. I will tell you my strange story at the appropriate time." Then we washed and, returning to the house, ate some boiled food and rested a while. Then the young man said to me, "Would you like to go for a walk in the Damascus Gardens?" I replied, "Yes, I would." He bade the servants take a few necessities, in addition to a roasted lamb and fruits, and we went to the gardens, where we enjoyed the sights for a while, then sat to eat. When we finished, they offered us some sweets and, after we had some, I was about to open the subject, when he anticipated me and said:

Doctor, I am a native of Mosul; when my grandfather died, he left behind ten sons, of whom my father was the eldest. When they grew up, all ten got married, and God blessed my father with me but did not bless his nine brothers with any children. So I grew up among my uncles.

*But morning overtook Shahrazad, and she lapsed into silence. Then Dinarzad said, "Sister, what a strange and entertaining story!" Shahrazad replied, "What is this compared with what I shall tell you tomorrow night if the king spares me and lets me live!"*

THE ONE HUNDRED AND THIRTY-SECOND NIGHT

*The following night Shahrazad said:*

I heard, O King, that the Jewish physician told the king of China that the young man said:

I had grown up and reached manhood, when one Friday I went with my father and my uncles to the Mosul mosque. After we performed the Friday prayers and the people went out, my father and my uncles sat in a circle, talking about the wonders of foreign lands and the marvels of various cities until they mentioned Cairo, and one of my uncles said, "Travelers say that there is nothing on the face of the earth fairer than Cairo," and from that moment I longed to see Cairo. Another disagreed, saying, "It is Baghdad that is Paradise and the capital of the world." But my father, who was the eldest, said, "He who has not seen Cairo has not seen the world. Its dust is gold, its women dolls, and its Nile a wonder, whose water is sweet and refreshing and whose clay is soft and cool, as the poet said:

> Enjoy today the flooding of your Nile,
> Whose waters on you their riches bestow.
> The Nile is but the tears I shed for you,
> A boon, which from my blighted eyes does flow.

If you saw its gardens, adorned with flowers and ornamented with all kinds of blossoms, if you saw the Nile Island with its many lovely sights, and if you saw the Ethiopian Pond, your eyes would be dazzled with their wonders. O how lovely is the sight of the green gardens, encircled by the waters of the Nile, like chrysolites set in silver sheets! How well the poet put it who said:

> O what a day by the Ethiopian Pond
> We spent between the shadows and the light,
> The water flashing amid the green plants,
> A sabre in an eye trembling with fright.
> We sat in a fine garden where the rays
> Embroidered and adorned that lovely sight,
> A garden woven for us by the clouds,
> Soft carpets made and spread for us to rest,
> As we sat passing the refreshing wine,
> Which of all drugs for sorrow works the best,
> Quaffing deep draughts from large and brimful cups
> For they alone can quench our burning thirst."

*But morning overtook Shahrazad, and she lapsed into silence. Then Dinarzad said, "Sister, what a strange and entertaining story!" Shahrazad replied, "What is this compared with what I shall tell you tomorrow night if the king spares me and lets me live!"*

THE ONE HUNDRED AND THIRTY-THIRD NIGHT

*The following night Shahrazad said:*

I heard, O King, that the Jewish physician told the king of China that the young man said:

My father went on to describe Cairo, and when he finished describing the Nile and the Ethiopian Pond, he said, "And what is this compared with the observatory and its charms, of which every approaching viewer says, 'This spot is full of wonders'; and if you speak of the night of the Nile-Flooding Feast, open the floodgates of words and release the bow; and if you see al-Rauda Park in the shade of the late afternoon, you will be thrilled with wonder and delight; and if you stand at the river bank, when the sun is sinking and the Nile puts on its coat of mail and shield, you will be refreshed by the deep and ample shade and gentle breeze." When I heard this description, my thoughts dwelt so much on Cairo that I was unable to sleep that night.

Some time later my uncles prepared merchandise for a trade journey to Cairo, and I went to my father and importuned him with tears until he prepared merchandise for me too and let me go with them, saying to them, "Don't let him go to Cairo, but leave him behind to sell his goods in Damascus." Having provided ourselves for the journey, we set out from Mosul and journeyed until we reached Aleppo, where we stayed for a few days. Then we pressed on until we reached Damascus, which I found to be a pleasant, peaceful, and prosperous city, abounding in trees and rivers and birds, like a garden in Paradise, and abounding in "fruits of all kinds," like one of the gardens in Rudwan.[5] We stayed in one of the caravansaries, to my delight, while my uncles sold my goods at a profit of five dinars for each dinar. Then they left me and went on to Egypt, while I stayed in Damascus, in a large house, known as the house of Sudun 'Abd al-Rahman, which I rented for two dinars a month. It had a marble hall, a storeroom, an extra room with cupboards, and a fountain with water running day and night. I lived there, spending my money on feasting and drinking, until I had squandered most of it.

One day, as I sat at the door of my lodging, there came up a young lady so finely dressed that I have seen none better. I invited her to come in and could hardly believe it when she actually accepted.

*But morning overtook Shahrazad, and she lapsed into silence. Then Dinarzad said, "Sister, what a strange and entertaining story!" Shahrazad replied, "What is this compared with what I shall tell you tomorrow night if the king spares me and lets me live!"*

---

5. Literally, "the gardens of the blessed" — Paradise.

## THE ONE HUNDRED AND THIRTY-FOURTH NIGHT

*The following night Shahrazad said:*

I heard, O happy King, that the Jewish physician told the king of China that the young man said:

When she entered, I felt bound to honor the invitation, and I went in and closed the door behind us. When she sat and raised her veil and took off her cloak, I saw that she was extremely beautiful, like a painted moon, and her love took hold of my heart. I went out and bought from a special shop a tray of the most delicate foods and fruits, as well as wine and whatever was needed for the occasion. We ate, and when it got dark, I lighted the candles and set up the cups, and we drank until we were drunk. Then I slept with her and spent the best of nights. In the morning, I offered her ten dinars, but she frowned and said, "Shame on you, man from Mosul, to think that you can have me for gold or money!" Then taking out ten dinars herself, she swore that if I did not take them, she would never come back, saying, "Darling, expect me again in three days, between sundown and nightfall, and take these ten dinars to prepare a banquet similar to this." Then she bade me good-bye and went away, taking my heart with her, while I could hardly wait for the three days to go by.

On the appointed day, I prepared a banquet to my liking, and she came after sundown, wearing high wooden shoes, a black head-cloth, and a bonnet and exhaling sweet perfumes. We ate and drank and dallied and laughed, and when it got dark, I lighted the candles, and we drank until we got drunk. Then I slept with her, and when she arose in the morning, she gave me ten dinars and, saying, "We will meet as usual," went away.

Three days later I again prepared a banquet, and when she came as usual, we sat and ate and dallied and conversed. When it got dark and we sat to drink, she said, "My lord, by God, am I not beautiful?" I replied, "Yes, by God, you are." She said, "Will you then allow me to bring with me a young lady who is even more beautiful and younger than I, so that she may play, laugh, and enjoy herself, for she has been sequestered for a long time, and she has asked to go out and spend the night with me?" I replied, "By God, yes." In the morning, she gave me fifteen dinars and, saying "Buy more provisions, for we will have a new guest when we meet as usual," went away. On the third day I prepared a banquet.

*But morning overtook Shahrazad, and she lapsed into silence.*
*Then Dinarzad said, "Sister, what a strange and entertaining story!"*
*Shahrazad replied, "What is this compared with what I shall tell*
*you tomorrow night if the king spares me and lets me live!"*

### THE ONE HUNDRED AND THIRTY-FIFTH NIGHT

*The following night Shahrazad said:*

I heard that the Jewish physician told the king of China that the
young man said:

Soon after sundown, she came with a girl, as we had agreed on.
I received them with pleasure and delight and lighted the candles,
and when the girl unveiled herself, she revealed a face that re-
dounded to "the Glory of God, the Best of Creators." Then we sat
down to eat, and I kept feeding the new girl, while she looked at
me and smiled, and when we finished eating and I set the wine
and the fruits and sweets before them, I drank with her, while she
smiled and winked at me as I gazed on her, all-consumed with love.
My friend, seeing that the girl's eyes were fixed on mine and mine
on hers, laughed and asked playfully, "My darling, isn't this girl,
whom I have brought you, more beautiful and charming than I?"
I replied, "By God, yes, she is." She asked, "Would you like to sleep
with her?" I replied, "Yes, by God, I would like to." She said, "After
all, she is only a visitor here tonight, while I am always here." Then
girding herself, she rose in the middle of the night and prepared
our bed, and I took the girl in my arms and slept with her that
night, while my friend prepared a bed for herself in the extra room
and slept there alone.

When I awoke in the morning, I found myself drenched and
thought that I was wet with perspiration. I sat up and tried to rouse
the girl, but when I shook her by the shoulders, her head rolled
off, and I realized that she had been slain. I lost my senses and,
crying out, "O gracious Protector," sprang up, and the world began
to turn black before my eyes. Then I looked for my friend, and
when I could not find her, I realized that it was she who, out of
jealousy, had murdered the girl. I said to myself, "There is no power
and no strength, save in God, the Almighty, the Magnificent. What
shall I do now?" I thought for a while and finally said to myself,
"I am afraid that the murdered girl's family will look for her; no
one is safe from the treachery of women." Then I took off my clothes

and dug a hole in the middle of the hall and, placing the girl with all her jewelry in it, covered it back with earth and replaced the slabs of the marble pavement. Then I put on clean clothes and, taking what was left of my money in a small box, locked up the house and left. I took courage, went to the landlord, and paid him a year's rent, saying "I am going to join my uncles in Cairo." Then I paid for my voyage at the king's caravansary and departed.

*But morning overtook Shahrazad, and she lapsed into silence. Then Dinarzad said, "Sister, what a strange and entertaining story!" Shahrazad replied, "What is this compared with what I shall tell you tomorrow night if the king spares me and lets me live!"*

### THE ONE HUNDRED AND THIRTY-SIXTH NIGHT

*The following night Shahrazad said:*

I heard, O King of the age, that the Jewish physician told the king of China that the young man said:

I set out on my journey, and God granted me safe passage, and I reached Cairo. When I met my uncles, I found that they had already sold their goods on credit. They were glad to see me but surprised at my arrival. I said to them, "You were gone for too long, and I yearned to see you." But I did not tell them that I had any money with me. I stayed with them, enjoying Cairo and its sights, and began to spend the rest of my money, squandering it on feasting and drinking. When the time drew near for my uncles' departure, I hid myself from them, and when they looked for me but could not find me, they said, "He must have gone back to Damascus," and departed, and I came out of hiding and lived in Cairo for three years, sending every year to the landlord in Damascus the rent for the house, until at last I had squandered all my money and had nothing left but the fare for the journey back.

I paid the fare and set out, and God granted me safe passage, and I reached Damascus. I dismounted at the house, where the landlord, who was a jeweler, received me gladly. I unsealed the lock, opened the door, and went in. When I swept the house and wiped it clean, I found under the bed, where I had slept with the murdered girl, a gold necklace set with ten gemstones that boggled the mind. When I saw it, I recognized it, picked it up and, holding it in my hand, wept for a long time. Then, having cleaned the house,

I placed the furniture as it was before. I stayed at home for a couple of days, then went to the bath, rested, and put on fresh clothes. By then I had absolutely no money left. Driven by fate and tempted by the devil, I took the necklace, wrapped it in a handkerchief, and, carrying it to the market, handed it to a broker. When he saw it, he kissed my hand and said, "By God, this is fine; by God, this is a fine and fortunate way to start business. O what a blessed morning!" Then he took me to the shop of my landlord, who made me sit by his side.

We waited until the market was full, and the broker took the necklace, offered it secretly, and without my knowledge got two thousand dinars for it. He returned to me, saying, "Sir, we thought that the necklace was gold, but it turned out to be fake, and I was offered a thousand dirhams for it. Will you accept the offer?" I replied, "Yes, I accept, for I know that it was brass." When the broker heard my reply, he realized that there was a problem with the necklace and struck a bargain with the chief merchant, who went to the chief of the police and told him that the necklace had been stolen from him and that the thief had been apprehended, dressed as a merchant.

Suddenly, calamity fell upon me, for as I sat in the shop, the officers seized me unawares and took me to the chief of the police. When he asked me about the necklace, I told him what I had told the broker, and he laughed, thinking that I had stolen it, and before I knew it, I was stripped and beaten with rods until, smarting from the blows, I lied, saying, "Yes, I stole it." After they wrote down my confession, they cut off my hand, and when they seared it with boiling oil, I fainted and remained unconscious for half of that day. Then they gave me wine to drink, and my landlord carried me away and said to me, "My son, being a nice young man of substance and means, why did you have to steal? When you steal from people, none will have mercy on you. Son, you stand convicted; leave my house and find yourself another lodging; go in peace." I felt disappointed and said to him, "Sir, I wonder whether you can give me three days to find another place." He replied, "Very well," and left me, sad and worried, wondering, "If I go back home with my hand cut off, how shall I face my people and convince them that I am innocent?" and I wept bitterly.

*But morning overtook Shahrazad, and she lapsed into silence. Then Dinarzad said, "Sister, what a strange and entertaining story!" Shahrazad replied, "What is this compared with what I shall tell you tomorrow night if I live!"*

### THE ONE HUNDRED AND THIRTY-SEVENTH NIGHT

*The following night Shahrazad said:*

I heard, O happy King, that the Jewish physician told the king of China that the young man said:

I was ill for two days, and on the third day I suddenly found my landlord and the chief merchant, who had bought the necklace from me and accused me of stealing it from him, standing at my door, with five police officers standing on guard. I asked them, "What is the matter?" but they bound me at once and put around my neck a collar attached to a chain, saying, "The necklace that was with you belongs to the governor of Damascus, who told us that for three years it had been missing, together with his daughter." When I heard what they said, my heart sank within me, and I went with them, with a cut-off hand. So I covered my face, saying to myself, "I will tell the governor my true story, and if he wishes, let him kill me, and if he wishes, let him pardon me."

They brought me to the governor and made me stand before him, and when he looked at me, he said, "Unbind him. Is he the one who took my necklace to the market to sell?" They replied, "Yes, he is." He said, "He did not steal it; why did you cut off his hand unjustly? Poor fellow!" When I heard this, I took heart and said to him, "My lord, by God, I did not steal the necklace, but they slandered me, and this merchant, claiming that the necklace belonged to him and accusing me of stealing it, took me to the chief of the police and when the chief had me beaten with rods, I smarted from the blows and lied against myself." The governor said, "Don't be afraid." Then he sentenced the chief merchant who had taken the necklace from me, saying to him, "Pay him indemnity for his hand, or I will beat you until I flay your hide." And he cried out to the officers, who dragged the merchant away, while I remained with the governor. He said to me, "My son, speak the truth and tell me the story of the necklace and how you came by it. Don't lie, and be truthful, for the truth will make you free." I replied, "By God, this has been my intention." Then I related to him in detail what had happened to me and the young lady and how she had brought with her the girl who owned the necklace and had murdered her at night, out of jealousy. When he heard my story, he shook his head, wrung his hands, and, with tears in his eyes, said, "To God we belong and to Him we return." Then turning to me, he said, "My son, let me explain everything to you. It so happened that . . ."

*But morning overtook Shahrazad, and she lapsed into silence. Then Dinarzad said to her sister, "What a strange and entertaining story!" Shahrazad replied, "What is this compared with what I shall tell you tomorrow night if the king spares me and lets me live!"*

THE ONE HUNDRED AND THIRTY-EIGHTH NIGHT

*The following night Shahrazad said:*

I heard, O happy King, that the Jewish physician told the king of China that the young man said:

The governor said, "The first young lady who came to you was my eldest daughter. I brought her up in strict seclusion, then married her to her cousin in Cairo. Then he died, and she came back to me, having learned bad habits there. She visited you three or four times and at last brought you her sister, my middle daughter. They were sisters from the same mother, and they loved each other and could not bear to be without each other even for a single hour. When the elder sister was having her affair with you, she revealed the secret to her sister, who desired to visit you with her; so she asked for your permission and brought her to you. But she got jealous of her and murdered her and returned home, without letting me know anything. When we sat down to eat that day, and I looked for my daughter but could not find her, I inquired after her from her elder sister and found her crying and grieving for her. She said to me, 'Father, at the time of the call to prayer, she suddenly put on her clothes and jewelry, including her necklace, wrapped herself in her cloak, and went out.' I kept waiting for her, day and night, without telling anyone, for fear of scandal, while her elder sister, who had murdered her, kept weeping for her, refusing to eat or drink, saying 'I will never stop weeping for her until I die,' until she worried us and made our lives miserable. Finally, when she could not bear it any longer, she killed herself, and I continued to grieve more and more for her. This is what happened. If you look at what happens to the likes of you and me, you will agree that 'this life is all vanity and that man is but a transient image, which vanishes as soon as it appears.'

"Now, my son, I would like you not to disobey me. Today, what had been foreordained for you came to pass, and your hand was cut off unjustly, but now I would like you to accept my offer and marry my youngest daughter, for she is born of a different mother. I will provide you with the dowry and will give you clothes and money, settle an allowance on you, and treat you like my son. What do you say?" I replied, "My lord, how could I hope for such a good fortune? Yes, I accept." Then he took he at once to his house, sent for the witnesses, and married me to his daughter, and I went in to her. Moreover, he got me a large indemnity from the chief merchant and continued to hold me in the highest esteem. When at the beginning of this year news reached me that my father had died, I told the governor and he obtained from the king in Egypt an edict and sent it with a courier, who went to Mosul and brought me back all the money my father had left me, and now I am living in all prosperity. This, then, is the cause of hiding my right hand, begging your pardon, doctor!

His story amazed me, and I stayed with him until he went to the bath a second time and returned to his wife. He gave me a considerable sum of money and, providing me for my journey, bade me good-bye and sent me on my way. I left him and journeyed eastward until I reached Baghdad. Then I traveled in Persia and finally came to your city, where I have lived contentedly until my last night's adventure with the roguish hunchback. Isn't this story more amazing than that of the hunchback?

*But morning overtook Shahrazad, and she lapsed into silence. Then Dinarzad said to her sister, "What a strange and entertaining story!" Shahrazad replied, "What is this compared with what I shall tell you tomorrow night if the king spares me and lets me live!"*

THE ONE HUNDRED AND THIRTY-NINTH NIGHT

*The following night Shahrazad said:*

I heard that when the king of China heard the Jewish physician's story, he shook his head and said, "No, by God, it is not stranger or more amazing than the story of the hunchback, and I must kill all four of you, for all of you plotted to kill the roguish hunchback, and you have told stories that were not more amazing than his. But there is still you, tailor, you who are the chief offender. Tell me a story that is more wonderful, more amazing, more diverting, and more entertaining than that of the hunchback, or I will kill you all." The tailor replied, "Very well":

# [The Tailor's Tale:
# The Lame Young Man from Baghdad
# and the Barber]

O King of the age, the most amazing thing that ever happened to me occurred yesterday, before I met the roguish hunchback. I was invited to an early morning banquet, together with about twenty companions from the city. As soon as the sun rose and they set food before us, the host entered with a handsome stranger, a perfectly beautiful young man, except that he was lame. We stood in salute, in deference to the host, and the young man was about to sit down when, seeing among us a man who was a barber by profession, he refused to sit and started to leave. But the host stopped him and adjured him, asking, "Why do you enter my house and leave at once?" The young man replied, "For God's sake, my lord, don't hinder me. The cause is that ill-omened, ill-behaved, bungling, shameful, and pernicious old barber." When we and the host heard this description of the barber, we took a look at him and began to feel an aversion for him.

*But morning overtook Shahrazad, and she lapsed into silence. Then Dinarzad said to her sister, "What a strange and entertaining story!" Shahrazad replied, "What is this compared with what I shall tell you tomorrow night if I stay alive!"*

THE ONE HUNDRED AND FORTIETH NIGHT

*The following night Shahrazad said:*

I heard, O happy King, that the tailor said to the king of China:

When we heard this description of the barber, we said, "None of us will be able to eat and enjoy himself, unless the young man tells us about the barber." The young man said, "O fellows, I had an adventure with this barber in my native city of Baghdad, and he was in fact the cause of my breaking my leg and becoming lame. I have sworn never to sit in the same place or live in the same city

with him, and because of him I left Baghdad and settled in this
city. Now suddenly, I find him here with you. Not another night
shall pass before I depart from here." We begged him to sit down
and tell us what had happened between him and the barber, in
Baghdad, while the barber turned pale and bowed his head. The
young man said:

My father was one of the richest men of Baghdad, and God had
blessed him with no other child but myself. When I grew up and
reached manhood, he died, and the Almighty God took him under
His mercy. He left me great wealth, and I began to dress handsomely and to live the best of lives. It happened that God had made
me a hater of women, and one day, as I was walking along one
of the streets of Baghdad, a group of women blocked my way and
I fled from them into a blind alley. I had not sat long, when a
window opened and there appeared, tending some flowers in the
window, a young lady, as radiant as the moon and so beautiful that
I have never seen one more beautiful. When she saw me, she smiled,
setting my heart on fire, and my hatred of women was changed
to love. I continued sitting there, lost to the world till close to sundown, when the judge of the city, riding a she-mule, came by, dismounted, and entered the young lady's house, leading me to guess
that he was her father. I went home in sorrow and fell on my bed,
consumed with passion. My relatives came in and wondered what
was the matter with me, but I did not reply. I remained like this
for several days until they began to lament over me.

One day an old woman came in to see me and, looking at me,
guessed at once what was the matter with me. She sat down at my
head, spoke gently to me, and said, "Son, be cheerful; tell me what
ails you, and I will help you get what you desire." Her words soothed
my heart and we sat talking.

*But morning overtook Shahrazad, and she lapsed into silence.
Then Dinarzad said, "Sister, what a strange and entertaining story!"
Shahrazad replied, "What is this compared with what I shall tell
you tomorrow night if the king spares me and lets me live!"*

THE ONE HUNDRED AND FORTY-FIRST NIGHT

*The following night Shahrazad said:*

I heard, O King, that the tailor told the king of China that the
young man said to the guests:

The old woman gazed on me and recited the following verses:

No, by her radiant brow and rosy cheeks,
My eyes I turned not when she left the place,
But like an eyeless man, I rolled along,
In my confusion, stumbling in her trace.
She was a nimble deer, well-used to run,
A cruel mistress, with a heart of stone.
She set my heart and soul on hellish fire
And I became a misfit, alien and alone,
Cheeks in the dust and eyes flowing with tears,
Mourning the old days and love I did crave.
Helpless I grieve, but what avail the sighs?
I am dead without her, though not in my grave,
Haunted by everlasting memories
Of her face that showed neither joy nor rage.
Heart, break with grief and let my soul expire,
O heart of silver in a marble cage!
Consumed with love, impatient with my fate,
I watch my rivals pressing in their turn,
Unable to reproach them for their love.
O will the good old days ever return?
How can my soul forbear or how forget
Her slender body and her lovely face,
Which like the shining sun dazzled the world
As I held her in an ardent embrace
And in the dark tasted the night's delight,
Lying on green grass that felt like the down
That graces tender, plump, and rosy cheeks,
Fondling her cheeks like silk of high renown,
Clutching them as a miser clutches gold,
Feeling their softness like silk stuffed with flowers
Or with a tender heart throbbing unseen!
O let the watchman come; she had redeemed my hours!
My love is constant; I have never changed,
Unlike the others, never turned away,
But always loved and will forever love;
Keeping the pledge with honor is my way.
I swore that if I died from grief, I would not plead;
A stoic lover does not need to sigh,
And I am not a heedless lover, quick to blame
Or to betray, for none knows love as I.
We lived in bliss and boundless happiness
Until I thought our Eden safe from blight,
Thought we would stay secure and never part.
Now all has died and vanished from my sight.
Alas for the days with that black-eyed deer!

If they return and bring her back to me,
I pledge eternal fasting all my days.
For without her I will an outcast be,
Living love's victim to eternity.


*But morning overtook Shahrazad, and she lapsed into silence.
Then Dinarzad said, "Sister, what an entertaining story!" Shahrazad
replied, "What is that compared with what I shall tell you tomorrow
night if I live!"*

THE ONE HUNDRED AND FORTY-SECOND NIGHT

*The following night Shahrazad said:*

I heard, O happy King, that the tailor told the king of China
that the young man said to the guests:

Then the old woman said to me, "Son, tell me your story." When
I told her, she said, "Son, that young lady is the daughter of the
judge of Baghdad, and she is kept in strict seclusion. The place
where you saw her is her private room, which she occupies by herself
alone, while her parents live in the great hall below. I often visit
her, and I will undertake to help you, for you will not get to her
but through me. Gird your loins." When I heard her words, I was
encouraged and began to eat and drink, to the satisfaction of my
family.

The old woman left and came back the following morning, crest-
fallen, and said, "Son, don't ask how I fared with the young lady
when I mentioned you to her. The last thing she said about you
was, 'Wretched woman, if you don't stop this talk, I will punish
you as you deserve, and if you ever mention him again, I will tell
my father.' But by God, son, I must try her again, even if I suffer
for it." When I heard what she said, I felt even worse than before
and kept repeating, "Alas, how cruel is love!" The old woman visited
me every day, while my illness dragged on, until all the physicians
and sages and my entire family began to despair of my recovery.

One day the old woman came in and, sitting at my head, whispered to me, out of the hearing of my family, "You must give me
a reward for good news." When I heard her words, I sat up and
said, "The reward is yours." She said, "My lord, I went yesterday
to the young lady, who welcomed me and, seeing that I was brokenhearted and tearful, asked, 'O aunt, what is the matter with you,
and why are you unhappy?' I replied tearfully, 'My lady, I have

just come from a sick young man, who has been lying, now conscious, now unconscious. His family has given up on him, and he will surely perish because of you.' She asked, as she began to feel pity, 'What is he to you?' I replied, 'He is my son. He saw you some time ago, at your window, watering your flowers, and when he looked at your face and lovely hand, his heart was captivated, and he fell madly in love with you. These were the verses he recited:

> By the rare treasure of your lovely face,
> Don't kill your lover with your cruel disdain.
> His heart is intoxicated with love,
> His wasting body racked and torn with pain.
> By your supple, curving, and graceful frame,
> Your mouth that puts the perfect pearls to shame,
> The piercing arrow from your arching brows
> That found my heart without missing the aim,
> Your slender, melting waist, which is as frail
> As the sad lover who pines for you,
> By the enchanting star of ambergris,
> Gracing your cheek, your victim mercy show.
> And by your curling sidelocks, have pity,
> Be tender, and give him your love divine,
> For by the pearls between your coral lips,
> By your sweet mouth and its delicious wine,
> Your belly, folded in poetic lines
> That lacerate my heart; O painful dream!
> And by your legs, which brought me death and doom,
> Only your love can your lover redeem.

But, my lady, when he sent me to you last time, I fared badly at your hands.'"

*But morning overtook Shahrazad, and she lapsed into silence. Then Dinarzad said to her sister, "What a strange and entertaining story!" Shahrazad replied, "What is this compared with what I shall tell you tomorrow night if the king spares me and lets me live!" The king said to himself, "By God, I will not kill her until I hear the rest of the hunchback's story."*

### THE ONE HUNDRED AND FORTY-THIRD NIGHT

*The following night Shahrazad said:*

I heard, O happy King, that the tailor told the king of China that the young man said to the guests:

The old woman said, "'O my lady, I fared badly at your hands, and when I went back to him and acquainted him with your reply, he got worse and remained bedridden until I thought that he would surely die and gave him up for lost.' The young lady turned pale and asked, 'Is all this because of me?' I replied, 'Yes, by God, my lady; what is your command?' She replied, 'Let him come here on Friday, before the noon prayer, and when he arrives, I will come down, open the door, and take him upstairs to my room, where he can visit with me for a while and then leave, before my father comes back.'" O fellows, when I heard the old woman's words, my anguish ceased. Then she sat at my head and said, "God willing, be ready on Friday." Then she received the reward I owed her and departed, leaving me completely recovered, to the delight of my family.

I kept waiting, and on Friday the old woman came in and inquired after my health, and I replied that I was hale and hearty. Then I rose, put on my clothes, and scented myself with perfumes and incense. The old woman asked me, "Why don't you go to the bath and wash off the traces of your illness?" I replied, "I have no desire to go to the bath, and I have already washed myself with water, but I do want a barber to shave my head." Then I turned to the servant and said to him, "Get me a sensible and discreet barber who will not give me a headache with his chatter." The servant went out and returned with this wretched old barber. When he entered, he greeted me and I returned his greeting. Then he said to me, "My lord, I see that you are emaciated." I replied, "I have been ill." He said, "May God be kind to you and make you well." I said, "May God hear your prayer." He said, "My lord, be cheerful, for your recovery is at hand," adding, "O my lord, do you want me to shave your head or to let blood?"[6] I said, "Shave my head at once and spare me from your raving, for I am still weak from my illness."

*But morning overtook Shahrazad, and she lapsed into silence. Then Dinarzad said to her sister, "What a strange and entertaining story!" Shahrazad replied, "What is this compared with what I shall tell you tomorrow night if the king spares me and lets me live!"*

---

6. To this day, in certain parts of the Middle East, barbers function as surgeons and dentists.

ـبـابـ

## THE ONE HUNDRED AND FORTY-FOURTH NIGHT

*The following night Shahrazad said:*

I heard, O happy King, that the tailor told the king of China that the young man said to the guests:

I said to the barber, "I am still weak from my illness." Then he put his hand in his leather bag and took out an astrolabe[7] with seven plates inlaid with silver and, going into the courtyard, held the instrument up to the sun's rays and looked for some time. Then he said to me, "O my lord, eight degrees and six minutes have elapsed of this day, which is Friday, the eighteenth of Safar, in the six hundred and fifty-third year of Hijra and the seven thousand three hundred and twentieth year of the Alexander era, and the planet now in the ascendant, according to the mathematical calculations on the astrolabe, is Mars, which is in conjunction with Mercury, a conjunction that is favorable for cutting hair. I can also see that you intend to meet another person, and for that the time is inauspicious and ill-advised." I said to him, "By God, fellow, you are pestering me and wearying me with your wretched auguries. I have not brought you here to read the stars, but to shave my head. Proceed at once to perform what I have brought you for, or get out and let me call for another barber to shave my head." He said, "By God, my lord, 'even if you had cooked it in milk, it wouldn't have turned out better.' You have asked for a barber, and God has sent you a barber who is also an astrologer and a physician, versed in the arts of alchemy, astrology, grammar, lexicography, logic, scholastic disputation, rhetoric, arithmetic, algebra, and history, as well as the traditions of the Prophet, according to Muslim and al-Bukhari.[8] I have read many books and digested them, I have had experience of affairs and understood them, and I have studied all sciences and crafts and mastered them. In short, I have tried and mastered everything. It behooves you to give thanks to the Almighty God for what He has sent you and to praise Him for what He has bestowed on you. Follow my advice today, and obey the stars. I offer it to you free of charge, for it is nothing, considering my affection and esteem for you. Your father loved me because of my discretion; therefore, my service is obligatory to you."

7. Instrument used formerly by astrologers for ascertaining the positions of the heavenly bodies.
8. Two of the compilers of the sayings of the prophet Muhammad.

When I heard his speech, I said to him, "You will surely be the death of me today."

*But morning overtook Shahrazad, and she lapsed into silence. Then Dinarzad said to her sister, "What a strange and entertaining story!" Shahrazad replied, "What is this compared with what I shall tell you tomorrow night if the king spares me and lets me live!"*

THE ONE HUNDRED AND FORTY-FIFTH NIGHT

*The following night Shahrazad said:*

I heard, O happy King, that the tailor told the king of China that the young man said to the guests:

The barber added, "Am I not the one whom, because of my taciturnity, people call the Silent One? My eldest brother is called al-Baqbuq [the Prater], the second al-Haddar [the Babbler], the third al-Buqaybiq [the Gabbler], the fourth al-Kiuz al-Aswani [the Stone Mug], the fifth al-Nashshar [the Braggart], the sixth Shaqayiq [the Noisy], while I, because of my taciturnity, al-Samit [the Silent One]." The barber kept talking until I got exasperated and angrily said to my servant, "For the sake of the Almighty God, give him four dinars and let him go. I do not wish to have my head shaved today." When the barber heard my words, he said to me, "O my lord, what kind of talk is this? I swear that I am under an obligation not to accept any money from you until I have served you, and indeed I must serve you, for it is my duty to help you and fulfill your need; and I don't care whether I get paid or not. If you, my lord, don't know my worth, I know yours and know what you deserve because of the esteem I hold for your father." Then he recited the following verses:

> I came one day to my lord to let blood,
> But found out that the season was not good
> And sat and talked of many prodigies
> And my store of knowledge before him strewed.
> Pleased with my talk, he turned and said to me,
> "You are beyond compare, O mine of lore!"
> I said, "O lord of men, you are the source,
> Bestowing wisdom from your boundless store,
> O lord of grace and all munificence,
> O treasure house of knowledge, wit, and sense!"

[He added, "When I recited these same verses to your father], he was pleased and cried out to the servant, saying, 'Give him a hundred and three dinars and a robe of honor,' and the servant did as he bade. Then I read the signs and, finding the moment auspicious, let blood. When that was done, I could not help asking him, 'By God, my lord, what made you bid the servant give me a hundred and three dinars?' He replied, 'One dinar was for your astrological observation, another for your entertaining conversation, the third for the bloodletting, and the remaining hundred and the robe of honor for your praise of me.'" The barber went on and on until I got so angry that I burst out, crying "May God show no mercy to my father for knowing the likes of you."

*But morning overtook Shahrazad, and she lapsed into silence. Then Dinarzad said to her sister, "What a strange and entertaining story!" Shahrazad replied, "What is this compared with what I shall tell you tomorrow night if I am alive!"*

THE ONE HUNDRED AND FORTY-SIXTH NIGHT

*The following night Shahrazad said:*

I heard, O happy King, that the tailor told the king of China that the young man told the guests:

I said to the barber, "For God's sake, spare me your chatter, for I am going to be late." But he laughed and said, "There is no god but God. Glory be to Him who changes not. My lord, I must conclude that your illness has changed you from what you used to be, for I see that you have become foolish, while people usually become wiser, as they grow older. I have heard the poet say:

> Comfort the poor with money, if you can,
> And God's recompense will be yours by right.
> Want is a dire affliction, hard to cure,
> But money can improve a sorry sight.
> And if you meet your fellows, wish them peace,
> And show your parents their due reverence.
> How oft have they, sleepless, waited for you,
> Praying to God to keep his vigilance!

In any case, you are excused, but I worry about you. You should know that your father and grandfather did nothing without consulting me, for it is said, 'He who takes counsel shall not be disappointed,' and 'He who has no mentor will never be a mentor.' And the poet says:

> Before you proceed to do anything,
> Consult a mature man ere venturing.

Indeed, you will find none more experienced than I, and I am here, standing on my feet, ready to serve you. I am not annoyed with you; why should you be annoyed with me?" I said to him, "By God, fellow, you have talked too much; all I want from you is to shave my head and be done with it." He said, "I know that my lord is displeased with me, but I do not hold it against you." I said to him, "My appointment is drawing near; for the sake of the Almighty God, fellow, shave my head and go." And I tore my clothes. When he saw me do this, he took the razor and, sharpening it, came up to me, shaved a few hairs, then held his hand back and said, "My lord, haste is of the devil, for the poet says:

> Be careful and restrain your hasty wish;
> Be merciful to all, and they will mercy show.
> The hand of God is above every hand,
> And every tyrant shall another know.

My lord, I don't think that you know my worth, for you are unaware of my knowledge, wisdom, and high merit." I replied, "Stop meddling, for you have pestered me enough." He said, "My lord, it seems to me that you are in a hurry." I replied, "Yes, yes, yes!" He said, "Don't be in a hurry, for haste is of the devil and leads to regret. I am worried about you, and I would like you to let me know what it is you intend to do, for I fear that it might prove harmful to you. There are still three hours left to the end of prayer," adding, "However, I don't wish to be in doubt about this but I must know for certain the exact time, for speech, when it is conjectural, is flawed, especially in one like me, whose merit is plain and known among men; and it does not befit me to base my statements on conjecture, as do the common sort of astrologers." Then he threw down the razor, went out . . .

*But morning overtook Shahrazad, and she lapsed into silence. Then Dinarzad said to her sister, "What a strange and entertaining story!" Shahrazad replied, "What is this compared with what I shall tell you tomorrow night if the king spares me and lets me live!"*

## THE ONE HUNDRED AND FORTY-SEVENTH NIGHT

*The following night Shahrazad said:*

I heard, O happy King, that the tailor told the king of China that the young man said to the guests:

The barber threw down the razor, went out with the astrolabe, and came back, counting on his fingers, and said, "According to the learned and wise mathematicians and astrologers, there are exactly three hours left to the end of prayer, neither more nor less." I said to him, "For God's sake, fellow, hold your tongue, for you have tormented me enough." So this cursed fellow took the razor, shaved a few hairs, and said, "By God, I don't know the cause of your haste, and I am concerned about it. You would do better to tell me, for your father and grandfather — may God have mercy on them — did nothing without consulting me."

When I realized that I was not going to get rid of him, I said to myself, "Noon is approaching, and I wish to go to the young lady before the people return from the mosque. If I am delayed much longer, I will not be able to get to her." Then I said to him, "Be quick and stop jabbering, for I have to go to a party at the house of one of my friends." When he heard me speak of a party, he said, "This day of yours is a blessed one for me; you have reminded me that yesterday I invited a group of friends, and I have forgotten to provide something for them to eat till now. What a disgrace in their eyes!" I replied, "Don't worry about it. I have told you that I am going to a party today. All the food and drink in my house shall be yours, if you hurry and shave my head." He said, "God bless you, but tell me what you are giving me, so that I may know and inform my guests." I replied, "I have five different dishes, ten fried chickens, and a roasted lamb." He said, "Bring them out, so that I may see them." I bade one of my servants buy all that and bring it back quickly. The servant did as I bade him, and when the barber saw the food, he said, "My lord, the food is here, but there is no wine." I said to him, "I have two flagons of wine." He said, "Have them brought out." I said to the servant, "Bring them," and when he did, the barber said, "O what an excellent fellow, what a generous soul, and what a noble pedigree! We have the food and wine, but there remain [the perfume and the incense]."

I brought him a box containing five dinars' worth of aloewood, ambergris, and musk, and as time was running out, I said to him,

"For God's sake, take the whole box and finish shaving my head."
But he replied, "By God, I will not take it until I see the contents,
one by one." I bade the servant open the box, and the barber threw
down the astrolabe, sat down, and began to turn over the contents,
before accepting them. Meanwhile, I waited, with most of my head
still unshaven, until I choked with exasperation. Then taking the
razor, he came up to me and shaved a little hair, reciting the following verses:

> The growing boy follows his father's suit,
> Just as the tree grows firmly from its root.

Then he added, "By God, my lord, I don't know whether to thank
you or thank your father, for my party owes itself entirely to your
generosity. May God preserve it and preserve you. None of my
friends is worthy of it; yet they are all decent men, such as Zentut
the bathkeeper and Sali' the corndealer and Sallut the beanseller
and Akrasha the grocer and Sa'id the cameldriver and Suwaid the
porter and Hamid the garbageman and Abu-Makarish the bath-
attendant and Qusaim the watchman and Karim the groom. There
is not one among them who is disagreeable, contentious, meddlesome or troublesome. Each has his own dance, which he dances,
and his verses, which he sings. But their best quality is that they
are like your servant and slave; they neither meddle nor talk too
much. The bathkeeper sings enchantingly to the little drum and
dances and says, 'I am going out, mother, to fill my jar.' As for
the corndealer . . ."

*But morning overtook Shahrazad, and she lapsed into silence.
Then Dinarzad said to her sister, "What a strange and entertain-
ing story!" Shahrazad replied, "What is this compared with what
I shall tell you tomorrow night if the king spares me and lets me live!"*

### THE ONE HUNDRED AND FORTY-EIGHTH NIGHT

*The following night, Shahrazad said:*

I heard, O happy King, that the tailor told the king of China
that the young man said to the guests:

The barber said, "The corndealer sings better than the nightingale
and dances and says, 'O wailing mistress, you have not done badly,'
which makes the men laugh until their hearts burst from laughter.

As for the garbageman, he dances to the tambourine and charms even the birds, as he sings, 'News from my neighbor is locked in a chest.' He is a clever, deft, spirited, quick-witted, and refined fellow, of whose virtues I like to say:

> O my life for a handsome garbageman,
> Whose boughlike gait has set my heart on fire!
> Fate blessed me with him one night, and I said,
> Feeling the ebb and flow of my desire,
> 'You have inflamed my heart,' and he replied,
> 'No wonder that a scavenger can light the pyre!'

Indeed, every one of these men is accomplished in knowing how to divert the mind with mirth and fun. Perhaps my lord would like to join us today and postpone going to his friends, as he had intended, for you still show traces of illness and you may meet there some meddlesome and very talkative people or may encounter a busybody who will give you a headache, while you are still weak from illness."

I said to him, "You have not failed in giving me your good advice," and, in spite of my anger, I laughed, adding, "Perhaps some other time, the Almighty God willing. Finish my business and go in God's peace and enjoy yourself with your friends and companions, for they are waiting for you." He said, "My lord, I only wish to introduce you to the company of these nice fellows, among whom there is not one meddlesome or garrulous man, for since I reached manhood, I have never been able to tolerate the company of a man who meddles in what concerns him not or who is not, like myself, a man of few words. If you were once to spend some time with them, you would forsake all your friends." I said, "May God grant you joy with them. I must visit you and enjoy their company one of these days." He said, "I wish it were today, but if you are determined not to come with me but to go to your friends today, then let me take to my guests what you have kindly given me for them and leave them to eat and drink without me, while I return to you and go with you to your friends, for there is no formality between me and my friends to prevent me from leaving them and returning to you." I replied, "There is no power and no strength, save in God, the Almighty, the Magnificent. Go to your friends and enjoy yourself with them, and let me go to mine and be with them this day, for they are waiting for me." The barber said, "My lord, God forbid that I leave you and let you go alone." I said, "The party I am going to is private, and you will not be able to get in." He said, "My lord, I believe that you are going to meet a woman and that if you were really going to a party, you would take me with you, for it is the like of me that brings color to places of entertainment, parties, celebrations, and festivals. And if you are planning to be alone with some woman, I am the fittest . . ."

*But morning overtook Shahrazad, and she lapsed into silence. Then Dinarzad said to her sister, "What a strange and entertaining story!" Shahrazad said, "What is this compared with what I shall tell you if I stay alive!"*

### THE ONE HUNDRED AND FORTY-NINTH NIGHT

*The following night Shahrazad said:*

I heard, O happy King, that the tailor told the king of China that the young man said to the guests:

The barber said, "I am the fittest of all men to help you in your plan and to see that no one sees you entering the place and puts you in jeopardy, for in Baghdad one cannot do anything of the kind, especially on a day like this and in a city whose chief of the police is very powerful, severe, and sharp-tempered." I said to him, "Damn you, wretched old man! Aren't you ashamed to speak to me like this?" He replied, "You silly man, you ask me whether I am not ashamed, yet you hide from me your plan, which I know for certain, while all I wanted was to help you today." Fearful lest my family and neighbors should hear the barber's talk and I be exposed, I remained silent, while he finished shaving my head. By then it was almost noon, and the first and second exhortations to prayer were over and the hour of prayer had come. I said to him, "Take the food and drink to your friends, while I wait for your return and take you with me." I kept trying to cajole and outsmart the cursed fellow, hoping that he would leave me, but he replied, "I think that you are trying to trick me and go alone and cast yourself in some peril from which there is no escape. For God's sake, for God's sake, don't leave until I come back and go with you, so that I may watch for you and see that you don't fall into a trap." I replied, "Very well, but don't be late." Then he took all that I had given him of food, drink, roast lamb, and perfume and went out. But the cursed fellow sent everything to his house with a porter and hid himself in an alley.

As for me, I rose at once, for the announcers of prayer had already chanted the salutations, dressed myself, and went out in a hurry until I came to the house where I had seen the young lady—I did not realize that the cursed barber had followed me. I found the door open, and when I went in, I found the old woman on her feet, waiting for me. I went upstairs to the young lady's room, but hardly had I gone in, when the master of the house returned from the mosque and, entering the house, closed the door behind him. I looked out from the window and saw this cursed barber sitting by the door and said to myself, "How did that devil find me out?" At that moment, as God had decreed my undoing, it happened that a maid had committed some offense for which the master of the house beat her. So she screamed, and when a male slave came to rescue her, the judge beat him also, and the slave too began to scream. The cursed barber concluded that it was I whom the judge was beating and began to tear his clothes, throw dust on his head, and cry out for help. The people began to gather around him, while he kept crying out, "My master is being murdered in the judge's house." Then he ran, shrieking, toward my house, followed by the crowd, and told my family and servants. Before I knew it, they arrived, with torn clothes and disheveled hair, crying out, "Alas for our master!" with the barber at their head, in a sorry state, tearing his clothes and screaming.

*But morning overtook Shahrazad, and she lapsed into silence. Then Dinarzad said to her sister, "Sister, what a strange and entertaining story!" Shahrazad replied, "What is this compared with what I shall tell you if the king spares me and lets me live!"*

THE ONE HUNDRED AND FIFTIETH NIGHT

*The following night Shahrazad said:*

It is related, O happy King, that the tailor told the king of China that the young man said to the guests:

My relatives kept crying out, "Alas for our murdered one, alas for our murdered one," while a crowd gathered around them, until the judge, hearing the uproar and the screaming at his door, said to one of his servants, "Go and see what is the matter." The servant went out and came back, saying, "O my lord, there are more than ten thousand men and women at the door, crying out, 'Alas for our murdered one,' and pointing to our house." When the judge heard this, he became apprehensive and worried and, opening the door, went out and saw a great crowd of people. He was amazed and said, "O people, what is the matter?" They replied, "O cursed man, O pig, you have killed our master." He said, "What has your master done to me that I should kill him? My house is open to you." The barber said, "You beat him with a rod and I heard him just now screaming inside the house." The judge repeated, "What has your master done to me that I should beat him, and what brings him into my house?" The barber replied, "Don't be perverse, vile old man. I know everything. Your daughter is in love with him and he with her, and when you found them out, you bade your servants beat him. By God, none shall judge between us and you but the caliph, unless you bring out our master to his relatives, before I go in and bring him out myself and put you to shame." The judge stood blushing and tongue-tied before the crowd and could only mumble, "If you are speaking the truth, come in and fetch him." The barber pushed forward and entered the house.

When I saw the barber enter the house, I looked for an exit or a means of escape or a place to hide but saw none, save a large chest that stood in the room. I got into the chest, pulled the lid down on me, and held my breath. When the barber came into the room, he searched, looking right and left and, seeing nothing but the chest in which I was hiding, placed it on his head and left with it in a hurry. At this I lost my mind and, feeling certain that he would not let me alone, took courage and, opening the chest, threw myself to the ground and broke my leg. I opened the door and saw a great crowd of people. Now I happened to have a good sum of money hidden in my sleeve for such a day; so I took the money out and began to scatter it among the crowd, and while they were busy scrambling for it, I fled, running right and left through the alleys of Baghdad, while the cursed barber, whom nothing could divert, kept running after me from place to place.

*But morning overtook Shahrazad, and she lapsed into silence. Then Dinarzad said to her sister, "What a strange and entertaining story!" Shahrazad replied, "What is this compared with what I shall tell you tomorrow night if I stay alive!"*

### THE ONE HUNDRED AND FIFTY-FIRST NIGHT

*The following night Shahrazad said:*

I heard, O happy King, that the tailor told the king of China that the young man said to the guests:

I kept running, while the barber ran and shouted after me, "They would have killed and bereft me of my benefactor and the benefactor of my family, my children, and my friends, but praise be to God who made me triumph over them and helped me deliver my lord from their hands." Then he asked me, "My lord, where do you want to go now? If God had not sent me to you, you would not have escaped destruction at their hands, for no one else could have saved you. How long can I live to protect you? By God, you have nearly undone me by your desire and foolish decision to go alone. But I will not reproach you for your foolishness, for you are a rash and ignorant bumbler."

The young man continued:

As if the barber was not satisfied with what he had inflicted on me, he kept pursuing me and shouting after me through the streets of Baghdad until I lost all patience and in my rage and fury against him took refuge in a caravansary inside the market and sought the protection of the owner, who finally drove the barber away. Then I sat in one of the shops and thought to myself, "If I return home, I will never be able to get rid of this cursed fellow, and he will be with me day and night, while I can't stand even the look of him." So I sent out at once for witnesses and made a will, dividing the greater part of my money among my family, and appointed a guardian over them, bidding him sell the house and be in charge of the old and the young. Then, in order to get rid of this pander, I took some money with me and set out on that very day from the caravansary until I reached this country and settled in your city, where I have been living for some time. When you favored me with your invitation and I came here, whom should I see but this cursed barber, seated in the place of honor? How can I then enjoy myself in the company of this fellow who brought all this upon me, causing me to break my leg, leave my family and my home and country, and go into exile? Now I have run into him again, here at your place.

The young man refused to sit down and join us. When we heard what happened to the young man at the hands of the barber, we were very much amazed and entertained by the story, and we asked the barber, "Is what the young man says about you true? And why did you do it?" He raised his head and replied, "Fellows, I did it out of my wisdom, good sense, and humanity. Were it not for me, he would have perished, for none but I was responsible for his escape. It was good that he suffered in his leg and not in his life.

I endured so much just to do a favor to one who does not deserve it. By God, of all my six brothers—I am the seventh—there is none less talkative, less meddlesome, or wiser than I. I will tell you now about an incident that happened to me, in order to prove to you that, unlike all my brothers, I am neither meddlesome nor talkative."

## [The Barber's Tale]

I was living in Baghdad, in the days of al-Mustansir Billah[9] son of al-Mustazi Billah. Baghdad at that time was where the caliph resided. He loved the humble and the poor and associated with the learned and the pious. One day it happened that he was angry with a group of ten men and commanded the chief of the police of Baghdad to bring them before him on a feast day.

*But morning overtook Shahrazad, and she lapsed into silence. Then Dinarzad said to her sister, "Sister, what a strange and amazing story!" Shahrazad replied, "What is this compared with what I shall tell you tomorrow night if the king spares me and lets me live!"*

THE ONE HUNDRED AND FIFTY-SECOND NIGHT

*The following night Shahrazad said:*

I heard, O happy King, that the tailor told the king of China that the barber said to the guests:

The caliph ordered the chief of the police of Baghdad to bring before him at a feast ten men who had formed a band of robbers and made the road unsafe. The chief went out and, capturing them, embarked with them in a boat. When I saw them, I said to myself, "By God, these people have met for a party, and I think that they are going to spend the day on this boat, eating and drinking, and none shall be their companion but I." So, fellows, out of a sense of fellowship, as well as good sense, I slipped into the boat with them. They crossed the river, and as soon as they reached the opposite bank in Baghdad, there came police officers and guards with chains, which they put around the necks of the robbers, as well as mine, but because of my courtesy and reticence, fellows, I did not

9. A late Abbasid caliph who ruled from A.D. 1226 to 1242.

choose to speak and remained silent. Then they dragged us in chains and brought us before the Commander of the Faithful, who bade the heads of the ten robbers be struck off. The executioner came forward and, making us kneel before him on the leather mat of execution, drew his sword and struck off one head after another, until all ten were beheaded and none was left but myself. The caliph looked at me and said to the executioner, "You, you have struck off only nine heads." The executioner replied, "O Commander of the Faithful, God forbid that I should behead only nine, when you bade me behead ten." The caliph said, "This is the tenth, sitting before you." The executioner replied, "How can that be, how can that be! By your bounty, my lord, I have killed ten." So they counted the heads and found ten. Then the caliph looked at me and said, "You, what made you remain silent at such a time, and how did you come to be in the company of these murderers? You are advanced in years but retarded in understanding." When I heard the words of the Commander of the Faithful, I said, "O Commander of the Faithful, I am the Silent One, and I have attained of science and philosophy, wisdom and refinement, eloquent speech and repartee what no one has ever attained. The gravity of my apprehension, the keenness of my comprehension, the precision of my method, the greatness of my humanity and commitment, and the extent of my taciturnity are boundless and hard to attain. Yesterday I saw these ten men heading for a boat and, thinking that they were going to have a party, joined them and embarked with them. As soon as we crossed the river and disembarked, they met their fate. All my life, I have dealt kindly with people, but they repay me in the worst way."

When the caliph heard my words, he laughed until he fell on his back, realizing that I was no meddler, but a man of great generosity and few words, contrary to what I have been accused of by this young man, who has repaid me so badly, after I saved him from horrors. Then the caliph asked me, "Silent One, are your six brothers like you?" I replied, "May they perish and disappear if they are like me, act like me, or look like me. Each of my six brothers, O Commander of the Faithful, is afflicted with a bodily defect. One is one-eyed, another paraplegic, a third hunchbacked, a fourth blind, a fifth cropped of the ears, and a sixth cropped of the lips. You must not think that I am a man of many words, but I would like to show you that I am a man of greater worth and fewer words than my brothers, each of whom has a tale of how he came by his defect.

"The eldest was a tailor . . ."

*But morning overtook Shahrazad, and she lapsed into silence. Then Dinarzad said to her sister, "What a strange and entertaining story!" Shahrazad replied, "What is this compared with what I shall tell you tomorrow night if I stay alive!"*

### THE ONE HUNDRED AND FIFTY-THIRD NIGHT

*The following night Shahrazad said:*

It is related, O happy King, that the tailor told the king of China that the barber told the guests that he said to the caliph:

#### [The Tale of the First Brother, the Hunchbacked Tailor]

The eldest was a tailor who worked in Baghdad, in a rented shop, opposite the house of a very rich man, who had a mill in the lower part of his house. One day, as my brother the hunchback sat sewing in his shop, he happened to raise his head and saw at the bay window a lady like the rising moon, looking at the people below. When he saw her, his heart was set on fire, and he kept gazing at the window all day long till evening, when he gave up and went home sadly. The following morning he came to the shop, sat in his place, and kept gazing as before. A while later she came to the window to look at the people, as usual, and when he saw her, he fell into a swoon. Then he came to himself and went home, in a sad state. On the third day, as he was sitting in his usual place, the lady noticed that his eyes were riveted on her and smiled at him, and he smiled back. Then she withdrew and sent her maid to him with a piece of fine linen wrapped in a handkerchief. The maid said to him, "My lady sends you greetings and asks you to do her a favor and cut out a blouse from this fabric and sew it for her." He replied, "My friend, I hear and obey." Then he cut out the cloth and finished sewing it the same day.

Early the following day the maid came to him and said, "My lady sends you greetings and would like to know how you have passed the night, for she herself has not tasted sleep, thinking of you. Now she bids you cut and sew a pair of trousers to wear with her blouse." He replied, "I hear and obey," and began to cut out the trousers and sew them diligently. A while later, the lady appeared at the window, greeted him, and did not let him leave until he finished the trousers and dispatched them to her. Then he went home, confused and unable to buy supper; so he borrowed some money from a neighbor and bought some food.

The following morning, as soon as he arrived at the shop, the maid came by and said, "My master wishes to see you." When he heard her mention her master, he was terrified, thinking that her master had found out about him. But the maid said, "Don't be afraid. Nothing but good will come of this. My lady would like you to get acquainted with my master." My brother felt happy, and when he went in, he greeted the husband, and the husband returned the greeting and handed him a very large piece of Dabiqi linen,[1] saying, "Make this into shirts for me."

*But morning overtook Shahrazad, and she lapsed into silence. Then Dinarzad said, "Sister, what a strange and entertaining story!" Shahrazad replied, "What is this compared with what I shall tell you tomorrow night if the king spares me and lets me live!"*

THE ONE HUNDRED AND FIFTY-FOURTH NIGHT

*The following night Shahrazad said:*

I heard, O happy King, that the tailor told the king of China that the barber told the guests that he said to the caliph:

The husband said to my brother, "Make this into shirts for me." My brother fell to work and cut out twenty shirts and as many trousers by nightfall, without stopping to eat. Then the husband asked my brother, "What is your fee?" My brother replied, "Twenty dirhams' worth." The husband yelled at the maid, saying, "Bring the scales." At that moment the lady approached, seemingly angry at my brother for accepting the money, and he, realizing how she felt, said, "By God, I will take nothing from you." He took his work and went out, although he was sorely in need of money, and for three days all he ate was two loaves of bread and almost died from hunger.

Then the maid came to him and asked, "What have you done?" He replied, "They are finished," and, carrying them, went with her to the husband, who proceeded to pay my brother his fee, but my brother, afraid of the lady, said, "I will take nothing." Then he went home and spent the night without sleep from hunger. When he came to his shop the next morning, the maid came to him and said, "My master wishes to speak with you." He went to the husband, who

---

1. Dubaiq is a city in Egypt known for its fine linen.

said, "I would like you to make me some robes." So he cut out five robes and went home, feeling miserable, for he was broke and hungry. When he finished sewing the robes, he took them to the husband, who praised his work and called for a purse. My brother put out his hand to take it, but the lady signaled to him from behind her husband not to take anything. So he said to the husband, "My lord, there is no hurry; there is time." Then he went out, sighing both for the money and the lady. He was beset by five things: love, destitution, hunger, nakedness, and toil; nonetheless, he kept up his resolve. The fact of the matter was that the lady, without letting my brother know, had told her husband about the situation and my brother's infatuation with her, and they had agreed to take advantage of him and make him sew for them for nothing, so that whenever he brought the finished work and the husband was about to pay him, she would keep her eye on him and forbid him to take the money.

Some time later they tricked him and married him to their maid, but when he wanted to go in to her, they said to him, "Sleep in the mill tonight, and tomorrow you will consummate your marriage." My brother lay alone in the mill, and in the middle of the night, the miller, who had been sent by the husband, came in, saying, "What is the matter with this wretched mule? He stopped turning, and there is much wheat to be ground." He filled the hoppers with grain, and going to my brother with a rope, tied him to the yoke.

*But morning overtook Shahrazad, and she lapsed into silence. Then Dinarzad said to her sister, "What a strange and entertaining story!" Shahrazad replied, "What is this compared with what I shall tell you tomorrow night if the king spares me and lets me live!"*

THE ONE HUNDRED AND FIFTY-FIFTH NIGHT

*The following night Shahrazad said:*

I heard, O happy King, that the tailor told the king of China that the barber told the guests that he said to the caliph:

The miller tied my brother to the yoke and kept hitting him on the legs, while my brother kept turning the mill and grinding the wheat. And whenever he wanted to rest, the miller, pretending that he did not know that he was hitting a human being, would hit him and say, "You seem to have eaten too much, you wretched mule."

At daybreak the miller went away and left my brother still tied to the yoke and almost dead. Soon the maid came to him and said, "I am sorry for what has happened to you; my lady was unable to sleep last night, worrying about you." But he could not find the tongue to answer her because of the toil and the beating.

Then he went home, and soon the fortuneteller who had earlier written down his horoscope came to him and greeted him, saying "May God preserve your life. I see in your looks the signs of dalliance, kisses, and bliss." My brother replied, "May God curse you for a liar, you man with a thousand horns. By God, I did nothing all night but turn the mill, in place of the mule." Then he told him what had happened to him, and the fortuneteller said, "Your star does not agree with hers." Then my brother went to his shop, hoping that someone might bring him something to sew, by which he might earn his subsistence.

Soon the maid came to him and said, "My lady wishes to speak with you," but he replied, "I will have no more to do with you people." The maid went back and told her lady, who, before my brother knew it, put her head out of the window, weeping and saying, "My darling, what is the matter with you?" But he did not reply. Then she swore to him that she was innocent of what had happened to him, and when he saw her beauty and charm, he forgot what had happened to him and was glad to see her.

A few days later, the maid came to him and said, "My lady sends you greetings and would like you to know that her husband will spend the night at the home of one of his friends. When he leaves, come to us and spend the night with her." But the fact of the matter was that the husband had said to his wife, "It seems that the tailor has given up on you." She replied, "Let me play another trick on him and ridicule him before the entire city." But my brother did not know what was in store for him. As soon as it was dark, the maid came to him and took him to the house, and when the lady saw him, she said, "My lord, God knows how I have been longing for you."

*But morning overtook Shahrazad, and she lapsed into silence. Then Dinarzad said, "Sister, what a strange and entertaining story!" Shahrazad replied, "What is this compared with what I shall tell you tomorrow night if the king spares me and lets me live!"*

### THE ONE HUNDRED AND FIFTY-SIXTH NIGHT

*The following night Shahrazad said:*

I heard, O happy King, that the tailor told the king of China that the barber told the guests that he said to the caliph:

My brother said to the lady, "My lady, give me a quick kiss," but hardly had he spoken, when the husband emerged from a room, saying, "For shame! By God, I will not let you go until I deliver you to the chief of the police." My brother kept imploring him, but he would not listen and carried him to the chief, who gave him a hundred lashes and, mounting him on a camel, paraded him throughout the city, with a crier proclaiming "This is the punishment of those who trespass upon other people's wives." Then the prefect banished him from the city, and he left, not knowing where to go. But I went out after him and took care of him.

When he heard my story, the caliph laughed and said, "You have done well, O Silent One and man of few words!" and he bade me take a gift and go away. But I said, "By God, O Commander of the Faithful, I will take nothing, unless I tell you what happened to my other brothers."

#### [The Tale of the Second Brother, Baqbaqa the Paraplegic]

My second brother's name was Baqbaqa, and he was the paraplegic. One day, as he was going on some business, he was met by an old woman, who said, "Fellow, stop for a moment, so that I may propose something to you, and if my proposition pleases you, you may proceed with the help of the Almighty God." My brother stopped, and she said, "What I have to say is that I shall take you to a pleasant place, providing that you don't ask too many questions," adding "What do you say to a handsome house and a garden with running waters and fruits and clear wine and a face as lovely as the moon for you to embrace?" When my brother heard her words, he asked, "Is all of this in this world?" She replied, "Yes, it is all yours, if you behave sensibly and refrain from meddling and talking too much." He replied, "Very well." Then she walked, and he walked behind her, intent on following her instructions. Then she said, "The young lady to whom you are going likes to have her way and hates to be contradicted. If you follow her wishes, she will be yours." My brother said, "I will never contradict her in anything." Then he followed the old woman until she brought him to a mansion full of servants. When they saw him, they asked, "What are you doing here?" But the old lady replied, "Leave him alone; he is a workman, and we need him."

Then she brought him into a spacious yard, in the middle of which stood the loveliest of gardens, and seated him on a fine couch. Soon he heard a great commotion, and in came a troop of young ladies surrounding a lady as lovely as the full moon. When my brother saw her, he rose and bowed before her, and she welcomed him and bade him be seated. When he sat down, she turned to him and said, "God has chosen you and sent you as a blessing to us." My brother replied, "My lady, the blessing is all mine." Then she called for food, and they brought fine dishes. But as they ate, the lady could not stop laughing, and whenever my brother looked at her, she looked away from her maids, as if she was laughing at them, all the while showing my brother affection and jesting with him until he concluded that she was in love with him and that she would grant him his wish. When they finished eating, the wine was set before them, and there came ten young ladies as lovely as the moon, carrying lutes, who began to sing plaintive songs, which delighted my brother. Then the lady drank the cup, and my brother rose . . .

*But morning overtook Shahrazad, and she lapsed into silence. Then Dinarzad said to her sister, "What a strange and entertaining story!" Shahrazad replied, "What is this compared with what I shall tell you tomorrow night if the king spares me and lets me live!"*

THE ONE HUNDRED AND FIFTY-SEVENTH NIGHT

*The following night Shahrazad said:*

I heard, O happy King, that the tailor told the king of China that the barber told the guests that he said to the caliph:

My brother rose, but as he was drinking the cup in greeting, the lady gave him a slap on the neck. He drew back in anger, but as the old woman kept winking at him, he returned and the lady bade him sit. But she hit him again, and as if that was not enough, she ordered her maids to hit him too, all the while saying to the old woman, "I have never seen anything better than this," and the old woman replying, "Yes, by God, my lady." Then the lady ordered her maids to perfume my brother with incense and sprinkle rosewater on him; then she said to him, "May God reward you. You have entered my house and submitted to my condition, for whoever crosses me, I turn him away, but whoever is patient with me I grant him his wish." My brother replied, "My lady, I am your slave." Then she bade all her maids sing with loud voices, and they did as she bade.

Then she cried out to one of the maids, saying "Take my darling with you, take care of him, and bring him back to me soon." My brother rose to go with the maid, not knowing what was intended for him, and as the old woman rose to go with them, he said to her, "Tell me what she wishes this maid to do to me." The old woman replied, "Nothing but good. She wishes to dye your eyebrows and remove your mustaches." My brother said, "The dyeing of the eyebrows will come off with washing, but the plucking out of my mustaches will be hard on me." The old lady said, "Beware of crossing her, for her heart is set on you." So my brother submitted while the maid dyed his eyebrows and plucked out his mustaches. Then she went back to her lady, who said, "There is one more thing; shave his chin, so that he may be beardless." The maid returned to my brother and began to shave his beard, and the old woman said to him, "Be glad, for she would not have done this to you if she had not been passionately in love with you. Be patient, for you are about to have your wish." My brother submitted and sat patiently, while the maid shaved his beard.

Then she brought him to her mistress, who, delighted at the sight, laughed until she fell on her back and said to him, "My lord, you have won my heart with your good nature." Then she conjured him by her life to rise and dance, and he began to dance, while she and the maids grabbed everything around and threw it at him until he fell senseless from the pelting and hitting. When he came to himself, the old woman said to him, "You will have your wish."

*But morning overtook Shahrazad, and she lapsed into silence. Then Dinarzad said to her sister, "What a strange and entertaining story!" Shahrazad replied, "What is this compared with what I shall tell you tomorrow night if the king spares me and lets me live!"*

THE ONE HUNDRED AND FIFTY-EIGHTH NIGHT

*The following night Shahrazad said:*

I heard, O happy King, that the tailor told the king of China that the barber told the guests that he said to the caliph:

When my brother came to himself, the old woman said to him, "One more thing and you will have your wish; it is her habit, when she gets intoxicated, to let no one have her until he takes off his shirt and trousers and stands naked. Then she runs away, as if she is trying to escape, while he follows her from place to place until his penis hardens and becomes firmly erect. Then she stops and lets him have her," adding "Rise and take off your clothes." My brother took off all his clothes and stood stark naked. Then the lady herself took off her clothes, except for her trousers, and said to him, "If you want me, follow me until you catch me," adding "Start running," and she began to run from place to place, while, over-whelmed with desire, with his cock sticking straight up in the air, he ran after her like a madman. She entered a dark place and he followed her, stepping on a soft spot, which caved in under him, and before he knew it, he found himself in the middle of the leather market, where the traders were shouting their wares, buying and selling.

When they saw him in that condition, naked, without a beard, and with red eyebrows, they yelled and clapped their hands at him and beat him with hides on his naked body until he fell senseless. Then they set him on an ass and took him to the city gate. When the chief of the police arrived, he asked, "What is this?" They replied, "Lord, this fellow fell from the vizier's house, in this condition." The prefect gave him a hundred lashes and banished him from Baghdad. I went after him, O Commander of the Faithful, brought him back secretly into the city and arranged for his upkeep, and I wouldn't have done it were it not for my generous nature.

*But morning overtook Shahrazad, and she lapsed into silence. Then Dinarzad said to her sister, "What a strange and entertaining story!" Shahrazad replied, "What is this compared with what I shall tell you tomorrow night if the king spares me and lets me live!"*

THE ONE HUNDRED AND FIFTY-NINTH NIGHT

*The following night Shahrazad said:*

I heard, O happy King, that the tailor told the king of China that the barber told the guests that he said to the caliph:

*[The Tale of the Third Brother, Faqfaq the Blind]*

My third brother, O Commander of the Faithful, was blind. One day God led him to a great house, and he knocked at the door, hoping that the owner might respond and that he might then beg from him. When the owner asked, "Who is at the door?" my brother did not answer. Instead, he knocked again, and when the man asked for the second time, "Who is there?" he again did not answer. Then he hear the man repeat in a loud voice, "Who is there?" and when he still did not answer, he soon heard the man come to the door, open it, and say, "What do you want?" My brother replied, "Something, for the love of the Almighty God." The man asked, "Are you blind?" and my brother replied, "Yes." The man said, "Give me your hand." My brother put out his hand, thinking that the man would give him something. But the man seized it and, drawing him into the house, carried him up, from stair to stair, until they reached the housetop, my brother thinking all the while that the man would give him some food.

Then they sat down, and the man asked my brother, "What do you want, blind man?" My brother replied, "Something, for the love of the Almighty God." But the man said, "God help you." My brother asked, "Fellow, why didn't you tell me this downstairs?" The man replied, "You mean man, why didn't you answer me from the beginning?" My brother asked, "What do you want to do with me now?" The man answered, "I have nothing to give you." My brother said, "Then take me downstairs." But the man replied, "The way is open before you." My brother rose and began to descend the stairs until there remained only twenty steps between him and the door, when his foot slipped, and he rolled all the way down to the door and cut his head.

He went out, not knowing where he was, and met two of his comrades, who asked him, "How did you do today?" He replied, "Don't ask!" Then he told them what had happened to him, adding, "Brothers, I would like to take some of our joint money and spend some of it on myself." It happened that the owner of the house had, without my brother's knowledge, followed him and heard what he said, and when my brother went to his house and sat down to wait for his comrades, the owner of the house, again without his knowledge, entered after him. When his comrades arrived, he said to them, "Shut the door and search the place to make sure that there is no intruder here." The intruder, hearing this, rose, unperceived by the others, and clung to a rope that hung from the ceiling, so that when my brother's comrades searched the house, they found no one. Then they came back to my brother and asked him about his situation, and he told them that he needed his share of what they had collected. Each of them dug up what he had and placed it before my brother, who counted ten thousand dirhams, and after he took what he needed, they buried the rest in a corner of the room.

Then they set some food, and when they began to eat, my brother heard a stranger chewing beside him. He said to them, "By God, there is a stranger among us," and, stretching his hand, grabbed the intruder's hand, and while my brother caught hold of him, his comrades fell on the intruder, boxing and beating him. After they gave him beating enough, they cried out, "O Muslims, a thief has entered our house to steal our property!" When a large crowd began to gather, the intruder caught hold of them and, shutting his eyes, pretended to be blind, so that none would doubt him, accused them of what they had accused him, saying "I appeal to God and the king to judge between us." Suddenly the watchmen came and, seizing them, dragged them all, together with my brother, to the chief of the police, who had them brought before him and asked, "What is the matter with you?" The intruder, who was not blind, replied, "God bless the king. Even though you can see, you will not find out anything, except by torture. Begin by beating me; then beat this man, who is our chief," pointing to my brother. They threw the man down, O Commander of the Faithful, and gave him four hundred blows. When he began to smart under the blows . . .

*But morning overtook Shahrazad, and she lapsed into silence. Then Dinarzad said to her sister, "Sister, what a strange and enter-taining story! What an amazing story!" Shahrazad replied, "What is this compared with what I shall tell you tomorrow night if the king spares me and lets me live!" King Shahrayar said to himself, "By God, I will not kill her until I hear the rest of the story of the insufferable barber and his brothers and find out what happened between the king of China and the Jewish physician and the Chris-tian broker and the steward. Then I will kill her, as I did the others."*

THE ONE HUNDRED AND SIXTIETH NIGHT

*The following night Shahrazad said:*

I heard, O happy King, that the tailor told the king of China that the barber told the guests that he said to the caliph:

The chief of police gave the intruder four hundred blows on his arse, and when he began to smart, he opened one eye, and as the pain increased with the blows, he opened the other. The chief asked, "What is this, you devil?" The man replied, "Give me your seal ring of pardon and I will tell you what is going on." When the chief gave him the ring, he said, "My lord, we are four fellows who pretend to be blind, so that we may enter people's houses and gaze on their women and corrupt them. In this way, we have made ten thousand dirhams, but when I said to my comrades, 'Give me my share of two thousand and five hundred dirhams,' they refused and beat me and took away my money. I appeal to God and to you for protection, and it is better that you keep my share than they. If you wish to verify what I have said, beat each of them twice as much as you have beaten me, and they will surely open their eyes." The chief ordered the three to be beaten, starting with my brother, whom they tied to a ladder. Then he said to them, "You vicious men, do you deny God's gift to you and pretend to be blind?" My brother replied, "By God, by God, O lord, there is none among us who can see." But they beat him until he fainted. Then the intruder said to the chief, "Leave him until he revives; then beat him again, for he can stand more beating than I." The chief ordered the other two to be beaten, and each of them received more than three hundred blows, while the intruder kept saying, "Open your eyes, or you will be beaten anew."

At last he said to the chief, "Prince, send someone with me to fetch the money, for these fellows will not open their eyes, for fear of being exposed before the people." The chief sent someone to fetch the money, gave the intruder two thouand and five hundred dirhams, his supposed share, and took the rest for himself. Then he banished the three men from the city. I, O Commander of the Faithful, went out after my brother and, overtaking him, asked him about his plight, and he told me the story I have just related to you. I took him secretly back into the city and arranged for his upkeep, without letting anyone know.

When the caliph heard my story, he laughed and said, "Give him a gift and let him go." But I said to him, "By God, O Commander of the Faithful, I am a man of few words and great generosity, and I must relate to you the stories of my other brothers, in order to prove it to you."

### [The Tale of the Fourth Brother, the One-Eyed Butcher]

My fourth brother, the one-eyed one, was a butcher in Baghdad, who raised rams and sold meat. The prominent and the wealthy used to buy their meat from him, so that he acquired houses and property and amassed a great wealth. He continued to thrive for a long time until one day, as he was sitting in his shop, an old man with a long beard came up to him, gave him some money, and said, "Give me meat for this amount." My brother cut for him his money's worth of meat, and the old man went away. My brother looked at the silver coins the old man had given him and, finding them brilliantly white, put them aside by themselves. The old man continued to come to my brother for five months, and my brother continued to put the money he received from him into a separate chest.

One day he wanted to take out the money to buy some sheep, but when he opened the chest, he found nothing inside but paper cut round. He beat his head and cried out, and when the people gathered around him, he told them his story. Then he rose and, slaughtering a ram as usual, hung it up inside the shop. Then he cut off some pieces of meat and hung them up outside the shop, saying to himself, "Perhaps that wretched old man will come back." Soon up came the old man, holding his money in his hand. My brother rose and, catching hold of him, cried out, "O Muslims, come and hear what happened to me at the hands of this crooked old man!" When the old man heard his words, he asked him, "What do you prefer, to let go of me or to have me expose you before everybody?" My brother asked him, "Expose me for what?" The old man replied, "For selling human flesh for mutton." My brother said, "You are lying, you cursed man." The false old man cried out, "He has a man hanging up in his shop." My brother replied, "If you are telling the truth, my property and my life are forfeit." The old man said, "O fellow citizens, if you wish to prove the truth of my words, go into his shop." The people rushed into the shop, and instead of the ram, saw the carcass of a man hanging up there. They seized my brother, crying out, "O infidel! O villain!" and even his best friends began to beat him, saying to him, "You have given us human flesh to eat." Moreover, the old man struck him on the eye and put it out. Then they carried the carcass to the chief of the police, to whom the old man said, "Prince, we have brought you a man who slaughters people and sells their flesh for mutton. Carry out on him the justice of the Almighty God." My brother tried to tell the chief what the old man had done and how the silver pieces he received had turned out to be pieces of paper, but the chief would not listen and ordered him to be flogged, and he was given nearly five hundred painful blows. Then the chief confiscated everything, his money, his property, his sheep, and his shop, and had he not been able to offer a bribe, he would have been put to death. They paraded him for three days throughout the city and banished him.

My brother wandered until he came to a great city, where, being also a skilled cobbler, he opened a shop to earn his living. One day, as he went out on some business, he heard a clamor and the tramping of horses behind him, and when he inquired, he was told that the king was going out to hunt. He stopped to look at the king's handsome dress, when the king's eye chanced to meet his, and the king bowed his head, saying "May God protect me from the evil of this day," and, drawing the bridle, rode back, followed by all his men. Then he gave an order to his attendants, who seized my brother and gave him a painful beating until he nearly died, without telling him the reason. He returned to his shop in a sad state, and he went to see a man who was a servant in the king's household. Seeing my brother's condition, the man asked him, "What is the matter with you?" When my brother told the man what had happened to him, the man laughed until he fell on his back and said, "Friend, the king cannot endure the sight of a one-eyed man, especially if he is blind in the right eye, and he will not rest until he puts him to death." When my brother heard this explanation, he decided to run away.

*But morning overtook Shahrazad, and she lapsed into silence. Then Dinarzad said to her sister, "What a strange and entertaining story!" Shahrazad replied, "What is this compared with what I shall tell you tomorrow night if the king spares me and lets me live!"*

### THE ONE HUNDRED AND SIXTY-FIRST NIGHT

*The following night Shahrazad said:*

I heard, O happy King, that the tailor told the king of China that the barber told the guests that he said to the caliph:

My brother decided to run away from that city and go to a place where none would recognize him. He left, settled down in another city, and began to thrive until one day he went out to divert himself, when he heard the tramping of horses behind him. He exclaimed, "The judgment of God is upon me," and looking for a place to hide, found nothing but a closed door. When he pushed it, the door opened, and he fell forward, finding himself in a long hallway. But hardly had he advanced, when two men seized him and said, "Praise be to God, who has delivered you into our hands, O enemy of God. For three nights you have robbed us of peace and sleep and made us taste the agonies of death." My brother said, "Fellows, what is your problem?" They replied, "You have been tormenting us and plotting to kill the master of the house. Is it not enough that you and your friends have made him a beggar? Give us the knife with which you have been threatening us every night." Then they searched him and found a knife tucked in his belt. He said to them, "Fellows, for God's sake, treat me kindly, for my story is a strange one," saying to himself "I will tell them my tale," in the hope that they would let him go, but they paid no attention to him and refused to listen. Instead, they beat him and tore off his clothes and, finding on him the marks of former beating, said, "Cursed man, these are marks of punishment." Then they took my brother to the chief of the police, while my brother said to himself, "I am undone for my sins. Now no one can save me but the Almighty God." The chief said to my brother, "Villain, what made you enter their house and threaten them with death?" My brother replied, "I beg you, for God's sake, to listen to me and hear my story, before you hasten to condemn me." But the two men said to the chief, "Will you listen to a thief who beggars people, a man who bears the scars of punishment?" When the chief saw the scars on my brother's back, he said to him, "They would not have done this to you were it not for a grave crime." Then he sentenced him, and they gave him a hundred lashes and paraded him on a camel throughout the city, crying out, "This is the reward of those who break into people's houses." Then the chief banished my brother from the city, and he wandered until I went out after him and found him. When I questioned him, he told me his tale. Then I carried him secretly back to Baghdad and made him an allowance to live on. It was out of the utmost generosity that I treated my brothers in this fashion.

The caliph laughed until he fell on his back and ordered a gift for me. But I said, "By God, my lord, even though I am not a man of many words, I must complete the stories of my other brothers, so that our lord the caliph will be acquainted with all their tales and have them recorded and kept in his library, and so that he may discover that I am not a garrulous man, O our lord and caliph."

*But morning overtook Shahrazad, and she lapsed into silence. Then Dinarzad said to her sister, "What a strange and entertaining story!" Shahrazad replied, "What is this compared with what I shall tell you tomorrow night if I stay alive!"*

THE ONE HUNDRED AND SIXTY-SECOND NIGHT

*The following night Shahrazad said:*

I heard, O happy King, that the tailor told the king of China that the barber told the guests that he said to the caliph:

*[The Tale of the Fifth Brother, the Cropped of Ears]*

My fifth brother, the cropped of ears, was a poor man who used to beg by night and live by day on what he got. When our father, who was an old man, far advanced in years, fell sick and died, he left us seven hundred dirhams, which we divided equally among ourselves, each receiving one hundred dirhams. When my fifth brother received his share, he did not know what to do with it until he thought of buying glass of all kinds and selling it at a profit. He bought a hundred dirhams' worth of glass and, putting it in a large basket, sat to sell it next to a tailor's shop, which had a balustrade at the entrance. My brother leaned against the balustrade and sat, thinking to himself, "I know that I have a capital of a hundred dirhams' worth of glass, which I will sell for two hundred dirhams, with which I will buy more glass which I will sell for four hundred dirhams. I will continue to buy and sell until I have four thousand dirhams, then ten thousand, with which I will buy all kinds of jewels and perfumes and make a great profit. Then I will buy a fine house, together with slaves and horses, and I will eat and drink and carouse and bring every singing man and woman in the city to sing to me, for the Almighty God willing, my capital will be a hundred thousand dirhams."

All this went through his head, while the hundred dirhams' worth of glass sat in the basket before him. He continued, saying to himself, "As soon as I have amassed a hundred thousand dirhams, I will send out marriage brokers to demand for me in marriage the daughters of kings and viziers. In fact, I will ask for the hand of the vizier's daughter, for I have heard that she is singularly beautiful, that she is all perfection and grace. I will give her a dowry of a thousand dinars. If her father consents, well; if not, I will take her by force, in spite of him. When I return home, I will buy ten little slaves as well as clothes fit for kings, and I will get me a saddle of gold and have it set with expensive jewels. Then I will ride and parade in the city, with slaves before me and behind me, while the people salute me and invoke blessings on me. When I go to see the vizier, with slaves on my right and left, he will rise in greeting and, seating me in his place, will sit below me because I am his son-in-law. I will have with me two slaves carrying purses, each with a thouand dinars, one for the dowry, the other as a present, so that the vizier may know my generosity, my magnanimity, and my disdain for the world. Then I will return to my house, and if someone comes to me from the bride, I will give him money and bestow on him a robe of honor, but if he brings me a present, I will not accept it, but will return it, for I will maintain my dignity. Then I will prepare my house and ask them to make the bride ready, and when she is ready, I will bid them lead her to me in a procession. When it is time to unveil the bride, I will put on my best clothes and sit on a seat of silk brocade and lean on a cushion, turning neither right nor left, because of my sense of propriety, and my reticence, gravity, and wisdom. My bride will stand before me like the full moon, in her robes and ornaments, and I, out of a sense of self-respect, dignity, and pride, will not look at her until all those who are present will say to me, 'O our lord and master, your wife and slave stands before you. Be kind to her and grant her a glance, for standing hurts her.' After they kiss the ground before me many times, I will raise my head, give her one look, and bend my head again. They they will take her away, and I will rise and change my clothes for a finer suit. When they bring the bride for the second time, in her second dress, I will not look at her until they stand before me and implore me many times. Then I will give her a quick look, then look down again. I will continue to do this until they finish displaying her."

*But morning overtook Shahrazad, and she lapsed into silence. Then Dinarzad said to her sister, "What a strange and entertaining story!" Shahrazad replied, "What is this compared with what I shall tell you tomorrow night if the king spares me and lets me live!"*

THE ONE HUNDRED AND SIXTY-THIRD NIGHT

*The following night Shahrazad replied "Very well," and said:*

I heard, O happy King, that the tailor told the king of China that the barber told the guests that he said to the caliph:

All this went through my brother's mind. Then he went on, "I will continue to enjoy looking at the bride until they finish presenting her to me. Then I will order one of my servants to fetch a purse of five hundred dinars and, giving it to the attendants of the bride, command them to lead me to the bride chamber. When they lead her in and leave her alone with me, I will look at her and lie by her side, but I will ignore her and will not speak to her, so that she may say that I am a proud man. Then her mother will come in and kiss my hand and say, 'My lord, look at your servant and comfort her, for she craves your favor.' But I will not answer. When she sees this, she will kiss my feet many times and say, 'My lord, my daughter is a young lady who has never seen a man before, and if you disdain her, you will break her heart. Turn to her, speak to her, and comfort her.' Then her mother will give her a cup of wine and say to her, 'Entreat your lord to drink.' When the bride comes to me, I will let her stand, while I recline on a cushion embroidered with gold and silver, and will proudly disdain to look at her, so that she may say that I am an honorable and self-respecting man. I will let her stand until she feels humiliated and learns that I am her master. Then she will say to me, 'My lord, for God's sake, don't refuse the cup from my hand, for I am your servant.' But I will not speak to her, and she will press me, saying, 'You must drink,' and put the cup to my lips. Then I will shake my fist in her face and kick her with my foot like that." So saying, he kicked with his foot and knocked over the basket of glass, which, resting high, fell to the ground, and everything in it was broken.

The tailor [who had overheard some of my brother's conversation with himself] cried out, "All this comes of your pride, you dirty pimp. By God, if it was within my power, I would have you beaten a hundred times and paraded throughout the city." At that moment, O Commander of the Faithful, my brother began to beat on his face, tear his clothes, and weep. The people who were going to the Friday prayers saw him, and some of them pitied him, while others paid no attention to him, as he stood bereft both of capital and profit.

While he wept, a beautiful lady, riding on a she-mule with a saddle of gold and attended by servants, passed by, filling the air with the odor of musk. When she saw my brother weeping in his plight, she felt pity for him and, inquiring about him, was told that he had had a basket of glass, by which he was trying to make a living, but that it had got broken, and that this was the cause of his grief. The lady called one of her servants and said to him, "Give him whatever you have with you," and the servant gave my brother a purse in which he found five hundred dinars. When he saw the money, he almost died of joy and, invoking blessings upon the lady, returned to his house a rich man.

As he sat thinking, he heard a knocking at the door, and when he asked, "Who is it?" a woman answered, "My brother, I would like to have a word with you." He rushed and, opening the door, saw an old woman he did not know. She said to him, "Son, the time of prayer is near, and I have not yet performed my ablutions. I would like you to let me do so in your house." My brother replied, "I hear and obey." Then he asked her to come in, and when she was inside, he gave her a ewer for her ablutions and sat down, still beside himself with joy at the money, which he began to stuff inside his clothes. As he finished doing this, the old woman, finishing her prayers, came near where he sat and prayed a two-bow prayer. Then she invoked blessings on him.

*But morning overtook Shahrazad, and she lapsed into silence. Then Dinarzad said to her sister, "What a strange and entertaining story!" Shahrazad replied, "What is this compared with what I shall tell you tomorrow night if I stay alive!"*

THE ONE HUNDRED AND SIXTY-FOURTH NIGHT

*The following night Shahrazad said:*

I heard, O happy King, that the tailor told the king of China that the barber told the guests that he said to the caliph:

When the old woman finished her prayer and invoked blessings on him, he thanked her and, pulling out two dinars, gave them to her, saying to himself, "This is an offering from me." At this, she exclaimed, "How strange! Why do you look at me as if I was a beggar? Take your money and keep it for yourself, for I don't need it; however, I do have for you in this city a woman who has wealth, beauty, and charm." My brother asked, "How could I get such a woman?" The old woman replied, "Take all your money and follow me, and when you are with her, spare neither fair words nor amiability, and you will enjoy her beauty and her wealth to your heart's content." My brother took all his money and went with the old woman, so happy that he could hardly believe himself.

He followed her until she came to the door of a mansion, and when she knocked, the door was opened by a Greek slave-girl. The old woman entered and bade my brother follow her, and he entered a spacious hall, spread with carpets and hung with curtains. He sat down, placed the money before him, and, taking off his turban, put it on his knee. Soon in came a young lady, so beautiful and so richly dressed that none better was ever seen. He rose to his feet, and when she looked at him, she smiled in his face and was glad to see him. Then she bade the door be shut and, taking him by the hand, led him to a private room, where she seated him and, sitting beside him, dallied with him for a while. Then she rose and, saying, "Wait until I come back," went away.

He sat by himself, when suddenly a great black slave came in, with a sword in his hand, and said to him, "Damn you, what are you doing here?" My brother was tongue-tied and could not answer. The black slave seized him and, stripping him of his clothes, struck him with the flat of the sword and left him half paralyzed. Then he kept striking him, so severely that my brother fell unconscious. The hideous slave concluded that he was dead, and my brother

heard him say, "Where is the salt-woman?" and in came a maid
with a large dish full of salt. Then the black slave began to stuff
my brother's wounds with salt until he fainted again.

When he came to himself, he lay motionless, for fear that the
black slave would discover that he was alive and finish him off. Then
the maid went away, and the black slave cried out, "Where is the
cellar-woman?" and in came the old woman, who took my brother
by the feet and dragged him away and, opening a cellar door, threw
him down on a heap of dead bodies. There he remained unconscious, without stirring, for two whole days, but the Almighty and
Glorious God made the salt the cause of saving his life, for it stopped
the flow of blood. As soon as he found himself able to move, he
crept fearfully out of the cellar and made his way to the hallway,
where he hid till early morning. When the old woman went out
in quest of another prey, he went out behind her, without her
knowledge, and headed home. There he treated himself for a month
until he recovered. Meanwhile he kept a constant watch on the old
woman, while she took one man after another and led them to that
house. But my brother said nothing. When he regained his health
and recovered his strength, he took a piece of cloth and made it
into a bag, which he filled with glass.

*But morning overtook Shahrazad, and she lapsed into silence.
Then Dinarzad said, "Sister, what a strange and entertaining story!"
Shahrazad replied, "What is this compared with what I shall tell
you tomorrow night if the king spares me and lets me live!"*

### THE ONE HUNDRED AND SIXTY-FIFTH NIGHT

*The following night Shahrazad said:*

I heard, O happy King, that the tailor told the king of China
that the barber told the guests that he said to the caliph:

He put the glass in the bag and tied it to his waist. Then he disguised himself as a Persian, so that nobody would recognize him,
and hid a sword under his clothes. When he saw the old woman,
he said to her, with a Persian accent, "Old lady, I am a stranger
here. Do you have a pair of scales large enough to weigh five hundred dinars? I will give you some of it for your trouble." The old
woman replied, "O Persian, my son is a money changer, and he
has all kinds of scales. Come with me before he goes out to his

shop, and he will weigh your gold." My brother said to her, "Lead the way." She led him until she came to the house, and when she knocked at the door, the young lady herself came out and opened it. The old woman smiled in her face and said, "I have brought you a fat piece of meat today." The young lady, taking my brother by the hand, led him into the house and sat with him for a while. Then she rose and, saying to him, "Wait until I come back," went away.

As soon as she left, the cursed black slave came in, with a bare sword in his hand, and said to my brother, "Get up, cursed man!" He sprang behind the slave and, drawing the sword that was hidden under his clothes, struck him and made his head fly away from his body. Then he dragged him by the heels to the cellar and cried out, "Where is the salt-woman?" The maid came with the dish of salt and, seeing my brother with the sword in his hand, turned to run away, but he caught up with her and struck off her head. Then he called out, "Where is the cellar-woman?" and when the old woman came in, my brother looked at her and said, "Do you recognize me, you wicked old woman?" She replied, "No, my lord." He said, "I am the one in whose house you prayed and whom you lured here." She said, "Spare me." But he paid no attention to her and struck her with the sword, cutting her in four.

Then he went in search of the young lady, and when she saw him, she lost her mind and asked for mercy. He promised to spare her and asked, "And you, how did you come to be with this black slave?" She replied, "I was a slave to a merchant, and the old woman used to visit me until we became intimate friends. One day she said to me, 'We have at our house today a wedding, the like of which was never seen, and I would like you to be there.' I replied, 'I hear and obey.' Then I rose and, putting on my clothes and jewelry and taking with me a purse with a hundred dinars, followed her until she brought me to this house and bade me enter. As soon as I went in, this black slave seized me, and I have been in this situation for three years, due to the treachery of the old woman. May God curse her!" My brother asked, "Does the black slave keep any money or possessions in this house?" She replied, "Yes, he has plenty, and if you can carry it away, do so with God's help." Then she took my brother and opened for him several chests full of purses, and while he stood there, not knowing what to do, she said to him, "Leave me here and go and bring men to carry the money." He went out at once and hired ten men, but when he returned, he found the door open, and when he went in, he was surprised to find that the young lady had disappeared with the purses, leaving very little money behind, and realized that she had tricked him. He took whatever money was left and, opening the closets, carried away all the clothes, leaving nothing in the house, and spent a happy night.

When he got up in the morning, he found at his door twenty policemen, who seized him, saying "The chief of the police wants you." He implored them to give him time to go into the house, but they would not let him, and although he offered them money and kept imploring and throwing himself at their feet until he was weary, they would not listen. They tied his hands fast behind his back and carried him off. On the way, they were met by one of my brother's old friends, and my brother clung to him and implored him to assist him and help deliver him from the hands of these policemen and their officers. The friend, glad to intercede on his behalf, inquired what was the matter, and the officers replied, "The chief of the police has ordered us to bring this man before him and, having found him and seized him, we are on our way to our superior the chief, according to his orders." My brother's friend said to them, "Good fellows, I will get from him whatever you wish and desire for your trouble. Release him and tell your superior the chief that you could not find him." But they refused and dragged my brother on his face to the chief of the police.

*But morning overtook Shahrazad, and she lapsed into silence. Then Dinarzad said, "Sister, what a strange and entertaining story!" Shahrazad replied, "What is this compared with what I shall tell you tomorrow night if I stay alive!"*

### THE ONE HUNDRED AND SIXTY-SIXTH NIGHT

*The following night Shahrazad said:*

I heard, O happy King, that the tailor told the king of China that the barber told the guests that he said to the caliph:

When the chief saw my brother, he asked him, "Where did you get all these possessions?" My brother replied, "Grant me immunity first," and the chief said, "Granted." Then my brother told him about his adventure with the old woman and the flight of the young lady from beginning to end, adding, "Whatever I took is still in my possession. Take what you wish, and leave me enough to live on." But the chief sent his men and officers, and they took all the money and clothes and, fearing lest the matter should reach the king, he summoned my brother again and said to him, "Leave this city, or

I will have you put to death." My brother replied, "I hear and obey," and set out for another city. On the way some thieves set upon him and stripped him of his clothes. When I heard of his plight, I took some clothes and went out after him, clothed him, and brought him secretly into the city to join his brothers.

### [The Tale of the Sixth Brother, the Cropped of Lips]

My sixth brother, the cropped of lips, was first rich but later became poor. One day, as he went out looking for something to eat, he came to a handsome house, with a wide entrance and a high gate, guarded by attendants and servants. When he asked one of them who was the owner of the house, he was told that the owner was one of the Barmaki family. He approached the doorkeepers and asked them for alms, and they said to him, "Enter, and our master will give you what you want." He entered and, passing through a very long hallway, found himself in a lovely mansion that was spread with carpets and hung with curtains and in the middle of which stood a garden, the like of which he had never seen before. He stood for a while, perplexed, not knowing where to go; then he proceeded toward the door of a reception room, and when he entered, he saw at the upper end a handsome man with a fine beard. He approached the man, who, when he saw my brother, welcomed him and inquired about his health, and my brother told him that he was in need of charity. When he heard my brother's words, he showed great sadness and, grabbing his clothes, rent them, exclaiming, "How can you be hungry while I live in this city? I cannot endure this." And he promised my brother all the best. Then he said, "You must eat with me." My brother replied, "My lord, I cannot wait, for I am very hungry."

Then the man cried out, "Boy, bring the ewer and the basin, so that we may wash our hands," and said to my brother, "Go ahead and wash your hands." But my brother saw neither ewer nor anything else, yet the man gestured as if he was washing his hands. Then he cried out, "Bring the table," and motioned with his hand. Again my brother saw nothing, but the host said to him, "By my life, eat and don't be bashful," and, gesturing with his hand as if he was eating, kept saying to my brother, "By my life, have more, for I know how famished you are." My brother too began to gesture as if he was eating something, while the host kept saying to him, "By my life, have some more. Look how white and delicious this bread is!" Again my brother could see nothing and, saying to himself, "This man likes to have fun with people and play tricks on them," replied, "My lord, never in my life have I seen whiter or better-tasting bread." The host said, "I paid five hundred dinars for the slave-girl who baked it for me."

*But morning overtook Shahrazad, and she lapsed into silence. Then Dinarzad said, "Sister, what an amusing and entertaining story!" Shahrazad replied, "What is this compared with what I shall tell you tomorrow night if the king spares me and lets me live!"*

THE ONE HUNDRED AND SIXTY-SEVENTH NIGHT

*The following night Shahrazad said:*

I heard, O happy King, that the tailor told the king of China that the barber told the guests that he said to the caliph:

Then the host cried out, "Boy, bring the meat porridge first, and don't spare the butter." Then he said to my brother, "My guest, by God, have you seen a better porridge? By my life, eat and don't be bashful." Then he cried out again, "Boy, bring the fatted goose stew in vinegar sauce," and said to my brother, "Eat, for I know that you are hungry and in need of food." My brother began to move his jaws, as if he was chewing, while the host kept calling for dish after dish and inviting my brother to eat, although nothing appeared. Then he cried out, "Boy, bring us the marinated fat chickens," and said to my brother, "My guest, by my life, these chickens have been fattened on pistachio nuts; eat, for you have never tasted anything like them." My brother replied, "My lord, they are indeed delicious." Then the host began to put his hand to my brother's mouth, as if to feed him, and continued to expatiate on dish after dish, while my brother, who was starving, craved for a bite of plain barley bread. Then the host cried out, "Bring the fried meats," and asked my brother, "Have you ever tasted anything more delicious than the seasoning of these dishes? Have some more and don't be bashful." My brother replied, "My lord, I have had enough food." The host cried out, "Take this dish away and bring the sweets," and said to my brother, "Eat of this almond conserve, for it is excellent; eat of these fritters. By my life, let me give you this fritter, for it is dripping with syrup." My brother said, "My lord, may I never lose you," and asked him about the abundance of musk in the fritters. The host replied, "It is my custom to make them this way," while my brother kept moving his jaws. Then the host cried out, "We have had enough of this; bring us the almond jelly," and said to my brother, "Eat and don't be bashful." My brother replied, "I am full; I can eat no more."

Then the host asked, "My guest, if you are full, then would you like to drink some wine and be merry?" My brother said to himself, "Enough. I will do something to him that will cure him of these antics." Then the host cried out, "Bring the wine," and, giving my brother a cup, said, "Drink it and let me know how you like it." My brother replied, "It has a good aroma, but I am used to drinking a different wine." The host cried out, "Give him another kind," and saying to my brother, "Health and pleasure to you," pretended to drink a toast. My brother, pretending to be already drunk, replied, "My lord, I cannot drink any more." But as the host insisted, my brother, still pretending to be drunk, raised his arm until the white of his armpit appeared and suddenly hit the host on the back of the neck with a slap so hard that the place resounded with it. Then he gave him another slap, and the host exclaimed, "What is this, you vile man?" My brother replied, "My lord, you have admitted your slave into your house, fed him, and given him wine to drink until he became drunk and unmannerly. You should be the first to tolerate his foolishness and pardon his offense." When the host heard my brother's reply, he laughed heartily and said, "Fellow, I have been making fun of people for a long time, but never till now have I met one who has the wit and ability to humor me like you. I do pardon you."

*But morning overtook Shahrazad, and she lapsed into silence. Then Dinarzad said to her sister, "What a strange and entertaining story!" Shahrazad replied, "What is this compared with what I shall tell you tomorrow night if the king spares me and lets me live!"*

THE ONE HUNDRED AND SIXTY-EIGHTH NIGHT

*The following night Shahrazad said:*

I heard, O happy King, that the tailor told the king of China that the barber told the guests that he said to the caliph:

The host said to my brother, "I do pardon you. Be a real companion to me and never leave me." Then he summoned several servants and ordered them to set a real table, which they laid with all the dishes mentioned, and my brother and the host ate until they were satisfied. Then they moved to the drinking chamber, where they found young ladies like moons, who played all kinds of musical instruments and sang all kinds of songs. There they drank until they got drunk. The host felt a great affection for my brother, treated him as intimately as a brother, and bestowed on him a robe of honor.

Next morning, they resumed their eating and drinking, and they continued to carouse for ten full days. Afterward the Barmaki entrusted his affairs to my brother, who managed his estate for twenty years. But when the man died — Glory be to the Living who dies not — the king seized all his property, including that of my brother, leaving him a helpless pauper.

My brother left the city and wandered all alone until some bedouins set upon him on the road and, capturing him, brought him to their camp. Then his captor began to beat him, saying, "Ransom yourself with money," while my brother wept and said, "My lord, I have no money, not even one dirham. I am your captive; do with me what you wish." The bedouin took out a knife and cut off my brother's lips, still trying to get him to pay.

It happened that the bedouin had a pretty wife, who, whenever her husband left, used to make advances to my brother and try to entice him, but he refused her until one day she succeeded, and he came to her and began to pet her, when suddenly the husband came in and, seeing my brother, said to him, "Damn you, are you trying to debauch my wife?" Then he took out his knife and cut off my brother's male organ. Then he carried him on a camel and cast him at the side of a hill, where he was found by some travelers, who recognized him and gave him food and drink. When they informed me about him, I went to him, carried him back to Baghdad, and made him an allowance to live on.

Here I stand before you, O Commander of the Faithful, and it would have been wrong of me to leave without letting you know about the six brothers I am supporting.

When the caliph had heard the entire account of my brothers' adventures, he laughed heartily and said, "You are right, Silent One; you are neither a meddlesome nor a talkative man; but leave this city at once and settle in another." Then he banished me, and I went from country to country until I heard of his death and the succession of another caliph. Then I returned to Baghdad and found all my brothers dead and afterward met this young man, to whom I did the greatest of favors, for without me, he would have been killed, but he repaid me in the worst of ways, leaving the city and running away from me. I wandered in many countries until I chanced to meet him here. Now he accuses me of what is foreign to my nature, spreading lies about me and claiming that I am a garrulous man.

*But morning overtook Shahrazad, and she lapsed into silence. Then Dinarzad said to her sister, "What a strange and entertaining story!" Shahrazad replied, "What is this compared with what I shall tell you tomorrow night if the king spares me and lets me live!"*

### THE ONE HUNDRED AND SIXTY-NINTH NIGHT

*The following night Dinarzad said to her sister Shahrazad, "Sister, if you are not sleepy, tell us one of your lovely little tales to while away the night." The king added, "Finish the story of the roguish hunchback." Shahrazad replied, "Very well."*

I heard, O King of the age, that the tailor said to the king of China:

Yesterday, when we heard the barber's story and realized that he was a garrulous fellow who had wronged the young man, we seized him, bound him, and locked him up. Then we sat and enjoyed the banquet till late afternoon. When I left and came home, my wife scowled, and said, "You have been roaming around and partying all day, while I have been sequestered at home. If you don't take me out now, I will leave you." I took her out and we entertained ourselves till nightfall. When we returned home, we met the roguish hunchback, who was very drunk. I invited him to our house, bought fish, and we sat down to eat. When we were almost finished, I took the last piece, which happened to have a bone, crammed it into his mouth, and held it shut. He choked, his eyes bulged, and he stopped breathing. I rose and boxed him on the back, but the piece lodged in his throat and he died. I carried him and contrived to get rid of him in the house of this Jewish physician, who contrived to cast him into the house of the steward, who contrived to throw him in the way of the Christian broker. This then is the story of my adventure yesterday. Isn't it more amazing and extraordinary than the hunchback's story?

When the king of China heard the tailor's words, he shook his head with wonder and delight and said, "Indeed, the story of the young man and the meddlesome barber is better and more entertaining than the story of the hunchback." Then he ordered one of his chamberlains to go with the tailor and fetch the barber from his place of confinement, saying, "I would like to see and hear for myself this silent barber, who has saved you all from me. Then we will bury this roguish hunchback, for he has been dead since yesterday evening, and we will build him a tomb." The chamberlain and the tailor departed at once and returned with the barber. When the king of China looked at him, he saw a very old man, more than ninety years of age, with a white beard and eyebrows, floppy ears, a long nose, and a simpleminded look. The king laughed at his appearance and said to him, "Silent One, I would like you to tell us one of your tales." The barber said "O King of the age, why are this Christian, this Jew, this Muslim, and this dead hunchback before you, and what is the cause of this gathering?" The king of China replied, laughing, "Why do you ask?" The barber answered, "I ask so that your Majesty may know that I am no meddler and that I am innocent of the charge of being garrulous, for I am called the Silent One."

*But morning overtook Shahrazad, and she lapsed into silence. Then Dinarzad said, "Sister, what a strange and entertaining story!" Shahrazad replied, "What is this compared with what I shall tell you tomorrow night if the king spares me and lets me live!"*

## THE ONE HUNDRED AND SEVENTIETH NIGHT

*The following night Shahrazad said:*

I heard, O King, that the king of China bade the barber be told the story of the hunchback. When he heard the story, the barber shook his head and said, "This is amazing. Uncover for me this hunchback." Then he sat down and, taking the hunchback's head in his lap, looked at his face and burst out laughing until he fell on his back. Then he exclaimed, "How amazing! To every death there is a cause, but the story of this hunchback deserves to be recorded in letters of gold." Those present were puzzled by his words, and the king of China asked him, "What do you mean, Silent One?" The barber replied, "By your bounty, there is still life in this hunchback." Then he untied a leather bag from his belt and, opening it, took out a jar of ointment and applied it liberally to the hunchback's neck. Then he took an iron stick and, inserting it into the hunchback's mouth, pried open his jaw. Then he took out a pair of tweezers, thrust them down the hunchback's throat, and drew out the piece of fish with the bone, soaked in blood. Suddenly the hunchback sneezed and stood up, rubbing his face with his hand.

The king and all those present marveled at the story of this roguish hunchback and how he lay unconscious for a full night and a day until God sent him this barber, who saved his life. Then the king of China commanded that the story of the barber and the hunchback be recorded, and he bestowed robes of honor on the steward, the tailor, the Christian, and the Jew and sent them away. As for the barber, he bestowed on him a robe of honor, assigned him a regular allowance, and made him his companion, and they continued to enjoy each other's company until they were overtaken by death, the destroyer of delights.

*But morning overtook Shahrazad, and she lapsed into silence. Then Dinarzad said to her sister, "What a strange and entertaining story!" Shahrazad replied, "What is this compared with what I shall tell you tomorrow night if I live! It will be the story of Abu al-Hasan Ali Ibn-Tahir al-'Attar and Nur al-Din Ali ibn-Bakkar and what happened to him and the caliph's slave-girl Shams al-Nahar. It is a story that will entertain the listener and delight the one who is fortunate to hear it."*

THE ONE HUNDRED AND SEVENTY-FIRST NIGHT

*The following night Dinarzad said to her sister Shahrazad, "Sister, if you are not sleepy, tell us one of your lovely little tales to while away the night." King Shahrayar added, "Let it be the story of Abu al-Hasan Ali ibn-Tahir al-'Attar and Nur al-Din Ali ibn-Bakkar and what happened between him and the slave-girl Shams al-Nahar." Shahrazad replied, "With the greatest pleasure":*

# [THE STORY OF NUR AL-DIN ALI IBN-BAKKAR AND THE SLAVE-GIRL SHAMS AL-NAHAR]

I heard, O happy King, that once there lived in the city of Baghdad a druggist named Abu al-Hasan ibn-Tahir, who was a man of wealth and high status. He was truthful, well-mannered, friendly, and well-liked everywhere. He used to enter the caliph's palace, for most of the caliph's women and concubines used to go to him to fill their needs. He was also patronized by the sons of princes and notable men, one of whom was a descendant of the kings of Persia, a young man named Nur al-Din Ali ibn-Bakkar. This young man was endowed by God with every virtue, perfect beauty and grace, eloquence and sweetness of tongue, wisdom and nobility, generosity and modesty, manliness and chivalry. He was so much attached to Abu al-Hasan ibn-Tahir that he could not bear to leave him even for a moment.

It chanced one day that as he sat with Abu al-Hasan in his shop there came up ten full-bosomed virgins, looking like moons, with a young lady riding on a gray she-mule with trappings of red silk set with gems and pearls. Her beauty, which put the full moon to shame, radiated over all her attendants, for she was like her of whom the poet said:

> She was created flawless, as she wished,
> In beauty's mold, all charm and perfect grace,
> As if her body was a liquid pearl,
> In every part of which the moon to trace.
> Equaled by none she stood, the musk her scent,
> The bough her figure, and the moon her face.

She captivated the mind with her graceful features and her beautiful eyes. When she reached the shop of Abu al-Hasan ibn-Tahir and dismounted, he rose and, kissing the ground before her, seated her on a silk cushion with gold stripes and stood in attendance. She adjured him to sit down, and he sat below her, while she began to demand what she wanted. When Ali ibn-Bakkar saw her, he was beside himself with confusion, and his face flushed and turned pale, and as he tried to get up and go, in deference to her, he almost swooned. She gave him a flirtatious look with her narcissus eyes and with a sweet smile said, "My lord, I come to you, and when I please you, you run away from me." He kissed the ground before her and replied, "When I saw you, I lost my senses, for as the poet says:

> She is the sun that in the heaven dwells;
> Console your heart and let it patient be,
> For neither can you to the sun ascend,
> Nor can she descend from heaven to thee."

She smiled, and her mouth glittered more brightly than a flash of lightning, and she said, "Abu al-Hasan, where did you find this young man and where does he come from?" Abu al-Hasan replied, "His name is Ali ibn-Bakkar, and he is a descendant of kings." She asked, "Is he Persian?" He answered, "Yes, my lady." She said, 'When this maid of mine comes to you, take him with you and come to visit us, so that I may entertain you and him at home and so that he may not blame us and say that there are no generous people in Baghdad. For niggardliness is the worst vice in man. Do you hear what I am saying to you? If you fail to come, I will be displeased with you and will never speak with you again." Abu al-Hasan replied, "My lady, far be it from me to disobey you, and may God preserve me from your displeasure." Then she rose at once and, having captivated their minds and captured their hearts, rode away, leaving Ali ibn-Bakkar behind, not knowing whether he was in heaven or on earth.

As soon as the day ended, the maid came and said, "My lord Abu al-Hasan, let us go . . ."

*But morning overtook Shahrazad, and she lapsed into silence. Then Dinarzad said, "Sister, what a strange and entertaining story!" Shahrazad replied, "What is this compared with what I shall tell you tomorrow night if I live!"*

THE ONE HUNDRED AND SEVENTY-SECOND NIGHT

*The following night Shahrazad said:*

When the maid came, she said, "My lord Abu al-Hasan, my mistress Shams al-Nahar, the favorite of the Commander of the Faithful, Harun al-Rashid, bids you and my lord Nur al-Din Ali, in the name of God, to come to her." Abu al-Hasan rose, saying to Nur al-Din Ali, "Very well, my lord, let us go." They disguised themselves and followed the girl at a distance until she entered the caliph's palace and brought them to the lodging of Shams al-Nahar, where the young man found himself in a room that looked like a chamber in Paradise, furnished with couches, cushions, and pillows, the like of which he had never seen before. After he and Abu al-Hasan were seated and settled in their places, the black maid set a table before them and waited on them. The young man ate and marveled at the fine food: suckling lambs, fatted chickens, and other birds, such as grouse, quail, and pigeons, the jar full of assorted pickles, and all the candies.

What followed next I shall relate in Abu al-Hasan's own words:[2]

---

2. This story has three narrators: Shahrazad; the druggist, Abu al-Hasan; and the jeweler; it shifts back and forth from one narrator to another.

"When we had had our fill of such delicious food and fine drink, they brought us two gilded basins, and we washed our hands. Then they brought incense, with which we perfumed ourselves. Then they brought rosewater scented with musk in bowls of gilded crystal, encircled with carved figures of camphor and ambergris and set with all kinds of jewels, and after we scented ourselves, we returned to our couches. Then the maid asked us to rise and we rose and she led us to another chamber. When she opened the door, we found ourselves in a room covered with a silk carpet, under a dome that rested on a hundred pillars, at the base of each of which stood a bird or a beast dipped in gold. We sat and began to admire the carpet, which, with its gold ground and patterns of white and red roses, repeated the colors and patterns of the dome. In the room, resting on tables, there were more than a hundred trays of crystal and gold, set with all kinds of jewels. At the upper end of the room, numerous lovely couches, covered with fabrics of various colors, stood, each before an arched window that opened on a garden. The garden looked as if it had the same carpet for a floor cover. There the water flowed from a large pond to a smaller one surrounded by sweet basil, lilies, and narcissus in pots of inlaid gold. The thickly intertwined branches were heavy with ripe fruits, so that whenever the windy host passed through them, the fruits dropped on the water, while birds of all kinds swooped down after them, clapping their wings and singing. To the right and left of the pond stood couches of sandalwood covered with silver, and on each couch reclined a damsel more dazzling than the sun, wearing a gorgeous dress and holding a lute or some other musical instrument to her bosom. The damsels' music blended with the cooing of the birds, and the wafting wind joined the rippling water, as the breeze blew, lifting a rose here and downing a fruit there. With dazzled eyes and minds, we contemplated such great means and reflected on such abundant blessings and, turning from the garden with the pond to the room with the dome, we enjoyed the loveliness of the garden, the gracefulness of the art, and the magnificence of the endeavor and marveled at the grandeur of the sight and the beauty of the scene."

Then Ali ibn-Bakkar turned to Abu al-Hasan and said, "My lord, a rational, perceptive, wise, and cultivated man, who is good of heart and sharp of wit, can't help but like, desire, enjoy, prefer, marvel, and find this scene fascinating, especially if he were in my place and felt as I feel. Since it was only through beauty that fate brought me to my predicament and visited me with this affliction, and since this is, as you often say, the plight of the commissioned, and since nothing I have seen here prevents me from speaking, I would like to know what is the intention of the commissioner[3] and who it is who dares speak openly, especially to one of such a great power and such a great estate?"

*But morning overtook Shahrazad, and she lapsed into silence. Then Dinarzad said, "Sister, what a strange and entertaining story!" Shahrazad replied, "What is this compared with what I shall tell you tomorrow if the king spares me and lets me live! It will be more amazing and more entertaining."*

THE ONE HUNDRED AND SEVENTY-THIRD NIGHT

*The following night Shahrazad said:*

I heard, O happy King, that when Nur al-Din Ali said this, his companion replied, "I have no knowledge of her intention; nor do I know her well enough to make inferences and discover the true state of things. But we are almost there, and you will soon find out the situation and discover the mystery; besides, so far we have seen nothing but what is wonderful and heard nothing but what is delightful."

Abu al-Hasan related, "As we were talking to each other, the black girl came and ordered the reclining damsels to sing, and one of them tuned her lute and sang these verses:

> Smitten with love and ignorant of love,
> My poor forsaken heart burned with desire.
> No sin did I commit, save that my tears
> In spite of me revealed my secret fire.

The young man cried out, 'Bravo! This is wonderful!' Then she sang:

> With little hope I long and pine for thee,
> And what avails even the great when they desire?
> My ardent sighs of passion rise to thee,
> As if the coldest breath is blazing fire.

Nur al-Din Ali breathed a deep sign and said, 'Excellent! Bravo! You have sung with perfection!' Then he repeated the lines and with tears in his eyes said, 'Sing some more,' and the damsel sang these verses:

---

3. "Commissioner" and "commissioned": Shams al-Nahar and Nur al-Din respectively.

> O you, whose love grows deeply in my breast,
> Reign in my heart and rule as you desire,
> A lonely heart that pines and wastes away,
> Where cold disdain is but tormenting fire.
> Reap what you sow then, either good or ill;
> The lover's lot is but the martyr's pyre.

Nur al-Din Ali wept and kept repeating the lines for a while, when suddenly the damsels leapt from their places and, tuning their instruments, burst with one voice into song, with these lines:

> Glory to God who caused this moon to rise,
> Bringing together lover with lover.
> For who has seen the sun and moon at once
> In Eden or on earth; who has ever?

We looked in their direction and saw the first maid, who had come to my shop and brought us here, standing at the far end of the garden, while ten maidservants came in, carrying a large silver couch, placed it among the trees, and stood waiting in front of it. They were followed by twenty damsels like moons, wearing all kinds of jewelry and carrying various musical instruments. They moved in a procession, singing the same melody in unison, until they reached the couch, and arranging themselves on each side, continued to play so well that we began to feel that the whole place was swaying with their beautiful music. Then in came a group of ten damsels who were beautiful beyond description and who wore vestments and jewels that matched their beauty and charm, and they stood by the door, while another group just like them walked in and among them walked Shams al-Nahar."

*But morning overtook Shahrazad, and she lapsed into silence. Then Dinarzad said to her sister, "What a strange and entertaining story!" Shahrazad replied, "What is this compared with what I shall tell you tomorrow night if the king spares me and lets me live! It will be stranger, more amazing, and more entertaining."*

THE ONE HUNDRED AND SEVENTY-FOURTH NIGHT

I heard, O happy King, that the young ladies stood by the door, while another group just like them walked in, and among them walked Shams al-Nahar. The young ladies clung to her, while she moved, scarved with her abundant hair, dressed in a delicate, gold-embroidered blue robe that revealed the clothes and precious stones she wore underneath. She advanced, as the sun emerges from the clouds, with a proud and coquettish gait until she reached the couch and seated herself there, while the young man gazed on her and bit the tips of his fingers until he nearly cut them off. He turned to the druggist and said, "A man needs no explanation after seeing, nor harbors doubt after knowing." Then he recited these verses:

> She, she alone is the source of my pain,
> My unrequited love and love's long moan.
> Since first my eyes saw her enchanting face,
> Restless my soul has been and no peace known.
> O poor soul, for God's sake, depart in peace
> And let my wasting body lie alone.

Then he said to the druggist, "You would have dealt more kindly with me and done me a great favor to have forewarned me of the situation, so that I might have prepared and taught myself to be patient," and he wept bitterly and stood helpless before him. Abu al-Hasan related, "I replied, 'I meant you nothing but good, but I did not tell you the truth about her for fear that your love and longing for her would be so overpowering as to hinder you from meeting her and being with her. But take courage and be of good cheer; be sensible; cherish her, think well of her, and do not reproach her, for she is well-disposed toward you.' Nur al-Din Ali asked, 'Who is she?' I replied, 'She is Shams al-Nahar, a slave-girl of Harun al-Rashid, and this place where you are now is his new palace, known as the Palace of Paradise. I plotted and found a way to bring the two of you together. Now the outcome is in the hands of the Almighty God. Let us pray to Him for a happy ending.' Ali ibn-Bakkar stood speechless for a while and then said, 'Excessive caution drives us to love ourselves and crave to preserve it. But I am already in peril, and it is all the same to me whether I am destroyed by almighty love or by a mighty king.' Then he was silent again.

"Suddenly, as he stood at the window, Shams al-Nahar looked at him. Their faces flushed with rapture and their movements expressed their hidden, overwhelming passion, and even though they were speechless, they spoke with the language of love and disclosed their secret to each other. For a long time she gazed on him and he gazed on her; then she bade the first group of damsels return to their couches and sit down, and they did so. Then she signaled to the maids, and each of them brought a couch and placed it before one of the windows of the room in which we were. Then she bade the girls who were standing in attendance sit down on these couches, and when they did, she turned to one of them and said, 'Sing a song,' and the girl tuned her lute and sang these verses:

> As lover yearned for lover,
> Their hearts beating as one,
> They drank from love's sweet river,
> And when the two were done,
> On love's shore they stood and said,
> With bitter tears, 'Above,
> Of this the fates are guilty,
> Not those below who love.'

"The girl sang a melody that excites even the meek and heals the sick, a melody that moved Nur al-Din Ali ibn-Bakkar, who turned to her and said, 'Sing these lines:

> My unrequited love
> Has drowned my eyes with tears.
> O my joy, my idol,
> O wish of all my years,
> Have pity on a man
> Who, hopeless, mourns alone,
> Who keeps love in his heart
> And moans with love's sad moan.'"

*But morning overtook Shahrazad, and she lapsed into silence. Then Dinarzad said to her sister, "What a strange and entertaining story!" Shahrazad replied, "What is this compared with what I shall tell you tomorrow night if I stay alive!"*

THE ONE HUNDRED AND SEVENTY-FIFTH NIGHT

*The following night Shahrazad said:*

I heard, O happy King, that Abu al-Hasan said, "The damsel sang the verses that the young man asked her to sing, in a sweet melody, and when she finished, Shams al-Nahar turned to another damsel and said, 'Sing on my behalf these lines:

> I sigh for one who, had he shared my love
> And felt the pain I feel, would have gone mad.
> I raise my voice to God, not to a man
> Who knows no mercy, whose hard heart is bad.
> If men or demons felt the love I feel,
> Both men and demons would such love anneal.'

She sang a tender melody and sang it so well that the young man turned to another damsel and said, 'Sing on my behalf these lines:

> By your eyes smitten, for your love he yearns
> And without patience he does sigh and moan.
> You are his only wish in all the world,
> For which he suffers and pines, you alone,
> You who possess a soft body that bends
> Tenderly boughlike and a heart of stone.'

The damsel sang with tenderness and delicacy, and when she finished, Shams al-Nahar sighed deeply and said to the damsel nearest to her, 'Sing another song,' and the damsel sang these lines:

> If you remain deaf to my moans,
> Nor can you to me mercy show,
> I will not with patience endure,
> For how much patience to allow?
> My cheerless and slow-burning heart
> But for you would have burst aglow.

The damsel sang, while the two lovers, flushed with passion, heaved with ecstasy and trembled with delight. Then, Ali ibn-Bakkar turned to a damsel near him and said, 'Sing on my behalf these lines:

> The time of union is too brief
> For such coquettish air,
> For you are fair and such delay
> Does not befit the fair.'

And while the damsel sang, Nur al-Din Ali followed up her song with tears and moans.

"When Shams al-Nahar heard Ali ibn-Bakkar's words and saw his actions, she rose at last and headed for the room. He too rose and with hands outstretched met her at the door, and they embraced. Never in my life have I beheld two lovelier lovers, for never before have I seen a sun embrace a moon. Suddenly they felt weak and began to swoon, while the damsels rushed to them and carried them to the far end of the room. Then they brought rosewater scented with powdered musk and sprinkled them with it until they revived and regained consciousness." Then Shams al-Nahar looked to the right and left and, not finding the druggist, who had hidden himself behind a couch, asked, "Where is Abu al-Hasan?" The druggist came out from hiding, and when she saw him, she greeted him and welcomed him, saying . . .

*But morning overtook Shahrazad, and she lapsed into silence. Then Dinarzad said to her sister, "What a strange and entertaining story!" Shahrazad replied, "What is this compared with what I shall tell you tomorrow night if I live!"*

## THE ONE HUNDRED AND SEVENTY-SIXTH NIGHT

*The following night Shahrazad said:*

I heard, O happy King, that Shams al-Nahar thanked the drug-gist, Abu al-Hasan ibn-Tahir, saying, "My gratitude prompts me to reward you for your exceeding kindness, for the bow of your generosity has hit every mark and left no favor untouched." Abu al-Hasan bowed his head shyly and invoked blessings upon her. Then turning to young ibn-Bakkar, she said, "May you overcome all obstacles to love and attain all your heart's desires. Place your trust in God alone, submit to His will and decree, and bear your burden patiently." He replied, "My lady, being with you and look-ing at you neither consoles me nor extinguishes the fire of my heart, and I declare that I will never stop loving you until the day I die; for your love, which has mastered my soul, will never die, as long as my heart continues to beat." Then he wept and made her weep with him, and their tears, like unstrung pearls, ran down their cheeks, which flushed like twin roses wet in the rain. Abu al-Hasan al-'Attar exclaimed, "Your case is marvelous, and your condition is strange and interesting. If this is what you do while you are to-gether, what will you do when you part? Enjoy yourselves and forget trouble and pain, for the moments of love are furtive and short-lived."

The two stopped weeping, and Shams al-Nahar made a signal to the first girl, who departed hurriedly and returned with two maids bearing a silver tray. They set the tray before the guests, and Shams al-Nahar turned to them and said, "There is nothing more fitting after conversation and fun than enjoying a meal together. Please, help yourselves." They began to eat, and Shams al-Nahar and Nur al-Din Ali fed each other until they were satisfied. Then the maid removed the tray and set a basin of silver and a ewer of gold before them, and after they washed their hands, they returned to their places.

Then Shams al-Nahar made a signal to the girl, who disappeared briefly and returned with three maids bearing three gold trays, each bearing a different kind of wine in a flagon of cut crystal, which they set before Shams al-Nahar and the guests. Then Shams al-Nahar ordered ten maids to stand in attendance and ten singing girls to join them and dismissed the rest. She took a cup and, fill-ing it, turned to one of the girls and said, "Sing a song," and the girl sang these verses:

> My life for him who greeted back with smiles,
> Turning despair into a happy hope.
> When he appeared, I could no longer hide
> My secret love from my critic nor cope.
> My tears of passion pressed between us twain,
> As if for him they too felt lovers' pain.

Shams al-Nahar drank off the cup and, taking another, kissed it and gave it to her beloved Ali ibn-Bakkar, who took it and kissed it too. Then she said to another girl, "Sing a song," and the girl sang these verses:

> My flowing tears resembled the red wine,
> And my eyes brimmed e'en as the brimming cup.
> By God, I know not whether 'tis wine they shed,
> Or whether it is on my tears I sup.

The young man drank off the cup; then Shams al-Nahar took another and, filling it, kissed it and gave it to Abu al-Hasan ibn-Tahir, who took it from her hand and kissed it. Then she reached out and snatched a lute from one of the girls, saying, "Abu al-Hasan, none but myself shall sing over this cup, for you deserve much more than this tribute." Then she sang these verses:

> Oddly, his flowing tears course down his cheeks,
> And painful passion burns within his heart,
> Fearing to lose her; thus he always weeps
> Whether they are together or apart.

The two men were stricken with wonder and transported with delight, and as he listened to her excellent voice, which blended with the sound of the strings, and to her perfect art, the young man felt as if a bird had stolen his wings and had left him helplessly swaying with the music from side to side.

While they were enjoying themselves, up came a girl, flying like a bee and shaking like a palm tree, and said, "O my lady, 'Afif ad Masrur and Wasif and others of the Commander of the Faithful's eunuchs are at the door." Fearing that they had been discovered, the two guests nearly collapsed with anxiety and alarm and almost died of fright and terror. The moon of their delight had set, and the stars of their happiness had vanished. But Shams al-Nahar laughed . . .

*But morning overtook Shahrazad, and she lapsed into silence. Then Dinarzad said to her sister, "What a strange and entertaining story!" Shahrazad replied, "What is this compared with what I shall tell you tomorrow night if the king spares me and lets me live!"*

## THE ONE HUNDRED AND SEVENTY-SEVENTH NIGHT

*The following night Shahrazad said:*

I heard, O happy King, that when Ali ibn-Bakkar and his friend
Abu al-Hasan al-'Attar heard what the girl said, they were terrified.
But Shams al-Nahar laughed and said to the girl, "Stall them while
we cover our tracks." Abu al-Hasan related later what happened
next: "Still looking at the young man, Shams al-Nahar forced herself
to rise and, bidding the doors of the alcove be shut and the drapes
be drawn upon us, she closed the doors of the hall behind her and
went out into the garden. Then she bade the other couches be
removed, seated herself on her couch, and bade one of her damsels
sit and rub her feet. Then she said to one of the maids, 'Give them
permission to come in.' The three chief eunuchs came in with twenty
other eunuchs, all dressed in elegant and beautiful uniforms, girdled
with golden belts and girded with swords. They saluted in the best
of manners, and Shams al-Nahar saluted back and received them
with respect and good cheer. Then turning to Masrur, she asked,
'What is your wish?' He replied, 'The Commander of the Faithful
salutes you and inquires after your health. He longs to see you and
sends me to inform you that this has been such a joyous day that
he wishes to culminate his joy by seeing you and spending the night
with you in your quarters. Adorn your apartment and make yourself ready to receive him.' She kissed the ground before him and
said, 'I hear and obey the command of God and the Commander
of the Faithful.' Then she turned to the damsel and bid her bring
the housekeepers, who came and busied themselves around the
garden and the apartment, for although the apartment was perfectly
ready with carpets, drapes, and everything else, Shams al-Nahar
wanted to make a show of her compliance with the command. Then
she said to the eunuchs, 'Go with God's protection and care and
tell the Commander of the Faithful what you have seen, so that
he may wait a while until I arrange the furniture and make the
place ready.'"

The eunuchs left hurriedly, and Shams al-Nahar rose and went
to her beloved and his friend, who looked like startled birds. She
embraced Nur al-Din Ali, pressing him hard to her breast, and wept
bitterly. He said to her, "O my lady, this separation will lead to
my destruction and death. May God grant me patience until I see
you again, and may He grant me another opportunity to be with
you." She replied, "You yourself will leave safely; your passion will

remain concealed, your love will be safeguarded, and no one will know how you feel. I, however, will face doom and destruction, for the caliph expects what he is used to from me, something in which I can no longer satisfy him because of my great love for you and my grief at parting from you. With what voice shall I sing for him and with what heart shall I face him and take care of him? With what strength shall I serve him, with what mind shall I speak with those who will come with him, and with what wit shall I exceed them in gaining his favor?" Abu al-Hasan al-'Attar said to her, "I implore you to steel yourself and be as patient as you can tonight, and may the Beneficent God unite you again."

He related later, "While we were conversing, up came a damsel who said, 'The eunuchs are approaching, while you are still standing here.' Shams al-Nahar replied, 'Listen you, hurry and take them upstairs to the gallery overlooking the garden, and when it gets dark, help them go home graciously.' The damsel replied, 'I hear and obey.'" Then Shams al-Nahar bade them good-bye and left, hardly able to walk, while her maid took the two men to the upstairs gallery, which had many chambers, with one side overlooking the garden and another overlooking the Tigris River. She seated them and, closing the door on them, left them until it was dark.

*But morning overtook Shahrazad, and she lapsed into silence. Then Dinarzad said to her sister, "What a strange and entertaining story!" Shahrazad replied, "What is this compared with what I shall tell you tomorrow night if the king spares me and lets me live!"*

THE ONE HUNDRED AND SEVENTY-EIGHTH NIGHT

*The following night Dinarzad said to her sister Shahrazad, "Tell us the rest of the story." Shahrazad replied, "Very well":*

I heard, O happy King, that the girl seated them in the gallery and went away, and they remained seated until it was dark, not knowing what to do or how to get away. Suddenly, as they were looking, into the garden came more than a hundred eunuchs who looked like bridegrooms dressed with colorful costumes, girdled with gold belts, and girded with swords. With them came more than one hundred pages, each bearing a camphor candle, and with them came the Caliph Harun al-Rashid, swaying between Masrur and Wasif, intoxicated. He was followed by twenty girls as lovely as the sun, wearing the finest clothes and adorned with jewels that glittered around their necks and on their heads. They were met under the trees by Shams al-Nahar, followed by girls bearing musical instruments. When she kissed the ground before the caliph, he said to her, "Welcome, my joy, my life's bliss, and my heart's delight." Then he leaned on her arm and walked with her until he reached the silver couch, where he seated himself. Then they set the other couches before him by the sides of the ponds, and he bade the girls who came with him be seated, and each of them sat in her proper place, while Shams al-Nahar sat on a chair beside him.

After he enjoyed the sights of the garden for a while, he bade the drapes of the alcove be drawn open and bade the candles be placed to his right and left, so that the dark became light and the night day, while the pages began to bring in the wine service. Abu al-Hasan related later: "I saw jewels the likes of which had never before graced my eyes or even my imagination, dazzling my mind and making my heart beat with excitement, until I thought that I was in a dream, while Ali ibn-Bakkar, feeling weak and dejected, lay prostrate on the ground, loath to see what I saw and depressed to think what I thought. I said to him, 'Do you see the caliph?' and he replied, 'He is the cause of our misfortune, and I am certain to perish, but I will be undone only by what has overcome me, love and the separation after union, the danger of the situation and the impossibility of escape, as well as my own fear and helplessness. May God the Deliverer deliver me from my predicament.' I replied, 'There is no recourse but to be patient until the Almighty God sends you relief.' Then he turned to look at the scene again.

"When everything was readied before the Caliph Harun al-Rashid, he turned to one of the damsels who had come with him and said, 'Sweetheart, sing me a song.' The damsel played the lute and sang the following verses:

> If water can turn cheeks into green fields,
> My tears might have covered my cheeks with green,
> Reflecting the same tincture in their flow,
> Turning my face into a verdant scene,
> Except that I have shed nothing but tears
> When my departing soul bade me adieu
> And, finding no relief but death, I said,
> 'Welcome, O death,' when the hour nearer drew."

The two men looked and saw that Shams al-Nahar was so agitated that she slumped and fell off the chair to the ground, while the girls rushed to her and lifted her up. Abu al-Hasan said to himself, "Fate has proved kind to them both, by treating them equally." But, aware of the grave danger, he was overwhelmed with alarm. Presently, the girl came and said, "Rise, for we do not have much leeway, and I fear that all hell will break loose tonight." The druggist asked her, "Who can arouse this young man in his condition?" The girl sprinkled Nur al-Din Ali's face with rosewater and rubbed his hands until he came to himself. His friend the druggist said to him, "Wake up at once or you will destroy us with you." Then they carried him and went down with him from the gallery, and the girl, opening a small iron gate, brought them out to a jetty on the river. She clapped her hands softly, and a rowboat appeared with a boatman, who rowed until the boat touched the jetty. Abu al-Hasan related later, "As we entered the boat, the young lover, stretching one hand toward the palace and the young lady's apartment and placing the other on his heart, recited in a faint voice the following verses:

> I stretched one feeble hand to bid adieu
> And placed the other on my burning heart.
> But let this nourishment be not my last,
> Nor this parting keep us always apart.

"The boatman rowed us away, together with the damsel."

*But morning overtook Shahrazad, and she lapsed into silence. Then Dinarzad said to her sister, "What a strange and entertaining story!" Shahrazad replied, "What is this compared with what I shall tell you tomorrow night if the king spares me and lets me live! It will be even stranger and more amazing."*

THE ONE HUNDRED AND SEVENTY-NINTH NIGHT

*The following night Shahrazad said:*

I heard, O happy King, that the young man recited the verses, and the boatman rowed until they crossed the river and reached the opposite side. The two men disembarked, but the girl took leave of them, saying "I cannot go with you beyond this point." Then she departed, leaving Nur al-Din Ali prostrate on the ground before Abu al-Hasan, unable to stand on his feet. Abu al-Hasan said to him, "My lord, our lives are not safe here, for I fear that we may be prey to robbers," and he kept reproaching him and remonstrating with him until he rose at last and proceeded with him, hardly able to walk.

It happened that Abu al-Hasan al-'Attar had some friends who lived on that side of the city; so he went to the house of one of them, whom he trusted and with whom he felt intimate, and knocked at the door. The friend came out quickly, and when he saw Abu al-Hasan, he was extremely pleased. Abu al-Hasan related later: "He brought us into his house, and when we were seated, he asked, 'Where have you been, my lord?' I replied, 'I had a business deal with a certain individual, and when I heard that he had designs on my money as well as that of other people, I went to him tonight in the company of this gentleman,' pointing to Ali ibn-Bakkar and adding, 'I took him with me for fear that the man would get wind of my intention and hide from me. But in spite of my efforts, I was unable to catch him or find out where he was; so I returned and, feeling sorry for this exhausted gentleman, not knowing where else to go, and looking forward to the pleasure of your company, I took the liberty of coming to you.'" The host treated them with the utmost attention and generosity, and they stayed with him the rest of the night.

As soon as it was dawn, they headed for the riverbank and, taking a rowboat, crossed to the other side. They landed and went to the house of Abu al-Hasan, who conjured Ali ibn-Bakkar to go in with him. As soon as Ali ibn-Bakkar went in, he collapsed on the bed, suffering from longing, grief, and exhaustion. The two men slept a while, and when Abu al-Hasan awoke, he ordered the servants to spread the furnishings. He related later: "I said to myself, 'Let me entertain him and distract him, for I know very well the torment he feels for leaving his beloved behind.' Then I thanked God for my deliverance from danger and pledged alms in gratitude.

"When the young man awoke and sat up, I said to him, 'Refresh yourself.'" Ali ibn-Bakkar called for water, and when the servants brought it, he rose and, performing his ablutions, prayed the obligatory prayers, which he had missed the past day and night. Then he tried to find solace and console himself by talking with his friend. When Abu al-Hasan saw this, he turned to him and said, "My lord, it would be better for you in your condition to stay with me tonight, so that you may make merry with me, enjoy the entertainment and diversion, and relieve yourself from the anguish of your love and longing, and perhaps God will send you relief from your affliction." Ali ibn-Bakkar replied, "Do as you wish, for I will not contradict you." Abu al-Hasan related later, "I summoned his servants, invited his friends, and brought a singing woman. We spent the time together till nightfall, and when the candles were lit and the moment was propitious, the singing woman sang these verses:

> Fate pierced me with a deadly dart
> And left me of my love bereft,
> Sick and impatient with my lot,
> The sorry lot I did expect.

"When Ali ibn-Bakkar heard the singer's words, he swooned down and remained unconscious until I despaired of him. But at daybreak he came to himself." Then he asked to go home, and Abu al-Hasan al-'Attar did not try to prevent him, for fear of the consequences. The servants brought the young man's she-mule, and he rode home, accompanied by Abu al-Hasan, who related later, "When I saw him safe at home, I thanked the Almighty God. Glorious be His Name." Abu al-Hasan stayed with him for a while and tried to comfort him, but when he saw that the young man could not control himself but remained distracted and unresponsive, he rose to take his leave.

*But morning overtook Shahrazad, and she lapsed into silence. Then Dinarzad said to her sister, "What a strange and entertaining story!" Shahrazad replied, "What is this compared with what I shall tell you tomorrow night if the king spares me and lets me live! It will be even stranger than this."*

THE ONE HUNDRED AND EIGHTIETH NIGHT

*The following night Shahrazad said:*

I heard, O happy King, that when Abu al-Hasan rose to take his leave, Ali ibn-Bakkar said to him, "Brother, perhaps you will get some news from my beloved, for I saw how she was, and we must find out what happened to her afterward." Abu al-Hasan replied, "Her maid is bound to come and tell us about her." Then he left Ali ibn-Bakkar and went to his shop, and there he waited for the maid, but she did not come. He spent the night in his own house, and the next morning, after he performed his ablutions and prayers, he went to Ali ibn-Bakkar's house. When he went in, he found him lying in bed, surrounded by all sorts of people and by physicians, each of whom was examining him and prescribing something or other. Abu al-Hasan related later: "When he saw me, he hearkened to me with a glad look and a faint smile. After I made the proper salutation, I told him how much I had missed him, inquired about his health and how he had passed the night, and sat with him until everyone left. Then I turned to him and asked, 'Why this congregation?' He replied, 'The servants spread the word that I was sick, and the people came to see me and, being weak, I lay in bed and was powerless to turn them back. But have you seen the maid?' I replied, 'No, I have not seen her, but she will come today.'" Ali ibn-Bakkar wept bitterly until Abu al-Hasan finally said

312    THE ARABIAN NIGHTS

to him, "Stop weeping, conceal your secret from everyone, and avoid
scandal." But he continued to weep and recited the following verses:

> I hid my love, but it grew stronger still
> And made me weak, revealing what I hid.
> And when I saw my tears betray my love
> I wept without shame and myself outdid,
> The more revealing what my eyes concealed,
> Except that more by far lay within sealed.

Then he added, "Life has dealt me a blow I did not need, and
now there is nothing easier for me than death, for it will bring me
relief from my suffering and release me from my affliction." Abu
al-Hasan replied, "May God protect you and grant you a remedy.
You are not the first one to undergo such an ordeal or the only
one to suffer such a wrong." He conversed with him for a while,
then went to the market and opened his shop.

Hardly had he sat down when up came the maid. Abu al-Hasan
related later, "She greeted me, looking withered and dejected. I said
to her, 'You are very welcome. I have been worried about you and
waiting for news from you; how is your lady? As for us, here is
what happened to us.'" And he told her all that had passed. She
marveled and, sighing, said, "My lady fared much worse. When
you left, I kept worrying about you, hardly believing that you had
escaped. When I went back, I found my mistress lying prostrate
in the alcove, unable to speak or to respond, while the Commander
of the Faithful sat by her head, not knowing what ailed her and
finding none who could explain. She remained in this condition,
surrounded by her maids, some of whom rejoiced and some of whom
wept for her. When she came to herself, al-Rashid asked her, 'O
Shams al-Nahar, what ails you?' When she heard his words, she
kissed his feet and said to him, 'May God make me your ransom,
O Commander of the Faithful. I had an attack of the bile, which
set my body on fire and made me faint.' The caliph asked, 'What
have you eaten today?' She replied by inventing something and,
pretending to have recovered, called for wine, drank it, and begged
the Commander of the Faithful to resume his merrymaking. The
caliph returned to his place and bade her sit with him and be at
ease, and she did as he bade. Then I went up to her, and when
she asked me about the two of you, I told her what had happened
to you, and when I repeated the verses that Ali ibn-Bakkar had
recited, she wept. Then a girl, called the Lover's Eyes, sang the
following verses:

> Life has forsooth not been sweet after you;
> I wonder how you have fared after me!

> If my loss you don't mourn with bitter tears,
> Over your cruel loss my tears should blood be.

"When Shams al-Nahar heard the song, she swooned again, and I tried to revive her."

*But morning overtook Shahrazad, and she lapsed into silence. Then Dinarzad said to her sister, "What a strange and entertaining story!" Shahrazad replied, "What is this compared with what I shall tell you tomorrow night if I stay alive!"*

### THE ONE HUNDRED AND EIGHTY-FIRST NIGHT

*The following night Shahrazad said:*

I heard, O happy King, that the maid said to Abu al-Hasan, "I tried to revive her, rubbing her feet and spinkling her with rose-water. When she came to herself, I said to her, 'Tonight you are going to bring ruin on yourself and on all your household. By the life of your beloved, steel yourself and be patient, even though you are going through hell.' She replied, 'Can anything happen to me worse than death, which will deliver me from my torment?' While we conversed, another girl, called Dawn of the Forlorn, began to sing the following verses:

> 'Patience,' they said, 'may consolation bring.'
> 'Without him,' I replied, 'how can I patience find?
> For at our last embrace we pledged to cut
> The cords of patience with the oaths that bind.'

"When Shams al-Nahar heard the song, she swooned again, and the Commander of the Faithful noticed her and rushed to her, and when he looked at her, she seemed almost dead. He bade the wine be removed and each girl return to her chamber, while he spent the rest of the night with Shams al-Nahar, who remained unconscious.

"When she awoke in the morning, the Commander of the Faithful, not knowing what ailed her and unaware of her passion, summoned the physicians and ordered them to treat her. He stayed with her until he thought that she was beginning to feel better. Then he left a group of his concubines and maids with her and returned to his quarters, still concerned about her health. As soon as it was morning, she bade me go to you and bring her news of my lord Ali ibn-Bakkar."

When Abu al-Hasan heard what the maid said, he replied, "I have already told you what happened to Ali ibn-Bakkar and how he feels. Convey my greetings to Shams al-Nahar; do all you can to counsel her; and spare no effort to keep her secret hidden. I myself will acquaint the young man with what you have told me about her." The girl thanked Abu al-Hasan, took her leave, and departed.

Abu al-Hasan related later: "I spent the rest of the day buying and selling. Then I went to Ali ibn-Bakkar, and when I entered, I found him in the same condition in which I had left him. He welcomed me and, looking dismayed, said, 'My lord, I did not dispatch anyone to reassure you, knowing the burden that I have placed on you and for which I shall be beholden to you to the end of my days.' I replied, 'Leave this talk. Could I ransom you with my life, I would give my life for you, and could I protect you with my eyes, I would give my eyes for you. Today Shams al-Nahar's maid came to see me.'" Then Abu al-Hasan repeated to him what the maid had told him. But the young man's torment grew worse, and he fretted, lamented, and wept, wondering what to do in the face of this great misfortune. Then he asked Abu al-Hasan to spend the night with him, and Abu al-Hasan did so, but he slept very little.

As soon as it was dawn, Abu al-Hasan left the young man and went to his shop, where he found the maid already waiting for him. When he saw her, he did not open the shop but went directly to her. She made a sign of salutation to him, conveyed her lady's greetings, and asked, "How is my lord Ali ibn-Bakkar?" He replied, "He is the same. How is your lady?" She said, "She is worse. She wrote him a letter and, giving it to me, said, 'Bring an answer and do whatever Abu al-Hasan bids you.'" Abu al-Hasan related later, "I took her with me and, returning to the young man's house, went in to see him."

*But morning overtook Shahrazad, and she lapsed into silence. Then Dinarzad said to her sister, "What a strange and entertaining story!" Shahrazad replied, "What is this compared with what I shall tell you tomorrow night if I stay alive!"*

## THE ONE HUNDRED AND EIGHTY-SECOND NIGHT

I heard, O happy King, that when Shams al-Nahar's maid came to Abu al-Hasan al-'Attar, he took her with him and returned to the house of Ali ibn-Bakkar and, leaving her standing at the door, went in to see him. When the young man saw him, he inquired,

"What is the news?" Abu al-Hasan, giving him a wink, replied, "All is well. A friend of yours has sent his maid with a letter expressing his longing for you and explaining the reason for his delay, as you will see for yourself. Will you give her permission to come in to see you?" Ali ibn-Bakkar replied, "Very well." Then one of his servants went out and brought her in. As soon as Ali ibn-Bakkar saw her, he recognized her and rejoiced and, moving toward her, gave her a wink and asked, "How is your master? May God grant him health and recovery." She took out the letter and gave it to him, and he took it and, kissing it, read it, then gave it to Abu al-Hasan, with a trembling hand.

Abu al-Hasan related later, "When I looked at the letter, I found the following:

In the name of the Almighty God:

> Answer the one who brings you news of me
> And let his words suffice you for my sight.
> You left me with a heart mad with desire
> And eyes that sleepless stay throughout the night.
> I bear with patience my unhappy lot,
> For who can avoid the cruel blows of fate?
> Be glad: you will be always in my heart
> And you will always my thoughts dominate.
> Look at your body wasting with desire
> And you will know how mine burns with love's fire.

O my lord, were it not for my desire to acquaint you with my suffering for your sake, with the torments of your absence and my longing for you, I would have wisely refrained from speaking with my tongue or writing with my hand to lay open my heart and reveal the anguish of my body and soul, for an eyewitness's account needs no further explanation. In a word, I sit with sleepless eyes and anxious thoughts, with restless heart and confused mind, aware of nothing but my stricken body and my aching, lacerated soul. I feel as if I have never been well or free from distress, as if I have never seen a single lovely sight or lived a single happy day. O would that I were dead or forgotten, or would that I complained only to one who shares my plight or wept only before one who shares my tears, saying:

> Alas, with you I have not had my wish,
> Nor had the pleasure your favor to woo.
> Parted we were by fate, and now alone
> I sit and shed my bitter tears for you.

May the Almighty God reunite all yearning lovers and unite us again. In the meantime, write me some words to keep me company, and bless me with your precious answer to aid me and comfort me. And wait with becoming patience until God grants us a way to meet again. Peace be with Abu al-Hasan.

"What I read was so heartfelt that it would have moved even a light heart, let alone a heavy one, and I was so touched that I almost began to read it aloud, revealing everything, were it not for my fear of exposure. I said to Ali ibn-Bakkar, 'This writer has written a beautiful, tender, and moving letter. Give him a prompt reply and write him a beautiful letter.' Ali ibn-Bakkar replied with a faint voice, 'With what hand shall I write and with what voice shall I lament and mourn? For she has added sickness to my sickness and death to my death.' Then he sat up and, taking a sheet of paper, said . . ."

*But morning overtook Shahrazad, and she lapsed into silence. Then Dinarzad said to her sister, "What a strange and entertaining story!" Shahrazad replied, "What is this compared with what I shall tell you tomorrow night if the king spares me and lets me live!"*

## THE ONE HUNDRED AND EIGHTY-THIRD NIGHT

*The following night Shahrazad said:*

I heard, O happy King, that Ali ibn-Bakkar sat up and, taking a sheet of paper, said to Abu al-Hasan, "Hold the letter open before me." Abu al-Hasan held it, while Ali ibn-Bakkar proceeded, now reading Shams al-Nahar's letter and replying, now pausing to weep, until he finished writing. Then he gave the letter to Abu al-Hasan, saying, "Read it and give it to the girl." Abu al-Hasan related later: "I took it and read the following:

In the Name of God the Compassionate, the Merciful:

> A love letter has come to me
> From the moon, a gift of light,
> Whose words increase in loveliness,
> Like the blossoms of delight.
> It has lightened my heavy load
> And eased my sore affliction,
> Which had, O lady, cast my heart
> Between pity and caution.
> O lady, you know my great love

And you know my great desire,
My eyes that sleepless burn with love
My heart that lies on the pyre,
My tears that never cease to flow
And my everburning fire.
O by my sacred love for you,
By my unholy wish, I say
That my poor heart has love for none
Harbored, since you went away.

O my lady, your letter has reached me, bringing rest to a mind worn out with passion and desire and healing to a wounded heart torn by sickness and grief. It has delighted the eyes and gladdened the heart with its beautiful bloom, and after long silence and worry, it has moved the tongue to speak. The more I contemplated its words and understood their meaning, the more I enjoyed what I read, and the more I read and reread what with unequaled art it expressed, the more relief I felt. For I have been suffering all the torments of separation, a raging passion and an incurable sickness, an overwhelming desire and an all-consuming longing. Indeed, I feel as the poet says:

With saddened feelings and with helpless thoughts,
With sleepless eyes and with exhausted frame,
With confused heart and with demented mind,
With patience gone but loneliness the same,
I feel that I, after you did retreat,
In every grievance have tasted defeat.

No complaint can extinguish the fire of passion, but it may console one whom longing consumes and separation destroys until he quenches his desire in reunion and finds the means to recovery. Peace be with you.

"The words of the letter stirred my soul and tore my vitals, moving me so deeply that I was numb with pain and making me weep so much that I could not stop without a great effort. Finally I gave the letter to the girl, and when she took it, Ali ibn-Bakkar said to her, 'Come closer.' She stepped forward, and he said to her, 'Convey my greetings to your master, acquaint him with my sickness and grief and with my love for him, which is in my flesh and bones, and tell him that I am a miserable man whom life has dealt with heavy blows,' and he asked her to fly to her master with the answer; then he began to cry and made me and the girl cry with him. I took my leave of him and went out with the girl, who was still crying." Abu al-Hasan walked with her part of the way and took his leave and went to his shop.

*But morning overtook Shahrazad, and she lapsed into silence.*
*Then Dinarzad said to her sister, "What a strange and entertain-*
*ing story!" Shahrazad replied, "What is this compared with what*
*I shall tell you tomorrow night if the king spares me and lets me live!"*

### THE ONE HUNDRED AND EIGHTY-FOURTH NIGHT

*The following night Shahrazad said:*

I heard, O happy King, that when Abu al-Hasan took his leave
of the girl and went to his shop, feeling depressed, he began to think
about his situation and what the two lovers had done to him, and
he became convinced that because of them he was going to lose
his business, ruin himself, and come to no good. He continued in
such thoughts the rest of that day and night. The next day he went
to visit Ali ibn-Bakkar and found people congregated there as usual.
He waited until everybody left, and he approached Ali ibn-Bakkar
and asked him how he felt. When he began to complain, Abu al-
Hasan said to him, "Listen! I have never seen or heard of one like
you in your love. Such torment, sickness, and weariness befit the
case of one whose lover is insincere and unfaithful, whereas the
woman you love and wish to possess loves you and wishes to be
with you. What would happen to you if the one you loved was contrary, disdainful, and perfidious? If you continue like this, your
case will be discovered and you will be exposed. Rise, mix with
people, and keep yourself busy. Go riding, exercise, and keep your
heart at bay, or else you will surely destroy yourself." Abu al-Hasan
related later: "Having trust in me, he listened to my advice and
thanked me, and I took my leave and went to my shop. What he
did afterward, I was not to find out until much later.

"It happened that I had a friend, a jeweler by trade, who used
to visit me in my shop and who knew of my involvement in the
affair between Ali ibn-Bakkar and Shams al-Nahar. One day he
asked me about her, and I answered him evasively, saying, 'All I
know is that she is not herself. I am keeping nothing from you,
save perhaps what only God knows. But yesterday I resolved on
a plan on which I would like to consult you. As you know, I am
a well-known man, with much dealing among the notables, both
men and women, and I fear that the affair of these two may be
disclosed and may become the cause of my death, the seizure of
my goods, and the ruin of my family. Nor can I disengage from
them after having spent such good times with them; therefore, I

have resolved to settle my debts, set my affairs in order, and prepare myself to go to the city of Basra, where I will live, unknown to anyone, until I see how God determines their fate and what comes of their affair. For love has so possessed them that it will not leave them alone until they perish. Their go-between is a maid who till now has kept their secret, but I fear that she may get vexed with them or find herself in a fix and divulge their secret, make the affair public, and cause my ruin. Should this happen, my own daring and rash meddling would be the cause of my destruction and death, for I have no excuse before God or man.'"

Abu al-Hasan's friend replied, "You have acquainted me with a grave matter, the like of which should worry the discerning and frighten the wise. Your resolve is a sound one; may God protect you from the harm you dread and reward you with a good solution." The jeweler related later, "Abu al-Hasan asked me to keep this conversation secret."

*But morning overtook Shahrazad, and she lapsed into silence. Then Dinarzad said to her sister, "What a strange and entertaining story!" Shahrazad replied, "What is this compared with what I shall tell you tomorrow night if I stay alive!"*

THE ONE HUNDRED AND EIGHTY-FIFTH NIGHT

*The following night Shahrazad said:*

I heard, O happy King, that the druggist related later, "After I told the jeweler my plan and asked him to keep it secret, I prepared myself at once and set out for Basra."

Four days later, the jeweler came to the shop and found it closed. He related later: "Then I began to think of a way to gain Ali ibn-Bakkar's confidence, and, going to his house, I said to one of his servants, 'Ask your master Ali ibn-Bakkar to grant me leave to go in.' The leave was granted, and when I went in, I found Ali ibn-Bakkar lying back on a pillow. When he saw me, he raised himself and, standing up, received me with a cheerful mien and bade me welcome. I inquired about his health and apologized for the delay of my visit, and he thanked me profusely and said, 'Perhaps there is something you would like me to give you or do for you?' I replied, 'For some time there has been between me and Abu al-Hasan al-'Attar—may God save him—a business as well as a personal relationship based on friendship and mutual affection. I have liked him and trusted him and have confided in him and received his confidence. It happened that I had to be away from him for several days on some business with some colleagues, and when I came back and went to his shop as usual, I found it closed and was told by one of his neighbors that he had gone to Basra on some business that required his personal attention. But I am not satisfied with this explanation, and, knowing what close friends you two have been, tell me truly and in detail all you know, for I have come to you to plead, investigate, and find out.' When Ali ibn-Bakkar heard what I said, his color changed, and, looking visibly shaken, he replied, 'I have never heard or had any inkling of his departure until you told me. What you say, if it is true, makes me feel sobered, alarmed, discouraged, and worn-out.' Then he sobbed and recited the following verses:

I used to weep for errors of the past,
While those I love were present with me still,
But now that fate has taken them away,
I shed my tears for them and always will.
The tears of no man can like mine be said
To be shared by the living and the dead.

"He lowered his head pensively, and a while later he turned to one of his servants and said, 'Go to Abu al-Hasan ibn-Tahir's house and inquire whether he is at home or whether, as has been claimed, he is gone on a journey. If so, find out where he went and for what purpose.' The servant went out, while I sat conversing with Ali ibn-Bakkar, who seemed perplexed as he asked and answered questions, now paying attention to me, now listening absentmindedly. After a while, the servant came back and said, 'My lord, when I inquired about Abu al-Hasan, his people told me that he went to Basra two days ago. There I saw a girl standing at the door, and she too was inquiring about him. When she saw me, she recognized me, although I myself did not recognize her. She inquired whether I was a servant of Ali ibn-Bakkar, and I said that I was. Then she claimed that she was carrying a message for you from one who is the dearest to you. She is now standing at the door.' Ali ibn-Bakkar said 'Bring her in,'" and in came a girl whom the jeweler recognized from an earlier description of her by Abu al-Hasan ibn-Tahir al-'Attar, except that she looked even lovelier. She advanced and greeted Ali ibn-Bakkar.

*But morning overtook Shahrazad, and she lapsed into silence. Then Dinarzad said to her sister, "What a strange and entertaining story!" Shahrazad replied, "What is this compared with what*

*I shall tell you tomorrow night if the king spares me and lets me
live! It will be even stranger than this."*

THE ONE HUNDRED AND EIGHTY-SIXTH NIGHT

*The following night Shahrazad said:*

I heard, O happy King, that when the maid came in, she greeted
Ali ibn-Bakkar and, coming close to him, talked to him privately,
while he swore and exclaimed from time to time that he had no
knowledge of what she claimed. Then she took her leave and went
away, leaving him like a madman in Hell. The jeweler related later:
"As soon as I found the opportunity to speak, I said to him, 'Doubt-
less, some members of the caliph's household have some dealings
with you or some claim upon you.' He asked, 'How do you know?'
I replied, 'I know by this maid.' He asked, 'To whom does she
belong?' I replied, 'She belongs to Shams al-Nahar, the slave-girl
of the Caliph al-Rashid, who has none dearer, wiser, lovelier, or
livelier than her. A few days ago the same maid showed me a letter
that she suspected to have been addressed to her lady by one of
her lady's maids.' Then I repeated to him the contents of the letter,
and he was so upset and worried that I feared that he was going
to collapse. But he recovered his composure and said, 'I conjure
you by God to tell me truly how you know the girl.' I replied, 'Do
not press me.' He said, 'I will not leave you until you tell me the
truth.' I replied, 'I will tell you all, so that I may not cross you or
keep any secret from you, so that you may not entertain suspicion
and wrong impressions of me, and so that you may not feel diffi-
dence, apprehension, or anxiety; moreover, I swear to you by God
that, as long as I live, I will never reveal your secrets or betray your
confidence, never mislead you or keep any advice from you.' He
said, 'Tell me what you know,' and I told him everything from
beginning to end, adding, 'All this I did for no reason save my
affection for you and my concern and compassion for your suffering. It is my wish to place myself and my possessions at your service
and to be your friend, in place of your other friend, your ally against
the rest of the world, and your confidant and comforter. So take
heart and be cheerful,' and I repeated the oath. He responded by
invoking blessings on me and said, 'I do not know what to say, save
to trust in your generosity and to commend you to God.' Then he
recited the following verses:

If I claim to be patient since she went away,
May tears and loud lament give me the lie.
I wonder whether 'tis for a mere friend
Or for my true love that I mourn and cry
With bitter tears that flow and pour fore'er
For a banished friend or distant lover.

"When he finished, he remained silent for a while; then he asked me, 'Do you know what that girl said?' I replied, 'No, I do not.' He said, 'She claimed that I had been in collusion with Abu al-Hasan and that it was I who had instigated him to go to Basra. She refused to listen to my protestation and persisted in accusing me and chiding me. Now I do not know what to do in Abu al-Hasan's absence, for she liked him, listened to him, and accepted his word.' I replied, 'If I understand the situation correctly, I will take care of the problem.' He said, 'How can you, when she bolts away like a wild beast?' I replied, 'I will do my best to support you and help you and to resolve the problem in every way possible, without exposing you, causing you any distress, or bringing you any harm, with the help of the Kind, the Beneficent, and the Almighty God. Do not worry, for, by God, I will do everything possible to help you fulfill your wish.' Then I asked leave to depart, and he said, 'My lord, you have treated me with singular kindness, and you have offered me your help freely and without hesitation. You understand my situation; make me an offering of your friendship and a gift of your intimacy, and I will rely on your honor to keep my secret and depend on your support to help me attain my wish.' Then he embraced me and I kissed him, as we bade each other farewell."

*But morning overtook Shahrazad, and she lapsed into silence. Then Dinarzad said to her sister, "What a strange and entertaining story!" Shahrazad replied, "What is this compared with what I shall tell you tomorrow night if the king spares me and lets me live! It will be even stranger than this."*

### THE ONE HUNDRED AND EIGHTY-SEVENTH NIGHT

*The following night Shahrazad said:*

I heard, O happy King, that the jeweler said, "I bade him farewell and went out, not knowing where to go, what to do, or how to manage to let the girl know that I was in on the secret of the two lovers. As I went along, pondering the matter, I saw a letter lying on the road. I picked it up, and opening it, found the following:

In the name of God, the Compassionate, the Merciful:

> My envoy came bringing me hope and joy,
> But I surmised that he misunderstood.
> Therefore, instead of joy, my grief increased,
> Knowing that he mistook bad news for good.

O my lord — may God preserve you — you yourself may know the cause of breaking the bonds of trust between us and interrupting our correspondence. If the fault is yours, I will remain faithful, and if you are inconstant, I will forbear, forgive, and remain constant. If you succeeded in instigating our friend to depart, then you have succeeded in winning a loving companion, a confidant, and a loyal bosom-friend. Indeed, I am not the first one to lose her way and suffer weariness or to desire something and be doomed to failure. May the Almighty God grant me a quick remedy and a speedy relief. Peace be with you.

"While I read the letter in astonishment, wondering who could have dropped it, the maid approached, looking right and left in perplexity and alarm and, seeing the letter in my hand, came up to me and said, 'O my lord, this is the letter I dropped. Be kind and give it back to me.' I did not answer her but walked on, and she followed me until I came to my house and entered, and she entered behind me. When I was seated, she approached me and said, 'Listen! This letter is of no use to you, since you do not know from whom it came or to whom it is going. Why do you hang on to it and refuse to give it back to me?' I replied, 'Calm down, sit quietly, and listen.' When she sat down, I asked her, 'Is this letter not in the handwriting of your mistress Shams al-Nahar, and is it not for Ali ibn-Bakkar?' Her face turned ashen, and she burst out in alarm. 'He has exposed us and exposed himself; his feverish passion must have made him delirious, and he must have talked about his love to his friends and companions, without being careful about whom to trust with the truth and without thinking about the consequences.'

"Then she rose to go, but, thinking that her departure in that condition might bring injury and harm to Ali ibn-Bakkar, I said, 'Listen! The heart bears witness that one must and can conceal, disavow, or deny every secret, save for love, for one feels most pressed to reveal it and seek advice from others, in order to relieve its torments; besides, love has its telltale signs that make it hard to conceal. You have wrongfully suspected Abu al-Hasan and accused him of an offense of which he is innocent. As for Ali ibn-Bakkar, he has never betrayed your confidence, revealed your secret, or behaved ungraciously. Yet you reward him with accusations and distrust. I will acquaint you with something that will justify his behavior, relieve your anxiety, and please you, but first you must give me a firm pledge that you will hide nothing of your lady's affair from me. I am a man who keeps a secret, stands firm under stress, fulfills diligently the obligations of friendship, and follows the rules of manliness and the code of chivalry in everything I undertake and every task I assume.' When she heard my words, she sighed and said, 'None loses a secret in your trust and no one suffers disappointment under your care. You are in possession of a treasure that should not be entrusted save to the one for whom it was meant and to whom it was sent. But proceed with your explanation, and if you tell me the truth, as God and His angels are my witness . . .'"

*But morning overtook Shahrazad, and she lapsed into silence. Then Dinarzad said to her sister, "What a strange and entertaining story!" Shahrazad replied, "What is this compared with what I shall tell you tomorrow night if the king spares me and lets me live!"*

### THE ONE HUNDRED AND EIGHTY-EIGHTH NIGHT

*The following night Shahrazad said:*

I heard, O happy King, that the girl said to the jeweler, "If you tell me the truth, I too, as God is my witness, will tell you the truth and entrust my lady's secret to your care." The jeweler related later: "I told her what I had told young Ali ibn-Bakkar, how I acted with Abu al-Hasan ibn-Tahir until I won him over, how I went to see Ali ibn-Bakkar, and how I found the letter that she had dropped, adding, 'All of this shows my good will in this affair in which I have been reluctant to meddle.' The girl was astonished, and she enjoined me to swear again to keep the secret of the lovers, while I too made her swear to hide nothing of their affair from me. Then she took the letter and, sealing it up, said, 'I will tell him that it was given to me sealed and that I would like him to seal his own answer with his own seal, so that I may assume no responsibility. I will go to him now, get his answer, and stop to see you before I take it to Shams al-Nahar.' Then she bade me good-bye, and went away, leaving my heart on fire.

"But she was not gone for long before she returned with a sealed letter, which read:

In the Name of God, the Compassionate, the Merciful:

> Our messenger, who did our secrets keep,
> Has now in anger betrayed me and you.
> Choose then for messenger one we can trust,
> One who shuns falsehood and loves to be true.

I have neither committed a breach nor betrayed a trust, neither broken a vow nor severed a friendship. I have met with nothing but affliction after parting nor ever parted from sorrow; nor have I received any news or found any trace of the one you have mentioned. I long to be with my love, but the one I love is far away, and I desire reunion, but how can a lover attain his desire? You will know from my looks my disposition, from my disposition my plight, and from my words my sad state. Peace be with you.

"When I read the letter, I wept." The girl, who shared the jeweler's feeling and wept with him, said, "Do not meet with Ali ibn-Bakkar or leave your house until I return to you tomorrow. He suspects me and he is to be excused, and I in turn have suspected him and I too am to be excused, as I will explain later. I will endeavor in every way possible to bring you together with my lady, whom I left lying prostrate, awaiting news from his confidant." Then the girl departed.

The jeweler related later: "The next day she came in, looking cheerful. I asked her, 'What is the news?' She replied, 'I went to my lady and showed her the letter, and when she seemed upset and worried, I said to her that she should not worry, fear, or grieve that Abu al-Hasan's absence would harm her relationship with Ali ibn-Bakkar, adding that I had found another man to take his place. Then I told her about your friendship with Abu al-Hasan and how you gained his confidence, about your relationship with Ali ibn-Bakkar, and about our understanding and how in my distraction I lost the letter, how you found it, and how you agreed to keep the affair secret. When she heard my account, she was astonished and said that she wished to hear it from your own mouth, so that she might find comfort, assure herself of your commitment, and confirm your resolve to carry out what you had kindly offered to do. So get ready to go with me to her, with God's blessing and help.'"

When the jeweler heard the girl's words, he saw that what she proposed was a grave matter, not to be undertaken lightly or entered into rashly, and he said to her, "You should know that I am not a man of high rank like Abu al-Hasan, who used his wares for an excuse to enter the caliph's palace. Indeed, when he used to relate to me what he did there, I used to tremble with fear. If your lady wishes to speak with me, it must be in a place other than the

Commander of the Faithful's palace, for I do not have the heart for such an undertaking." He persisted in refusing to go with her, while she kept encouraging him and assuring him of protection and safety. But each time he rose to go with her, his legs failed him and his hands trembled. Finally the girl said to him, "Never mind; she will come to you, but do not stir from your place."

She went away in a hurry; then she came back and said, "Beware that none should be with you in the house, for he may tell." The jeweler related later: "I replied, 'There is no one with me.' Then with the utmost caution, she went out and returned, followed by a lady who was followed by two maids. When the lady entered, her perfume filled the house and her beauty lighted it, and when I saw her, I sprang to my feet and, offering her a cushion, seated her and sat before her. She sat without speaking until she was rested, and she unveiled her face, and I thought that it was the full moon or the rising sun. Then she turned to the girl with a weak motion and asked, 'Is this the man?' The girl replied, 'Yes he is.' I greeted her, and she returned my greeting in the best of manners and said, 'Our confidence in you moved us to come to you, entrust you with our secret, and count on your silence. May you be worthy of such confidence and trust, for you seem to be a man of honor, loyalty, and generosity. Then she inquired about my situation, my family, and my friends, and I acquainted her with my circumstances, adding, 'You should know, my lady, that I have another house that I have set apart for entertaining my friends and colleagues, and there is nothing there save what I have told your maid.' Then she questioned me about my involvement in the affair, and I told her, and when I finished, she sighed, expressing sadness for the loss of Abu al-Hasan, and invoked blessings on him. Then she said, 'You should know that the minds of men are alike in desires, although different in situation and purpose, and although men are diverse in their pursuits, no task is accomplished without speech, no wish is fulfilled without endeavor, and no rest is enjoyed without toil.'"

*But morning overtook Shahrazad, and she lapsed into silence. Then Dinarzad said, "Sister, what an entertaining story!" Shahrazad replied, "What is this compared with what I shall tell you tomorrow night if the king spares me and lets me live!"*

لیاله

## THE ONE HUNDRED AND EIGHTY-NINTH NIGHT

*The following night Shahrazad said:*

I heard, O happy King, that Shams al-Nahar admonished the jeweler, adding, "'No secret is confided without trust nor is an endeavor undertaken without ability; no success is achieved save with the help of the generous, nor is a serious matter entrusted save to a man of nobility and honor. Each man deserves to be thanked according to the kindliness of his intentions, the extent of his application, and the efficacy of his deeds. As for you, no man exceeds you in humanity and generosity. You know my secret, understand my situation, and see that I have been driven beyond my endurance. This girl, as you well know, I hold in trust and high favor, for she keeps my counsel and transacts my affairs; therefore, trust her in everything she tells you or asks you to do, and you will be pleased; besides, you will be safe from any danger, for we will not ask you to come to any place before making sure that it is secure. She will bring you news from me and act as our go-between.' Then she rose, hardly able to stand, and I saw her to the door of the house and returned, having seen of her beauty, witnessed of her actions, and heard of her speech what dazzled my eyes and captivated my mind.

"Then I changed my clothes and went to Ali ibn-Bakkar's house. His servants rushed toward me from all directions and brought me to him. I found him lying prostrate on the bed, and when he saw me, he said, 'Welcome! You have tarried too long and added worry to my worries. I have not closed my eyes since I saw you last. Yesterday the girl came to me with a sealed letter,' and he went on to tell me all that had passed, adding, 'I am perplexed and my patience fails me, for I have neither the knowledge nor the power to find relief, for Abu al-Hasan was of great help and comfort to me because she knew him and liked him.' I laughed and he said, 'Why do you laugh at my tears and the tale of my trial and woe?' Then he recited the following verses:

> He who laughs at my tears would now have wept,
> Had he suffered like me the pain I know,
> For none can feel compassion for the damned,
> Save one like him who knows protracted woe."

When the jeweler heard this, he told Ali ibn-Bakkar all that had passed since the jeweler left him, and when he finished, Ali ibn-Bakkar wept bitterly and said, "In any event I am lost; may God grant me a speedy end, for I have lost all satisfaction, all patience, and all resolve, and were it not for you, I would have wasted away with passion and died of sorrow. You will be my comforter in my affliction until God's will is done, for His are the grace and the blessing and His are the thanks and the praise. I will be your slave at your mercy, and I will contradict you in nothing but follow you in everything." The jeweler related later: "I said to him, 'O my lord, nothing will quench this fire, save your reunion, but this must not be in my house, which is exposed to danger and harmful consequences, but in another more suitable place of mine, which I prefer for the purpose. There the two of you will meet to converse, complain to each other of your suffering, and renew your vows, and you will be all by yourselves.' He replied, 'Do what you wish.' I stayed with him that night, entertaining him with conversation, till daybreak."

*But morning overtook Shahrazad, and she lapsed into silence. Then Dinarzad said to her sister, "Sister, what a strange and entertaining story!" Shahrazad replied, "What is this compared with what I shall tell you tomorrow night if the king spares me and lets me live!"*

THE ONE HUNDRED AND NINETIETH NIGHT

*The following night Shahrazad said:*

It is related, O happy King, that the jeweler said: "I stayed with him that night and in the morning returned to my house and hardly had I sat down, when the maidservant arrived. I told her what had passed between Ali ibn-Bakkar and myself, and she said, 'It is better if we meet at our place.' I replied, 'My place is safer.' She said, 'You are right. I will go to my lady, tell her what you have said, and convey to her your invitation.' She went out and, returning soon, said, 'Go to your other house and make it ready.' Then she took out a purse and, giving it to me, said, 'Use this money to buy food and drink.' But I swore that I would never touch it, and she took the purse back and departed.

"I was still annoyed at her behavior, when I went to my other house. I took with me all the utensils in my possession, borrowed from every friend all sorts of fine vessels of gold and silver, carpets, drapes, and whatever else was needed, bought all the necessary provisions, and had everything ready. When the girl came and saw what I had done, she was pleased. I said to her, 'Go now to Ali ibn-Bakkar and bring him here secretly.' She went out and brought him back, finely dressed and looking all delicacy and grace. I received him with respect and courtesy and, seating him on a couch, set before him the most marvelous vessels and sat talking with him.

"The girl went away and returned after the evening prayer with Shams al-Nahar, attended only by two maids. When the two lovers saw each other, they were so overcome with passion that they stood still; then they fell down in a swoon. It was a terrible sight. I endeavored to revive him on one side, while the girl endeavored to revive Shams al-Nahar on the other until they came to themselves. When they regained some strength, they talked with each other for a while in a faint voice. Then I offered them some wine and they drank, and I set food before them and they ate. Then they fell to thanking me, and I asked them whether they would like some more wine and they said that they would. So I took them to another room, where they sat to drink, forgot their worries, enjoyed themselves, and grew merry, all the while feeling astonished and pleased with what I had done for them. Then Shams al-Nahar asked me, 'Do you have a lute or some other musical instrument?' I replied, 'Yes, indeed,' and brought her a lute. She took it and, tuning it, played and sang with consummate skill."

*But morning overtook Shahrazad, and she lapsed into silence. Then Dinarzad said, "Sister, what a strange and entertaining story!" Shahrazad replied, "What is this compared with what I shall tell you tomorrow night if the king spares me and lets me live!"*

### THE ONE HUNDRED AND NINETY-FIRST NIGHT

*The following night Shahrazad said:*

I heard, O happy King, that the jeweler said: "Shams al-Nahar took the lute and, tuning it, played and sang with consummate skill the following verses:

> If you are a true messenger,
> Deliver and be coy no more.
> Say nothing save for my love's news,
> And let the truth my joy restore.
> And if he did deign to reply,
> Even without him I will live,
> For with coyness he gains such charm
> That I will his coyness forgive.

Then she sang these verses:

> I lay sleepless as if in love with lack of sleep,
> And pined as if pining was made for me,
> As my tears coursed over my burning cheeks,
> Who can at once in fire and water be?

"Her singing was so lovely that I had never heard anything like it before. But suddenly we heard terrifying noises and screams and felt as if the house was going to cave in under us. Then a servant, whom I had ordered to stand at the door of the house, rushed in and said, 'Some unknown men have broken the door and are raiding the house,' and, while a maid screamed from the rooftop, ten masked men, wearing swords and holding daggers, followed by ten more, attacked us. When I saw them, I ran out of the house and sought refuge in the house of one of my neighbors, and when I heard an uproar in my house, I concluded that the two lovers were found out and that they were being seized by the chief of police, and I remained in hiding till midnight."

The jeweler did not dare to leave his hiding place, and when the master of the house came down and saw someone he did not recognize hiding in a corner of the hallway, he retreated with fright and returned with a drawn sword and asked, "Who are you?" The jeweler replied, "I am your friend so and so." The man threw the sword away and said to the jeweler, "I am sorry for what has happened to you. May the Generous God restore your substance." The jeweler said, "O my lord, tell me who were the men who raided my house." The man replied, "They are the same men who robbed so and so and killed so and so. Yesterday they saw you bring in many fine and valuable utensils, and they plotted to rob you. I think that they have either kidnapped your guest or killed him."

Then the two men went to the jeweler's house, and when they entered, they found it stripped of everything and completely devastated, with broken doors and torn-out windows. The sight stunned the jeweler and broke his heart, and when he pondered upon his plight, what had happened to him and what he had done to himself, he began to worry about how to break the news to the friends from whom he had borrowed all the gold and silver utensils and how to make excuses to them. He also worried about Shams al-Nahar and Ali ibn-Bakkar and feared lest the caliph should find out about them from one of the maids and put him to death. He turned to his neighbor and asked, "My friend, what shall I do and what do you advise?" The man replied, "Be patient, keep calm, and trust in the Almighty God, for these same robbers have murdered some members of the household of the prefect of the police as well as the caliph's own guard. The police are looking for them and patroling the streets, but no one has yet found them or dared to confront them, because there are so many of them." Accordingly, the jeweler called on God to protect him from harm and went home.

*But morning overtook Shahrazad, and she lapsed into silence. Then Dinarzad said to her sister, "What a strange and entertaining story!" Shahrazad replied, "What is this compared with what I shall tell you tomorrow night if the king spares me and lets me live!"*

THE ONE HUNDRED AND NINETY-SECOND NIGHT

I heard, O happy King, that the jeweler called on God to protect him from harm and went home, saying to himself, "What has happened to me is just what Abu al-Hasan feared." Soon the people began to rush to him from all sides, some consoling him, some saying nothing, and others demanding their goods, while he thanked some, explained to some, and defended himself to others, feeling so unhappy that he did not touch any food all day.

While the jeweler remained in this condition, one of his servants came in and said, "My lord, there is a man at the door asking for you, a stranger whom I have never seen before." When the jeweler went out, the man greeted him and said, "I have something to tell you." The jeweler said, "Come in." But the man replied, "No, let us go to your other house." The jeweler said, "Do I have any other house left?" The man replied, "I know your plight and I bring you comfort." The jeweler related later: "I said to myself, 'I will go with him wherever he wishes.' Then we went out and walked on until we came to my other house. But when he saw it, he said, 'This house has no door, and we cannot sit here. Let us go somewhere else.' Then he took me from place to place, without stopping at any, until the night overtook us." The jeweler followed the man in bewilderment, without asking any questions, until they reached the open country and found themselves at the riverbank. Then the man said, "Follow me," and began to run, and the jeweler, summoning all his strength, ran after him until they came to a boat. They got into the boat, and the boatman rowed them to the other side, where they landed. Then the man took the jeweler by the hand and led him to a long street that he had neither trodden before nor known to which part of Baghdad it belonged.

Soon the man stopped at a door, opened it, and, taking the jeweler in, locked it with a large iron key and brought him before ten men dressed alike. The jeweler greeted them, and they returned his greeting and bade him be seated, and he sat down, suffering from exhaustion and fright. Then they brought him some cold water with which he washed his hands and face and gave him some wine, which he drank. Then they brought food, and they all ate together.

The jeweler said to himself, "If they had meant me any harm, they would not have eaten with me." After they washed their hands, they returned to their places, and when the jeweler took his seat before them, they asked him, "Do you know us?" He replied, "I do not know you, nor do I know the man who brought me here or where we are." They said, "Tell us your case without lying." The jeweler said, "My case is strange; do you know anything about it?" They replied, "Yes, it was we who took your goods yesterday and carried off your friend and the girl who was in your house." The jeweler said, "My God save you! Where are my friend and the girl?" They pointed to two doors facing them and said, "They are there, each in a separate room. They insisted that none besides you should know of their situation, and since then we have never met them or questioned them. Their fine attire has puzzled us and stopped us from killing them. Tell us the truth about them, and do not worry about yourself or them."

*But morning overtook Shahrazad, and she lapsed into silence. Then Dinarzad said to her sister, "What a strange and entertaining story!" Shahrazad replied, "What is this compared with what I shall tell you tomorrow night if the king spares me and lets me live!"*

### THE ONE HUNDRED AND NINETY-THIRD NIGHT

*The following night Shahrazad said:*

I heard, O happy King, that when the jeweler heard what they said, he almost died of fright and said to them, "If generosity was lost, none would harbor it but you; if there existed a secret one fears to reveal, none would keep it but you; and if one faced a difficult problem, none would solve it but you." He went on to expatiate in his praise until he saw that it would be more expedient and more useful to tell the truth at once than to conceal it, particularly since it was bound to come out eventually. So he told them the whole story, and when he finished, they asked, "Is this young man then Ali ibn-Bakkar and this young woman Shams al-Nahar?" He replied, "Yes, I have told you everything and kept nothing from you." They were upset and, expressing regret, went to the two lovers and apologized to them. The jeweler related later: "Then they said to me, 'Part of what we took from your house is gone, but here is what is left of it,' and they gave me back most of the gold and silver utensils, saying, 'We will carry them to your other house.'

"Then they divided themselves into two groups, one to go with me, the other with the two lovers, who stood, almost died of fright, but their fear and desire to escape made them move and leave the house. As we walked, I turned to them and asked, 'What happened to the girl and to your two maids?' Shams al-Nahar replied, 'I know nothing about them.' The men led us until we came to the river-bank. Then they made us get into the same boat and rowed us to the other side. We landed, but no sooner had we stood on firm ground than we found ourselves surrounded by a group of horse-men. The robbers leapt into the boat like eagles and flew away, while we stood motionless on the shore. The horsemen asked, 'Who are you?' and after some hesitation I replied, 'We were kidnapped yesterday by these robbers, but we implored them meekly until they took pity on us and released us, as you have seen.' They looked at me and Ali ibn-Bakkar and Shams al-Nahar and said, 'You are not telling the truth. Tell us who you are, what are your names, and in what quarter you live.' I did not know what to answer, but Shams al-Nahar took the captain of the troop aside, and as soon as she spoke with him, he dismounted and, setting her on his horse, began to lead it along by the bridle. Two of his men did the same with Ali ibn-Bakkar and myself, and we rode on until we reached a spot on the riverbank where the captain called out to someone who came pulling two boats. The captain made the two lovers and myself get into one, while his men got into the other. Then the boatmen rowed us until, feeling almost dead from fright, we reached the caliph's palace [where the captain disembarked with Shams al-Nahar], then motioned to the boatman, who rowed us across the river to a spot that led to our quarter. We landed with two guards appointed for our protection, and when we reached Ali ibn-Bakkar's house, the two guards bade us good-bye. As soon as they were gone, we collapsed on the spot and lay fast asleep through that night and the next day. When I came to myself, it was nightfall, and I saw Ali ibn-Bakkar lying motionless, with the men and women of his house-hold weeping over him. When they saw that I was awake, they made me sit up and said, 'Tell us what has happened to him, for you are the cause of his misfortune and ruin.' I said, 'O people . . .'"

But morning overtook Shahrazad, and she lapsed into silence. Then Dinarzad said to her sister, "What a strange and entertaining story!" Shahrazad replied, "What is this compared with what I shall tell you tomorrow night if the king spares me and lets me live!"

## THE ONE HUNDRED AND NINETY-FOURTH NIGHT

*The following night Shahrazad replied to her sister, "Yes, I will continue the story":*

I heard, O happy King, that the jeweler said: "When they questioned me about Ali ibn-Bakkar, I said, 'O people, do not press me, for his story cannot be told in public.' But while I was imploring them and trying to make them afraid of scandal, Ali ibn-Bakkar moved in his bed. The assembled people rejoiced, and some of them departed, while others stayed. But they refused to let me go home and do as I pleased. They sprinkled his face with rosewater scented with powdered musk, and when he came to himself, they began to question him, but he was too weak to answer and motioned to them to let me go home.

"I went out, hardly believing in my escape, and came home, supported by two men. When my people saw me, they cried and beat their faces, but I motioned to them to stop. They did, and I sent the two men away and went to sleep. I slept the whole night, and when I awoke, I found my family, children, and friends standing around me. They asked, 'What has happened to you!' I called for water and washed my face and hands; then I called for wine and drank it, then changed my clothes and, after thanking my visitors, said, 'Wine overcame me and made me feel sick.' When the people left, I apologized to my family and promised to replace what they had lost. They told me that some of the goods had been returned already, that someone had thrown them into the hallway and disappeared in a hurry. For two days, I lay quietly at home and was unable to do much.

"When I began to regain my strength, I went to the bath, still very much worried about the young man and the young lady. I did not dare to go near his house or visit any place, for fear of meeting him, for I had repented to God of my former conduct, given alms in gratitude for my safety, and reconciled myself to my loss.

"Then I thought of going to a certain place to visit some friends and divert myself, for my ordeal had taken a heavy toll on me. I went out, remonstrating with myself, until I came to the cloth market and sat there for a while with a friend of mine. When I rose to go, I saw a woman standing before me, and when I looked at her closely, I recognized Shams al-Nahar's maid. At that moment the world turned dark before my eyes, and I hurried away in a terrible fright, while she pursued me, saying, 'My lord, stop and listen to what I have to say to you,' but whenever I wanted to stop and speak with her, I was seized with fear until I reached a mosque in an unfrequented spot and went in. She went in after me and, expressing sorrow for me, asked me about my condition. I told her all that had happened to myself and to Ali ibn-Bakkar, then said, 'Tell me what happened to you personally and what happened to your lady after she left us.'

"She replied, 'As for myself, when I saw the men, fearing that they were the caliph's officers who came to seize me and my mistress forthwith and take us to our ruin, I and the two maids fled over the rooftops from place to place until we took refuge with some people who took pity on us and helped us reach our place early in the morning, in the sorriest of plights. We concealed the situation, and I waited anxiously till nightfall, when I opened the river-gate and, calling the same boatman, said to him, 'Damn it, go search the river and see if you can find a boat with a woman inside.' At midnight I saw a boat approaching the gate, with one man rowing, another standing up, and a woman lying in a corner. When the boat touched the jetty and the woman landed, I was surprised to see that it was my lady, and I rejoiced in her safety.'"

*But morning overtook Shahrazad, and she lapsed into silence. Then Dinarzad said to her sister, "What a strange and entertaining story!" Shahrazad replied, "What is this compared with what I shall tell you tomorrow night if the king spares me and lets me live! It will be stranger and more amazing."*

### THE ONE HUNDRED AND NINETY-FIFTH NIGHT

*The following night Shahrazad said:*

I heard, O happy King, that the girl said to the jeweler, "When I saw her, I rejoiced in her safety and went to help her. She bade me give the man who had brought her a thousand dinars, and I thanked him and gave him the very purse that I had brought you and that you had refused to take. Then he departed and I returned and locked the gate. Then I and two maidservants carried Shams al-Nahar, who was almost dead from exhaustion, and laid her on her bed. She slept the rest of that night and the following day, while I forbade the maidservants from going in.

"At last she awoke, as if she had risen from the dead, and I sprinkled her face with rosewater scented with musk, washed her hands and feet, and changed her clothes. Then I made her drink some wine and after a great effort persuaded her to eat some food. As soon as she began to regain some energy, I remonstrated with her and said, 'You have suffered enough, and you have been close to death.' She said, 'Death would have been easier to me than what I have suffered. I was sure that I was going to be killed, and I gave myself up for lost. When the robbers took us from the jeweler's house, they asked me who I was, and I said that I was a singing girl; then they asked my beloved, and he replied that he was one of the common people. Then they took us to their place, and it was nothing but fear that gave us the strength to walk with them.

"'But when we were with them in their place and they looked at me and at my jewelry, they did not believe me and said that no singing girl could have such jewelry and asked me to tell them the truth. When I refused, they turned to my beloved and, saying that his attire was not that of a common man, asked him who he really was. When he and I remained silent, they asked us to tell them who was the owner of the house. When we replied that he was so and so, one of them said that he knew him and knew where he lived, adding that with luck he would bring him back immediately. Then they agreed to set me in one room by myself and my beloved in another room by himself, and their chief asked us to rest there without fear until they found out who we were, assuring us that our lives and possessions would be safe.

"'Then their comrade went out and brought that man (meaning you), and when he revealed to them who we were, they apologized and went out at once and, bringing a boat, put us in it and rowed us to the other side. There the captain of the night patrol fell upon us, and I motioned him aside and said to him that I was so and so and that I had had too much to drink and had gone to visit some ladyfriends of mine, when these men, with whom I met these two gentlemen, came by and brought us all here. Then I added that I had the wherewithal to reward him, and he dismounted and placed me on his horse and bade his men do the same with Ali ibn-Bakkar and the jeweler. At last I arrived, as you saw, without knowing what happened to Ali ibn-Bakkar or the jeweler. My heart is on fire for them, especially for the jeweler, who had lost his goods. Take some money and go to him and inquire about Ali ibn-Bakkar.' I chided her and warned her to be careful, saying, 'Fear God, give up this intrigue, and instead console yourself with patience. But she was angry at my words and yelled at me. So I left her and, going out to look for you, came to your house—I did not dare to go to Ali ibn-Bakkar. Now I stand here to serve you; please accept the money, for your need is evident, since you must compensate your friends for their loss." The jeweler related later, "I rose and walked out with her until we came to a certain place and she said, 'Wait here until I come back.'"

*But morning overtook Shahrazad, and she lapsed into silence. Then Dinarzad said to her sister Shahrazad, "Sister, what a strange and entertaining story!" Shahrazad replied, "What is this compared with what I shall tell you tomorrow night!"*

THE ONE HUNDRED AND NINETY-SIXTH NIGHT

*The following night Shahrazad said:*

I heard, O happy King, that the jeweler said: "The girl said, 'Wait here until I come back.' Then she returned, carrying a heavy bag of money and, giving it to me, said, 'Go, and may God protect you. Where shall we meet?' I replied, 'Come to my house. In the meantime I will work hard to find Ali ibn-Bakkar and arrange for you to meet him.' All that money made my task seem very easy. She said, 'I am afraid that you may not be able to find him and meet with him and that I too may not be able to find you.' I said, 'Come to my other house. I will go there immediately, replace the doors, and secure the place, so that we may meet there safely. She took her leave, and I carried the money home and, counting it, found it two thousand dinars and felt happy. Then I gave part of it to my family and part to my creditors. Then I took my servants with me to the other house and summoned workmen, who restored the doors and windows and made them even better than before. Then I left two maids there to keep an eye on the house and two others to act as servants and, having forgotten my mishap and regained my confidence, went out and headed to Ali ibn-Bakkar's house.

"When I arrived, his servants met me, and one of them bade me welcome, kissed my hand, and took me in. When I entered, I saw Ali ibn-Bakkar lying in bed, unable to speak. I sat down at his side and held his hand. He opened his eyes and said, 'Welcome!' and, forcing himself to sit up, added, 'I thank God to see you again.' Then little by little I made him stand up and take a few steps. Then he changed his clothes and drank some wine. All this he did to please me. Then I talked to him about the situation, and when I saw that he was beginning to feel better, I said, 'I kow your aspiration. Be of good cheer, for nothing has recently happened in this regard but what will comfort you and please you.' He signaled to the servants,

who withdrew; and he said, 'Have you forgotten what happened
to us?' But he apologized and asked me to tell him the news, and
I told him all that had happened to me after I left him and all that
had happened to Shams al-Nahar. He thanked the Almighty God
and praised Him and said, 'What a wonderful woman and what
perfect generosity!'"

*But morning overtook Shahrazad, and she lapsed into silence.*
*Then Dinarzad said, "Sister, what a strange and entertaining story!"*
*Shahrazad replied, "What is this compared with what I shall tell*
*you tomorrow night if the king spares me and lets me live!"*

### THE ONE HUNDRED AND NINETY-SEVENTH NIGHT

*The following night Shahrazad said:*

I heard, O happy King, that the jeweler said: "When I told Ali
ibn-Bakkar about the money that Shams al-Nahar had given me,
he said, 'What a wonderful woman and what perfect generosity!'
adding, 'I will replace all the utensils and other goods you lost.' Then
he turned to his steward and gave him an order, and the steward
brought in carpets, drapes, and utensils of gold and silver, which
exceeded what I had lost, and gave them all to me. I felt embarrassed, thanked him for his generosity, and added, 'Making the two
of you happy is dearer to me than all the goods you have given
me. Out of my love for you I will even throw myself into peril for
your sake.'

"I stayed with him the rest of that day and night, while he lay
weak and wan and kept sighing and weeping. When the day began
to break, he said to me, 'You should know that there is an end to
everything and the end of love is either death or enjoyment. I am
nearer to death, which is easier and better than this. I wish that
I had found fulfillment, relief, and rest, or that my sorrow had put
an end to my miserable life. This was our second meeting, and
if you help us to meet again, the same thing, as you know, will
happen. How can I bear to go through this agony for the third time,
particularly since I have no excuse before anyone, after such warning from Him to whom belongs the honor and the glory, the
Benevolent God who has saved us from scandal? I am at a loss and
I do not know how to find a way out of this predicament, and were
it not that I fear God, I would hasten my death, knowing that both

she and I are doomed to perish, although not before our appointed hour.' Then he wept bitterly and recited the following verses:

> How can the sad do anything but weep?
> I yearn to let you know my love, and mourn,
> And wake all night, as if the night has said,
> 'O stars, stay fixed and do not heed the morn.'

"I said to him, 'O my lord, steel yourself, bear calmly both joy and sorrow alike, and be patient.' He looked at me and recited the following verses:

> Have his eyes grown accustomed to their tears
> Or has his sorrow his patience undone?
> He used to keep his secrets to himself,
> But his sore eyes have broadcast everyone,
> For every time he tries to check his tears,
> The world checks him and with love interferes.

I said to him, 'I would like to go to the house. It may be that the maid will bring some news.' He said, 'Very well, but please come back quickly, for you see in what condition I am.'

"I went to the house, and hardly had I sat down, when the maid came, trembling and crying and looking disconcerted, frightened, and dazed. I asked her, 'What is the matter with you?' She replied, 'What we feared has fallen on us suddenly. When I left you yesterday and returned to my lady, I found her bidding one of the maids who were with us the other night be beaten. The girl ran away, escaping through a door that happened to be open, but one of the gatekeepers, appointed to guard the concubines in our quarters, stopped her, gave her shelter, and treated her kindly. Then he availed himself of the opportunity and questioned her, and she let drop some hints about what we did the first and second nights. He took her at once to the Commander of the Faithful, who interrogated her until she confessed. Yesterday the caliph ordered that my lady be removed to his own quarters and set over her twenty eunuchs to guard her, and since then he has not visited her or let her know the reason for her removal. At last, as one thing led to another, I succeeded in finding a way to come out. But I do not know what to do or how to help her or help myself, for she has none trustier than me or worthier of her trust.'"

*But morning overtook Shahrazad, and she lapsed into silence. Then Dinarzad said to her sister, "What a strange and entertaining story!" Shahrazad replied, "What is this compared with what I shall tell you tomorrow night if the king spares me and lets me live!"*

## THE ONE HUNDRED AND NINETY-EIGHTH NIGHT

I heard, O happy King, that the jeweler said: "The maid said
to me, 'Go to Ali ibn-Bakkar and warn him to be on guard until
we find a way out of this situation or, if we fail, at least to escape
with his own life and possessions.' This news was such a blow to
me that I could not find the strength to stand up. But after she left,
I hurried to Ali ibn-Bakkar and said to him, 'Gird yourself, summon
your courage, gather your wits; then compose yourself and shake
off your languor, prostration, and debility, for there has been a grave
development that could cause the destruction of your life and your
property.' He was alarmed and his color changed and he said to
me, 'O my friend, you have worried me terribly. Tell me everything
plainly.' I said to him, 'Such and such things have happened, and
you are surely lost.' He sat dazed for a while, looking as if his soul
had left his body; then he recovered and asked, 'What shall I do?'
I replied, 'Take of your possessions what is valuable and of your
servants those you trust, and I will do the same and head with you
to al-Anbar before the end of the day.' He jumped like a madman
and, now walking, now stumbling, prepared himself as well as he
could, made his excuse to his family, and, giving them his instructions, left the house.

"We set out for al-Anbar and journeyed the rest of the day and
most of the night till close to daybreak, when we unloaded and,
tying the legs of our camels, lay down to sleep, forgetting to keep
watch. Suddenly we were attacked by robbers, who took our camels,
our possessions, and all the money hidden in our belts, killed all
our servants and, stripping us naked, made off with everything,
leaving us in the worst of plights. Then Ali ibn-Bakkar asked me,
'Which is better, this or death?' I replied, 'What can we do? It is
God's will and decree.' We walked on till morning, when we came
to a mosque and took refuge there, two destitute strangers who knew
no one. We sat in a corner all that day and night, without hearing
anything or seeing anyone, man or woman. But when it was morning, a man suddenly came and after performing his prayers, turned
to us and said . . ."

*But morning overtook Shahrazad, and she lapsed into silence.
Then Dinarzad said to her sister, "What a strange and entertain-
ing story!" Shahrazad replied, "What is this compared with what
I shall tell you tomorrow night if the king spares me and lets me live!"*

THE ONE HUNDRED AND NINETY-NINTH NIGHT

*The following night Shahrazad said:*

I heard, O happy King, that the jeweler said, "Suddenly a man
came in and after performing his prayers, turned to us and said,
'Greetings, and may God preserve you. Are you strangers?' We
replied, 'Yes, we are. We have been robbed, and we know no one
to go to.' He asked us, 'Will you come home with me?' I turned
to Ali ibn-Bakkar and said, 'Let us go with him, for I am afraid
that someone may enter the mosque and recognize us; besides, we
are strangers here and have nowhere else to go.' He replied, 'Do
as you wish.' The man asked, 'Well, what do you say?' Then he
took off part of his clothes and covered us, saying, 'Let us take
advantage of this early hour and go now.'

"We went out with him, and when we reached his house, he
knocked at the door, and a little servant came out and opened
it. We entered after our host, who called for a parcel containing
clothes and white cloth for turbans and gave them to us. We put
on the clothes, made ourselves turbans, and sat down. Soon a maid
brought in a tray of food and said, 'Eat, with the blessing of the
Almighty God.' We ate a little, and the girl took away the tray.
We remained with our host till nightfall, when Ali ibn-Bakkar sighed
deeply and said to me sadly, 'You know that I am surely going to
die. I have a charge to give you, namely, that when I die, you will
go to my mother and ask her to come here to have me washed and
prepared for burial. And tell her to bear my loss with patience.'"

*But morning overtook Shahrazad, and she lapsed into silence.
Then Dinarzad said, "Sister, what a strange and entertaining story!"
Shahrazad replied, "What is this compared with what I shall tell
you tomorrow night if the king spares me and lets me live!"*

THE TWO HUNDREDTH NIGHT

*The following night Shahrazad said:*

I heard, O happy King, that the jeweler said, "Ali ibn-Bakkar
charged me and asked me to tell his mother to bear his loss with

patience. Then he fell in a swoon and remained unconscious for
a long time, and when he came to himself, he heard a girl singing
the following verses:

> Adversity has hastened our parting,
> After our happy love and joyful life.
> Such parting after joy is bitter pain;
> Would that a lover were spared such a strife.
> Death's agony but a short moment lasts,
> But parting's pain stays always in the heart.
> God has allowed all lovers to unite,
> But has condemned me and kept us apart.

"When he heard these verses, he groaned and his soul left his
body. Then I wrapped him in a shroud and committed his body
to the care of our host.

"Two days later I journeyed, in the company of some people;
then I reached Baghdad and entered my house. Then I went to
Ali ibn-Bakkar's house, and when his servants saw me, they came
up to me and greeted me. I bade them ask leave of his mother for
me to see her, and she gave me leave, and I went in and greeted
her. After I sat for a while, I said to her, 'May God bless you and
be kind to you. The Almighty God orders the life of man according to His command, and none can escape His will and decree.'
When she heard my words, she wept bitterly and said, 'For God's
sake, tell me: is my son dead?' But I could not reply, for I was choking with sobs and tears. Her grief was so great that she fell down
in a swoon, and the maids rushed in, without veils, and propped
her up. When she came to herself, she asked me, 'What happened
to my son?' I replied, 'Such and such things happened to him, and
I am very sorry for him, for, by God, he was my best and dearest
friend.' When I finished telling her everything, she said, 'He should
have confided his secret to me. Did he give you any charge?' I
replied, 'Yes, he did,' and, giving her his instructions, left her wailing
and crying with her maids.

"I went out, dazed with grief and blinded with tears, thinking
of his youth and recalling the days when I used to visit him, and
as I was walking and crying, a woman suddenly grabbed my hand.
I looked at her and recognized Shams al-Nahar's maid, dressed in
black and looking grief-stricken. When I saw her in this condition,
I wept and sobbed more bitterly and made her weep with me. We
walked on until we came to my other house, and when we were
inside, I asked her, 'Have you heard the news of Ali ibn-Bakkar?'
She replied, 'No, by God,' and I told her, and we both wept again.
Then I asked her, 'What further affliction caused your lady's death?'
She replied, 'The Commander of the Faithful, as I told you, had

her removed to his own quarters, but, thinking the accusations absurd, he did not confront her with them because of his love and compassion for her. Indeed, he told her that she was the finest, the most virtuous, the most innocent of her enemies' accusations, and the dearest of all the people to him. Then he ordered for her a beautiful room decorated with gold, and this filled her with alarm and fright.

"'One evening, as he sat to drink and carouse as usual, he summoned his concubines, bidding them be seated in their places, and made Shams al-Nahar sit by his side, in order to show them her status among them and her place in his heart. She sat there, absent-mindedly, feeling weak and numb, and her words betrayed her apprehension and fear of what the caliph would do. Then one of the girls sang the following verses:

Sad love called for my tears, and they replied,
And o'er my burning cheeks they fell and flowed
Until my eyes, grown weary of the charge,
Hid what I wished to show and what lay hidden showed.
How can I hope my passion to conceal,
When my love's torment everyone can see?
After my darling, death is to me sweet;
I wonder how he would fare after me!

"'When Shams al-Nahar heard these verses, she lost control, burst into tears, and fell down in a swoon. The caliph threw the cup from his hand and drew her to him, but she was already dead. He cried out, and the girls joined him with their cries, and he bade all the vessels and all the musical instruments in the place be broken, and they were broken. Then he hurried out, having bidden her be carried to his private chamber, where he stayed with her the rest of the night. When it was morning, he bade her be washed, wrapped in a shroud, and buried. But he never inquired about her case.' Then the maid said to me, 'I beg you, in God's name, to let me know the day of the arrival of Ali ibn-Bakkar's body and his burial.' I asked her, 'Where can I find you?' She replied, 'The Commander of the Faithful freed all her women, including myself, and I am now staying at her tomb in such and such a place.' Then I went out with her to the cemetery, visited the tomb, and departed.

"On the fourth day Ali ibn-Bakkar's body arrived in Baghdad from al-Anbar, and people of all classes, both men and women, including myself, went out to meet him. It was a day the like of which I had never seen in Baghdad. Shams al-Nahar's maid joined Ali ibn-Bakkar's family in the procession, surpassing in grief both young and old, as she mourned and lamented with a voice that wracked the soul and broke the heart until they reached the cemetery and buried him. From that time on, I have never ceased to visit his tomb. This then is the story of Ali ibn-Bakkar and Shams al-Nahar."

*But morning overtook Shahrazad, and she lapsed into silence. Then her sister said, "What an entertaining story!" Shahrazad replied, "Tomorrow night I will tell you a strange and charming tale, a marvelous tale that will entertain you, the Almighty God willing."*

THE TWO HUNDRED AND FIRST NIGHT

*The following night Dinarzad said to her sister Shahrazad, "Sister, if you are not sleepy, tell us one of your lovely little tales to while away the night." Shahrazad replied, "I hear and obey":*

# [THE STORY OF THE SLAVE-GIRL ANIS AL-JALIS AND NUR AL-DIN ALI IBN-KHAQAN]

It is related—but God knows and sees best what lies hidden in the old accounts of bygone peoples and times—that there was once in Basra a king who cherished the poor and needy and was a popular leader. He was as bountiful as the sea, so that even the proud were glad to be his servants and even the days and nights awaited his command, for he was a man who rejoiced in sharing his wealth with those who served him. He was like him of whom the poet said:

He is a king who, when the foe assaults,
Answers with angry, trenchant, deadly blows,
Hewing the horsemen down, row after row,
As he on their felled bodies his mark draws.
The lines are carved by the swords and the spears,
And the horses heave in a sea of blood
That flows from nostrils, heads, and vital parts,
A sea where the spears are masts, the broad swords,
Inked with blood, sails, and the white helmets pearls.
Three torrents he unleashes from each fingertip
And with each torrent a thousand lions hurls.
Time swore a man his equal to create,
But Time has lied and must now expiate.

His name was Muhammad ibn-Sulaiman al-Zainabi, and he had
two viziers, one called al-Mu'in ibn-Sawi and the other Fadl al-Din
ibn-Khaqan. Fadl al-Din was the most generous man of his time,
equaled by none in purity of heart and nobility of conduct, so that
all the people were united in loving him, and the women at home
wished him long life, for he prevented evil and did good, just as
the poet said of him:

> He is a noble and a godly man
> Who helps a friend and thereby pleases life,
> For never knocked a supplicant at his door,
> Without obtaining relief from strife.

Al-Mu'in ibn-Sawi, on the contrary, was the most avaricious, the
meanest, the most vicious, and the most foolish of men, who always
spoke vilely and acted shamefully. He was more cunning than a
fox and more vicious than a dog, just as one of the poets said of him:

> He is a mean and wretched infidel,
> Who preys on everyone who comes and goes,
> That on his body not a single hair
> But its existence to a victim owes.

And as much as the people loved Fadl al-Din ibn-Khaqan, so much
did they hate al-Mu'in ibn-Sawi.

As it had been foreordained, one day, as King Muhammad ibn-
Sulaiman al-Zainabi sat on his throne, surrounded by his officers
of state, he cried out to his vizier Fadl ibn-Khaqan, saying "Fadl
al-Din, I wish to have a slave-girl of unsurpassed beauty, wisdom,
and refinement, one who is all perfection and grace." His courtiers
and chief counselors said, "Such a girl is not to be had for less than
ten thousand dinars." When the king heard this, he cried out to
his treasurer and said, "Give ten thousand dinars to Fadl al-Din
ibn-Khaqan." The treasurer did so, and the vizier went away, having received the king's orders to employ brokers, to go to the market
every day, and to see to it that no beautiful girl worth more than
ten thousand dinars should be sold without being first shown to
the vizier. Accordingly, the brokers showed every girl to the vizier
before selling her.

*But morning overtook Shahrazad, and she lapsed into silence.
Then Dinarzad said to her sister, "What a strange and entertain-
ing story!" Shahrazad replied, "What is this compared with what
I shall tell you tomorrow night if the king spares me and lets me live!"*

## THE TWO HUNDRED AND SECOND NIGHT

*The following night Shahrazad said:*

I heard, O happy King, that the brokers showed every girl to
the vizier before selling her, but none pleased him until one day
a broker came to him and, finding him about to mount his horse,
on his way to the royal palace, caught hold of his stirrup and recited
the following verses:

> Without you everything would have been dust,
> But your great bounties have restored the state.
> O vanquisher of foes, O hope and trust,
> O fortunate vizier, O man of fate!

Then he said to the vizier, "O Grand Vizier, she who has been
demanded by the noble order is here." The vizier said, "Bring her
to me." The broker went away and soon returned with a girl who
was about five feet tall, with a slender waist, heavy hips, swelling
breasts, smooth cheeks, and black eyes. She was sweet youth itself,
with a figure more elegant than the bending, blossoming bough,
dewy lips sweeter than syrup, and a voice softer than the morning
breeze. She was just as a poet said of her:

> With face as lovely as the dazzling moon,
> In beauty she excels the antelopes and deer.
> The Glorious God has given her honor, fame,
> Virtue, a golden shape, and all the graces dear.
> Seven stars shine on her heavenly face
> To guard her cheeks and all intruders bar,
> So that if one dares steal an impish look,
> At once she shoots him with a falling star.

When the vizier saw her, he was exceedingly pleased with her
and, turning to the broker, asked, "What is the price of this girl?"
The broker replied, "O my lord, her price is ten thousand dinars,
and her owner swears that the sum will not cover the cost of the
chickens she has eaten, the wine she has drunk, and the robes of
honor bestowed on her teacher; for she has learned Arabic grammar and syntax, enunciation and penmanship, jurisprudence and
medicine, and the explication of the Quran, as well as the art of
playing on every musical instrument." The vizier said, "Bring me
her master." The broker brought him immediately, and he turned
out to be a Persian, an old man whom time had ravaged, leaving
him like a sick eagle or a ruined wall, so debilitated that he could

be drawn by a hair or made to stumble on a lotus seed. He was like him of whom the poet said:

> Time made me tremble; ah! how sore that was,
> For with his might does time all mortals stalk.
> I used to walk without becoming tired;
> Today I tire although I never walk.

The vizier asked him, "Old man, will you sell the girl to King Muhammad ibn-Sulaiman al-Zainabi for ten thousand dinars?" The Persian replied, "Yes by God, for it is my duty to let him have her even without money." The vizier sent for the money and, counting ten thousand dinars, gave it to the Persian.

Then the broker turned to the vizier and said . . .

*But morning overtook Shahrazad, and she lapsed into silence. Then Dinarzad said to her sister, "What a strange and entertaining story!" Shahrazad replied, "What is this compared with what I shall tell you tomorrow night if the king spares me and lets me live!"*

THE TWO HUNDRED AND THIRD NIGHT

*The following night Shahrazad said:*

I heard, O happy King, that the broker turned to the vizier and said, "If my lord the vizier permits me, I have something to say." The vizier replied, "Speak." The broker said, "In my opinion, you should not take the girl to the king today, for she has just arrived from a journey and the change of air seems to have bothered her. Keep her in your palace for fifteen days until she regains her good looks. Then send her to the bath, dress her in the finest of clothes, and take her to the king, and that will be more to your advantage." The vizier considered the man's advice and, finding it to be right, took the girl to his palace, lodged her in a private chamber in the inner quarters, and offered her a generous daily allowance of chickens, wine, and fine clothes, and she lived this way for a while.

It happened that the vizier had a son like the full moon, with a radiant face, rosy cheeks covered with down like tender myrtle, and a mole like a disk of ambergris. He was like him of whom the poet said:

> He is a moon who slays with charming looks,
> A bough who captivates the heart with his rare grace.
> Fair is his person, spearlike is his shape,

Jet black are his locks, golden is his face,
Hard is his heart, and slender is his waist;
Alas, why can't they each other replace?
Had his heart been as tender as his waist,
He would never have wronged and let his lovers smart.
O you who blame me for his love, forbear,
For he has full possession of my heart.
The fault lies with my heart and with my eye,
So none should be blamed for my pain but I.

The young man knew nothing about the affair of the girl, and his father cautioned her, saying "O my daughter, you should know that I have bought you for none save King Muhammad ibn-Sulaiman al-Zainabi and that I have a devil of a son who has slept with every girl in the neighborhood. So be on your guard against him and beware of letting him see your face or hear your voice. Now you know what to do." She replied, "I hear and obey," and the vizier departed.

As it had been foreordained, it chanced a few days later that the girl went to the bath in the palace, where one of the maids washed her. The bath lent her even greater beauty and grace, and when she came out, she was dressed in an attire befitting her youthful charm. Then she went to the vizier's wife and kissed her hand, and the lady said, "Anis al-Jalis, may the bath bring you blessing!" She replied, "May God send you all the joy and blessing." The lady asked her, "Anis al-Jalis, how did you find the bath?" She replied, "My lady, it is fine; at this moment the water is just right and lacks nothing save your presence." The lady said to her waiting women, "Let us go to the bath, for I have not been in for some days." They replied, "Our lady, you spoke what has been on our minds." Saying, "Very well, let us go," the lady rose and her waiting women rose with her, and they went to the bath, while Anis al-Jalis went to her chamber with two little maids whom the vizier's wife had ordered to stand at the door, saying, "Be on guard and do not let anyone come near the chamber."

While Anis al-Jalis sat resting in her chamber after the exertions of the bath, Nur al-Din Ali, the vizier's son, entered his mother's apartment, and when he saw the two maids sitting by the door, he asked them about his mother, and they replied . . .

*But morning overtook Shahrazad, and she lapsed into silence. Then Dinarzad said to her sister, "What a strange and entertaining story!" Shahrazad replied, "What is this compared with what I shall tell you tomorrow night if the king spares me and lets me live!"*

## THE TWO HUNDRED AND FOURTH NIGHT

*The following night Shahrazad replied, "Very well," and said:*

I heard, O happy King, that Nur al-Din asked the two maids about his mother, and they replied, "She went to the bath." When Anis al-Jalis heard Nur al-Din, she said to herself, "I wonder what the young man who is talking looks like and if he is the one they warned me about." She ran, still fresh from the bath, and, going to the door, looked at Nur al-Din, and when she saw that he was like the full moon, she sighed. Nur al-Din, chancing to turn his head, saw Anis al-Jalis, and when he looked on her, he too sighed, as each fell in to the snares of love for the other. Then he went up to the two little maids and yelled at them, and they fled from him in fear and stood at a distance to see what he would do. He went to the door of the chamber and, opening it, entered and asked Anis al-Jalis, "Are you the one whom my father bought for me?" She replied, "Yes, by God, my lord, I am the one." So Nur al-Din, who was drunk, went to her, took her legs, and pressed them to his sides, while she locked her arms around his neck and began to give him adept and passionate kisses, and he at once undid her trousers and took her virginity. When the little maids saw what happened, they cried out and screamed, while Nur al-Din, fearing the consequences of his action, got up and fled.

When the vizier's wife heard the cries, she came out of the bath in a hurry to see what was causing the commotion in the house. She came up to the two maids and said, "Woe to you, what is the matter?" They replied, "Our lord Nur al-Din came and beat us, and since we were unable to stop him, we fled, while he entered Anis al-Jalis's chamber and embraced her for a while, but we don't know what he did afterward, except that he came out running." The vizier's wife went into Anis al-Jalis's chamber and asked her, "O my daughter, what happened to you?" Anis al-Jalis replied, "O my lady, as I was sitting here, a handsome young man suddenly came in and asked me, 'Aren't you the one whom my father bought for me?' and I replied, 'Yes,' for, by God, my lady, I thought that he was telling the truth. Then he came up to me and embraced me." The vizier's wife asked, "Did he do you know what to you?" Anis al-Jalis replied, "Yes, but he did it only three times." The vizier's wife said, "I hope that you will not have to pay for this!" and she and the maids began to cry and beat their faces, for they feared that Nur al-Din's father would kill him.

While they were in this condition, the vizier came in and asked, "Damn it, what is the matter?" But nobody dared tell him what had happened. He came up to his wife.

*But morning overtook Shahrazad, and she lapsed into silence. Then Dinarzad said to her sister, "What a strange and entertaining story!" Shahrazad replied, "What is this compared with what I shall tell you tomorrow night if I stay alive!"*

THE TWO HUNDRED AND FIFTH NIGHT

*The following night Shahrazad said:*

I heard, O happy King, that the vizier came up to his wife and said, "Tell me the truth." She replied, "I will not tell you until you swear that you will do whatever I say." He said, "Very well." She said, "Your son went in to Anis al-Jalis and took her virginity." When the vizier heard his wife's words, he sagged down to the ground, beat his face until his nose began to bleed, and plucked out the wisps of his beard. His wife said to him, "My lord, you are killing yourself. I will give you ten thousand dinars, the price of the girl, from my own money." But he raised his head and said to her, "Damn it, I don't need her price. I am afraid of losing both my life and my possessions." She asked, "My lord, how so?" He replied, "Don't you know that our enemy al-Mu'in ibn-Sawi is lying in wait for us, and when he hears of the affair, he will go to the king and say to him, 'O my lord, your vizier, who, according to you, loves you and cares for your welfare, has taken ten thousand dinars from you and bought a girl, whose like was never seen, but when he saw her, he liked her and said to his son, "Take this girl for yourself, for you deserve her more than the king." So, my lord, the young man took her and took her virginity and she is now with him.' Then the king will reply, 'You are lying,' and the vizier will say, 'With your leave, I will bring the slave-girl to you.' The king will order him to do so, and he will come, attack us, and take the girl to the king, who will question her, and she will not be able to deny what has happened. Then the vizier will say to the king, 'O my lord, I have done this only so that you may know that I give you true counsel and care for your welfare. By God, my lord, I have not been fortunate, yet everybody is jealous of me.' When the king hears this, he will give orders to kill me and plunder my property." When his wife heard this, she said to him, "My lord, don't you know that God's graces are hidden from us?" He replied, "Yes." She added, "O my lord, commit yourself to the Almighty God, and I will pray to him that none will discover the affair of the girl or hear anything about it, for, my lord, 'The Master of what lies hidden controls what lies hidden.'" When the vizier heard his wife's words, he calmed down and drank a cup of wine.

As for Nur al-Din, fearing the consequences of the affair, he spent the whole day in the gardens and places of entertainment, away from his companions, and came back at night. When he knocked, the maids opened the door for him, and he went to sleep but left before daylight. He lived like this for a whole month, without showing his face to his father, until his mother said to her husband, "My lord, you have lost the girl and now you are going to lose your own son. If things continue like this, he will run away." The vizier asked, "What shall we do?" She replied, "My lord, stay awake and wait for him tonight, and when he comes home late at night, seize him and scare him, and I will rescue him from you. Then you will make your peace with him and give him the girl, for she loves him and he loves her, and I will pay you her price."

The vizier waited until his son came home, and when he heard him knocking at the door, he rose and hid in a dark corner, while the maids opened the door. When the young man entered, he suddenly felt someone seize him and throw him down to the ground, and when he raised his head to see who had done this to him, he saw his father.

*But morning overtook Shahrazad, and she lapsed into silence. Then Dinarzad said to her sister, "What a strange, amazing, and entertaining story!" Shahrazad replied, "What is this compared with what I shall tell you tomorrow night if the king spares me and lets me live!"*

### THE TWO HUNDRED AND SIXTH NIGHT

*The following night Shahrazad said:*

I heard, O happy King, that the young man saw that the man who had thrown him down was his father, who then knelt on his breast and pulled out a knife as if to cut his throat. At that moment the vizier's wife came up from behind and said, "What do you want to do with him?" He replied, "I want to kill him." Nur al-Din asked, "My lord, do you find it so easy to kill me?" His father looked at

him, and, as the divine power moved him and his eyes filled with
tears, he said, "Son, do you find it so easy to make me lose my
life and my possessions?" The young man replied, "O my lord, the
poet says:

> Pardon my crime, for every mighty judge
> Is used to mercy some offenders show.
> I stand before you, guilty of all sins,
> But you the ways of grace and mercy know.
> For he who seeks forgiveness from above
> Should pardon the offenders here below."

When he heard this, the vizier felt compassion for his son and rose
up from his chest. Then Nur al-Din kissed his father's hands and
feet, and his father said to him, "O Nur al-Din, if I knew that you
would treat Anis al-Jalis fairly, I would give her to you." Nur al-
Din asked, "My lord, how do you wish me to treat her?" His father
replied, "Do not take an additional wife, or abuse her, or sell her."
Nur al-Din replied, "My lord, I swear to you," and he swore to do
none of these things. Then he went in to Anis al-Jalis and for a
whole year lived with her the happiest of lives, while God caused
the king to forget the affair of the slave-girl. Meanwhile al-Mu'in
ibn-Sawi was unable to speak of the affair because of the intimacy
of the Vizier Fadl al-Din with the king.

One day, at the end of the year, the Vizier Fadl al-din went to
the bath and, coming out, still in perspiration, caught a chill, became feverish, and took to his bed. When he got worse, until he
was no longer able to sleep, he called his son, and when the son
came, his father wept and said, "O my son, you should know that
fortune is allotted, that life is allocated, and that everyone must
die. The poet says:

> I am mortal and know that I must die;
> Glory to the eternal Lord and King.
> He is no king who is subject to death;
> The sovereignty is His who fears no mortal thing.

"O my son, I have no charge to give you, save to fear God, to
weigh the consequences of your actions, and to look after Anis al-
Jalis." Nur al-Din said, "O my father, who can be like you, you
who are known for your good deeds and the blessings invoked upon
them from the pulpits?" His father replied, "O my son, I pray for
God's acceptance." Then his death throes began, and when he ex-
pired, the cries of the women of his household filled the palace. The
king received the news, and when the citizens heard of the death
of the vizier Fadl al-Din ibn-Khaqan, everyone cried, the children
in their schools, the men in their mosques, and the women in their

homes. Then Nur al-Din proceeded to prepare his father for burial, and all the citizens, headed by the princes, viziers, and officers of state, attended. The young man gave him the most lavish preparations, and when he was buried, a poet mourned him with the following verses:

> On Thursday I left my dear ones for good,
> And my friends washed me on a slab of wood,
> And stripped me of the clothes that I had on
> And made me other than my own clothes don
> And on four shoulders carried me away
> And in the mosque did on my body pray;
> A standing prayer on me they performed,
> As all my friends around my body swarmed.
> At last they took me to a vaulted hut
> Whose door will to the end of time stay shut.

After his father was buried, Nur al-Din returned with his family and friends, still weeping and sobbing, as if to say:

> On Thursday night I bade adieu and stayed,
> While they departed and left me alone,
> Taking my soul with them, and when I said,
> "Return," it answered, "How can I go on
> In a body reduced to rotting bones,
> A frame where both the flesh and blood are gone,
> Where the eyes are blinded by bitter tears,
> And the ears hear not, being as deaf as stone?"

He continued to mourn his father deeply for a long time. One day . . .

*But morning overtook Shahrazad, and she lapsed into silence. Then Dinarzad said to her sister, "What a strange and entertaining story!" Shahrazad replied, "What is this compared with what I shall tell you tomorrow night if the king spares me and lets me live!"*

THE TWO HUNDRED AND SEVENTH NIGHT

*The following night Shahrazad replied, "Very well," and said:*

I heard, O happy King, that one day, as the vizier's son Nur al-Din sat in his father's palace, there was a knock at the door. He rose and, opening the door, found one of his father's friends and companions, who kissed his hand and said to him, "My lord, he who has left the like of you is not dead. My lord Nur al-Din Ali, take comfort, be cheerful, and stop mourning." So Nur al-Din rose and went to the guest hall and, transporting there whatever he needed for entertainment, invited his friends, ten of the sons of merchants, and asked his girl Anis al-Jalis to join him. Then he began to eat and drink, giving one banquet after another and dispensing gifts, favors, and honors until his steward came to him one day and said, "My lord Nur al-Din, have you not heard the saying 'He who spends without reckoning, becomes poor without knowing it'? My lord, this enormous expense and lavish giving will erode even mountains." When Nur al-Din heard his steward's words, he looked at him and said, "I will not listen to one word of yours. Haven't you heard the poet say:

> If I have wealth and be not liberal,
> May my hand wither and my foot be stilled.
> Show me the niggard who has glory won;
> Show me the man who by giving was killed."

Nur al-Din added, "It is my wish that if you have enough for my morning meal, worry me not about my supper a great deal." The steward said, "Is this what you wish?" Nur al-Din replied, "Yes." Then the steward left him and went away while he continued to pursue his pleasures and his lavish ways, so that if someone chanced to say to him, "My lord Nur al-Din, such and such an orchard of yours is lovely," he would reply, "It is yours as an irrevocable gift from a friend," and if the man asked for the deed, he would not hesitate to give it to him; if another said to him, "Such and such a house," another, "My lord, that other house," and a third, "Such and such a bath," he would give them all to them. In this way he lived an entire year, giving daily banquets, one in the morning, a second in the evening, and a third at midnight.

One day, as he sat listening to Anis al-Jalis sing these verses:

> You thought well of the days when they were good,
> Oblivious to the ills fate brings to one.
> You were deluded by the peaceful nights,
> Yet in the peace of night does sorrow stun,

there was knocking at the door. One of the guests said, "My lord Nur al-Din, there is knocking . . ."

*But morning overtook Shahrazad, and she lapsed into silence. Then Dinarzad said to her sister, "What a strange and entertaining story!" Shahrazad replied, "What is this compared with what I shall tell you tomorrow night if the king spares me and lets me live!"*

اليلة

## THE TWO HUNDRED AND EIGHTH NIGHT

*The following night Shahrazad said:*

I heard, O happy King, that one of the guests said, "There is knocking at the door." So Nur al-Din Ali rose and went to the door, but, without knowing it, he was followed by one of his companions. When he opened the door, he found the steward standing there, and when he asked him, "What is the matter?" the steward replied, "My lord, what I feared has come to pass." Nur al-Din asked, "How so?" The steward replied, "To put it briefly, you should know that there is not even a dirham's worth left of your possessions in my hands; here is the record of what was entrusted to your servant in my lord's own handwriting." When Nur al-Din heard this, he bowed his head and said, "This is God's wish, for there is no power, save in God."

As soon as the man who had secretly followed Nur al-Din heard what the steward said, he returned to his companions and said to them, "You should consider what to do, for Nur al-Din is bankrupt and destitute." They replied, "We will not stay with him." Meanwhile Nur al-Din dismissed the steward and returned to them with a troubled look. Then one of them rose and, turning to him, said, "My lord, perhaps you will give me leave to depart." Nur al-Din asked, "For what reason?" The man replied, "My wife is due to give birth today, and I cannot be absent from her and wish to be with her." Nur al-Din gave him leave, and another rose, made an excuse, and departed. Then each in turn gave excuse until all ten companions were gone and Nur al-Din was left alone.

Then he called Anis al-Jalis, and when she came, he said to her, "O Anis al-Jalis, do you see what has happened to me?" and he related to her what the steward had told him. She said, "My lord, your family and friends have warned you, but you refused to listen. O my lord, some nights ago I intended to speak to you about the matter, but I heard you recite these verses:

> If fortune befriend you be kind to all,
> Before she slips away and lets you down.
> Munificence will not undo it if she smile,
> And avarice will not preserve it if she frown.

When I heard you, I kept quiet and decided not to open the subject." Nur al-Din said to her, "O Anis al-Jalis, you know that I have spent my money on none save my ten friends, and I don't think that they will leave me destitute." She replied, "By God, my lord, they will never help you." Nur al-Din said, "I will rise at once and go to them and maybe I will get enough from them to use as capital to trade with and leave off idle pursuits."

Then Nur al-Din rose and went until he came to a certain street, where all his ten companions happened to live. He went to the first door, and when he knocked, a maid came out and asked, "Who are you?" He replied, "O girl, say to your master, 'My lord Nur al-Din Ali ibn-Khaqan stands at the door and wishes to kiss your hand and greet you.'" The girl went in and told her master, who yelled at her, saying, "Go out and say to him, 'My master is not at home,'" and the girl came out and said to Nur al-Din, "My master is not at home." Nur al-Din said to himself . . .

*But morning overtook Shahrazad, and she lapsed into silence. Then Dinarzad said to her sister, "What a strange and entertaining story!" Shahrazad replied, "What is this compared with what I shall tell you tomorrow night if the king spares me and lets me live!"*

### The Two Hundred and Ninth Night

*The following night Shahrazad said:*

I heard, O happy King, that Nur al-Din said to himself, "Though this fellow is a bastard who has turned me away, another may not be so." Then he went to the second door, and when he knocked, a maid came out, and he repeated what he had said to the first girl. She disappeared, then returned, saying, "Sir, he ain't here." Nur al-Din smiled and said to himself, "Maybe I will find another who will help me." So he went to the third door, saying to himself, "I will send him the same message." But when the third turned him away too, he regretted coming, wept, and recited the following verses:

> When affluent, a man is like a tree,
> Round which people collect as long as fruit they see.
> But when the fruit is gone, they turn away
> And leave the tree to dust and misery.
> Perish the people of this age; not one
> In ten can as a friend be counted on.

Then Nur al-Din returned to Anis al-Jalis, feeling even more depressed than before, and she said to him, "My lord, do you believe me now?" He replied, "By God, not one of them would take any notice of me or ask me in." She said, "My lord, sell some of the furniture and utensils in the house until the Almighty, Exalted, and Glorious God provides." So Nur al-Din began to sell the articles, little by little, and to live on the proceeds until there was nothing left. Then he turned to Anis al-Jalis and asked, "What is left to sell now?" She replied, "O my lord, it is my advice that you should rise at once and take me down to the market and sell me. You know that your father bought me for ten thousand dinars; perhaps the Exalted and Glorious God will help you get close to this amount for me, and if it is his will to reunite us, we will meet again." Nur al-Din replied, "O Anis al-Jalis, by God, I cannot endure to be parted from you one single hour." She said, "By God, my lord, nor can I; but necessity compels, as the poet says:

> Necessity compels us to resort
> Sometimes to ways that decent men oppose.
> No man forces himself to do a thing,
> Except what is dictated by the cause."

Then Nur al-Din rose and took Anis al-Jalis with him, with his tears running profusely over his cheeks, as if to say:

> Stay and give me a final look before we part,
> So that I may console my heart, which wastes away.
> But if you deem this burdensome, I'd rather die
> Of love than on you such a burden lay.

When Nur al-Din entered the market with Anis al-Jalis, he delivered her to one of the brokers, saying to him, "Haj Hasan, you should know the value of the girl you are going to auction." The broker replied, "O my lord Nur al-Din, your interest is protected," adding, "Isn't she Anis al-Jalis, whom your father bought some time ago for ten thousand dinars?" Nur al-Din replied, "Yes, she is." Then the broker looked around and, seeing that many merchants were still absent, waited until the market began to get very active and all kinds of girls were sold, Nubians, Europeans, Greeks, Circassians, Turks, Tartars, and others. When the broker saw that the market was very active, he rose and, going up to the merchants, cried out, "O merchants . . ."

*But morning overtook Shahrazad, and she lapsed into silence. Then Dinarzad said to her sister, "What a strange and entertaining story!" Shahrazad replied, "What is this compared with what I shall tell you tomorrow night if the king spares me and lets me live! It will be even stranger."*

### THE TWO HUNDRED AND TENTH NIGHT

*The following night Shahrazad replied, "Very well," and said:*

I heard, O happy King, that the broker cried out, "O merchants,
O men of wealth, not every round thing a walnut nor every long
thing a banana; not every red thing meat nor every white thing
fat. O merchants, I have here this unique pearl. What will you pay
for her and what is your opening bid?" One of them cried out, "Four
thousand dinars," and the broker opened the bidding at four thousand dinars, but while he was calling for bids, the Vizier al-Mu'in
ibn-Sawi happened to pass through the market and, seeing Nur al-
Din standing in a corner, said to himself, "I wonder what ibn-
Khaqan is doing here. Has this good-for-nothing anything left to
buy girls with?" Then he looked around and, seeing the broker in
the middle of the market, surrounded by the merchants, said to
himself, "If I am not mistaken, I think that Nur al-Din has become
penniless and has brought Anis al-Jalis down to the market to auction her off. O how soothing to my heart!" Then he called the broker,
who came and kissed the ground before him, and he said to him,
"Broker, show me the girl you are selling." The broker, who dared
not cross him, replied, "Yes, my lord, here she is, look at her," and
he showed him Anis al-Jalis, who pleased him very much. He said
to the broker, "Hasan, what is the bid on her?" The broker replied,
"My lord, I have an opening bid of four thousand dinars." Al-Mu'in
said, "I too bid four thousand dinars." When the merchants heard
this, they dared not bid against him, knowing his tyranny and
treachery. The vizier looked at the broker and said, "Damn it, what
are you waiting for? Go to Nur al-Din Ali and offer him four thousand dinars for her." The broker went to Nur al-Din and said to
him, "My lord, your girl is about to be sold for nothing." Nur al-
Din asked, "How so?" The broker replied, "I opened the bidding
at four thousand dinars, when that unfair tyrant al-Mu'in ibn-Sawi
passed through the market, and when he saw the girl, she pleased
him and he said to me, 'Go and offer four thousand dinars for her.'
I am sure, my lord, that he knows that she belongs to you, and
if he would pay you at once, it would still be all right, but knowing
how unfair he is, he will give you a written note on some of his
agents; then he will send someone to tell them to procrastinate and
give you nothing at this time, and whenever you go to them to ask
for your money, they will say to you, 'Very well, but come back
tomorrow.' They will do this to you day after day until, being as

self-respecting as you are, you will angrily snatch the note and tear it up and lose the money for the girl." When Nur al-Din heard the broker's words, he looked at him and asked, "What is to be done?" The broker replied, "My lord, I will give you a piece of advice that, if you follow, will be more to your advantage." Nur al-Din asked, "What is it?" The broker replied, "When I stand in the middle of the market, come to me at once and, taking the girl from my hand, slap her and say, 'O slut, see how I have fulfilled my pledge and brought you down to the market to sell you at auction, just as I had sworn that I would.' If you do this, the vizier, as well as the merchants, will be fooled and will believe that you brought the girl to the market only to fulfill a pledge." Nur al-Din replied, "This is good advice."

Then the broker left him and, returning to his place in the middle of the market, took Anis al-Jalis by the hand and, turning to al-Mu'in ibn-Sawi, said, "My lord, here comes her owner," as Nur al-Din came up to the broker and, snatching the girl from him, slapped her.

*But morning overtook Shahrazad, and she lapsed into silence. Then Dinarzad said to her sister, "What a strange and entertaining story!" Shahrazad replied, "What is this compared with what I shall tell you tomorrow night if the king spares me and lets me live!"*

### THE TWO HUNDRED AND ELEVENTH NIGHT

*The following night Shahrazad replied, "Very well" and said:*

I heard, O happy King, that Nur al-Din slapped Anis al-Jalis and said, "Damn you, see how I have brought you down to the market as I had sworn. Go back home and see to it that you don't repeat your bad habit. Woe to you, do I need your price to sell you? The furniture of my house would fetch many times your value, if I sold it." When the vizier heard this, he turned to Nur al-Din and said, "Damn you, have you anything left to sell for a single dinar or dirham?" and he advanced to hit him. Nur al-Din turned to the merchants, brokers, and shopkeepers, all of whom loved him, and said to them, "Were it not for you, I would kill him." They all responded with the same signal, meaning, "Do with him what you wish, for none of us will step between you." Nur al-Din, who was a stout young man, seized the vizier and, pulling him off his saddle, threw him to the ground and into a mudhole that happened to be there, and fell on him, slapping him and boxing him, with blows, one of which landed on his teeth and filled his mouth with blood. The vizier had with him ten Mamluks,[4] who, seeing their master treated in this fashion, grabbed the hilts of their swords and were about to draw them, attack Nur al-Din, and cut him to pieces. But the merchants and bystanders interposed and said to them, "One is a vizier and the other a vizier's son, and if by chance they make peace one day, you will be hated by both, or if by chance your master receives a blow, you will all die the worst of deaths. You will do wisely not to interfere."

When Nur al-Din finished beating the vizier, he took Anis al-Jalis and went home, and when the vizier finally got up, he was in three colors, the white of his clothes, the black of the mud, and the red of his blood. When he saw himself in this plight, he put a halter around his neck, held a bundle of grass in each hand, and began to run until he stood below the wall of the palace of King Muhammad ibn-Sulaiman al-Zainabi and cried out, "O King of the age, I am a man aggrieved." When the king heard the cry, he said, "Bring me the fellow who is shouting." When they brought him in and the king saw that it was his grand vizier, he asked him, "O Vizier, who has done this to you?" The vizier wept before the king and recited the following verses:

> Shall bad fortune oppress me while you live?
> Shall wolves eat me while you stand, a lion strong and
>     proud?
> Shall every thirsty man drink from your store,
> While I go thirsty, O rain-laden cloud?

Then he said, "My lord, all who care for your welfare and serve you fare this way." The king said, "Damn it, hurry and tell me how this happened and who mistreated you in this way; your sanctity is my sanctity." The vizier said, "My lord, I went today to the slave market to buy a cook, when I saw there a slave-girl whose beauty none has seen before and decided to buy her for my lord the king. When I asked the broker about her and about her owner, he replied that she belonged to Nur al-Din Ali ibn-Khaqan. Some time ago, my lord the king had given his father the vizier ten thousand dinars to buy a girl for my lord, but when the father bought her, she pleased him and he begrudged my lord the king and gave her to his son. When he died, his son sold everything until he had nothing left, and when he found himself penniless, he took her down to the market and gave her to a broker to sell. The broker started the auc-

4. See n. 2, p. 38.

tion, and the merchants bid against each other until the bidding reached four thousand dinars. At that point I said to Nur al-Din, 'O my son, take the four thousand dinars from me and let me buy this slave-girl for our lord the king, for he deserves her more than anyone else, especially since it was his money that had paid for her in the first place.' When he heard this, he looked at me and said . . .

*But morning overtook Shahrazad, and she lapsed into silence. Then Dinarzad said to her sister, "What a strange and entertaining story!" Shahrazad replied, "What is this compared with what I shall tell you tomorrow night if the king spares me and lets me live!"*

THE TWO HUNDRED AND TWELFTH NIGHT

*The following night Shahrazad said:*

I heard, O happy King, that the vizier al-Mu'in ibn-Sawi said to the king, "Nur al-Din looked at me and said, 'Wretched old man, I will sell her to a Christian or a Jew rather than to you.' I replied, 'Is this how you reward our lord the king for helping your father and myself thrive under his blessing?' When he heard me say this, he rose and, pulling me off my horse, began to beat me until he left me in this condition. All this happened to me solely because I strove to be true to you." Then the vizier threw himself on the ground and lay there, weeping, trembling, and pretending to swoon. When the king saw the vizier's condition and heard his story, the veins of his eyes bulged with anger, and he turned to the officers of state and, seeing forty armed guards standing on duty, said to them, "Go down to ibn-Khaqan's house and sack it and raze it; then bind him and drag him with the girl on their faces until you bring them to me." They replied, "We hear and obey," and they put on their outfits, preparing to go to Nur al-Din's house.

It happened that one of those present was one of the king's chamberlains, who was called 'Alam al-Din Sanjar. He had earlier been one of the Mamluks of Fadl al-Din ibn-Khaqan but had subsequently left his service for that of the king, who had advanced him and made him a chamberlain. When he saw the enemies intent on killing his master's son, he could not stand it; so he withdrew from the king's presence and, mounting his horse, rode until he came to Nur al-Din's house and knocked at the door. Nur al-Din came out to see who was there and, finding that it was the chamberlain

Sanjar, greeted him. But the chamberlain replied, "This is no time for greetings. As the poet says:

> If you suffer injustice, save yourself
> And leave the house behind to mourn its builder.
> Your country you'll replace by another,
> But for yourself you'll find no other self.
> Nor with a mission trust another man,
> For none is as loyal as you yourself.
> And did the lion not struggle by himself,
> He would not prowl with such a mighty mane."

Nur al-Din asked him, "'Alam al-Din, what is the matter?" 'Alam al-Din replied, "My lord Nur al-Din, rise and flee for your lives, you and the girl, for the vizier al-Mu'in ibn-Sawi has set a trap for you, and if you don't move quickly, you will fall into it. At this very moment the king has dispatched forty armed men to sack your house, bind you and the slave-girl, and bring you before him. I advise you to rise at once and flee with the girl, before they over-take you." Then 'Alam al-Din put his hand in his pouch and, find-ing there forty dinars, took them and gave them to Nur al-Din, saying, "My lord, take this money for your journey. If I had had more, I would have given it to you, but this is no time for self-reproach."

Nur al-Din went to Anis al-Jalis and told her what had happened, and her hands began to shake. Then the two of them fled at once, and God granted them cover until they came out of the city gate and reached the riverbank, where they saw a large ship with the captain standing on the middle, ready to sail.

*But morning overtook Shahrazad, and she lapsed into silence. Then Dinarzad said to her sister, "What a strange and entertain-ing story!" Shahrazad replied, "What is this compared with what I shall tell you tomorrow night if the king spares me and lets me live!"*

### THE TWO HUNDRED AND THIRTEENTH NIGHT

*The following night Shahrazad said:*

I heard, O happy King, that Nur al-Din saw the captain stand-ing on the middle of the ship and heard him saying, "O merchants, has any one of you anything else to do in the city? Think whether you have forgotten anything." Everyone replied, "O Captain, we have nothing left to do." Then Nur al-Din got on board with Anis al-Jalis and asked, "Where are you heading?" and when they replied, "Baghdad," he said, "Very well." Then the boat sailed and flew, as if the sails were wings, as the poet says:

> Look at a ship that's ravishing in sight,
> As she speeds like the lightning in her course,
> Or like a thirsty bird that swoops from high
> Down to the water with determined force.

Meanwhile the Mamluks, whom the king had dispatched, came to Nur al-Din's house and, forcing the door open, searched the whole place for him and Anis al-Jalis, but found neither trace nor news of them. After they demolished the house, they returned to the king and told him what they had done. The king said, "Search for him everywhere, and wherever you find him, bring him to me." They replied, "We hear and obey." Then he bestowed on the vizier a robe of honor and sent him home with comforting words, saying, "None shall avenge you but I." Then the king issued a proclamation against Nur al-Din, and the criers proclaimed throughout the city, "O ye people, it is the will of King Muhammad ibn-Sulaiman al-Zainabi that whoever brings the vizier's son Nur al-Din Ali to him shall receive a robe of honor and one thousand dinars. He who hides him or looks the other way knows what will happen to him."

In the meantime Nur al-Din and Anis al-Jalis sailed on before a fair wind, and God granted them safe passage, and they reached the city of Peace, Baghdad. The captain said to him, "O my lord, congratulations on your safe arrival. This city, which is teeming with people and full of life, is fair and peaceful. Winter has departed with its frost and spring has arrived with its roses; and now the streams are flowing, the flowers blooming, and the birds singing. It is like the city of which the poet said:

> Behold a peaceful city, free from fear,
> Whose wonders make it a gorgeous Heaven appear."

Nur al-Din gave the captain five dinars, then disembarked with Anis al-Jalis.

Then they wandered about until God led them to an alley surrounded by gardens. It was well-swept and watered, with long benches, hanging cooling pots full of cold water, and a hanging trellis, which ran the whole length of the alley and led to a garden gate, which was shut. Nur al-Din said, "O Anis al-Jalis, this is a nice place." She replied, "O my lord, for God's sake, let us sit down on this bench and rest for a while." So they sat on the bench, after they drank some water and washed their hands and faces, and as they were caressed by the breeze and heard the sounds that rose from the garden, the warbling of the birds, the cooing of the doves in the trees, and the murmur of the water in the streams, they began to feel drowsy and fell asleep.

That garden had no equal in all of Baghdad, for it belonged to the caliph Harun al-Rashid and was called the Garden of Delight, and in it there stood a palace called the Palace of Statues, to which he came whenever he was depressed. The palace was surrounded by eighty windows and eighty hanging lamps, each pair flanking a candelabra holding a large candle. When the caliph entered the palace, he used to order all the windows opened and the lamps and candelabras lighted and order Ishak al-Nadim[5] to sing for him, while he sat surrounded by concubines of all races until his care left him and he felt merry.

The keeper of the garden was an old man called Shaikh Ibrahim, a man for whom the caliph felt a great affection. Whenever Shaikh Ibrahim went out on some business in the city, he would find a group of pleasure-seekers and their whores congregating at the garden gate, and this used to pain him and make him angry. But he waited patiently until one day the caliph . . .

*But morning overtook Shahrazad, and she lapsed into silence. Then Dinarzad said to her sister, "What a strange and entertaining story!" Shahrazad replied, "What is this compared with what I shall tell you tomorrow night if the king spares me and lets me live!"*

THE TWO HUNDRED AND FOURTEENTH NIGHT

*The following night Shahrazad said:*

I heard, O happy King, that Ibrahim, the keeper of the garden, waited patiently until one day the caliph came and he informed him about the situation. The caliph said to him, "Whomever you find at the garden gate, do with him as you wish." It happened that Shaikh Ibrahim went out on some business in the city on the very day of Nur al-Din's arrival, and when he finished and returned, he found two people covered with a cloak and sleeping on a bench, beside the gate. He said to himself, "By God, this is fine! Don't these two know that the caliph has given me permission to kill anyone I catch here? I will make an example of them so that none may come near the gate in the future." He went into the garden and,

---

5. A famous musician and virtuoso of the lute who used to entertain Harun al-Rashid.

cutting a palm stick, came out and raised his arm until his armpit showed, and he was about to fall on them with heavy blows, when he considered and said to himself, "Ibrahim, you are about to beat these two, who may be strangers or travelers whom fate has brought here. Let me uncover their faces and find out who they may be." He threw away the stick and, stepping closer, uncovered their faces and saw that they were as bright as two shining moons, just like those of whom the poet said:

> I saw two sleeping, high above the stars,
> And wished that they would on my eyelids tread.
> "A distant crescent and a rising sun,
> A green bough and wild deer divine," I said.

When he saw them, he said to himself, "By God, they are a handsome pair." Then he covered their faces again and, going to Nur al-Din's feet, began to rub them. Nur al-Din awoke and, seeing a venerable old man rubbing his feet, felt embarrassed and, drawing them in, sat up and took the old man's hand and kissed it, saying, "Uncle, God forbid, and may He reward you!" Shaikh Ibrahim asked, "My son, where do you two come from?" Nur al-Din replied, "Shaikh, we are strangers." He said, "You are my honored guests. Will you not rise and come with me into the garden to relax and enjoy yourselves?" Nur al-Din asked, "Shaikh, to whom does this garden belong?" The old man, wishing to put them at ease and induce them to enter, replied, "I inherited it from my father. My son, I am inviting you in only so that you may forget your cares, relax, and enjoy yourselves." When Nur al-Din heard what Shaikh Ibrahim said, he thanked him and, rising together with Anis al-Jalis, followed him into the garden.

They entered through a vaulted gateway that looked like a gateway in Paradise and passed through a bower of trellised boughs overhung with vines bearing grapes of various colors, the red like rubies, the black like Abyssinian faces, and the white, which hung between the red and the black, like pearls between red coral and black fish. Then they found themselves in the garden, and what a garden! There they saw all manner of things, "in singles and in pairs." The birds sang all kinds of songs: the nightingale warbled with touching sweetness, the pigeon cooed plaintively, the thrush sang with a human voice, the lark answered the ringdove with harmonious strains, and the turtledove filled the air with melodies. The trees were laden with all manner of ripe fruits: pomegranates, sweet, sour, and sour-sweet; apples, sweet and wild; and Hebron plums as sweet as wine, whose color no eyes have seen and whose flavor no tongue can describe.

*But morning overtook Shahrazad, and she lapsed into silence.*
*Then Dinarzad said to her sister, "What a strange and entertain-*
*ing story!" Shahrazad replied, "What is this compared with what*
*I shall tell you tomorrow night if the king spares me and lets me live!"*

THE TWO HUNDRED AND FIFTEENTH NIGHT

*The following night Shahrazad said:*

I heard, O happy King, that when Nur al-Din looked at the
beautiful garden, it pleased him and delighted him and reminded
him of the happy times he used to spend with his friends and companions. He turned to the old man and said, "Shaikh, what is your
name?" He replied, "My name is Ibrahim." Nur al-Din said, "Shaikh
Ibrahim, by God, this is a beautiful garden. May the Almighty God
bless you with it. O Shaikh Ibrahim, you have already been kind
enough to invite us to your place, and we cannot allow ourselves
to demand any more from you, but take these two dinars and get
us some bread and meat and the like." Ibrahim was glad to take
the two dinars, saying to himself, "They will not eat more than ten
dirhams' worth, and I will keep the rest." Then the old man went
out and bought them plenty of good food.

In the meantime Nur al-Din and Anis al-Jalis went and walked
around, enjoying the garden, until, as it had been foreordained,
they came to the caliph's palace, which was called the Palace of
Statues. When they saw its beauty and stateliness, they wanted to
enter, but they could not. When Shaikh Ibrahim returned from the
market, Nur al-Din asked him, "Shaikh Ibrahim, haven't you said
that the garden belongs to you?" He replied, "Yes." Nur al-Din asked
again, "Then to whom does this palace belong?" The old man said
to himself, "If I say that the palace does not belong to me, they
will ask me to explain how so." So he replied, "My son, the palace
belongs to me too." Nur al-Din said, "Shaikh Ibrahim, we are your
guests and this palace is your place, yet you don't open it and invite
us in to see it." The old man, who felt embarrassed and duty-bound,
disappeared for a while, then returned with a big key, opened the
palace door, and said, "Please, come in." Then he led them through
the palace until they came to the elevated hall. When Nur al-Din
saw the windows, the hanging lamps, and the candelabras, he recalled his former parties and exclaimed to the old man, "By God,
this is a beautiful place!"

Then they sat and ate until they were satisfied. After they washed
their hands, Nur al-Din went to one of the windows and, opening

it, called out to Anis al-Jalis, who joined him to look at the trees laden with all kinds of fruits. Then Nur al-Din turned to the old man and said, "Shaikh, do you have anything to drink?" The old man replied, "My son, why do you wish to drink after you have already eaten? People usually drink before they eat." Nur al-Din said, "This drink people take after they eat." The old man exclaimed, "You don't mean wine?" Nur al-Din replied, "Yes, I do." The old man said, "My son, God forbid; I have made the Holy Pilgrimage thirteen times and I don't even mention the word." Nur al-Din said, "Let me say one word." The old man said, "O my son, say it." Nur al-Din said, "If that ass tied in the corner is cursed, will the curse fall on you?" The old man replied, "No." Nur al-Din said, "Then take these two dinars and these two dirhams, ride that ass, and go to the wineshop. Stand at a distance, and when a customer comes, call him and say to him, 'Take these two dirhams for yourself and buy me two good flagons of wine with these two dinars.' When he buys the wine and comes out of the wineshop, say to him, 'Place the wine in the saddlebag and set it on the ass,' and when he does it, drive the ass back, and we will unload the wine. This way you will neither touch it nor be dirtied or defiled by it." When the old man heard Nur al-Din's words, he laughed and said, "My son, by God, I have never met anyone wittier or more charming than you."

The old man did what Nur al-Din asked, and when he bought the wine and came back, Nur al-Din and Anis al-Jalis rose and unloaded it. Then Nur al-Din said to him, "Shaikh, we are in your charge and you have to bring us what we need." The old man asked, "My son, such as?" Nur al-Din replied, "Bring us from your storerooms the necessary wine service, utensils, and the like." The old man gave them the keys to the storerooms and cupboards and said, "Take out what you need, while I get you some fruits."

*But morning overtook Shahrazad, and she lapsed into silence. Then Dinarzad said to her sister, "What a strange and entertaining story!" Shahrazad replied, "What is this compared with what I shall tell you tomorrow night if the king spares me and lets me live!"*

THE TWO HUNDRED AND SIXTEENTH NIGHT

*The following night Shahrazad said:*

I heard, O happy King, that Shaikh Ibrahim said, "Take out what you need." Then Nur al-Din opened all the storerooms and cupboards and took out whatever he needed and desired, while the old

man brought them all kinds of fruits and flowers. Then Anis al-
Jalis proceeded to prepare the table, arranging the cups and beakers
and the gold and silver utensils of all shapes and the nuts and fruits,
and when everything was ready, they sat to carouse and drink. Nur
al-Din filled a cup and, turning to Anis al-Jalis, said, "Our journey
has proved most fortunate by coming to this garden," and recited
the following verses:

> O what a lovely and a perfect day,
> What charm, what joy, and what a total bliss!
> My right hand holds the cup, my left the moon;
> Why heed the one who censures me for this?

Then he drank with Anis al-Jalis until the day departed and night
descended. The old man returned to see whether they needed anything else from him. He stood at the door and, addressing Nur al-
Din, said, "My lord, by God, this is a happy day, for you have
honored me with your presence, as the poet says:

> If the house could know what has visited,
> It would rejoice and kiss the very dust,
> As if to say, 'Only the generous
> Has by his gifts such welcome merited.'"

Nur al-Din, who was drunk by now, replied, "O Shaikh Ibrahim,
far be it from you to be honored by the likes of us. By God, we
have imposed on your goodness and fully enjoyed your generosity."
Anis al-Jalis turned to her lord and said to him, "My lord Nur
al-Din, I wonder what will happen if we make Shaikh Ibrahim
drink?" He asked her, "By my life, can you?" She replied, "Yes,
by your life, I can." He asked her, "Damn it, how?" She replied,
"My lord, invite him and press him until he comes in and sits with
us. Then drink a cup and pretend to fall asleep and let me handle
the rest." When Nur al-Din heard Anis al-Jalis's words, he turned
to Shaikh Ibrahim and said to him, "Shaikh Ibrahim, is this how
people behave?" The old man replied, "How so, my son?" Nur al-
Din said, "We are your guests, yet you refuse to sit with us to entertain us with your conversation and help us while away the night."
Shaikh Ibrahim looked at these two, as the wine took hold of them,
and their cheeks flushed, their foreheads perspired, their eyes flirted,
and their hair became disheveled, and said to himself, "What is the
harm in sitting with them, and when will I again meet people like
them?" He entered and sat in the corner, but Nur al-Din said to
him, "By my life, you must come and sit with us." The old man
joined them and Nur al-Din drank the cup and lay down, making
the old man think that he had fallen asleep. Then Anis al-Jalis

turned to the old man and said, "See how he treats me!" The old man asked her, "What is the matter with him?" She replied, "He always drinks a little and falls asleep, leaving me all alone, with none to keep me company." As the old man began to weaken, she filled a cup and said, "By my life, be kind to me and drink." The old man took it and drank it off, and she filled a second cup and he drank it off too, saying, "This is enough." But she said, "'It is all the same whether it is one or one hundred,'" and gave him the third cup, which he drank off. Then she filled the fourth cup and gave it to him, and he was about to drink it, when Nur al-Din sat up.

*But morning overtook Shahrazad, and she lapsed into silence.*

THE TWO HUNDRED AND SEVENTEENTH NIGHT

*The following night Shahrazad said:*

I heard, O happy King, that the girl filled the fourth cup and gave it to the old man, and he was about to drink it, when Nur al-Din sat up and said, "Shaikh, what is this? Did I not invite you to drink, but you refused, saying 'I have forsworn drinking'?" The old man, who was embarrassed, replied, "It is not my fault." Nur al-Din laughed and they resumed their drinking. Then the girl whispered to Nur al-Din, "Drink, but don't entreat him to drink, and I will show you what he will do." When the two of them began to drink and carouse by themselves, the old man looked at them and asked, "What is this? Why do you give me nothing to drink?" and when they heard this, they burst out laughing. Then they drank and gave him to drink, well into the night. When half of the night was gone, the girl said, "I will go and light one of these candles." The old man said, "Do, but light only one." But she rose, lighted all the candles, and sat down again. A little later Nur al-Din asked the old man, "Will you do me a favor? Let me light one of these lamps." The old man replied, "Very well, but light only one." But Nur al-Din rose and lighted all the lamps, setting the palace ablaze with light. The old man, who was intoxicated by now, saying to them, "You are more playful than I," rose and opened all eighty windows.

As it had been foreordained, the caliph was at that moment seated at one of the palace windows overlooking the Tigris River and, chancing to turn his head, saw the Palace of Statues ablaze with light. He was furious and, summoning the Vizier Ja'far, looked at him angrily and said, "You dog of a vizier, has Baghdad been taken from me and you do not tell me?" Ja'far replied, "O Commander of the Faithful, by God, by God, these are harsh words." The caliph said, "You dog, if Baghdad was not taken from me, the palace would not be lighted and the windows would not be opened, for who would dare do such a thing unless the caliphate has been taken from me?" Ja'far, who was trembling with fear, said, "O Commander of the Faithful, who told you that the Palace of Statues was lighted and its windows opened?" The caliph said, "Damn you, come here and look." Ja'far went to the window and, looking toward the garden, found the palace blazing in the darkness of the night and, thinking that something must have happened to the keeper Ibrahim and wishing to make an excuse for him, said, "O Commander of the Faithful, Shaikh Ibrahim came to me last Friday and said, 'I wish to circumcise my sons during the Commander of the Faithful's lifetime and yours,' and when I asked him, 'What do you want?' he replied, 'The caliph's permission to hold the festival in the palace.' I said to him, 'Go and circumcise them, and I will tell the caliph when I see him.' But I forgot to tell you, O Commander of the Faithful." The caliph said, "Ja'far, I had thought that you had committed one offense against me, but now I find that you have committed two, first by failing to tell me, second by failing to understand what he really wanted. For he came and told you only to ask indirectly for some money to help him out with the expenses of the circumcision, yet you neither gave him any nor told me about him so that I might have given it to him myself." Ja'far replied, "O Commander of the Faithful, I was distracted." The caliph said, "By the tombs of my fathers and forefathers, I will not pass the rest of the night but with him, for it will be to our mutual advantage, his in that my presence will mollify and please him, mine in that I will meet the pious and holy men assembled there."

*But morning overtook Shahrazad, and she lapsed into silence.*

THE TWO HUNDRED AND EIGHTEENTH NIGHT

*The following night Shahrazad said:*

I heard, O happy King, that the caliph said to Ja'far, "I will meet the pious men assembled there." Ja'far said, "It is very late and the gathering is over by now." The caliph said, "I must go, regardless." Ja'far was silent, for he was perplexed and did not know what to do.

The caliph rose, as did Ja'far and Masrur the eunuch, and the three left the palace, disguised as merchants, and made their way through the streets of Baghdad until they came to the garden. The caliph went up to the gate and was surprised to find it open and said to Ja'far, "O Ja'far, Shaikh Ibrahim has, contrary to his habit, left the gate open to this hour; he must have been distracted by the festivities." Then they entered and crossed the garden until they stood before the palace. The caliph said to Ja'far, "I wish to watch them secretly before joining them, so that I may see what they are doing, for I hear neither their voices nor the mendicants'; nor do I hear their hymns to God. These men conduct themselves with great reverence."

Then he looked around and, seeing a tall tree, said to Ja'far, "This tree is the best, for its branches come near the windows. I will climb it and see what they are doing." He climbed the tree and moved from branch to branch until he reached one that came up to one of the windows. When he looked through the window, he saw a young man and a young lady who looked like two moons and saw Shaikh Ibrahim holding a wine cup in his hand and heard him say, "O mistress of fair women, wine without song is better left in the jug; the poet says:

> Pass round the wine in great and small cups too,
> As our two hands with this bright moon we link,
> And drink not without song, for 'tis well known
> Even the horses need whistling to drink."

When the caliph saw this, the veins of his eyes bulged with anger and he descended and said to Ja'far, "My eyes have seen the pious men assembled there. Do likewise and climb the tree and look at them, lest you miss their blessings." When Ja'far heard this, he was puzzled, but he climbed the tree, and when he looked in and saw Shaikh Ibrahim drinking with Nur al-Din and Anis al-Jalis, he turned pale and was sure that he was undone. When he came down and stood before the caliph, the caliph said to him, "Ja'far, it is good that we came in time for the circumcision." But Ja'far, out of embarrassment and fear, was unable to say a word. The caliph asked him, "I wonder who let these two in and how they dared trespass on my palace? But in beauty, the like of this young man and this young lady I have never seen." Ja'far, hoping to propitiate the caliph, replied, "You are right, O Commander of the Faithful." The caliph said, "O Ja'far, let us both climb the branch opposite the window and amuse ourselves by watching them carouse." Then the two climbed up to that branch and, looking through the window, heard the old man say to the girl, "O mistress of fair women, what else

do we need for this banquet?" She replied, "Shaikh, if you had some
musical instrument, our joy would be complete."

*But morning overtook Shahrazad, and she lapsed into silence.*

THE TWO HUNDRED AND NINETEENTH NIGHT

*The following night Shahrazad said:*

I heard, O happy King, that Anis al-Jalis replied, "If you had
some musical instrument, our joy would be complete." The old man
said, "I do," and rose to his feet. The caliph asked Ja'far, "What
is he going to bring?" Ja'far replied, "O Commander of the Faithful,
I do not know." The old man went out and soon returned with a
lute. When the caliph saw the lute, he recognized it as the one
belonging to Ishak al-Nadim and said to Ja'far, "Ja'far, this girl is
going to play the lute. By the tombs of my fathers and forefathers,
if she sings well, I will pardon them and hang you, but if she sings
badly, I will hang you all." Ja'far replied, "O God, let her sing badly!"
The caliph asked him, "Why so?" Ja'far replied, "Because if you
hang us together, we will entertain each other." The caliph laughed.
Then the girl tuned the lute and began to play a melancholy measure
so well that it filled their hearts with yearning and sadness. Then
she sang the following verses:

> You who rebuff us in love's misery,
> Whatever you do, we deserve the pain.
> Of you, for you, to you we do appeal,
> You who listen to all those who complain.
> Torment us not, we who pity deserve;
> Fear the Almighty and yourself restrain.
> We fear not that you'll glory in our death,
> But we fear that you will wrong us again.

The caliph said, "Ja'far, never in my life have I heard anything
lovelier." Ja'far, realizing that the caliph was no longer angry, replied, "You are right, O Commander of the Faithful." Then they
descended from the tree and the caliph said to Ja'far, "I wish to
join them and hear the girl sing before me." Ja'far replied, "If we
go in, we will spoil their pleasure and Shaikh Ibrahim will die of
fright on the spot." The caliph said, "I will not let him recognize
me." Then he left Ja'far standing and walked to the side overlooking the Tigris River.

While he was pondering what to do, he saw a fisherman fishing below the palace wall. It happened that the caliph had earlier heard a noise below the windows, and when he had asked the keeper of the garden Shaikh Ibrahim, "What is that noise?" the keeper had replied, "It is the voices of the fishermen," and the caliph had said to him, "If you let them in again, I will hang you." So the keeper had forbidden the fishermen from fishing there. But on that night a fisherman named Karim happened to pass by and, seeing the garden gate open, said to himself, "The keeper must have gone to sleep and forgot to shut the gate. I will carry my net and take advantage of his carelessness and go in and fish below the palace, for at this hour all is quiet and the fish are calm."

*But morning overtook Shahrazad, and she lapsed into silence.*

THE TWO HUNDRED AND TWENTIETH NIGHT

*The following night Shahrazad said:*

I heard, O happy King, that the fisherman happened to look back and suddenly saw the caliph. When he recognized him, his whole body began to tremble and he said, "O Commander of the Faithful, I did not do this because I took your commandment lightly, but because my poverty and need drove me to it." The caliph said, "Don't be afraid. Cast the net for me." The fisherman cast the net, and when he pulled it up, he found in it various kinds of fish. The caliph was pleased and said, "Pick out the salmon and clean them," and the fisherman did as he bade. Then the caliph said, "Fisherman, take off your clothes," and the fisherman took off a robe sewn in ninety patches and a turban. The caliph took the fisherman's clothes and put them on, saying to him, "Put on my clothes," and the fisherman did so. Then the caliph veiled his face and said to the fisherman, "Go on your business." Then he took a clean basket, covered the bottom with green leaves, and placed the fish inside. Then he went back and stood before Ja'far, who took him for a fisherman, but when the caliph began to laugh, Ja'far recognized him and asked, "Are you the Commander of the Faithful?" and he replied, "Yes," adding, "Stay here until I return."

Then the caliph went up to the palace door and knocked. Nur al-Din said, "Shaikh, there is knocking at the door." The old man cried out, "Who is there?" and the caliph replied, "I, Karim the fisherman. I heard that you had guests and brought you some fish."

When Nur al-Din and Anis al-Jalis heard the mention of the fish, they were glad, and she said to the old man, "For my sake, please open the door and let him bring us the fish." The old man rose and opened the door, and when the caliph entered and saluted, Shaikh Ibrahim said to him, "Welcome, you gambling thief! Show us what you have." The caliph showed them the fish, and the girl said, "By God, these are fine fish, but they would have been better if they had been fried." Shaikh Ibrahim said to the caliph, "Why didn't you bring us the fish ready fried; what shall we do with them? Go, fry them, and bring them back," and he yelled at him. The caliph went out running until he came up to Ja'far and said, "O Ja'far!" Ja'far asked, "What is the good news, O Commander of the Faithful?" The caliph replied, "They want the fish fried." Ja'far said, "I will fry them," but the caliph replied, "By the tombs of my fathers and forefathers, none shall fry them but I, with my own hands." Then the caliph went to the keeper's hut, where he found everything he needed, to the salt and marjoram. Then he placed the frying pan on the stove, poured in some sesame oil and, lighting the fire, placed the fish in the frying pan and fried them. Then he added lemons and radishes, carried the dish back to the palace, and set it before them. They all ate, and when they finished, Nur al-Din said to the caliph, "O fisherman, you have done us a good deed." Then he put his hand in his pocket and took out a paper purse.

*But morning overtook Shahrazad, and she lapsed into silence.*

THE TWO HUNDRED AND TWENTY-FIRST NIGHT

*The following night Shahrazad said:*

I heard, O happy King, that Nur al-Din took out a paper purse containing thirty dinars, which were the remainder of the money the chamberlain had given him before he fled, and said to the caliph, "O fisherman, excuse me, for this is all I have. By God, had I known you before I spent all my inheritance, I would have done away with the bitterness of poverty in your heart. Take this as a token of my good will." Then he threw the money to the caliph, who caught it and, kissing it, put it away. The caliph, whose only wish was to hear the girl sing, said to Nur al-Din, "My lord, you have rewarded me handsomely, but I would like you to do me one more favor and let the young lady sing a song for me." Nur al-Din said, "O Anis al-Jalis, sing something for the sake of this fisherman." Anis al-Jalis took the lute and, tuning it, played a measure, then sang the following verses:

> The fingers of the fair caressed the strings
> And ravished the soul with her dulcet lute
> And with her singing cured the very deaf
> And "Bravo!" cried out one who had been mute.

Then she played another measure, so beautifully that she dazzled their wits, and sang the following verses:

> When with your visit you honored our land,
> You filled the air with incense and dispelled the gloom;
> Therefore, with camphor, rosewater, and musk
> It well behooves me my house to perfume.

The caliph was delighted and said, "I have never heard anyone sing as well." Nur al-Din said to him, "Take her as a gift from me to you." Then he rose, intending to put on his robe and depart, but Anis al-Jalis turned to him and said, "Where are you going? If you must leave me, then stay a while and let me tell you how I feel." Then she recited the following verses:

> My memories and longing have tormented me
> Until they turned me into a poor ghost.
> O my darling, I have not forgot you;
> 'Am still the same, still to my torments host.
> If one was able to swim in his tears,
> I would be the first in my tears to swim.
> O you whose love has filled my brimming heart
> As wine fills up the wine cup to the brim,
> Whose love has wracked my body and my soul,
> The fate I dreaded has forced us apart.
> O Khaqan's son, O my sole wish and hope,
> Who will always reign and rule in my heart,
> For my sake you transgressed against our lord,
> To spend in exile the rest of your days.
> May God give you to me, even though you
> Gave me to Karim, who deserves the praise.

When the caliph heard her conclude, "You gave me to Karim . . ."

*But morning overtook Shahrazad, and she lapsed into silence.*

THE TWO HUNDRED AND TWENTY-SECOND NIGHT

*The following night Shahrazad said:*

When the caliph heard her conclude with the words, "You gave me to Karim," he turned to Nur al-Din and asked, "My lord, the girl said in her verses that you had transgressed against her lord and master. Against whom did you transgress, and who is it who has a claim on you?" Nur al-Din replied, "Fisherman, what has happened to me and to this girl is extraordinary." The caliph said, "Tell me your story." Nur al-Din asked, "Do you wish to hear it in prose or in verse?" The caliph replied, "O my lord, prose is words, but verse is strung pearls." Nur al-Din bowed his head and recited the following verses:

> O my dear friend, I can no longer sleep,
> And my grief has increased since I left home.
> I had a father once who loved me well,
> But left me and lay dead under a dome.
> Then after him misfortunes fell on me
> And with a broken heart have left me now.
> He had bought me a girl so beautiful
> That her fair figure put to shame the bough.
> Then I spent all my substance for her sake
> And lavished all I had on every friend.
> When all was gone, I put her up for sale,
> Forced by my dire need to that loathsome end.
> But when the auctioneer called out for bids
> And a vile old man was having his way,
> I was so furious that I angrily
> From the broker wrested the girl away,
> When that vile old man, out of pent-up hate,
> Gave me a blow that hurt and made me smart,
> But I fell on him with hard rights and lefts,
> Knocking him down, until I soothed my heart.
> Then I left and hastened back to my house
> And out of fear myself from my foes hid,
> And when the king sent men to have me seized,
> A great and wise chamberlain came and bid
> Me flee my native land and go abroad
> And leave behind my many envious foes.
> So we fled in the dead of night and came
> To Baghdad, where we found refuge from our woes.
> As we were banqueting and drinking here,

You came to visit unexpectedly.
And caught me with little money to give
For the fine gift you had given kindly.
But I give you, fisherman, my sole love,
And 'tis from my wish, hope, idol I part.
Accept then from me this, my precious gift,
Certain that I have given you my heart.

The caliph said, "My lord Nur al-Din, tell me the story in detail,"
and Nur al-Din told him the story from beginning to end. Then
the caliph asked him, "Where do you intend to go from here?" Nur
al-Din replied, "God's world is wide." The caliph said, "I will write
a letter to give to King Muhammad ibn-Sulaiman, and when he
reads it, he will no longer bother you or harm you."

*But morning overtook Shahrazad, and she lapsed into silence.*

### THE TWO HUNDRED AND TWENTY-THIRD NIGHT

*The following night Shahrazad said:*

I heard, O happy King, that the caliph, who was disguised as
a fisherman, said "I will write a letter to the king, and he will no
longer harm you." Nur al-Din asked, "Is there in the whole world
a fisherman who corresponds with kings?" The caliph replied, "The
king and I studied together under the same tutor. I was above him,
but he became a king, while I became a fisherman. Yet whenever
I write to ask him for a favor, he fulfills my wish." When Nur al-
Din heard this, he said, "Very well, write and show me." The caliph
took paper and ink and, after the invocation to God, wrote the
following:

> This letter is from Harun al-Rashid son of al-Mahdi to His High-
> ness Muhammad ibn-Sulaiman al-Zainabi, my cousin, seedling
> of my bounty, and shareholder in my estate. The bearer of this
> letter is Nur al-Din Ali son of ibn-Khaqan the vizier. As soon
> as you receive it, abdicate and let Nur al-Din Ali ibn-Khaqan
> take your place. Fail not to carry out my command, and peace
> be on you.

Then the caliph gave the letter to Nur al-Din, who took it, kissed
it, then put it in his turban and departed.

When Nur al-Din was gone, Ibrahim the keeper turned to the
caliph and said, "Enough, enough! You have brought us a couple

of fish worth no more than twenty fils,[6] yet you received a full
purse for them and now you intend to get the girl too." It happened
that when the caliph had earlier gone to fry the fish and bring them
back, he had said to Ja'far, "Go to my palace, bring back one of
my royal robes, and return with Masrur and four armed officers
and wait below the window. When you hear me cry out, 'Help,
help!' come up at once with the officers, dress me in the robe, and
stand in attendance," and Ja'far had done the caliph's bidding and
stood waiting below the window. When the old man spoke with
the caliph, the caliph replied, "Shaikh, I will give you half of the
money in the purse, but I will keep the girl." The old man said,
"By God, you will keep no more than one-half of the girl. As for
the purse, open it and let me see what is in it. If it is silver, take
a dirham for yourself and give me the rest, but if it is gold, give
it all to me, and for your fish I will give you a dirham's worth of
change, which I have in my pocket." The caliph replied, "I will give
you nothing." The old man took a porcelain plate and hurled it at
the caliph, who evaded it and let it smash against the wall. Then
the old man went into a storeroom to fetch a stick.

*But morning overtook Shahrazad, and she lapsed into silence.*

### The Two Hundred and Twenty-Fourth Night

*The following night Shahrazad said:*

I heard, O happy King, that the old man went into a storeroom
to fetch a stick with which to beat the fisherman, who was the caliph,
while the caliph cried out from the window, "Help, help!" and was
at once joined by Ja'far and the officers, who dressed him in his
royal robe, seated him on a chair, and stood in attendance. When
the old man came out of the storeroom with the stick, rushing toward
the fisherman, he was stunned to see instead the caliph seated on
a chair and Ja'far standing in attendance. He began to bite his nails
in bewilderment and to exclaim, "Am I asleep or awake?" The caliph
turned to him and said, "O Shaikh Ibrahim, what state do I see
you in?" The old man became sober at once and, rolling on the
ground, recited the following verses:

> Forgive my error, for it was a slip,
> And grant your slave, O lord, your clemency.

6. Small copper coins; in Iraq worth one-thousandth of a dinar.

I have confessed, as my own sin requires;
Where is the act expected of mercy?

The caliph forgave him and bade Anis al-Jalis be carried to the palace, where he assigned her a separate lodging and servants to attend her, saying to her, "You should know that I have sent your lord to be king in Basra, and, God willing, when I send him the order of investiture and the deed of bestowal, I will send you along."

In the meantime Nur al-Din ibn-Khaqan journeyed on until he reached Basra and went to the king's palace and gave the king the caliph's letter. When the king read it, he kissed it and stood up three times, saying, "I hear and obey God and the Commander of the Faithful." But when he was about to abdicate, the vizier arrived, and when the king showed him the letter, the vizier read it, then tore out the invocation to God, put it in his mouth, and chewed it. The king asked, "Why did you do that?" The vizier said, "My lord, did you think that this was the handwriting of the caliph?" The king asked, "Is it not?" The vizier replied, "No, by your life, O King of the age. It is nothing but a forgery by this devil. Would the caliph have sent him all by himself to assume the kingship without an order of investiture or a deed of bestowal?" The king asked, "What do you advise?" The vizier replied, "I advise you to hand this fellow over to me and wait, and if neither order of investiture nor deed of bestowal arrives, you will know that I am right and will punish him for what he did to me."

*But morning overtook Shahrazad, and she lapsed into silence.*

THE TWO HUNDRED AND TWENTY-FIFTH NIGHT

*The following night Shahrazad said:*

It is related, O happy King, that when the king heard the advice of the vizier ibn-Sawi, he replied, "Take him." The vizier took Nur al-Din, and when he brought him to his own palace, he shouted to his servants, "Throw him to the ground," and the servants threw him to the ground and beat him until he fainted. Then the vizier shackled him and threw him into jail, shouting to the jailer, whose name was Qutait, "Qutait, throw him into a deep cell and punish him." The jailer beat Nur al-Din well into the night, until he fainted, and when he came to himself in the dark, he recited the following verses:

> I will endure until I patience shock
> And God fulfills my fate and His decree.
> He who says that life is made of sweetness,
> A day more bitter than aloes will see.

Nur al-Din suffered the same treatment for ten days until the vizier decided to strike off his head. So he took some gifts and gave them to a group of unknown bedouins, saying, "Give these gifts to the king," and when they presented the gifts to the king, the vizier said, "My lord, these gifts were not meant for you but for Nur al-Din, the new king." The king replied, "You have reminded me of him. Bring him and let us strike off his head." The vizier said, "When he beat me that time, my enemies gloated. Will you permit me to proclaim in the city, 'Whoever wishes to watch the beheading of Nur al-Din Ali ibn-Khaqan, let him come to the royal palace'? Then the public will come to watch and I will be satisfied."

*But morning overtook Shahrazad, and she lapsed into silence.*

### THE TWO HUNDRED AND TWENTY-SIXTH NIGHT

*The following night Shahrazad replied, "Very well," and said:*

I heard, O happy King, that the vizier said, "And I will be satisfied." The king replied, "Do as you wish." The vizier departed and bade the crier make the proclamation, and the crier did, and when the people heard it, they mourned and wept for Nur al-Din.

Then the vizier went to the jail with ten Mamluks and said to the jailer, "Bring me that young prisoner." The jailer brought Nur al-Din, and when he opened his smarting eyes and saw his enemy the vizier preparing to kill him, he asked him, "Are you secure against fate; have you heard what the poet says?

> For long they ruled us arbitrarily,
> But suddenly vanished their powerful rule."

The vizier said, "Do you threaten me, you good-for-nothing? After I strike off your head, despite the people of Basra, let fate do with me what it will, for the poet says:

> He who outlives his foe one single day
> Will have attained his wish and had his way."

Then he ordered his attendants to set Nur al-Din on the back of a mule, and as they took him away, the people wept and, flocking around him, said, "O our lord Nur al-Din, even though we may endanger our lives, give us your permission and let each of us pick a stone and stone to death this wretched old vizier and his attendants and save you; and let whatever happens happen."

*But morning overtook Shahrazad, and she lapsed into silence.*

### The Two Hundred and Twenty-Seventh Night

*The following night Shahrazad said:*

I heard, O happy King, that the people said to Nur al-Din, "Let whatever happens happen." The attendants rode with Nur al-Din until they came below the palace walls. Then they made him kneel on the execution mat, and the executioner bandaged his eyes and, drawing his sword, asked him twice whether he had a last wish. Then he knelt before him and, removing the bandage from his eyes, said to him, "I am only a servant who does what he is told; I have no choice, and you will die as soon as the king gives the order." Nur al-Din looked to the right and left and, realizing that none could help him or save him and feeling very thirsty, recited the following verses:

> My life is spent and death is drawing near;
> Will no one help me and God's reward gain?
> Will no one pity me in my distress
> And with a cup of water ease my pain?
> Yet if I die thirsty, then I will die
> Like Ali's holy son[7] and martyrdom attain.

The people wept and the executioner rose and brought him a cup of water, but the vizier jumped up, knocked the cup from his hand, and broke it, screaming, "Strike off his head." The people cried out, "This is not lawful," when suddenly there arose a great cloud of dust that filled the air. The vizier repeated, "Strike off his head at once," but the king said, "Let us wait and see what is the matter."

That cloud of dust was raised by Ja'far and his retinue, and the reason of his coming was as follows:

*But morning overtook Shahrazad, and she lapsed into silence.*

---

7. al-Hussein, the grandson of the prophet Muhammad. He and his brother al-Hasan and their family were surrounded by the enemy near Kerbala in Iraq, deprived of water for days, then massacred.

### THE TWO HUNDRED AND TWENTY-EIGHTH NIGHT

*The following night Shahrazad replied, "Very well," and said:*

I heard, O happy King, that one night, as the caliph passed by one of the chambers in the palace, he heard someone reciting the following verses:

> Love's torment has wracked me, body and soul,
> Ever since cruel fate drove us far apart.
> God has allowed all lovers to unite,
> But has condemned my unrequited heart.

The caliph cried out, "Who is in the chamber?" and a woman replied, "O my lord, I am Anis al-Jalis, whose lord you sent to Basra to replace the Lord Muhammad ibn-Sulaiman as king." When the caliph heard this, he summoned Ja'far and said to him, "I have forgotten Nur al-Din Ali ibn-Khaqan and forgotten to send him the order of investiture and the deed of bestowal, and I fear that his enemy may have succeeded in killing him. Ride posthaste to Basra, and if you find him dead, hang the vizier, but if you find him alive, bring him with the king and the vizier to me, as you will find them, and do not tarry beyond the time necessary for the journey." Ja'far prepared himself at once and set out for Basra with his retinue.

*But morning overtook Shahrazad, and she lapsed into silence.*

### THE TWO HUNDRED AND TWENTY-NINTH NIGHT

*The following night Shahrazad replied, "Very well," and said:*

I heard, O happy King, that Ja'far set out at once and journeyed until he reached Basra at the very moment when, as I have described, the executioner stood with his drawn sword and was about to strike off Nur al-Din's head. Ja'far went up to the king, saluted him, and inquired what was the matter with Nur al-Din, and the king explained the situation. Then Ja'far bade Nur al-Din be brought before him, and they brought him with the execution mat and sword. Then he bade them untie him, and they did so, then bade them bind the vizier and tie a rope around his neck, and they did so. Then he took all three and journeyed until he reached the City of Peace and, going to the caliph, presented Nur al-Din to him and told him the story.

The caliph said to Nur al-Din, "Nur al-Din ibn-Khaqan, take this sword and strike off the head of your enemy with your own hand." Nur al-Din rose and, taking the sword, went up to the vizier, who said to him, "I did according to my nature; do according to yours." Nur al-Din threw the sword from his hand and said to the caliph, "O my lord, the poet says:

> I tricked him to forgive me for my breach,
> For noble minds are deceived by fair speech."

The caliph said, "Masrur, strike off his head yourself." Masrur went to the vizier and with one stroke severed his head from his body. Then the caliph turned to Nur al-Din ibn-Khaqan and said, "Ask for a boon from me." Nur al-Din replied, "I have no need of the kingship of Basra; all I desire is the honor of your companionship." The caliph reunited Nur al-Din with Anis al-Jalis, bestowed favors on him, and granted him his wish, making him one of his boon companions. Then Nur al-Din and Anis al-Jalis lived the happiest and most delightful of lives until they were overtaken by the breaker of ties and destroyer of delights. May God help us on that day!

*But morning overtook Shahrazad, and she lapsed into silence. Then Dinarzad said to her sister Shahrazad, "What a strange and entertaining story!" Shahrazad replied, "What is this compared with what I shall tell you tomorrow night if I stay alive! It will be even stranger and more amazing."*

THE TWO HUNDRED AND THIRTIETH NIGHT

*The following night Shahrazad said:*

# [THE STORY OF JULLANAR OF THE SEA]

I heard, O happy King, that there was once in Persia a great and mighty king whose capital was Khurasan. He ruled over so many provinces and cities and so many people that all the kings of Persia and all their armies paid him homage. He was a sensible, discerning, and pious man who judged fairly between the strong and the weak and treated the offenders with mercy, so that everyone near and far loved him and wished him long life, victory, and success. He had one hundred concubines of all races, each housed in her own apartment, but in all his life he had never been blessed with a son. He used to offer sacrifices, give alms, and do all kinds of favors and good deeds, praying to God to bless him with a son to bring him joy and inherit the kingdom after him. He used to say to himself, "I am afraid that I will die without a son and the kingdom will pass into the hands of strangers."

The slave-merchants knew that he enjoyed having many women and concubines, so that whenever they came by any slave-girl, they brought her to him, and if he liked her, he would buy her at the highest price, making the merchant rich. Then he would bestow on him a robe of honor as well as other favors, give him written orders that none should levy any duty or tax on him, and hold him in high esteem. Consequently, the slave-merchants came to him from various provinces and countries to present him with fine mistresses and concubines. But in spite of all these efforts, he remained depressed and anxious for a long time.

*But morning overtook Shahrazad, and she lapsed into silence.*

THE TWO HUNDRED AND THIRTY-FIRST NIGHT

*The following night Shahrazad said:*

I heard, O happy King, that in spite of all these efforts, the king remained depressed and anxious for a long time because he was getting old, without having been blessed with a son to inherit the kingdom after him.

One day, as he sat on the throne, with his vizier by his side, with the princes, lords of the realm, and notables sitting before him, and with the Mamluks and servants standing in attendance, a servant came in and said, "O King of the age, there is a merchant at the door, with a girl worthy of our lord the king. He wishes to present her to you, and if she pleases you, he will offer her to you. He says that there is none like her in beauty or charm." The king replied, "Bring him to me." The servant rose and returned with the merchant led by a chamberlain who presented him to the king. The merchant kissed the ground and bowed before the king, who engaged him in conversation and spoke amiably with him until he put him at ease, allaying the awe he felt in the presence of the king. Indeed, it is the mark of kings, sovereigns, and other leaders that when a messenger or a merchant stands before them on some business, they converse with him amiably to allay the awe he feels in their presence. At last the king turned to the merchant and asked . . .

*But morning overtook Shahrazad, and she lapsed into silence.*

### THE TWO HUNDRED AND THIRTY-SECOND NIGHT

It is related, O happy King, that the king at last turned to the merchant and asked, "Where is the girl whom you consider to be worthy of me?" The merchant replied, "She is beautiful and elegant beyond description, and she is standing at the door with the servants, awaiting your pleasure. With your leave, I will bring her at once." The king gave him leave, and when she came in, the king looked and saw a tall girl, as slender as a spear, wrapped in a silk cloak embroidered with gold. The king rose from his throne and, entering a private chamber, bade the merchant bring in the girl. The merchant brought her before the king, and when he unveiled her, the king looked on her and saw that she was brighter than a banner and more slender than a reed, for she put even the rising moon to shame, with hair hanging down to her anklets in seven tresses like horses' tails or the veil of the night, and with dark eyes, smooth cheeks, heavy hips, and slender waist. When the king saw her, he was dazzled by her beauty and grace, for she was like her of whom the poet said:

> When they unveiled her, I doted at once,
> As she stood there with calm and dignity,
> Neither too little nor too much, faultlessly formed,
> Wrapped tightly in her cloak, in total parity,
> Slender her figure and perfect her height,
> Her lovely body to perfection bred.
> Her hair trailed to the anklets and revealed
> The glory and the envy of her head.

*But morning overtook Shahrazad, and she lapsed into silence. Then Dinarzad said to her sister, "What a strange and entertaining story!" Shahrazad replied, "What is this compared with what I shall tell you tomorrow night if I stay alive!"*

## THE TWO HUNDRED AND THIRTY-THIRD NIGHT

*The following night Shahrazad said:*

It is related, O happy King, that when the king looked at the girl, he was dazzled by her beauty, captivated by her charm, and overwhelmed by love for her. He turned to the merchant and asked, "Shaikh, what is the price of this girl?" The merchant replied, "O King, I bought her from another merchant for two thousand dinars, and to this date I have traveled for three years and spent one thousand dinars on her to bring her to you, but your slave does not want any money for her; she is a gift to our lord the king." When the king heard this, he bestowed on him a robe of honor and ordered him ten thousand dinars and one of his choice horses. The merchant kissed the ground before him and departed.

Then the king committed the girl to the care of the nurses and attendants, saying to them, "Prepare her and leave her alone in one of my choice private apartments." They replied, "We hear and obey." Then they took care of her and brought her whatever she needed of servants, clothes, and food and drink. Then they took her to the bath and washed her, and when she came out, looking even more charming and beautiful, they dressed her in fine clothes and adorned her with jewelry worthy of her beauty and brought her to an apartment overlooking the sea. For at that time the king resided on the seashore, on an island called the White Island. When in the evening the king went in to her, he saw her standing at the window, looking at the sea, but although she noticed his presence, she neither paid attention to him nor showed him veneration, but continued to look at the sea, without even turning her head toward him. When the king saw this, he surmised that she came from ignorant people who had not taught her manners. But when he looked at her and saw her in her fine clothes and jewelry, which lent her greater beauty and charm and made her look like the twinkling stars or the shining sun, he said to himself, "Glory be to God who created you 'from a humble drop . . . in a safe haven.'" Then he went up to her, as she stood at the window, and embraced her. Then he sat down on the couch and, seating her on his knees, kissed her and marveled at her beauty and grace. Then he bade the maids bring food, and they set the food before him, in plates of gold and silver, worthy of a king and, placed in the middle of the table almond pastry in a platter of white crystal. Then the king ate and fed her with his hand, but, while she ate, she kept her head bowed down, without paying any attention to him or looking at him.

*But morning overtook Shahrazad, and she lapsed into silence.*

THE TWO HUNDRED AND THIRTY-FOURTH NIGHT

*The following night Shahrazad said:*

It is related, O happy King, that the king kept feeding her with his hand, while she kept her head bowed down, without paying any attention to him, looking at him, or speaking to him. He began to talk to her and asked her name, but she kept her head bowed down, without replying, speaking, or uttering a word or a single syllable until the maids removed the table and the king and the girl washed their hands. When the king saw that she did not speak or answer his questions, he said to himself, "Glory be to the Almighty God! How beautiful is this girl but how ignorant! Or else she is dumb, but none save the Exalted and Glorious God is perfect. Were she able to speak, she would be perfect." He felt very sorry for her, and when he inquired of the attendants about her silence, they replied, "O King, by God, she has never said a word to us or uttered a single syllable, but has remained silent, as you see."

Then he summoned his concubines, favorites, and other women and bade them entertain her with all kinds of music and songs. But when they played and sang, the king enjoyed it very much, while she, neither speaking nor smiling, kept her head bowed, looked at them silently, and sulked until she made the king depressed. He dismissed the women and remained alone with her. Then he took off his clothes, lay down in bed, and made her lie beside him. When he looked at her body and saw that it was as fair as pure silver, he was enthralled and felt a great love for her, and when he took her virginity, he discovered that she had been a virgin and he rejoiced and said to himself, "By God, it is amazing that a girl of such beauty and grace, who has been bought and sold as a slave, has remained a virgin. This is a mystery."

Thereafter, he devoted himself totally to her, as she began to assume and occupy a great place in his heart, and he forsook and neglected his favorites, concubines, and all other women and considered her his blessing and his lot in life. He lived with her an entire

year as if it were one day, yet she never spoke to him or uttered
a single word, and this was very hard on him.

One day he turned to her . . .

*But morning overtook Shahrazad, and she lapsed into silence.
Then Dinarzad said to her sister Shahrazad, "O sister, what a
strange and entertaining story!" Shahrazad replied, "What is this
compared with what I shall tell you tomorrow night if the king spares
me and lets me live! It will be even stranger."*

THE TWO HUNDRED AND THIRTY-FIFTH NIGHT

*The following night Shahrazad said:*

I heard, O happy King, that at the end of the year, during which
the king had grown infatuated and madly in love with the girl, he
turned to her one day and said, "O my heart's desire, by God, my
whole kingdom is not worth a grain of sand to me when I see you
unable to reply or speak to me, for you are dearer to me than my
eyes. I have forsaken my concubines, my favorites, and all my other
women and made you my lot in life, and I have been patient with
you and have been praying to the Almighty God to soften your heart
with pity and make you speak one word to me, if you are able to
speak. If you are dumb, let me know, in order that I may give up
hope. I pray God to bless me with a son from you to bring me joy
and inherit the kingdom after me, for I am lonely and forlorn, without relatives or anyone else to help me with the affairs of the kingdom, especially now that I am old and too weak to manage by myself
and take care of my people. My lady, if you are able to speak, for
God's sake, answer me, for my only wish is to hear one word from
you before I die." When the girl heard the king's words, she bowed
her head in thought, and, looking up, smiled in his face and said,
"O gallant King and valiant lion, may God exalt you and humble
your enemies, and may He give you long life and grant you every
wish. The Almighty God has accepted your pleadings and entreaties
and has answered your prayers. O King, I am bearing your child
and the time of my delivery is near, although I do not know whether
the child is a boy or a girl. Had it not been for the child, I would
not have answered you or spoken to you." When the king heard
her words, he was extremely happy and he embraced her and kissed
her face, saying, "O my lady, O my darling, God has granted me
two blessings and relieved me of two sorrows, the first, to hear you

speak after long silence, a wish dearer to me than my entire kingdom, the second, to hear you say that you are bearing my child."

Then he left her and sat on his throne and in a fit of happiness
bade his vizier distribute a hundred thousand dinars in alms to the
widows, the orphans, and the homeless, and to all the poor and
needy, and the vizier did as he bade. Then the king returned to
the girl and said, "O my lady and my heart's delight, how was it
that you spent a whole year, lying with me in the same bed day
and night, without speaking to me until today? How could you bear
it and what was the cause?" She replied, "O King, I am an exile
and a captive in a foreign land, with a broken heart aching for my
people, a woman all alone without father or brother."

*But morning overtook Shahrazad, and she lapsed into silence.
Then Dinarzad said to her sister, "O sister, what a strange and enter-
taining story!" Shahrazad replied, "What is this compared with what
I shall tell you tomorrow night if I stay alive!"*

### THE TWO HUNDRED AND THIRTY-SIXTH NIGHT

*The following night Shahrazad said:*

I heard, O happy King, that when the king heard her words,
he replied, "As for your saying that you are a brokenhearted woman
in a foreign land, where is the reason for it, since my entire kingdom
is in your hands and I am your slave? But, as for your saying that
you have a mother and a father and a brother, where are they and
what is your name?"

She replied, "I will tell you my name. I am called Jullanar of
the Sea. My father was a sea-king, who then died and left his kingdom to my mother, my brother, and myself, but another sea-king
defeated us and took the kingdom from us. My mother is descended
from the daughters of the sea, not the daughters of the land and
clay. My brother is called Sayih. One day I quarreled with him
and left, swearing by the Almighty God that I would throw myself
into the hands of a man of the land. I came out of the sea and sat
down on the shore of the Island of the Moon, where an old man
came up to me and, taking me to his house, tried to make love to
me. But I refused and hit him on the head, so hard that I almost
killed him! Then he took me out and sold me to that pious, fair,
and honorable merchant who bought me for two thousand dinars,
and brought me here and sold me to you. Had you not, O King,

offered me your kindness and love and preferred me over your favorites, concubines, and all other women, I would never have stayed with you even one single hour but would have thrown myself from this window into the sea and returned to my people. I was also too ashamed to return with child, for fear that my people would distrust me, think ill of me, and refuse to believe, even if I swore to them, that it was a king who had bought me with his money and made me his lot in life."

When the king heard her explanation, he thanked her and kissed her between the eyes and said, "By God, O my lady and my darling, if you leave me even for a single hour, I will die. But for God's sake, tell me how do the people of the sea walk there without sinking and dying?" She replied, "O King, we walk in water just as you people walk on land, without being wetted or hurt by the water," adding, "We do this by virtue of the words inscribed on the seal ring of God's prophet Solomon, son of David — Peace be on him — and stay dry without being touched by the water. You should know, O King, that the time of my delivery is near, and I therefore wish my mother, my uncle's daughters, and my brother to come so that they may see me with you and find out that I am bearing the child of one of the kings of the land, who has bought me with his money and treated me kindly, and so that I may make peace with them; besides, your women are daughters of the land who do not know how to assist in birth the daughters of the sea or how to help them or take care of them properly. Moreover, I wish them to come, so that you may satisfy yourself that I am truly a daughter of the sea and that my father was a king."

When the king heard her explanation, he replied . . .

*But morning overtook Shahrazad, and she lapsed into silence.*

THE TWO HUNDRED AND THIRTY-SEVENTH NIGHT

*The following night Shahrazad said:*

I heard, O happy King, that when the king heard Jullanar's explanation, he replied, "Do as you wish, and I will agree with whatever you do." She said, "You should also know, O King, that we walk in the sea and see the daylight and the sun and the sky and see the night and the moon and the stars, without being harmed at all. In the sea there are people of all types and creatures of all kinds, just as there are on land, and more." The king marveled at what she said. Then she took out from her bosom a case of Javanese aloewood and took out from it a bead of the same wood. Then she threw the bead into the fire, whistled, and spoke words that the king did not understand, and there arose a great cloud of smoke. She said to the king, "Rise and hide in a closet, so that you may see my brother, mother, and cousins without being seen by them, for I intend to bring them here and show you the Almighty God's marvelous handiwork and the forms He created in the sea." The king ran and, hiding in a closet, watched what she did.

No sooner had she finished her incantation than the sea began to foam and surge, and suddenly the water split asunder and a young man emerged. He had sprouting mustaches, rosy cheeks, and teeth as glittering as gems. He was more handsome than the moon and as lovely as his sister Jullanar. He was followed by a gray-haired old woman and five young ladies who looked like moons and resembled Jullanar in beauty. The king saw the old woman and the young man and young ladies . . .

*But morning overtook Shahrazad, and she lapsed into silence.*

THE TWO HUNDRED AND THIRTY-EIGHTH NIGHT

*The following night Shahrazad said:*

I heard, O happy King, that the king saw the old woman and the young man and young ladies walk on the surface of the water until they reached the palace, while Jullanar went to the window to receive them. When they saw her, they were happy and they leapt and flew like birds and in an instant stood beside her, embracing her tearfully and telling her how much they had missed her. Then they said to her, "O Jullanar, you have been away for three years, and we have been desolate without you, unable to enjoy food or drink." Jullanar kissed her brother's head and his hands and feet and did the same to her mother and her cousins. Then they sat for a while, expressing to each other how they had suffered during their separation. Then they questioned her about her present situation, with whom she was living, to whom the palace belonged, and who had brought her there. She said to them, "When I left you, I came out from the sea and sat on the shore of the Island of the Moon, where a man found me and sold me to a merchant who sold me to the king of this city for ten thousand dinars. I have had a happy life with him, for he has forsaken all his concubines and slave-girls on my account, has turned away even from the affairs of the kingdom, and has devoted himself to me." When her brother heard this, he said, "O sister, rise and let us return to our home and family." When the king heard what the brother said, he lost his senses from shock and fright, saying to himself, "I am afraid that she will listen to her brother, leave me, and cause my death by her departure, for I am madly in love with her, especially since she is bearing my child, and I will die of longing for her and for my son." But when Jullanar heard her brother's words, she laughed and said, "O brother, you should know that the man I am living with is a pious, generous, and honorable man who has never said one bad word to me, who has treated me kindly, and who has given me the best of lives."

*But morning overtook Shahrazad, and she lapsed into silence.*

### THE TWO HUNDRED AND THIRTY-NINTH NIGHT

*The following night Shahrazad said:*

I heard, O happy King, that Jullanar added, "I am bearing his child, and just as I am the daughter of a king, he too is a king and the son of a king. He has no son, but the Almighty God has been generous to me, and I pray to Him to bless us with a son to inherit his father's kingdom." When her brother and her mother and cousins heard this, they rejoiced and said to her, "You know your place in our heart; if you wish to stay here, we will gladly abide by your wish." She replied, "Yes, by God, I do." When the king heard this, he realized that she truly loved him and that she wished to stay with him and he was grateful to her and loved her even more.

Then Jullanar called for food, and the waiting women set the tables and laid on them all kinds of food, sweets, and fruits. They began to eat but soon said to her, "Your lord is a stranger whom you have praised to us because of your gratitude for his kindness to you and your love for him. We have entered his house without his leave and we have eaten his food, yet he has neither shown us himself nor eaten with us." They were so angry at the king that the fire flamed from their mouths as if from torches. When the king saw this, he was mad with terror, while Jullanar rose and, going into the closet, said to him, "O King, you have seen and heard how I praised you and how they wanted to carry me with them down to the sea and take me home." The king replied, "By God, I was

not sure of your love until this moment. May God reward you."
She replied, "O King, 'Is the reward of kindness anything but kindness'? You have treated me kindly and generously and you have
made me your lot in life; how can I bear to part from you?"

*But morning overtook Shahrazad, and she lapsed into silence.*

### THE TWO HUNDRED AND FORTIETH NIGHT

*The following night Shahrazad said:*

I heard, O happy King, that Jullanar said to the king, "How can
I bear to part from you? You should know that when I praised you
to my brother and mother and cousins, they felt a great affection
for you and desired to see you, saying, 'We will not leave until we
meet him and eat with him, so that his bread and salt may bind
us together.'" The king replied, "I hear and obey, but I am afraid
of them because of the fire I saw flaming from their mouths, for
although I was not near them, I almost died of fright." Jullanar
laughed and said, "Do not worry, for they do this only when they
are angry, and they got angry this time because I had invited them
to eat without you." Then she took the king by the hand and led
him to them, as they sat before the food, waiting for him. When
he came up to them, he greeted and welcomed them and they
greeted him back with utmost respect, sprang up to their feet, and
kissed the ground before him. Then they said to him, "O King of
the age, we have only one request for you; take care of this unique
pearl, Jullanar of the Sea, who is worthy of you just as you are
worthy of her. By God, all the kings of the sea sought her hand
in marriage, but we rejected them because we could not bear to
part from her even for a single moment. Had you not been a pious,
upright, honorable, and noble-hearted man, God would not have
blessed you with this queen. Glory be to Him who made you cherish
her and made her favor you and serve you, for you are like those
of whom the poet said:

> She is worthy of none but him,
> And he of none but her,
> That should another seek her hand,
> The earth would be astir."

The king thanked them and thanked Jullanar and sat to converse
and eat with them until they had had enough and washed their

hands. Then he lodged them in a private apartment where they lived for a full month, during which he never left their company for a single hour.

When the month had passed, Jullanar said, "The time of my delivery is at hand," and the king provided for her all the medicines and potions she needed for herself and her child. Then she went into labor and the women gathered around her, and the labor increased until the Almighty God granted her safe delivery, and she gave birth to a boy as lovely as the moon. When his mother looked at him, she was extremely happy to see him. Then her mother went to the king and announced the birth of his son.

*But morning overtook Shahrazad, and she lapsed into silence.*

## THE TWO HUNDRED AND FORTY-FIRST NIGHT

*The following night Shahrazad said:*

I heard, O happy King, that Jullanar's mother went to the king, and when she announced the birth of his son, he rejoiced and knelt in gratitude before the Almighty God. Then he bestowed robes of honor, distributed money, and gave gifts. When he was later asked, "What do you wish to name him?" he replied, "I name him Badr," and the boy was called Badr. Then the king bade the princes and chamberlains bid the people decorate the city, and he opened the jails and clothed the widows and orphans and gave alms to the poor and freed many Mamluks, as well as male and female slaves, and held celebrations and gave a magnificent banquet, to which he invited the select few as well as the general public. The celebrations lasted for ten full days.

On the eleventh day, as the king sat with Jullanar and her brother and mother and cousins, Jullanar's brother rose and, taking the newborn Badr, played with him, made him dance, then carried him in his arms, while the king and Jullanar looked at the boy and rejoiced. Suddenly her brother, taking them by surprise, flew with the boy out of the window, far from the shore, and dove with him into the sea. When the king saw the uncle take his son, plunge with him into the sea, and disappear, he let out a great cry, and his soul almost left his body. He tore his clothes and began to weep and wail. When Jullanar saw him in this condition, she said to him, "O King of the age, do not fear or weep for your son. I love him even more than you do, and he is with my brother, who does not mind the sea or fear drowning. If he thought that the boy would be in any danger, he would not have taken him there. Soon he will come back with your son safely, God the Almighty willing."

Soon the sea began to storm and surge and suddenly Sayih, the boy's uncle, emerged safely with the boy and flew into the room with the boy nestling in his arms as quietly as the moon. Then Sayih turned to the king and said, "I hope that you were not frightened when I dove with him into the sea." The king replied, "Yes, by God, Sayih, I thought that he would never return safely." Sayih said, "I took him there to pencil his eyes with a special kohl blessed by the words inscribed on the seal ring of Solomon son of David. When a child is born to us . . ."

*But morning overtook Shahrazad, and she lapsed into silence.*

THE TWO HUNDRED AND FORTY-SECOND NIGHT

*The following night Shahrazad said:*

I heard, O happy King, that Jullanar's brother Sayih said to the king, "When a child is born to us, we pencil his eyes, as I have told you. Now you need not fear for him to drown, suffocate, or be harmed in any way by water, for just as you walk on land, we walk in the sea." Then he pulled out from his pocket a sealed bag and, breaking the seal, emptied it, scattering strings of rubies and all kinds of jewels, in addition to three hundred emerald cabochons[8] and three hundred gemstones, as big as pigeon eggs, glittering like the sun. He said, "O King, these big gemstones are a gift for your little son Badr, and these rubies, emeralds, and other jewels are a gift from us to you, since we had not brought you any, being unaware of Jullanar's whereabouts or her situation. But now that we have met you and become one family, I have brought you this gift, and every little while I will bring you another like it, for these rubies and jewels are plentiful with us and I can easily get them, since I know their sources and whereabouts better than anyone else on land or in the sea." When the king saw these jewels, he was dazzled and wonderstruck, and he said, "One of these jewels is worth my whole kingdom." Then he thanked the young man Sayih and, turning to Queen Jullanar, said, "I am embarrassed before your brother, for he has generously given me this priceless gift that is

---

8. Gemstones cut with round unfaceted tops.

beyond the reach of anyone on earth." Queen Jullanar praised her husband and thanked her brother, who said, "O King of the age, it is you who have the prior claim on us, and it behooves us to thank you, for you have treated my sister kindly, and we have entered your dwelling and eaten your food. The poet says:

> Had I for Su'da's love before her wept,
> I would have solace found and never had to rue,
> But she wept first and made me weep and say,
> 'The credit to him who is first to act is due.'

And if we stand at your service, O King of the age, a thousand years, we would not repay you enough." The king thanked him profusely. They stayed with him forty days. Then Jullanar's brother Sayih rose and, kissing the ground before the king, said, "O King of the age, you have done us many favors, but we have imposed on your generosity and now we request one last favor. Grant us leave to depart, for we long for our home, family, and relatives. But we will never cease to serve you and serve my sister Jullanar. By the Omnipotent God, we are not happy to leave you, but what shall we do, since we have been reared in the sea and find uncongenial the life of the land?" When the king heard this, he rose to his feet and bade farewell to the young man and his mother and cousins, as did Jullanar, and they all wept because of the sorrow of separation and said, "We will visit you often." Then they rose and with one leap flew off, dove into the sea, and disappeared from sight, leaving the king in amazement.

The king continued to cherish Jullanar and treat her with the utmost generosity, while the boy grew and flourished and was catered to by many attendants. The king loved him exceedingly because he was very beautiful and because the older he grew, the more beautiful he became. His uncle and grandmother and cousins often came to visit the king, staying with him for a month or two, then going back home, while the boy continued to thrive, so that by the time he was fifteen, he was unequaled in charm, beauty, and perfect grace. By then he had learned grammar, lexicography, penmanship, history, and the Quran, as well as archery and spearplay.

*But morning overtook Shahrazad, and she lapsed into silence.*

## THE TWO HUNDRED AND FORTY-THIRD NIGHT

*The following night Shahrazad said:*

I heard, O happy King, that the boy had learned the skills of
chivalry, such as archery, spearplay, playing with the ball and
mallet,[9] and every other skill befitting the son of a king, so that
all the people of the city, men and women, spoke of none but him,
for he was like him of whom the poet said:

> His downy whiskers grew upon his cheeks
> Like a fine drawing that dazzled my sight.
> He was a lamp suspended from a chain
> Of ambergris, in the dark of the night.

When the boy had learned everything that befits a king, his father,
who loved him exceedingly, summoned the princes, the lords of
the realm, and the chief officers of state and made them take an
oath that they would make his son Badr king over them. They were
very happy to take the oath because they loved the old king very
much, for he was kind to everyone, spoke courteously, acted benevo-
lently, and never said anything that did not benefit the people. The
next day the king rode into the city with the princes, officers of state,
and troops until he entered the city square. Then he returned, and
when they drew near the royal palace, he and all the princes dismounted to wait on his son, while the new king continued to ride,
surrounded by attendants and preceded by officers, who announced
his progress, until they came to the entrance of the palace, where
he stopped and was assisted by his father and the princess to dismount. Then he sat on the throne, while his father stood before
him in the rank of a prince, and he issued edicts, adjudicated between the princes, deposed the unjust and appointed the just, and
ruled till close to midday. Then he descended from the throne and
went in to his mother Jullanar of the Sea, with the crown on his
head, looking like the moon. When his mother saw him, with the
king his father standing in attendance before him, she rose and,
kissing him, congratulated him on having assumed the kingship
and wished him and his father long life and victory over their
enemies. He sat with his mother and rested till the hour of the afternoon prayer. Then he rode with his father and the officers of state
to the city square, where he played with the ball and mallet till night-

9. A form of polo.

fall, then returned to the palace, attended by all the people. He did this every day.

*But morning overtook Shahrazad, and she lapsed into silence.*

### THE TWO HUNDRED AND FORTY-FOURTH NIGHT

*The following night Shahrazad said:*

I heard, O happy King, that during the first year King Badr used to go to the city square every day to play with the ball and mallet and return to sit on the throne to judge the people, doing justice to prince and beggar alike. In the second year he began to go hunting, to tour the cities and provinces under his rule, proclaiming peace and security, and to do what kings usually do. He was unique in his day in chivalry, valor, and fairness to his subjects.

One day the old king went to the bath and caught a chill and, becoming feverish, sensed that he was going to die and go to the next world. Then he got worse, and when he was on the verge of death, he called his son and charged him to take care of his kingdom and of his mother, as well as all his chief officers. Then he summoned all the princes, lords, and prominent men and made them once more swear a binding oath of allegiance to his son. He lingered a few days and died and was admitted to the mercy of the Almighty God. His son King Badr and Jullanar and all the princes and viziers and officers of state mourned over him, and they built him a tomb and buried him.

*But morning overtook Shahrazad, and she lapsed into silence.*

### THE TWO HUNDRED AND FORTY-FIFTH NIGHT

*The following night Shahrazad said:*

I heard, O happy King, that they buried him and mourned over him for a full month. Jullanar's brother and mother and cousins arrived and offered their condolences, saying, "O Jullanar, although your husband is dead, he has left this noble young man, this fierce lion and radiant moon." Then the lords and chief officers of state went in to Badr and said to him, "O King, mourning is unseemly, except for women. Stop distracting yourself over your father's death and distracting us with you, for he has passed away and 'everyone must die'; indeed, he who died and left a son like you is not dead." Then they entreated him and took him to the bath, and when he came out, he put on a fine robe embroidered with gold and adorned with rubies and other jewels and, placing the royal crown on his head, sat on the throne and took care of the affairs of the people, judging fairly between the strong and the weak and exacting from the prince the right of the beggar, so that all the people loved him and invoked blessings upon him. He lived in this fashion for a full year, while every now and then his relatives of the sea visited him and his mother, and he led a pleasant and a happy life.

One night his uncle came to see his sister Jullanar, and he greeted her and she rose, embraced him, and, seating him beside her, asked, "O my brother, how are you and how are my mother and cousins?" He replied, "They are fine and lack nothing save the sight of your face." Then she called for some food, and after they had eaten and the table had been removed, they began to chat. They spoke of King Badr, his beauty and elegance, his cultivation and wisdom, and his skill in horsemanship, while Badr himself lay reclining nearby. When he heard what his mother and uncle said, he continued to listen to them, pretending to be asleep.

Sayih said to his sister Jullanar, "Sister, your son is now sixteen years old and he is still unmarried, and I am afraid that something may happen to him before he has a son; therefore, it is my wish to marry him to one of the princesses of the sea, one who is his equal in beauty and grace." His sister Jullanar replied, "By God, brother, you are reminding me of something in which I have been negligent. Brother, I wonder who is worthy of him from among the daughters of the kings of the sea? Name them to me, for I know them all." Sayih proceeded to name them to her, while she kept saying, "I do not like her for my son; I will marry him only to a girl who is his equal in beauty and grace and piety and wisdom and cultivation and nobility and dominion and rank and pedigree." Her brother said, "By God, by God, I know none other of the daughters of the kings of the sea, for I have named more than one hundred and none of them pleases you. But, sister, find out whether your son is asleep or not." She replied, "He is asleep; why do you ask?" He said, "Sister, I have just thought of the daughter of one of the kings of the sea, one who is worthy of your son, but I am afraid to name her, lest he be awake and his heart be taken by her, for if we fail to win her easily, all of us, he and we and all the chief officers of state will have to work very hard and devote all our energies to that end, for the poet says:

> Love is at first nothing but harmless play,
> But, once entrenched, it takes your peace away."

When his sister heard this, she replied, "Brother, you are right, but tell me who she is and who is her father, for I know all the kings of the sea and their daughters, and if I judge her worthy of him, I will demand her for him in marriage from her father, even if I have to give all our possessions for her. Tell me who she is, for my son is asleep." He said, "I fear that he may be awake, for the poet says:

> [I loved her when I heard them her descry],
> For sometimes the ear loves before the eye."

Then he added, "Sister, no girl is worthy of your son save Jauhara, the daughter of King al-Shamandal, for she is his equal in beauty, charm, and grace, and there is none on land or in the sea who is sweeter or more delightful than she, with her rosy cheeks, radiant brow, and jewel-like teeth."

*But morning overtook Shahrazad, and she lapsed into silence.*

THE TWO HUNDRED AND FORTY-SIXTH NIGHT

*The following night Shahrazad said:*

I heard, O happy King, that Sayih said to his sister, "She has jewel-like teeth, sweet lips, black eyes, a soft body, heavy hips, and a slender waist. When she turns, she shames the deer, and when she sways, she makes jealous the willow bough." When Jullanar heard what her brother said, she replied, "Brother, you are right, for I have seen her many times when she was my companion, when we were children, but it has been eighteen years since I last saw her. Indeed, by God, none but she is worthy of my son, and none but he is worthy of her." King Badr, who was awake, heard what his mother and uncle said, and when he heard their description of Princess Jauhara, the daughter of King al-Shamandal, he fell in love with her at once, but he continued to pretend that he was asleep, even though his heart was on fire with love for her. Then Sayih turned to his sister Jullanar and said, "There is none among the kings of the land or sea who is more powerful, more proud, and more ill-tempered than al-Shamandal. So say nothing to your son about her until we demand her in marriage from her father. If he favors us with his assent, we will praise the Almighty God for His help, and if he refuses to give his daughter in marriage to

your son, we will keep quiet and seek another girl in marriage."
When Jullanar heard this, she replied, "This is an excellent idea,"
and they said no more on the subject, while the king spent the night
with his heart on fire with love for Princess Jauhara. But even
though he was on the burning coals of passion, he concealed his
feelings and said nothing of her to his mother and uncle.

Next morning the king and his uncle went to the bath and
washed, and when they came out, the servants gave them wine to
drink and set food before them, and the king and his uncle and
mother ate, until they were satisfied and washed their hands. Then
Sayih rose and said to the king and to his sister, "I will miss you,
but I beg your leave to return to my mother, for I have been with
you many days, and she is waiting and worrying about me." King
Badr bade his uncle Sayih farewell and, with his heart still on fire,
rode until he came to a meadow with a thicket of trees by the banks
of a running stream. When he saw the shade, he dismounted by
himself—for he had no retinue or servants with him—intending
to sleep, but he recalled his uncle's description of the princess and
her beauty and grace, and he wept bitterly.

It so happened, as it was foreordained, that when he had bidden
his uncle Sayih farewell and mounted his horse, his uncle looked
at him and, seeing that he did not look well, feared that the young
king had overheard their conversation, and he said to himself, "I
will follow Badr and see what he will do." So he followed him, and
when the king dismounted at the bank of the stream, his uncle hid
himself. So now, from his safe hiding place, he heard him recite
the following verses:

> Who will help me with a hard, full-hipped girl,
> Whose face is bright like the sun, nay brighter.
> My heart is her captive and willing slave,
> Lost in love for al-Shamandal's daughter.
> I will never forget her all my life;
> I will never love anyone but her.

When his uncle Sayih heard these verses, he wrung his hands
and said, "There is no power and no strength, save in God, the
Almighty, the Magnificent." Then he came out of his hiding and
said, "I have heard what you said. O my son, did you hear my conversation with your mother about Jauhara, last night?" King Badr
replied, "Yes, uncle, and as soon as I heard what you said about
her, I fell in love with her, and now my heart cleaves to her and
I cannot give her up." His uncle said, "O King, let us return to your
mother and inform her about the situation and tell her that I will
take you with me and demand the Princess Jauhara in marriage.
Then we will take our leave of her and depart, having informed

her, for I fear that if I take you with me without her leave and consent, she will reproach me, and indeed she will be right, for I will be the cause of her separation from you; moreover, the city will be left without a king, and your subjects will be left with none to govern them and look after them, and this will undermine your authority and cause you and your mother to lose the kingdom." When King Badr heard what his uncle said, he replied, "Uncle, I will not return to my mother and consult her in this matter because I know that if I return to consult her, she will not let me go with you. No, I will not return to her." And he wept before his uncle, adding, "I will go with you now without telling her, and I will return to her later." When Sayih heard what his nephew said, he was at a loss and said, "In any case, I can only pray to the Almighty God for help."

When he saw . . .

*But morning overtook Shahrazad, and she lapsed into silence.*

### THE TWO HUNDRED AND FORTY-SEVENTH NIGHT

*The following night Shahrazad said:*

I heard, O happy King, that when King Badr said to his uncle, "I must go with you," his uncle took off of his finger a seal ring engraved with one of the names of the Almighty God and said to him, "Put this ring on your finger, and it will protect you from the whales and other beasts of the sea." King Badr put the ring on his finger, and they plunged into the sea and fared on until they reached his uncle's palace. When he entered, he saw his grandmother seated with her relatives, and he greeted her and kissed her hand, while she rose and, embracing him, kissed him between the eyes, saying, "O my son, blessed is your coming. How is your mother Jullanar?" He replied, "O grandmother, she is well, and she sends greetings to you and to her cousins."

Then Sayih informed his mother that King Badr had fallen in love with Jauhara, al-Shamandal's daughter, as soon as he had heard of her, and told her the story from beginning to end, adding, "He has come with me, so that I may demand her for him in marriage from her father." When King Badr's grandmother heard what Sayih said, she was angry and upset, and she said to him, "Son, you have made a mistake in mentioning Princess Jauhara, al-Shamandal's daughter, before your nephew, for you know that al-Shamandal is an ill-tempered tyrant who is very proud and very foolish and that all the kings have demanded his daughter in marriage but he has rejected them all and dismissed them, saying, 'You are no match for my daughter in beauty or dominion.' I fear that if you demand her of her father, he will respond to you as he has responded to all the others, and we, given our self-respect, will return disappointed and embarrassed." When Sayih heard what his mother said, he asked her, "Mother, what is to be done? For King Badr fell in love with this girl when I mentioned her to my sister Jullanar, and he says, 'I must demand her of her father in marriage, even if I have to give my whole kingdom for her,' adding that if her father refuses to marry her to him, he will die of love and longing for her."

*But morning overtook Shahrazad, and she lapsed into silence.*

## THE TWO HUNDRED AND FORTY-EIGHTH NIGHT

*The following night Shahrazad said:*

I heard, O happy King, that Sayih said to his mother, "My nephew is superior to her, for his father was king of all the Persians and he is now their present king. Indeed, none but Jauhara is worthy of him, and none but he is worthy of her. I intend to take to her father necklaces of rubies and other jewels, a present worthy of him, and demand her in marriage. If he objects that he is a king, Badr is also a king, and a handsome king at that, with a greater kingdom, vaster dominion, and many more troops and followers. I must endeavor to fulfill his wish, even if it costs me my life, because I was the cause of his infatuation, and just as I plunged him in the ocean of love, so will I endeavor to marry him to the girl, and the Almighty God will help me in my endeavor." His mother replied, "Do as you wish, but when you speak with al-Shamandal, beware of offending him, for you know his pride and violent temper, and I fear that he will lay hands on you, for he has no respect for anyone." Sayih replied, "I hear and obey."

Then he took two bags full of precious necklaces, emerald cabochons, and rubies and diamonds, and, giving them to his servants to carry, set out for the palace of al-Shamandal. When he arrived, he asked for leave to see the king, and when leave was granted, he entered, kissed the ground before him, and greeted him in the best of manners. When the king saw him, he rose to return the greeting and bade him be seated. When he was seated, the king said to him, "Blessed is your coming. I have missed you in your absence. Tell me your wish, and I will grant it." Sayih rose and, kissing the ground once more before the king, said to him, "O King of the age, my errand is to the Almighty God and to the gallant king and valiant lion, whose fame has spread far and wide and whose praise has been sung in all the provinces and cities, for his justice, his forbearance, his mercy, his generosity, his kindness, and his graciousness." Then he opened the two bags and, emptying out the precious necklaces, the emerald cabochons, and the rubies and diamonds before the king, said to him, "O King, I hope that you will do me a favor and make me happy by accepting my present." King al-Shamandal replied, "There is neither reason nor explanation for such a present. What prompted you to give me this great treasure, and what do you expect in return? Explain your case and tell me your need. If it is in my power, I will grant it at once without further ado; and if I am unable to grant it, I will be excused, for 'God asks nothing of a soul beyond its means.'" Sayih rose and, kissing the ground before the king, said, "O King, my need is within your means; it is in your possession and within your power, for I am not mad enough to ask the king for a favor he is unable to grant."

*But morning overtook Shahrazad, and she lapsed into silence.*

### THE TWO HUNDRED AND FORTY-NINTH NIGHT

*The following night Shahrazad said:*

I heard, O happy King, that Sayih said to King al-Shamandal, "The sage says, 'If you wish to be denied, ask for what can't be supplied,' but my wish is one that the king is able to grant, for it is at his disposal and his to give." The king said, "Explain your case, tell me your need, and ask your wish." Sayih said, "O King of the age, I come to you as a suitor, seeking the unique pearl, the priceless jewel, and the glorious Princess Jauhara, daughter of our lord the king. O King, do not disappoint your suitor, but desire him who desires you." When the king heard this, he laughed in derision until he fell on his back. Then he said, "O Sayih, I thought you an excellent and wise young man who said nothing but what was reasonable and uttered nothing but what was sensible. What has possessed you and urged you to embark on such a grave venture and dangerous adventure, to seek in marriage the daughters of kings who rule over

cities and provinces and who command armies and retinues? Is your
self-esteem so high and your sense so little that you dare affront
me with such a demand?"

Sayih replied, "O King, may God guide you; I do not seek your
daughter for myself, and even if I did, I am her match and more,
for you know that my father was one of the kings of the sea, like
you, and that our kingdom has been taken from us. I seek her for
none other than King Badr, the king of Persia, whose might and
fame you know. If you object that you are a great king, King Badr
is a great king too, indeed greater, and if you object that your
daughter possesses beauty, charm, and grace, King Badr is more
beautiful, more charming, and more amiable. Indeed he has no
equal in discernment, fairness, courtesy, and generosity. If you
grant my request and give him your daughter in marriage, you will
have done the right thing and settled the matter, as any wise and
sensible man would do, but if you reject us and treat us arrogantly,
you will not have treated us properly or fairly. O King, you know
that Princess Jauhara, the daughter of our lord the king, must have
a husband, for the sage says, 'A girl needs a husband or a grave,'
and if you intend to marry her at all, my nephew is worthier of
her than any other man, but if you dislike us and refuse to have
anything to do with us, you will not find a better man." When King
al-Shamandal heard Sayih's words, he was so furious that he almost
lost his senses and his soul left his body. He said, "O dog, shall
the like of you dare speak to me like this and freely mention my
daughter's name in public gatherings, saying that your nephew is
a match for her? Who are you, who is your father, who is your
sister, who is your nephew, and who is his dog of a father that you
should speak such words to me and address me in this manner?
Guards, seize this good-for-nothing and strike off his head." The
guards drew their swords and attacked Sayih, who fled to the palace
gate, where he found his cousins, relatives, followers, and servants.

*But morning overtook Shahrazad, and she lapsed into silence.*

THE TWO HUNDRED AND FIFTIETH NIGHT

*The following night Shahrazad said:*

I heard, O happy King, that the young man fled to the palace
gate, where he found more than a thousand of his cousins, relatives, members of his entourage, followers, and servants, whom his

mother had sent to his aid, armed to the teeth, with coats of mail
and spears. When they saw him running, they asked him, "What
is the matter?" and he told them what had happened. When they
heard what he said, they realized that al-Shamandal was an ill-
tempered, arrogant man. They dismounted and, drawing their
swords, went in with him to al-Shamandal, whom they found seated
on his throne, still raging against Sayih, unaware of their coming
and surrounded by his guards, attendants, and servants, who were
unprepared for battle. When he saw Sayih's men enter with drawn
swords, he cried out to his men, "Damn you, away with the heads
of these dogs!" but before long his men were routed and he was
seized and bound. When his daughter Jauhara heard that her father
had been taken captive and his men and followers had been killed,
she fled from the palace to one of the islands and, climbing a tree,
hid herself there.

Earlier, when the two clans were still fighting, it happened that
some of Sayih's servants came to his mother and told her of the
battle, and when King Badr heard about it, he ran away in fear,
saying to himself, "All this turmoil is on my account, and none is
to answer for it but I." So he ran away, not knowing where to go,
until, as it had been foreordained, he came to the same island where
Jauhara had taken refuge and, being tired, stopped to rest at the
very tree in which she was hiding. He threw himself down, like a
dead man, and as he lay on his back to rest, he chanced to look
up and saw Princess Jauhara, who looked like the shining moon.
He said to himself, "Glory be to God who created this wonderful
form! Unless I am wrong, she must be Princess Jauhara. I think
that when she heard of the battle between her father and my uncle,
she fled to this island and hid in this tree. If she is not Princess
Jauhara herself, then she is one who is even more beautiful." He
pondered for a while, then said to himself, "I will seize her and question her, and if she is indeed Jauhara, I will ask her to marry me
and I will attain my wish." Then he spoke to her, saying, "O end
of all desire, who are you and who brought you here?" She looked
at him and, seeing that he was a young man as beautiful as the
full moon, with a slender figure and a sweet smile, said to him,
"O fair young man, I am Princess Jauhara, the daughter of King
al-Shamandal. I took refuge in this place because Sayih and his men
fought my father, killed most of his men, and bound him and took
him prisoner. I fled, fearing for my life."

*But morning overtook Shahrazad, and she lapsed into silence.*

### THE TWO HUNDRED AND FIFTY-FIRST NIGHT

*The following night Shahrazad said:*

I heard, O happy King, that Princess Jauhara said to King Badr, "Young man, I feared for my life and fled to this island." When Badr heard this, he marveled at this strange coincidence and said to himself, "There is no doubt now that my uncle Sayih has defeated King al-Shamandal," and he felt very happy, adding, "and there is no doubt that I have attained my aim and fulfilled my wish by the capture of her father." Then he looked at her and said to her, "O my lady, come down to me, for I am captured my your eyes and slain by your love. It was on your account and mine that these turmoils and broils took place, for I am Badr, king of Persia, and Sayih is my uncle, who came to your father to demand you in marriage for me. I have left my kingdom and my mother and relatives; I have parted from my friends and companions, and I have come far away from my country for your sake. Our meeting here is a rare coincidence. Come down to me and I will take you to your father's palace, ask my uncle Sayih to release him, and make you my lawful wife."

When Jauhara heard this, she said to herself, "Then it was on the account of this vile good-for-nothing and depraved coward that my father's army has been routed, his men have been killed, and he has been taken prisoner, and on his account that I have been driven far away from home to seek refuge on this island. If I do not find a way to foil him, this worthless fellow will overpower me and have his will of me, for he is in love, and the lover is not blamed for anything he does." So she deceived him with sweet words, acted coquettishly, and made eyes at him, saying, "O my lord, O my darling, are you indeed King Badr, the son of Jullanar of the Sea?" He replied, "Yes, my lady, I am." She said, "May God cut off my father's hand and take his kingdom from him and may He never grant him consolation or return from exile! How could he desire anyone more handsome, more elegant, or more suitable than you? By God, he has little sense or judgment," adding, "O King, if you love me a span, I love you two cubits, for I have fallen in the snares of your love and I am one of your victims. Your love for me has transferred itself to me, and what I feel for you now is manyfold greater than what you feel for me." Then she came down from the tree and, coming up to him, embraced him and kissed him, and his love and desire for her grew even greater. He did not doubt that she loved him and he trusted her and embraced her and kissed her, saying to himself, "By God, my uncle has not done justice to a fortieth part of her charm or a carat of her beauty."

*But morning overtook Shahrazad, and she lapsed into silence.*

### The Two Hundred and Fifty-Second Night

*The following night Shahrazad said:*

I heard, O happy King, that King Badr said to himself, "Or a carat of her beauty." Suddenly Jauhara pressed him to her bosom and, uttering words he could not understand, spat in his face and said, "Leave your human form, you vile good-for-nothing, and turn into a bird, the prettiest of birds, with white feathers and red bill and feet." Hardly had she spoken, when King Badr was suddenly transformed into the prettiest of birds, which shook itself and stood looking at Princess Jauhara.

It happened that Princess Jauhara had with her one of her maids, who was also hiding in the tree, and she said to her, "By God, if I did not fear for my father, who is his uncle's prisoner, I would kill him. May God never bless him or grant him good health! How unlucky was his coming to us, for all this trouble is due to him. Listen, girl, take him and carry him to the Island of Thirst; then leave him there and come back to me quickly." The girl took him in the form of a bird, carried him to the Island of Thirst, and was about to leave him there and return, when she said to herself, "By God, a young man of such beauty and grace does not deserve to die of thirst." So she took him to a large, green island, abounding in trees and fruits and streams and, leaving him there, returned to her mistress and told her that she had left him behind.

Meanwhile, when Sayih, King Badr's uncle, killed King al-Shamandal's guards and followers and took him prisoner, he searched for his daughter Jauhara but could not find her. Then he returned to his palace, or rather his mother's palace, and asked her, "Mother, where is my nephew King Badr?" She replied, "By God, son, I know nothing of him or his whereabouts, for when he heard that you had fought a battle with al-Shamandal, he feared for himself and ran away." When Sayih heard what his mother said, he grieved sorely for his nephew and said, "Mother, by God, this was all for nothing. You were negligent with King Badr, and I fear that he may perish or that one of King al-Shamandal's guards or his daughter Jauhara may catch him and kill him, and we may then have an unfortunate situation with his mother, for I took him with me without her permission." Then he dispatched officers and soldiers to search for King Badr throughout the sea, but they found no trace and heard no news of him, and they returned and told Sayih, compounding his worry and grief. So Sayih sat on al-Shamandal's throne and kept al-Shamandal prisoner but continued to grieve for King Badr.

*But morning overtook Shahrazad, and she lapsed into silence.*

THE TWO HUNDRED AND FIFTY-THIRD NIGHT

*The following night Shahrazad said:*

I heard, O happy King, that meanwhile Queen Jullanar waited for her son, after he had departed with his uncle, but when she waited for many days, without seeing him or hearing any news of him, she rose one day and, going down into the sea, headed to her mother's palace. When her mother saw her, she rose to greet her, embraced her, and kissed her, as did her cousins. Then she asked them whether her son King Badr had come down with his uncle Sayih. Her mother replied, "He came with his uncle, who took rubies and other jewels and, presenting them to al-Shamandal, demanded his daughter in marriage for your son, but al-Shamandal refused and attacked your brother with abusive words, and there ensued a battle between al-Shamandal and your brother, to whom I had sent a thousand horsemen, fully armed. Your brother defeated al-Shamandal, killing his officers and soldiers and taking him prisoner. When your son heard of the battle, before finding out that his uncle had won, he feared for himself, as it would seem, and ran away from here without my leave, and since then we have had no news of him." Then Jullanar asked about her brother Sayih, and her mother replied, "He is sitting on al-Shamandal's throne, and he has sent men in every direction to search for your son and Princess Jauhara."

When Jullanar heard her mother's reply, she grieved sorely for her son and wept, and she was furious against her brother Sayih for having taken her son down to the sea without her leave. Then she said to her mother, "O mother, I am worried about our kingdom, for I came to you without letting anyone know, and I fear that if I tarry, someone may maneuver against us and take the kingdom from us. I have no choice but to go back soon and manage the affairs there until the Almighty God resolves the matter. But do not forget my son Badr, or neglect his case, because if he dies, I will certainly die too, for I cannot live or enjoy life without him." Her mother replied, "With all my heart! O my daughter, do not ask how much I have suffered because of his absence and loss." Then she too sent men to look for King Badr.

*But morning overtook Shahrazad, and she lapsed into silence.*

THE TWO HUNDRED AND FIFTY-FOURTH NIGHT

*The following night Shahrazad said:*

I heard, O happy King, that Jullanar's mother sent men to search for King Badr, while his mother returned to her kingdom in tears, feeling sad and depressed.

As for Badr, when the maid took him to the island and left him there, as I have mentioned, he stayed there several days in the form of a bird, eating of its fruits and drinking of its waters, not knowing how to fly or where to go. One day, as he perched on a tree branch, there came a birdcatcher to the island, looking for game. When he drew close to King Badr and saw him in the form of a bird with white feathers and red bill and feet, which dazzled the eyes and bewildered the mind, he marveled at him and said to himself, "This is a lovely bird, the like of which in color and beauty I have never seen." Then he cast his net, caught it, and took it to the city, saying to himself, "I will sell it." Then he took it down to the market, where a man came by and asked him, "O catcher, how much is this bird?" The catcher asked him, "If you buy it, what will you do with it?" The man replied, "I will kill it and eat it." The catcher said, "Who could have the heart to kill this bird and eat it?" The man said, "You fool, what else is it good for?" The catcher said, "I intend to present it to the king, who will give me much more for it than its value and price and will divert himself by gazing on its beauty, while the most you would give me for it is a dirham; by God, I will not sell it to you even for a dinar."

Then the catcher went to the king's palace and waited there with the bird until the king saw him and, noticing the bird's white feathers and red bill and feet, was taken by its beauty and said to one of his servants, "If that bird is for sale, buy it." The servant came to the catcher and asked, "Will you sell this bird?" The catcher replied, "It is a gift from me to the king." The servant took the bird and brought it to the king, telling him what the catcher had said. The king said, "Go to him and give him ten dinars," and the catcher took the money, kissed the ground, and went away. Then the servant carried the bird to the king's palace and, placing it in a handsome cage, left with it food and water and hung it up.

When the king rode back and dismounted, he asked the servant, "Where is the bird? Bring it and let me look at it, for, by God, it is beautiful." The servant brought the bird and set it before the king.

*But morning overtook Shahrazad, and she lapsed into silence.*

THE TWO HUNDRED AND FIFTY-FIFTH NIGHT

*The following night Shahrazad said:*

I heard, O happy King, that the servant brought the cage and set it before the king and, seeing the food untouched, said, "O my lord, I left it this food, but it did not touch it, and I don't know what it will eat, so that I may feed it." But the king continued to gaze on the bird and marvel at its beauty. Then he called for food, and they laid the table before him, and he began to eat. When the bird saw the food and meat, it flew down from the cage and, perching on the table, ate of all that was before the king of bread, meat, sweets, and fruits. When the king saw what the bird ate, he and everyone present were surprised and taken aback, and he said to his attending officers and servants, "Never in all my life have I seen a bird eat like this one." Then he called for his wife to come and see the bird, and a servant went to her and said, "O my lady, the king wishes you to come and divert yourself with the sight of a bird he has bought, for when we brought the food, it flew down from its cage and, perching on the table, ate of all the dishes. O my lady, come and look at it, for it is a beauty and a wonder."

When the queen heard what the servant said, she came in a hurry, but when she saw the bird, she veiled her face and turned to go away. When the king saw his wife veil her face and turn to go away, he rose and said to her, "Why do you veil your face and turn away, when there is none here but the servants and your maids?" She replied, "O King, this is not a bird but a man." When the king heard what his wife said, he replied, "You are lying; how can a bird be a man? O how much my wife likes to joke!" She replied, "By God, I am not joking but telling you the truth. This bird is King Badr, the king of Persia and the son of Jullanar of the Sea."

*But morning overtook Shahrazad, and she lapsed into silence. Then Dinarzad said to her sister, "Sister, what a strange and entertaining story!" Shahrazad replied, "What is this compared with what I shall tell you tomorrow night if the king spares me and lets me live!"*

### THE TWO HUNDRED AND FIFTY-SIXTH NIGHT

*The following night Shahrazad said:*

I heard, O happy King, that the queen told the king that that bird was King Badr, the king of Persia, that his mother was Jullanar of the Sea, his uncle Sayih, and his grandmother Farasha, and that he had been cast under a spell by Princess Jauhara, the daughter of King al-Shamandal. Then she told him the story from beginning to end, how he had demanded Jauhara in marriage from her father, how her father had refused, and how his uncle Sayih had fought al-Shamandal, defeated him, and taken him prisoner. When the king heard the story, he was amazed and said to his wife, who was the greatest sorceress of her day, "For my sake, deliver him from the spell and do not leave him to suffer in this condition. May God cut off the hand of that harlot Jauhara! How little is her mercy and how great is her perfidy!" His wife said, "O King, say to him, 'King Badr, enter that room,'" and when the bird heard the king's words, it entered the room. Then the queen covered herself with a cloak, veiled her face, and, taking in her hand a bowl of water, entered the room. Then she pronounced over the water certain words that none understood and sprinkled the bird with it, saying, "By the power of these mighty names and solemn and holy oaths and by the Almighty God, Creator of heaven and earth, who allocates livelihood, allots the days of life, and resurrects the dead, leave your form as a bird and return to that in which God created you." Hardly had she finished, when the bird shook violently and became a man, and the king saw before him a handsome young man, than whom there was none lovelier on the face of the earth.

When Badr looked at himself, he said, "Glory be to God, the Creator of all creatures and the Master of their destiny!" Then he kissed the king's hands and feet and said to him, "My God reward you for this!" and the king kissed his head and said to him, "King

Badr, tell me your story from beginning to end." Then King Badr told him his entire story, concealing nothing, and the king was very much amazed. Then he said to King Badr, "King Badr, what do you intend to do now?" He replied, "O King of the age, I ask of your bounty a ship with a company of servants and other necessities to convey me to my home and kingdom, for I have been long absent from my mother and relatives and subjects, and I fear that if I tarry much longer, I will lose my kingdom; besides, I fear that my mother is either already dead because of my absence or in all likelihood dying of grief for me, not knowing where I am or whether I am alive or dead. My lord the king has kindly . . ."

*But morning overtook Shahrazad, and she lapsed into silence.*

THE TWO HUNDRED AND FIFTY-SEVENTH NIGHT

*The following night Shahrazad said:*

I heard, O happy King, that King Badr begged the king and queen to grant him one more favor and equip him for the journey. The king was moved by his beauty and eloquence and, feeling affection for him, said, "I hear and obey." Then he fitted out a ship for him, furnished it with all the necessities, and manned it with a company of his own servants.

King Badr bade him farewell, embarked, and set sail. He sailed before a fair wind for ten continuous days, but on the eleventh the wind began to blow harder, the sea raged, and the ship rose and fell so helplessly that the sailors were unable to control her. They drifted at the mercy of the waves until the ship hit a rock and broke up. Some men drowned and some escaped, while King Badr rode on one of the planks of the ship, after having almost drowned. For three days and nights he continued to rise and fall with the waves and to drift helplessly with the wind, not knowing in which direction he was going or where he was heading, until on the fourth day the waves cast him on the shore.

When he looked around, he saw a city as white as a fat dove, with high towers and beautiful buildings, built on the water, which was beating against its walls. When he saw the city, he rejoiced, for he was near death with hunger and thirst. He dismounted from the plank and tried to climb ashore to the city, but he was attacked by mules, asses, and horses, as countless as the grains of sand, which kicked him and prevented him from climbing. So he swam around to the other side of the city, but when he came out, he was surprised to find no one there and said to himself, "I wonder to whom this city belongs and why there is no king or inhabitants and whose are these mules, asses, horses, and cattle, which prevented me from climbing."

Then he walked aimlessly, musing on the situation, when suddenly he saw an old man.

*But morning overtook Shahrazad, and she lapsed into silence.*

### THE TWO HUNDRED AND FIFTY-EIGHTH NIGHT

*The following night Shahrazad said:*

I heard, O happy King, that King Badr suddenly saw an old man, a fava-bean seller, sitting in his shop. He greeted him and the old man returned the greeting and, seeing his handsome face, asked him, "Young man, where do you come from and who brought you to this city?" King Badr told him the whole story, and the old man was very much amazed and asked him, "My son, did you see anyone on the way?" King Badr replied, "Father, no, by God, I did not. Indeed, I was amazed to see the city without inhabitants." The old man said, "Son, come up into the shop, lest you perish." King Badr went up into the shop and sat at the upper end, and the old man rose and brought him some food, saying, "Son, stay inside the shop and eat. Glory be to Him who has saved you from that she-devil." King Badr was frightened, but he ate his fill and washed his hands. Then he turned to the old man and asked, "My lord, what is the meaning of your words? You have made me afraid of this city and its people." The old man replied, "Son, you should know that this city is called the City of the Magicians, and its queen is an enchantress who is as enchanting as the moon. All the beasts you saw were once men like you and me but are now enchanted, for whenever a young man like you enters the city, that blasphemous witch seizes him and enjoys him for forty days and . . ."

*But morning overtook Shahrazad, and she lapsed into silence.*

## THE TWO HUNDRED AND FIFTY-NINTH NIGHT

*The following night Shahrazad said:*

I heard, O happy King, that the old man said, "Then she casts a spell on him and turns him into a mule or an ass or one of the other beasts you saw. When any of the inhabitants of the city, who are sorcerers like her, wishes to go on an errand, he rides one of those beasts, who kicked you out of pity for you, to prevent you from climbing to the shore, lest she should cast a spell on you as she has done to them, for there is none who equals this cursed queen in the power of her magic. Her name is Lab, which means 'the Sun.'" When King Badr heard what the old man said, he was terrified and shook like a thunderbolt, saying to himself, "Hardly did I believe that I had been delivered from sorcery, when God cast me into the den of worse sorcerers." Then he pondered what to do. When the old man saw him trembling with fear, he said to him, "Son, go and sit at the door of the shop and see how many inhabitants there are in this city. Do not be afraid, for the queen and all the inhabitants respect me and like me and will not cause me any trouble." When King Badr heard what the old man said, he went and sat at the door of the shop to look at the people.

*But morning overtook Shahrazad, and she lapsed into silence.*

## THE TWO HUNDRED AND SIXTIETH NIGHT

*The following night Shahrazad said:*

I heard, O happy King, that when King Badr sat at the door of the shop to look at the people, he saw numberless people pass by. When they saw him, they marveled at his beauty and, coming up to the old man, asked "Shaikh, is this your most recent captive and prey?" He replied, "No, by God, he is my brother's son who lives far from here, and when I heard that his father was dead, I sent for him, so that I might see him and allay my grief." They said to him, "He is a handsome young man, but we fear for him from Queen Lab, lest she should turn against you and take him from you, for she loves handsome young men." The old man replied, "The queen will not cross me in anything, for she respects me and likes me, and when she hears that he is my nephew, she will not bother him, trouble him, or molest him." Then King Badr lived with the old man for a full month, eating and drinking, and the old man loved him exceedingly.

One day, as King Badr sat at the door of the shop as usual, there appeared a thousand officers riding Arabian horses with gilded saddles, dressed in all kinds of uniforms, girded with jeweled girdles, and holding drawn swords. When they passed by the shop, they saluted the old man and he returned their salute. Then they were followed by a thousand Mamluks dressed in the uniforms of attendants and holding drawn gilded swords, and when they passed by the old man, they saluted him and he returned their salute. Then they were followed by a thousand girls like moons, dressed in silk and satin robes embroidered with gold, and armed with shields and spears. In their midst rode the queen on an Arabian horse with a saddle of gold set with rubies and all kinds of jewels. The girls halted before the old man and saluted him, and he returned their salute. Then the queen came up to him and saluted him, and he rose and kissed the ground before her. Then she looked at him and said, "O Abu 'Abd-Allah, is this handsome, charming, and graceful young man your captive, and when did you catch him?" The old man replied, "No by God, O Queen, he is my brother's son, who had been long absent. When I could no longer live without seeing him, I brought him here to satisfy my longing and dispel my loneliness, for I love him very much; besides, I am an old man and his father is dead, and if he stays with me, he will help me during my lifetime and inherit my estate after my death." The queen replied . . .

*But morning overtook Shahrazad, and she lapsed into silence.*

THE TWO HUNDRED AND SIXTY-FIRST NIGHT

*The following night Shahrazad said:*

I heard, O happy King, that the queen said to the old man, "Father, will you give him to me as a gift, for I love him? By the fire and the light, by the hot wind and the cool shade, I will make him my lot in life. Do not fear for him, for I may harm everyone on the face of the earth, but I will not harm him, for you know the mutual esteem you and I hold for each other." The old man replied, "O my Queen, I can neither give him to you as a gift nor surrender him to you." She said, "By the fire and the light, by the

hot wind and the cool shade, and by my faith, I will not leave without him. I will not betray him or enchant him, and I will do only
what will please him." The old man, who did not dare cross her,
fearing for himself and for King Badr, secured an oath from her
that she would not harm the young man and that she would return
him as she received him. Then he said to her, "When you return
from the square tomorrow, I will give him to you." She thanked
him and returned to her palace.

Then the old man turned to King Badr and said, "This is the
woman I had feared and worried about, but she swore by her
Magian[1] faith that she would not harm you or enchant you, and
were it not that she respected me and liked me, she would have
taken you by force, for it is the custom of this blasphemous witch
and queen to do with strangers what I have already told you. May
God shame her and curse her and her great malice, wickedness,
and depravity." When King Badr heard what the old man said,
he replied, "My lord, by God, I am terrified of her, for I tasted
enchantment for an entire month, when Princess Jauhara, the
daughter of King al-Shamandal, cast a spell over me and made me
a lesson to others, until the wife of one of the kings delivered me
from the spell. I have tasted the most bitter torments and I know
how the enchanted suffers," and he wept. The old man felt sorry
for him and said to him, "Do not be afraid, for she may hurt even
her relatives, but she will not dare hurt me."

*But morning overtook Shahrazad, and she lapsed into silence.*

THE TWO HUNDRED AND SIXTY-SECOND NIGHT

*The following night Shahrazad said:*

I heard, O happy King, that the old man said to King Badr,
"She may hurt even her relatives, but she will not dare hurt me.
Have you not seen how her troops and retinue stood at my shop
and saluted me? By God, son, this infidel refuses to salute even
kings, yet whenever she passes by my shop, she stops to salute me
and speak with me, as you have seen and heard."

They slept that night, and when it was morning, Queen Lab came
with her girls, Mamluks, and attendants, who were armed with
swords and spears, stopped at the door of the shop, and saluted

1. See n. 1, p. 61.

the old man. He rose and kissed the ground before her, returning the salute. Then she said to him, "Father, fulfill your pledge and do at once what you have promised me." The old man replied, "Swear to me again that you will never harm him, enchant him, or do to him anything he abhors." She swore again by her faith and unveiled a face like the moon, saying, "Father, how you procrastinate in giving me your handsome nephew! Am I not more beautiful than he?" When King Badr saw her beauty, he was bewitched and said to himself, "By God, she is more beautiful than Jauhara. If she marries me, I will leave my kingdom and stay with her, without returning to my mother; if not, I will at least enjoy her in bed for forty days and nights, and I do not care if she enchants me or kills me afterward. By God, a single night with her is worth a lifetime." Then the old man took King Badr by the hand, saying to her, "Receive from me my nephew Badr and return him to me as you receive him. Do not harm him or take him away from me." She swore for the third time that she would not harm him or enchant him; then she ordered for Badr a handsome, saddled horse, bedecked with gold trappings, and gave the old man a thousand dinars.

*But morning overtook Shahrazad, and she lapsed into silence.*

THE TWO HUNDRED AND SIXTY-THIRD NIGHT

*The following night Shahrazad said:*

I heard, O happy King, that the queen gave the old fava-bean seller a thousand dinars and, saying "May God give you more," took King Badr and departed. He rode beside her, looking like the moon, and whenever the people looked at him and at his beauty, they felt sorry for him, saying "By God, such a handsome young man does not deserve to be enchanted by that cursed witch," while he rode silently, having committed himself to the Almighty God. They rode on to the palace, and when they reached the gate, the princes and nobles and servants dismounted and stood in attendance, while she and King Badr dismounted and sat on the throne. Then she dismissed all the princes and chamberlains and notables, and they kissed the ground before her and departed.

Then she took King Badr by the hand and with her maids and male servants went into the palace. It was like a palace in Paradise, with walls adorned with gold, with storerooms full of clothes and vessels, and with a beautiful garden in the middle, with a large pond and birds singing in all kinds of voices and tongues. When King Badr saw this opulent palace, he said to himself, "Glory be to God who in His generosity and clemency blesses those who worship other than Himself." Then Queen Lab sat at a window overlooking the garden, on a couch of ivory with high cushions, and, seating King Badr beside her, embraced him and kissed him. Then she called for food, and the maids brought a table of red gold set with jewels and pearls and spread with all kinds of food and sweets, and the queen and King Badr ate, until they were satisfied, and washed their hands. Then the maids brought the wine service, vessels of gold and silver and crystal, as well as dishes full of dried fruits and nuts, and flowers and perfumes. Then, at her order, they ushered in ten girls like moons, with all kinds of musical instruments in their hands.

Then the queen filled a cup and drank it off and filled another.

*But morning overtook Shahrazad, and she lapsed into silence.*

## THE TWO HUNDRED AND SIXTY-FOURTH NIGHT

*The following night Shahrazad said:*

I heard, O happy King, that the queen gave the cup to King Badr, who took it and drank it off, and they continued to drink until they began to get drunk. Then she ordered the girls to sing, and they sang all kinds of songs until King Badr imagined that the palace danced with him in delight, and he became lightheaded and happy and forgot his separation from home, saying to himself, "By God, this queen is young and beautiful, and I will never leave her, for her kingdom is vaster than mine and she is fairer than Princess Jauhara." He continued to drink till nightfall, when they lighted the candles and burned the incense until the banquet was as joyous as the one of which the poet said:

> O what a day we spent under the trees,
> Enjoying every pleasure and delight,
> The shining rivulet, the myrtle blue,
> The starry narcissus and roses bright,
> The glittering wine and the brimming cup
> And crackling incense rising in the light!

Queen Lab and King Badr continued to drink, while the singers sang, until most of the night was gone and the queen was completely drunk. Then she dismissed the singing women and, lying in bed, ordered King Badr to lie beside her. Then the maids took off all the clothes they had made him wear, except for a gold-embroidered shirt, like the one Queen Lab was left with, and the two spent the happiest of nights till the morning. Then Queen Lab rose and took King Badr to the bath inside the palace, and they washed themselves, and when they came out, the maids dressed them and brought them cups of wine, which they drank. Then she took King Badr by the hand and with her maids . . .

*But morning overtook Shahrazad, and she lapsed into silence.*

THE TWO HUNDRED AND SIXTY-FIFTH NIGHT

*The following night Shahrazad said:*

I heard, O happy King, that the queen took King Badr by the hand and with her maids came out of the bath and went to the banquet room, where they sat and rested for a while. Then the maids set food before them, and they ate and washed their hands. Then the maids removed the table and set the wine service and fruits and nuts and flowers before them, and they drank, while the singing women sang all kinds of melodies and songs till nightfall.

They continued to live like this, eating and drinking and kissing and playing, for forty days. Then Queen Lab asked King Badr, "Which is more enjoyable, this place or the shop of your uncle the fava-bean seller?" He replied, "O Queen, by God, this place is more enjoyable, for my uncle is a poor man." She laughed at his reply, and the two spent the happiest of nights in bed. But when he awoke in the morning, he did not find her beside him and asked himself, "Where could she have gone?" He felt lonely without her, and when he waited for her and she did not return, he arose from bed and, putting on his clothes, searched for her, and when he did not find her, he said to himself, "She may be in the garden." He went into the garden and came to a running stream, beside which he saw a black bird next to a white she-bird, under a large tree full of birds of various colors. He stood and watched the birds, without being seen by them, and saw the black bird leap and mount the white she-bird three times. Soon the she-bird turned into a woman, and when he looked at her closely, he saw that she was none other than Queen Lab, and he realized that the black bird was an enchanted man whom she loved and that she had turned into a she-bird so that the man could make love to her. King Badr was seized with jealousy, and he was resentful and angry with Queen Lab because of the black bird. He returned and lay down on the bed, and a little later she came to him and kissed him and joked with him, but when his anger mounted and he did not speak a single word to her, she guessed what was troubling him and was certain that he had seen the bird mount her. But she kept it to herself and said nothing.

When it was broad daylight, he said to her, "O Queen, I wish you to give me leave to go to my uncle's shop, for I have not laid eyes on him for forty days and I long to see him." She replied, "O Badr, go, but do not stay long, for I cannot bear to be without you or wait a single hour." He replied, "I hear and obey," and, mounting his horse, rode to the old man's shop.

*But morning overtook Shahrazad, and she lapsed into silence.*

### The Two Hundred and Sixty-Sixth Night

*The following night Shahrazad said:*

I heard, O happy King, that King Badr rode to the shop of the old fava-bean seller, who ran to greet him, welcomed him, and embraced him. Then he asked, "How have you fared with that infidel?" King Badr replied, "I was well, healthy, and happy till last night, when I awoke and did not see her by my side. When I arose and did not find her, I put on my clothes and searched for her until I went into the garden." Then he told him the story and how he had seen the black bird mount her. When the old man heard this, he said, "The cursed woman has started to play games. You should beware of her and should know that the birds on the tree were all young strangers whom she loved, enjoyed, then turned into birds. The black bird was one of her Mamluks, with whom she was madly in love, but when he cast his eye on one of her women, she cast a spell over him and turned him into a bird. Whenever she lusts for him, she turns herself into a she-bird and lets him mount her, for she still loves him. Now that she knows that you have found out, she will no longer be good to you, but fear nothing, since I will protect you, for there is none better skilled in magic than I, although I do not use it except when I have to. I have delivered many men from her hands, for she has no power over me and she fears me, as do the inhabitants of this city, who are fire worshippers

like her. Come back to me tomorrow, and tell me what she does
to you, for tonight she will prepare to destroy you. Dissemble with
her till tomorrow; then come back, and I will tell you what to do."
King Badr bade the old man farewell and returned to the queen.

He found her sitting and waiting for him, and when she saw him,
she rose to greet him and welcome him. Then the maids set food
before them, and they ate and washed their hands. Then they
brought them wine, and she drank and plied him with wine until
by midnight he was drunk and unconscious. When she saw him
in this condition, she said to him, "I conjure you by God and by
the god you worship, if I ask you a question, will you answer me
truthfully?" He, being unconscious and not knowing what he was
saying, replied, "Yes." She said, "O my lord and my darling, when
you looked and did not find me, did you not search for me until
you found me in the garden in the form of a white she-bird and
saw a black bird mount me, then saw me turn back into my human
form?" He replied, "Yes." She said, "That black bird was one of
my officers, whom I loved, but one day he cast his eye on one of
my women, and I became jealous and turned him into a bird and
killed the woman. But I cannot bear to be without him, and whenever I desire him, I turn myself into a she-bird and let him possess
me, as you have seen. It is because of this that you are jealous and
angry at me, yet, by the fire and the night, you love me and I love
you more than ever."

*But morning overtook Shahrazad, and she lapsed into silence.*

THE TWO HUNDRED AND SIXTY-SEVENTH NIGHT

*The following night Shahrazad said:*

I heard, O happy King, that the queen said to King Badr, "You
love me and I love you, for you are my lot in life." When he heard
this, he, being drunk, replied, "Yes, this is how I felt." Then she
embraced him and kissed him and, pretending to love him, lay down
to sleep, and he lay beside her. In the middle of the night, she rose
from bed, while Badr lay awake, pretending to be asleep, and
watched with one eye to see what she was doing. She took red sand
from a bag and spread it on the floor of the room, and it became
a running stream. Then she took out a handful of barley and strewed
it in the soil on the bank of the stream and watered it with the water
from the stream, and it turned into ears of barley. Then she reaped

the barley and ground it into meal. Then she laid the meal aside and, returning to bed, slept beside King Badr till the morning.

When it was morning, King Badr rose and, as soon as he washed his face, asked her leave to visit the old man. She gave him leave and he went to the old man and told him what he had seen. When the old man heard what he said, he laughed and said, "By God, this infidel is plotting mischief against you, but do not mind her." Then he gave him a half-pound of barley meal and said, "Take this with you, and when you arrive and she sees it, she will ask you, 'What will you do with this?' Say to her, 'An extra blessing is a blessing,' and eat some of it. Then she will bring you her own meal and say to you, 'Eat some of this.' But pretend to be eating of hers and eat of this instead. Beware, for if you eat as much as a dirham's weight or even a grain of hers, her spell will have power over you, and, knowing that you have eaten of her meal, she will cast her spell over you, bid you leave your human form, and turn you into any other form she pleases. But if you do not eat of it, you need not worry about her, for her magic will have no power over you and will fail to work on you. She will be abashed and tell you that she was teasing you and will make a show of affection and love, but all this will be nothing but abomination. Then make a show of love and say to her, 'O my lady and my darling, taste of my barley meal.' If she tastes even one grain of it, take water in your hand, throw it in her face, and bid her leave her form and turn into any form you please. Then leave her and come to me, and I will take care of you."

Then King Badr bade the old man farewell and, returning to the palace, went in to the queen. When she saw him, she said, "Welcome!" and she rose and kissed him, saying, "O my lord, you have tarried too long from me." He replied, "I have been with my uncle, who gave me some of this barley meal to eat." She replied, "We have better than this." Then she put his meal in one dish and hers in another and said to him, "Eat of this, for it is better than yours." He pretended to eat of it, and when she thought that he had done so, she took water in her hand and sprinkled him with it, saying, "Leave this form, you vile good-for-nothing, and turn into a mean, barren, ugly, lame mule." But he did not change, and when she saw that he did not change, she went up to him and kissed him, saying, "O my beloved, I was teasing you to see what you would say." He replied, "My lady, as long as you love me, nothing will change me toward you."

*But morning overtook Shahrazad, and she lapsed into silence.*

THE TWO HUNDRED AND SIXTY-EIGHTH NIGHT

*The following night Shahrazad said:*

I heard, O happy King, that King Badr said to the queen, "As
long as you love me, nothing will change me toward you, for I love
you even more than you love me. Eat of my barley meal." She took
a mouthful and ate it, and no sooner had it settled in her stomach
than she began to convulse. Then King Badr took water in his hand
and threw it in her face, saying, "Leave this form and turn into
a dappled she-mule," and she became at once a dappled she-mule.
When she saw herself in this condition, the tears rolled down her
face, and she began to rub her cheeks against his feet. He tried to
bridle her, but she would not let him; so he left her and went to
the old man and told him what had happened, and the old man
took out a bridle, saying, "Bridle her with this, for, when she sees
it, she will submit and let you bridle her." King Badr took the bridle
and returned to the queen, and when she saw him, she came up
to him, and he set the bit in her mouth, and, mounting her, he
rode from the palace to the old man's shop. When the old man saw
her, he said to her, "May God shame you, O cursed woman! Do
you see what He has done to you?" Then he said to King Badr,
"My son, it is time for you to leave this city. Ride her and go wherever you like, but beware of relinquishing the bridle to anyone."
King Badr thanked him and bade him farewell.

Then he rode on for three days until he came near a city, where
he met an attractive gray-headed old man, who asked him, "Son,
where are you coming from?" King Badr replied, "From the City
of the Magicians." The old man replied, "You are my guest," but
while they were conversing, up came an old woman, who, when
she looked at the she-mule, began to cry, saying, "This she-mule
resembles my son's she-mule, which is dead, and my heart aches
for her. O young man, for God's sake, sell her to me." King Badr
replied, "Mother, by God, I cannot sell her." She said, "For God's
sake, do not refuse me, for my son will surely die if I do not buy
him this she-mule," and she pressed him until he said to her, "I
will not sell her for less than a thousand dinars." She said to him,
"Say to me, 'She is sold to you for a thousand dinars.'" King Badr,
saying to himself, "Where could this old woman get a thousand
dinars? I will say that the she-mule is sold to her and see where
she will get the money," replied, "She is sold to you." When she
heard his words, she took out from her pocket a thousand dinars,

and when he saw the money, he said to her, "Mother, I was joking with you, for I cannot sell her." But the old man looked at him and said, "Son, you should know that none lies in this city, for whoever lies is put to death." King Badr dismounted from the she-mule . . .

*But morning overtook Shahrazad, and she lapsed into silence. Then Dinarzad said to her sister, "O sister, what a strange and entertaining story!" Shahrazad replied, "What is this compared with what I shall tell you tomorrow night if I stay alive!"*

### THE TWO HUNDRED AND SIXTY-NINTH NIGHT

*The following night Shahrazad said:*

I heard, O happy King, that King Badr dismounted from the she-mule and delivered her to the old woman, who, as soon as she received her, removed the bit from her mouth, took water in her hand, and sprinkled her with it, saying, "O my daughter, leave this form and return to your human form." The queen was at once restored to her original form, and the two women embraced and kissed each other. Then King Badr realized that the old woman was Queen Lab's mother and that he had been tricked, and he wanted to flee, but there was nowhere to go.

Then the old woman gave a loud whistle, and there appeared before her a demon, as huge as a mountain. She mounted on his back and placed her daughter behind her, and the demon, putting King Badr on his shoulder, flew off with them and soon brought them to the palace of Queen Lab. When the queen sat down on the throne, she looked at King Badr and said, "You worthless fellow, here I am; I have attained my wish and I will show you what I will do to you and to that wretched old fava-bean seller. O how many favors have I done him and how ill he has served me, for you succeeded with me only with his help!" Then she took water and sprinkled him with it, saying, "Leave this form and turn into the ugliest of birds," and he at once turned into an ugly bird. Then she put him in a cage and withheld from him all food and water.

But one of her women took pity on him and gave him food and water without the queen's knowledge. Then she went to the old man and told him what had happened and informed him that the queen intended to destroy his nephew. He thought it over, pondering what to do with the queen, and finally said, "I must take this city from her." Then he gave a loud whistle, and there appeared before him a demon with four wings, to whom he said, "O Barq, take this girl, who has pitied King Badr and given him food and water, and carry her to the city of Jullanar of the Sea and her mother Farasha, who are the most powerful magicians on the face of the earth, and tell them that King Badr is Queen Lab's captive."

The demon took her, and flying off with her, soon set her down on the roof of Queen Jullanar's palace. The girl descended from the roof and, going in to the queen, kissed the ground before her and told her what had happened to her son from beginning to end. Jullanar rose and kissed her face and thanked her. Then she ordered the drums to beat in the city in celebration and informed her family that King Badr had been found. Then Jullanar and her mother Farasha and her brother Sayih summoned all the tribes of demons and the troops of the sea, for the kings of the demons obeyed them ever since the capture of King al-Shamandal. Then they all flew up into the air and, descending on the City of the Magicians, attacked the city and the palace and killed all the inhabitants in the twinkling of an eye.

Then Jullanar asked the girl, "Where is my son?" The girl brought the cage and set it before her, and Jullanar took the bird out of the cage and, taking water in her hand, sprinkled the bird with it, saying, "Leave this form and return to your human form, by the power of the God of the world," and no sooner had she finished than King Badr changed into "a full-fledged man." Then she embraced him and wept, as did his uncle Sayih and his grandmother Farasha and his cousins, who fell on him, kissing his hands and feet. Then Jullanar sent for 'Abd-Allah, the old fava-bean seller, and when he presented himself to her, she thanked him for his kindness to her son and married him to the girl whom he had dispatched to her with King Badr's news.

*But morning overtook Shahrazad, and she lapsed into silence.*

### THE TWO HUNDRED AND SEVENTIETH NIGHT

*The following night Shahrazad said:*

I heard, O happy King, that the old man married the girl, as Jullanar had wished.

Then King Badr said to his mother, "O mother, nothing remains, except that I should get married and unite us all." His mother replied, "My son, this is an excellent idea, but wait until we inquire

who is suitable from among the daughters of the kings." His grandmother Farasha and his uncle Sayih and his cousins said, "O King
Badr, we will endeavor at once to get you what you desire." Then
each of them went out to search throughout the country, while
Jullanar sent out her waiting-women on the backs of demons, saying
to them, "Leave not a province or a city or a king's palace without
noting every beautiful girl there." When King Badr saw what his
mother Jullanar had done, he said to her, "Mother, stop this, for
none will satisfy me."

*But morning overtook Shahrazad, and she lapsed into silence.*

The Two Hundred and Seventy-First Night

*The following night Shahrazad said:*

I heard, O happy King, that King Badr said to his mother
Jullanar, "None will satisfy me, save Princess Jauhara, the daughter
of King al-Shamandal, for she is, like her name, truly a jewel." His
mother replied, "Son, she is yours." Then she sent at once for King
al-Shamandal, who was immediately brought and kissed the ground
before her. Then she sent for her son King Badr, informing him
that al-Shamandal was in her presence. King Badr came and bade
him welcome, and when he demanded his daughter Jauhara in
marriage, King al-Shamandal replied, "She is your servant and at
your disposal." Then he dispatched some of his officers, bidding
them go to his city, inform his daughter Jauhara that he was with
King Badr, and bring her back with him. The officers flew up into
the air and a while later returned with Princess Jauhara.

When she saw her father, she went up to him, embraced him,
and wept. Then he turned to her and said, "O my daughter, I have
given you in marriage to this gallant king and valiant lion, King
Badr, for he is the best, the most handsome, and the most exalted
man in this age, and none is worthy of him but you and none is
worthy of you but him." She replied, "O my father, I cannot disobey
you; do as you wish." So they summoned the legal witnesses and
drew up the marriage contract. Then they beat the drums in celebration and opened the prisons and clothed the widows and orphans
and bestowed robes of honor on the princes and lords of the realm.
Then they held a wedding feast, giving banquets and celebrating,
day and night, for ten days, at the end of which they unveiled the
bride in seven different robes. Then King Badr went in to Princess

Jauhara and took her virginity, and when he found that she had been a virgin, he rejoiced, and they loved one another exceedingly. Then he bestowed a robe of honor on her father King al-Shamandal, gave him riches, and sent him happy to his home and country. Then King Badr and his wife and mother and relatives continued to enjoy life until they were overtaken by the breaker of ties and destroyer of delights. And this is the completion and the end of their story.

## Translator's Postscript

Tradition has it that in the course of time Shahrazad bore Shahrayar three children and that, having learned to trust and love her, he spared her life and kept her as his queen.

# OTHER TITLES IN
# EVERYMAN'S LIBRARY

Everyman's Library, founded in 1906 and relaunched in 1991, aims to offer the most complete library in the English language of the world's classics. Each volume is printed in a classic typeface on acid-free, cream-wove paper with a sewn full cloth binding.